CWMARDY
&
WE LIVE

LIBRARY OF WALES

Lewis Jones was born in Clydach Vale in 1897. He started work underground at the age of twelve in the Cambrian Combine Colliery, which was central in the famous 1910-1911 strike that culminated in the Tonypandy riots. Jones absorbed the syndicalist philosophy of direct action and workers' control by which he was surrounded, and, in the Central Labour College which he attended in London from 1923 to 1925, the Marxism that led him to join the Communist Party. Jones became a full-time worker for the National Unemployed Workers' Movement, and led a number of the famous hunger marches of the 1930s from Wales to London. He was elected to the Glamorgan County Council in 1936, and died of a heart attack in 1939, after addressing numerous public meetings in support of the Spanish Republic. *Cwmardy* (1937) and *We Live* (1939) are his two epic novels of the experience of South Wales from the 1890s to the 1930s.

CWMARDY
&
WE LIVE

LEWIS JONES

LIBRARY OF WALES

Parthian
The Old Surgery
Napier Street
Cardigan
SA43 1ED
www.parthianbooks.co.uk

The Library of Wales is a Welsh Assembly Government
initiative which highlights and celebrates Wales' literary
heritage in the English language.

Published with the financial support of
the Welsh Books Council

www.libraryofwales.org

Series Editor: Dai Smith

First published in 1937 and 1939
© Lewis Jones 1937, 1939
Library of Wales edition published 2006
Foreword © Hywel Francis 2005
Publishing Editor: Penny Thomas
All Rights Reserved

Reprinted in 2010

ISBN 9 781902 638836

Cover design by Marc Jennings
Cover image: *The Coming Revolution* (1935) from a fresco by
Jack Hastings, by kind permission of the Marx Memorial Library

Printed and bound by Gomer Press, Llandysul, Ceredigion
Typeset by text@lloydrobson.com

LIBRARY OF WALES

FOREWORD

Some notable Welsh public figures were once asked to choose their heroes and give a radio lecture about them. The writer Gwyn Thomas chose Lewis Jones, a seemingly long-forgotten leader of the Rhondda's unemployed. Gwyn talked memorably about Lewis' refusal to jump through other people's hoops. All the time I puzzled over the phrase and what Gwyn intended it to mean – for Lewis.

Having been brought up in a 'communist' family I was not unfamiliar with the facts of Lewis Jones' remarkable life: Labour college student, imprisoned in 1926, Cambrian Colliery checkweighman, victimised union activist, leader of several hunger marches, remarkable orator, Communist councillor and proletarian novelist. He was even capable of holding an audience of over a thousand people for two and a half hours with his lecture 'The Social Significance of Sin'.

All that was packed into a life of just forty-two years. He died in 1939 on the day that he had addressed over thirty meetings in support of the besieged Spanish Republic. To many he was a hero and a martyr.

At about the same time as I heard Gwyn Thomas' radio broadcast I spoke to Billy Griffiths, close friend and comrade of Lewis, who had served in the International Brigades in Spain. Imagine, he suggested, the British Communist leader Harry Pollitt coming into Judge's Hall, Tonypandy. The packed hall would of course stand in respect. Imagine, then, he said, attending the Seventh World Congress of the Communist International in Moscow in 1935. Stalin arrives. The thousands in attendance rise. Everyone except Lewis, who was one of the small band of British delegates. He was sent home in disgrace and disciplined by the British Communist Party. Some say he was overwhelmed with emotion and could not rise; others said he was too busy reading a novel or a comic and could not be bothered. I prefer to accept a further explanation: he did not believe in the cult of personality and believed that no one should be worshipped, least of all Stalin. Some say he was capable of all three responses. Take your own pick. Certainly, for me, the deeper reason and how Lewis manifested it fits best.

He was a maverick in the best sense of the word. Born illegitimate, he was shaped by riotous and cosmopolitan Tonypandy. He married young, enjoyed the company of men and women, could never be a party 'apparatchik' and would never jump through other people's hoops. His was a discordant revolutionary voice like that of Federico Garcia Lorca, Aneurin Bevan and Antonio Gramsci.

I still remember sitting with Billy Griffiths in his home in Dunraven Street, Tonypandy in November 1969, in the very room where Communist Party meetings took place in the 1930s – meetings that are so vividly described in Lewis' two novels. Billy Griffiths spoke with difficulty, as he was suffering badly from emphysema. Among all the interviews I did as an historian, his description of Lewis Jones remains the most powerful evocation of one man's purpose in life, and it explains why Lewis Jones the novelist is important to us today:

> His main quality I think was love of people and compassion, it superseded everything else. I have seen Lewis... sitting down listening to two old people telling him about their troubles, and tears running down his cheeks. That's the kind of man he was, he felt it, it was for him more than logic. The rules that could do nothing for these people had to be broken, understand? .... I remember recruiting people, we had a meeting here for some people to go to Spain. We used to have a long table here and Lewis sat in by there, by the fire, and I was trying to interest people to go to Spain.... And when they had gone out, Lewis got up in the end, he couldn't stand it any more, he said: 'You've no right, to do that, to get the young boys to go there and die...' You see it was more important than the politics, [it] was the humanism and compassion... it was this that people loved about him....

His powerfully evocative speeches painted such vivid pictures of his people's individual and collective struggles it was thought that he would make a natural novelist. That was the view of Arthur Horner, the President of the South Wales Miners' Federation. Lewis acknowledged this in his foreword to *Cwmardy*, referring to Horner as 'my friend and comrade... whose fertile brain conceived the idea that I should write it'. According to Lewis,

Arthur Horner 'suggested that the full meaning of life in the Welsh mining areas could be expressed for the general reader more truthfully and vividly if treated imaginatively'.

And that, expressed in Lewis' own words, is the essence of both the work and the man for us today. He was the 'people's remembrancer' who had also contributed actively to the people's chronicle. In that sense Lewis Jones is unique in the political culture of Wales in the twentieth century, standing alongside only Saunders Lewis (and what an intriguing contrast) in combining political activism with literary aspirations and, indeed, with literary achievement. The difference between the two, however, was that Lewis Jones was directly of the Welsh working class and gave voice to their pain and suffering. For that reason he stands apart from all other activists and writers in that remarkable generation of self-educated working class men and women, the organic intellectuals who provided local and national leadership for communities broken by economic depression. He was *the* organic intellectual of the South Wales valleys in the inter-war period.

I suppose the people in *Cwmardy* and *We Live* have resonance for me because I feel I knew many of them. Big Jim, Len, Siân were an amalgam of many of Lewis' friends. I knew *them* too – albeit a generation later. Jack Jones, the Rhondda miners' agent, and Will Paynter, later general secretary of the NUM, were both International Brigaders, and frequent visitors to our home. Mavis Llewellyn and Annie Powell, schoolteachers and councillors both, were also well known to me because they too were my father's 'friends and comrades'. They all come alive again when I read Lewis' two novels. My first acquaintance with the novels, in the late 1960s, occurred when I was beginning my research into the Welshmen who fought fascism in Spain by joining the International Brigades. It was at this time I met Dai Smith. We read the books at the same time. Fresh from New York, he was hoping for a Joseph Conrad; I was looking for a Will Paynter. The characters for him were somewhat stereotyped; for me they were 'flesh and blood'.

The only conversation which compares with the one I had with Billy Griffiths in 1969 was one I had with Mavis Llewellyn in 1972. Lewis and Mavis had been 'close' in a way that was a problem in the puritanical communist world of the South Wales valleys in the 1930s. Mavis explained to me that when Lewis died *We Live* was incomplete. The last two chapters – 'A Party Decision' and 'A Letter from Spain' – were essentially hers, and that is why the voice is softer, more poignant, more reflective. The description of the relationship between Mary and Len is a description of their own relationship.

When in the 1970s and 1980s I wrote about the political pressures and sacrifices of those who went to Spain, and argued that there was an 'inner party conscription', my research was disputed by some in the Communist Party, but the survivors from Spain only needed to point to their tribune, Lewis Jones, for confirmation of that truth, and for confirmation of the deep and troubled circumstances that had made it true.

'The full meaning of life' is surely given in these novels.

I agree with Gwyn Thomas' words to me on the occasion of a Llafur Day School in the Rhondda which first re-launched the novels back in 1978: 'Any residual dust left from the passing of that astonishing star should be cherished.' Cult of the personality? Read the books and judge for yourself.

Hywel Francis

CWMARDY

AN EVENING IN CWMARDY

Big Jim, known to civil servants and army authorities as James Roberts, stopped abruptly and let his eyes roam over the splendour of the mountain landscape. A coat hung uncouthly from his arm and a soft breeze played on the hairy chest that showed beneath his open red-flannel shirt.

His small son, Len, stood near by wondering what had caused this sudden halt. He saw Big Jim open his mouth as if about to say something, but instead of words came a smacking sound and a large mass of tobacco-stained saliva.

The lad, whose wavy hair shadowed his sad eyes, watched the spittle twirl in the air before it fouled the grass at his feet. Len looked at the massive body that made his own feel puny while Big Jim remained pensively motionless.

Father and son remained silent for some minutes, the former looking like a Wild West desperado with the red silk scarf dangling loosely from his neck. His soap-stiffened moustaches gave him a fierce, reckless appearance which Len thought romantic.

The lad eventually grew impatient with the silence.

'What be you waiting for, dad?' he asked, his wistful eyes searching for the face that towered above him.

The plaintive voice rose to Big Jim's ears like a bubble. He looked down on his son and sighed. 'I be just thinking, Len bach,' he started, his deep voice tinged with pathos, ''bout the days long ago, when I did use to walk the fields of the North before ever I come down here to work in the pits.'

The man sighed again, bit his moustache, and sat on a little mound nearby. Len wormed his way to his father's knee, and the pair silently looked before them at the miles of undulating highland which buried itself in the shimmering haze that marked the encircling distant sea. Here and there the landscape was splashed with patches of purple heather and rich brown bracken whose blended colours stood out boldly in the telescopic clarity of the midsummer evening.

Browsing sheep languidly chewed their way from patch to patch, while larks lifted their song into the blue recesses of the sky. Even the clear air conspired to produce an aspect of tranquil serenity on the mountain top. Rising and falling in tiny semi-visible globules of heat, the air played an irresponsible hide-and-seek with the bladed grass.

The two solitary humans were affected in different ways by the pacific scene. It softly recalled to the rough, toil-scarred miner the days of his youth. But young Len had no such solid memories to be awakened. In their place he felt a vague emotional hunger that made him sad. He turned on his stomach and lay full length on the grass before his father, who was meditatively moving a huge lump of tobacco from check to cheek, occasionally spitting its gravy-like juice into the air.

The lad strained his eyes towards the distant channel. He wondered what the ships it held looked like, and vainly tried to magnify the black spots that dotted the ribbony gleam. A hoarse grunt from Big Jim brought Len to his haunches. 'Huh,' said the former, trying to twist the reveries from his mind by twirling his moustaches, 'this bit of mountain by here, Len bach, is where King Rhys did have his head chopped off.' The statement was resonant with rolling r's. Big Jim waited in confident anticipation of a comment from his son.

Len looked at him with wistful interest. 'For what did they chop his head off, dad?' he asked.

'Oh,' was Jim's slow reply, 'I be not quite sure now, boy bach, but I 'spect they did do it 'cause he was a bad man and that was the only way to bring him to his senses.'

Len thought a moment before asking, 'Well, how was he a bad man and who did chop his head off for it?'

This put Jim out of his depth, but he tried to recover the position by saying as he scratched his head, 'I don't hardly 'member now, boy bach. You see, it did happen a long time ago, ay, hundreds of years ago, and I can't pull things back to my mind these days as I used to.'

He turned the subject sharply. 'Do you see that red grass over there?' he asked, pointing a huge forefinger vaguely into the distance. Len looked into the desired direction and fancied he saw the red patch.

'Ay,' he said, 'you do mean that place where the sheep is, dad?'

'That be it. Well, by there a big battle was once fought between the Cymro and the English. A awful lot of blood was spilt that day and the grass have been red with it ever since.'

Len wanted to ask further questions, but Big Jim lifted him to his feet before they could be made articulate. 'Come,' he muttered to his son, 'it be getting late and your mam will be wondering where we be.' The pair sauntered slowly across the mountain top that was already crimsoning in the rays spread by the setting sun. Len watched the deepening hues and wondered where they went when darkness fell.

Father and son soon reached the mountain crest, where they again sat down so that the former could have another smoke before descending into the valley. Len knew his father took some time to enjoy a pipe-full of tobacco and resigned himself to the consequent wait. Lying on his stomach the lad surveyed the valley beneath.

His eyes looked down upon the belt of smoke that hung halfway up the mountain like a blanket blotting out everything beneath. The lad watched the billowing cauldron break and twist into ever-changing forms in the clutches of the evening breeze. They swirled into bubbling eddies that brought to his mind thoughts of the broth he had often seen his mother make over the open fireplace of their home.

'Look, dad,' he uttered excitedly, 'i'n't it like the cawl

mam do make if soot was to fall in it from the chimney?'

The analogy tickled Big Jim. 'Ho ho!' he guffawed. 'That be good, muniferni. When I do tell your mam what you have said her belly will shake with laughing. Ho, ho, ho!'

Len could not see the joke, and let his eyes follow the sheep-track winding its way down the mountain breast like a tortuous vein. He saw where it buried itself in the murk and hid as if ashamed of its eventual destination. It was just there, Len knew, that the grass ceased to be green.

Big Jim still showed no signs of moving, although the sun had already dipped half its red orb behind the mountain and was now sending scarlet gleams across the black blanket that was the valley's sky. Father and son gazed at the changing panorama in silence, their bodies tingling to the palpitating throb of the pit engines that came to them from below. Its vibrant rhythm broke through the air with the monotonous regularity of a ticking clock, and Len felt the vibration soak into his flesh. A muffled hum of voices muted in an incoherent chorus mingled with the throb.

For long minutes the pair lay while the glow from the dipping sun melted into the black pall and became a deeper red. At last Big Jim knocked the burning ashes from his pipe and rose to his feet. 'Come,' he commanded the entranced Len, 'I got to see Dai Cannon, my butty, so we will go down the long way, past the pits.' Len followed obediently, being always eager to get near the pit that stood at the top end of the valley.

Carefully threading their way down the steep path, they entered the belt of smoke and were soon standing at the foot of the mountain against which the grimy pit-head machinery, buildings, and gear stood out with grim grotesqueness.

Len's eyes widened at sight of the forbidding black power-houses and the lake of feeding water near them. A score of pipes with tiny holes intersected this latter and sent bubbling sprays of boiling water into the air, where each became a miniature rainbow before falling back into the lake.

Len could not take his eyes from this effervescent, sparkling cascade. 'Is all the colours in the world by there, dad?' he asked wonderingly.

Big Jim coughed and blew his nose. 'Ay, I think they all be there, boy bach,' he answered doubtfully. 'But,' he added, 'you did ought to see it first thing in the morning when the sun be rising. Ah, that be a sight for sore eyes.'

Len thought a moment before saying, 'When I grow up and start to work I will be able to see it in the morning, 'on't I, dad?'

'Ay, ay, my boy,' answered Big Jim; adding under his breath, 'When you start to work you 'on't want to see it.' Len did not hear this.

The thought of working in the pit sent ripples through his flesh and made him anxious to grow up quickly. He looked at the trellised ironwork of the pit-head frames, to which the power-houses made such an appropriate background, and sighed longingly. The gleaming rail-tracks which radiated from the pit-head down the valley towards the invisible sea seemed, in his imaginative eyes, to be like veins of quickly coursing blood. Big Jim broke into his thoughts with the command, 'Follow me, and be careful how you do tread.'

Len followed the imprints of his father's feet in the powdery coal-dust which thickly coated everything. He passed great piles of logs, some of which were covered with reddish rough bark, while others, slippery and smooth, looked indecent in their nakedness. Big Jim replied to his query on the contrast: 'Those big heavy uns, with bark, be Frenchmen. You know, those who do bring the onions every year,' he exclaimed. 'The other ones, that do look like wet sausages, be from Norway.'

Without another word the pair made their way carefully past the numerous obstacles that cluttered the colliery surface. In a short time they reached the straddling pit-frames, whose huge wheeled heads broke into the dark shadows which sat on the red-streaked haze of smoke and steam surrounding the pit-shaft.

Big Jim allowed Len to look over the little gate into the cylindrical hole that seemed to dangle like a black blob from the wire ropes that threaded it. The immensity of the drop made the lad draw his breath sharply. It was the first time he had been so near to the shaft. Big Jim said, 'Watch this now,' and spat a mouthful of saliva halfway across the shaft, where it remained suspended for a moment before beginning its twisting fall into the hole that swallowed it from sight. Len watched it as long as he could, straining his eyes to follow the falling object into the depths of the pit.

His eyes became sore, and he turned to his father to ask in an awed voice: 'How deep be it, dad?'

The latter answered casually, 'Oh, 'bout two thousand feet or thereabouts, I s'pose.'

The lad stood amazed for a moment, then asked, 'Be it the deepest pit in the world?'

'Duw, duw, no,' replied his father. 'It be the deepest about here, but there be pits, mun, that do go down for miles in some parts of the world. I 'member myself,' he continued reminiscently, 'when I was in South Africa, a pit that go down half a mile. Of course,' he added apologetically, 'it be only niggers that do work down there; us white men be the bosses.'

Len thought deeply over this as they made their way towards the long wooden bridge that separated the pits from the rest of the valley. Halfway across he stopped and looked over the parapet at the oily river far below, which noisily gurgled in angry whirlpools around every rock that stemmed its progress. 'It do look like it is quarrelling with itself,' he commented. Big Jim said nothing, but led the way over the bridge to the long wooden building near its end, one half of which was a stable and the other half the home of Dai Cannon.

The lad felt his feet sink with a squelch into the dust-blackened manure that covered the ground. The stench of this and of hot horseflesh stung his nostrils after the clean air of the mountain. He sneezed, then stretched himself and peered through the little window into the stable. The sweaty horses stamping their feet and clanging their head-chains, thrilled him. He flattened his nose on the pane to get a better view, and would have remained there indefinitely had not Big Jim shouted sharply, 'Come on, Len bach. You be hellish nosey today, in't you?'

Len reluctantly left the window and followed his father

to the doorway of the house. Jim rapped the door with his great knuckles. His knock was answered by a short, round-shouldered man with dark hair and a dough-coloured face. The heavy, drooping moustache that hung over his mouth failed to hide the thick, moist underlip. One hand was thrust down his trousers between the heavy belt and stomach, while his black-rimmed eyes gave the face a sepulchral appearance.

This was Dafydd Jones, known to all the workmen as Dai Cannon, a name given him because of his explosive eloquence. A self-taught man, he could quote the Bible chapter and verse, and although he spoke the idioms of the pit with his workmates, he possessed an extensive vocabulary that enabled him to talk on equal terms with anyone when the occasion demanded. Each Sunday he occupied the pulpit in the little tin chapel, and his rusty clothes redolent and shiny with the drippings from upturned tankards, did not detract from the pungent vehemence of his sermons.

Dai stepped into the manured roadway, where his pot-bellied rotundity and humped shoulders contrasted queerly with the erect bulk of Big Jim.

'Huh,' he grunted, 'I had give you up and was thinking to prepare my sermon for next Sunday. S'pose I will have to leave it there now that you have come at last.' Jim gruffly started to explain the delay, but Dai airily brushed him aside with the remark: 'Tut, tut. Don't waste your breath, mun, you will want it later on.'

He invited Jim and Len into the wooden shack while he put his coat on, but the former refused. 'Me and Len will

11

wait by here,' he declared. Dai did not argue the matter but went inside and shortly returned with his coat on.

The queerly contrasting trio then made their way to Main Street, that led from the pits down the hill to the village of Cwmardy. Main Street was the shopping and social centre of the village that had grown with the pits. It contained the few shops, the numerous chapels, and the three drinking dens that the village boasted of. The turreted church was jostled on one side by the police station and on the other by the Boar's Head public house. There were no pavements, and the roads in winter were slimy with black mud, while during the summer they were heavy with powdered coal-dust.

Len had to quicken the pace of his short legs to keep up with his father and Dai. The occasional people they passed with a sibilant 'Nos da' salutation looked like black shadows in the deepening dusk of the unlit street. For some distance the three walked in silence before Dai muttered: 'It do look as if they 'on't clear that fall for another couple of days, Jim.' Len pricked his ears interestedly. Talk of the pits and work always excited him.

'No,' replied Big Jim morosely, 'and no bloody wonder. I never seen such a fall in all my born days. It come down like water, and nothing on earth could ever stop it. I was 'specting every minute to see the grass from the mountain mixed up in the stones.'

Dai grunted acquiescence and added, 'Ah well, it's a bad boot that have got no leather at all. You will be able to take the old 'ooman out and make up for what you done at the school opening yesterday.'

12

Big Jim stopped and looked down at his mate in amazement. 'Well, muniferni,' he grunted, 'that be a dirty back-hander! After me saving you and Bill Bristol from simpling yourselves before all those people, you do turn round and blame me! Huh,' he spat into the road, 'that be the thanks a man do get for looking after his butties.'

Dai said nothing to the charge made against him, and the three proceeded on their way without further conversation until they reached the village square, in the centre of which was a brick structure known as the Fountain, although the only water it ever held was that which fell on it from the clouds.

One corner of the Square was occupied by the general stores and bakehouse of Mr. Evans Cardi, while on the opposite side of the street stood the shop of Ben the Barber. This was where the villagers shed their hair and their viewpoints. It was the local parliament, where the problems of the pit and the village were debated by the miners.

Ben the Barber welcomed everyone to his shop. He had a tongue as sharp as his razors and delighted in provoking arguments among the men. This was not a difficult task, and Ben participated in the numerous debates with a kind of gleeful vindictiveness, pouncing with cunning skill upon all weak points.

Big Jim and Dai remained outside this shop for a little while before the former bent down to Len and asked, 'Be you 'fraid to go home by yourself, Len bach?' The lad looked at the dark opening at the side of the general stores. It led up the mountain at right angles to Main Street until it reached the eight houses called Sunny Bank.

It was in one of these houses that Big Jim and his family lived. To Len the tiny twinkling lights from the windows looked like faraway stars.

He swallowed a nervous lump that had risen in his throat before replying, 'No, dad, I be not afraid to go up by myself if you will wait by here till I be halfway.'

'Good lad,' replied Big Jim, digging his hand deep into his trousers pocket. 'Here, take this ha'penny and me and Dai will wait till we know that you be safe.' Without another word Len turned and started his way up the hill. The darkness swallowed him before he had taken ten strides.

Big Jim and his friend waited in silence until they heard a shrill long-drawn shout, 'I be all right now, dad. So long.' Satisfied, both turned and walked into Ben the Barber's.

The echoes of Len's voice had hardly died in the night when its stillness was broken by another, harsh and piercing: 'Len-n-n,' it wailed, 'where be you? Come to your mam quick.'

The lad recognised his mother's voice. 'I be coming, mam,' he shouted back reassuringly.

In a few minutes he reached the doorway of the house, where his mother awaited him, her head wrapped in a heavy woollen shawl. She had been on the point of searching for him when his voice reached her as he shouted to his father. She now caught the lad fussily to her and hurried him indoors. Here she removed the shawl that hid her haggard face and big-boned body, with its slightly stooping shoulders. Care-dulled eyes made her look older than she really was.

Len sat on the chair facing his sister, who was toasting

14

bread before the open fire. 'Where have you been so long, Len bach?' asked his mother, her usually harsh voice now soft and husky. 'Mam have been awful worried 'bout you.' Len told her of the trip round the mountain and the pits. When he had finished the recital she asked sharply, 'Where did your father go after you did leave him?'

'They went into Ben the Barber's,' replied Len, 'and dad did say he 'ood'n't be long.'

'Long, indeed,' Siân snorted; 'it is time for every decent man who do think anything of his fambly to be in his own house this time of the night. Much he do think of his home and his children,' she went on with rising temper, 'to leave a little innocent boy like you to come up the black hill by yourself. How do he know,' she demanded of no one in particular, 'that you have not fall into the gutter and broked your little neck? Huh! Call hisself a father indeed!'

Len said nothing. He looked at Jane, his sister, five years older than himself. Even in the candlelight she had a vague charm. Her fair, clustering hair enhanced the brightness of her eyes and the paleness of her thin face. Jane was her parents' first-born. She now rose to her feet and pulled the toasted bread off the fork, saying to her mother, 'There now, mam fach, don't upset yourself. Dad will be home all right. Now jest sit down while I do make supper for you.'

Len watched her take down the ill-assorted dishes from the huge box-like dresser that hid one side of the small kitchen. The cracked mirror in its centre grinned at the candlelight. One of the three shelves which constituted the dresser was filled with loose fortnightly volumes of 'The

15

History of the Boer War'. These, despite their finger-soiled pages and torn covers, were sacred to the family. No visitor could leave the house without first being shown the three separate places in which the name of Big Jim was mentioned.

Big Jim had joined the militia just prior to Jane's birth and immediately the Boer War was declared had volunteered for active service, becoming batman to an officer whom he always declared to be a certain general.

Siân, left to take care of young Jane the best she could, washed and sewed clothes for other people. When Jim returned she had a home of sorts awaiting him, but the toil and worry of this period had left ineffaceable marks upon her body and her temper. Strong-willed and faithful, she was proud of the fact that her people belonged to the valley before the pits were ever thought of.

Jim had courted her with whirlwind impetuosity, his magnificent body sweeping away all her preconceived notions of love-making. Many people asserted that he ran away to the war to escape from Jane, the consequence of his courtship, but Jim always repudiated the suggestion with indignation and offered to fight anyone who repeated it.

After his return from the war Siân often begged him to 'clean' her by marriage, but he always evaded this issue by asserting that the children tied him to her with stronger bonds than any marriage lines. Siân, however, never accepted this plea. She never tired of reminding him that he had 'dirtied' her and was not man enough to do the right thing in the eyes of God. Big Jim, arrogant and tempestuous, feared nothing on earth except Siân in her tantrums.

Len waited patiently for his supper. He crouched nearer the large open fireplace that sent heat up the chimney and smoke into the kitchen. At last supper was ready, and the three drew their chairs to the table.

Meanwhile Big Jim and Dai Cannon had entered the shop of Ben the Barber. The lather boy, Charlie the Cripple, smiled widely at their appearance. The lad, being more or less a prisoner because of his disability, enjoyed the company of adults, and liked nothing better than to listen to the older wags exchanging reminiscences of the days when the valley was a place of wooded beauty with just one street, Sunny Bank, looking down upon it.

Charlie would sigh when the old men lauded the green-plastered slopes now buried beneath monstrous conical masses of pit residue. Some of them remembered the sewer-impregnated river, shining with oily outpourings from the pit, when it was a sparkling stream nursing trout in its cobbled bed. These tales were romance to the crippled lad, but he also liked to listen to the boisterous breeziness of Big Jim's quaintly spoken English.

Everyone in the crowded and smoke-filled room moved up when the newcomers entered. Ben the Barber paused, holding an open razor over the lathered face of Will Smallbeer. When the pair were seated Ben coughed before saying, as he went on shaving his customer, 'To continue where I left off when we were interrupted, stupid as you workmen are, you nevertheless provide the real power in the world today. I know,' he added quickly, his sharp, thin voice rising when he saw Dai Cannon squirming on the bench, 'that no one looking at your dull faces would

17

believe this. But there, seeing is not always believing.'

Will Smallbeer rubbed his nose vigorously with the back of his hand. 'What in hell be you talking about, mun?' he croaked hoarsely. 'Do you mean to tell us that old T.I. Williams, the coalowner, who have now been made Lord Cwmardy, have got no power or brains? Tut! Where be your bloody sense, mun? Look at Mr. Hicks, our general manager. Do you say that he be not a clever man? Huh! Where be the power of a man who do work in the pit all the week and then haven't got 'nough to have couple of pints on a Saturday after he pay his lodgings? Huh!' he snorted in conclusion and with a triumphant glance around. 'If you do call that bloody sense, I give in.'

Ben turned to Dai Cannon with a sneering smile. 'There,' he said, 'the oracle has spoken and he's knocked you all flat.'

Dai knew the symptoms and accepted the challenge. He gave a retching cough, wiped the product into the sanded floor with his boot, then spoke in a ponderous voice. 'Power and brains are not the monopoly of any people or class,' he said. 'We must admit there are some brains among the masters, and certainly a lot of power, but there are also brains with some of the workmen, although they have no power. Take myself or Ezra Jones, our leader,' he went on. 'Both of us are workmen and both of us are clever. This doesn't mean, however, that all workmen or all masters are clever. You have only to look at Will Smallbeer to see that.'

The latter jumped to his feet with a snarl. 'Don't you try to simple a better man than yourself can ever be,' he shouted. Little lumps of saliva mixed with the lather on his moustache.

'I might look a bit twp to you beggars,' he continued, 'but I can hold my own with any of you in the pit.'

Big Jim immediately bridled up at this. He was regarded as the strongest and best-skilled man in the pit, and took pride in the fact. 'What nonsense you be talking, Will bach,' he growled patronisingly. 'Why, mun, I could work the hands off ten men like you any bloody day, muniferni, and you do all know it well. There be no man in Cwmardy can take a tool out of my hands.'

Ben swept his razor across the strop as if he was slicing a man's head off. 'Huh,' he grunted. 'Hark at the brains oozing out! There'll be a hell of a mess on my floor after this unless you're more careful. Here you are, bragging how clever you are, and all you can brag about is how much work you do. Ha-ha! Not a word about the money you get for your work! Now I know why you come to me on Sunday mornings for a haircut and shave on tick. It's men like you the masters want. Give them men with brains from their shoulders down and they have no need for any brains themselves. Ha-ha! Huh, you make me sick.' Saying which he spat contemptuously on the floor.

There was silence for a while after this outburst before Bill Bristol, his thin face quivering, took up the argument. 'There be'ant no need to get excited,' he declared. 'To me it seems us have got to have masters and us have got to have workmen. Without masters us cawn't have pits, without pits us cawn't have wages, and without wages us cawn't have beer and baccy and grub. That's how I see the business,' he concluded. The argument continued for some time longer until Big Jim and Dai left to make their way

19

across the road to the Boar's Head.

Long before his father had left the beer-stenched bar Len was curled up in the bed he shared with Jane. He watched her slowly undressing, his own small body hidden beneath the bedclothes. In many ways he was a queer lad for his age. He had neither the physique nor the desire to participate in the boisterous games of the neighbouring boys. His greatest pal was Jane and his greatest pleasure he found in the occasional rambles over the mountain with his father. Apart from this, his natural tendency to introspection made him seek solitude, where he could allow his vivid imagination to wander without interruption.

These practices made him older than his years, and he thought more than he spoke. He was, however, devoted to his parents. He loved and respected his mother's quaint, affectionate firmness and thought his father only one step removed from God and Bob Fitzsimmons the fighter.

As he watched Jane undressing his mind again traversed the mountains. He wondered how many were really killed in the battle his father had mentioned, and if it were true that the grass was dyed with blood ever since. Drowsily he moved up for Jane and nestled closely to her warm body. Imperceptibly he floated from thought to thought until he was suddenly brought back to the bedroom by a loud rattle at the front door. He sprang to his haunches in alarm, but lay down again when he heard his mother patter to the door to open it for Big Jim.

Jim looked worried and irritable as he made his way past Siân into the kitchen. He sat heavily on the stool near the fire and looked around slowly. The flickering candlelight sent hot grease down the sides of the brass holder. The dimness got on Jim's nerves.

'I'n't there no oil in the house, Siân bach,' he asked, 'that you have got to use corpse lights?' Siân paid no heed to his surly question. In a short while he continued, 'Here I be in the dark of the pit all day and now I can't get light in my own house. Muniferni! No wonder men do go to the 'sylum before their time.' He spat into the fire. Siân heard the spittle sizzle in the flames.

A few minutes' silence followed before Jim asked, 'Where be our Jane? Out gallivanting, I s'pose,' he answered himself.

Siân replied sharply, 'No, she be not out. The gel is in bed where you ought to be long ago instead of sitting on your backside in other people's places, then coming home here full of grunts.'

She paused a moment, swallowed hard, then went on with increasing bitterness. 'That's how all you men be. Always thinking of your own comforts. Never do you think of me, slaving my fingers to the bone trying to keep the children tidy and the house clean.'

Jim made no reply. He was sorry now for what he had said, because he knew Siân was getting into her stride. He stretched his long body towards the table and picked up a piece of toast. Before he could recover his position the stool overbalanced and he lay ignominiously on the sanded floor with his head under the table. This was too much for his dignity. 'Arglwydd mawr, fenyw!' he roared as he scrambled to his feet. 'Be you trying to kill me or what, pulling the stool from under me like that? Do you think I be a crot of a boy to be played with, eh?'

21

Siân gave him a blistering glare before muttering in a gloomy tone, as if she were pronouncing a curse: 'Sure as God is your judge, James, you will be sorry for your words one day. You sit by there like a great bear and do not move a finger to help me or yourself. Not satisfied with this, when you be too drunk to sit on the stool you put the blame on me for falling off it. Ach,' she continued, her voice rising higher with every sentence, 'out all night I ought to leave you. That 'ood be good enough for the likes of you. Fine man you be, indeed, to rear a fambly of children who haven't got a shirt to their little backs while you do spend your money in the public house and put silks and satins on that slut of a landlady.'

Big Jim shook his head at this sneer and started to plead. 'Leave me alone, Siân bach,' he begged; 'don't go on to me no more now.'

'Don't go on to you, indeed,' retorted Siân, continuing her indictment. 'Oh, God bach,' she wailed into the air 'what for did I ever take a man like this? Here I be, day in and day out, trying to rear my children clean and 'spectable so that no one can point a finger at them, and after it all this lout do bring disgrace and shame on us all. Oh dear, dear, what have I done?' She turned to Big Jim with flashing eyes. 'Pity the good Lord didn't strike you dead when you was in Africa!' she cried.

Her last words brought tears to Len's eyes. He heard no more after this and knew his father had fallen to sleep in the chair. The lad cuddled closer to Jane and was himself asleep when Siân crept upstairs for blankets with which to cover her snoring spouse.

Her naked feet squashed the black beetles that plastered the kitchen floor at night, but she paid no heed to these as she again ascended the stairs to her bedroom.

LEN GOES
TO SCHOOL

Len woke earlier than usual next morning. He sat up in bed and shook Jane by the shoulder. 'Come, Jane,' he said, 'I've got to start school today and it be time for us to get up.'

Jane slowly shook the sleep from her eyes in response to his request. She rose and dressed while he remained squatting in bed. When she had finished they both proceeded downstairs, Len clad only in his shirt. The contact of the cold stone stairs with his bare feet sent shivers up his spine, and he was glad to get near the kitchen fire. Big Jim and Siân were already down, the latter busily preparing breakfast.

Halfway through the meal Big Jim, his mouth full of toasted bread, muttered to Len: 'Well, boy bach, you be a big man today, starting school, eh?' The lad merely nodded his head in reply. He was not over-excited at the prospect of attending the school which had been built across the gutter that separated Sunny Bank from the village. He had spent much of his time in this gutter, driving tunnels into its sides at the risk of his life under the impression that he was acting like a collier. Or sometimes, for a change, he had transformed the hole into a 'tent', by simply putting a piece of sacking across its mouth, and on these occasions he would peer carefully through the sacking to look for imaginary Red Indians.

During the winter, snow often filled the gutter, and Len loved to impress his 'photo' in its soft, alluring surface by lying prostrate in the snow with his arms and legs spread-eagled. This made him soaking wet, a fact that disturbed Siân much more than it did her son, but all her pleadings and threats had failed to rob the lad of this exquisite pleasure, and now the school had effaced his beloved gutter.

After breakfast Jane helped Len to dress in the new velvet suit specially bought for the occasion. The blue material showed up the boyishness of his long face and clustering brown hair. Siân's eyes filled with tears as she looked at the lad. Pride in her son quickened the beats of her heart and, turning to Big Jim, she remarked: 'Duw. Our boy do look fine today, don't he, James bach?'

'Ay,' replied her spouse. 'He do that, my gel. But what can you expect from the son of Big Jim, eh?' And twirling his moustaches arrogantly, he continued: 'Some day you will be so good a man as your father, Len bach, and that be saying something, i'n't it, Siân?' turning to his partner.

The flattery helped to lift Len out of his despondent mood, and his spirits became more in accord with the boisterous excitement of the other lads who accompanied him down the hill for the first day at the new school. His dislike of the building that had robbed him of the pleasures of the gutter was permeated with a faint curiosity. He wondered what would be expected of him in the school. But neither Jane nor any or the inhabitants could enlighten him, because this was the valley's first school.

When Len reached the schoolyard he was paraded with the other children and marched into the classroom. He was surprised to find girls present. This possibility had never entered his mind, and the fact made him resentful, an emotion which increased when he found that the teacher was young woman who did not look much older than Jane.

The lad was told to sit at the same desk as Ron, the son of Mr. Evans Cardi, who, as Len later found out, was about the same age as himself. But all resemblance between the two lads ended there. Ron was robust, ruddy, and well-fed. He kept boasting to Len with boyish candour that his father only intended him to remain at the school until he was old enough to go to college. Len was suitably thrilled at this information, although he had not the slightest idea what a college was. His initial nervousness had evaporated in the bright freshness of the classroom, with its interesting pictures of battles and kings.

During the days that passed Len took a greater interest in his classmates. Among them was one who particularly attracted his attention. Her sombre eyes, frail body, and dark, wavy hair fascinated him, and he discovered that she was Mary, the daughter of Ezra Jones, the miners' leader in Cwmardy.

In the months that followed Len proved he had a capacity for absorbing his lessons. He was particularly fond of history, and revelled in the stories of the conquest of India and America by the British. But nothing gave him greater pleasure than to read and hear of the Boer War. He felt he had a living link with this through his father. His natural quickness soon took him ahead of the other pupils with the exception of Mary, who in a quiet, unobtrusive way, seemed to devour the lessons and tenaciously retain all the knowledge she gathered. The mutual mental alertness brought the two youngsters into closer bonds of friendship, and often, accompanied by Ron, they spent the evenings after school hours scouring the mountains for birds' nests. Sometimes the two lads failed to present themselves for school although they had left home for this purpose, and on such occasions they would go for long rambles through the murk of the valley into the clear air of the country a few miles away.

Once away from the valley and the school Len and Ron, with boyish exuberance, thrilled to the joys of exploration. The fact they were missing school without their parents' knowledge or consent put an edge to the pleasure they found in exploring the many noisy little streams. Sometimes they caught little tiddlers which they proudly imagined were trout, and with a kind of patronising pride they always showed these to Mary, who refused to accompany them on their illicit expeditions.

One day, unknown to Len, the schoolmaster sent for Siân, who, donning her woollen shawl, obeyed the request with some trepidation. At the school gates she paused awhile to gather her breath before entering, her mind full of queries.

It appeared that the master had been waiting for Siân, because immediately she knocked at the door he opened it for her. 'Good day, Mrs. Roberts,' he said, his face grimmer than usual. 'Come in.' The manner of his invitation increased Siân's nervousness. She sensed that it had something to do with Len, but had no idea what it could be.

After ushering Siân to the chair opposite the master seated himself at the desk and immediately came to the point. 'I have asked you down, Mrs. Roberts,' he said, 'to discuss Len, your son.'

Siân stiffened a little in the chair, but made no reply. 'Yes,' he went on, 'I am very worried about him.' He looked at her quizzically for a moment before saying: 'I hope I am right in believing that you want him to be a good scholar and a credit to yourself, his father, and the school, Mrs. Roberts?'

The flustered woman nodded her head dumbly. 'I thought so,' asserted the master; 'and, this being the fact, I cannot understand why Len loses school so often.'

Siân bridled up immediately at this. 'Lose school?' she asked incredulously. 'Who do say my boy lose school? Why, he be here every day like a clock ever since he started. Huh! Be very careful what you do say, my man! 'Member there be still a law, even for the poor.'

Mr. Vincent, the master, was taken aback for a moment by this indignant outburst. When he had recovered he tried to placate her. 'Now, now, Mrs. Roberts,' he exclaimed, 'there is no need to get excited or angry. You have confirmed my suspicions that Len has been absenting himself from school without your knowledge.'

Siân's lower jaw dropped in astonishment, but after some seconds she snapped her teeth together. 'I don't believe my boy 'ood do such a thing,' she asserted definitely. 'I 'oodn't believe no man, not even if he went down on his bended knees before my eyes.'

There could be no mistaking that all argument would be futile, and the schoolmaster said no more. He rose and left the room. In a very short time he returned with Len at his side, obviously frightened. Siân drew the lad to her and both of them stood facing Mr. Vincent. Len looked scared, but his mother's whole demeanour was defiant. 'Well,' she demanded, 'what do you want, now you have got my boy here?'

Mr. Vincent looked at Len. His eyes were hard and cold. 'Tell your mother,' he said, 'where you were yesterday.' Len shuddered at the question and his face went white. The silence became heavy and the room oppressive to mother and son. Siân's eyes misted during the prolonged silence, but her cheek muscles twitched although no word was said till Mr. Vincent instructed Len to go back to the classroom. The boy shivered coldly as the door closed behind him. Slowly, with his head bent, he took his seat in the class, blind to the eyes that stared at him curiously.

At the first opportunity Ron whispered, 'What was the matter, Len?'

'It is about our mitching from school yesterday,' the downcast Len replied. 'My mother is in the master's room.'

Ron chuckled, 'Yes, I know,' he said, 'the master was in our house last night, but my father told him not to worry because I wouldn't be here much longer.'

This was small consolation to Len, who was conjecturing what was happening between his mother and the master. He paid little attention to what the teacher was saying during the next ten minutes, but lifted his head with a start when he heard the door open.

Mr. Vincent stood framed in the doorway, his face grim and hard. He carried a long cane in his hands, the sight of which fascinated Len. He wondered if his mother had gone home, and hope kindled in his heart as he thought she might have remained in the master's room.

The boy hardly heard the harsh command, 'Len Roberts, come out here. Let the whole class see you.' When he responded, he seemed to rise from his seat without personal volition, and equally automatic was his stride as he walked to the front of the class. Something cold clutched at his heart. He knew with increasing certainty that he was about to be punished before all his schoolmates.

Never in his life had he been physically beaten, and the immediate probability that it was about to happen appalled him. Only five yards separated him from the master who had become his tormentor, but it appeared five years to the lad as he slowly walked forward. He tried to shout for his mother, but no sound left his mouth. His face was strained and set when at last he reached the master's side, who turned him round to face the class. Len kept his head down, and Mr. Vincent began to address the pupils.

'You see before you,' he said, 'a boy who has lied to his mother, not in words but in deeds. He led her to believe he was coming to school when he already knew he had no intention of doing so.' The silence in the classroom was made more deadly by the sharp voice.

'What can you think of a boy who deludes his best friend, his mother?' the master went on remorselessly. Each word stung Len like a lash. He felt they were unfair and untrue. All he had done was in a spirit of adventure, with no thought of lying, and the consciousness of this steeled him and determined him not to cry.

As Mr. Vincent went on, 'A boy who can do a thing like this will grow up a vagabond and a man without honour unless he is checked in time,' Len looked at Mary, and her eyes seemed to shine with disbelief as she returned his glance.

The master ended his homily with the words, 'Hold your hand out, Roberts,' and Len dazedly did as he was bade, his eyes fixed on the rising cane.

He saw it suddenly stop ascending and heard it swish as it swept down upon his outstretched hand. Without conscious thought he withdrew his hand a split second before the cane reached it. The stick met Mr. Vincent's shin-bone with a resounding thwack, and he clutched the injured limb. Suddenly Ron began laughing, and in a few seconds all the children in the room had followed suit. The teacher vainly shouted for order, fluttering between the seats and cuffing everyone who came within her reach, but Len remained standing, aghast at what he had done. He looked apologetically at Mr. Vincent as the latter continued to rub his leg. Then suddenly, without a word of warning, the master began to slash the cane across the boy's face, heedless of where the blows fell.

The children's laughter died as suddenly as it had started. Each of them watched with increasing childish horror the flash of the quivering cane as it rose, to fall in quicker and heavier slashes. Mary rose to her feet and shouted, 'Stop it, you coward! Hit someone as big as yourself.'

After the first unexpected blow on his face, Len bent his head, only to feel the back of his neck burn with the next slash of the cane. Spontaneously his hands went to his head. The burning pain spread from his neck to his knuckles, and in a short time his whole body felt as if it were on fire. Whimpering and only half-conscious of what he was doing, Len staggered about in an effort to escape the twirling cane. 'Oh, mam, mam,' he shouted, 'come and stop him! He's killing me!' In the pain of the blows he failed to see Mary fling an ink bottle at Mr. Vincent. It caught him behind the ear, and the ink spattered all over his face and collar. Spluttering with anger, the master stopped chastising Len, and slowly wiping his hand over his face, looked around at the class. Every pupil sat motionless and every eye looked straight in front. Mr. Vincent started forward towards the boy nearest him, hesitated a moment, then, without another word or glance, left the room.

Immediately the master had left the children jumped on the seats and desks, singing and shouting, and it was a considerable time before the harassed teacher could restore quiet. Throughout the hubbub, however, Len remained silent. He was wondering if his mother had authorised the beating, and the very suspicion, although it was unfounded, hardened the lad and determined him to say nothing to his family. He felt he was doubly hurt, by the cane and by his mother, for before he left the school for home he was firmly convinced that his mother knew what the master had done, and the thought stung him much more than the cane.

Len's mother did not speak to him that night, and he went to bed earlier than usual. His mind was a turmoil of emotions that kept him turning and tossing for hours. He saw the school in a new light. It had become a monster that was going to rob him of his mountain rambles and the free existence he was accustomed to, and memory of the hiding he had received filled him with a hot resentment. For hours his brain was confused with conflicting thoughts, until imperceptibly they became focused on chains. He saw chains all round him. They seemed to hold him down and fetter his every movement, and he broke into perspiration. He thought of books. They floated before his eyes through the links in the chains, in a multiplicity of shapes and colours, and he saw in the open, flashing pages pictures of ships and engines, cowboys and kings. The fast-moving leaves slowed down and changed to canes. Long, sinewy sticks that bent and twanged. They fell on his back with stinging slashes at each of which they quivered and hummed with laughter. He jumped up in bed shouting, 'Oh Mam, mam, stop him. He will kill me!'

Siân rushed into his bedroom and caught him in her arms. 'There, there, boy bach,' she crooned into his ear, 'don't cry no more at those old dreams. Mam be with you, and you can venture you be safe so long as her eyes be open.' She remained with the lad till he fell asleep.

In the weeks that followed Len came to hate the school and everything connected with it. Despite this, at the end of the first year he shared top place with Mary. He read his report sheet to his parents that evening.

Big Jim and Siân were rather awed by this educational achievement of their son. Jim prophesied that one day Len be a 'big scholar.'

'Ay,' replied Siân, 'I knowed that before he started school. Let us hope he 'ont forget his poor old mam and dad when he be up in the world.'

Jim snorted at this. He regarded it as a reflection upon himself. 'What?' he exclaimed. 'Think you that the son of Jim the Big will ever forget his people and his butties? Never on your life, my gel.'

Siân looked at him sharply, then said, 'You do know full well, James, that my words did have no such meaning as you do put into them. But there,' she added, 'talking to you be like talking to a sledge. I do only waste my time by saying anything to you.'

She turned to Len before the surprised Jim could reply. 'You must keep pitching in, my boy,' she told him; 'then perhaps one day you will win a scholarship and go to college like Ron, although his father be paying for him.'

Len looked at her with alarm in his eyes. 'No, mam,' he said slowly, 'I don't want to go to any schools after I finish this one. What I want is to go to work with dad in the pit as soon as I be old enough.'

'That be the spirit!' declared Jim. Siân only sighed.

THE CHAPEL
EXCURSION
TO THE SEASIDE

Usually on Sundays Jane woke Len early. The whole family, with the exception of Big Jim, regularly attended the service in the little tin chapel at the end of the street on the Sabbath. The services were conducted by Dai Cannon, and Len enjoyed them.

He liked to see the preacher's moustaches quiver as he thundered of blood and brimstone. It was known to all the villagers that Dai's sermons were always better and his vehemence greater the more beer he had consumed on the Saturday night.

His lurid language and flowing eloquence always lifted his listeners into ecstasies of fervour, which found vent in the singing of hymns. The blended harmony of the voices gave Len special pleasure, although the hymns often saddened him.

One Sunday at the conclusion of the service, Mr. Evans Cardi, who was the senior deacon, announced that the chapel anniversary fell during the following week.

'We expect,' he stated, in his ponderous manner, 'that all our brothers and sisters with their children will attend for the procession through the streets. We shall take our collecting boxes with us and all the money we gather will go towards our excursion to the seaside in the summer.'

This announcement was received with great excitement by the congregation. During the few days that remained before the anniversary the womenfolk patched and cleaned their dresses in readiness. Those who could afford it bought new ones.

When the great day arrived Siân arrayed herself in the black cape she had bought twenty years before. This and Big Jim's 'best suit' were only brought from their hiding-place in the box under the bed for special events. Jane dressed herself in a flower-patterned linen frock whose simplicity set off the firm beauty of her body. Excitement put a colour in her cheeks and a glow in her eyes that outdid the colours in her dress.

The two women, Len accompanying them, made their way to the little chapel, where most of the other people were already gathered in little groups, chatting and slyly eyeing the dresses of the newcomers.

Len's inquisitive eyes were immediately attracted to the great silk banner that rested against the wall. Imprinted in yellow on its scarlet background was the representation of an angel looking with piteous eyes upon a box that looked like a horse trough. Above this touching scene were the words 'Cwmardy Primitive Methodist Church' and beneath it 'Glory be to God.'

The preliminaries were soon completed. Four young men took the banner and carried it to the front. Dai Cannon and the deacons fell in immediately behind, followed by the remainder of the congregation. The procession of brightly clothed figures made a pretty sight as it slowly wound its way round the village. In each street it stopped and sang hymns to the people who filled the doorways, and who always gave liberally to the collectors when they came round after the singing.

Before the procession had gone far the light frocks and pinafores were soiled and smudged in the smoke-infested atmosphere. But no one paid any attention to this, least of all Len and Ron, who walked together.

Having circled all the streets in the village, the procession made its way towards the long drive which led to the Big House where Mr. Hicks, the general manager of the pits, lived. This was in the centre of a wooded patch on the mountain breast. It overlooked the valley and the pits. Lord Cwmardy had originally built it for his own use, but had let it as the official residence of the pit manager after his own elevation to the peerage.

Len looked in amazement at the huge house, with its verandas and rolling lawns. He was intrigued by the lake that glistened a little lower down in the grounds.

'I wonder if ships could sail on that?' he asked Ron.

'Of course they can,' replied the latter in a contemptuous whisper, 'it's over a hundred feet deep. I know because my father told me.'

They had no time for further conversation before the signal was given and the choristers lifted their voices to the lilting hymn which always saddened Len. Mr. Hicks' housekeeper and a number of young people listened from the veranda to the singing. When several tunes had been sung the housekeeper flung down a shilling and ceremoniously shepherded her charges into the house.

On the way home Len heard one of the men who had carried the banner say to his mate: 'Stingy old cow! She's well in with Hicks, and I bet he gave her more than that, only the mean bitch kept it for herself.' Len edged away from the conversation.

Big Jim was awaiting them when they arrived home. He had supper already laid. Anniversary day was the only one in the year when he regarded it as an obligation upon himself to remain in and watch the house. Although he never went to chapel himself he had a deep respect for the opinions of those who did, which was one of the reasons why he was so attached to Dai Cannon.

The long trudge had tired Len, and he was not sorry when bedtime came and he ascended the stairs with Jane. The fatigue left him when he lay down and the excitement of the day began to quicken his blood. He watched Jane undressing. His eyes shone with unusual interest. For the first time he consciously noticed that Jane's breasts were different from his, and wondered why this was so. He knew his mother had big breasts because he had seen them when she was suckling the little brother who had since died of fits. But this did not solve the problem that was now consuming Len. Jane had not had a baby like his mother, yet her breasts were big.

When the young girl came into bed he cuddled up to her, and soon fell to sleep with his hand on her bosom and his mind full of queries.

The spring imperceptibly floated into summer and the day for the chapel excursion drew nearer. The children became restless with excitement. Siân had insisted that Big Jim should remain home from work on this day 'out of respect to the chapel and the children' as she cogently remarked to him. There had been no argument against this, and the whole family became embroiled in the preparations. Siân did the necessary patching, sewing, washing, and pressing. Jane cleaned the house from top to bottom, including the rarely used parlour. Big Jim slyly put aside each week little sums of money of which Siân knew nothing.

Len failed to sleep the night preceding the eagerly awaited day, and responded immediately Siân called him at six o'clock. Excitedly shaking Jane before leaving the bed, he hurried downstairs, where he found his mother preparing breakfast while Big Jim shaved. The latter was nearly bent in two trying to catch a glimpse of his face in the tiny cracked mirror which was the only one in the house.

During breakfast Big Jim kept on making humorous remarks. 'It's a lovely fine day for the 'scursion,' he said, looking out of the window at the sun trying to force its way through the clouds of smoke and dust from the pits. 'Like old times,' he added turning to Siân, 'when you and me was courting, eh? Ha-ha!' He laughed happily. 'Do you 'member the outings we used to have then, Siân bach?' he asked. Before she could reply he turned to Jane and Len with the remark, 'Them was the days. Never will be any like them again. Your mam was worth looking at then.' He caught Siân's eyes and hurriedly continued, 'Not that she be bad looking now, mind you. Only in those days she did have your wavy hair, Len, and her face was 'xactly like Jane's do look now. Eh? What say you, Siân bach?' he inquired.

The latter said nothing, although the subtle flattery brought a gleam to her tired eyes.

After breakfast Jim made his way towards the stairs with a mumbled, 'Well, I 'spose I must go up the bedroom now to fetch my best boots.' His attempt to appear casual was hopelessly lost in the mumbled words.

Siân hastily interjected, 'No, no, James bach. There be no need for you to go up. Jane will fetch the boots for you.'

Jim gave her a scared look, then pulled himself together to say with heavy dignity: 'What think you I be, fenyw? Think you I do want a crot of a gel to tend on me? No, thank you, I will manage to tend on myself.' He proceeded up the stairs while Siân put the finishing touches to Len's dressing and Jane cleared the table.

Some little time later, when they were all ready, a noise overhead reminded them that Big Jim was still upstairs. Siân flurriedly called out: 'Come on, James. You be a long time putting on your boots, i'n't you? We will be late unless you do hurry up.' A wicked little pucker twisted her mouth when she added as an afterthought: 'You haven't lost anything, have you?'

Back came the answer in a gruff, shaking rumble: 'Lost, muniferni? Lost? What think you I have got to lose, fenyw?'

The shuffling went on for a little time longer, and Siân was on her way up the stairs when they heard Jim slowly and heavily descending. His white face was haggard when he entered the kitchen and the ends of his moustache drooped pitifully. The buoyant spirits that had preceded his entry into the bedroom had been left there.

No one said a word as Siân straightened his tie and brushed the dust from the knees of his best trousers. Jim submitted meekly, although the flesh on his cheeks twitched as if invisible strings were drawing it into tiny knots. Little drops of perspiration dripped from his chin on to the high collar, which he had only worn as a special concession to maintain the dignity of the family in the eyes of the chapel deacons.

Having made all ready, Siân took a final look around the kitchen. Satisfied with what she saw, she dug her hand into the bosom of her dress and pulled out a purse. Carefully concealing its contents from Big Jim, she withdrew some silver, which she handed him with the remark: 'Here, take this, James bach, not for you to go 'bout with your finger in your mouth today.'

Jim looked at the money in his hand. His eyes were bulged and glassy. A deep suspicion began to shape in his mind that this was the money he had been looking for but failed to find. He half opened his mouth as if about to say something, then closed it again with an audible snap.

Swallowing back the lump in his throat, he caught Len by the hand and gruffly said, 'Come on or we will lose the train.'

It was over two miles to the little railway station, but the little family, each one consumed with different thoughts and emotions, covered the distance before they were aware of it.

At the station they fell into the long queue of people who were slowly filing past the two chapel deacons at the doorway, who exchanged their vouchers for tickets.

Big Jim kept mumbling to himself at the delay. Siân asked, 'What be the matter with you, mun? Do you 'spect the deacons to deal special with you and let you go on in front of all the people who have been here before you?'

Big Jim made no reply other than to glance at her with glaring eyes. Siân took no notice of his surliness.

She caught Len's hand and bent down to murmur in his ear, 'Your father be in a awful state all of a sudden, i'n't he?'

Len had noticed nothing out of the way but answered, 'Perhaps he be bad, mam.' Siân chuckled wickedly at this.

In a short time they passed the deacons and entered the little hut which was the railway station. It was packed with people, bags, and baskets. Each family carried its own provisions for the day. The excitement in the crowded room affected the little children. The bigger ones laughed and chattered, while the babies struggled and cried in the woollen shawls which held them to their mothers' bodies. Numerous breasts were openly exposed as women tried to quiet the cries. The atmosphere became increasingly hot and moist as the people overflowed from the tin hut on to the platform.

Siân suddenly missed Jane. Urging Len and Jim to follow her, she went out and paraded up and down the platform until she eventually found her daughter and Evan the Overman's son sitting close together on a fish barrow.

44

Near them a number of young men were playing 'devil's cards' as Siân called them. She turned Len away from the scene and called Jane to her with the words: 'Come from there, Jane. I'n't you shamed of yourself, sitting there brazen as brass? Time 'nough for you to sit with men in a railway station when you be married.' Jane pouted, but obeyed and left the young man sitting sheepishly alone.

The people began fussily to gather their bags, baskets, and children in readiness for the train that was now due. It arrived puffing and blowing as though impressed by its own importance. The wooden-seated carriages were soon full of perspiring people. Young couples sat on each other's knees while the older children sat on the floor.

After much running about by railway officials, who were unaccustomed to so much traffic, the train slowly rattled out of the station.

Len remained standing at the window, his nose pressed flat against the cool glass that soon was streaming with moisture. He watched the country fly past, while miles of coal wagons seemed to float by like a river.

It was the first time he had ever left his home in the valley, and the amazing newness of the experience, together with the splendour of the ever-changing countryside, made him oblivious to the terrific heat in the over-laden carriage.

The train ran some distance along the coast before reaching its destination. The vista of sea and ships thus exposed sent Len's blood coursing madly.

Never before had he seen ships, and his only sight of the sea had been the glimpses he occasionally had from the mountain top of its glistening ribbon-like winding

45

round the coast. Its close proximity now gripped him like a dream. When the train arrived at the seaside station the sweat-soaked people poured out on the platform as if emptied from a steaming oven. Little children howled in the misery of damp clothes as their already wearied parents hurried them through the irritating sands to the beach. Here everyone sat down. The glare of the sun, flung back by the sea, blinded pit-darkened eyes for a while and forced tears where none were meant.

A nearby steam organ started to play. It filled the hot air with raucous noise, but the people soon caught its vague refrain and accompanied it with lusty singing. This stimulated their flagging spirits, and in a short time the receding tide was followed by bare-footed adults and children.

Big Jim and his family spread a newspaper on the sand and began eating the food that Siân had packed. Len thought he had never tasted anything so delicious, although the sand gritted in the tinned meat and bread beneath his teeth. After the meal Len commenced undressing. He wanted to play naked in the water, but Siân stopped him. 'Duw, duw, boy bach,' she asked, 'do you want to catch your death of cold?'

The disappointed lad had to be content with paddling his stockingless feet. He played at this for some hours, his eyes longingly wandering across the waves whose edges swirled in cooling bubbly frothiness about his legs. He sensed the power of the ever-recurring sweep and felt an aching urge to ride its crests and hollows, which he mentally likened to his beloved hills and vales. The illimitable distance of the rolling sea awed him, and he wondered what the horizon was hiding. The occasional black stripes on its surface, which he knew were ships, seemed to cling to the dim distance as if stuck there.

His mother called him away from his thoughts and he returned to where his parents and Jane were sprawling on the sand. Siân wiped the moisture from his legs with the newspaper they had used as a tablecloth. Big Jim rose ponderously to his feet and announced he was going for a walk. Siân knew where he was going, but, since it was a holiday, contented herself with saying: 'All right. Take care of yourself, and watch you o'n't get drunk. Member the deacons be all eyes.'

Jim glanced back and replied: 'You trust me for that, my gel. Think you I have got no sense, mun? Huh!' Saying which he went on his way and was soon lost to sight.

Jim had been gone some time when Jane asked her mother if she also could take a stroll. 'Certainly,' answered Siân. 'You have been a good gel, today. But mind you don't go far.' Jane rose, arranged her disordered dress, and casually strolled off, the sun playing on her fair hair and pink-clad body.

For some time after the departure of the pair Len lay motionless at his mother's side, his mind still centred on the ships he wanted to explore. He noticed that they all made their slow way past the headland that jutted into the sea on the right. Wondering if they were all gathered there, he suddenly sat up.

'What be the matter with you, boy bach?' his mother inquired.

'I wish Ron was here,' was his enigmatic reply.

Siân looked at him a moment in bewilderment before asking, 'Why, Len bach, i'n't you satisfied to have your old mam with you?'

Len felt the reproach in her voice and hastened to explain that if Ron were present they could walk across to the headland that hid the ships. Siân sensed his mood and struggled to her feet, saying, 'Come, my boy, you and me can walk so far as that. Huh! I 'member the time I could walk thirty miles without flinching and then carry a sack of coal from the tip.'

Len joyfully jumped to his feet. He picked up the empty basket and followed his mother through the soft sand that soon filled their boots and burned their feet. It was late in the afternoon and the sun, free of clouds, focused its rays upon the beach with sleep-inducing intensity. Len's youthful exuberance, however, invigorated Siân. They steadily plodded around the recumbent people who sprawled about the shore. In half an hour they had left the sands behind and were walking alongside the golf-links and green-clad dunes. Courting couples took advantage of the seclusion offered by the latter.

Len's enthusiasm kept him ahead of Siân, even though her feet were now free from encumbering sand. He peeped into the dunes. What he saw set his brain whirling with questioning thoughts. He remembered Jane undressing and saw her panting breasts. The conjured picture sent little tickling ripples through his flesh. He thought he had unravelled the problem of the difference between girl's breasts and his own. What he had seen demonstrated that the former were larger so that men could play with and caress them.

This train of thought robbed his feet of direction and he wandered aimlessly from dune to dune, his musings accelerated by the occupants of each. Immersed in a tumult of emotions, Len paid no further heed to his surroundings until he stumbled sharply and heard a small scream followed by a flash of something white. Thus suddenly brought to himself, he glanced into the dune over whose edge he had nearly tumbled, and saw a young girl twist hurriedly from the embracing arms of her companion while she vainly tried to hide a pink garment behind her back. The lad's eyes were drawn to the disarranged dress that partially exposed the warm breast which the young man had been caressing. Len looked at the white face and recognised his sister.

An instantaneous stab like a hot flame burned through his body, bringing tears to his eyes. For a moment he remained motionless, then burst out, 'Oh, Jane bach, what be you doing?' His embarrassed sister made no reply and turned her head away. The lad's mind suddenly turned to his mother trudging along behind. 'Quick,' he said, 'mam is coming.' The girl sprang to her feet as if impelled by an electric current. She hurriedly arranged her clothes, then remembered the pink garment behind her. A quick blush spread over her white face. Her companion felt the urgency of the situation and turned his back to her.

Trembling in every limb, Jane hastily pulled the betraying garment over her sand-encrusted shoes while Len gulped back his tears and helped to arrange her dress. The toilet was hardly completed when Siân came panting to the edge of the dune. The loss of Len from her sight had put her into a quiver of nervousness. Perspiration poured down her face as she slowly recovered her breath and took in the scene beneath her.

Turning her weary eyes from Len she looked at Jane and immediately noted the pallor of the girl's face. Half unconsciously she noticed the impression of bodies on the soft crushed grass. The fidgeting youth near by attracted her attention. She recognised him as Evan the Overman's son, the young man who had sat with Jane in the station while they were waiting for the train.

Jane felt years roll away before she heard her mother's voice float quietly down from an interminable distance. Something seemed to quiver through its customary harshness and mellow it. 'What have you been doing, Jane bach?' Siân asked plaintively.

Len edged closer to his deathly white sister as she replied in a frightened whisper, 'Nothing, mam, nothing.' Siân stood motionless for a moment, her eyes full of fear. Then she beckoned the young people to her with an awkward gesture.

The agitated youth had been silent during the scene, but he now jumped forward. 'There is nothing wrong, Mrs. Roberts,' he blurted out hysterically. 'Me and Jane only come here to have a little chat away from the noise of the crowd. Don't think wrong about us. You have been young yourself once.'

His demeanour belied his plea, and Siân knew he was lying. Choking back her tears, she replied, 'All right, boy bach, all right. May time prove that you be speaking the truth.'

No more was said. Siân beckoned Len and Jane to follow

her, and the trio left the young man where he stood. During the slow trudge back to the sands Siân tried to beat back the fears that tumbled to her mind with increasing torment. The day for her had come to a sudden end. Mentally she battled with herself whether she should communicate her fears to Big Jim.

Len, holding his mother's hand, walked dumbly by her side. He wondered what had happened to make her look so sad and old. Unable to find an answer, he turned his thoughts to Jane. The hot flame again seared his body when he remembered the bared breast and the young man caressing it. The fact grieved him, although he had not the slightest knowledge of its import.

Jane, tight-lipped and with nerves twitching hysterically, looked piteously at her mother. But the latter, absorbed in her own misery, paid no attention. Immersed in themselves yet thinking of each other, the three eventually reached the spot where Big Jim lay fast asleep, with his mouth wide open and his legs spread loosely in an obscene sprawl. His cheek was cut, while one eye was swollen and discoloured.

Siân glanced over her mate quickly, noting the contented twist on his face. She stooped and lifted Jim's huge hands and saw the knuckles were torn and blooded. Hazily Siân wondered what had happened, but her mind still wrestled with the main problem. Should she tell him? Perhaps, after all, she thought, nothing had really occurred between Jane and the youth. Even if it had, perhaps nothing would come of it. Thus she argued with herself. Her thoughts tore and gashed her infinitely more deeply than the wounds did Jim's hands. Shaking him gently, she called, 'Wake up, James bach, wake up.'

Turning on his side and drawing his knees up, he drowsily murmured, 'Plenty of time, 'nghariad i, the hooter haven't gone yet. Let me be for a bit.'

'No, no!' burst out Siân frantically. 'I want you, James bach. You must wake up now.' The urgency in her voice jerked him out of his beer-laden slumber. Rubbing the sun glare from his undamaged eye and licking his damp moustache, he sat up with a grunt.

He immediately sensed something was wrong with Siân and assumed it had to do with the fight he had engaged in during the afternoon. He started an apologetic explanation. 'It was not my fault, Siân bach,' he began, 'I didn't want to fight, but I couldn't leave my butties down, could I?' The last was a plaintive query.

Siân sadly studied his face. Already she felt stronger and more confident. 'Did you win?' she asked.

'Win? Of course I did,' he replied, as though the very question were an insult. 'Have anybody ever seen big Jim losing?'

Heedless of the boast, she quietly dragged from him all she wanted to know of the afternoon's events. The recital helped to deaden the pain in her heart and decided her to tell him nothing about Jane until something transpired.

They still had some time to wait before the arrival of the excursion train to take them back to the valleys. This they spent on the sands with the rest of the people, most of whom were already worn out. The air resounded to the noise of screaming children, which helped to further irritate nerves already frayed by the excitement and fuss of the gruelling day.

At last the time for the return train arrived. Perspiring parents dragged and carried howling children to the railway station and packed the waiting carriages. Len, feeling himself stifling in the breath-laden compartment, tried to open the window, but was stopped by Siân, 'for fear of the draught' as she said.

The journey home was agonising, and everyone was glad when the train eventually puffed into Cwmardy. Len felt the smoky, noisome air of the valley to be the sweetest he had ever breathed. The walk up the hill to Sunny Bank was a silent one. None of them wanted supper that night.

Len and Jane went to bed before their parents. The lad watched his sister stripping off her clothes. Her audible sighs sent the memory of the events of the day surging through him. Without knowing why, he felt a vague pity for her that seemed to deepen when she dropped the white nightdress over her slender body. His tear-misted eyes saw a thousand rainbows dance around the dim flame of the candle. Speechless, he waited until she came to bed and pressed the hot wick of the candle into the oily grease with a piece of paper.

Len gathered courage in the ensuing darkness. He nestled his body to her warm flesh and said, 'Don't worry, Jane bach. I 'on't tell mam what I seen.' Jane made no reply but he felt the heavy sobs that shook her shudder through him beneath the bedclothes. They broke down his boyish restraint, and he jumped up in bed, tears rolling down his cheeks.

Jane reached up in the gloom and drew his wavy head to her bosom, which he clasped with a loving tenderness. The dormant mother-love rushed in waves over her body at the touch of his sweat-moistened hand. Twisting on her side she huddled him back under the bedclothes, taking care not to remove his hand. In this posture they both cried themselves to sleep.

THE DEATH
OF JANE

For many months the events of the excursion day dominated young Len's mind. Since their return home he fancied the house had become gloomier. His parents spoke in whispers whenever he was about, and he could not escape the tormenting thought that these changes were in some way due to Jane. He began to observe that his sister was each week becoming more mopy and haggard. At night his wandering hands stole over her stomach and breasts, and he noticed that the former was swelling while the latter were growing heavier. Watching like a cat, he noticed that Jane spent a long time in the lavatory each morning and he sometimes heard her retching painfully in sickness.

Deep in his immature heart Len felt something terrible was happening, and an undefinable fear began to grow on him. One night, some months after the excursion, he fell to sleep in the armchair near the kitchen fire. He was awakened by a soft murmur of voices. Without raising his head Len slyly opened his eyes. The only light in the kitchen was a deep glow from the fire, around which his parents and Mrs. Thomas, the next-door neighbour, were sitting. Shutting his eyes again, the lad listened to the conversation. 'Yes,' he heard his mother say bitterly, 'I am 'specting it to happen in six weeks from now.' She groaned, then continued, 'To think my poor gel have got to go through this and he have not been near her yet. Anybody would think she was muck.'

She stopped again while Mrs. Thomas tried to console her.

'Don't worry, Mrs. Roberts bach,' she said. 'God will pay him back.'

There was a moment's silence before the neighbour asked, as if seeking a loophole, 'Be you sure of your dates?'

'Sure?' burst out Siân passionately. 'Was I not there the day it did happen?' She stopped, then moaned in a sudden spasm of grief. 'Oh, God bach, I would sooner if you did strike her dead at my feet the day she was born, than for her to come to this. The first of my children, too. Day in and day out have I slaved to rear them 'spectable and to put the fear of God into their little hearts. And now to come to this.' Her voice broke in a pitiful wail.

For some minutes there was another deep silence, which was broken by Siân. She sprang to her feet and shouted in a voice vibrant with passion and hate, 'Be a man, Big Jim!' Jim sat up as if jerked by a rope at her words. 'Yes,' she spat at him, 'be a man for once. You can fight in a public house for other people, fight now for your own flesh and blood.' Jim sat silent and motionless, his eyes staring into the fire as she continued tauntingly: 'But no. You would sooner sit on your backside by there, biting your nails. It is easier than hiding your only daughter from the storm Evan the Overman's son have made for her.'

Big Jim's continued silence enraged her. 'Have you no tongue that you do not answer me?' she howled, heedless of her words. 'Why don't you rise from your backside and go to Evan the Overman? Get out, Big Jim. Go, tell Evan the Overman that his son have dirtied your daughter.' Her voice softened a little as she beseeched, 'Be a man, James. Put on your coat and make Evan's boy do the right thing by our gel before it be too late.'

Big Jim looked up from the fire to her haggard face, the lines in which were so deep that they appeared to have been chiselled in. A deep, impotent grief filled his heart. He understood Siân's anger but wondered how he could ask another to marry his daughter when he was himself not married to her mother. He loved his children with the blind devotion of an animal and it hurt him to the bone that this thing had happened. The disgrace which the event would bring upon the family disturbed him very little. What he feared was the possibility of something happening to Jane.

'Don't worry, Siân bach,' he muttered, his puzzlement evident in his tone. 'I be not dead yet, and I can still keep my children without asking other men to do it for me.'

Len choked back the sobs that gathered in his throat as his father went on. 'These hands that have stood the

57

biggest timbers in the pit, this body that have lifted the heaviest trams, are still strong enough to work to fill another mouth. Yes,' he went on, while his tear-glistened eyes looked directly into Siân's, 'Jane's baby will be so dear to me as is Jane herself, whether it be made on a mountain or in a bed.'

Siân began to sob. Mrs. Thomas attempted to console the grief-stricken woman. Taking Siân's bowed head into her arms, she murmured, 'There, there, Mrs. Roberts bach, don't take it so hard to your heart. Everything will come all right in God's good time.'

The weeping woman raised her head, and the red glow from the flames turned the tears trickling down her cheeks into blood. Turning to Big Jim she said softly, as though talking to a child: 'I know, James bach, that it will never have a better father than you. But think of the shame on our daughter, on all of us. In God's eyes she is not clean and people will point on her baby and say "Look at Big Jim's girl, she have got a bastard by Evan the Overman's son".'

Jim's huge frame stiffened and quivered at the words, which acted like an electric current. For some seconds he fought silently to control himself, then, rising slowly from the chair, he stood erect before the two women. He breathed quickly and his voice was harsh as a saw when he said, 'If ever I do hear another living body say that, it do mean that my life will end upon a hangman's rope.' Saying which, he brought his fist down upon the table with a crash that startled Len from his feigned sleep.

No more was said until the lad had finished supper and was sent to bed. Here he strained his ears to listen, but nothing reached him other than a faint indistinct murmur. Disappointed, he turned to Jane and woke her from her restless sleep. Nestling closely to her in the semi-darkness of the candle-lit room, he mumbled hesitantly, 'I know what be the matter with you, Jane. You be going to have a baby bastard.'

Jane sprang to her haunches, the nightdress slipping from her shoulders, and glared at the frightened lad. For a moment it seemed she was going to strike him, but she suddenly caught him in her arms and pressed his face to her naked, palpitating bosom. The smell of her flesh and the pulsing of her heart tingled Len's senses as her tears moistened his hair. 'Oh Len, Len,' she moaned rocking him backwards and forwards in her grief, 'what shall I do? I have got a good mind to go up the feeder and end it all.' He tried to soothe her, but Jane continued fatalistically, 'Mam will kill me when she knows.'

Len had been alarmed at her despairing outburst, but he brightened up at this. 'Don't worry 'bout that,' he told her confidently, 'mam do know 'bout it already, Jane bach.'

Frantically the girl probed every word of the conversation from him. When he repeated his father's statements she burst into sobs again, saying, 'He is too good for me. Many fathers would put me out on the streets.'

Len started convulsively and raised himself on his elbows. 'Oh no, he 'oodn't,' he retorted vehemently; 'and if he did,' he added manfully, 'I 'ood keep you. I will be starting to work very soon now.'

She cuddled him to her and sighed, 'There now, Len bach, go to sleep, it will soon be all over.' Sleep, however, was out of the question for both of them. Jane sobbed softly all night, while Len wondered how the baby that was coming would be born. The definite knowledge of what was wrong made his mind a little easier, though he could not understand how it happened or what it meant. The surreptitious manner in which he had obtained the information determined him that the matter was a big secret and must not be mentioned to his schoolmates. With this thought in his mind he dozed off.

Big Jim returned from work the following morning without making his usual call at the Boar's Head. While he bathed Siân fetched his best clothes from the box under the bed. Preparing herself as he dressed, she warned Len and Jane: 'You two children stop in till me and dad come back. We 'ont be very long.'

Jane looked at her mother. Her eyes were appealingly pitiful. She sensed where they were going, but did not have the courage to ask them to desist.

Len noticed the look and a gnawing pain tugged at his heart as he wondered what was the matter. Big Jim, carefully soaping his moustaches, appeared too preoccupied to observe anything. As he picked up the bowler hat and followed Siân to the door, he huskily muttered over his shoulder: 'Don't you worry, gel bach; everything will come all right in the end.'

His head bowed, like a man on the way to the scaffold, he accompanied Siân down the little street that led to Main Street. He inclined to lag behind as they drew nearer the house of Evan the Overman, and several times Siân had to urge him to walk faster. Her eyes glistened wetly.

When they eventually reached their destination there was a momentary pause before Siân timidly lifted the bright brass knocker which adorned the door. Big Jim stood in the muddy roadway, his whole demeanour betraying the awkward misery he felt. At the second rap the door was opened by the young man who had been with Jane on the day of the excursion. It was the first time Siân had seen him since the incident on the dunes. His sudden appearance now drained the blood from her face and her eyes seemed to grow bigger and wetter.

Speechless with emotion, she listened to the stuttering words of the youth, who was obviously as upset and surprised as herself. 'Hallo,' he stammered, 'come to see me, I 'spose?' He hesitated while her sunken eyes bored a sharp, nervous pain into his head. Turning his head away from the burning gleam, he gathered his thoughts and blurted out, 'I believe I know what you have come about. It is about your Jane.'

Neither Jim or Siân replied. 'Well,' continued the disconcerted young man, 'it is no good coming to me. I am not the man you want to look for. Jane have been courting dozens before me.' He stopped again, his eyes still averted, and then burst out as if the words were boiling in his throat, 'I am not the first chap who have been with her.'

Big Jim, who had been silently fidgeting in the roadway during this monologue, stepped sharply towards the door at these words. His body was taut and his moustaches twitched. 'That will do,' he said curtly, in a quivering voice. 'Me and my wife have not come here to see you, and we want to hear no more from you. We have come to see your father, Evan the Overman.' The young man paled at the threat in Jim's voice. Stuttering more than ever, he hastily retreated into the passage, saying, 'Oh, all right, Mr. Roberts. I didn't mean any harm. I will tell my father you want him.' Shutting the door behind him, he left the old couple in the roadway.

Siân looked at Jim's set face and warned him, 'Now, 'member, James bach, no nonsense. You keep your temper and leave the talking to me. We have come here to get justice for our gel and not to use our fists.' Before Jim could reply the door opened.

Facing them stood a short, thickset man with a sallow face and heavy, overhanging eyebrows. This was Evan the Overman. He was an official at the pit where Big Jim worked. In common with other officials, his function was supposed to be that of watching over the workmen's safety, but the colliery company regarded this as secondary to output, and the ability of the officials was measured by the amount of coal they could wring from the area and the men in their charge.

Evan the Overman's attitude was domineering when he said, without any preamble, 'I understand you want to see me particular.'

Siân replied to him. 'Yes, Evan,' she said, 'we do want to see you very particular.' Without another word he beckoned them in and led the way to the parlour.

The old couple carefully wiped their muddy boots on the coconut mat before entering. The mat bore the word 'Welcome'. Even in her perturbation Siân noted the gaudy brassiness of the room as she sat gingerly on the edge of the plush settee. Big Jim remained standing until Evan invited him to sit. This Jim did, precariously perching the unaccustomed bowler hat on his knee.

When they were all seated the official opened the conversation. 'Hmm,' he began ponderously, 'I believe I know what you have come about, James. I believe I am right in saying it is about your Jane, isn't it?' Receiving no reply to his question, he continued, 'I have been told Jane is going to have a baby and that she do blame my son for it.'

Bridling at the sneer in his voice, Siân interrupted him. 'Yes,' she said, 'that be quite right. Jane be going to have a baby by your Evan.'

The outspoken assertion and the manner in which she made it startled the two men for a moment. Siân went on in a softer voice: 'We have come to ask you, as a God-fearing man, Evan, to make your son clean the gel he have dirtied. You have knowed me and James for many years now and, although James is only a collier and do like his drop of beer, you do know us to be 'spectable people not ashamed to look nobody in the face. Yes,' she went on proudly, 'we don't owe a penny to no man and nobody do need be ashamed to have our Jane for a wife. I know we be poor, but she have been reared 'spectable and clean, thank God.' She paused a moment to swallow, then continued: 'Yes, Evan, we have come to ask you to make your son do the right thing.' Her voice faltered on the last sentence and it sounded like a plaint.

For some moments nothing else was said. Then the overman rose heavily to his feet and walked slowly to the door. He opened it and shouted, 'Evan, come here.' In a very short time the young man entered, sheepishly avoiding the eyes that scanned his face. 'You know what we have been talking about,' his father began. 'James and Siân do blame you for the baby that is coming to their Jane, and they want you to marry her. What have you got to say about it?' His words were a command.

Seconds elapsed before the youth made any response. The three parents anxiously watched him, each seeming ready to catch the words when they dropped from his lips. At last he started speaking. His voice was low and he kept looking at the floor. 'I do admit I have been with Jane,' he started, 'but only once and that was when we went away with the chapel.' He stopped a moment. No one moved and he continued, his breath quickening. 'She was courting regular with another chap before that. I have got witnesses to prove it.' He raised his head and looked at his father. Encouraged by the quick gleam of interest he saw in the latter's eyes, he failed to notice the horror in Siân's or the spasmodic twitching of Big Jim's face muscles. The young man chose his next words like bullets which he shot venomously at Jim and Siân. 'You can't trap me with this,' he rattled out in jerks. 'You have got the wrong bird this time. You are only blaming me because my father is an official. But it is no good looking for the right man in this house; he don't live here.'

Each word struck Siân with an impact that quivered through her body. She hid her drawn face in her hands. Hot tears trickled like molten glass through her fingers. Immersed in her own grief, she did not see Big Jim spring to his feet, his panting chest emphasising the magnitude of his bulk.

He stood motionless, the pallor of his face giving greater heat to the glow in his eyes. When he at last spoke the deep tremor in his voice made Siân shudder and raise her tear-stained face. 'Oh,' said Jim, with callous deliberation, 'so the son of Evan do class my gel a whore. Eh? The man who have used my daughter do now call her a prostitute.' He paused to battle with his passion, then spat out, 'Look well to yourself, man, before talking 'bout other people. Before you start to run other women down, look well to your own mother.'

Siân sensed the drift of his words and tried to stop him. She wailed through her tears, 'Don't say no more, James bach, for the sake of God.'

Jim waved her aside and paid no attention to Evan the Overman cowering in the chair. Completely dominating the situation, he nailed the trembling youth with his eyes and went on: 'Too late now. Too late. When you hurt my gel, you do put poison in my heart. Poison that have got to be spit out. And if it do kill anyone, who am I to try and stop it?' He paused again with a visible tremble, gulped hard and then continued: 'You say that your father is an official. Yes, that is true. But you don't tell us how he came to be one. Answer that, Evan bach, before you open your mouth again. But, there,' he went on raspingly, without waiting for a reply, 'perhaps you don't know.'

Apart from Jim's voice the room was silent. Siân sat rigid, her bottom jaw hanging loosely. Evan the Overman had buried his face in his arms, while his son stood motionless and helpless before the glaring eyes of Big Jim.

The young man trembled as Jim continued: 'Let me help

you. Do you believe your father was made an official because he was a good workman? Ha-ha!' The laugh did not sound out of place. It was deep and bitter, giving coherence to the words that followed. 'No, of course not. I could work his hands off, but I have not been made an official. No, my boy, it is not *that* you have to brag about. Your father did not have the job of overman because of the work he have done himself.' Jim's voice began to rise as he said, 'No; it is not there you will find the answer. Your father was made an official because when Williams, the under-manager, come here first he did lodge with your father and mother. Yes,' he burst out passionately, his voice palpitating with the contempt that consumed him, 'your father did sell his wife's body for an overman's job.'

The usually arrogant colliery official slumped forward in the chair. His heaving shoulders betrayed what his covered face was hiding. Young Evan cowered, with staring eyes, against the door post. Big Jim lifted Siân from the settee and stood with her in the middle of the room.

Pride and passion deepened his voice: 'You do tell me to look somewhere else. Yes, I can. But you look first, my boy, to your own face and see if you can find the likeness of Evan the Overman there. Huh. That is one thing you will never see. I am sorry for you. The son of such a man as your father is not fit to enter the family of Jim the Big. I would sooner find the father of my gel's babby in the gutter than in this house.'

Jim's voice became softer as he said: 'But there be no need for me to look anywhere. I am man enough to father my daughter's babby as I have fathered her. I ask no man to make or to keep my children.'

Neither father or son opened their mouth as Jim made his terrible indictment. The room became cold as a vault of resurrected corpses. Siân, almost overcome by the ruthless, devastating words of her mate, trembled from head to foot. She was thankful when his great arm encircled her waist and he led her to the door, saying aloud, 'Come, Siân bach. Let us leave this painted muckhole and the rubbish that do live in it. Our Jane do still belong to us and her babby is ours.'

Big Jim paused as they passed the young man at the door. His voice vibrated with a sudden spasm of passion and hate. 'Do you hear me?' he shouted.

Neither of the stricken, shamefaced men looked up as he went on: 'Now both of you 'member this. The father of Jane's babby do not live in this house. If ever I hear a word that it do, that day will I come back and pull it about your ears brick by brick.' With this he slammed the door, sternly bade Siân dry her tears, and with his arm through hers proudly marched past the neighbours who had seen them enter the house and had waited in anticipation of a rowdy scene.

Words were not necessary to explain the result of the interview. Siân's tear-stained face told it.

The couple found Len and Jane awaiting them when they arrived home. Jane looked in her mother's eyes and burst into sobs when she read the message they contained. Jim turned at the pitiful wail. 'That will do,' he said abruptly, 'there is to be no more crying in this house.' He waited until Jane had somewhat controlled herself, then added more softly, 'Sit down and wipe your eyes, my little gel. Now, listen to me. The little babby you are going to bring into the world belong to no one but the people in this house. It will be ours and no one else's. There will be no wedding before it is born, and its father is not Evan the Overman's son. Do you understand my words, Jane bach?' he queried, a world of love in his voice.

Jane's face went ghastly white and her eyes dilated, but she made no reply other than to nod her head dumbly.

Siân went to the girl. 'What your father do tell you be quite right,' she told her. 'Your sin will fall on all of us, but the good Lord will help us to carry it.'

She gathered her daughter into her arms, murmuring as their tears melted together, 'Don't cry, 'nghariad bach i. Mam be with you.' Rocking the weeping girl in her lap like a baby, she broke into a soft haunting Welsh lullaby. She crooned the words into her daughter's ears as she had done seventeen years before, when suckling her:

> Cariwch, medd Dafydd,
> Fy nhelyn i mi
> Ceisiaf cyn marw
> Roi tôn arni hi.

> Bring to me,
> Said dying David,
> My harp,
> That I may play another tune
> Before I die.

The mournful words, clothed in minor tones, soaked into Jane's pent-up emotions, soothing their pain and calming their tumult.

She pressed her body closer to her mother's and sank slowly into a soft sleep interspersed with irregular sighs. Big Jim, with infinite tenderness, lifted the girl from Siân's lap and carried her to bed.

All the while Len had looked and listened in bewilderment. He did not understand what marriage was, but that Evan the Overman's son, whom he now knew had done something terrible to Jane, would not marry her struck him as an affront to the family. Whatever had happened to transform his sister from a happy girl to a morose, malformed young woman, Len did not know. But he knew from what he had heard that Evan bach was responsible and that he was now evading the consequences. The knowledge that all the family was suffering as a result tormented Len for a long time. At school he became even more taciturn than usual, refusing all Ron's attempts to draw him into a conversation or a game. He began wandering the mountains alone, boots and stockings slung around his shoulders. He roamed aimlessly through the grass while his mind pondered the problem of Jane.

In this way the weeks went by. Each week he observed her body become more misshapen and her face more haggard. Her eyes alarmed him. They were dull and full of impatient grief. Len felt the atmosphere in the house change. His parents no longer quarrelled, and when they spoke it was in quiet whispers as if they were afraid the walls would hear what they were saying. Jim no longer burst his grumbling way into the house. Neither did he frequent the Boar's Head with his mate, Dai Cannon. When he came home from work he moped in the armchair near the fire until it was time to go to bed.

Siân was the only member of the family who maintained the ordinary routine, and even she, Len observed, did more sewing than was usual. The changed domestic environment affected the lad deeply and developed in him a hatred of the man he thought responsible. In his mind the problem now appeared perfectly simple. If Evan the Overman's son married Jane everyone would be happy, he thought.

The simplicity of the solution made him wonder why Evan did not apply it. During the nights when he lay alongside his sobbing sister, he clenched his fists and wished he were big enough to force the cause of all the trouble do the right thing.

The snatches of conversation he picked up in the kitchen from his mother and Mrs. Thomas, the neighbour, led him to believe that the only thing that prevented young Evan marrying Jane was the fact he was an official's son and not an ordinary workman like Big Jim. This idea grew on Len. He pondered long over the distinction between officials in the pit and workmen. It struck him as monstrously unfair that this distinction in status should break up his home life and make his people sad. The hatred he felt for Evan the Overman's son slowly diffused itself into a hatred of all those classed as officials. He began to regard them as enemies. He was too young and immature to appreciate the subtle divisions deliberately developed between the colliery staff of officials and the workmen, and came to believe that all officials had, of necessity, to be cruel.

Jane no longer went outside the house. Occasionally and for no apparent reason she burst into hysterical sobs that shook her body. In her eyes grew the dull glazed look of a hunted animal that, even as it runs, knows there is no escape.

Very early one morning, when the sun still had some hours to travel before it peeped over the mountains into the valley, Len was awakened by his father. He vaguely heard Jane toss and moan as Big Jim wrapped his trembling form in a blanket and carried him down into the kitchen. Len was placed in the armchair while his father sat on the stool near the fire. Big Jim bade the lad go to sleep, but the strangeness of the proceedings brushed all sleep from Len's eyes. He looked about him. The kitchen was full of shadows and the big boiler on the fire only added to the number. Len saw the water it contained bubbling and sparkling in the beams from the oil-lamp. He wondered what it was for and where his mother was.

The front door opened with a sudden clang and Siân came in accompanied by Mrs. Thomas. The former's head and shoulders were swathed in the big woollen shawl, but Len's eyes did not see this. They were riveted on the black bag Mrs. Thomas carried. He had often heard that babies came in such bags as that.

Siân muttered something to the crouching Jim, who immediately got up from the stool and began pacing the kitchen with bent head and hands behind his back. Len watched his mother dip an unlit candle into the fire flames and heard her hurried footsteps shuffle up the stairs. Mrs.

71

Thomas remained downstairs and filled a large pan with the hot water from the boiler. In a short time Siân returned to the kitchen. She took up the pan of hot water and with a whispered 'Don't worry, James bach, everything will come all right,' accompanied Mrs. Thomas back up the stairs.

Big Jim stopped his restless pacing. He stood still, while his huge body began a soft, regular swaying as though trying to soothe a child cradled in his arms.

The silence and definiteness with which everything was done frightened Len. He felt like crying. The black bag had made him aware that the unusual happenings had to do with Jane. Lying perfectly still on the armchair, he let his mind drift. He saw Jane as she was prior to the excursion; then before his eyes drifted a picture of her horribly bloated body as he had seen it the previous night. Tears blurred his vision and coursed down his cheeks. The hatred he felt for officials ran through his blood like fire, and he began thinking of the form his revenge would take when he grew up.

Closing his tired eyes, the lad tried to ease the torment in his mind, but the continual shuffling overhead made this impossible. His active imagination likened it to the sound of doom walking through the darkness and slyly sweeping up its victims. Suddenly a dreadful scream brought him in one leap from the chair to his father's side. Whimpering and trembling, he clung to Jim's legs, the quiver of which mingled with that in his own body. Len's upturned, pitiful eyes asked mutely what was wrong, but Big Jim, himself seared with anguish, made no reply other than to stroke the lad's hair. The action pacified Len somewhat. The scream died down in gasping moans, through which he heard Jane's pain-drenched plea: 'Oh, let me die, mam. Let me die.' The lad felt his father's legs stiffen at the words, but he did not feel the tear that fell on his hair.

Shortly after this Mrs. Thomas came down for more boiling water. Her return to the bedroom was followed by more screams and their culminating moans. This went on for hours, and Len felt the night would never end. He longed for daylight to steal its way through the drawn blinds. Every second became an embodied nightmare.

The sound of his mother's harsh cough as she came down the stairs eased the tension. Her sweaty face was a lump of shiny shadows. She murmured tiredly to Big Jim: 'You had better get ready for work, James bach. The time be going on. You have got nothing to worry about,' she said as an afterthought. Without a word Jim drew from under the table the box that contained his working clothes.

Len went back on the armchair while his father dressed and Siân toasted some bread. The pit-grimed clothes which Jim drew on his naked body filled the small kitchen with dried coal-dust, which settled in layers on everything. The bubbling water in the boiler lapped up the black dust and made it into soft mud.

When he had finished dressing Big Jim drew his chair to the table and poured the hot tea Siân handed him into a saucer from which he sucked it in audible gulps. He left the flame-scorched toast untouched. After the second cup of tea he rose and without a word made for the door. At the foot of the stairs he hesitated and squared his drooping shoulders to the sigh that seeped up from his heart.

For a moment he stood motionless, then, with a muttered 'Good morning,' turned towards the doorway that led to the day then being spawned. His eyes were blind to the black-bordered red streaks that ran across the sky at the bottom of the valley. They resembled the blood-streams of birth. His ears were deaf to the loudly shrieking pit hooters that raped the early morning air with violent echoes. He paid no attention to their frenzied demand that he hurry to the pit. Imperceptibly his body melted into the silent, shadowy line of men that wound its way up the hill to the colliery.

After Jim's departure Siân sat on the stool before the fire. She rocked herself backwards and forwards, quietly groaning with every movement. Len watched her for some time. He wished she would stop the rocking that threatened to put her head in the flames with each forward motion. Thought of this possibility unnerved him, and he was on the point of speaking when he heard her murmur to herself: 'Oh, Jane bach, Jane bach, it will be all over on you, 'nghariad i, very soon now. You will never come through this. Ah,' she went on softly, 'it do seem only yesterday you was suckling on my breast.' The memory brought tears to her eyes. She stopped her rocking and sobbed despairingly, 'O God, what have I done that you should make my little gel suffer?' Receiving no answer to her supplication, she resumed her rocking until a sound overhead took her hurriedly up the stairs.

Len eased his legs on the chair and sank into an uneasy doze. When he woke daylight had already yellowed the undrawn window blinds. His mother sat at the table, her head pillowed in her arms and her shoulders shaking convulsively. Len looked in amazement at the tall, cadaverous man who stood near. He knew it was the doctor and wondered what he was doing in the kitchen. The lad turned his eyes again towards his weeping mother. The connection between the tears and the doctor suddenly flashed into his mind. Panic-stricken he rushed towards the man, shouting and weeping, 'What have you done to our mam? Oh, mam, mam,' he wailed, 'what have he done?'

Siân took the hysterical lad on her lap. His frenzy calmed her own grief. 'There, there, Len bach,' she crooned, 'you must be quiet or you will wake Jane.' The last words were more a sob than a statement. The doctor beckoned Mrs. Thomas to accompany him to the door, which they closed behind them.

Very shortly Mrs. Thomas returned and fussily put her arms round Siân's shoulders. 'It be no good worrying now, Mrs. Roberts bach,' she said. 'The good Lord do always know what is best. Poor little Jane is out of her pain now, and is resting safe where there be no temptation.' Siân did not reply. Mrs. Thomas continued: 'Don't you bother 'bout anything. l will see to the laying out and James can go to the undertaker's when he come home from work. I will take all the dirty clothes with me now and have a couple of hours' sleep, then I will come back and put things in order for you.' Siân nodded her head, dumbly acquiescent.

When Jim returned from the pit late in the afternoon the blinds in every house of the street told him what had happened before he reached his own. Speechless with grief, he bathed and donned his clean clothes. Siân appeared oblivious to his presence until he carried the tub into the backyard. When he returned to the kitchen he caught her to him and kissed her hair. She broke down completely under the caress, and it was some minutes before he could calm her.

He succeeded eventually and remained silent while she stared into the fire. Presently she raised her head and began speaking in a low sing-song tone: 'Our little Jane have left us, James. Yes. Left us for ever and we will never again hear her voice in this kitchen.' She paused a moment and swallowed hard. When she continued it was more to herself than anyone else. 'Often have I been harsh to you, Jane bach. But I did never mean it.' She turned to Jim, who was getting alarmed at her attitude. 'She was our only gel,' she said, peering into his tear-misted eyes. 'Yes, our only gel. And now she have been taken from us. O God,' she burst out in sudden passion, 'why for did you make her suffer so much before taking her? Could you not have spared her pain?' She paused again, as if afraid of her thoughts, then went on challengingly: 'You did desert my little gel when she needed you most. You have done the same as Evan the Overman's son done. You left her when she wanted you. Ach,' she went on harshly, 'what have our little Jane done that she should be deserted by everybody? She have never done no wrong. And yet Evan bach do go happy and free on his way while my little gel is stiff and cold upstairs.'

There was silence for a while and Jim thought the outburst was over, until Siân gave another sigh and continued her slow, despairing monologue: 'Our little gel did mean no harm that day at the seaside,' she moaned.

'She was young and clean as the driven snow. Yet look what she have had to suffer, while him who was the cause of it did lie safe and sound in bed sleeping through her agony. And now all her pain have been for nothing.'

Siân grasped the silent Jim by the shoulders. Slowly and deliberately, letting every word soak into his ears before proceeding with the next, she said, 'All my life I have prayed to my God. Every Sunday I have gone to His chapel. In everything I have tried to live in His ways. Yes. I loved him. And yet the first time I do ask Him for mercy He do turn against me.'

Her voice was cold and her face was bitter as the clash between faith and anguish tore at her vitals. She gave a deep sigh and said as though resigned to her fate: 'When God do desert his children there be nothing fair in this world and nothing more to look forward to.'

Jim sensed the impending breakdown implied in the last words. 'Sh-h-h,' he warned her soothingly. 'This do come to everybody in their turn, Siân bach.' She looked at him sadly, her eyes already dark with mourning.

Later Len saw his father don the best suit and go out. No word was said or explanation made. Mrs. Thomas came in during his absence and occupied herself in the little parlour at the side of the kitchen. Len tried several times to make his way upstairs with the intention of seeing Jane, but on each occasion he was prevented.

When Big Jim returned to the house he was accompanied by a tall, thin-faced, black-coated stranger. Mrs. Thomas gave Len a penny and told him to go out for a while until the strange man left. The lad made his way up the mountain behind the house, stamping a tear into the sod with each aimless stride. Darkness was beginning to blanket the valley in a black shroud when Len came back to his home. The light in the parlour window surprised him. He had never seen one there before.

He found the house full of neighbours, all of whom were talking in subdued whispers. Len went straight to his mother, who sat crouched on the stool, and asked what was in the parlour. Siân looked at him dazedly for a moment before replying: 'Nothing much, Len bach, nothing much. You shall see in the morning.' Her voice sounded empty as an upturned bucket.

After supper Mrs. Thomas took the lad upstairs to the bedroom. Len looked at the empty bed. A peculiar smell rose from it. He asked Mrs. Thomas, who was fussily arranging the clothes, 'Where be our Jane then? I thought she was in bed.'

The woman readily replied, 'You go to bed, Len bach, and don't bother your little head. Jane is safe enough, you can venture.'

Len was not satisfied, but he said no more as she tucked him beneath the bedclothes. The peculiar smell seemed to be thicker here and he thought it hung more heavily around him. Weary, his mind full of worrying notions, he soon fell to sleep.

Next day Len found the house even more silent than it had been during the past few months. In addition he felt something eerie creep into his bones. Tiny bubbles of perspiration covered his body; each one felt like the icy point of a needle. Mrs. Thomas was still there. She seemed to be in complete charge of the household. Whenever Len tried to get near his mother, the well-meaning neighbour always prevented him. 'Don't bother your mam now, Len bach,' she said; 'she have got enough on her plate as it is.' The lad could not understand the reason for this, but he obediently submitted.

After dinner Mrs. Thomas told Big Jim, 'We can go in now, James. You had better take the boy with you.' Jim rose from the table and caught Len's hand. As they approached the parlour door the boy felt he was on the verge of some great adventure. His heart missed a beat, then jumped more quickly into action at the sound of the raised latch. He thrust his perspiring hand more deeply into the engulfing fist of his father as they entered the parlour.

Len noticed immediately the two long candles wasting their flames in the daylight mellowed by the drawn window blinds. The white-covered chairs puzzled him even while he wondered what the long yellow box on the table in the centre of the room was for. He instinctively knew that the funny-shaped plank of wood standing upright near the fire grate belonged to the box. The shining shield near its top stared at him like a lonely, glaring eye.

The lad pressed his body more tightly to the rigid leg of his father. He turned his head away from the shield and waited. Len knew something else was to come, but had no idea what it was until he heard Mrs. Thomas murmur quietly, her apron to her eyes, 'Don't she look lovely, Mr. Roberts?'

Like a flash Len knew what was in the box. Before he could say anything Big Jim bent down and lifted him from the floor. With awestruck eyes the boy looked down into the interior of what he now knew to be a coffin. Jane lay there, more still and silent than he had ever seen her.

Her body was clothed in a white lace and looked longer than when Len had last seen it. Her hands were waxy mirrors reflecting the blue tracery of all their veins. They were folded across her breast. One hand grasped a bunch of red roses that cast a blush over her smooth, white face, which seemed to smile into Len's downcast eyes.

Cuddled to Jane's side was the body of the baby that had killed her. Its tiny face looked like a blob of paste. Len felt a sudden urge to again caress Jane with his hands. He wanted to run them over the smooth contours of her breasts. Lumps of saliva rose to his throat. He swallowed them back in gulps and began to struggle hysterically in his father's grip. No tears came to his eyes as he continued the vain fight against Big Jim, but the feeling of impotence eventually conquered him and the emotional storm abated, leaving him panting on his father's shoulder.

Jim let him recover his breath, then slowly lowered him to the coffin until his lips touched those of his silent, smiling sister. Len shuddered at their cold clamminess. He tried to warm them with his breath. Jim saw the boy's hands wander through Jane's hair, and lifted him away before he could clasp her head.

Together father and son looked down for a few moments longer. Neither said a word. Their tears fused before reaching the dead face, whose smile seemed to soften at the burning touch. Big Jim turned away at last and the pair went quietly out, followed by Mrs. Thomas, who closed the parlour door softly behind them.

Five days after Jane had died Len was again taken in to see her. This was to be the last occasion before they screwed the coffin down ready for the funeral next day. As before, Big Jim lifted his son above the edge. Len looked down and a look of horror filled his eyes. Jane's beautiful face was gone. In its place was a dirty yellow mask with snarling lips that curled back from shiny white teeth. A blackened penny grinned at him mockingly from each of her eyes. The roses had died and were now withered blotches on the white lace of her shroud. Dark blobs filled the places where her cheeks had been. The tiny shrunken form at her side was covered. A fusty smell rose from the coffin and reminded Len of the odour in his bed the night after Jane had died. An acid-tasting lump rose to his throat. It made him feel sick. Turning his head away he hid his burning face on Jim's neck. In this manner both went back into the kitchen.

All that night the horror of what he had seen sunk more deeply into Len's mind. The awful face chased him in his sleep. Always it was grinning before his eyes. It refused to go away. Fumes came from its mouth and entered his nose. He felt himself choking and screamed to Jane for help, pressing tightly to his body the pillow on which her head used to rest. But the horrid face with its coin-covered eyes and drawn lips followed him. He started fighting it away when he heard it say, 'Don't you know me, Len bach? I am Jane, your sister. Why do you drive me from you?'

Len stopped his frantic struggles and looked again.

The pennies melted and made way for bright blue eyes.

The lips closed in and the cheeks filled out. Len's heart thrilled. He laughed happily and pressed the face of his sister to his lips. The short stiff hair on it hurt him. He looked again and found he had been kissing Evan the Overman's son. His body quivered with disgust and he threw the face from him with all his might. It rebounded back upon the bed and again it was the face of the coffin.

Len heard his father's voice ask from an interminable distance, 'What be the matter with you, Len bach? Perhaps you had better come to sleep with me and your mam.' Jim felt the steaming body of the lad dampen his flannel shirt as he carried him into Siân's bedroom. Finding comfort in his parents' presence, Len fell into a deep, lethargic sleep.

Next morning he was awakened early. 'You must get up now, Len bach,' said Mrs. Thomas, shaking him gently.

Len looked around and asked bewilderedly, 'Where be mam and dad, then?'

'They be downstairs,' was the impatient reply. 'Come now, there's a good boy. It be the day of the funeral today and we have got a lot to do.'

Len rose sluggishly and went down the stone stairs to the kitchen. He was followed by the exhortation, 'Don't you worry your mam today, boy bach. She have got plenty to go on with as it is and she do want plenty of quiet now.'

As the day wore on relatives, friends and neighbours crowded into the small kitchen. The women all began weeping sympathetically when they saw the dry-eyed Siân sitting silently on her stool. The black apron she wore deepened the pallor of her face. Her dull eyes looked vacant, giving the impression that she had given up searching for something she wanted urgently to know. But Big Jim, who had somewhat recovered his composure, twirled his moustaches in the old bombastic manner and tried to put everyone at their ease by assuming a nonchalance that deceived no one.

Everyone, apart from members of the family, ate dinner with a quiet, respectful gusto. When this was over Len was dressed in a brand-new black suit, which, like Big Jim's mourning suit, was to be paid for later out of the insurance money. He noticed that everyone now became excitedly expectant in a subdued way. Hushed whispers filled the kitchen with a droning sound, and he wondered what was the matter, but did not like to ask anyone.

The lad pulled the drawn window-curtains a little to one side so that he could see into the street. He saw a large number of men about the house. Most of them he knew to be his father's workmates and drinking pals. They were all dressed in black or blue suits which had obviously been taken from long hiding in drawers and cupboards, and above the starched linen collars their necks were red and sweaty.

When Len heard the door-latch rattle he turned his head from the window and saw Dai Cannon walk in. The people in the house became momentarily silent as Dai entered. He wore his 'pulpit costume', as he called it. Long wear had rusted its original blackness. The lobes of his ears were pressed upwards by the high collar. His face was sombre when he approached Big Jim.

He shook his mate's hand with a muttered 'Hard luck,

butty,' then made his way towards Siân. The hitherto dry-eyed woman began to sob as soon as she saw him. The tears overflowed and streamed down her face. This visible agony made all the other women present weep, while the men, swallowing hard, looked on awkwardly, all of them trying to appear unconcerned.

Dai patted the grief-stricken Siân on her head. 'There, there, my gel,' he consoled, 'it have come to you as it must come to all of us some time or another. Try to bear up the best you can, Siân bach, you still have the others to think of.'

With this he turned away and asked Mrs. Thomas for the Bible. She told him it was in the parlour and that everything was ready to start.

Dai led the way out of the kitchen, followed by Big Jim, Siân, and Len, then the relatives and as many of the neighbours as could squeeze into the little parlour. Len kept close to his parents at the head of the coffin, while Dai Cannon undid the heavy brass clasps of the family Bible, which contained the written history of the bereaved family. With sure fingers the preacher found the page he wanted. His ponderous voice started in a hoarse undertone, gaining in volume and in tempo as he warmed to his theme. With the skill of an Inquisition torturer Dai Cannon used the poor, covered body as a claw with which he tore the hearts of his listeners. He left them red-eyed, gasping with pain and grief, and when he had accomplished this he finished. There was a brief hush, broken only by an occasional sob, then they all slowly made their way back into the kitchen.

Dai went to the door and beckoned to some of the waiting men, who immediately came forward. The undertaker opened the parlour window and the men pushed the coffin into sight of the people who crowded the small street. Here it was grasped by willing hands and placed upon a trestle.

The people gathered round while Dai Cannon, his sleek black hair shining even in the foggy murk of the valley, mumbled a few hardly audible words. A voice began the rising cadences of a hymn. Other voices followed and soon everyone had joined in the mournful lay which was their farewell to Jane and her baby.

The last husky notes had not finished floating in the thick atmosphere before the men filed off in twos before the bier, leaving six of their number to carry the bare box and its contents on their shoulders.

Big Jim, holding Len by the hand, walked immediately behind the coffin. Following father and son came the other male members of the family in the order of their relationship, and in this fashion the long line began its slow trek down the valley towards the distant cemetery, Len carrying the little bunch of white flowers thrust into his hand by Mrs. Thomas.

As the mourners left the street they shivered to an unearthly wail that followed them, and seemed to hammer the air into sharp points that stuck in their quivering nerves. 'Oh, Jane bach, Jane bach, come back to me. They be taking you from your mam for ever.' The wail died down for a moment, then rose to a horrible scream. 'Bring her back to me, you jawled!' it demanded. 'Don't rob me of my only gel. Oh, Jane, Jane.'

Len looked at his father, but Big Jim's face was hidden in the shadows of his drooping shoulders. As the funeral made its way down Main Street, men coming home from the pits stayed their weary feet and doffed their caps till the coffin had passed. The coal-blackened faces made their eyes appear like white, liquid balls.

Evan the Overman and his son ran up a side-lane when they saw the funeral approaching. Ben the Barber and the landlord of the Boar's Head had drawn the blinds of their establishments out of respect for Big Jim.

At regular intervals the men who carried the coffin were changed by others who fell out from the front. Len walked like a person in a dream. His mind failed to co-ordinate impressions until he reached the cemetery gates and the single, sonorous 'dong' of the bell shook him from his stupor. His dazed eyes singled out the marble monuments each the symbol of a corpse, an advertisement of decay. He stared hard at every coffin-shaped earth-mound whose only ornament was a withered bunch of flowers dead as the body it marked.

Len knew now that Jane and her baby had gone for ever, but he still wondered what was going to be done to them. The cortege stopped while he was thinking, and Big Jim led him through the silent ranks of bare-headed men to the edge of Jane's grave.

Still clasping his father's hand, Len looked down into the freshly dug, water-sogged hole. He began to cry, and throughout the ceremony that followed he only dimly comprehended the beautiful panegyric that Dai Cannon was pouring out upon the dead daughter of his mate. After

86

the hymn that followed the closing words Len looked again into the hole. This time it was not empty. The coffin seemed to float in the water that reached half-way up its sides. Len threw the little bunch of flowers into the grave. He wanted them to drop on the coffin, but they fell into the water surrounding it. This turned his tears into sobs and Jim hurried him away.

Len never remembered going home. He sat moping in the corner while the relatives and friends busily consumed the ham and other food specially bought for and peculiar to the occasion. When the repast was over the relatives and friends quietly took their leave, each whispering a few condolences to Siân as they went. Then Len and his parents were left alone with their thoughts and their memories. The tears that fell on the sanded floor did not break the silence that followed, but at last Big Jim rose and, tenderly lifting the worn-out Siân to her feet, led her upstairs.

Len followed with scarcely a sound, and that night he missed Jane more than ever as he pictured her warm body and recalled conversations with her. During the months that followed he dreaded remaining in the house. Incidents and words constantly brought Jane back to his mind, and he would go off to the mountains and wander aimlessly over their slopes. Often he would lie down on the mountain and cry himself to sleep, waking when the coldness of dusk pierced his clothes, but he no longer found any pleasure in the rambles down the valley after and during school hours. The death of Jane had marked the end of his boyhood.

THE EXPLOSION

Though the death of his daughter had shaken Big Jim, he soon took up the usual routine of his life. When he had money he spent it in the Boar's Head, more often than not finishing the night with a fight. When he and Dai had no money they spent their evenings arguing in Ben the Barber's shop, and the main topic of discussion sooner or later always centred around the pits. It appeared that conditions were becoming worse. Mr. Hicks, the general manager, was pressing the men for more coal, while the officials, under his direction, were refusing to pay for work the men claimed they had already done.

Len heard the repercussions of what was happening in the pits each alternate Saturday, when his father brought home the pay for the preceding fortnight's work. When Big Jim had what he regarded as a good pay, he always enjoyed a little smoke after dinner and before bathing. But when he had a smaller pay packet than he expected or thought he deserved, he would bath first, then after dinner casually throw his wages on the table with an offhanded remark, 'There you be, Siân bach. That be all I can do for you this week, my gel.'

On one such occasion Siân slowly counted the money over, while Jim carefully soaped his moustache. After the first count her lips tightened ominously and she went over the coins once more. Then she looked up. 'Some little mistake by here, i'n't there, James bach?' she asked quietly.

Jim looked at her with feigned surprise. 'Mistake? Of course not, my gel,' he replied. Then he added, 'Not that I know of anyway. Let us count it again; perhaps it is you that have made the mistake. Ha-ha.' He laughed lamely, in spite of a big effort to appear unconcerned.

Together they recounted the money scattered on the table. When this was done Jim looked at Siân uneasily. 'There you are,' he said with forced jocularity. 'What did I tell you? It is you who have made the mistake, my gel.' He stopped a moment, then finished with, 'I knowed there be nothing wrong with the pay.'

Siân bridled up. 'Nothing wrong?' she exclaimed incredulously. 'Nothing wrong, you say? Man alive, if there be nothing wrong with the pay then there must be something wrong with you. Or,' she added slyly, 'perhaps you be starting your 'scursion tricks again.'

Jim coloured up. 'For shame, Siân bach,' he said reproachfully. 'You didn't ought throw that up to my face. You do know it was only a little joke on my part.' His temper began to rise. 'What the hell can I help if the pay be small?' he burst out vehemently. 'Arglwydd mawr, I do work hard enough for it.'

A short silence followed this outburst. It was broken by Jim, who began to wheedle. 'Come, 'nghariad i, give me my pocket money. I have promised faithful to meet Dai Cannon tonight on very 'portant business.'

Siân interrupted him brusquely. 'Ah, I did think so,' she said. 'Dai. 'Portant business. Anything but your home. How do you think I be going to keep all of us on this money? Bah, boy's money! I 'ood be shamed to bring it home if I was you.'

Jim dreaded the bitter onslaught of her tongue, but he braved it for the sake of his pocket money. He tried blustering. 'Come, come, fenyw,' he uttered sharply, 'there be no need for all this fuss and nonsense. You can't always 'spect to have big money. I will have a good place next week, then things will be better.'

Siân took no notice of his bluster. 'Big money! Next week!' she twitted harshly, her eyes beginning to glitter. 'You will say next that I have been squandering the pay. If anybody did hear you, man, they 'ood swear I had put you ears over heels in debt.'

She began to weep into her canvas apron. 'What good be next week to me?' she asked plaintively. 'We have got to live till then, and don't forget, James,' she put in as a final shot, 'that you be a big-eating man.'

Big Jim looked at her, his eyes at once desperate and despairing. He was ashamed of the pay himself, but was too proud to admit it. Siân had beaten him in the argument and he had no more to say. He put on his coat with a hopeless gesture and walked to the door, making as much noise as possible on the way.

Siân raised her head from the apron. 'Where be you going?' she asked.

The tone of her query put new hope into Jim. Quietly, as if weary and overcome with care, he replied, 'Not far, Siân bach. Only just down the road to have a shave from Ben the Barber.'

'But you have got no money,' she retorted.

Jim saw his opportunity and jumped at it. 'No; I do know that well 'nough, 'nghariad bach i,' he said; 'but Ben be very good to me when he do know I be down and out.'

Siân pricked up her ears at this. Her face reddened.

'Don't you dare, James Roberts, to simple me before any man,' she commanded. 'We have gone through worse times than this and we still be alive.'

Jim knew he had conquered and gravely murmured, as she handed him some money, 'I did know you 'oodn't leave me down when it come to the push, Siân bach. You be so good as gold, though your words do come so hard as brass sometimes.'

With this he went out, promising he would not be late.

Siân remained at the table planning how best to share the pay between the various debts that had accumulated during the past fortnight. Len wrote the items down at her dictation. Several times she made him change them, but at last she seemed satisfied and rose to her feet. Len fetched the heavy woollen shawl from behind the door. She swathed this round her head and shoulders and bade Len follow her.

Both of them enjoyed these Saturday night shopping expeditions. The women of the village used the general stores of Mr. Evans Cardi to retail gossip while the obliging Mr. Evans attended to their requirements.

This night the chief item of gossip was the bad times. 'Yes, my gel,' Mrs. Thomas told Siân, loud enough for everyone in the stores to hear, 'things be getting worse from day to day. How they 'spect people to live on the money they pay our men, the good Lord alone knows.'

A murmur of assent spread round the counter.

'Ay,' responded Siân, 'you be quite right. I member the time we could put a few shillings by our side every fortnight, but we have to pay it out now as it come in, and then we haven't got 'nough to go round half our time.'

The conversation became general. One woman who had a house full of children remarked, 'It be 'bout time our men did something. What with small money and the children coming every year, life be not worth living. The pits is going to pieces,' she added bitterly: 'they will never again be like they used to.'

After a while Siân gathered up the groceries Mr. Evans had placed in a big paper bag for her. She handed this to Len with the remark, 'We had better go now, boy bach, to make supper ready against your father come home.'

The street looked dark and forbidding after the warm, glaring oil-lamps in the stores and a slight drizzle made the road muddy underfoot.

Len and his mother had reached the lane that led up the mountain to Sunny Bank when they heard an uproar in Main Street, which they had left behind. 'Some drunken men fighting again, I 'spose,' commented Siân casually. 'Fitter if they went home to their famblies.'

She continued on her way. Suddenly she pulled up short and turned her head towards the street. Above the uproar rose the great voice of Big Jim. 'Let him come on,' she heard him roar. 'Think you I be 'fraid of any man, let alone a bloody Bristolian?'

Siân hurriedly retraced her steps, Len following with the groceries. Outside the Boar's Head they saw a crowd of people stretching across the street, swaying spasmodically to the accompaniment of excited shouts. 'Fair play there! Keep the ring clear! No up and down.'

Siân pulled the shawl more tightly round her head and forced her way towards the centre, Len following closely at her heels. He heard a woman scream at the top of her voice: 'O God, they be killing each other. Police! Police!'

A man near her growled, 'What the hell be the matter on you, fenyw. Get off home if you don't like to see a fight. Don't worry 'bout the police.' He added, 'I 'spect he is snooping round the back-streets looking for burglars that are not there, ha-ha. You can venture you 'on't see him here,' he concluded.

Smacking thuds followed by loud grunts frightened Len, and he would have run away had it not been for his mother. When she stopped pressing through the crowd he drew to her side and saw the ring made by the people. In the centre his father and Bill Bristol, both naked to the waist, were punching away at each other with every ounce of energy concentrated in their fists.

Len saw the blood spurt from Bill's face as Big Jim's

fist caught him squarely on the nose. A gasp went through the crowd, echoing the impact of the blow. Bill Bristol staggered back, and willing hands held him erect. Someone offered a knee as a stool, and Bill was made to sit on this while the blood was mopped from his face with his own shirt.

Meanwhile Big Jim had turned to Dai Cannon. 'That have finished it,' he said: 'you might as well leave me have my shirt and coat now.'

He began to pull on his shirt when he heard a sudden shout: 'Good old Bill! That's what you want, guts! Play for his belly and you'll soon have him down. The bigger they are the harder they fall.'

Like a flash Big Jim twisted the shirt off his head and half turned to meet his antagonist. But he was too late to check the headlong rush of the recovered Bill. The latter dodged the fist flung at him like a thunderbolt and buried his lowered head deep into Jim's belly.

Big Jim's mouth was forced open with an agonising gasp by the violently expelled wind. The quivering knees slowly contorted themselves into a subsiding movement and Jim's body collapsed like a deflated concertina, but his brain remained perfectly conscious and clear although his muscles were paralysed by the impact. He tore at the air with his lips as he tried to gulp it into his lungs, where it rattled like a bag of marbles.

Siân bent over her fallen spouse and reproachfully taunted him. 'What be you doing down by there, James bach?' she asked him. 'Fancy lying in the gutter with the only decent suit you have got. Ach! Call yourself a man!

Why, I could buy your sort for ten a penny.'

The gibe sent an electric quiver through Jim's body, giving it new and sudden life. He sprang to his feet with a bound and a muttered curse.

Bill Bristol, surprised at the quick recovery, sprang forward and met Jim half-way. He tried to repeat the same tactic as before, and literally flung himself, like a bullet, head first at Jim's body. But the latter had learned a bitter lesson. He stepped a little to one side as Bill reached him and his huge fist streaked in and out once like a snake's tongue. The thud of the terrible blow clotted the blood in Len's veins. He saw the horrible jerk that seemed to tear Bill's head from his shoulders. He watched the body straighten like a released spring and flatten itself on the wet earth.

The excited people in the crowd knew the prostrate man would fight no more that night, and anxious hands helped him to recover while Dai Cannon helped Jim don his shirt and coat.

Siân, her eyes shining, kept nagging. 'For shame, James,' she said. 'Do you call yourself a 'spectable man, fighting like a blackguard on Main Street? Just the same the blood of Bill Bristol could be on your head this night. What do you think people will say 'bout me? I will be too shamed to raise my head in chapel again.'

Jim grunted an inaudible answer and walked over to the recovering Bill, who after some further assiduous attention, stood dazedly on his feet. Jim caught his arm and led him back to where Dai Cannon was earnestly talking to Siân. The latter was saying when they reached her, 'All right, David, I will give James half an hour.

96

William did ought to be better by then. But 'member,' she exclaimed, turning to Jim, 'no more nonsense. If butties can't have a pint together without fighting, then they better left it there altogether.'

Without more words Dai and Jim made their way through the open door of the Boar's Head, and most of the men in the crowd followed them.

Len and his mother trudged quietly up the black hill. The oil-lamps shining through the windows of Sunny Bank invited them to hurry through the drizzle, and both were glad when they reached the house. Siân busied herself fanning the dying fire into flame while Len sat moodily in the corner, and as soon as he had finished his supper he went straight to bed.

Next day in chapel Len watched his mother carefully. He expected to see her with drooping head after the events of the previous night, but both she and Dai Cannon appeared to have forgotten what had occurred.

The sermon was based on the text, 'If he strike thee on one cheek, turn to him the other'. In deep tones Dai rolled out his message to the congregation, and at the end of the service the women declared to each other that they had never heard such a beautiful and inspiring sermon.

Throughout the day Len failed to tear from his eyes the sight of Bill Bristol's blood-spattered face. Physical brutality was repugnant to the lad. He tried to imagine how Bill felt when Jim's fist smashed into his nose.

The thought made him shudder coldly, and for the remainder of the day he remained silent and aloof.

Since Jane's death Len had become increasingly morbid

and introspective, and that night in bed his thoughts ran riot. He pictured Jane as he used to see her and wondered what Evan the Overman's son had done to give her the baby from which she died. His warm body tossed restlessly about the lonely bed as his imagination fluttered between mental images. Pressing Jane's pillow closely to him, he longed again for her presence, but this only made him think of the muddied grave, and as his mind drifted from one morbid thought to another he fell at last into an uneasy sleep.

He slept for some hours before waking to the roar of a thunder-clap. The intense darkness made him doubt if his eyes were open. In the act of putting his fingers to them he saw the blazing flash of lightning that filled the bedroom with a ghostly blue haze. It went in a second and left the room darker than ever. The pursuing thunder frightened him, and he tried to hide from its crackling roar by burying his head beneath the bedclothes. But the thunder followed.

The fitful lightning flashes and the rising tumult quickened Len's emotions. He felt afraid. Quivers ran up and down his flesh and he broke out into a sweat. He wound the bedclothes more tightly about him, thinking their warmth would provide protection from the noisy storm, but, though the school books told him that thunder was harmless, he was more afraid of its clamouring roar than of the knife-like flashes that cut the night in two.

Swathed in the blanket, his nerves tense with anticipation, he waited for the next crash. He heard the initial ear-shattering crack, but the usual rolling rumbles that chased it were drowned in an unearthly roar that made the house tremble and for a moment the air was full of little flaming bubbles that suddenly spluttered out and left the world dark and still as if all existence had ended.

Len sprang out of bed and rushed screaming to his mother's room. He found her moaning as she tried to light the candle with a match that quivered in her hand, while Big Jim, clad only in a shirt, stood peering through the window as if the universe were centred in his eyes. The glow from the sputtering candle filled the bedroom with moving shadows, and Len stopped screaming. The hushed silence that followed was broken by a hoarse groan from Siân.

'Oh, James bach, James bach,' she muttered in a shuddering undertone, as if scared of her own voice, 'the pit have blowed up.'

Jim, still at the window, did not answer. He saw the lights that suddenly appeared at every window in the street glimmer like corpse candles upon the raindrops, and suddenly springing towards the bed he snatched his trousers from the rail, and with frenzied fingers began pulling the garment over his naked legs.

Simultaneously Siân got out of bed, still moaning to herself. As she also began hurriedly to dress, she asked him: 'Where be you going?' Receiving no reply, she cried out, 'Oh, God bach, you be going to your death, James.'

By the time she had wrapped the woollen shawl about her head Jim had already rushed down the stairs. Turning to Len, she lifted the terror-stricken lad into the bed. Then, with a murmured, 'Be a good boy, Len bach; mam 'on't be long,' she tucked him in and followed Jim down the stairs and out of the house.

The street was already full of half-clad, white-faced men and women. They paid no heed to the driving rain that beat on to their shivering bodies or the lightning that sizzled through the air and bathed the valley in sulphuric blue. Each street was a tributary, pouring men and women into the main stream of people rushing madly up the hill to the scene of the explosion. Only children, hysterical with fear, were left behind in the houses.

The rain slashed savagely at streaming faces, while the thunder cracked and rumbled in angry roars, but the people were oblivious to the cruelty of the elements. As if drawn by magnets, they flung themselves into the storm, defeating all its attempts to prevent them from reaching the pit. At every street the living stream of distracted human beings gained impetus and numbers, and the clang of their hobnailed boots challenged the jealous mumbling of the thunder.

No words were spoken now. Nothing mattered but to reach the pit. Slowly the long, uphill drag against the storm began to take toll of the weaker and the aged. Gasping and coughing under the terrible physical and emotional strain, they had to give way to the stronger and more agile, who forged to the front. Big Jim, who had burst his way through the querulous crowd, was at the head of the long-drawn, hurrying procession. Siân, panting and spitting thick clots of saliva that filled her mouth, was close on his heels. For every stride he took she had to take two.

Her legs dragged on her thighs like lead. The pain in her body reminded her of the times when she had to carry sacks of coal on her back. Then she had felt her body being squeezed into her feet. Now she felt her feet tearing her body from her head. She stumbled and moaned, but, closing her eyes, she followed her feet, which automatically rose and fell and drew her on. She felt her body go numb from the exhaustion, and was glad, because her brain cleared as a consequence. When Big Jim led the rush over the flimsy wooden bridge that spanned the ravine separating the pit from the village, Siân was still close to him.

The crude structure became a bridge of sighs that echoed the trampling feet stumbling across it, and the thin cordon of police and pit officials at the end was brushed aside like soot by the rushing people. Mr. Hicks, the general manager of the pit, howled, 'Keep back. Keep back. Everything is all right.' His howls became wails and were lost in the storm. None of the rain-drenched people heard what he said, as with deadly certainty they plunged towards the pit, from whose mouth belched the fumes generated by the explosion.

When they reached the pit-head everything became confusion for some minutes. The storm redoubled its efforts to dominate the scene. Men shouted incoherently to each other, women screamed and moaned. Everyone gave orders that no one obeyed.

Ezra Jones, the miners' leader, who was already on the pit-head, beckoned Big Jim to him. Ezra's short, thickset body and stern face looked as hard as the coal from which he forced a livelihood. Jim forced his way forward, Siân still following. 'Jim,' said Ezra, his cold voice quivering a little, 'we must get these people away from the pit-head.' Big Jim nodded agreement. He looked around the excited crowd and realised if something were not done quickly the women would become hysterical and panicky. He went back into the thick of the crowd, urging men here and there to the front. When he returned he found the biggest men of the village circling the pit-head, keeping the others behind them.

The storm gave added terror and significance to the scene. Its crooked lightning cynically blinded the staring eyes, then played in blue streaks round the trellised steelwork of the pit-head gears. The lightning used the red glare from the open furnaces as a frame for itself, then mockingly withdrew for a moment into black obscurity, to return unexpectedly a moment later with ten times greater ferocity. Thunder wantonly joined in the game. Its unholy laughter rolled and crackled, tearing the air in a devil's chorus of reverberating echoes, that died down the valley only to be born again, with greater vigour, at the pit.

Heedless of the clamour, Big Jim and Ezra strengthened the cordon of men around the pit. Mr. Hicks, putty-faced and panting, was allowed through. Siân kept near the rim of the cordon, never taking her eyes from Big Jim.

The three men held a hurried consultation with certain of the other workmen, and when it was ended Big Jim's great voice rang out above the storm.

'Rescue brigade and first-aid men to the front!'

The ring immediately opened to admit the men who obeyed the command. Scores of volunteers rushed to carry out the next order that someone should fetch the rescue apparatus from the stores, where it had been rotting unattended for years, but apart from an occasional moan no voice could be heard except that which was giving the orders.

It was now discovered that the pit cage had been smashed into the side of the shaft by the force of the explosion, and the splintered steel was dangling like ravelled cloth from the threaded rope that held it. After another hurried conference it was decided that the only thing to do was to make use of the discarded sinking-bucket, rusting a quarter of a mile away from the coal screens, and soon a score of men were pushing and rolling the bucket towards the pit, while others disentangled what remained of the cage.

Suddenly a woman's piercing scream rang clear through the turmoil. It rose in ascending, agonising shrieks. 'O God, spare him for me! Let him come back home.'

Siân shivered icily as a crash of thunder swallowed the pitiful plea. For the first time that night she forced her eyes away from Big Jim, and looked at the distraught young woman near by, who had fallen on her knees into the black mud and was tearing loose her rain-soddened hair. The woman's mouth opened and shut like a frog's, but no sound came from it. Siân flung her shawl over the woman's heaving shoulders and, bending down, tried to lift her from the mud. 'Come, my gel,' she murmured, 'don't take it like this now. Perhaps everything will come all right for you and all your tears will be wasted.'

The woman appeared not to hear, and began screaming again. Siân shook her roughly, at the same time blinking back the tears from her own eyes. 'That will do,' she said. 'You must act like a 'ooman, not like a child, at this time. 'Member, you might need all of your strength before this night be gone over your head.'

103

Other women came to Siân's assistance. They lifted the shaking form bodily from the mud and led her gently away, leaving the storm to silence the gasping wails that bubbled wetly from her lips. Once more Siân turned her attention to Big Jim, flinging back the wet hair from her eyes and wringing it into a knot at the back of her neck, but Big Jim and his mates had paid no attention to the incident. Franticly, they continued their efforts to fix the bucket to the rope, and finally the sure, hurrying fingers completed the transference.

Ezra began drawing the weird-looking rescue apparatus over his head, but without a word of explanation Big Jim and some of the other men took it from him. Sharp words followed between them, Ezra claiming the right to go down the shaft with the first group. They did not argue, but hurriedly taking a vote, decided that Ezra had to remain on the surface.

The bucket was now dangling over the fearful, steaming hole, slowly circling round itself and round the shaft at the same time, like a ghastly pendulum, the dual motion being caused by the absence of guide ropes to steady it. Soon a number of men, wearing rescue apparatus and led by Big Jim, wormed their way across the black gap that separated them from the oscillating bucket, and climbing in stood jammed erect, their masks making them look like inhuman creatures from some abysmal world. Then, as the bucket slowly sank into the fuming mouth of the pit, Siân forced her way through the cordon. Her face shone white even through the black grime that covered it. Both hands were pressed with tense hardness to her chest. Her voice came in gasps as she shouted, 'Stop a minute! Stop a minute!'

Someone caught her by the shoulders and held her back. Siân turned round with a snarl. 'Keep your dirty hands off me!' she shouted. 'Who be you to dare stop me going with my man?' Her eyes were too misty to see who gripped her. She wasn't even aware there was more than one.

Siân battled grimly to break away from the impeding grasp. 'Let me go,' she screamed, kicking out wildly, 'my place be with my man.'

But finding her struggles were of no avail, she suddenly relaxed. 'It be all right now,' she announced. 'Please forgive me, I know I have done wrong' and her eyes were dry and hard, as they stared at the bucket that was now nearly out of sight.

Its slow descent was followed by a soft groan from thousands of parched throats. The groan became a mass moan which kept time with the motion of the bucket and its human cargo as it slithered out of sight, leaving nothing but the snaky rope to mark its existence. Imperceptibly the moan took shape, was given form. Deeper than the sea, it nestled a path through the voids in the thunder. Sometimes it was subdued by the fiercely crashing roars, but it always returned to ride their crests, until at last it swept a clear road of domination above the storm. At once a prayer and a challenge, the old Welsh hymn burned its fiery way into the hearts of the grieving men and women on the pit-head, melting their sobs into music which mastered the tempest and rang down the valley of doom. Mournfully the cadences of the hymn, harmonised in the common agony, broke the air into emotional vibrations.

Beth sydd imi yn y byd
Ond gorthrymderau mawr o hyd.

What in this world for me
But great grief and agony.

The pit had become in one night a crematorium surrounded by thousands of mourning people.

In the meantime Big Jim and his rescue brigade, speechless under their rescue gear, were swinging giddily from side to side of the shaft. Thick, swirling fumes gave them the impression they were slowly falling through dense clouds, and during the descent the bucket swung with exceptional force into the side, nearly tumbling two of the men out into the black depths beneath. As it was impossible to give vocal orders Big Jim did the next best thing, and placed his hands out rigid before him over the side of the bucket. Each of the other men followed suit, and their hands made a buttress between the bucket and the sides.

Slowly, shrouded in a green halo spread by the gleam of the safety lamps hanging from their belts upon the fumes that enveloped them, the rescue men sank into the pit. Although they appeared cool and calm, inwardly they quivered with dread of what they were about to see, for every one of them was an experienced miner who had practically been reared in the pit and knew all its moods and powers.

At last the bucket bumped sharply on the shaft bottom and the interminable descent was over.

The lamp lights seemed to fling the foggy fumes back

into their eyes and made them blinder than the darkness. The men shut their eyes tightly and lowered the lamps until they nearly touched the floor. After some minutes they opened their eyes again and were able to distinguish objects.

Big Jim walked in front, while the others lined themselves across the breadth of the roadway so that nothing should escape their joint observation, and in this way they proceeded, with infinite slowness, further into the pit. After about ten minutes of this, during which the atmosphere got more dense and hot each second, Big Jim called a sudden halt. His lips formed themselves into a 'sh-h-h' which no one heard. He realised this, and raised his finger to his mouth as if seeking to enjoin silence where all was still. The men, however, understood what he meant and stood rigidly erect, straining their ears to catch any sound that should break through their masks.

From a seeming distance of miles they heard a crackling noise as if some huge fire was feeding itself on an incalculable supply of what it needed. Sweat poured down the men's strained flesh in streams. It was hot, like boiling water.

One of the men could stand the strain no longer, and dragging the helmet from his head, heard for one second the roar of the fire. Then everything was lost in the cough that tore his lungs. He gasped for air, every gasp choking him more firmly. He felt his lungs tearing and tasted the blood that rushed to his throat and mouth. But he never knew that Big Jim had sprung forward and jammed the helmet back on his head.

When Big Jim raised himself from the prostrate man he shook his head sadly, and the small group, now one man less, walked slowly on. Here and there they had to clamber over falls of roof and hot steel girders, their hearts pumping madly and their heads bursting inside the helmets that covered them. They inhaled the putrid air inside their masks with gasping swallows, like sufferers from tonsillitis.

When they reached the stables Big Jim again halted. Falling on his knees he began to feverishly turn over the black blotches that lay in queer heaps upon the ground. The other men followed suit. When they stood erect again their legs were trembling and their stomachs felt sick. They had found the first victims of the explosion.

At the pit-head the people waited. Every eye was focused upon the rope that had ceased moving long before. Its stillness told the people that Big Jim and his men were still searching. For all who watched it it had become the centre of creation, as hour after hour they waited, their voices becoming mute and their faces set into unnatural hardness. Patience lost meaning and time had no existence in the common urge to know what was happening in the black depths of the pit.

The sun was struggling to push its new-born rays through the cloud-crusted murk of the valley when the iron knocker at the pit-head suddenly clanged. The dead silence that instantly followed the solitary knell was more eerie than the thunder rumbling dismally in the distance.

At the second clang the people shivered as if icicles had pierced their flesh. The tension was eased by the spontaneous quiver, and a tremor of suppressed excitement ran through the throng. A warm glow stole over their cold bodies, and anxiously the waiting people strained their ears to catch the third signal announcing that someone or something was ready to ascend from below. When the sharp command came everyone shuddered with sudden apprehension. They dreaded that the ascending bucket contained someone belonging to themselves.

Siân drew the rain-shrunken shawl, which had been returned, more tightly around her shoulders. The hair again hung loose in wet wisps about her face. Fixing her eyes upon the rope that was slowly beginning to move, she mused audibly, 'I wonder what it be bringing up?'

A gleam flashed in her eyes as she thought, 'Perhaps my James be dangling from its end.'

She felt the rope was moving too slowly. She wanted it to hasten so that everyone could see what the bucket held, but in the same instant she banished the thought from her head. 'No-no,' she murmured, 'bad news do travel quick enough without us wishing it to come quicker.'

The same impulses filled the other people, as the rope weaved a slow path around the huge wheel above their heads. Men mentally measured the rate of the rope against the depth of the pit, and unspoken thoughts told everyone that the bucket was near the surface. A restless, impatient movement again ran through the crowd like quicksilver. Face looked at face in mute appeal and saw nothing but the black-grimed shadow of itself. The ring of men around the pit-head closed in nearer, and stood ready to grasp the bucket and whatever it contained immediately it reached the surface.

Sensing the developing panic, Ezra called out in his

cold, harsh voice, 'Steady, boys. Cool heads now.' The calm, sensible words eased the tension and soothed hysterical emotions, and when at last the bucket broke through the black void of the pit-mouth willing hands hurriedly pulled it to the side.

The sole human occupant was gently lifted out. While some men unstrapped the encumbering rescue apparatus from his shoulders, others removed the misshapen, brattice-covered lumps dumped in the bottom of the bucket like sacks of red cement. Eight of these were drawn out, tenderly straightened on the waiting stretchers, and immediately carried to the manager's office on the other side of the bridge. Silently the people opened their ranks to make way for the passing corpses, for although not a limb could be seen everyone knew that Big Jim and his men had made sure of the first victims of the explosion.

Sad-eyed women, their wet skirts sticking to their legs, followed the procession of stretchers across the bridge to the temporary mortuary in the office. But most of the men remained at the pit-head where Ezra and Mr. Hicks were questioning the rescue man, who had now recovered from his exhaustion. He reported that the stables near the pit bottom were a mass of impassable flames, and that a huge fall of roof further on prevented penetration into the inner workings. The eight men already brought up had been found huddled together near the stables, as if seeking to protect each other from the blast that swept the mine.

When he reported the terrible death of the rescue man everyone present was shocked. They vividly pictured the horrible details of the tragedy.

The rescue man brought them back to the task on hand when he added that it was impossible for Big Jim and his mates to remain below much longer, as the after-damp was already beginning to intrude its poisonous breath inside the gas-masks.

To stress his warning the iron knocker clanged an urgent message to the surface. Ezra hastily strapped the rescue apparatus to his own shoulders and stepped into the bucket. The rope again commenced its twirling motion as it dropped the bucket with its solitary occupant into the shaft.

Police and extra rescue men, hurriedly drafted in from other places, cleared the colliery yard of the people not directly engaged in rescue world.

Siân and a number of other women steadfastly refused to move. 'What do you think I be?' asked Siân when they attempted to remove her. 'Think you I be slut enough to go crying across the bridge while my man be down in that hell? No,' she declared with adamant determination, 'there be no man or devil in this or any other world can shift me from by here until I see my James safe and sound.'

Further unpleasantness was prevented by the appearance of the bucket and all those who had descended the shaft after the explosion.

Siân ran forward and threw her arms around Jim's neck. 'Thank God,' she whispered in his ear. 'I be satisfied now that I know you be all right.

Jim said nothing, but squeezed her tightly for a moment before entering the little shack at the pit-head where his mates and the other responsible people were.

111

While the police cordoned off all approaches to the pit, Big Jim made his report. 'We will have to tackle it from two ends,' he said. 'Some will have to work their way through from the pits the other side of the mountain, while some of us be driving through the fall of roof this end.'

'But before we can do anything,' he added, 'we will first of all have to smother the fire in the stable. It will all have to be done in very short shifts, because the heat and smoke be unbearable.'

Ezra and Mr. Hicks now took charge of the operations, while Jim and his mates made their way to the office. Here they found the mass of people who had been urged from the pit-head. Inside the office attempts were being made to identify the bodies already brought up. Jim helped in this. The corpses were stripped stark naked and searched for birth marks, while other means of identification were sought in the clothes. Big Jim, examining the pockets of a pair of trousers he picked up from the floor, pulled out a brass tobacco pouch containing some loose tobacco and a shilling and exclaimed excitedly, 'This do belong to Shoni Jones, Cap-du.'

The name flew from mouth to mouth until it was stopped by a wild scream when it reached the ears of the widow. Willing and tender hands led her away.

It was agreed by the man in charge that the bodies not identified should be left where they were for a while. The body of Shoni Cap-du was replaced on a stretcher and covered with some brattice-cloth.

Headed by what was left of Shoni Cap-du and the dead rescue man, the wet, grief-stricken people wearily made their way down Main Street to their homes. The frenzied rush through the storm on the previous night together with the agonising wait at the pit-head had exhausted them in mind and body, and their grief was sharpened by the uncertainty of the actual casualties and by the knowledge that it would take a considerable time to clear the pit and find the full extent and effects of the explosion. Families with missing men mourned even while they tried to persuade themselves that remote possibilities were probabilities.

Jim and Siân found Len crouched over the dead embers of the fire. The big, bright eyes that looked into theirs when they entered showed that the lad had cried himself dry in a fury of impotent fears, but neither of them had given him a thought during the terror of the night. Siân was immediately penitent. She stooped down and gathered the lad to her wet clothes, crooning in his ear, 'There, there, 'nghariad bach i. Don't cry no more. Mam 'o'n't leave you alone never again.'

Big Jim interrupted her. 'Where be your sense, fenyw?' he exclaimed. 'You leave him alone to frighten his little self to death all night, and now that you do find him alive after all you do want him to die of pewmonia from your wet clothes.'

Thus reminded of her condition, Siân began to build the fire into a huge blaze while Big Jim coaxed from the usually reticent Len a recital of what he had felt during the night.

When his parents had left him, Len, already frightened by the storm, had let his imagination run riot. Like all other miners' children, he knew that explosions meant death and destruction. And once he had gripped this fact

113

it was easy for his fertile mind, egged on by the storm and the horrible loneliness, to conjure up pictures of burned and mangled bodies. He had seen his father among the dead, his body shredded into blood-dripping pieces.

Siân had remained silent up to this point, but she now sensed that the lad was working himself up into an emotional climax. She checked the recital with the abrupt announcement, 'Come, the two of you, and have something hot in your insides.'

Big Jim ate nothing throughout the meal. Siân mused more than she ate. 'There be many a poor dab gone to meet his God before his time this night,' she said, half crying. 'I wonder, James bach, if there be any we do know among them?'

Jim did not reply. He knew most of the men working in the pit when the explosion occurred, and he knew from what he had seen that only a miracle could bring any of them from it alive, but he did not believe in miracles. The fall of roof, while big enough to prevent ingress to the workings, had failed to subdue the sound of crackling flames or to prevent the heavy, poisonous fumes percolating through.

As Big Jim's thoughts jumped from name to name, linking each with an incident or characteristic relating to it, he muttered, abstractedly, 'Poor old Shoni Cap-du 'on't drink any more pints in the Boar's Head.'

He was silent a moment, and Siân looked at him quietly. At length he exclaimed, in a somewhat louder voice: 'Duw, duw. Who 'ood think the old pit 'ood blow up so sudden? But there,' he added, as an afterthought, 'I have knowed there have been something the matter with her for a long time now.'

114

He ceased his musings, and Siân handed him a cup of tea. 'Have this now, James bach,' she coaxed. 'Then try to have a bit of a rest.'

Big Jim took her advice but found sleep impossible, and in a very short time his impatient restlessness took him to Ben the Barber's.

The little back room was crowded with men discussing the explosion and its victims. Ben was unusually silent in face of the catastrophe that had swept the pit. He felt keenly the immensity of the grief that was to follow. The men moved up to make place for Jim's huge bulk. They had already been commenting upon his daring initiative during the preceding night. Young Charlie the Cripple kept close to Jim when the latter sat on the bench.

Big Jim turned towards Dai Cannon, who was sitting in his customary place near the fire. Jim noisily retched some mucus from his chest to his mouth and spat it on the floor before saying, 'Well, boys, it have come at last, as it was bound to come sooner or later.'

He paused a moment, as if expecting Dai or one of the others to say something. Finding that no one responded, he went on, wiping the back of his hand across his mouth. 'Huh. If us all spoke the truth us would all say that we 'spected it to come. Ach! No man can drag coal from the face like hair, and leave his gobs empty, without something being bound to happen. No; you leave the gobs empty of muck and they will soon fill with gas.'

Jim stopped a moment again, then burst out with a passionate oath, his voice resounding with the vehemence of his conviction. 'Arglwydd mawr! That's all they do think 'bout these days is coal, coal, and still more coal. Blast safety. That don't count. Blow the men to hell, but give the big boss coal.'

He was now roaring in his fury, and every word brought more saliva on his moustache. 'Don't us all know that the pit have been getting worse every day?' he demanded. 'The officials did know so good as us men, but they never took any notice. Bah! What do us men count? We be cheaper than chickens.'

Big Jim subsided into silence. After a brief spell during which everyone appeared to be thinking hard over Jim's words, Dai Cannon took up the subject. His deep voice trembled with emotion as he said, 'There is much in what Jim says. Yes, very much. But it's no good us talking like that now. What we have got to do is get those boys up as quick as we can, dead or alive, and put the old pit a bit shipshape again. All of our talk or all of our tears 'on't bring our butties back to us.'

While this discussion was taking place Ezra, Mr. Hicks, and Lord Cwmardy, who had hurried specially from London to the scene of the disaster, were planning the rescue operations. They divided the twenty-four hours into shifts of two hours each, and allocated the men necessary for them.

Big Jim was allowed to come and go to the pit as he liked. He worked practically night and day. His strength, example, and experience spurred on the other men and gave added energy to their flagging bodies.

The men worked in the most intolerable conditions. Excessive heat and the foetid atmosphere melted their flesh and left them like empty sacks at the end of their short

116

shifts. The bodies they discovered each day were simply ghastly lumps of greasy putrefaction. Very few could be identified. In a short time it became known to the people of the valley that the explosion had left no survivors.

THE INQUEST
AND BURIAL

The people of Cwmardy were full of excitement. Sad-eyed women, their arms folded inside their aprons, stood on the street corners and discussed the rumour spreading round the village like wildfire. In Ben the Barber's shop nothing else was talked of. No one seemed to know where the rumour emanated from, but those who were bereaved by the explosion already regarded it as Gospel truth, and the day before the inquest on the first eight bodies brought up the flaming pit, matters reached a head in Sunny Bank.

Big Jim, his legs stretched obscenely towards the fire, was about to doze off when Siân asked him, apropos of nothing, 'Do you think there be any truth in it, James bach?'

Jim looked at her, blank surprise in his eyes, before appealing to Len. 'Now what do you think of that?' he asked the lad. 'Your mother 'spect me to read her mind while she do keep her tongue between her teeth and her eyes shut.'

Len did not answer, although he wondered what his mother was driving at. Jim turned and addressed himself directly to her, saying, 'Now tell me, fenyw, what exactly do you want me to tell you?'

Siân took umbrage at his tone. 'There you go again,' she complained. 'I can't ask you a simple question unless you do go and lose your temper. You do talk to me, James, like as if I was a dog under your feet.'

This somewhat softened Jim's asperity. The terrific strain of the rescue work was beginning to fray his nerves.

'There, there, merch i,' he consoled her. 'Don't take no notice of me, mun. I be tired. Tell me what you do want to know.'

Siân responded immediately. 'I was only asking you, James bach, if you do believe all this talk going about.'

Jim tried to keep his patience. 'What talk, my gel?' he asked.

'Oh, I thought you had heard,' she replied. 'They do say that the 'splosion was made by one of the men who did open his lamp on the sly to have a whiff.'

Jim sprang to his feet with an oath and banged his fist violently upon the table. His curses were eloquent testimony that he did not believe the rumour.

Siân tried to placate him. 'Well, well,' she said, 'there be no need for you to go to all this fuss. I be only telling you what everybody else be talking about.'

'Ach!' he snarled. 'Fitter if everybody looked after their own bloody business and let the dead rest in peace.'

Saying which, he flung on his coat and left the house without more ado.

Next morning Siân opened the box under the bed and took out the suit she had bought Jim for Jane's funeral. Ready tears sparkled in her eyes as she put the clothes to air on the rod beneath the mantelpiece.

Jim, immersed in his thoughts, had recovered from his temper of the previous evening. 'Last time you put these on,' Siân reminded him, 'was when we did bury our Jane bach. Nothing have been right since she have gone.' She wiped her eyes on the canvas apron.

'Ay, ay, merch i,' retorted Jim ponderously, 'that be quite true. But it be no good worrying 'bout it now,' he added resignedly.

Abruptly changing the subject, he asked, more to himself than Siân: 'I wonder what I will have to say in the inquest this afternoon. They do tell me these lawyer chaps be awful clever and can put into your mouth words you don't want to say and don't mean. Ezra did tell me yesterday to be very careful how I do answer the questions.'

The nervous tone betrayed his uneasiness. Siân tried to encourage him. 'Pooh-pooh!' she exclaimed confidently. 'Don't tell me that Big Jim be 'fraid of any man that do wear a frocktail coat and a black wig.' She had never been in any court of law, but had been told by her neighbours that this was the uniform of justice. 'All you got to do,' she continued, 'is to speak the truth. Truth will stand before man or God.' She hesitated a moment to see what effect this had on Jim, then added: 'Don't be 'fraid, James bach, I will come with you.'

Jim jumped from his seat. 'No-no, my gel,' he hastily said. 'Don't you worry 'bout me. I will look after myself. And even if I couldn't,' he added, 'they 'oodn't let you in with me, 'cause you are not a witness, see.'

No more was said as Jim prepared himself for the inquest. Siân gave the final touches to his clothes and bade him as he left: 'Now, 'member, James, you don't owe a single ha'penny to a living soul and can hold your head up before any man.'

The inquest was to be held in the large room of the Boar's Head which, ordinarily, was only used on Saturday nights. When Jim arrived at the public house a large number of his workmates tried to detain him with questions, but he evaded them and hurried into the large, rambling building. To reach the inquest room he had to pass through the public bar, where Dai Cannon and several more of his mates were drinking beer.

Twirling his moustaches, Jim refused with a pathetic smile Dai's invitation to have one before he went in. 'No thanks,' he said sadly. 'You do know I have got very 'portant business to see to first and Siân have told me you can be had up for contempt of court if you go to a inquest with the smell of beer on your breath.'

'Oh, well,' Dai replied, 'if that be the case you had better go in and get it over as quick as you can.'

Jim winked feebly as he passed on through the bar. The policeman at the door of the big room let him through without any question. Big Jim, already damp with nervousness, entered and sat down gingerly on the bench nearest him, and looking around the room he recognised many of the men who stood chatting in groups. Among others he saw Ezra, Mr. Hicks, Evan the Overman, and certain relatives of the deceased men. The pompous-looking, well-dressed men in the front he assumed to be lawyers and clerks.

Jim was heartened by the presence of Ezra, the miners' leader, and was glad when he strolled across the room and sat next to him. In a low whisper, which softened the habitual harshness of his voice, Ezra tried to reassure the perturbed Jim.

'You have no need to be nervous,' he said.

Jim swelled out his mighty chest. 'Huh,' he boasted. 'Big Jim be not afraid. Don't forget, Ezra, I fight in the Boer War, and a man who done that have no need to be afraid of a few spaniels like them by there,' pointing to the well-dressed men.

Ezra smiled quietly and waited. After a few moments' silence he said, 'I am glad to hear that, Jim, because I understand they are going to try to put the blame for the explosion upon Shoni Cap-Du.'

He felt Jim move on the seat, but went on as if he had noticed nothing, 'You can scotch this effort if you speak the truth and stick to it through thick and thin.'

Big Jim had no time to reply before the proceedings opened. He stood on his feet with the others in sympathy for the victims. Then for what seemed ages he hazily tried to follow Ezra's subdued comments on the evidence given by various people. But most of his attention was devoted to swallowing the hard lump that persistently rose in his throat, and this nervous reaction, coupled with his poor grasp of English, robbed him of any coherent knowledge of the proceedings.

He vaguely recognised Mr. Evans Cardi among the twelve sitting to the right of the coroner, and even while he tried to listen, he wondered why it was there were no miners among the jurymen. He heard a faraway voice call for 'Mr. James Roberts,' but it did not occur to him that the name was his until Ezra nudged him sharply and muttered, 'Your turn now. Pull yourself together; speak the truth and watch me.'

Jim rose slowly to his feet, his white face set like a man about to hear sentence of death passed on him. His huge bulk dominated the room, but he was unaware of this as he walked towards the important-looking men sitting at the table. When he reached the table he stood irresolutely for some seconds with perspiration gathering in little beads about his collar. It irritated him, and he aimlessly inserted his finger between his collar and wet neck, while everyone present gazed at him with interest.

The stern-looking man opposite began asking questions. Jim replied in a husky, tremulous voice which contrasted strangely with his usual deep and boisterous tones. He felt his face muscles twitching, and it was only with great difficulty that he managed to control them. When he spoke the words stuck in his parched throat and he had to cough to get them out of his mouth. The strange sound of his voice made him even more nervous, and he looked supplicatingly at Ezra, whose encouraging glance and confident demeanour heartened him.

The coroner, having completed the usual formal inquiries,

was followed by an insignificant looking man who began to re-examine Jim. He had a squeaky voice and a bombastic manner, to which Jim took an immediate dislike, and with every answer he gave his initial nervousness progressively evaporated.

'Yes, sir,' he said in answer to a question. 'I be the first man down the pit after the explosion and the first to come across the dead bodies.' Jim's voice was now nearly normal and resonant.

His interrogator struck a pose before saying impressively, 'Now, Mr. Roberts, I want you to tell us exactly what you saw when you reached the bodies.'

Big Jim's mind spontaneously flashed back and a shudder passed through his body. What he had seen again floated before his eyes like a horrible picture. The contorted bodies charred and unrecognisable, appeared, like fantastic shadows about the courtroom.

Suddenly Jim jerked his great body erect. He remembered Ezra's words and the rumour spreading round the village. 'Arglwydd,' he thought, 'this man be trying to trap me to put the blame on Shoni Cap-du.' And he murmured to himself, 'Not if Big Jim can help it.'

The fact that he was about to defend his dead mates steeled his nerves and gave him greater courage, and giving a quick glance round the room, he began.

'When we reached the pit bottom, me and the other boys did have to go very slow and careful because of the thick after-damp, and we didn't know how the gas-masks would act, because they had been in the stores for years.'

He stopped a second, drew in his breath sharply, and

continued. 'After we had gone 'bout fifty yards from the pit bottom and was just by the mouth of the stable where we first heard the fire, I fancy I see something in front. It looked black and limp, as if a lot of brattice had been blowed into one heap.'

Jim swallowed a mouthful of saliva, then resumed. 'When we reached it we did find it was not brattice but the bodies of our poor dead butties. They was lying round 'xactly as if they had been struck by lightning. Duw,' he added sadly, 'it was awful, mun, to see your butties lying cold like that.'

He was interrupted before he could continue further. 'Ahem. Very good, Mr. Roberts, and no doubt very interesting,' said his cross-examiner. 'But we want to know what you saw, not what you felt. Now tell me. When you came across the bodies, did you see any lamps?'

Jim's dislike for the man immediately increased. He realised that the questioner was trying to get an admission from him, and although he did not mind this, he objected to the method used. Some of the questions appeared to his practical mind as irrelevant and silly, and in answering the last one he made no attempt to conceal his contempt.

'Of course we did see lamps,' he said. 'Do you ever 'spect to see sensible men in a pit without them? Huh. Any fool can answer that question and only a fool would ask it.'

His opponent was discomposed by this reply and the twitter that circled round the courtroom.

'Is that so?' he commented sharply, his squeaky voice rising to a falsetto. 'Then perhaps you will tell us if you examined the lamps you say you saw?'

126

Big Jim nodded a brief affirmative.

'Now tell us if you saw something wrong with any of the lamps.'

Big Jim hesitated and looked across at Ezra, who sat immobile and detached on the corner of the bench. Ezra's quick eyeflick seemed to flash the message: 'Speak the truth and stick to it.'

Jim cleared his throat and answered, 'Yes. There was something wrong with them.'

Everyone in the room held his breath. The cross-examiner looked knowingly at the coroner, as if saying, 'He was a bit awkward, but we've got it at last.'

Big Jim continued: 'All the lamps was in the dark, because their flames had been blowed out by the blast of the explosion.'

He stopped at this. The tension in the room eased. The little interrogator was red-faced and angry at being thwarted in this manner. He shot his next questions quickly and viciously.

'Were any of the lamps damaged?'

'No.'

'How do you know?'

'Because I did examine each of them.'

'Did you know John Jones?'

'Yes. We did call him Shoni Cap-du.'

'Never mind what you call him. Tell me if you found anything wrong with his lamp.'

Jim's temper flared up at the trend of the questions. 'Ho,' he shouted, his voice booming through the room like a drum. 'So that's the way the wind be blowing, is it?

Well, let me tell you straight from the shoulder that Shoni's lamp was under his left leg. I did pull it from there with my own hands, and the only thing that was wrong with it was that the handle was twisted a little bit.'

A deep silence followed these words, spoken so vehemently in defence of the dead man. But Jim's questioner seemed oblivious of the impression created. He took a paper package from the table and unwrapped it to show a miner's oil-lamp with a twisted handle. He handed this to Jim with the words: 'Is that the lamp you took from under John Jones's leg?'

Jim took the lamp in his hand, turning the pot that contained the oil as he did so. The pot gave under the pressure and Jim, surprise in his whole appearance, kept on turning until the pot came away from the top of the lamp. If the wick were now lighted it would be naked to the air.

He looked at the separated parts, and his eyes half-closed as he concentrated his mind on the problem. The remorse-less voice of his interlocutor pursued him. 'Is that the lamp you took from beneath John Jones's leg?' it asked again.

Big Jim looked once more towards Ezra before he replied. Again he saw the same message in the hard face: 'Speak the truth and stick to it.'

In a firm voice he answered: 'It is the same lamp, and yet it isn't. Something have happened to it since it was in my hands before.'

He paused, then went on more confidently. 'The first thing a miner will do whenever he get a lamp in his hand is to twist the pot, just like I did with this one. It do come natural to us, and I know I did twist Shoni's lamp when I picked it up from under his leg.'

His voice rose sharply. 'Somebody have been mucking about with this lamp since I brought it up the pit,' he challenged.

The slow, cold smile that crossed Ezra's face seemed to say, 'Good lad, Jim. Stick to it.'

The lamp was now handed to the jurymen, each of whom scrutinised it as if he were acquainted with all its parts and secrets.

While they were doing this Jim was pulled back to the issue by a question sharply barked at him. 'If you don't think the lamp was responsible for the explosion, can you, as a practical man and an experienced miner, advance another theory as to the probable cause?'

A puzzled frown puckered Jim's forehead. He shook his head slowly, then asked, ''Scuse me, 'ont' you? But will you please tell me what you do mean by the last part of your words? You see,' he added apologetically, 'I be not much of a English-speaking man and some of your words do come strange to my ears.'

The coroner helped him and put the questions more plainly. 'What you are being asked, Mr. Roberts,' he explained, 'is if you don't believe the lamp caused the explosion, then what else do you think could have caused it?'

Jim thought deeply for some moments, then said very deliberately: 'No; I don't believe the 'splosion started back where we found Shoni Cap-Du at all. It be my belief, sure as God be my judge, that it did start somewhere in the face. I do know for sure that there was tons of gas back in the empty gobs, and just one little spark from a mandril would be 'nough to blow the whole lot up.

'However that might be,' he added solemnly, 'I am so sure as this hand is fast to me this minute,' he held his huge scarred hand out for all to see, 'that the 'splosion was not made by the lamp.'

This answer, which caused a murmur of interest to pass through the room, was followed by another question. 'What makes you so positive that the lamp had nothing to do with the explosion?'

Jim chose his words carefully as he replied: 'If that lamp made the 'splosion because the pot was unscrewed, then it 'ood have been unscrewed when I found it. If Shoni Cap-du put the flame to the gas, then he 'ood have been blowed to pieces before ever he 'ood have time to screw the pot back on. More than that,' he continued, with rising temper, 'no man without the key could open that lamp unless he smashed it open, and here it is as perfect as on the day it was first made.'

While the people in the room whispered excitedly to each other at Jim's concluding remarks, the coroner invited that worthy to resume his seat.

When the whispering had ceased the coroner summed up the evidence. 'Accidents such as this,' he said, 'however regrettable they may be, are an inevitable outcome of modern coalmining. In the present case every care seems to have been taken by the management to ensure the maximum of safety. Yet, in spite of all efforts to keep the pit reasonably free from danger, this terrible catastrophe occurs.'

He coughed ponderously before continuing. 'Were it not for the open lamp found after the explosion, one could very well consider it to be purely and simply an act of God. But this discovery is of particular significance, and appears to point to the fact that the terrible tragedy was due to the deliberate or foolish action of John Jones. We shall, of course, never know the real truth of the matter, but while I am impressed with the evidence of Mr. Roberts, I cannot for the life of me imagine what interest or motive the management could have in opening the lamp after it came up the pit.'

He stopped to clear his throat and concluded, 'No; I cannot accept that theory. In my opinion the explosion was caused by an act of foolish negligence on the part of a workman.'

The jurymen had all craned their necks forward as an indication that they were listening attentively, and without leaving the court they returned a verdict in accordance with the coroner's directions.

Big Jim was furious and would have sprung to his feet in protest had it not been for Ezra's restraining hand. The two workmen were surrounded immediately they appeared in the street. Ezra said very little, but Big Jim, his moustaches twitching with indignation, could not curb his rash temper.

'Just fancy,' he roared, 'blaming a poor dead man, who can't answer back, for the 'splosion.'

A cry of 'Shame!' spread through the crowd as Jim went on, 'All of us do know what caused it. If the gobs had been pinned as they ought to be, there 'ood have been no blow-up. Ach,' he continued dismally, 'us don't count no longer. Coal be more 'portant than us now.'

'Ay,' came a voice from the crowd. 'You be quite right,

Big Jim. What do hundred men count for 'longside a hundred trams of coal? Men be cheap 'nough these days, and will soon be dear at ten a penny.'

Someone laughed at this quip. But the laugh sounded flat and was not taken up.

Immediately after the inquest the people of the village made preparations to bury their dead. Very few of those brought up the pit could be identified, but this difficulty was easily overcome by those in charge. Each body not identified was allocated to some family on the basis of a button or some such fictitious clue. This method served two useful purposes. It saved unnecessary and useless investigation and it also eased the grief of the relatives, who were led to believe that the inflated, flame-seared mass of rotten flesh encased in an odour-proof shell in the parlour belonged to them.

The first group of fifty-nine bodies brought up the pit was buried together in a common grave.

On the day of the mass burial the atmosphere weighed heavy upon the people of Cwmardy. Each house was a casket of sobs and sighs. All window-blinds were drawn and businesses closed down for the day. The people in each street followed the coarse wooden coffin they believed contained their own relative or friend and the coffins were covered with crude wreaths that glistened with the tears of the donors.

All the sombre wooden boxes with their flowery coverings were carried to the village square and laid side by side. When all was ready Dai Cannon lifted his squat body into the solitary bowl of the Fountain. His pale face

132

was made whiter by the shiny blackness of his hair. He looked dignified and impressive to the people from the height of his platform in the bowl.

Dai waited a few moments to get a grip on his feelings. Then his deep, sonorous voice began to float over the silent throng who waited, sad and patient, below him.

'The good God has given and the good God has taken away,' he chanted. 'He has taken loved ones from relatives, husbands from wives, and fathers from children. He has left our valley full of widows, orphans, and grieving parents, all of whom have nothing but sad memories, which cannot ease their pain. The Lord has given the pit power to destroy men's bodies, but has kept to Himself the power to preserve people's souls.'

His voice rose till it rang through the black air like the wailing chords of a harmonium.

'O, Lord, you seem so cruel to Your children this day. They, in their grief, do not understand Your infinite mercy and tenderness. They, in their sorrow, do not know that You do all things for the best. They see only the coffined remains of those they love, and cannot see the purified souls now nestling to Your bosom. You have said, "Through fire to eternal bliss." The bodies which held the souls you now hold in Your blessed care have been through the fires of the pit and deserve the best that heaven can provide.

'Give strength and courage, O Lord,' he exhorted, his voice falling in emotional waves upon the bowed heads of the people, 'to those of Your children now suffering the horrors of earthly parting from those they loved best. Give

133

them solace in their grief. Put soothing balm in their aching hearts. Let them feel that their loss has brought them nearer Thee. Cast from the minds of these women and children all thoughts of this week of death and devastation. O God, we do pray Thee to sow again in our valley the peace and happiness that we knew before the explosion.'

Tonefully his words wormed their way into tormented hearts, tearing them into agonising shreds. Sobs mingled with moans and made a death dirge as he continued his plea, and when he finished practically everyone was weeping, open and unashamed.

Len, standing near Big Jim, wept in a fervour of self-pity. The words brought Jane vividly to his mind. He wondered how she now looked in her coffin and shuddered at the recollection of the last glimpse he had of her. Siân, tears streaming down her face, kept rocking her body backwards and forwards, moaning painfully all the while. Big Jim blew his nose throughout the service, wiping it with the back of his hand.

When Dai Cannon finished Len stopped weeping and looked about him. He saw Ezra standing near the Fountain. The man's eyes were hard and dry and a cynical smile played around the corners of his lips. Len had seen very little of the miners' leader, although, like all the other children, he had heard much about him.

After the service Ezra quietly took charge. He whispered directions to Dai Cannon, who immediately transmitted them to the people.

Six men, already appointed, took hold of each coffin. Their hard and horny hands seemed to caress the boxes they lifted to their shoulders. The fifty-nine coffins, carried on three hundred and fifty-four broad shoulders, lay head to foot in one long line. Behind each coffin came the mourners who thought it contained the remains belonging to them. All the other people fell in behind this procession of dead bodies and relatives. Men walked seven and eight abreast in the middle of the road, while the women and children walked on the sides. Dai Cannon, Mr. Hicks, Mr. Evans Cardi, and Big Jim walked immediately in front of the first coffin. Len fell in with his mother among the women.

The choir from Dai Cannon's chapel started to sing the hymn that had conquered the storm on the night of the explosion. Its plaintive melody, palpitating and mellowed with grief, rose above the housetops of the village and crept slowly up the sides of the surrounding mountains, whence it drifted back, matured music, to cover the valley with a blanket of shivering sound. The echoes re-entered the throats where they had originated and were reborn, more resonant and rounded, to be thrown again with greater vigour and clarity into the air. Here they hung, harmonising with the slow-moving funeral feet.

Dogs in the side-streets sat disconsolately on their haunches and gave voice to the dread that suddenly consumed them. Len felt the voices soak their music into his flesh in emotional vibrations. His eyes filled when they caught sight of the anaemic flowers carried by the chapel children as tokens of love, respect, and loss, and he began to think of what his father had told him about the mad rush up the hill on the night of the explosion. He compared it to this slow-moving march down the same hill to the cemetery, and ideas tumbled over each other in his imagination as he pondered over the problem of life and death.

The hill became a symbol to him. He saw it as a belt taking live men up to the pit, then bringing them down dead to the cemetery. The pit became an ogre to him. He likened it to some inhuman monster that fed on men and spewed up their mangled bodies to be buried in the graveyard. He conjured the hill and the pit as common enemies of the people, working in connivance to destroy them. Suddenly the words of Dai Cannon recurred to him, 'The good God has given and the good God has taken away', and he wondered what they meant. Did they mean that the pit was not to be blamed and that God was responsible for destroying the men whose bodies were encased in the boxes before him? If so, he mused, then perhaps God had killed Jane, and not Evan the Overman's son, as Siân had said. His brain twirled in a vortex of conflicting and seemingly insoluble problems that made his head ache long before the funeral reached the cemetery gates, and he closed his eyes, clinging tightly to his mother's hand, letting her lead him on.

LEN STARTS
TO WORK

Six months had passed since the air of the valley had been shattered by the explosion. All the bodies that could be brought up the pit had been taken by the people to the distant cemetery. The remaining hundred or so were left as cindered dust in various parts of the colliery. Imperceptibly the explosion had sunk from the surface of men's minds and become a memory, though in many homes it was a black one. The explosion distress fund that had been organised throughout the country immediately following upon the catastrophe was now declared to be running low, and the widows and orphans were informed that their relief scales would have to be reduced as a consequence.

One day Big Jim came home from his repairing work at the colliery, and after dinner casually told Siân: 'Well, gel bach, we will be starting to fill coal in the old pit next

137

week once again.'

Siân turned to him. 'That be good news,' she said.

'Ay, but I have got even better than that. I have arranged with Williams, the under-manager, for our Len to start work with me next week.'

Len sat up in his chair with a start and looked at his father with wide-opened eyes that sparkled with interest.

'Aye, aye. It be quite true. You be starting to work with me next week. Your mam wanted you to keep in school, but since you be not willing for that there be nothing left but for you to work.'

The week following this brief announcement Len was so excited he hardly knew what he was doing, He told his mother one day: 'I'm glad, mam, that I'm starting to work. School's no good to me, I can't learn enough there. I want to be with dad in the pit. I'm not afraid. The other boys have told me it's not so bad when you get used to it.' And, looking slyly at his mother, he added: 'They get pocket-money from their mothers on top of trumps from their butties.'

Siân pretended not to notice, but a tiny smile flickered for a moment on the corners of her mouth.

Len became a hero in the eyes of his schoolmates. He made them envious with tales of what he intended to do, the things he would buy, the places he would visit when he started work. He conjured up for them a romantic vista of what work meant, and the days went by so slowly he thought the week would never end. But at last the final night arrived.

His mother had bought him the usual white-duck

trousers that marked the end of his boyish breeches. The large tin box and jack, to carry his food and water, were given to him by his father, who had already used them for years. Siân sent him to bed early, intending him to get plenty of sleep. Excitement and anticipation, however, prevented this and he was still awake when the first morning hooter blew at five o'clock. About ten minutes later his mother called him. She had already lit the fire and had breakfast waiting. Big Jim was half dressed in his pit clothes when Len entered the kitchen. The lad soon clothed himself in his strange rig-out, and sat down to drink a cup of tea, for food was out of the question in the state to which he had worked himself. When the half-past five hooter gave the signal that it was time they were off, Siân passionately pressed her son to her body. She kissed him tenderly and whispered in his ear, 'Do everything your dad do tell you, my boy. Don't move from his side. You be starting today what only the grave can steal you from.' She said this more to herself than anyone else and put the canvas apron to her eyes. Then shaking her head sharply, she turned to Jim.

'I know you will take care of him, James. 'Member he be only a baby after all, the only one us have got left.' With another hungry kiss she sent them into the dark, wet street with a 'Good morning' that stuck in her throat and was never uttered.

The rain poured down as Len and his father, like a giant and a pigmy, trudged up the hill towards the pits. Jim made his son walk as closely behind him as possible. It was some time before Len realised this was done to shield him from the main force of the rain driving down the valley. His head bent to the drops that evaded his father's body, Len vaguely noticed the long string of silent men, like shadows, making their way in the same direction as himself. Each of them, dragging his feet, used the man immediately in front to shelter him from the rain.

Len followed his father across the bridge into the cabin where authoritative-looking men scanned him over curiously as if he were a calf.

'So this be the boy, James?' asked the most officious.

'Ay, this be him,' responded Jim, whereupon Len had to write his name and age in a big book.

He took a round piece of metal handed him by one of the men, who told him, 'Take care of that, my lad; it is your lamp check with your number on it.'

A few further words passed between the group before Jim led the way to the lamp room, a long corrugated-iron structure containing hundreds of lighted lamps arranged on a series of trestles. Len followed his father to one of the pigeon-holes, where Jim handed in the check and received a lamp in exchange. Len did the same and at once felt himself a man, although the lamp dangling from his hand nearly touched the floor. They left the lamp room and walked to a cabin, where another man with an air of authority examined the lamps. Having unscrewed the top and blown all round the pots, he handed them back with a final twist of the bottom, to ensure that the lamps were stuck fast.

Big Jim and his son left the cabin and went straight to the pit-head. The shaft in which Len was to work was called the 'upcast', because all the air from the pit was

140

sucked up through it by a fan of huge dimensions. To prevent the air being drawn up before it had time to circulate all round the workings, the shaft was closed in with heavy wooden 'droppers', only leaving a space for the rope to wind its way through, so that when the two cages were in the pit the air howled and screamed through this tiny outlet.

Len was rather frightened by the terrible tumult on the pit-head, and he had to shout to make himself heard above the din. While they were standing in the queue waiting to go down, he felt for his father's hand and pressed it to his side in a gesture of love and confidence, but Big Jim, sensing the boy's mood, said nothing, thinking to himself that the lad had to 'find his own feet.'

When the ascending cage lifted the wooden barriers from the pit-top the released gusts of heated air rushed through with a roar. Jim cautiously led his son over the little gap between the cage and the pit edge. Eighteen other men and boys followed before the man in charge declared that the box was full and placed a thin iron bar across the entrance. This was a measure of precaution supposed to prevent the men falling out.

Once inside the cage, Len held his breath and waited. He heard the knocker clang three times, and the tinkling of a bell far away in the engine-house. Then suddenly he felt the floor of the cage press against his feet as it lifted off the stanchions that held it to the pit-head, and in another second the breath was torn from his lungs by the sudden drop as the cage plunged its way into the depths of the pit.

Even in his panic Len heard the clatter of the droppers

falling into place above him, and he felt that a door had been bolted between himself and the world. Regaining his wind after the initial shock he put his arms round his father's leg, finding courage in the human contact it provided in the black, falling void. Warm air rushed past the cage with wicked squeals, and just as Len was beginning to get accustomed to the sensation of dropping, the bottom of the cage again pressed against his feet. This was due to the brakes in the engine-room being applied to the great winding drums and marked the half-way line between the pit bottom and the surface. The lad felt the cage rising under him and wondered why they were returning to the pit-head, but before he had time to think it out the cage, with a few preliminary jerks, jarred on the planks that covered the water sump at the bottom of the pit.

The men slowly got out, Len behind his father. His curious eyes noticed at once that the little lamps appeared to give out a greater light here than they did on the surface, due to the more limited space they had to illuminate. He was also surprised that he could see underground as well as he could above, for he forgot there was no daylight when he left the pit-head and that his eyes were already inured to the darkness before he descended. He stumbled against a rail and glanced around the semi-elliptical passage-way that led from the pit bottom. Looking behind, he saw a similar passage going in the opposite direction, the other side of the pit, then, threading his way carefully between the long line of coal-laden trams on the one side and an equally long line of empty ones on the other, he eventually came to the end of

142

this double roadway.

'Look where you be going to now, Len bach,' advised Big Jim, as they turned off into a narrow and gloomier passage.

'There's different this place do look, dad, without no whitewash on the sides.'

'Never you mind about the sides. You watch these ropes in the roadway.'

Len took his father's advice and kept his eyes glued upon the ropes. Not another word was said until they came to a large cabin dug into the side of the roadway, where their lamps were again taken from them and tested.

Big Jim received certain instructions from the man in the cabin, and Len listened to their talk of 'shots' and 'rippings'. After receiving instructions and having their lamps returned to them, Big Jim remarked to Len: 'Come on. We have got a hell of a plateful for today, so you'll have to look sharp.' Without a word Len followed his father. The roadway was becoming narrower and lower with every stride, and steel girders gave way to timber as supports for the roof.

In his anxiety to keep pace with Big Jim Len had no time for talking; it was his father who broke the silence.

'Are you all right, Len?'

Len started at the sound of Jim's voice. 'Ay. I'm all right, dad. How much further have we got to go?' he asked tremulously.

'We got a good bit to go yet.'

'Have we come two miles so far?'

'Thereabouts, boy bach,' replied Jim, turning to Len. 'You don't feel tired, do you?'

143

'Of course not,' bragged the lad, forgetting the tired ache in his legs and pulling himself to his full height.

Jim walked on again. 'Many is the time I have tramped this old roadway,' he mused. 'Duw, duw, I be sure to have done hundreds of miles along it.'

They proceeded in silence for a while, Big Jim thinking of the good old days that had gone, while Len thought of the days that were to come. Suddenly the former warned: 'Look out by here, Len bach. This be a nasty old trip.'

Len continued down the steep road that reminded him of the path leading from the mountain top.

'I 'member coming over this trip once with old Dai Cannon,' said Jim, 'when all of a sudden we did hear a rush behind us. Dai and me stopped like statues for a minute. But not for long. The rush come louder and louder and, muniferni, you did ought to see us jump for the side. Ha-ha! Dai gived one howl, mun, and before I did know what was happening he fell back on 'is arse in the middle of the road. Ha-ha-ha! Arglwydd mawr, boy, I was bound to laugh, mun, if Dai did kill me for it. Arglwydd, you should have seed the look he did give me! "That's right," he did say, "laugh you silly beggar. Go on. Enjoy yourself although I have broked my bloody neck".'

Jim burst out into another uproarious guffaw at the memory. When this had subsided Len asked: 'But what was the matter, dad?'

'Why, some of the horses, coming down from the top of the trip, got a little bit restless and was stamping their feet like hell. 'Oops a daisy, we did think, the devils be running wild. Dai jumped for the side and bumped right into a low piece of timber, and that was why he did land flat on his arse. Ha-ha!'

The descent now became even steeper. Len compared it to the sheer mountain drop near the quarry, and the thought made him long for the first time that morning to be back again in the sun. He had never dreamed of this interminable tramp in the darkness of the pit. Thinking of the world above prompted him to ask: 'How far be we down, dad?'

'They do say 'bout two thousand feet. But never mind 'bout that, now. You look after yourself; the roof be getting pretty low by here.'

Jim was walking with his body bent nearly double and Len, taking the tip, dug his chin deep into his chest and bent his head low. After a while they came to a part of the road where the roof was higher. Jim, knowing the spot, straightened his body and walked erect, but Len, fearing to raise his head, was not aware of this and walked on in solemn silence with his head bowed like a man in a funeral. The ropes beneath the lad's feet were moving when Jim called out, 'Come into this manhole, boy bach.'

Len hurried into the tiny hole in the side of the roadway and squeezed himself alongside his father in the limited space. 'What's the matter, dad?' he asked, thinking that something serious was about to happen.

'It's only the journey,' Jim assured him. 'You see those ropes by there,' pointing into the roadway, where the ropes were slithering along like snakes, one sizzling along the ground while the other ripped through the air nearly to the height of the roof, 'Well, those do belong to the journey.'

Len hesitated a moment, then asked, as a low rumbling

145

sound came to his ears from the distance, 'What's that noise, then, dad?'

Jim started to explain when thirty empty trams rushed past the manhole with a deafening clatter. The terrific din sent Len cowering against his father's legs. Without further explanation, Jim caught the lad by the arm and drew him out of the hole. 'Come quick,' he shouted above the rattle of the receding trams, 'let us get to the parting before the full journey come out.'

Len did not understand the meaning of these instructions, but he obediently ran headlong after his father. Gasping and perspiring, they stopped after they had run about a quarter of a mile. Still panting from his exertions, Len noticed that the roadway had widened and was blocked by two strings of trains, one of which was empty, the other full of coal.

Safe in another manhole, the lad watched with interest two men change the rope from the string of empty trams and place it on the full ones. When the change was completed he heard a whistle blow further on, and one of the men near him responded to the signal by rasping the two thin wires above his head with the blade of a knife. The wires connected with the engine-house at the bottom of the pit. The ropes began to move and slowly tightened on the first tram of the string, then the others, attached to it with steel shackles, were drawn forward with increasing speed and clamour until the last was lost to sight in the darkness of the roadway.

Len and Jim emerged from the manhole and again continued their walk, the former beginning to think that it was to be endless. He noticed places where huge holes gaped in the roof. At other places he saw large masses of stone overhanging into the roadway without any visible support.

He turned to his father and asked in a quavering voice, 'Be that safe, dad?'

'Safe? Ay, boy, safe as houses. It will take more than Gabriel's trumpet to blow that down.'

Len was too fatigued to ask any further questions. He was glad when Big Jim stopped and said, 'Here we be. Strip off and get yourself ready. A little whiff will dry up all that sweat on you.'

Len's exhaustion vanished with the knowledge that the interminable trudge was over and that he was now in his father's working place. He started to pull off his coat, when Jim interrupted him testily. 'Not by there, boy bach. Shift under those timbers, where you will be safe.'

Len did as he was told, and putting his box and jack carefully at the foot of a strong-looking prop, he pulled off his coat and shirt. He paused at this until he saw Jim pull off the singlet next his skin; then he did the same, and immediately felt the air beat more cool and pleasantly upon his naked chest.

'Duw, that be nice, dad,' he said, revived by the contact.

'Huh,' grunted Jim. 'Take the tools off the bar. Here be the key.'

Len did so, then, with a shovel in his hands, he followed his father on hands and knees through the coalface. The glistening coal, reflecting the gleam from the two lamps, fascinated Len. He watched Jim crawl, practically on his stomach, up the long stretch of the coalface until only the dim light of his lamp was visible. Scared to be left alone, the lad followed, only to be gruffly ordered back.

'You keep by that empty tram and don't move till I tell you.'

Len turned back and for the first time gave conscious thought to the tram. It stood end on to the clear-cut roof, or 'rippings', which had to be blown down as the coalface advanced, so that the tram could follow the coal.

A deep feeling of loneliness enveloped Len as he wondered what would happen if his father were not near and he were left entirely on his own. All round him he could hear little movements, as if the place were alive. He had an uncanny feeling that the roof was moving, and each creak of the timbers, as they unwillingly took the weight of the settling strata, sent a quiver through his body. He had yet to learn that the pit had a life of its own, that it was never still or silent, but was always moving and moaning in response to the atmosphere and pressure.

Suddenly he felt a burning sensation on his stomach. His hand flashed to the spot automatically, his fingers clutched some object and tore it away, and opening his hand he saw a huge red insect with innumerable hairy legs and hard, shiny wings. Although crushed in his convulsive grip, the ghastly legs still beat the air, and looking down at his belly, he saw a thin stream of blood running down it where the cockroach had gripped the flesh and torn it away. A sick giddiness swept over the lad for a moment, while the perspiration burst from every pore in his body, lathering it in a mixture of coal-dust and moisture, but

148

before he could recover from the shock he heard his father crawling back. This proof that he was not alone encouraged the lad and he was smiling when Big Jim emerged on the roadway.

'We will work in the right hand cut today, Len bach,' he said, 'so that we can free the whole face for tomorrow.'

Len did not understand the technique underlying the remark, but he asked with assumed indifference, 'What be I to do, dad?'

Jim replied: 'You will come up the cut with me and throw the coal back towards the tram.'

The lad obeyed, and followed his father, and for hours he worked on his knees with the back of his head rubbing against the roof. He began mentally counting each shovelful of coal his father cut and which he had to throw back to the tram. His arms grew heavy as lead, cramp caught him in his bent legs, and his back felt as though it were broken. The coal-dust that filled the air got into his nose and eyes. It made him sneeze and blink and, working into the sweat-opened pores of his body, set up an intolerable irritation. He felt it impossible to lift another shovelful of the coal he now detested, but somehow he kept on, until at last his father said: 'That will do for now. Let's go back and get a bit of tommy.'

The lad dragged his weary, painful limbs back into the roadway, where he stretched himself full length in the dust. He saw his heart pumping against the bones of his naked chest, and felt pins and needles run through his flesh in spasms of excruciating agony.

Big Jim, sensing what was happening, urged him to his

149

feet. 'Come on. Get up before you go stiff.'

With infinite care Len dragged his limbs together and slowly rose to his feet. He opened his food box and sat down. The bread and butter looked dirty and unappetising, but the water in his jack was like nectar. Jim stopped him before he had emptied the tin of its contents. 'Don't do that again or you will get cramp in your belly. Get on with your food.'

The lad tried to obey, but the hundreds of savage-looking cockroaches that buzzed and fussed around turned his stomach, while the dust he had already swallowed curdled in his inside.

After a while Big Jim rose and made his way back up the face, telling Len: 'You stop there till I shout for you. A bit of a whiff 'on't do you any harm now.'

During the rest the lad slowly recovered from his exhaustion. The black dust under his body seemed softer and more sweet to him then than even the green grass on his beloved mountain, and his mind wandered to the end of the shift. Before his eyes floated a picture of the envious glances of his schoolmates when they saw him striding, black-faced, down the hill in his working clothes. He saw the glad look in his mother's eyes as he walked into the little kitchen, having finished his day's work. Already he began to count the pocket-money he would have in a fortnight's time, and speculated how best to spend it.

Deeply immersed in these pleasant contemplations, Len dozed off into a heavy sleep. Jim's deep voice seemed miles away when he shouted, 'Right you are, Len bach; come up and start chucking this coal back.'

Len came back to reality with a start and made his way up the coalface he already hated with every fibre in his body. He worked in a semi-conscious state, only faintly aware of the three or four occasions when the haulier and his horse noisily changed the full tram of coal for an empty one. When the fireman came round and chatted with Jim he waited respectfully on his knees, wishing fervently that the man would stop there till the end of the shift. But he had ceased to take any interest in what was happening. His brain was numbed with the physical exhaustion that again consumed him even though his father had been careful to limit the amount of work to a minimum.

The poor lad, accustomed to the fresh air of the mountain, felt the foul atmosphere of the pit beginning to choke him. He thought again of his mother, and now wished he had listened to her advice and tried the examination for the secondary school. Young Mary, Ezra's daughter, had done so and passed successfully, although she was no better scholar than he. Too late now, he thought to himself, half weeping; now he had started in the pit he had to continue. He wondered if the rain had stopped up above; it seemed years since he had left its refreshing coolness. He was sorry now he had ever grumbled at the rain, and was willing for it to pour down for ever as long as he was on the surface to see it.

Tears involuntarily gushed to his eyes and he was on the point of bursting into sobs when a terrific crash shook the whole earth. For a moment he stood paralysed with fear, then he rushed headlong with a wild scream towards his father. Big Jim caught the terror-stricken, hysterical lad to him.

'Duw, duw, mun, don't ever let it be said that the son of Big Jim is frightened by a noise. That was only gas and squeeze busting inside the coal, mun. There, there, now, don't be 'fraid no more.'

It took Len some time to control his quivering flesh. The crash had sent the memory of the explosion flashing through his mind, and in a split second he had seen himself in the place of the bodies he had watched being buried on the day of the funeral.

Jim made the lad rest back on the roadway again until, some half-hour later, he took him down the roadway to fetch some timber. Here Len saw another lad with his adult mate engaged in the same task. The sight of someone his own age immediately restored his confidence. His natural taciturn unsociability evaporated with the new contact in the new environment. While the two men were chatting and selecting the timber they wanted, Len shyly asked the strange lad, 'How long you been working?'

'Oh,' was the casual, off-handed reply, 'a long time now, butty. More than six months, I believe, though I can't 'member 'xactly, because it be so long ago.' Saying which, he took a lump of chewing-gum from his mouth and spat noisily into an empty tram near him.

'Well, what do you think of the bloody hole?' patronisingly.

'Not so bad,' lied Len, trying to forget the torments of the day.

'Huh. I'm only sticking it till I'm old enough to get a horse.'

'Get a horse?' queried Len amazedly.

'Ay, ay, that's it. I'm going to be a haulier.'

'Oh, I see. Like that man who do bring the horse to fetch our full trams out?'

'You got it, butty. And, by Christ, can't I handle them!' warming to his subject. 'Take a tip from a old hand, butty, never take no bloody nonsense from them. When they turn twp or stupid, a sprag will always bring them to their senses.'

He accompanied these remarks with a clicking sound and a practical demonstration which left Len staring with admiration. The budding haulier put the chewing-gum back into his mouth with a grimace and remarked, 'This bloody stuff be getting too weak for me now; I will have to start chewing 'bacca soon.'

Len felt he would like to have a say: 'I only started to work today,' he said hesitantly.

'Be that so? Ah well, never mind, you'll soon get used to it when you have worked so long as me.'

Their conversation was interrupted by the man with Big Jim.

'What the hell be you blabbing 'bout by there?' he demanded. 'Why don't you come and give me a hand with this blasted timber?'

'All right, all right, keep your wool on,' the lad said casually, and turning to Len, he hurriedly whispered: 'That's my butty. I 'spose I'd better go and give him a hand. Come out same time as me tonight – we be working next place to you. My name is Will Evans. So long.' With this he and his mate left, each with one end of a long nine-foot prop on his shoulder.

Shortly after this finishing time came and Len gathered all the tools together, his father showing him how to put them securely on the tool bar.

He dressed in quick time, the clothes sticking to his steaming body, and as he envisaged his triumphant entry into the house all his old pride began to surge through him again. To make sure his face was quite black he rubbed it vigorously with his dusty cap.

On the way out he told his father of the request made by Will, the lad in the next working place. Big Jim took him round to it, and they both waited for the others to finish; then the two men and their boys went out together, the former in front.

Len felt elated as he retraced his steps along the roadway that in the morning had seemed like the pathway to hell. He chattered incessantly and already felt he was an old hand in the pit. His new-found mate let him ramble on for a while, then broke in with the question: 'Do you know Sam Dangler?'

Len shook his head negatively.

'Huh, you have missed a treat. That's a haulier for you, mun. You ought to see him handling the rough 'uns.' He stopped half-way up the trip. 'This is how he do do it,' he remarked, catching hold of an imaginary rein. 'Whoa boy, whoa! Ah, bite you sod, would you?' giving a sharp tug and pressing his body back as though he were pulling the non-existent rein. 'Take that, you bloody cow!' hitting the air with a short piece of timber. 'Whoa, boy. Steady now. Ah, that's got you. Come to your senses, have you?' He flung the sprag into the roadway triumphantly and remarked: 'That's how Sam Dangler do conquer um, see?' A moment's pause, then: 'He's a devil. All the horses do

154

know him, and after a week he have very near got them talking. I'm going to be like him one day. He do have more trumps off the colliers than any haulier in the pit.'

He broke off here to take Len on the side and whisper in his ear: 'You want to watch your old man on pay day. Tell him straight from the beginning that if he want you to work he have got to give you trumps. Huh. Fathers be the worst butties going. They do think their own sons be bloody slaves and do never think of trumping 'em. Oh, no. They do pocket that their bloody selves and the old 'ooman don't have a smell of it. You listen to me,' he continued sagely. 'Don't let any butty make out of you unless he pay you for it, father or no father.'

A voice drifted down to the two lads from the top of the trip: 'Will-o! What the bloody hell be you hanging like a shirt behind there for?'

They hurriedly continued their way, and eventually overtook their mates on the pit bottom, where they had to wait a while in the queue before they were bundled into the cage.

The sound of the iron knocker, announcing to the men on the surface that all was ready, came to Len's ears like the chime of sweet-tolling bells. The cage sprang up the shaft like a projectile released from a mighty catapult, and in a matter of breathless minutes the roar of the air beating against the droppers drowned every other sound. There was a clamouring rush as the chains caught the covering and Len once more saw the light of day.

Although it was not a bright day, the light hurt Len's eyes, and he had to close them for a while. Will waited for him, then led the way to the lamp room, where they exchanged their lamps for the numbered metal discs. Having done this, Will led the way to some iron girders near by and began poking his fingers into the crevices. His movements became more vigorous and excited and his face grew red.

Len noticed this and asked timidly, 'Be there anything the matter, Will?'

'Matter? Matter to hell!' exploded Will. 'Some dirty swine have pinched my fag. I put it by here this morning before going down, and now the bloody thing is gone. Ah,' he grunted viciously, twisting his cap in his hands, 'if I only had him by here now I'd wring his dirty neck.' He gulped something down his throat and turned to Len. There was a pathetic look in his eyes when he said, 'Butty, that is the worst thing a man can ever do. To pinch a fag is worse than pinching grub. Huh. Hanging be too good for a man who do a thing like that.'

Some other lads now approached and listened interestedly to Will's tirade against the unknown thief. One of them eventually handed over a piece of cigarette that he had been smoking himself, and the little party made their way homewards. Seeing all the other lads enjoying their cigarettes made Len feel out of place, and he decided he must learn to smoke as soon as possible.

He took his place in the long line of men that streamed homewards down the hill, and looked surreptitiously into every window to see the reflection of his coal-blackened face. The eyes which looked back at him seemed twice their usual size in the dark frames.

When he reached home he found Siân busily fussing around with the dinner. Len never felt so proud in his life. Pulling off his coat, he put it in the box under the table and jovially remarked, 'Hallo, mam. Here I be, safe and sound.'

Siân did not look up from her task as she answered in a voice that quivered a little: 'Ay, I see you are, Len bach, thank God. How did you like it?'

Len forgot all the pains and terrors of the day when he replied, 'All right, mam. It be not so bad and I have made a new butty.'

He proceeded to retail the events of the day. When he had finished Siân beckoned him to wash his hands in the bowl of water she had ready. This done, he drew his chair to the table and voraciously ate the kipper and potatoes she had cooked him.

He had nearly finished his dinner when Big Jim came in, and explained to Siân he had called in to have a pint of beer to clear his throat. He always claimed, and believed, that if he did not have this pint of beer he would be unable to eat his dinner, because of the coal-dust that coated his lungs.

After dinner Siân fetched in the wooden tub made out of half a big barrel. Jim lifted the boiler from the fire and poured its contents into the tub, while Siân cooled it with cold water. Len quickly stripped to his waist while his father enjoyed a smoke, and was thrilled at the fact this was the first time in his life he had bathed with the top half of his body over the tub.

While he wiped his head and shoulders Jim followed him into the tub; then, when the latter had finished, Len got in naked to wash his bottom half. He enjoyed the sensation of the warm water running down his legs and lingered in the tub until Jim said: 'You be in there long enough to swim round it, boy bach. Come out and give your father a chance.'

Big Jim had hardly started rubbing soap into his legs when the door opened and Mrs. Thomas, their neighbour came in.

'Can you lend me a bucket of coal till mine do come from the pit?' she asked, taking no notice of Jim's magnificent nude body.

'Certainly, gel fach, go out the back and fetch it,' he replied, completely unabashed by her appearance.

By the time Mrs. Thomas had filled her bucket of coal Len had dressed, and when she re-entered the kitchen he was peering at his face in the cracked mirror. The two black rings of coal-dust that circled his eyes made them show up vividly against his white face, but though he rubbed them with the towel until the rims were sore, he could not remove them entirely. Later in the evening when he walked through Main Street he was proud of the black rings, because they showed to all and sundry that he had started to work.

That night he slept without any coaxing and was still fast asleep when the hooters blasted the air with their warning call at five o'clock. Siân had to call the lad a few times before he completely awoke and slowly drew his legs from beneath the bedclothes.

The second day in the pit was much the same as the first, but this time he took more notice of what happened

158

during the shift. When finishing time came he was even more tired and sore than on the first day, but in spite of this he arranged to meet Will by the Fountain in the evening. After dinner, however, he fell asleep while he was bathing, with his head over the tub. Siân tenderly finished washing him, after which Jim carried him to bed like a child. Although the appointment with Will was not kept, a strong friendship developed between them, which gradually forced from Len's mind all thought of Ron, his old schoolmate.

Will taught him much about the pit and its ways, and the knowledge so gained helped Len to avoid many a fright he would otherwise have had. In time he learned to hew coal and stand timber without the help of his father. He came to understand the struggle between himself and the coalface, and he pitted his brains against the strata, using the lie of the coal and the pressure of the roof to help him win the coal from the face with the minimum expenditure of energy. He learned the exact angle to stand his timbers so that they would bear the maximum weight of roof and side, and which part of the roof to shatter with a shot to bring only what he wanted to the floor.

In this manner, quietly and stealthily, the pit became the dominating factor in his life. Each morning, wet or fine, well or indisposed, he had to struggle out of bed at exactly the same time, join the same never-ending silent flow of men to the pit, and travel the same ever-lengthening pit roadway. He came to hate the hooter, whose blast he had to obey if he were not to suffer loss of food and pocket-money. He saw the walk to the pit in the mornings as one long queue from which he dropped in the evening only to catch up with again the next day. Slowly he came to regard himself as a slave and the pit as his owner, and his old taciturnity again grew in him as he brooded over these matters in the months that followed. Not that he had any objection to the work, but the thought that he was tied to the pit horrified him. His workmates noticed the growing unsociability. They thought it due to a love affair, and cracked smutty jokes at his expense.

'Have you got a dose, or what, Len?' Will asked him one morning.

'Dose? What dose do you mean?' Len replied, colouring up.

But the only answer he was vouchsafed was, 'Well, if you haven't, you ought to marry the bloody wench.'

Len said no more, but the conversation made him even more introspective and morose.

One evening after work Len wandered aimlessly down to the village, and, having nothing else to do, he ambled into Ben the Barber's, which happened to be practically empty. He asked Ben for the loan of a newspaper, but after scanning the headlines for a few minutes and finding nothing to excite his interest, he dug his hands deeply into his trousers pockets, thanked Ben, and shuffled to the door.

It was opened as he reached it, and a well-set-up young man about his own age entered. Len would have passed, but the stranger deliberately obstructed him.

'Len Roberts, if I am not mistaken?' inquired the newcomer.

'Ay, that's me,' replied Len, beginning to take an interest in his well-dressed questioner. He pulled his hands from his pockets and drew himself to his full height. 'Did you want me?'

'Ah, I see you have forgotten all about your old schoolmate. I'm Ron Evans. Don't you know me?'

Len stood on one side, surprise in his eyes. 'Well, well, just fancy, Ron. Who would have expected you? Duw, you have altered a lot since our schooldays.'

'Yes, and you haven't remained the same, either. I see you have started work and didn't go to the secondary school after all,' looking meaningly at the rims of Len's eyes.

'Ay. I have been working going on three years now.'

'Are you going anywhere particular tonight, Len?'

'No. I only come down here to have a hour or two out of the house.'

'Will you come with me for a stroll, then?' Ron suggested.

Len agreed, and the two sauntered together along the Main Street and up the steep stony path that led to the mountain.

Ron talked volubly all the way, and Len was suitably impressed by his tales of college life. But try as he would, Ron could not get Len to talk of the pit. The latter felt it would be a waste of time talking of the pit to a fellow who was so obviously out of touch with such life. Dusk lengthened their shadows as the two friends retraced their steps to the village. Ron was jubilant at the fact he had renewed an old acquaintanceship, and Len was pleased because Ron had promised to give him some books to read.

This unexpected walk was the prelude to many while

161

Ron was home on vacation, and when he returned to college he remained true to his promise and gave Len a number of books which dealt with a subject called socialism.

Len had not the slightest idea what this was apart from the occasional remarks he had heard in the pit to the effect that socialism was some method of sharing other people's property. Ron sent a letter from college explaining what the books were really about and what the subject really meant. The colourful manner of his explanations stimulated Len's interest. He felt here was a key to the problem troubling his mind.

Len devoted his spare time to the books, but most of the contents he did not fully understand, and those parts he could fathom only served to deepen his disappointment. Mentally he cursed the ignorance that prevented his understanding all that the books contained, yet, in spite of this, the little knowledge that he gained revived his interest in the pits and in his workmates. He dimly began to see them in a new light, although he failed to appreciate the real basis for this. And in addition there was awakening within him a vague physical urge that made him feel more sentimental and philosophical.

The hard work and long hours, combined with his mental and physical turmoil, began to take toll of Len's strength. He became dispirited and a weakening lassitude crept over his body. Big Jim noticed the symptoms in the pit when Len, though his body was steaming with perspiration, continued to shiver as if he were cold. He decided to speak to Siân about the matter.

The opportunity came one evening when Siân was

swilling the wet working clothes, while Jim sat in his usual place with his legs stretched towards the fire. Len had gone to bed directly after bathing, complaining that he was tired.

'Hem,' Jim started. 'Have you noticed anything wrong with our Len this last few days, Siân bach?'

Siân looked up sharply from the tub, her face red with exertion. 'What do you mean?' she asked. 'Do you say the boy be bad?'

Jim nodded assent.

Siân rose from the tub wringing the soap suds from her hands. 'What make you think that, James?'

'Oh, nothing much, only I fancy he be getting very weak and miserable. He couldn't lift a lump of coal into the tram today, and I do know that if he was well he could bloody eat it.'

Siân said nothing and Jim went on: 'Not only that, but he was sweating like a pig today and was shivering at the same time, as if he had pewmonia.'

'Ha,' interrupted Siân, 'so that be why he went straight to bed, eh? Do you think we had better send for the doctor, James?'

Jim spat heavily into the fire before answering contemptuously: 'Doctor, mun jawli! What good would they be? What the boy do want is a good whiff and some boiled beer. Sweat it out, see, Siân bach. That be the thing for a cold.'

'I don't know so much 'bout the beer,' replied Siân, 'but I be sure he 'on't go to work tomorrow. No, nor he 'on't go till he be quite well.' She sat down on the stool near Jim, her eyes full of tears. 'I 'ood sooner have him sit by the fire by there all the days of his life,' she asserted, 'than to see him lie by the side of Jane bach and her babby in the cemetery.'

Jim said no more.

The following morning Len did not wake till nine o'clock, four hours too late for the pit. His head throbbed even as he wondered what was wrong, for Siân had never slept late before and he could not understand why she should have done so this day.

He shouted to her and noticed that his voice was thin and weak and that it cost him an effort to raise it. He heard her shuffling feet patter up the stairs in response to his call, and she came into the bedroom with a basin in her hand.

'Here you be, Len bach,' she murmured. 'Mam have brought some gruel for you. Now you must drink it all down like a good boy and you will soon be well again.'

Len did not like gruel, but he felt too weak to argue, and obediently swallowed the hot, thick fluid. Siân tucked the clothes around him although he was already perspiring.

'There you be,' she said, 'you must be a good boy for mam now, and go to sleep.'

Len dozed off into a semi-conscious state.

He remained in bed a month before he was able to go down to the kitchen again. During this period Jim and Siân often quarrelled over his illness. Each day in the pit Jim received advice as to the best recipe for curing Len, the favourite one being a quart of stout, treated with a red-hot poker and thickened with nutmeg. Jim was convinced that this treatment would cure his son, but Siân was equally convinced it would kill him, and for hours they nagged each other on the matter, each trying to persuade the other.

During his convalescence Len was visited by his workmates, the younger of whom brought him fruit while the elder, belonging to Jim's circle, brought him flagons of beer under their coats without Siân knowing. But she always discovered these before Len had the opportunity of informing his father of their whereabouts.

One day when Len was well on the way to recovery, Jim saw Siân emptying one of the flagons down the sink. He jumped to his feet from the armchair in which he was sprawling and with one stride reached the back door, but when he saw the last dregs trickling from the upturned bottle in Siân's hand, he could only open his eyes in a pitiful stare. He grasped the flagon, looking at it hard for some moments while the ends of his moustache twitched convulsively, and then turning reproachfully to Siân, asked her: 'Have you no shame, fenyw, that you pour good money down the sink like that?'

Siân glared at him a while before replying. 'Shame?' she queried indignantly. 'You talk to me of shame? Ha-ha! You, who did let your drunken butties bring beer to your innocent dying son and let them try to poison him behind my back!'

Jim did not expect this outburst and retreated shamefacedly into the kitchen. 'Come, come, Siân bach,' he mumbled, 'you have got no need to say such a thing to my face.'

He would have continued but for a peevish interruption from Len, who exclaimed, 'Oh, leave it there, dad. Don't start quarrelling over nothing.' And at this they both stopped arguing.

Len read again the letter he had received that morning from Ron. It asked about his progress with the books and commented on certain political matters, and he spent the remainder of the day answering it.

A few days later Siân allowed him to take a short stroll up the mountain. She put Jim's overcoat over his shoulders, whence it dangled to his feet, and but for the fact that he flatly refused, threatening to remain at home if she insisted, she would have wrapped her shawl round him as well.

'I don't know what the world be coming to,' she complained. 'Children don't no longer trust their mothers to know what be best for them.' But eventually she let him go with the warning: 'Now, 'member, Len bach, if you will be longer than a hour mam will be after you.' Len promised he would return within the prescribed time, knowing that if he did not she would waken the valley with long-drawn cries for 'Len-n-n-n.'

Each day after this first attempt he continued his excursions up the mountain. He felt his body regaining strength and in a short time began to talk of restarting work. His parents tried to dissuade him, but Len was aware, in spite of attempts to hide the fact, that the loss of his wages was playing havoc with the domestic budget and that Siân was getting more deeply into debt each week. One day he walked to the colliery office and notified the officials that he was now fit and well.

He was told to start with his father next morning.

THE PIT CLAIMS
ANOTHER VICTIM

The Saturday following his return to work, as he had no wages to draw, Siân agreed that Len should approach the management for an advance on the security of the work he had already performed. He did so, and was granted the equivalent of three days' wages. He was aware that the advance given was actually a mortgage upon his body, but he saw no other alternative in view of the debts that had accumulated during his illness.

Siân paid off the sundry little creditors with the money but was unable to diminish the bulk she owed Mr. Evans Cardi for groceries. The latter was very agreeable about it when Siân informed him of the position.

'I understand, Mrs. Roberts,' he said. 'Things will come better by and by. Perhaps you will be able to settle it next week, now that Len have started to work again.'

Len was rather worried over the whole business. For one thing, he did not want his family to be indebted to Ron's father, but the main cause of his worry was the fact that, after working for more than three years, he was unable to meet the financial emergency of an illness. The books he had been reading, in addition to improving his vocabulary, had also explained why the family could not meet the obligations incurred during his enforced period of idleness. The knowledge made him very bitter, especially when, on the following pay-day the advance made him was deducted from his wages.

Tired and irritable, he mentioned the matter to his parents one night.

'It's a shame,' he started, addressing both of them, 'that you two have to suffer because I have been too bad to go to work.'

Big Jim merely grunted. 'Ho, ay. That's just how it be in this old world, boy bach. It have always been the same ever since I can 'member, and it always will be the same.'

The casual, off-hand nature of the reply drove Len frantic. His experiences since starting work had made him emotionally more volatile, and he sprang to his feet with a curse, the first they had ever heard him utter. His face was white with passion.

'Holy Christ, dad,' he burst out, 'how can you sit by there and talk so comfortable about it? You talk as if we are nothing but cattle, mun. Look at yourself. You have been working in the pit for over thirty years and are supposed to be one of the best workmen there. Yet what are you now? The body you are so proud of is breaking up before our eyes, 'in't it, mam?' he pleaded, turning to Siân, who continued to look at him dazedly without answering.

'Yes,' Len went on, 'and not only that, but it is breaking your spirit if your words are anything to go by.'

Jim half rose from his chair at this, but Len paid no attention.

'Look at me,' he said passionately. 'I have been working over three years. Yet when I lose a month's work because I'm too bad to go to the pit, we get in arrears with the rent and have to owe money for food.'

He paused a moment, overcome with emotion. And when he continued in a sad voice the muscles of his face were twitching visibly.

'Cattle are not treated like us. A farmer takes care of his cow when it is bad, but we be no use to anybody.' His voice rose in a sudden frenzy of passion. 'No, not even to our bloody selves when we fail to drag our bodies up the hill to the blasted pit.'

His voice dropped. 'Oh, mam. I couldn't help falling bad, could I? Yet you have got to suffer because of it. You once said, dad,' turning to his father again, 'that when you came to the pits first you had five golden sovereigns in your pocket. Since then you have spent a hard life and have given your wonderful body to the pit. And now, after all these years, instead of having five sovereigns in your pocket we owe five for food and rent.' His voice began to rise again and a little quiver ran through it. 'Think of it – a lifetime of hard work ending in debt. Mam do quarrel with you sometimes because you do have a pint or two of beer. Christ almighty, don't you deserve it? Or is it only work we have got to live for.

'Oh, dad and mam,' he cried in despair, 'I am sorry if I have hurt you, but think. You two are getting on and are beginning to look back. I have got to start where you finish, and I must look ahead, not behind.'

He seemed to lose his thoughts for a minute and swallowed hard before turning to his mother beseechingly. 'Oh, mam bach. Look at our dad. He's the finest working man that ever went down a pit. He do take pride in his work and do never lose a shift, but because I, his son, do go bad for a month he have got to go in debt. It's not right. It's not fair. There's something wrong somewhere.'

He bent his head on the table and his parents looked at him with a loving pity. Presently Big Jim spat in the fire and said, 'Don't worry, Len bach. You be not quite right in your head after that bout of illness, yet.'

And Siân broke in: 'Ay, and you be reading too many of those old books, too. They 'on't do you any good.'

Jim stopped her as Len raised his head from the table. 'It be not that,' he said, before Len could say anything. 'You listen to your old man, Len bach, and don't worry your head 'bout anything. When you do fail Big Jim be still here, strong as ever even if I do have a few pints now and agen.'

Len looked at both the old people and felt something tug at his heart. He opened his mouth to say something, but shut it again without speaking.

That evening he met Will, his workmate, who coaxed him into the Boar's Head, where, as he explained, he had some winnings to pick up. Len waited until Will returned with the man he was looking for, and the three sat down while the bookie called for a pint of beer apiece. Len was still feeling the effects of his outburst and only required a little coaxing to drink up the first pint of beer he had ever tasted. He did not like the taste, but the warm glow it sent through his body was pleasing and helped to dissipate his anger, and as the conversation became more lively, the first was followed by a second and a third.

Len could drink no more after this. The stuff rose back into his throat and the room seemed to be twisting around him, but in spite of this physical discomfort, the glow still pervaded his body with a languorous warmth, and his brain moved more quickly and in pleasant channels.

He never remembered how he reached home that night or how he got into bed, but next morning when he woke his mouth was dry and his head throbbed.

Siân asked, 'Why did you go straight to bed last night, Len bach? Was you bad?'

He was thankful she did not suspect, and told her, 'No, mam; I was only a bit tired.'

Once in the pit, however, he soon sweated out the aftermath of the beer and felt really well again. At this time he and his father were working with many other men and boys on a long stretch of coalface called a 'barry'. During the dinner break, when all the men were gathered together, a discussion started about a shortage of timber from which they were suffering.

'Ay,' said Jim, 'this be the third day now. The fireman do know all about it, but not a bloody stick have I seen yet.'

'That's quite right,' interjected Bill Bristol. 'They can't say they don't know nothing about it, because I told the fireman myself this morning. I suppose the sods will not send timber down till we are all buried.'

'Ay,' said Scottie, 'and they'll not need to wait verra long. My bloody place is just on the floor now.'

Will took up the discussion. 'That be true. The whole rotten barry be on the move now, and once this top do start to work nothing in blue hell will give us time to get out before we are all squashed flat as bloody black pats.'

All the men nodded agreement with Will's crude observation as they chewed their food and brushed the cockroaches off the boxes that held it.

Len had been silently listening to the talk. The men's casual appreciation of the deadly possibilities arising from the timber shortage made him think deeply. He wondered if it were sheer bravery that made the men and boys talk so calmly about the possibility of a horrible death awaiting them in the next few hours. He pondered over this while the men carried on the conversation, and eventually came to the conclusion it was not only bravery that made them talk in the way they did. He felt there existed a callous indifference among them, bred in their knowledge that the pit held their fate in its power and that death and destruction could come suddenly in a thousand different ways. He sensed this feeling, in himself, and realised that if he pondered over the possible deaths awaiting him, he would never muster sufficient courage to descend the pit again. But his thoughts were interrupted by the booming voice of his father.

'Boys,' he said, 'we have got to make our minds up. Either we do stop by here until the timbers come or we do shut our chops and get on with the work. I'n't that it, Len?' he asked, turning to his son.

Big Jim was always decisive in a crisis. He divided all problems into two straight opposites and demanded the acceptance of one or the other without the slightest regard for compromise. He was precisely the same in his public-house affairs. Either a man wanted to fight or he did not. For Jim, that was the end of it.

Len knew of this characteristic, and he was wary.

'Perhaps we can find some other way out for the best,' he answered hesitantly. 'What about one of us going back for the fireman now, before we start to work. He ought to know by now when we can 'spect to have the timber in.'

'But what if he don't know?' shouted Will. 'What do you say we do then?'

Len thought hard for a moment, then said, 'I believe the best thing we can do if the fireman don't know when we can get the timber, is to sit down by here until it comes to us.'

There was some discussion on this suggestion. A few of the workmen wanted to continue working, pending the reply of the fireman. Others were opposed to this. Len considered the danger to be immediate and not ultimate, and re-entered the argument with this in mind.

'If we start now, and one of us gets killed, we won't be able to use the timber when it comes.'

The logic of this statement appealed to the men's humour and their common sense. Big Jim insisted upon every man voting, 'so that everything be square and above board,' as he explained. Two men were sent to notify the fireman of their decision. The remainder whiled away the time with

173

obscene jokes and smutty yarns that, for some undefined reason, reminded Jim of his adventures in the Boer War.

'We was coming out of the old farmhouse,' he related, 'when I seed a black 'ooman, naked as a dog, on a tump 'bout hundred yards away. Duw, duw, she was the first 'ooman us had seen for years, and the sun that hot we was full of tickles all the time. We all winked to her, but she take no notice, mun. Then I shout, 'Dere 'ma. Arglwydd mawr.' She didn't half run then. All of us did race after her like mad. But I was a good runner then, and did soon leave 'em all standing. But funny thing, mun, she did leave me standing. I did go like hell, but all I could see was her little black arse shining in the sun like a brass button, before she did turn round and shout, "Toodle-oo!"'

All, except Len, enjoyed this little anecdote, but he regarded it as sacrilege for his father to talk smut. Before he had time to say anything, however, lights appeared back on the roadway and everyone became silent as they drew nearer.

The fireman was obviously uneasy. 'Well, boys,' he asked, 'what are you doing here? Dinner-time is up and you all ought to be back in your places.'

No one answered, so the fireman resumed, this time more harshly: 'You all know that the output was down yesterday and that Mr. Hicks have said if we don't get more coal from this barry we will have to shut it down.'

The men looked at each other sheepishly, much of their courage vanishing at this threat to their livelihood. They would probably have returned to their working places without another word had not Will shouted out: 'What the blasting hell be the barry to us? We don't own it, do we? Mr. Hicks do claim it belongs to him, so let him look after the bloody hole. The only thing that do belong to us is our bloody lives, and that be all we have got to look after.'

This heartened the men and they maintained their stand.

Len rose diffidently to his feet. 'Will have hit the nail on the head, boys. If Mr. Hicks wants to shut the barry, that be his business. What we have got to do is to watch we are not buried in the barry for ever, which we will be very soon if we don't get timber.' There was an audible murmur of approval at this statement.

The fireman felt the tide going against him, and started to cajole: 'I have told you that I'm doing all I can to get timbers for you as soon as possible. There will very likely be some on the next journey. Now be reasonable and get back to your work, boys bach, and I will see that everything will come all right.'

'That's my eye of a bloody yarn,' said Bill Bristol. 'We have heard that tale before during the last fortnight. It's like the battles Big Jim used to fight in the Boer War, always finishing miles further back than where they started.'

Jim started to his feet at this insult, but the fireman, exasperated by his failure to get the men back to work, interrupted. 'Hell fire! Do you 'spect me to shit bloody timber for you?'

A voice from outside the circle of light shouted, 'No. And even if you did it 'ood be no good to us, because nothing from you would be of any use to anybody.'

Len felt the air grow tense, and knew the men were now in the mood for defying anything the fireman ordered. Turning to the latter, he said: 'Perhaps it 'ood be better, Shenkin, if you went back the road for five minutes to give the boys a chance to talk the thing over.'

The irate fireman bridled up immediately. 'What,' he shouted, at the top of his voice, 'you want me, the fireman of this district, to go back on the road? Never in your life! Huh. Who ever heard of such bloody cheek? What do you you take me for, a bloody doorboy or what? If men haven't got guts enough to talk open and free before another man, that is their own look-out.'

Again from outside the ring of light came the voice: 'You be bragging hell of a lot, today, i'n't you, Shenkin? Nobody said you was a man. Ach. There be no more bloody man in you than there be in a dog's arse.'

This stung the fireman into a fury. 'What,' he howled, saliva trickling down the corners of his mouth, 'cheek me, would you? Defy me, eh? Easy you can do that when you hide your dirty bloody face in the dark. But I know you. Oh, ay. I know who you be by your voice, don't forget. No man have ever got the better of me yet. Do you know,' he asked them all, 'that a fireman in a pit is like a captain on a ship? He have got, by law, to be obeyed. The law is on his side and you men must do as I order. If you are not ready to do that, then out you go, the bloody lot of you. And don't none of you ever come back, either.'

This sudden and unexpected ultimatum alarmed the men, particularly those with big families. Len saw through the fireman's attempt to split the ranks, and knew they were all in a tight corner. Capitulation at this moment would leave them no alternative but to go back to the untimbered face, hoping for the best, until timber came. And for this he was not prepared. On the other hand, if they refused there was nothing else for it but to leave the pit for good.

He looked around the perturbed men before him. They were all thinking hard and hoping someone would tell them what to do. Len glanced at the fireman and saw the triumphant smirk on his face, and for some reason or other the sneer gave him the counter-move to the fireman's threat. Turning sharply, he shouted: 'Go round the other barries, Will, and tell all the men to come down by here. Tell them there be a dispute on and that Shenkin have ordered us out because we 'on't work without timber.'

Like a flash the men grasped the astuteness of the move. The fireman knew that the other colliers were also short of timber and that they would follow such a lead as this. He grew alarmed. If the agitation spread there was every likelihood of all the men in the pit going on strike, and rather than face this possibility he gave way with a bad grace.

'All right. I didn't mean what I said 'bout going out, but we must have a little bit of order sometimes or everything will be upside down. You can hold your meeting, but don't be too long, and give me a shout when you are ready.'

His eyes glinted viciously in the light of the lamps as he went back. The men waited until he was out of hearing before excitedly starting the discussion.

Len had already planned what was to be done. 'Look here, boys,' he said. 'When me and the old man was going out yesterday I noticed some good timber loose on the other side of the parting. What if we tell Shenkin we are willing to go back and fetch that for the barry if he will give us an extra half-turn each for our trouble?'

This appeared a brilliant idea to the men. It solved the immediate problem of timber and at the same time took the offensive out of the fireman's hands. In addition it meant more money on pay-day. Without hesitation they all agreed to stand for this.

Big Jim shouted for Shenkin, who soon came panting up the roadway. 'Well, have you made your minds up? What are you going to do? I hope you are going to be sensible for once.' His voice was like a rasp. Bill Bristol reported the outcome of the discussion. The fireman scratched his head for a while, then asked, 'How far back is these timbers you are talking about?' Jim told him, whereupon Shenkin said: 'Very well, boys. If you fetch that timber I will put five trams of muck in for each of you on measuring day.'

This was not equal to the half-turn asked by the men, but they saw the compromise as a victory and accepted. They fetched the few timbers that were available and shared them equally. All of them were elated, for this was the first time they had been together in a conflict with the officials of the pit, and the victory gave them confidence in each other.

In the minds of all of them Len was automatically promoted to leadership of their affairs in the barry.

Having had their timber, the coalface soon became a hive, each man hurrying to make good the time lost in the dispute.

Towards the end of the shift, the enclosed air of the

barry shook to a sudden crash, which was followed by a loud cry: 'Quick, boys, quick! Bill is under a fall.'

Flinging down their tools anywhere, the men instantly responded, tearing along in their headlong scramble to get to the scene of the accident. When they reached it they saw at a glance what had happened. Bill Bristol had been digging a hole in the floor ready for the last prop he intended standing that day. He must have been bending over this hole when the roof had crashed down upon him, and now only his feet and one clenched hand were visible. Without a moment's pause the men began tearing at the debris that had buried their mate. Big Jim worked his hands beneath a huge stone that had fallen flatwise. Straining his gigantic muscles till they stood out in knots, he gasped out: 'Now, boys, put that prop under.' It was the one Bill intended using to protect himself from the roof that had now fallen.

'Careful, now,' went on Jim, 'not too far or you might put it on poor old Bill. Right. Now, all together.'

With one concerted lift the stone was heaved over in a mighty jerk. Jim flung himself on his stomach and hurriedly scraped away the loose rubble until his fingers felt the flesh of his crushed workmate. He put his arms gently beneath the poor mangled body and lifted it carefully away from the fallen roof.

The men helped Big Jim to carry Bill back to the comparative safety of the roadway, where they laid him down, tenderly as breasting mothers, on the hastily arranged coats and shirts. Two of the men ran back for a stretcher, while the others cut away the injured man's bloodstained clothing. Blood spurted from the contorted limbs as, with infinite care, they were examined by the men. The whites of Bill's eyes were turned up in a ghastly glitter, and he groaned deep in his throat. Jim gave him some water to drink, but nothing more could be done until the stretcher came. The men stood around silent and sad while Jim rested the dying man's head on his arm. Presently he groaned again, and his lips shaped as if he were trying to say something. Big Jim bent down. 'There, there. Don't excite yourself, Bill bach,' he whispered, with a lump in his throat as he lied: 'You haven't had much, mun. Just a scratch or two, and a bruise here and there. Duw, duw, you will soon be all over the old 'ooman as strong as ever.'

Bill made no movement other than with his lips, but he failed to utter anything, and all that came from his mouth was a thick stream of blood and saliva. His eyes now seemed to have become normal again, and he looked at Jim with a deep intensity as though he were concentrating all his energies and thoughts in an attempt to say something. Jim bent his head nearer the bloodied lips, but the only thing that came was a horrible gibbering of the mouth. The men looked on helplessly, their faces full of grief and sadness, until at last they saw Bill's body quiver, then suddenly stiffen. They had known after the first brief examination that his back was broken.

The men who had run to fetch the stretcher came panting back, accompanied by the fireman. The latter was given details of the accident while the body was placed on the stretcher and covered completely with coats and a sheet of brattice as a final blanket. Then four of the men grasped the stretcher in lowered hands and led the slow procession to the pit bottom, each man taking it in turn to carry the lifeless body of his mate.

As the file of stooping men made their way forward no one spoke a word until they met Mr. Williams, the under-manager.

'Who is it, boys?'

'Bill Bristol.'

'Well, well. Pity. A splendid workman, too. It's always the best that go. Pity, pity. Try not to be longer than you can help, boys, not to keep the journey waiting too long. Well, well.'

The men continued their slow trudge. The whole pit seemed to hold its breath, and the usual clamour was stilled. Yet as if the warm air had whispered the news in every ear, everyone in the pit knew what had happened, and at the pit bottom everything was in readiness. All approaches to the cage had been cleared and the cage itself hung waiting. Ten men filed in with the corpse, lining it five aside like a guard of honour. The iron knocker clanged six times, announcing to those on the surface the presence of death, and the cage, now become a coffin, was drawn slowly to the pit-head. Men on the surface hushed their voices as they waited for it and stood respectfully to one side while the body and its escort came out.

Big Jim sent Len off in front of them to acquaint the widow of what had occurred. This was regarded by the men as the most unpleasant job they could undertake, and many of them stated they would sooner be on a stretcher themselves than have the task of telling someone else it

181

was coming. But much as he disliked it, Len regarded the task as a duty that had to be fulfilled, and handing his box, jack, and lamp to his father, he ran without coat or cap towards the home of Bill Bristol.

At the corner of the street where Bill had lived he stopped, and standing for a few minutes panting and gasping, he wondered how he was going to break the news. Neighbours were already flocking to the doorways as though drawn by some invisible magnet. All of them knew intuitively, as soon as they saw Len, that an accident had occurred, and though Len tried to walk casually up the street, every woman went white as he approached. Only when he had passed did the colour come back to their cheeks and, feeling themselves spared, every woman became immediately solicitous for her neighbour.

By the time Len reached the house he was looking for all the women in the street were with him, many of them already in tears. He knocked softly on the closed door, fearing that a loud sound would advertise his message, and as he waited he felt his heart beating painfully at his ribs.

The knock was answered by a pretty young woman holding a baby at her breast, while another dragged at her skirts. Len recognised Bill's wife at once. As soon as she saw him, her face went white as a death-mask with blue streaks and black shadows painted across it. She looked slowly from Len to the neighbouring women, then back to him. His coatless form and wild eyes struck her like a physical blow.

Something seemed to choke her for a moment, but she swallowed hard and gasped: 'For God's sake don't tell me something have happened to our Bill.'

Len gulped back the sour saliva that gathered in his mouth before replying. 'Ay. Bill have had a little tap. He will soon be all right and you have got no need to worry.'

She glared into his eyes and clutched her children more closely to her. 'Tell me the truth, man,' she demanded. 'Don't you dare to lie to me. Oh, God,' she added, bursting into hysterical sobs, 'Bill is dead. I can see it in your eyes. Oh, Bill, Bill! Oh, my little babies!'

Len said no more. The neighbours took the children from the grieving woman and led her weeping back into the house.

Meanwhile the procession of half-clothed, black-faced men from the pit grew longer with every stride as miners returning home from work fell in behind the corpse. News of the accident trickled through the doors of each house long before the mournful cortege passed it. The stretcher betrayed the dead body by the fact that the face was covered, and whispers of 'Who is it?' floated quietly from one side of the street to the other. Tradesmen drew down their blinds till it passed and publicans closed their doors. The pit had claimed another victim and everyone mourned the latest sacrifice.

Big Jim and two other men remained behind in the house to wash the shattered limbs and lay the body out on the parlour table ready for the coffin.

Next day in work the men of the barry hardly spoke to each other. The blood-spattered stones had been cleared away by the night-shift and the coalface was ready for work immediately the day-shift returned. This cold planning by

183

the management to ensure that whatever happened to the men there should be no hitch in the production of coal drove Len frantic. Throughout the morning he kept on working without saying a word to his father, although inwardly he was impotently fuming.

During the dinner hour, when all the men were gathered together, he could contain himself no longer. He spat a lump of half-chewed moist bread from his mouth and let his temper grip him.

'Holy Christ. This isn't a pit, but a slaughterhouse,' he began. 'The officials are more like butchers than men. They measure coal without giving a thought to our flesh. They think, they dream, they live for coal, while we die for it. Coal – that's the thing. Get it. Drag it out by its roots. Do what you damn well like with it, but get it.

'Ay,' he went on more calmly, 'I believe that coal has come to be greater than God to the officials, and they now measure our lives by the trams of coal we can fill for them. Can't you see it, boys?' he asked, his passion again getting the upper hand. 'Firing hell, we don't count! If we had timber a couple of minutes sooner yesterday, Bill 'ood be eating food with us now and cracking his jokes. Instead of that he be lying dead with his body cut to pieces and the bosses have already planned how to make up for the coal they lost yesterday.'

His rage overcame him and he subsided into silence.

For the remainder of the week the men plodded to work like dumb animals each morning, answering with their bodies when the hooter called. But on the day of Bill's funeral, though the hooter blasted the air as usual, no one

184

answered its hysterical screams. It kept blowing and bellowing like an animal robbed of its food, and still no one answered, until at last its noisy shrieks faded into a wail and died out. The men had determined not to go to the pit on the day of Bill's funeral. They had to bury their dead.

CWMARDY
PREPARES
FOR ACTION

During the next few months big changes took place in the valley. The colliery company had extended its interests and now controlled the other groups of pits. As a result of this transaction Lord Cwmardy called a meeting of the directors and various pit managers at the Big House. While these were assembling he looked through the open French window at the pits he controlled and the valley he dominated. His black hair carried little tufts of grey at the sides, but his square, clean-shaven face was as hard as the coal he owned. When he turned from the window and took a chair next his daughter-secretary at the end of the table, everyone present became silent. They were aware that drastic changes of policy and personnel would accompany the merger which Lord Cwmardy had so cleverly negotiated, and each of them wondered how he would be affected.

187

When Cwmardy spoke his words dropped into his listeners' ears like icicles on a hot body. He accused the managers of lack of interest in their work, insisting that their friendly handling of the men was ruining the pits and the company. Some of the officials tried to remonstrate, but he abruptly checked them.

'You have come here to listen, not to talk,' he told them. He spoke for more than an hour before introducing to them the sharp-faced grey-moustached man who sat unobtrusively at the far end of the table.

'This is Mr. Higgins,' he announced. 'In future Mr. Hicks will look after the practical and technical running of our affairs, but Mr. Higgins will work in close co-operation with him and will be directly representative of the financial interests of the company in the day-to-day operations of the collieries. That is all, gentlemen,' he concluded. 'But before you go we will drink to the future prosperity of our undertaking,' and filling their glasses, they all rose and echoed the toast.

In the meantime Len also had developed. He attended the night-school recently organised by the Council in order to study mining, and most of his spare time he spent in the bedroom with his books.

Siân warned him: 'No good will come from all this reading, Len bach. The Lord have put into your head all that it be good for you to know, and if you go beyond that you will be sure to land up in the 'sylum, like your poor old uncle John, God help him.'

But Len took no heed of her grave warnings. He kept on at his studies and passed examinations which theoretically qualified him to take up a position as a colliery manager if he so desired. But this was the furthest thought from his mind. His heart revolted at the idea of becoming an official, for deep in him was still the memory of Jane's death and the official's son who was supposed to be responsible for it. But even apart from this emotional reaction, his experiences in the pit had embittered him against the officials as a caste. He regarded them as something distinct from the ordinary workmen and felt it would be an act of betrayal to his family, to himself, and to the men in the barry if he left the ranks of his workmates.

News of the amalgamation soon spread from pit to pit and became the main topic of discussion. The older workmen were apprehensive of the move and their feelings were neatly summed up one night in the Boar's Head by Big Jim.

'Mark my words, boys bach,' he warned them. 'Old Lord Cwmardy haven't done this for our sakes. Oh no. You can bet the buttons on your shirt that he have got something up his sleeve that 'on't do us any good.'

The pits resounded with furious discussion each day. Many of the younger miners were inclined to regard the merger in a more favourable light than Big Jim, some of them arguing that the amalgamation would eliminate competition and so lead to more wages.

One Saturday when the men were returning from work the village crier met them at the end of the bridge. Shouting at the top of his voice, he announced there was to be a special mass-meeting of all workmen on Sunday afternoon. The announcement created a stir in the valley and there were very few public-house fights that night, as the men were too busy discussing the meeting on the morrow. Many of them remembered that the last time such a meeting had been held it was followed by a strike of hauliers.

When Sunday afternoon came Big Jim and Len made their way to the huge old barn where the meeting was to be held. They found it packed with workmen, and Big Jim had to use all his weight to force a way in, Len crushed to his side in the press. Ezra Jones, the miners' leader, sat by himself on the improvised platform waiting for the hubbub to die down. The hall was thick with tobacco fumes when he rose to his feet and advanced to the front of the stage. He looked exactly as Len had first seen him at the funeral of the explosion victims. His solid, square body fitted his stern face and made a complete picture of rugged determination. There was something powerful and dominating in the man's presence, and when he raised his hand in the authoritative gesture that Len still remembered, the tumult of voices in the hall faded away. Ezra waited until everyone was perfectly quiet and then, his voice as hard and stern as his face, began to speak.

'Fellow workmen, I have taken the responsibility upon myself for calling you together today. You will decide for yourselves if I was justified in doing this after I have reported the purpose of the meeting. Many of us believe we should meet like this more often. Maybe what follows from this meeting may make that not only possible but necessary.' Loud shouts interrupted him.

'That's right. We ought to meet more often.'

'Good old Ezra! Get it off your chest.'

This was followed by a prolonged stamping of feet, but

190

when this had ceased Ezra went on to explain that the colliery company, through Mr. Higgins, was no longer going to pay for the small coal filled by the men. In future the only payment made would be for large coal. 'That is the exact message I have to give you from the company,' he concluded, 'and that is why I have called you together. You can now ask what questions you like and discuss the matter for yourselves.'

With this he sat down abruptly. The hall was immediately in an uproar. Men asked each other a hundred different questions and made a hundred different statements that were lost in the general din. But eventually a voice forced itself above all the others.

'Can I ask a question, Mr. Chairman?' it asked.

'Yes, if you want to,' was the curt reply.

'Well, can you tell us how much small coal we fill in each tram?'

Everyone became silent as Ezra, without rising from his chair, answered, 'Yes. About forty percent – that is, nearly half.'

A groan echoed throughout the hall, and another workman rose to his feet. He was tall and austere-looking, as became a deacon of Calfaria, the biggest chapel in Cwmardy and the one much favoured by the colliery management and officials.

'Does Mr. Hicks really mean to do this thing to us? Is he serious in what he says? It will mean a big loss to all of us, and I was thinking perhaps Mr. Hicks is going to make the loss good in some other way, maybe by giving us a bigger price for large coal.'

191

The chairman rose to his feet. 'Yes, Mr. Hicks and Mr. Higgins are prepared to consider something in that direction. On the old price-list for through and through we had a shilling for every ton of coal we filled, large and small. Now we are offered one and threepence for every ton of large but nothing at all for small coal. This means that where we used to earn a pound, the same amount of coal will now give us fifteen shillings.'

The men were dumbfounded as they closely followed Ezra's statement. As the meaning of the offer sank home to them the hall became a bedlam, and everyone broke into abuse.

'Dirty old swine!'

'How the hell do he think we are going to live?'

'Let him come and do his own dirty work!'

'Better starve out than in!'

'Let him get to hell and find his workmen there!'

Len sat silent and morose. He was astounded by the proposition. More or less subconsciously his mind searched for favourable possibilities in the situation.

To his father's terse comment, 'Only one thing we can do, take it or fight,' his only reply was, 'Wait a minute, let's see how the men take it. There might be some way out which we can't think of for a minute.'

He sensed the implications of the ultimatum, and pictured the men in the barry, already overworked on the present basis, slogging themselves to a standstill to make up in extra output what they lost by the lower price-list. He saw his own home where, working full-time as he and his father were doing, they could barely pay their way, and he tried to imagine what domestic conditions would be like if they failed to make good their present wages by harder work.

A deep hush brought his thoughts back to the meeting. He looked around and saw Dai Cannon standing on a bench directly opposite him. The man's beer-drenched suit and bedraggled moustache, under which the bottom lip hung loosely, attracted attention. He stood above the seated workers and looked a picture of disgust and defiance. His voice was deep and booming when he spoke.

'Mr. Chairman and fellow workmen, at last the octopus is closing his tentacles about the living bodies of our women and children. Like a gloating vulture, the hireling of the company is waiting to fill our valley with the sighs and sobs of starving people.' He lifted his eyes and hands to the ceiling and went on in this strain with increasing passion and vehemence in each phrase he uttered. The men were on their feet cheering wildly when he concluded with the words: 'If we are to starve let it be in the sun with God's pure air around us. If we are to die let it be fighting like the slaves of old Rome. I stand, like Moses, for my people.'

Big Jim, a puzzled frown on his face, bent to Len and said, 'By Christ, old Dai is a good speaker, mun, but what did he mean by octopus's testicles?'

Len hurriedly corrected him, without taking his eyes off the speaker. Dai knew he had struck the right note and sat down contentedly, his wet lower lip more conspicuous than ever. Presently, when the tumult had become hushed, Ezra rose from his chair. 'That's a good speech of Dai's,' he said with quiet irony. 'As usual he has told us what to do, but has not told us how to do it. It is quite easy for us all to get excited and enthusiastic, but that alone won't

193

take us far against this company. Whatever we think is necessary to safeguard our conditions will have to be planned out in cold blood.' He sat down again, leaving the men to think out the problem. Speaker after speaker got to his feet and contributed to the discussion that followed.

Len listened attentively to everyone. He felt there was a lot in what Ezra had said, but thought he could have been more helpfully critical of Dai's speech instead of brushing it aside as he had done. During the discussion he had already, in a hazy way, seen how the ravelled threads could be separated, but he wanted to be sure before plunging. At last he satisfied himself that the way was clear and tremblingly rising to his feet he asked for the floor. Big Jim looked at him with open mouth and was about to say something when Ezra nodded acquiescence. In a shaking, squeaky voice Len asked: 'Does this new price-list affect the workmen in the other pits taken over by the company?' Ezra again nodded a curt assent, and Len's thoughts immediately cleared, for the reply showed him the counter to the company's threat. Clearing his throat, he told the meeting: 'If that is so, as far as I can see there are two things to be done if we are to succeed in this fight.' His voice became more confident and resonant as he continued: 'While I agree with all that Dai Cannon has said, I don't believe he has gone far enough. What I mean is this. The old price-list made it possible for us to earn some sort of a living, but the new one will make this impossible. If this be so, then we should demand from the company a minimum wage that will guarantee we won't starve under the new list.' Ezra had leaned forward when

194

Len began propounding his policy, and the workmen, who grasped its import immediately, applauded loudly. Len went on: 'But how to get this is the problem. We can depend on it that the company will fight, because this is a principle that affects every miner and owner in the country. That is why we must look for support right from the start, and where better can we look for this than among our neighbours, who are suffering under the same company as us and facing the same attack? I believe we should send somebody from this meeting to our butties in the other pits under the company and ask them to come with us to a mass-meeting of the workmen from all the pits.'

He stuttered here, tried to go on, then gave it up and sat down. For a second the hall was perfectly quiet. Then uproar broke out as the men grasped the logic of the arguments. The shouting and applause continued for many minutes, while Big Jim looked round the hall, nodding his head all the time as if saying, 'There you be, you beggars, what think you of that? Big Jim's boy, see?'

Len, sitting next to him, hardly heard the cheering, his face was pale with nervousness and he bent his head in a vain attempt to stop the thumping of his heart. Ezra at last succeeded in restoring order.

'I think that our young friend has cleared the way for us,' he said. 'If fight there is to be, then we bring our allies into it from the start.' He strained his eyes to peer through the smoky atmosphere. 'I am not sure – the smoke is rather heavy – but I believe the last speaker is Big Jim's boy.'

Again the cheering, broke out, and despite Len's efforts to restrain him, Big Jim got to his feet and shouted

'Ay, ay, Mishter Cadeirydd, you be quite right. Big Jim's boy.'

Once the way forward was clear the men soon disposed of the steps to be taken, and the meeting closed with the singing of a Welsh anthem. The excited and chattering men streamed into the street and, breaking up into groups, continued the discussion as they made their way homewards. During the intervening week approaches were made to the other workmen in the valley, and it was agreed to hold a joint mass-meeting on the following Sunday.

Two matters now dominated the minds of the people, the coming strike, which they regarded as inevitable, and the coronation of the new king that was shortly to take place. This latter was the cause of much speculation. Will told Len, as they trudged to the pit one morning, 'The new king will never be so good as his old man was.'

'What makes you think that?'

'Well,' replied Will, 'by all accounts the old man was a hell of a bird, a proper sport by all accounts and different to the rest of 'em. He'd have a bit of fun with the best, and they tell me he was hot bloody stuff with the gels.'

Len did not seem to be paying much attention, so Will brought out what he regarded as a broadside. 'More than that, your old man told me that if it wasn't for the last king us 'ood have been at war with the bloody Shermans long ago. Now he's gone it will be bound to come off one day.'

Len merely murmured abstractedly: 'They're all the same, Will bach, they all carry out the orders given to them by our masters.'

Will snorted contemptuously. 'Huh! That be all balls.'

196

His mate did not reply for a while, then said, 'Don't let us bother our heads about the new king now. What do you think is going to happen in the meeting Sunday?' and with this began an argument that continued throughout the day in the pit.

Len listened avidly to everything that was said about Ezra, and found out that he had once worked on the other side of the mountain before he was blacklisted by the company and driven from his home. This had made him bitter and cynical, but since coming to the valley his dour determination and dominating personality had made him respected and admired by the workmen.

Listening to the instances of Ezra's staunchness and loyalty related by Big Jim, Len was thrilled, for he was now of an age when his vague ideas were beginning to find a coherence. Although very emotional, he yet had a capacity for deep thinking, and what he now needed was someone who could inspire him, a person whose words and actions would serve as a focus for his thoughts, a man he could look up to as an example.

More or less subconsciously, Len began to accept Ezra as a leader to be followed and trusted.

CWMARDY GOES
INTO ACTION

When Sunday came the weather was bright and the sky cloudless. The atmosphere was free from the weekday thrum of the pits and the smoke of the huge stacks, and this accounted for the strange hush that enveloped the valley as, up at the Big House, two men gazed silently through the window into the shimmering air that separated them from the mass of people gathered on the rubbish dump near the pit.

'They will assuredly strike,' Mr. Higgins told Mr. Hicks as they withdrew from the window.

'You may depend upon that,' replied the general manager, pouring himself a generous dose of whisky. 'But we have one consolation. They can't remain out long, because they have practically no organisation and no finance to maintain them for any length of time. More than that, they have no leaders.'

Mr. Higgins looked up at this last remark. 'I don't know

199

so much about that. This man Ezra Jones strikes me as a pretty stubborn type, and he seems to wield a great deal of influence with the men.'

'That's true,' murmured Mr. Hicks hesitantly. 'We were warned about him before he came to the village and were very foolish to have permitted him to start work at our pit.'

Mr. Higgins interrupted him rather abruptly. 'What are the possibilities of placing him on the staff?' he asked.

'Absolutely impossible. The man is incorruptible. All we can do now, if the men are foolish enough to strike, is to ensure that it is a short one. We must close every possible avenue of finance to them and use whatever measures are necessary to show them how silly their conduct is. We are fortunate in this last respect, Mr. Higgins, in that we have a representative majority in both the district and county councils. This will enable us to proceed constitutionally in the desired directions.'

Down on the rubbish dump thousands of miners and their womenfolk were waiting for the meeting to begin. They became accustomed to the putrid stench of decaying matter that rose from the nearby river, and it ceased to sting their nostrils. A lorry in the centre of the huge mass of people held Ezra and some other men. Presently a glorious baritone voice lifted itself from the throng in the lilting melody of an old Welsh hymn. Its strains floated over the crowd like a shawl encircling a child. The people lost their individual identities in the vibrating rhythm of the tune, which impelled their emotions into expression through bonds of vocal unity. In a matter of seconds every voice had taken up the refrain. The music rippled round the mountains in caressing billows that fell back upon themselves and then ran wistfully down the valley, the power in the men's deep voices carrying with it the tender soprano of the womenfolk.

The men on the platform stood with bared heads and took part in the singing until it finished, when they all, with the exception of Ezra, sat down. The latter waited with bent head until the last echoes ebbed into silence down the valley, then with an imperative wave of his hand he commanded attention. Each of the thousands of eyes was fixed upon him when his cold voice split the air as he reported all that had happened since the previous meeting. With steady calculation he built his case against the company and eventually concluded with the words: 'That is the position, fellow workmen, either we fight or starve. You will yourselves decide which.'

For a minute after his voice had ceased the whole world seemed to slumber, then it awoke to a terrific shout that rattled and throbbed in the blood of the people present. It ascended in increasing crescendos, pushing itself up the mountain with brazen resonance until it banged itself against the windows of the Big House.

'Strike! Strike!'

'Better starve out than in!'

'Strike! Strike!'

Ezra, white-faced and tight-lipped, stood motionless on the lorry waiting for the storm to abate. He knew the men and their moods, and was aware that no power on earth other than complete capitulation by the company could now avert a strike. But he felt neither pity for the company nor sympathy for the people. His heart had been broken with the breaking of his home, an event which had sent his wife to a premature death. His eyes looked blankly over the mass of heads before him as he unemotionally pictured the immediate future and concentrated his mind on the dominating need for defeating Lord Cwmardy and the company. After a while he raised his hand again.

'Men and women of our valley,' he began, 'no need to ask, is there peace or war? You have declared for war. So be it. Now let every man and woman stand solid in the fight, for we shall need every atom of energy and determination if we are to win.'

For the first time his eyes shone with hard glints as though he gloated over something long desired and now obtained. The gleam strengthened as someone struck up the strains of a Welsh battle hymn in which everyone joined. The meeting ended to the strains of the stirring song, and the people returned excitedly to their homes.

Len had been silent all the while. Overawed by the huge crowd of people and the tremendous upsurge of feeling, he had dumbly followed the proceedings, and that night he lay awake for long hours wondering what would be the outcome of the whole business. He knew the issue had now widened beyond the question of small coal and had become the vastly bigger and more important one of a minimum wage. He saw that the initiative had been taken out of the hands of the company, who were now thrown upon the defensive, and, although proud of the part he had played, he was sensible enough to realise that such a development was inevitable even had he not spoken at the initial meeting.

Next morning not a man other than officials presented himself at the pits. But in the afternoon each of them was surrounded by hundreds of men and women. The weather was beautifully fine and warm and the valley looked as peaceful as a hamlet in the Alps. The people joked with the police, most of whom they knew, while at the same time they jealously scrutinised everyone who approached the colliery. During the evening separate pit meetings were held and committees elected, from which representatives were chosen for a central committee that controlled all the pits. To this committee Len was elected.

The strike had dragged on for two weeks without any move being made by the company before Len realised that the men could not win on the present basis of operations. He had many ideas on the matter, but felt rather nervous of expressing them before the seasoned veterans of the committee. Particularly was he shy and diffident in Ezra's presence. The manner in which the latter had handled the decisive meeting greatly impressed him, and he began to look upon Ezra as the greatest man he had ever seen or read of. Despite this hesitancy, the thought persisted that something must be done, and he eventually made up his mind to seek an interview with the miners' leader. 'After all,' he thought to himself, when coming to this decision, 'he can't eat me. The most he can do is order me out of the house.'

Len's nervous rap on the door was answered by Ezra in person. The lad looked up to him for some moments as though he had suddenly lost his tongue. The elder man broke the silence.

'Hello,' he asked, 'what's brought you here, Len? But

come in. We can talk better inside.' The welcome and interest in Ezra's voice heartened him, and he felt more at ease when he sat down in a room lined with bookshelves. He had never before seen so many books at one time and would have liked to go round reading the titles, but Ezra gave him no opportunity. The man's keen, dark eyes seemed to bore into him and he again began to feel uncomfortable, but he swallowed his rising chagrin and went direct into the matter troubling his mind.

'I have come to see you, Mr. Jones, about our strike. We have now been out for a fortnight and I feel that unless we do something we will be beat.' He stopped abruptly as if he had unloaded himself of all he had come to say.

Ezra tried to help him. 'Well, Len, my boy. What ideas are troubling you? I would like to know what you are thinking, because I, also, have been disturbed by the way in which the strike is drifting.'

Len was pleased and encouraged by the implied compliment, and in a very short time his initial embarrassment was banished as he talked of the things he thought should be done. Ezra listened attentively until he had finished, and for some moments, that seemed like hours to Len, he sat deep in thought.

At last he rose from the chair and looked in a queer way at the young man. 'I am glad you came to me, Len, and I want to say before I go any further that I don't like being called Mr. Jones. My name is Ezra to all the workmen and it is the same to you.' Len looked a little startled at this but had no time to make any comment as the miners' leader went on. 'There is a great deal in what you have said. Yes, a great deal. But to my mind there are even more important things than the steps you are suggesting, all of which I agree with, by the way. For instance, Len,' he asked, looking directly into his eyes, 'have you thought what the next move of the company is likely to be?'

Len shook his head negatively.

'Well, you see, my boy, when you enter a fight such as we are in now we must always try to see at least two moves ahead. We must always try to anticipate what the enemy is thinking and what he intends doing. To begin with, do you think for a moment the company is prepared to let the strike drift on indefinitely without taking measures to bring it to an end? No, of course not,' he answered himself. 'Each day the strike lasts means further loss to the owners, and they are no more anxious than we are to prolong the strike. Just as you have been thinking of methods to strengthen the strike, so have they been thinking of ways and means to break it and drive our men back to the pits. Our job is to find out how they intend doing this. Yes, that is the problem.'

Len listened avidly to all he had to say and felt the ruthless strength of the man even in his words.

'I am glad you came to see me,' Ezra concluded, 'and shall always be pleased to welcome you in my house. I know,' he added somewhat wistfully, 'that you think me a hard man, but there are reasons for this. In any case I shall always be glad to help young men like yourself who take an interest in the affairs of the people. You had better let me raise the matters you mention in the committee. They will have a better chance of being accepted.'

Len unhesitatingly agreed to this and, after a moment's awkward pause, Ezra diverted the conversation into other channels. He talked of Big Jim and related little anecdotes in an inimitable manner that simply convulsed Len, who had never thought this stern man could be so human. Presently Ezra called into the kitchen, 'Mary, my dear, I have a visitor here and I want you to make a cup of tea for him.'

The answer came back in a sharp girlish voice: 'It's already done, dad. Shall I bring it into the parlour or will you have it in the kitchen?'

There was a soft look in Ezra's dark eyes when he replied, 'Len and I will come into the kitchen, Mary.'

Len had seen very little of Mary since their school-days, and understood she had been away from home a great deal, although he did not know why.

He shyly took the slim outstretched hand as Ezra introduced him, and looked into her eyes. At first they appeared too big for her small, well-defined, straight features and he could not determine their colour. Her aquiline nose was rather long when compared with the remainder of her face and her small body gave the impression it was an incidental appendage to her eyes. Even Len's slim body looked robust beside hers. She had very little colour except in her hair, which was a shiny brown whose gleaming sheen and accompanying shadows found a reflective pool in her eyes. Mary invited him to take a chair, at the same time sitting on a stool near her father. It was obvious they were devoted to each other, and as Ezra continued his reminiscences she joined in with occasional remarks. Len felt himself in a new world. The time seemed to fly, and when at last the time came to take his leave there was real regret in his voice as he thanked them for their kindness. They both accompanied him to the door, where he thanked them again. He felt strangely elated as he made his way home to Sunny Bank.

That night in the committee Ezra surveyed the strike situation. The committee-men realised that the strike had gone on for a fortnight without any real effort being made to organise the struggle, and there was a serious discussion as to the number of safety men permitted to work in the pits. A resolution involving the withdrawal of the safety men was agreed to. This business having been disposed of, the men considered the proposals Len had made to Ezra during the afternoon. They included sending emissaries throughout the land to gather finance and win sympathy, the establishment of food kitchens, publicity, sports and concert departments, and the organisation of methodical picketing at the pits. This latter was considered of primary importance in view of the decision to withdraw all the safety men and officials.

The decisions of the committee were given to the mass-meeting next day, at which all the adults in the valley, with the exception of the bedridden, attended. Ezra, as usual, conducted the proceedings.

Mary strolled among the women, the sun, dazzling through her hair, giving her face a brightness that made it attractive. She felt proud of her father, as she watched him focus the attention of the workers to the points at issue. He stood perfectly still on the lorry and his face in no way betrayed his feelings while the multitude of people roared their assent to the proposals. After the recommendations had been vociferously accepted, Mary heard his calm voice call out the names of the men who were to act as emissaries in other areas. Each name was greeted with bursts of cheering, and when the last of these had died down, Ezra turned to where he had seen Len standing near Big Jim.

Without any preamble he announced: 'I now call upon Len, the son of Big Jim, to say a few words to us.'

Len was stunned by the unexpected suddenness of what virtually amounted to a command. His face paled and he felt the air heavy and humid about his body. He started to stammer something when, in the centre of the huge grey blob of faces that confronted him, he saw Mary.

It seemed to him her eyes were filled with pity, and the thought that this was so stung him into a frenzy. Without further hesitation he flung himself on a flood of words into the silence that had followed Ezra's announcement. The words spilled from his mouth in a torrent that left little drips of saliva on his lips, each word pulsing with the tremor that shook him. For some minutes he stumbled on, unconscious of the import of his remarks, until the situation began to grip him. Then his sentences became more coherent and started to flow with an eloquence which gained added power in the natural music of his voice. He spoke of Ezra as one would speak of God.

'We are being led into battle by one who knows all that the battle means and all that we must do to win it. There in the Big House,' he pointed dramatically towards the mountain, 'are the people who have brought us to this pass. If they are looking down on us now they see us as solid as ever.'

He urged the people to be steadfast and true and to follow Ezra with faith and loyalty, and concluded with the exhortation: 'It may be a long strike. It may be hard and bitter, but whatever comes, if we stand together and stick to Ezra we will be as sure of victory as we are that the sun rises in the bottom of our valley and sets over the pit.' He stood motionless with his arm upraised and his head thrown back as if he were seeking inspiration from the sky. Then he burst out: 'He who follows Ezra captures victory. Let those who want victory shout it till the mountains carry its echoes to those who are waiting in the Big House.'

Like an avalanche the roar shook the air: 'For Ezra and victory.'

A sudden rush took the miners' leader by surprise and, before he could avoid it, he was lifted into the air and carried triumphantly through the streets in a spontaneous demonstration of loyalty and determination.

Later that night, while Ezra was in a deep meditation that had already lasted some time, Mary quietly asked him: 'Why did you call on Len to speak, dad? You knew he was shy and not used to it.'

Her father looked quizzically into her eyes. 'Why do you ask, my dear?'

'Oh, there's no definite reason at all, only I wondered why you did so unusual a thing when you knew the men had already shown they agreed with you. In any case,' she added with a little confused blush, 'I don't see why you chose the man you did.'

She stopped, then went on quickly before Ezra could intervene. 'Don't think I'm nosey, daddy dear. I'm only concerned for your sake. You have so many enemies who would like to buy or destroy you. I know, dear, they can never buy you, but I'm sometimes afraid they will use your own friends to destroy you. That is why I want you to be strong in yourself without having to depend on others.' Her head drooped on his chest and a lump rose to his throat as he ran his fingers gently through her hair and around her face till they came to her burning ears and began playing absently with the lobes, as he had always done in moments of great bitterness or loneliness when caressing his wife.

The action was now quite unconscious, but it reflected his mood, and Mary, aware of this, raised her head and murmured, 'There you go again, daddy. Wandering round an empty world. But you are not lonely. How can you be with all these wonderful people who look up to and follow you? How can you be lonely when you have me?'

Ezra looked at her again, his eyes sad and heavy.

'No, I cannot be lonely while I have you, although you are all that I have got. The people who today carried me on their shoulders would, with equal willingness and fervour, in different circumstances trample my body into the mud. One day, my dear,' he went on slowly as if he were deeply cogitating, 'you will learn there is only one way to lead, and that is the way the people want to go. Once try to take them away from this, they destroy you. When you are not prepared to go their way, they desert you. They deserted me before and left me to the mercy of enemies who smashed my home and killed your mother. That is why you are left today with a crusty old man as a father to take care of and worry about.'

He gulped hard and abruptly changed the subject. 'You ask why I called upon young Len to speak. It was because I wanted to do two things: I wanted to know how deep he is in the events of the strike and I also wanted to know the extent of my influence over him. It is necessary that I should know both these things, because the future is full of unexpected happenings and if a leader wants to survive them he must have some knowledge of their drift before they actually occur. That's all, my dear,' reaching for his pipe.

The intimacy was at an end.

ACTION DEEPENS

Late one night Mr. Evans Cardi was surprised to hear a hurried knock at his front door. He hastened down to open it and found Mary waiting on the step.

'Duw's annwyl y byd, Mary bach. What has brought you here at this time of the night?' asked the old man anxiously.

'May I come in, Mr. Evans? I would like to talk to you privately if you can spare the time.'

'By all means, my gel. But tell me quick, what's the matter?'

'There's nothing the matter, Mr. Evans,' Mary assured him as he led her into the parlour beside the shop.

She took the proffered chair and went into the business straight away. She explained she had just come from the canteen committee, which was anxious to start the feeding centres as soon as possible but did not have the necessary means. In view of this she had been invited to approach Mr. Evans to solicit his help in providing foodstuffs on credit till the money came in from the outside areas now being canvassed by the strikers' representatives.

Mary had little trouble in coming to an agreement with the old man, and without more ado took her leave, making the lateness of the hour an excuse for not waiting to see Mrs. Evans. She had hardly gone a hundred yards, however, when she heard someone hurriedly running behind her. As the steps came nearer, she stood still, wondering who it could be, and for a moment fear clutched at her heart and she felt like running back to the safety of the shop.

The running footsteps tip-tapped even more quickly on the roadway and Mary was on the point of dashing wildly down the street when she heard a girl's voice gasp out: 'Miss Mary. Miss Mary. Wait for me.'

Mary remained motionless as if turned to stone. She had no idea who was calling her until the runner overtook her, struggling to regain her breath, and she recognised the servant girl from the Big House, evidently in a state of great agitation.

'Well, Lizzie, what on earth is the matter?' she asked, her voice betraying the surprise she felt and her heart pounding madly with the temporary fright.

'Oh, Mary, they are going to do something awful tomorrow,' the girl managed to say, almost bursting into tears. 'Those black swine up there,' pointing to the Big House, 'I heard them with my own ears. They were sitting in the lounge planning what they are going to do about the strike. The hell's scum that they are!' She was so overcome for a moment by the depth of her feeling that she stood mute and trembling, and Mary grew impatient.

'But what have they planned, Lizzie? For God's sake let's have some sense.'

'They are going to bring policemen from all over the country into Cwmardy to drive our men back to work. I heard them say it. Good job I saw you coming from Evans Cardi. You can tell your father all about it now.

'No, no, Lizzie,' said Mary, beginning to grasp the situation, 'you come along with me and tell father yourself.' And taking the girl by the arm, Mary led her, half walking, half running, to the house where Ezra sat anxiously waiting.

It was only a matter of minutes before the miners' leader had drawn from the girl the whole story of Mr. Higgins' sudden journey to the city, of the stormy scene on his return, and the orders that all the officials were to present themselves for work irrespective of what the strikers thought or did. Having satisfied himself, he bade Mary make tea for the girl and, taking his cap from its peg, he quietly left the house.

Next morning as the sun was sending its red beams across the valley, the pickets specially selected by Ezra during the previous night surrounded the pit. Ezra, Len, and Big Jim stood together when the first group of officials approached. As usual the pickets closed in to scrutinise if they were *bona fide* safety men, and Ezra noticed in the group four men who were not regarded as being necessary to the safety of the pit.

Accompanied by Len and Big Jim he pushed his way through the pickets and addressed the men concerned.

215

'The decision today remains as it did yesterday,' he remarked. 'No officials below the rank of overman can go down this pit. There is no need to argue the matter. I advise those of you who are not entitled to act as safety men to return home.'

Not a single official moved. The police who had been scattered loosely about drew together as though they had received a signal. The atmosphere became tense and many of the officials turned pale with nervousness. Their orders had been clear and explicit. They had to go down the pit in spite of the pickets.

One of them, noticing the movement of the police, gathered courage, and turning to Ezra said abruptly, 'It is none of our business what the strikers decide. Our duty is to keep the pits in a state where they can be worked again. That is what we intend doing. I ask you to withdraw your men and let us get on with our work.'

Big Jim, who was standing near, took umbrage at this last remark. 'Duty! Work!' he exclaimed contemptuously. 'What in hell be you talking about, mun? Only the other day you was a workman yourself, and not the best of them, too. What do you want down the pits now when we be fighting for a living? I know these pits so good, if not better than any man. There be no need for half of you devils down there.' He broke his statement off short.

One of the officials howled: 'Look out there, the bloody lot of you, or I'll blow your rotten brains out.' And the steel barrel of a pistol flashed in the sun like a streak of blood.

As the official advanced with the pistol quivering in his hand, the men tumbled hastily back over one another.

'Look out there! Clear the way!' he bellowed hoarsely. 'The first man who tries to stop us will get his blasted brains splashed on the ground.'

A tremor ran through the ranks of the pickets. They saw all their plans being suddenly and easily defeated, as they fell back helpless in the face of the slowly circling pistol, that seemed to leer through its bore at each of them in turn. The circle they had formed round the officials broke, and Ezra, feeling the tension, murmured, 'Steady, boys, no panic and don't do anything silly.'

The officials were nearly clear of the pickets when a fist, seemingly flung from nowhere, struck the man with the pistol a terrific blow that flattened him, silent and senseless, on the roadway.

A howl like the roar of a lion burst from Big Jim. 'Good old Africa,' he shouted his eyes glinting with excitement, 'the man who can fight Boers can fight blacklegs any day.' In two strides he broke through the ranks of the now frightened officials and called upon the strikers. 'Hold 'em tight, boys bach. Hold 'em tight!' His words and quick action electrified the pickets, and in a twinkling the officials were again surrounded.

The sudden movement with its complete reversal of the position made the latter think they were in danger of physical harm. They hastily dragged lead piping, wooden clubs, and other weapons from their pockets and commenced frenziedly hitting out at the strikers. In a moment everyone was fighting furiously. Grunts followed howls and screams as fists, boots, and weapons made violent contact with flesh and bone. The police tried to force their way into the centre, where Big Jim was fighting to ward off any harm to Len and Ezra. But the strikers saw the move and closed around the trio in such a way that a compact mass of men stood between them and the police.

The affray ended as suddenly as it had started. First one and then another of the officials struggled back down the hill to their homes, and in a few minutes they had all disappeared, including the one with the pistol. Big Jim, towering above the pickets, laughed happily although blood dripped from his nose on his moustache. The police had followed the officials and the strikers were left in sole command of the colliery yard, and though a few suffered from cuts and bruises no one was seriously injured.

Len's heart throbbed with excitement and pride, and he kept as near as possible to his father and Ezra. The latter, with his coat torn, and capless, stood on the steps of the colliery office, and looking around him waited for the excitement to die down a little, then said: 'Well boys, we have, thanks to Big Jim, beaten the first move of the company.' The strikers gave a resounding cheer, while Big Jim with a dignified gesture solemnly twirled the ends of his long moustache. When the cheers had died down Ezra went on. 'We have beaten the first move, but God alone knows what their next step is going to be. The best thing we can do now is to go home altogether and hold a mass-meeting this afternoon.'

Very little was said during the march down the hill, but everyone walked with a jubilant spring that seemed to repeat in every step: 'We have won the first round, first round, first round.'

After the wildly enthusiastic meeting that afternoon the word 'blackleg' went flashing from mouth to mouth. It captured the people's imagination. No one, least of all Big Jim himself, had any idea why the term was appropriate, but it was sufficient to everyone that it conveyed to their minds in a simple manner the significance of all personal actions detrimental to their strike.

Later that night when Siân was preparing for bed she was surprised to see Big Jim and Len making preparations to leave the house. She said nothing about the unusual and unexpected procedure of the two men, but Big Jim fidgeted uncomfortably when he caught the burning look in her eyes. As they were ready to leave she asked Len in what she intended to be a casual, off-hand manner: 'Going out late tonight 'in't you, Len bach? Be there something special on?'

Getting no answer, she addressed herself cuttingly to Jim. 'Anybody with any sense would think it was time for all decent peoples to be going to bed, not thinking at this hour of going gallivanting about the place. You can't be up to no good.'

Jim blushed, but made no reply to the taunt. The silence made Siân even more uneasy. She turned pleadingly to Len. 'Tell your mam, 'nghariad i, where be you going. Don't say that you don't trust your own mother that have reared you.'

Len saw she was bravely trying to squeeze back her tears, and his love for her forced him to say, 'Don't worry, mam bach. You go to bed and sleep sound. Me and dad 'on't be long, we are only going to see the boys about the soup kitchen tomorrow. You see,' he added as a bright afterthought, 'we have got to get some planks to make tables and benches.'

Siân knew he was lying, but she said no more. The two men bade her good night as they went through the door into the darkness. She waited a few moments after they had left, then hurriedly put the heavy woollen shawl over her head and followed them. Throughout the night she dogged their steps, and she did not return home till the early hours of the morning.

Next day when the people of the village went about their business they were amazed to see splashed upon the walls of each official's house a word painted in huge black letters: 'Blackleg'. On the door of Evan the Overman's, house was the single word 'Skab'. Throughout the day the groups of men and women discussed the sensational action. They wondered how it had been so silently and effectively carried out. Many speculations were made, but no names were ever mentioned.

During the afternoon the strikers were astounded to see hundreds of police in military formation parade the streets of the valley, and the committee was again called to discuss this new development.

Ezra's pale face went a shade whiter when reports were given that police drafted from all parts of the country were being barracked at each of the pit-heads and in the public houses. The hint given him by Lizzie the servant girl had somewhat prepared him for this, but the fact they were actually in the valley upset him. He knew it was bound to happen sooner or later, but the speed with which it had been organised took him by surprise. He listened attentively to the reports and the muttered whispers that accompanied them.

All the committee-men were uneasy. They felt that something unusual, something beyond their experience was about to happen in the valley. They had seen the strike in the first instance as a more or less sharp battle in which each side tried to call the other's bluff. Most of them had even been prepared for a long-drawn-out struggle of endurance in which victory depended upon the amount of support they could get for the strikers. None of them, apart from Ezra and possibly Len, had foreseen the possibility of this new move by the company.

Their bewilderment was summed up in the words of Dai Cannon: 'But they have no bloody right to bring police in from outside. The duty of the police is to stop stealing and to catch murderers. Nobody is stealing here and nobody have yet been killed. Whoever asked for them to come here had no bloody business to do it. We know how to carry on a strike without interference from outside.'

It was slowly dawning in the minds of these raw, untutored strike leaders that in preventing officials from working they were hitting the owners in their weakest part. What they failed to understand was why, when the advantage was with them, the police should be placed at the disposal of the owners. They all knew that the testing time had now come. Either they must capitulate after a month's struggle or go on to victory despite all opposition and whatever the consequences. They decided to go on, and at the mass-meeting to which they announced their decision, the committee were greeted with prolonged cheering.

The weeks went by more or less uneventfully. The men in each pit had organised football and other teams. Matches of all descriptions were played every day amid scenes of great excitement and partisanship. Mary organised a dramatic society and concert party. She was particularly interested in the former, and proved herself to possess considerable dramatic talent; and her natural appearance and moods gave life to the characters she portrayed.

These activities did much to rouse Mary from her insular subjectivity, and she watched carefully her father's direction of the strike and its reactions upon him. She got to understand him much better and noticed with perturbation that the longer the strike lasted the more moody and taciturn he became. She knew that, cynically bitter though he was, the developments in the strike worried him, but she never by word or deed tried to hasten the time when he would unburden himself to her. With the infinite patience of a mother watching over her convalescing child, she waited, happy in the knowledge that her strike activities were a source of pleasure and of pride to him.

The weather continued to be gloriously fine. For the first time in many years the sun showed itself clear and heartening in the shimmering atmosphere that quivered on the mountain top like skeins of hair. The wearing throb of the pit had already become a memory. Pit horses, grazing and playing in the fields, oozed the content they felt, even though their pit-blinded eyes were sightless. Children went light-heartedly to school as if the world had suddenly become beautiful. The drabness of the valley no longer lived in their minds. Like the horses, they only felt the immediate; and most of them had already forgotten how the valley looked and sounded before the strike.

Each evening parties of youthful men and women made their way up the mountain paths and drank in romance with the grass-sweetened air. The mountain became to the young people a vast bed which nestled their bodies to its breast in a voluptuous embrace. Under the star-sprinkled sky it became a bridal chamber, and when dusk at last fell the youth of the valley whispered into listening ears the innermost thoughts of their hearts and shared together the intimacies of their bodies. In the small hours of the morning their voices filled the air with melody.

At the head of the village the pit stood brooding in its enforced silence, scowling like an immobile death's head on the peaceful streets and people; and the Big House was the scene of many confidential discussions. On one occasion a tall uniformed man with an authoritative air consulted in secret with Mr. Hicks and Mr. Higgins for nearly two hours. But the strikers knew nothing of this. Nevertheless one night shortly afterwards, when they were parading the streets of the village as usual, they noticed that whenever they gathered in groups for a chat or to look into the shop-windows they were gruffly ordered to move on by the police. Scores of uniformed men were moving about the streets and the least hesitation on the part of the strikers to obey their arbitrary instructions was met by the harsh command: 'Now then, you there, move on when you are told, and none of your damned nonsense.'

The strikers had hitherto been accustomed to a measure of affability from the police, and the suddenly changed attitude disturbed them. Harassed from point to point, they gravitated slowly towards the Square, which, as always on important occasions, became the centre of attraction. And soon, despite the efforts of the police to break up all groups and keep them on the move, it was filled with a mass of excited people.

Len, who had been spending a couple of hours with Jim at the free entertainment organised by Mary, noticed something unusual in the air directly he came out, but seeing nothing wrong he paid little attention. Siân stopped before reaching the Square to look in a shop-window, whispering something to Big Jim that Len did not catch. But he saw a policeman who had suddenly appeared nudge her sharply with his elbow and order them all to move on. Before he had a chance to say or do anything Big Jim's fist flashed out like a thunderbolt, and the policeman tumbled over as though he had been struck by a battering ram.

The action seemed like an electric current that set hell loose, in a moment some of the crowd began smashing plate-glass windows. Almost immediately, above the shattering crash a voice screamed, 'Charge!' and as a solid phalanx of police rushed from nowhere into the Square, the crowd began to sway like wheat in the wind. Batons rose and fell with smashing regularity, and the contact of clubs and heavy boots on living flesh brought men and women in sickening tumbles to the ground. Like wildfire the fight spread down the street and into the distance, its progress marked by the crashing shop-windows and the screams and moans of the injured lying in the roadway.

That night, when at last the streets were empty and the windows darkened, posses of uniformed men paraded the back lanes. Sometimes they would burst their way into a darkened house, and their entry would be followed by the sound of curses and crashes, and then suddenly silence.

Len, tired and worried by the day's event, was just dropping off to sleep when he heard a terrific rap on the back door. He jumped out of bed and was about to make his way downstairs when Jim and Siân overtook him on the landing. 'I 'spect they be after me,' whispered Jim hoarsely. He crept quietly down the stairs, pulling on his trousers as he went, followed by Siân's instructions: 'Make your way to Ezra's. We will keep them here as long as we can.' No one heard the front door open or close as he went out, and after a few minutes Siân, grasping Len tightly by the arm, led him to the back door. Her long flannel nightdress clung round her legs as she feverishly stumbled her way forward.

Len took the lighted candle and, from force of habit, held it up when she shouted: 'Hello. Who's there this time of the night?'

'Open in the name of the law,' came the gruff answer.

'I have never in my life opened my door at this time of the night to nobody, not till I know who it is,' said Siân, all the while seeking to kill time. 'Who are you?'

'The police.'

'Oh dear. Oh dear,' moaned Siân. 'What for do you want in my house? For more than thirty years I have lived here and not a policeman have ever had cause to come inside my door.'

The rapping on the outside became more vigorous and a voice shouted, 'Are you going to open this blasted door or must we break it down?'

225

Realising she could save no more time, Siân fumbled at the bolts, grunting audibly the while, 'Duw, duw. Can't you wait a minute dyn jawl?'

Len said nothing, but his quivering limbs betrayed the extent of his emotions. Eventually Siân opened the door and the little kitchen filled immediately with policemen.

One, who appeared to be the chief, stood in the centre of the room and solemnly stated: 'We have information that leads us to believe you have property in this house that has been looted from the shops tonight.'

'What say you, man?' flared Siân indignantly. 'Do you call me a fief? Me, who have reared my children 'spectable and tidy, thank God. Better be careful what you say, my man, or I will call the police to you for slandering my character.'

Len could not help smiling to himself, but his mother heedlessly fumed on: 'Never in my life have I heard such impudence! For a man to call me a baggage and a fief before my own face in my own kitchen – it be more than any 'ooman can stand!'

She would have kept on, but was cut short by the curt order to search the house. The first man to obey was one with an ugly cut on his lip and a big bruise on his jaw, whom Len recognised as the policeman Big Jim had struck when the riot started. Although no one was seriously looking for any stolen material, they went through the pretence of searching the house from top to bottom, Siân, following them wherever they went, threatening to have the law on each of them in turn.

Failing to find what they were searching for, the chief again approached Siân. 'Where is your husband?' he demanded.

'How on earth do you 'spect me to know where he be? Do your wife know where you be? No. Once a man have got a hat on his head he have got a roof on him, and the good Lord knows when you will see him again. But there,' she sighed dismally, 'all men be the same.'

At this the chief, giving it up in disgust, ordered his men out, and when the last one had gone Siân hastily bolted the door again and drew Len to her. 'Do you think your father did get safe to Ezra's?' she queried.

Len nodded hesitantly to reassure her, but staring towards the front door, said: 'I had better go and see to make sure.'

But Siân caught him before he could move. 'Not a living soul do leave this house tonight again,' she asserted. 'If anyone go out now they will be followed by those men, see, Len bach.'

He nodded assent and they went upstairs to bed, but neither slept as they waited for Big Jim's knock at the door. That night he did not return.

Siân, anxious because of Jim's non-appearance, sent Len out early next morning to pick up what news was available. At each street corner he found groups of people discussing in subdued voices the events of the previous night, everyone adding something new to the recital, but he continued on his way to Main Street, where he found large numbers of strikers waiting for some word or instruction from the strike committee. Many of them carried bruises and gashes that deepened the pallor of their faces, and blood was still seeping through some of the bandages. When they asked him for information Len shook his head negatively.

'You will more than likely find all the news you want in the papers,' he said, and passed on to Ezra's house.

At Ben the Barber's he stopped to look at the paper. Ben watched him as he hurriedly scanned the pages before asking slyly: 'What are you looking for that your brow is so furrowed?'

'I was hoping to see something about what happened last night, but all I can see is this,' Len answered, throwing the paper down. 'Reports and pictures of the coronation. Have you got another?'

'No. In any case, didn't you have enough of the riot last night without wanting to read about it today again?' But as Len did not answer, Ben picked the newspaper from the floor, and pointing to some photographs, went on in a satirical voice: 'Look here, what better would your eyes like to see than this beautiful coach made of solid gold. See this magnificent crown of gems and rejoice at such skilful manipulation of wealth. You talk of your puny riots and futile strike when staring at you from the paper are a hundred thousand resplendent troops equipped with arms. Talk of the justice of your case,' he went on mockingly. 'Read here of the million people who, last night, while you and your sort were smashing up the town, were howling deliriously in support of their newly crowned monarch.'

Len fidgeted restlessly, although he was aware of Ben's propensity to sarcasm. Without noticing him the barber went on: 'Ay. You say your people are fighting for a living wage. Read here of how other people, who also want a living wage, spend the little that is given them in jubilation over another's power. Ach,' he concluded, as he spat on the floor, 'the bloody lot of you make me sick.'

No more was said for some moments until Ben, as if repenting of his harsh words, said, 'If you want news of your strike, look at the stop-press on the back page.'

Len took the paper and his face went white as he read:

HOOLIGANS SMASH UP TOWN
POLICE DRAW BATONS IN SELF DEFENCE

As we go to press reports are coming in of outrages at Cwmardy. Strikers loot shops. Much damage to property. Police persuasion fails to restore order. Wild crowds attack police. Batons drawn. Many casualties.

Ben smiled sarcastically at Len's attempts to swallow back his rising rage. 'You understand what you are now and you also know what happened last night.'

'But it's all lies. It's not true,' Len blurted out.

Ben looked at him reproachfully. 'The papers never lie, my boy. What you see in black and white is truth, and you must always believe it.'

Without another word Len left the shop, and when he reached Ezra's house his temper was still burning and his mind was absorbed in the new lesson he was learning. Running through his contempt for the newspapers was a thread of worry about Jim's whereabouts. His timid knock was answered by Mary, who invited him in.

Ezra, who sat near the fire, looked around as Len entered but said nothing until Mary had prepared a cup of tea for each of them. Then, without looking at Len, he asked: 'Well, what has happened?'

Len felt hurt by the casual tone of the query. More so because it told him that his father had not been at Ezra's during the night. He choked back the lump that suddenly rose to his throat and began relating, in a husky voice, the events of the night. As he spoke of Jim's part in the fight Mary listened attentively with sparkling eyes, but Ezra appeared to be paying no attention. The memory of what had occurred, however, warmed Len's imagination and he soon became lost in the recital. The blood pounded through his veins, and as he lived the fight again, his musical voice gave harmony and rhythm to his story. When he indignantly related the newspaper report Ezra smiled grimly, but neither he nor Mary moved for some minutes after Len had finished.

Mary was the first to break the awkward silence. Rising to her feet, she said, 'Dad, we must find Big Jim.'

Ezra nodded slowly. 'Yes my, dear, you are right. But first things first.' And, turning to Len and looking him up and down, he went on, his voice cold as steel: 'You must tell all the committee-men to be at the agreed place two hours from now. Tell them to be careful how they get there and to let no one know there is a meeting. On your way back call at the pit criers' and tell them to remain at home until they hear from us.' As his words became more sharp and incisive Len felt again the overwhelming power of the man sweep over him, and without a word he left the house and proceeded on his mission.

After he had gone Ezra paced the length of the kitchen

several times before pausing suddenly by the fireplace. He rested his elbow on the mantelpiece, holding his head in the cupped palm of his hand. Mary knew from experience that his mind was now finally and irrevocably made up on some matter, and that conversation would be unwelcome. She therefore busied herself in clearing away the teacups and washing-up, and when she had finished sat patiently waiting for him to speak. Some minutes elapsed before he bent down and took her by the shoulders, looking deeply into her eyes. They looked back at him gleaming with solicitude and love, and as if to himself he murmured: 'Yes my dear, exactly as I had expected, so it has happened. Right has always been, and always will be, determined by might. There can never be one law that is at once good for the tiger and the lamb. Neither can there be one law that binds together the interests of workmen and owners. No one can blame the tiger for using his claws and teeth to destroy his victim. Nor can anyone blame the company for using the means at its disposal to safeguard its interests. That is what both claws and batons exist for.'

He broke off and resumed his pacing, without noticing the expression of doubt that flashed across Mary's face as he made the last assertion. Presently he came back to her, and she felt the familiar caress of his fingers trickle through her hair till they touched the small, pinkish lobes of her ears. She felt the love of his touch and cuddled her head between his chest and his arm.

'Go on, dad dear,' she whispered gently. 'Tell me. You surely haven't yet finished what you were going to say?'

As she had anticipated, he at once continued: 'If the

231

tiger is justified in using his claws, his victim is entitled to use everything to defend itself and defeat the enemy that is seeking its destruction. Yes,' he repeated, 'that is so. If the company takes the initiative and uses its claws, we can't complain. What we have now to do is to see what is necessary to prevent the claws hurting us, and if we can't do this, then we have to find some way of causing greater hurt to the company than it does to us. That is the only course left to us now.'

He stopped abruptly and fetched his cap and coat from the hall. Near the door he turned to her, and said: 'When I come back we shall have taken decisions that will determine the course of the strike for good or evil. In the meantime, dear, don't worry about Big Jim. If I know him at all he is perfectly safe.'

That evening messengers were sent around the picket leaders with instructions that not a single man was to go down any of the pits until the committee gave further orders. This was the strikers' reprisal for the attack by the police on the previous night.

Meanwhile Ezra and a deputation from the committee went to interview Mr. Hicks and Mr. Higgins. The latter, who accused Ezra of fomenting disorder, asked him: 'Do you intend that the pits shall be so damaged that they can never be reopened again?'

Ezra looked him in the eyes and replied: 'The pits are no longer any concern of ours. You represent those who claim ownership and it is your business to do what you will with them. The business of this deputation is to safeguard the men and women we represent. Neither myself nor any other member of the deputation desires any harm to the pits. Too many of our men have died in making them what they are. On the other hand, we hope you desire no harm to our people. Our mission here is simple. Withdraw the police and we will permit the safety men to work.'

'That,' replied Mr. Higgins, 'is impossible. The matter is entirely out of our hands. The police are under the control of the authorities and have nothing at all to do with the company.' And, as Mr. Hicks nodded approval, he went on with a sanctimonious smirk: 'Probably the riotous disorders of last night and yesterday morning, when numbers of our officials were seriously injured while attempting to do their duty, influenced the authorities and led them to take the necessary measures to protect law-abiding people.'

He seemed to warm to this theme and would have continued, but Ezra brusquely interrupted with the remark: 'We are not here to discuss your theories, Mr. Higgins. I think I speak for my colleagues when I say we want an answer to our offer. We are prepared to allow your safety men to work if you notify the authorities that the extra police are unnecessary and must be withdrawn. When you talk of the few bruises suffered by some of your officials, I would remind you of the scores of our people who were severely manhandled last night.'

Mr. Higgins muttered an excuse and beckoned his colleague to the far corner of the drawing-room, where the two men considered the proposition put by the deputation. As they carried on a conversation in low voices, a discussion developed amongst the men. Len wanted to know how far Mr. Higgins was correct in stating that the company was not responsible for the police, but Ezra brushed the question curtly aside. 'We were sent here to get the police withdrawn, not to argue responsibility,' he declared. Some of the deputation, however, disagreed with this, and one of them asked how, if the company was not responsible for bringing the police in, they could be responsible for taking them out. Ezra coldly replied: 'That is not our concern. If they want safety men, it's their duty and not ours to remove the obstacles that prevent them working. Our mandate is clear. Don't let us lose sight of that in attempting to find excuses for the company.'

This veiled sneer closed the discussion, and at the same time the company representatives returned from their consultation.

Mr. Higgins again took on the role of spokesman: 'It appears, Mr. Jones, that your deputation is determined to give a free hand to all the unruly and disorderly elements in the valley, even if it means the destruction of the pits. In these circumstances we do not feel justified in asking the authorities to reconsider the position. You will understand, gentlemen,' turning towards each striker in turn, 'that it is the desire of the company, in the interests of the men themselves, that everything shall be done to ensure that the pits restart normally immediately this unfortunate dispute is ended. And I may say, as far as the company is concerned, we are adamant on this. Goodnight.'

It was clear that further argument was useless and, without another word, Ezra led his men out.

In the valley people were still talking about the events of the previous night. Practically every street contained someone who had been more or less injured in the affray, and when Len reached home after the deputation had dispersed, he found Big Jim the centre of a group in Sunny Bank.

Len was pleased to hear his father reporting how he had eluded the police. 'Ay,' Jim boasted, 'it will take a good man to catch me. You see, I been used to dodging Boers on their own ground, and any man who goes through that do learn a few tricks, I tell you.'

'But tell us how you did it,' came a voice from the crowd.

'That be easy enough. When I went out through the front door there was just enough light to see any shadows that be hanging about. I could see that there was plenty of police between me and Ezra's house, where I did think to make for, so I had to double back on my tracks. By this time the police was all over the place like black pats, and I was just beginning to think it was all up the spout when I did suddenly think of old Will Smallbeer's chicken hutch. I gived one dive and landed in on my head. I don't 'member what shape the door is in, but it can't be very solid by now. Only two chickens he have got, but they did make more bloody noise than all the brass bands in the army. And me wanting quiet, see, not for the police to know where I be hiding. I lighted a match on the quiet and saw where they was. It wasn't long before I had 'em one under each arm and gagged 'em proper with my coat.'

Everyone, including Len, laughed at this anecdote, but Jim, changing the subject, began to speak of the baton charge. It was a matter of honour to the people in the valley that the Square belonged to them and that no one could turn them from it, and a harsh note stole into his voice as he said: 'We got beat on our own little dung-heap last night, by God! They 'ood never have done it if they wasn't so bloody sly.'

That night, as though by some inaudible command, most of the able-bodied strikers made their way in casual groups to the Square, but except for the more adventurous, the women remained at home. By midnight the Square was thronged with people. No one seemed to know what they were there for, yet every group of ten or so appeared to have a leader. There was complete absence of shouting and hilarity, but the night air quivered in the drone of five thousand whispering voices, and presently, without a command or a shouted order, the strikers slowly formed themselves into a procession which threaded its way like smoke towards the pits.

Every voice was now silent, even the drone of whispered talking had ceased, and the only sound that disturbed the peaceful air was the shuffle of heavy-booted feet and the sharp clang of iron hobnails on the stony road. Suddenly, when the head of the procession was already a quarter of a mile on the way to the pit, there was a rush upon those in the rear who had not yet left the Square. Hearing shouts and screams, the strikers in front turned to see what had happened behind them. The scurry of their twisting feet sounded above the din, but the darkness was too heavy to permit sight and the only news was spread by the deepening moans and the wild undulations that swept along the ranks like waves.

As the foremost strikers, pressing back upon each other, tried to force their way back to the rear, the tumult and trampling became wilder and more desperate until the pressure was eased as sections of the men broke from the main body and turned up the little side-lane that circled round to the Square. Only those in the immediate vicinity saw them go, and before anyone had time to conjecture about the manoeuvre, a whistle pierced the air with three distinct blasts, which were immediately followed by a roar from the front and the wild clamour of galloping horses.

For a second the men in the procession froze into immobility. They did not know what was happening. Nothing could be seen. Nothing could be felt but the increasing undulations that marked the fighting at the rear. The world at that moment seemed to be dominated by the horrifying trample of unseen horses' hoofs bearing down on the front ranks of strikers, and as the hoofs tore into their flesh the air was filled with screams. Above the moans and thuds an anguished cry, 'We are trapped,' swelled to a hysterical roar, and in a moment everything had become mad tumult as clubs swished down on unprotected heads. In the hearts of all the strikers there was one over-whelming desire – for light. Light to see what was actually happening. Light to fight back. Light to see the enemy.

The horses had torn through to the centre of the procession, leaving behind them a trail of bleeding bodies, and it seemed that the one-sided fight was already over when a soft red glow, deepening in intensity, dissolved the darkness. It came from the pit. It grew wider and brighter, spreading its crimson wings over the valley like a red glare from hell, and at once the men realised that someone had set the power-house on fire. They paid no attention to the fellows lying on the ground, but concentrated on the column of horses rearing and plunging in the roadway, that was bounded on one side by a high stone wall, on the other by a stout wooden fence separating the road from the pit and the burning power-house. As the glow quickly grew to a flame that showed up everything in crimson relief, the panting men and frightened horses in the centre of the procession could be seen, mixed together like dough in which the yeast was fermenting. But there was no sight or sound of the men who had turned up the little side-lane. Their existence was forgotten.

In the houses of the village lights that had been extinguished suddenly flared into new life. Women, already dressed, came tumbling out of their doorways and rushed screaming and cursing towards the Square. Above the tumult could be heard the voice of Big Jim booming instructions to tear up the fences, and in a matter of seconds every man had dashed across the road and provided himself with an improvised weapon.

Again the commanding voice rang out: 'Pick your man and bring him down.'

Big Jim had now assumed command, and as the strikers instinctively rallied their forces and rushed headlong down the narrow roadway towards their separate objectives, the tumult rose to even greater volume. Shouts and curses mingled with groans and cries, while cracking thuds joined in the chorus. Horses driven mad by ripping spurs reared their forefeet into the air like hammers that methodically broke down the barrier of human bodies before them. Here and there bleeding men tore a rider from his mount, and his screams would end abruptly.

The pressure of the horses was too great for the strikers, and they slowly beat a track for themselves over the heads and bodies of the men. The eyes of the mounted police were anxiously fixed on the Square, and they gradually drew nearer, ready to join the ranks of the foot-police who were already in possession. If they succeeded in this manoeuvre it meant that the strikers were trapped in a cul-de-sac with the police concentrated in the only outlet.

The strikers fought desperately to prevent this fusion of forces, but the sticks they had torn from the fence were too short to make efficient weapons against the mounted men, and each minute the battle lasted made the trap more secure. Suddenly, however, as they were on the point of giving up hope, they heard a mad roar from the hill that led to the opposite side of the Square. They looked anxiously in the direction of the sound and saw a compact body of men rushing down the hill to fling itself with wild impetuosity upon the surprised police. The horses screamed horribly as the sharpened points of long broom-handles were plunged into their soft sides, and they kicked out frantically in all directions, dislodging their riders, who became easy victims of those who were waiting to get them on the ground. This reinforcing body of strikers was that which had slipped up the side-lane when the first charge took place. They had gathered all the children's marbles they could lay hands on and now scattered these under the feet of the horses, bringing them crashing to the ground.

The sweeping suddenness of the attack disorganised the police, who ran like rabbits for refuge in the neighbouring side-streets. But here women were waiting for them with buckets of water and slops, which they emptied on to them from the bedroom windows. Gradually the police were driven from the Square, which was left in the possession of the strikers.

Ezra at once climbed up to a precarious platform on the Fountain, where he stood supported by the great arms of Big Jim, and surveyed the scene. Jim's face was streaming with blood, but he paid no heed to the wound from which it flowed, being much more concerned about the absence of Len, whom he had not seen since the fight began. A deep silence that contrasted eerily with the previous clamour fell over the Square as the strikers waited for Ezra.

Clearing his throat, he began to speak, warning them that the battle was not over yet and that unless they stood firm it would be lost. The police were reforming their ranks, cutting them off from their own wounded. They could not allow this, and he suggested that a message should be sent to the chief of police asking that the wounded of both sides might be collected and brought to the surgery. Twenty men would be enough to bring them all in, he said, and then, raising his voice, concluded:

'If he agrees, well and good. If not we must fight for it. Is it agreed we send a message to the chief?'

A roar of assent swept through the air like a tidal wave.

'Will anyone volunteer?'

'Ay, I be just the man for that,' shouted Big Jim above all the other voices.

Ezra hurriedly wrote a note and with this in one hand and a blood-stained handkerchief in the other, Big Jim made his way to the spot where the police were regathering and concentrating their forces. But he had only gone about two hundred yards when he was suddenly surrounded by police who sprang upon him from the darkness of a side-lane. 'Hold on boys,' roared Jim waving his handkerchief wildly as he saw their threatening demeanour and the loosely twirling truncheons that seemed to itch with desire to land on his head. 'I have got a special message for your chief if you will be good enough to take me to him.'

After some muttering among themselves the police, with apparent disappointment, hemmed him in and curtly ordered him to 'Get going.' They led him to where the main body of police was concentrated, and as the little group approached a tall, military-looking man stepped forward.

'Who are you?' he asked harshly.

'My name is Mishter Roberts, known to everybody as Big Jim. Old soldier. Served through the Boer War with the old 41st and proud of it. I have got a letter here from our leader.'

The police chief silently held out his hand for the message. A slow smile crept across his face as he read it. As an old soldier he appreciated Jim's courage and also the request made by the strikers, and turning to one of his subordinates he remarked: 'Evidently these men regard this as a war and expect the mutual courtesies of such.' Then, turning to Big Jim, 'So you are an old soldier, eh?'

'Ay, sir, and a reservist. Seven years with the old 41st, the best line regiment in the British Army and most battle honours.'

He drew himself up smartly to the full height of his magnificent body and saluted. The chief acknowledged the salute.

'Tell your leader that the request is granted. I hope to see you again in better times, Mr. Roberts.'

With another salute Big Jim turned sharply on his heel and marched back through the open ranks of police.

His old war days had risen vividly to his mind. Everything that had happened during the night had assisted in reviving habits and memories of his old life, and when he reached the Square he gave a gasp of pleasured surprise as the strikers made a clear path for him to the Fountain, where he saw Len and his mate, Will, chatting excitedly to Ezra.

Both young men were black with mud and coal-dust and their clothing was in tatters, but Ezra seemed pleased with what they were telling him.

Big Jim strolled up, still in his military mood, coughed and smartly saluted before reporting: 'Your request is granted, sir.' The strikers around looked at him in amazement and Len stared at him with open mouth.

The momentary silence jerked Jim to his senses. 'Arglwydd mawr,' he roared, 'be I bloody mad or what?'

No one replied, so he turned on Len.

'It's your fault, worrying a poor man as you be. Where the hell you been all night?'

'Not far, dad. I'll tell you all about it again.'

This somewhat mollified Jim, and he stood sheepishly on one side while Ezra gave orders to the selected men to bring in the wounded. All the roads and lanes near the Square were scoured and in a very short time the casualties had been brought to the little surgery which now looked like a miniature hospital. Those awaiting treatment and those already treated were lined up in a queue of lying and sitting bodies on the road outside the surgery. The queue was over a hundred yards long.

By the time the police had been marshalled and marched back to their barracks in the public houses and on the pit-heads, the sun was already peeping over the mountain into the turmoiled valley, and when the last of them had disappeared, Ezra again climbed on to the Fountain plinth. As he faced the strikers he felt buoyed up by their spirit of confidence and determination, and he spoke to them proudly, praising their courage. The night that was now dying, they would remember till the day of their death. It had been a test and they had proved their strength, but it was not yet over, he warned them.

'We must not think we have now won the fight. No; the fight is now really beginning. But we can talk of that later. First we must go home with our injured; and we will go home all together. Remember, unity is always strength.'

And in spite of their exhaustion and suffering, the strikers raised a cheer that crackled in the morning air as Big Jim and Ezra led the reformed ranks up the hill.

When Ezra reached home, Mary had a big fire and tea waiting for him. She took his cap and coat and put them away while he washed his black hands and face. This done, he sat down and drank the tea in gulps, heedless of its boiling heat. He emptied the cup, then turned to the fire, looking into its depths as if seeking an answer there to the problems that were rising in his mind.

Mary sensed her father's mood and sighed softly. She was impatient to know what had happened. All night she had paced the little kitchen wondering if he were safe. Often during the long hours she had felt an overwhelming urge to get out into the streets to see for herself. Yet she had refrained from doing so because she knew that the sight of herself would distract Ezra's attention from the serious things in hand. Patiently sitting on the stool near his chair, she had to exercise all her will-power to prevent herself asking him questions. Presently, with a sigh, he muttered something to himself which she failed to distinguish, and, seeming to hesitate, turned from the fire and looked at her. Then, for the first time in many years, he caught her passionately to him and kissed her tenderly.

'My dear,' he murmured, 'I wonder where it is all going to end. How long can hungry men stand up to physical violence? The first charge last night told me how men can be out-manoeuvred and how all our plans can be shattered by an unexpected action. Do you know, my dear,' he continued in a soft voice, while his fingers played with her hair, 'that when we fail to anticipate things it means that men's bodies, their flesh, have to suffer? Bravery isn't enough in a strike. Often what we call bravery is merely an act of desperation committed in a moment of sheer fear.' He stopped short, then, as though recollecting something, went on. 'But no. Not all brave deeds are acts of desperation. Big Jim last night did a brave thing in cold blood. Young Len and his mate also did something that required nerve and courage, and they did it without the stiffening of noise and company.' Mary fidgeted on her stool, but kept on listening without interrupting. 'Yes. All of them fought and all of them are brave. But to what end? What has been started must be continued in one way or another, and right will work itself out on the basis of might. The company will not give way after last night's events; they will continue trying to force their officials into the pit.' He jerked his head spasmodically: 'Yes. That's the word, "force",' he said, as if he had discovered a solution to the problem troubling him, and again he looked into the flaming depths of the fire. The word seemed to conjure up a picture in his mind that found life in the leaping flames, and he suddenly sprang from his chair.

Mary watched him pacing the kitchen. She felt a vague ache in her heart. Her mind bubbled with involuntary questions, one of which continually posed itself before her. 'Is he weakening?' she asked herself, and immediately tried to brush the thought from her mind with a toss of the head.

Ezra stopped his pacing and stood with his dark, gloomy eyes burning into hers. When he spoke the words rattled in his throat.

'I wonder where it is all going to lead. We should have known in the first place what was bound to happen sooner or later, that we could never carry the strike through peacefully. My own experience should have told me that the company would move heaven and earth to defeat the men. The owners don't care that we are only fighting for a livelihood, and will use any means to their hands to get us back on their own terms. What matters it to them the months of misery, pain, and suffering that our people have endured? To them these are added weapons with which to break us.'

His voice became a snarl as he talked of the company. He stopped, and Mary flung her arms round him as she searched his face through her tears. 'Dad,' she said, with more confidence than she felt, 'our people will win. They must win. Right and justice are on our side.'

Ezra smiled bitterly. 'The company claim the same thing, my dear, and are prepared to prove their argument by force. What worries me is the future. Dare I continue the strike and all that it means indefinitely, and at the end be forced to accept perhaps even worse terms than are offered now? Or had we better give in and avoid further injury and misery?'

Mary looked at him, alarm large in her eyes. It was obvious to her that the suspicions she had tried to banish were being confirmed. 'No, no, dad,' she cried. 'You must not give in. I know our people are suffering. I know they are short of food and aren't strong enough to stand up to these monstrous policemen that are being imported. But we've not lost yet. You know the support our men are winning all over the country. Money is coming in greater amounts for our food kitchens. No: we can carry on a long time yet.'

Ezra looked at her intently as she spoke, and he seemed to gather strength from her words.

While this discussion was taking place, Len was sitting at home listening to Big Jim telling Siân of the riot. 'What

246

a lovely fight! Nearly so good as one I 'member 'gainst the Boers when we put the old farmhouse on fire.' He twirled his moustache and looked quizzically at Len before asking, 'Who put the power-house on fire, boy bach?'

But, receiving no reply, he went on: 'That be a clever move, Siân, who ever done it. It comed just when us was all beat and the jawled horses was trampling our brains out. Duw, duw! You ought to have heard the row, gel bach! 'Nough to make your hair stand on end.'

Siân looked at him admiringly, but Len was absorbed in his own thoughts. His mind flashed back to the climb over the high fence when neither he nor Will, his mate, dared whisper as they dropped the other side. He wondered again, as he crawled in memory through the river, if each shuffle forward would end in a hole from which he would never rise. Dread of the possibility even now made him shudder. He remembered whispering to Will, 'Are you there, Will bach?' and receiving a grunt, followed by a muffled 'Blast it,' in reply, as Will's knee jerked into a stone.

He smiled at the memory, and Siân, observing his expression, asked, 'What be you laughing at, Len bach?'

Len readily related the story of his adventures to his parents, who listened with deep attention.

'When we got over the fence to the side of the river nearest to the pits, me and Will was right out of breath. We sat down for a bit to get it back. I could hear Will draw it in through his teeth as if he was sucking water.' They all laughed at the analogy, and he continued: 'Will asked me quietly, "Which bloody way now, Len?" I told him. But all the same I wasn't quite sure myself, and I was

247

wishing we had a bit of light.'

'Ay,' broke in Jim, 'that is what we was short of, too.'

'Well, we crawled on our hands and knees to the pit. I remember both of us shivering with fright when we got near to it. Rats ran under our legs and we could see their eyes shining wicked and cruel when they peeped from between the timbers on the colliery yard. I put my hand on one of them and squashed it flat before I knew what was there. Ugh! It was cold and wet. I gave a little scream, I couldn't help it, when I heard the rat go "squelch" under my hand. Will jumped into the air and called me everything under his breath. At last we came to a big building that was blacker than the night. Both of us knew that this was the power-house, and now we was close to it we was more afraid than ever in case there was some policemen left inside to watch it. Will crawled round and squinted in through the windows, none of which had glass in them. When he came back I knew everything was all right.

'The two of us knew exactly what we had to do, but neither of us, somehow, was willing to start. At last Will gave a shaky, squeaky little laugh and said to me, "Well, us might as well get it over, Len bach." I didn't answer him for a minute. From over the river we could hear the sounds of the battle. They floated to us like waves in the wind. The screams made us shiver, and Will said to me, "Cold, 'in't it, Len?" We crawled inside the power-house, more to get away from the noise of the riot than anything else. When we came back out flames followed us with wicked crackles as if they was laughing at some big joke.'

Len said no more. He was torn between pride in what he had done and fear that the wrong people would find out who had done it.

SOLDIERS ARE SENT
TO THE VALLEY

One day shortly after the riot on the Square a conference was held in the Big House at which four people were present: Lord Cwmardy, Mr. Higgins, the chief of police, and another man with wheezing breath and a thick gold chain across his stomach. Lord Cwmardy was pointing out to the others that once the strikers succeeded in stopping the safety men the company would have no alternative other than to grant their demands, and he added, 'I need not tell you, gentlemen, that this would have disastrous effects upon our undertaking and is a project we dare not face.' Then, turning to the man with the chain-imprisoned paunch, he went on, 'To give way to this display of intimidation and force, Alderman, would be tantamount to condoning anarchy and disorder. Such a thing is inconceivable, and that is why, with the consent of the proper authorities, I have asked you here today.'

'Quite right, my lord, quite right,' wheezed the alderman. 'What do you say, chief?' turning to the police chief.

The latter stood up and shrugged his shoulders. 'I am here to see that the peace is kept and to ensure that those men who desire to work shall do so without molestation. That is what my men are for.'

Then, as Mr. Higgins did not say a word, Lord Cwmardy nodded his head sententiously and said in a tone of finality: 'Well, gentlemen, it seems we are all agreed and all that remains is to work out the precise steps necessary to preserve peace in the valley.'

While this conference was taking place the pickets on their way to the pit-head found for the first time that their entry was barred. Scores of police were cordoned across the road, while each group of officials was escorted by posses of additional police. As the latter passed through the streets they were greeted with cat-calls and shouts from the women and children, 'Blacklegs!' 'Scabs!' 'Traitors!' being the favourite epithets. The officials walked with lowered heads between their uniformed escort. They were ashamed or shy, for they had worked among these people all their lives and it now hurt some of them that they had to act as open enemies of the strikers. But they could see no alternative. They had to obey instructions or lose their positions, while many of them felt the strikers should not have gone to the length of wanting to leave the pit to the mercy of the waters.

The strikers, however, appeared to think differently as

they waited for the guarded officials who were silently escorted as far as the first rank of the picket lines, where they halted while Ezra and his colleagues consulted the officer in charge.

Big Jim kept his eyes on the man who had drawn the pistol on the first occasion. The argument between Ezra and the police officer ended abruptly when the latter suddenly snarled, 'Make way there.'

Not a striker moved, and the policeman lifted his hand high in the air as a signal. His men immediately obeyed, and, drawing their dangling batons, began hitting down the strikers nearest them without the slightest warning.

Big Jim saw Len and Ezra tumbled over, and, setting up a howl, he threw himself bodily towards the stricken men. In a flash the colliery yard became a battle-ground, the police trying to force the officials to the pit while the strikers fought to prevent them. But slowly the pickets were pressed back by repeated police charges until, with one accord, as though the same thought had struck each of them simultaneously, they broke up and rushed headlong over the bridge towards the pit.

For a moment the police stood stock-still in stupefied amazement, then they gathered their forces together and, with the officials in the middle, made a concerted dash after the strikers. For fifty yards they raced across the bridge without meeting any opposition, but just as it seemed the strikers were making for the mountain and leaving the way clear for their pursuers, they suddenly stopped and began hurriedly clambering up the walled coal-heaps near the end of the bridge.

The police rushed on with wild, exultant shouts, confident that the strikers were now trapped, but before they had gone a further ten yards they were met by a fierce shower of coal-lumps that smashed into their faces and their bodies. Numbers of them dropped to the ground like logs. Others, blood streaming down their faces, staggered to the rear screaming with pain and fury. When the charge was halted the strikers were still between the officials and the pit where, in spite of several efforts made to dislodge them, they remained. The men now knew they were in an impregnable position and were determined to hold it at all costs. This fact eventually forced itself upon the police chief and he reluctantly ordered his men to pick up the injured and retire.

The roar that accompanied their retreat ran down between the mountains like rain, and the strikers, arming themselves with pieces of timber and iron scraps that littered the colliery yard, marshalled their forces and marched down the valley, picking up their own wounded on the way. Their jubilation was increased when they discovered that no one was seriously hurt and their battle song electrified Cwmardy with news of the victory. Women and children, together with the pickets on other shifts, poured into the streets and swelled the volume of marching feet. Tramp, tramp, tramp they went, down the valley to the Square.

Outside the house of each official on the route the people stopped for a while, shouting and singing, after which they reformed their ranks and proceeded on their way. There was no leadership now and everyone did what

254

the mood impelled. By the time the demonstration reached the house of Evan the Overman he was frantic with fear and injured pride. He watched the procession from his bedroom window and cursed wildly as it slowly passed his door. But the fact that no one seemed to take any notice of him drove him mad and he howled at the top of his voice: 'Get back to your kennels, dogs, and leave decent men rest.'

For a fraction of time the people stood in petrified silence. Then a shower of stones darkened the air and crashed through the windows of the overman's house. A moment later a dozen young strikers forced their way through the front door, to return in a very short time with a quivering, white-faced man helplessly squirming in their midst.

'I didn't mean anything,' he screamed when he saw the mass of set, stern faces before him. 'Oh, God, think of my poor wife and children.'

The people were very quiet now. They silently opened their ranks to make way for the wailing official, and he was led right to the centre of the throng, where Siân and Big Jim stood like statues awaiting him. From the back of the crowd burst a sudden cry: 'To the river! Take him down to the river. He should have thought of his wife and kids before.'

The cry became a shout that grew in volume and spread until it seemed to empty from the sky. 'To the river... the river.'

As the threat penetrated Evan's twitching senses he turned piteously to Siân. 'Don't let them drown me. Oh, don't let them drown me,' he gasped in a whisper, the words oozing out slowly with the saliva that stuck in frothy bubbles on the edges of his moustache.

255

Siân's face was as pale as his own. She looked at him scornfully, her eyes blazing with contempt, then, turning to the crowd, she shouted in a shrill falsetto that sounded like the dry 'gawk' of a vulture sighting its victim: 'Don't anybody touch him. Wait till I come back. He do belong to me.' She tore up the street towards her own house, the people spontaneously making way for her, and in a few minutes she returned, panting for breath and carrying something white in her clenched hand.

'Here,' she cried, 'don't hurt him. Don't no one of you dirty your hands with such muck. Help me to put this shimmy on his stinking body, then we can march down the street agen,' and she held up the nightdress she had fetched. The idea fired the imagination of the strikers, and willing hands helped to place the garment over the head of the shivering Evan, so that it covered him from his shoulders to his feet. Then the ranks reformed again with Siân and Big Jim on either side of the white-draped, shame-faced figure. Siân gurgled in her throat and she felt her heart swell with every stride the demonstration made as she soaked in the full measure of her vengeance. She had grasped the possibilities in the situation immediately she saw Evan in the hands of the strikers, and the nightdress in which she had robed her enemy belonged to the dead daughter his son had besmirched. With burning eyes she stooped down to look into his face, stimulating his dragging feet with taunts.

'Proud man you did ought to be today, Evan, wearing my Jane bach's nightdress. Let your eyes see it. Don't it look nice and white and clean, like her little body did

256

before you and yours did send it rotting to the grave.' The helpless official shivered in the blast of her words. Something gripped her by the throat and she stopped to cough, then, with greater bitterness, went on: 'You do 'member, Jane bach, don't you, Evan? She did used to pass your house to chapel. Yes, of course, you be bound to 'member her.'

When Evan made no reply she changed her line. 'Look you, mun,' she rasped through her teeth, 'what revenge you have now. Often have your wife's nightdress covered the naked backside of Williams the manager; today Jane's do cover your body over your clothes.' Big Jim listened in silence, biting the drooping ends of his moustache, but when the overman quivered beneath this last taunt he felt in his heart that Siân was too cruel, yet he dared not try to thwart her in her present mood.

Oblivious to everyone but her prey, Siân continued: 'They do tell me that your son be going to get married. Well, well. How nice it will be for his wife.' She paused a moment and blinked, something hot was burning in her eyes, then bent her head again till it was level with Evan's face. 'I wonder if the poor gel do know that her coming husband did send my daughter to the grave with his baby lying cold by her side in the coffin.'

The overman stumbled and Siân hastened to put her hand under his arm to help him along. 'There, there, Evan bach, perhaps you be a little bit tired or perhaps you can see again poor Jane's body as it did pass your window on its way to the grave.'

The memory forced the tears to her eyes and she

suddenly loosened his arm and turned her head away from him. She could say no more, and Big Jim, taking her by the waist, solicitously led her on.

The strikers paraded every street with their exhibit, but no attempt was made to injure him in any way, and very few of the jeering shouts and cat-calls were directed to him personally. When at last the strikers retraced their steps to Evan's house the noise of their coming floated before them, and as they reached their destination the door was violently drawn open to reveal a dark-eyed, comely woman trembling with passion. She gave one flashing glance at her husband to make sure he was safe, then, grabbing him by the arm as one would grab a cat by its scruff, she spat viciously towards the strikers and screamed to the women among them: 'It would be fitter if you stopped at home and washed your dirty faces, you stinking cows!' Then she slammed the door against the people as they rushed towards it.

Siân pushed her way through the crowd of women who were angrily beating the door with their boots and fists, and, putting her mouth to the keyhole, she shouted with all the strength of her cracked voice, 'We have brought your bread-basket safe back home to you. Take care of him now that you have got him. Your bed-warmer will come later on, when no one be looking.'

This sneer placated the angry women, who looked upon it as a vindication of their personal honour, but the people remained some time longer outside the house, singing and shouting, before they finally dispersed to their homes.

Len did not accompany the others. He and Will accepted

Ezra's invitation to call at his house for a chat. The older man's interest in the two lads had deepened since the firing of the power-house and Len was frequently summoned to the house and taken into his confidence.

For the greater part of the evening Ezra sat back and smiled quietly at the eager chatter of the young folk. Len and Will were anxious to talk of the demonstrations and battles, while Mary was equally anxious to talk of the food-kitchens that were now in operation. Will, with his usual irresponsible exuberance, eventually dominated the conversation for a time with a tale about the concert party that had been touring the surrounding towns gathering support for the strikers.

'Ay,' he said, 'our Ianto went to Pantglas with 'em. He be a pretty good singer, you see, and have won prizes at the Eisteddfods.'

'Never mind about the prizes,' broke in Mary eagerly, 'get on with the story, Will. Tell us what happened at Pantglas.'

'Well, they did have it pretty tight all day and there wasn't much hopes of sending much back to the soup-kitchens, so they did hold a meeting and made their minds up to go round the streets singing like as if it was Christmas. They gived the collecting-box for our Ianto to go round the doors with. They went to one grand street and sang till they was blue in their faces, but not one answer did Ianto get at the doors. At last a kid come up and told him he 'ood have to go round the backs because the kitchens where the people lived was behind. So round the backs they went, cursing all the way; then they sang all their songs over agen, our Ianto knocking at

259

a door till he rubbed the bones out of his hands. But no answer came and they all got their hair off. "Open the bloody door, mun, and go in!" they bawled. So my brother rises the latch and steps in bold as brass, and where do you think he found hisself?... In the bloody lavatory. Ha, ha, ha!'

They all laughed at the crude narrative. 'I would have liked to see Ianto's face,' chuckled Mary. 'Do you know I saw the funniest thing today. You remember those barrels of apples sent to the canteen yesterday? Well, we decided to ask some of our women to make jam from them, and this morning when I was going down the canteen I saw little Maggie Coch sitting in the gutter hugging an armful of jam-jars. "Hello, Maggie," I asked, "where have you been?" "Down the cemetery to fetch these pots for mam to put jam in," she answered.'

They continued to cap each others' stories for some time longer, until Will jumped to his feet in a flurry and announced, 'Duw, duw, I must go. I got to see the boys 'bout sticks for the canteen fires.'

'I must be off, too,' said Len, also rising, but Ezra stopped him.

'If you have nothing important on, Len, I would like you to stop here with Mary while I do a little business.'

'Perhaps,' said Mary slyly, when she noticed Len's hesitation, 'he has a sweetheart somewhere he wants to see.'

The blood rushed to Len's face. 'No-no, Miss Mary; I have no time for girls. There are bigger and more important things than that facing us now,' he retorted with such vehemence that Mary was completely taken aback. But Ezra, looking at the young couple with a queer, half-sad smile, beckoned Will to follow him, and left the house.

Mary soon recovered her composure and, standing boldly before him, she asked in a challenging voice: 'Perhaps you don't think women worth bothering about, eh?'

Len started forward at what he knew was an accusation, but he pulled himself together and twisted his lips into a smile. 'No, it is not that. I love my mother. I loved our Jane. I love all those women who are with us in the strike. Who could help loving them?' he demanded passionately.

There was a moment's silence during which the only sound was Len's heavy breathing. Neither dared look at the other during this tense pause until Len, regaining a grip on his emotions, slowly raised his eyes and, seeing the sad expression on Mary's face, said in softened tones: 'But to go courting is another thing.'

She looked at him directly, her sympathy encouraging him to continue, and he went on: 'I know our boys do go courting up in the mountain and in the back lanes. My butties have told me all about it, but that isn't all there is to love, is it?' he asked, as if beseeching her assent. Mary made no reply, so he continued: 'I have seen my father's dog, which is the best scrapper in the valley, follow a bitch about all day and let her do as she like with him. But that isn't love, is it?'

The essential innocence of Len's words appalled her, even while for some reason unknown to herself she thrilled at their significance, and her eyes melted when she asked in a low voice: 'Well, what do you think love is, Len?'

He looked at her for some moments as though he were trying to see through her eyes into her mind. His mouth became dry and he ran his tongue over his lips before hesitantly replying: 'I don't know. It puzzles me. Sometimes I feel something burning me up and I can't sleep. As I lie awake in the nights and think, all the time, do what I will, my mind goes back to all the girls I have known.' He seemed to be talking to himself.

Mary asked timidly: 'But isn't there one girl who comes to your mind more often than the others?'

Len turned his eyes away from her and swallowed hard before replying: 'Yes, there's one girl I think about more than anyone else. But what's the good in talking about that?' he asked petulantly, trying to shake something from his mind. She waited for him to go on. 'I am not much of a scholar since I left school, but the strike is teaching me lots of things I would never have learnt without it. The boys in work talk of girls as the owners talk of us. The owners make us slaves in the pit and our men make their women slaves in the house. I've seen my father come home after a week's work and chuck his small pay on the kitchen table, chucking his worries with it at the same time. My mother had the job of running the home and rearing him and me on money that wasn't half enough to pay the bills. Yes. A man's worries finish in the pit. Once he comes home it is the woman who has to carry the burden.'

Mary listened attentively, intrigued by the new direction of his thoughts. 'Ay,' he went on, 'I have heard my butties talk about women exactly as if they were cattle – to be taken up the mountains and then laughed at in the pit. If that is love, I don't want it.' His next words came with a rush that was pregnant with pride and indignation. 'Look at our women today. They are on the picket lines with us, they are in the riots. It is they who give our men guts to carry on. And it is because of this I love them all. You ask if I think more of one than the others. Yes, I do.' His voice became stern. 'I think of you night and day, in the meetings and on the pickets. You haunt me like a spirit. But not in the way men talk in the pit. I want to be with you so that we can talk about the strike together. There is so much to be done and I am so weak when I am by myself. I feel if you were with me all the time both of us could do so much more just because we were doing it together. Sometimes when I am lonely I think of you, and my body goes warm as I imagine that you are close enough for me to whisper in your ear all the thoughts that crowd into my mind. Ach,' he concluded lamely, 'what's the good of it all? You are only laughing at me.'

Throughout the recital Mary had listened in amazement, but now she pulled herself together. Unconsciously she had drawn nearer to him and had to look up to see his face. 'I am not laughing, Len. What you have said is too serious for that. You have made me think a lot by what you've said, and I don't quite know where I stand.'

She hesitated, and was glad when a knock, which she knew was her father's, sounded on the door. As he came into the room he glanced at the young couple, and Len, mumbling an excuse, quickly left the house.

Once outside the door Len, in a maze of emotions, stumbled down the street unaware of any direction until he found himself facing Siân in the kitchen. His mother was obviously agitated. 'Oh, Len bach, thank God that

263

you have come. Me and your father have been worried awful 'bout you,' she greeted him.

'Why worry about me, mam? But there, you are excited after getting your own back on Evan the Overman.'

'Don't poke fun at your old mam, my boy. You are laughing all right now, but you 'ont laugh when the soldiers be here.'

Len straightened up in shocked surprise. 'Soldiers? What soldiers?' he asked excitedly.

Siân turned appealingly to Big Jim. 'Tell the boy, James, not sit by there as if you have lost your tongue.' Jim rose from his chair, crossed to Len, and laid a great hand heavily on his shoulder.

'I thought you 'ood have heard the talk in the village, boy bach. They do say that the sodgers is on their way to Cwmardy,' he said, adding with greater vehemence: 'But I don't believe the bastards. I don't believe them.'

Siân chimed in spiritedly: 'What do us want sodgers here for? Sure to goodness, haven't us got 'nough old police here now?'

Len grasped the situation but said nothing to further agitate his parents.

Some days later the committee sent Ezra to make inquiries why the troops were being sent to Cwmardy. His return was anxiously awaited, and long before the train was due a huge crowd of strikers had gathered at the station. Len caught sight of Mary and they kept together while they waited. A restless, impatient excitement ran through the crowd when the puffing train was heard in the distance. Ezra's face was more stern than usual when he stepped from the carriage, and although the strikers gave him a rousing cheer, for some reason this soon died down and a queer kind of half silence followed as he led the way through the crowded station. The people's exuberance sounded flat and hollow as they marched through the Main Street, whose shop-windows, covered with corrugated iron sheets, looked like bandaged eyes. When the procession reached his house Ezra instructed the committee-men to enter, and turning to address the main body of strikers, advised them to go home quietly. They silently obeyed and throughout the valley the air seemed to breathe a deathly sort of menace that caused children to cry and dogs to howl without apparent reason.

The committee sent Len to fetch his father, and in a short time both entered the parlour where the meeting was to be held. Big Jim proudly twirled his moustache, nodding familiarly to those present, before taking the chair that was offered him. No one objected to Mary, who shyly took a stool near her father, while Len stood erect with his elbow on the mantelpiece. When everyone was settled Ezra rose from his chair at the end of the table. His face was haggard and his voice was deep and heavy when he reported the result of his interview with the authorities. Once he was interrupted by a murmur that sounded more like a snarl, and Big Jim rising to his full height with inflated chest, solemnly declared: 'I have fought and died for my King and country, and I 'ont let any man, whether he be a Home Secretary or any other kind of secretary, call me a hooligan.'

Ezra quietened him with a glance and continued his

report. 'They told me the whole British army would be used if necessary to restore law and order in our valley,' he said. He waited a moment and felt Mary's hand steal softly into his own.

Big Jim gave a sarcastic guffaw. 'Ho-ho. If it did take the devils a regiment of sodgers with cannons to shift Peter the Painter from a house, they will want more than all their army and bloody navy too to shift us, muniferni!'

A general laugh followed this remark, but Ezra did not participate. He scrutinised the faces of the committee-men and lowered his voice to announce that Lord Cwmardy had made a final offer of an additional threepence per ton of large coal. Having done this he passed his hand slowly over his brow, then, rising suddenly from the chair, he left the table, saying to the bewildered men as he walked towards the door, 'Now make your minds up quickly as to what you are going to do.'

A momentary silence followed before Len's voice, sounding far away and strange, broke the awkward stillness. 'But, Ezra, you can't leave us like this, you haven't told us what you think we should do.'

A muffled chorus of 'Ay, let's hear what you have got to say,' followed this appeal, and all eyes turned expectantly towards Ezra, who had stopped at the door.

The miners' leader turned round sharply and faced them almost accusingly. 'Isn't it time you started to think a little for yourselves?' he snapped. 'I am sick and tired of your "See what Ezra says," "Go and ask Ezra." Now Ezra asks, what do *you* think?'

His voice broke, but after a moment he recovered

himself and faced the astonished men again. 'Forgive me, boys. I didn't mean all I said. You see, the responsibility is too great for one man. Here we are, offered more than the Company intended to give us. If we don't accept it the soldiers will be used against our people and after weeks or months of further misery and fight we may be forced back without the extra threepence even. I cannot take the responsibility. That's why I ask you to decide for yourselves.'

None of the men said a word, and it was again left to Len to be their spokesman. He walked slowly towards Ezra. 'Look here, Ezra, we have followed you faithfully during the strike, have always obeyed your orders, carried out your commands. Don't tell us now that you are to desert us when we need you most.' Ezra's head sank on his chest and his voice appeared to come from deep in his stomach.

'Very well. I will tell you my opinion. I believe we should accept. Half a loaf is better than nothing.' His mouth closed with an audible snap.

Len quietly made his way back to the mantelpiece and spoke to the crestfallen, despondent committee-men. His voice was a little high and carried a tone of sadness: 'Friends, don't take any notice of what Ezra says. He is tired and worried after all he has done. But we, who have not done or worried half so much as him, can see the whole position differently. I believe the offer the company is now making is a sign of their own fear and despair.' His voice became more strong and spirited. He outlined the steps the company had taken to break the strike. 'But in spite of it all, our strike is still solid,' he said.

'Hear, hear, Len,' his listeners applauded as they

showed signs of renewed confidence.

Len continued: 'I believe, friends, this new offer is a bribe; they want to buy us back to the pit on half of what we ask. We asked for bread and butter and, in the words of Ezra himself, they offer us half a loaf.'

Ezra, again seated by Mary, shuffled his feet uneasily, but Mary's dilated eyes were on Len.

'Bah!' he said contemptuously. 'Not one of us dare to tell our women "The strike is over. Half a loaf is better than nothing." No; if we did such a thing they would turn us from the door in scorn. They would tell us that we were afraid of a Home Secretary we have never seen. Who is this Home Secretary,' he asked in a sudden outburst of passion, 'this man who calls us hooligans and savages? Is he a working man? Have he ever worked down a pit? Have his mother been put in a county court because he have been too bad to work for a week or two? Not on your life!' he answered. 'He don't belong to us, that's why he sends his soldiers here to drive us back to the pit. Ha. But he'll never beat our men that way. If we are to die, let it be fighting in the clean air that the pit has robbed us of for so long. Better to die like that than as Bill Bristol did, or die of starvation by an empty grate in the back kitchen.'

His voice now rose into powerful resonance as he drove home his convictions. 'They claim they own the pits. All right. Let them come and work the coal themselves if they want it. Let them sweat and pant till their bodies twist in knots as ours have. Let them timber holes whose top they can't see and cut ribs in coal like solid steel. Oh, boys,' he exclaimed confidently, 'we have no need to be downhearted. They will do none of these things. While it is true our bodies belong to the pit, so also is it true that this makes us masters of the pit. It can't live without us. When we are not there to feed it with our flesh, to work life into it with our sweat and blood, it lies quiet like a paralysed thing that can do nothing but moan. The soldiers are here. Good. Let the company use them to work the pit. Soldiers can shoot. Soldiers can kill. But soldiers can't drive us back to work if we all stand together. My father has been a soldier, yet none of us are afraid of him, because we know he is one of us. Neither need we be afraid of the others. Let us tell our people to have no fear. Let us tell the soldiers the justice of our case and we will beat the company yet.'

As Len finished his passionate indictment the room became electrified. Ezra raised his head from the table on which it had drooped. His eyes were heavy and bloodshot as though from loss of sleep, and his voice was hoarse when he said: 'I think we can all learn from the spirit of Len's words. There is hope even now. Let us get on with the business, with no more talk of calling the strike off. We have nothing to be ashamed of and nothing to fear. Forget the words I used just now. I was tired and a disheartened man, but now I have new life and strength. I take it we all agree to urge our people to remain solid and staunch as ever?'

A loud 'Ay' came from everyone present, and with this the meeting came to an end. The committee-men hurried to the canteens for their tea, but Len was too much concerned about Ezra's attitude to think of food. He took the path to the mountain, where he could find the loneliness he desired to help him solve the problems tumbling in his mind.

Ezra's outburst at the committee had given the young man a terrible shock. He felt that the miners' leader, whom he had regarded as the greatest man in the valley, had been prepared to betray the strike. Failing to find a satisfactory answer, his doubts multiplied and his confidence became weaker. He wished he could talk to Mary about the matter, but knew she would curl up like a hedgehog immediately he broached the subject.

Still hounded by these thoughts and chased by his fears, he was wandering aimlessly over the grassy slopes when, arising from a dingle, he heard voices lustily singing:

> 'We are strikers from Cwmardy,
> Fighting for a living wage,
> And we do not mean to surrender
> To the terror of the age,'

Before the strikers' song had ended Len found himself facing the singers, Will and three other young men from the village who were obviously unnerved at being confronted so unexpectedly. Fidgeting uneasily, each tried to conceal a sack under his coat, but Len saw their confusion and the peculiar bulge along the leg of Will's trousers.

His curiosity prompted him to ask, 'What are you up to, boys?'

Will, to whom they all turned, answered: 'Nothing, Len. We be only out for a stroll.'

270

Len shook his head disparagingly. 'Come on Will, you can't kid me.'

'Well if you be so bloody nosey as all that, why not come with us? You will soon see for yourself.'

Len asked no further questions and with Will in the lead the little group made its way up the mountain-side until it came to one of the numerous mine levels that scarred its crest. Here they stopped for a while and as the dusk was beginning to settle on the valley one of them began laying a trail of potato peelings outside the mouth of the level. Another lengthened the trail inside, while the third hid nearby. Without a word Will led Len into the cavern, and in perfect silence they all waited.

Len had not the faintest idea what all these careful and secretive preparations were for, and was about to ask Will for an explanation when the latter, as if anticipating his words, whispered, 'Sh-h-h-h. There's something coming.' Looking towards the level mouth, which looked like a circle of dim light, Len saw the dark shape of a sheep slowly following the trail of potato peelings. He held his breath as in a flash it came to him what the expedition was for and what was to be done.

The sheep drew steadily nearer the level as it chewed its way forward, oblivious to the eyes that watched its every step with eager excitement. Suddenly there was a wild rush as the watchers outside the level flung themselves headlong towards the surprised animal, which turned head-on to meet the rush. Someone gave a pained gasp, 'Hold his bloody head, mun! Turn him back or he'll be away. Ah-h!'

Will flung himself upon the animal in a rough rugby tackle, grasping its legs and, with a sharp twist, threw it upon its back.

The young men dragged the poor animal, gasping and snorting, into the level near Len, one of them lighting the miner's lamp he carried on his belt. For some minutes they sat on the sheep, waiting to recover their breath. At last one of them said, 'Come on, boys. Let's get on with it or we'll be here all blasted night.' Unable to turn his eyes away, Len saw the gleam of the flame on the knife that Will drew from the leg of his trousers, and as Will drew the blade across the sheep's throat, it seemed to be beseeching him with piteous eyes that glared glassily in the glow from the lamp. The poor beast struggled as the steel bit more deeply into its neck and blood poured from the opening wound as Will, ignorant of butchering technique, sawed and hacked at the mutilated throat. The animal's struggles were unavailing, and when the knife eventually cut through the windpipe they ceased entirely.

Len felt faint, and sharp dazzles swirled before his eyes. He wanted to be sick, but fear of ridicule helped him to swallow back what had risen to his throat, and presently, when the sheep had been cut up and dripping bundles of meat had been shoved into sacks, the entrails were buried in the level and they all went outside. On the way down the mountain they met other groups of men laden as they were, and next day the strikers had roast mutton and potatoes for their dinner at the canteens.

Towards the end of the week Cwmardy resounded to the rhythmic march of military feet. The people watched the impressive parade without comment, their faces hard and bitter as they saw the glitter of naked bayonets in the sun. The soldiers were camped in the spacious grounds of the Big House.

Hardly had the resentful excitement aroused by the arrival of the soldiers died down when news arrived at the committee that strike-breakers had been introduced into one of the pits. On one of his early-morning rambles Big Jim made the discovery, and at once communicated the knowledge to Len, who conveyed it to Ezra. A secret meeting of the committee was summoned, and it was decided that on a particular day all the strikers should march to the pit.

This sudden and unexpected development made Len forget all his previous doubts and revitalised his blood. He shared the work of preparation for the march with the other men, and went from door to door to acquaint the strikers of the final plans.

When the day arrived Ezra and Big Jim were the first on the Square, where they waited while the strikers sauntered in casually, most of them, remembering past experiences, carrying mandril shafts and other improvised defensive weapons. The streets leading to the Square soon became packed with people, and the excitement rose as the mass became more dense. Len kept near his father and Ezra, who, despite his habitual coldness, looked haggard and hot, with his lips drawn tightly across the teeth.

By common, though unspoken, accord, the women had been kept in the side-streets off the Square, and presently without a warning word, the miners' leader and Big Jim led off towards the pit where the strike-breakers were working. The towering head of Big Jim, visible to everyone, was recognised as the mark they were to follow, and steadily the human mass, hemmed in by the walls that skirted the road, made its way towards the bend that hid the pit from sight. The strikers heralded their approach with loud shouts:

'Out with the blacklegs!'

'Down with the scabs!'

'Clear our valley of strike-breakers!'

The slogans rang like cannon salutes up and down the ranks, pounding tumultuously at the air.

Len felt the deadly power of the weight behind him. It gave him strength and courage until the first ranks, with quickening impetus, swept round the bend and confronted the deep cordons of police, batons ready poised, drawn across the road. Then he felt himself hesitate with an involuntary checking of his stride, but the pressure lifted him forward and burst him, with the others, through the solid cordon like a hot ray of the sun through snow. He sensed rather than saw batons rise and fall with deadly precision and regularity, and heard the dull thuds that followed each descent. Before he could completely grasp all that was happening the air was full of screams and groans from stricken men. In the mad, chaotic whirl of bodies he lost sight of Big Jim and Ezra, and his eyes went dark as he fought frantically to get back to the thick of the strikers. Something struck him on the cheek, cutting it to the bone, but he paid no heed to the blood that followed the blow. Dimly he saw a poised baton falling. He ducked his head sharply, but staggered as it met his shoulder with a crack that seemed to crush the bones. Staggering on his knees, he felt a muscular paralysis run down his side, deadening his arm and leg, but, dazed and blinded, he forced himself to his feet and weakly fought his way back.

Vaguely above the din he heard the roar of his father's voice. The sound gave him greater strength, and in a short time he was again at Big Jim's side in the midst of the strikers, although he never knew how he got there. By this time the police had reformed their ranks and once more stood between the strikers and the pit. They made repeated charges in an effort to drive the people back to the Square, each charge being fiercely combated, but inch by inch the police gained ground, the narrowness of the street giving them every advantage, because the main body of strikers could not actually enter the fight. In spite of this, the resistance grew more determined and frenzied, and it became a hand-to-hand fight in which everyone had to fend for himself. Police and strikers grappled with each other when the pressure became too great to strike blows. All who fell or were struck down were trampled upon in the mad fury of the battle, until the roadway was covered with still and squirming bodies.

Just when it seemed the police must give way to the tremendous weight their ranks suddenly opened and disclosed a large body of soldiers running forward at the double, rifles clenched tightly to their sides. The strikers fell back before this new threat and, without any resistance, allowed the troops to reach the Fountain where, as though he had dropped from the clouds, Mr. Hicks, closely guarded by police and soldiers, drew a long paper from his pocket and began to read. Though they could not hear a word the strikers knew he was reading the Riot Act. With a wild howl of rage they rushed for the Fountain, drowning the words of the general manager in a snarl of fury and hate. In a moment the battle became more intense and bitter than ever. The officer in charge of the troops was seen to open his mouth, but no one heard what he said. The only sound that came to their ears was the sharp crack of the volley that the soldiers fired. Twice it smashed the air round the Square to fragments, before the echoes bounded from mountain to mountain as though seeking to escape from Cwmardy and to soften the thud of the eleven strikers who fell to the earth as if struck by gigantic sledgehammers.

In the long, deathly silence that followed the volleys one of the shot men rolled, with weak, funny squirms, over on his side. His fingers tore into the roadway as, with infinite slowness, he twisted his head and looked at the dumbstruck mass of people. A geyser of hot blood squirted from his neck and sent thin veins of steam into the still air.

Len, who was standing quite near, gazed fascinatedly at the squirming form with its white, blood-stained face. He saw the lips slowly shape to the word 'mam' before the limbs relaxed and the body flattened to the road. Something snapped in Len's brain. With a wild, inhuman scream he flung himself beside the prostrate striker, and he remembered no more until he felt himself being lifted by the arms and led up the hill, to the accompaniment of a low wail from the people.

The latter, as soon as they had recovered from the

shock of the shooting, had picked up their dead and wounded and were now marching away from the Square. The dragging rattle of their hobnailed boots harmonised with the moans of their dying comrades.

They took the dead and wounded to their respective homes, then, motivated by a common silent urge, the people made their way to the banks of the mountain. When they arrived at their destination the committee-men, led by Ezra, walked quietly to the centre, like mourners in a funeral. Ezra's head was bowed and his shoulders hunched as he confronted the men and women he had led for so long. His white face twitched. The man's mind was focused on the shooting and the bodies he had seen lying still in the dust of the road as though already asking to be buried in the earth. Not even in his most calculating moods had Ezra anticipated such an outcome to the strike.

Lifting his heavy head he looked slowly about him. Horror and grief were stamped on the faces he saw. Tears were tumbling down Len's bloody face, making his wounds burn, and Ezra, seeing them, sensed that they sprang from an overpowering temper and not alone from grief. With a superhuman effort he forced himself to speak, but his words, when they came, were those of a man who had lost grip upon himself. They were words squeezed from a broken heart. The roar of the volley had blasted his confidence and shattered what faith he had in the ability of the men to win the strike.

'My poor friends,' he said in a low, sad voice, 'we have arrived at the saddest moment of our lives. The strike which we began with so much hope and power, with so much confidence and faith, has brought us nothing but misery, injury, and, now, death. The forces against us are so many and so great that they can smash our determination by bludgeon and bullet in the name of law and order. I don't know what we can do. We must have time to think. I don't believe we can carry on much longer.'

His voice broke and came to a halt, but the silence that followed Ezra's statement seemed to electrify Len. Swaying slightly, he raised his arms excitedly in the air.

'Never say die,' he shouted at the top of his voice, yet hardly hearing himself. 'We can't expect to fight a battle without suffering hurt, and we can't expect to win the strike without beating the company and all that it brings against us. We can grieve for our poor butties who have been battered and shot, but to give in now will be to betray all the principles for which they have suffered and died.' A sob rose to his throat, but he struggled on. 'Let them blow and blast, but never let them force us back to the pit without what we have fought for.' Then, finding it impossible to continue, he openly burst into tears that were lost in the roar from the people: 'To the end! To the end! No giving way now!'

Later that day Mary found her father in the parlour with his head pillowed on his bent arms which rested on the table. Deep sobs shook his shoulders and, hearing them, she withdrew and left him alone with his grief and shadows.

In the weeks that followed the initial bitterness of the shooting wore away and the strikers began to fraternise with the soldiers. In the public houses and on the streets the latter shamefacedly tried to excuse their action, and for the most part their explanations were accepted. Strikers' daughters took to the mountains arm-in-arm with the young soldiers and told them all about the strike.

While this was developing some of the strikers banded themselves together and each night raided the houses of particular officials. No trace of these men could be found next day after the injured man or his relatives had reported to the authorities. No striker asked questions. Even Siân no longer paid attention to the nightly absences of Len and his father, and she refrained from questioning when they returned in the early hours of the morning. The raids took place in the most unexpected quarters and never at the same times, so that the guards placed round particular houses were useless, as the raids always took place elsewhere.

Gradually the officials became stricken with fear and the management failed to persuade or coerce them to the pits, with the result that the directors had to reconsider the whole position and decided to grant the men's demands rather than lose the pits entirely. A conference was held at the Big House to which the committee was invited. Here Lord Cwmardy grimly announced that the men could restart as soon as they were ready and that the Government was introducing a minimum wage act. This was in the tenth month of the strike.

News of the victory was conveyed to the people at a mass-meeting on the rubbish dump where they had first declared for strike. The roar that followed the announcement swept the news down the valley like a raging fire, and the windows of the Big House quivered in the victorious tremulo.

THE PIT THROBS
AGAIN

Ezra in the period following the shooting had aged considerably, and he was no longer so assertive and cynical. The people greeted him with a storm of cheers that continued for many minutes before culminating in song. The joy of victory was boiling in the strikers. Thunderous applause and wild flinging of caps into the air followed the reading of the terms.

Ezra finished with a peroration: 'We are left as victors, but some of our friends and mates will never work or live among us again. Yet if they could only see us now they would pride themselves, for they have played a determining part in winning the fight for those they have left behind.'

Mary, who had refused to go on the platform, listened in silence to her father's words. They appeared enigmatic to her when she related them to other words she had heard him utter. Nevertheless, her eyes glistened with pride as she felt the power and control of the man. She stood on her toes and tried to look over the dense throng. A man near by sensed her need and lifted her small body in his arms so that she could get a better view of the teeming mass of people. Her heart stirred when she saw the lined and haggard faces covered with smiles, and she felt the victory more than counterbalanced the tribulations that preceded it. The friendly worker lowered her to the ground as a further roar of cheers announced the conclusion of the meeting. The Big House frowned down upon the exultant mass as though disapproving of its wild, victorious exuberance when the people lined up for the march to their homes.

From the pits a deep throb was already beginning to beat through the valley, as if the engines were starting to laugh because the men were coming back to work.

For the next few days the people of Cwmardy celebrated the victory while the pits were being made ready for their return. All the chapels held special services, the public houses gave free beer for one night, and Mary organised a victory concert. Everyone was consumed with the desire to help and please.

Even Big Jim succumbed to the general mood, and accompanied Siân to the little tin chapel where Dai Cannon was preaching a sermon on the text 'Render unto Caesar the things that are Caesar's'. The sermon lacked nothing in fervour and vehemence from the fact that Dai and Jim had spent the previous night in the Boar's Head drinking everyone's health at the expense of the landlord.

The schools closed for a day and the children, spotless in their specially washed linens and voiles, paraded the streets, their teachers marshalling the procession. Shopkeepers hailed the victory with bunting which transformed Main Street into a bright and colourful thoroughfare.

It took a week before the examiners completed their scrutiny of the workings. The people anxiously awaited the final report. They regarded the pits as living things and wondered how they had fared during the long stoppage. The report showed that very little harm had been done, and in a very short time the valley began to vibrate again as the pit developed its old life and power. The sun once more became a thing of the past, an orb that shone somewhere above the murk that was Cwmardy's heritage from the pit. But the people enjoyed this transformation, for the smoke and throb meant work, wages, life.

After full resumption of work had taken place the weeks soon lengthened into months, but the passage of time did not eradicate the great lessons of the strike from the minds of the men and their leaders. Ezra and the committee took full advantage of the fruits of victory to draw the men into permanent organisation. Ezra told Len one day: 'The committee can only hold power and control when it is directly representative of the men. The seat of strength is not on the surface or in our meetings, it is in the pit itself.' Len's doubts of Ezra's integrity and motives were once more dispelled by the manner in which the latter had smoothed out the complications following upon the strike and his dynamic drive to keep the men organised. The man's spirit and determination spurred Len on.

A few nights later Len held a conversation with his father as a result of which Siân was instructed to call them very early for work the next morning.

They were first on the pit-head, and the fireman who tested their lamps was very curious. 'Early this morning, i'n't you, boys?' he asked.

'Ay mun,' Jim replied casually. 'The old 'ooman was in her tantrums and me and Len was glad to get out of it.'

The official appeared to accept the explanation as *bona fide*, and said no more. In a few minutes the two men were down the shaft and on their way to the district in which they worked. Instead, however, of proceeding as usual direct to their own barry, they remained on the four-railed engine parting, to which all the coal trains filled in the district were drawn by horses. This parting was wider than the ordinary roadways and contained two parallel sets of rails. Here all the trams were shackled together in journeys of twenty to thirty, and hauled to the pit bottom by the three-mile-long wire ropes attached to the haulage engine. The various headings and roadways in the district branched off from this parting, and it was, therefore, the farthest point towards the coalface which all the men working in the district had to pass. Here father and son waited.

The restless squeaking of the roof-pressed timbers, the hurried scuttling of mice and cockroaches, the tiny avalanches of rubble that trickled down the sides reminded Len of his first day in the pit. He felt again that the pit had life, that it was always moving and muttering. His eyes tried to pierce through the darkness that edged on the brief rim of light cast by the safety lamps, and he

284

wondered if the grave held a heavier pall than that solid blackness. A horrible feeling of loneliness engulfed him in a tight grip, although his father was near placidly chewing a lump of tobacco and squirting its juice at the mice which came within range. Len tried to tear himself from this mood and started to think of the interminable roadways and passages that intersected the pit like knotted arteries. In a short time, he mused, men would be circulating in these like blood, giving a hurried, palpitating life to the pit that now seemed restlessly sleeping. His meditations were disturbed by a hum of voices heralding the approach of miners through the black, encircling belt. The hum was soon followed by a glow, and in a very short time some men were looking in surprise at Len and his father.

Will Smallbeer, the pit-battered, crotchety old miner who for many years had made it a matter of personal honour to be first workman down the pit, broke the short silence.

'Well, I'm damned,' he gasped, his deep Welsh accent emphasising the deep resentment he felt at this trespass upon his rights. 'Are you two living here now? Didn't you go home last night, or have you no bloody home to go to?'

Big Jim immediately took umbrage at his tone. 'What be the matter with you, mun?' he demanded spitefully. 'Think you that you do own the bloody pit?'

Len intervened before Will could take up the implied challenge. 'It's all right, boys,' he said. 'Me and dad have come down early today at the orders of the committee. They want us all to hold a meeting this morning before we go on to our working places.'

Will Smallbeer grunted. 'Huh. Why in hell didn't Big Jim

say that, then, instead of making a long speech?'

Jim's jaw dropped in sheer surprise. 'Arglwydd mawr!' he roared, but he caught Len's eye and closed his mouth with an audible snap.

Will turned with an air of triumph to the other men who had come with him. 'May as well sit down by here, boys, till the other lazy beggars come, I s'pose,' he mumbled.

They all, with the exception of Big Jim, sat down on the damp roadsides. Jim strode backwards and forwards, his hands behind his back, muttering what sounded like curses under his moustache. Len watched him carefully, fearful that he would precipitate an argument with Will. If Jim had this in mind he was prevented from putting it into effect by the arrival of more men, who, after a brief consultation, also squatted down. Within half an hour all the men working in the district were gathered on the parting. Hauliers, holding their horses' heads, stood on the outskirts of the circle when Len got into an empty tram and started to speak.

'Fellow workmen,' he began, his voice ringing in the confined space, 'it has been decided by those who led us through the strike that we must now hang together in such a way that an injury to one is an injury to all.' He stopped a moment while he tried to recollect what followed in the speech he had carefully prepared and which he had repeated to himself a dozen times. Failing to recall it, he cleared his throat to give the impression that the pause was due to something sticking there, then went on. 'What I mean is this. We won the strike because we were united and organised, but we can easily lose all we have won if we go back to the old way of every man for himself.'

He was interrupted by a shout. 'Spit it out, Len bach. Tell us what you be trying to say.'

Big Jim took up the cudgels. 'Don't you try to be clever against my boy,' he shouted threateningly. 'Haven't you got sense enough to see he do want us to join the federashon and for us to pick a man to be our re–re–rep—' He failed at the word and finished 'Our spokesman on the committee, mun.'

A cheer greeted the end of his remarks and the men agreed they should all join the union. Will Smallbeer said nothing one way or another. This matter settled, Len asked for a representative upon the committee. Immediately pandemonium broke loose. The hauliers at the rear demanded a special representative for themselves on the plea that they were key men. Tom Morgan, their spokesman, put the case. 'Where would you colliers be,' he asked, 'if it wasn't for us hauliers? You do know you would be all to hell. Me have only to take our horses back to the stable and you colliers can put your tools on the bar and clear off home.' The other workmen saw the truth of this, and after a heated discussion during which many hard and personal things were said it was decided that Len and Tom Morgan should represent the district upon the committee.

Len, pleased with what had been accomplished, was about to make a laudatory peroration when the fireman and Evan the Overman, panting and fuming with rage, pushed themselves through the crowd.

'What the flaming hell is this?' asked the latter. 'A bloody circus or a pit, or what?' No one answered him, and this infuriated him still further. 'Hi,' he shouted at Len, 'you in that blasted tram. Who in firing hell do think you are? Since when have you become the manager of this pit, eh?'

Still there was no reply, and the only sound was a shuffling of feet as the men drew nearer. The fireman, who had left all the speaking to his superior, grew nervous when he noticed the movement. He looked around and saw faces as shadows rather than features in the light of the small-flamed lamps. But the overman, oblivious to everything but his temper, continued to fume and threaten. 'Come on,' he ordered Len, 'get out of that bloody tram and up the pit you go. I won't have none of this damn nonsense here.'

Len started as though the words were a physical blow. From his vantage point he looked at the white, shadowy faces of his workmates. Something in their demeanour gave him courage. 'All right,' he shouted. 'You heard what he said, boys. I am to go up the pit. Good. How many of you are coming with me?'

In a flash every lamp was lifted into the air, and babel broke out with the action. Through the clamour a staccato voice shouted: 'Let's put the old bastard in the water-bosh before we go. We've had enough trouble with him in the strike. Now we can get a bit of our own back.' The cry was taken up and the overman hurriedly scrambled into the tram to avoid the rush that was made.

Len, shouting himself hoarse, at last managed to quell the noise. 'Don't do anything rash, boys,' he begged. 'It will only make matters worse if we hurt him.'

The men stopped and one of them shouted: 'Ay, that's right. Getting our own back be like pissing against the wind.'

A loud shout of laughter greeted this sally, during which

Len began to leave the tram. He already had one leg over its side when the overman grasped his arm. 'Do they all mean to go out?' he asked, his voice hoarse with incredulity.

'Of course they do,' replied Len. 'You watch them and you'll see.'

But before he could draw his other leg over the side Evan the Overman again spoke. 'But what in hell for, Len bach?' He paused, then started to plead. 'Come, come, Len bach. I was only joking, mun. Ha-ha. Fancy taking me serious. Ho-ho. Well, well, Len bach, I thought you had more sense than that, mun. Tell them everything is all right and they can go on to their work.' His words tumbled over each other and his laughter sounded flat. Len looked at him for a moment, thinking the man had gone mad, then, suddenly realising that the men's determination to return home had smashed the official's pugnacious authority, he got back into the tram.

His arms waved wildly and his voice broke with excitement as he yelled: 'Fellow workmen. The overman has withdrawn his words and all of us can go to our places. From today on we will know what to do, and this parting shall be our meeting place where the trouble of one shall be the trouble of all.' A wild shout followed his words, and the men excitedly made their way to their working places.

That evening after work Len could not eat his food and bath quickly enough. Siân scolded him for his haste. 'You will get cramp in your stomach, sure as God is in heaven, one day, gulping your food down like that.'

Len smiled. 'It's all right, mam. It will take more than a bit of grub to hurt me.'

289

Siân tossed her head when she retorted: 'Hmm. I don't know so much about that, indeed, my boy. Your poor old mamgu was a much stronger body than you, but it was pitiful to see her the last days. God help her.'

Jim squirmed restlessly in his chair, being always afraid of something starting Siân off on reminiscences of her long-deceased mother. Len finished eating as quickly as possible and, with his dark, wavy hair still damp, made his way to Ezra's house.

With shining eyes he looked into Mary's big grey ones as he asked for her father. Her emaciated body looked even smaller than usual and a pain tugged at his heart when he followed her into the kitchen, where Ezra was reading some papers.

The shadow cast over Len by Mary's appearance was soon dissipated in the bubbling enthusiasm with which he related the events of the day. At the end of the recital Ezra nodded his head in satisfaction.

'Very good, Len; you have now seen where power lies and what it is.'

Mary made some hot tea while the others were conversing. This and Len's contagious elation thawed the older man's taciturnity. Stretching his feet towards the fire and running his fingers through Mary's hair, he began to speak in an unusually soft voice.

'Yes, my children, power is both great and terrible. It is great when it is held by yourself, but it is terrible when it is held by your enemies.'

The two young people looked at each other, neither of them quite following the drift of his mood, but they said nothing as Ezra went on, more to himself than to them: 'There were some occasions during the strike when I feared power was passing out of our hands into those of the company. On the night of the big riot and the days following the shooting, I felt it would be better to capitulate to power than be crushed by it.'

Mary's eyes widened at these remarks and, although she had not the slightest doubt of his ultimate courage, they reminded her of his favourite adage: 'Always think two moves ahead before you make a single move yourself. Always try to find out what the enemy is thinking.'

Len was more emotional than Mary, and when in the presence of someone who could dominate his impulses, he was less inclined to critical analysis. His mind was now concentrated on Ezra's words and their import in relation to the day's events, and he failed to link them up with incidents that had disturbed him during the strike. He had carried many gods in his life, but never one had he held to with the tenacity with which he held on to Ezra.

When he returned home Len ate a frugal supper and went straight to bed with a simple 'Goodnight' to his parents. As he tossed about in his bed, Ezra's words kept recurring to his mind, preventing sleep. Through them, like a burning thread, ran thoughts of Mary. He wondered what was the matter with her and longed to see the body under her clothes. He likened her to Jane, but failed to imagine the small body carrying robust breasts like his sister. At such intimate thoughts he felt his face warming as the blood went pounding to his head. At length he fell into an uneasy sleep and dreamed that he and Mary were walking over the mountain hand in hand. He saw Jane waving to them, beckoning them on. They started to run, but Mary stumbled and fell. Stooping to pick her up, he saw her clasped in the arms of Evan the Overman's son, one breast hanging loose and flaccid through her blouse. Len moaned and tossed in his sleep as the dream gripped him, and he woke the next morning feeling heavy and lethargic, while his head throbbed painfully.

During the weeks that followed the main topic in the pits was the 'federashon', as the men called it. Most of them had already joined, but a few of the older ones remained independent and adamant to all approaches. Will Smallbeer, now working in the same barry as Len and his father, was one of the most stubborn. To all Len's enticements he replied: 'What think you, Len? Do you think I slog my guts out every day in the week, first man down and last man up, in order to keep lazy beggars in collars and ties idle on top of the pit? Huh, not me.'

Len tried to point out the value of organisation and the lessons to be learned from the strike, but he was always met with: 'Don't you worry 'bout me, boy bach. I have always looked after myself, ay, before the napkins was off your backside, and I will do so till me and the old 'ooman peg out. I have got no man but myself to thank for anything. Let those who want a federashon have it, I say. But I be one of those who can manage by myself, thank you.'

The old man's attitude worried Len, and he reported it to the committee. As a result of this he went to work early the next morning and visited all the men of the barry in their working places, but he passed that of Will Smallbeer without saying a word, though the old workman shouted, 'Good morning. How be?' as he passed. Will spat on a heap of small coal, then turned to the man in the next working place and asked conversationally: 'What be the matter with him this morning? Got out of bed the wrong side, I 'spect.' The man thus addressed did not answer.

Will looked up from the huge lump of coal he was hoisting to his knees, preparatory to jerking it into the empty tram, his body naked from the waist up sweating and shining with the strain. 'Huh,' he grunted. 'Everybody bloody deaf this morning or what?' Still receiving no reply, he swore at the top of his voice. 'Be you all bleeding mad? But perhaps you do think to worry me with your quiet. Huh. Don't forget old Will Smallbeer have beat better men than you before breakfast in the morning. Ay,' he howled into the silence, 'and spit 'em out as easy as that,' retching a prodigious mass of mucus from his chest and spitting it into the tram.

Big Jim started his way up the barry at the challenge, but Len caught him in time and drew him back to his own place, and though Will's curses continued to dribble down the barry no one paid any heed to him. Everyone was concentrated on filling his tram of coal in the shortest space of time. A number of horse-drawn empty trams rattled and clanged in the distance. When the haulier arrived with these he unhitched the horse with a 'Whoa. Come here back,' and began pulling the full ones singly out of the barry.

When all the full ones had been withdrawn the men came down the barry to help each other shove the empty

293

ones up the steep incline to their respective working places. Will Smallbeer worked the top place but one, and when it came his turn to have a tram the men left it at the working place below his without saying a word.

Will, his eyes bulging with amazement, the sweat pouring off his nose and down his moustache, looked dully after the retreating lamps. Carefully turning so that his bare back was against the cold iron of the tram, he spread-eagled his feet and, jamming them against a sleeper, waited for the men to return, thinking they had made a mistake. In a short time he heard the clankety-clang of the next tram being pushed up the barry. This again stopped lower down, and the men once more made their way back for the next.

'Hi, boys, you have made a mistake, my tram isn't in the right place,' he howled, but no one paid the least attention. Will tensed his body to the weight of the tram he was holding and his muscles swelled with the effort. Sweat and fury bathed him, and the tram felt so cold on his back that he was convinced it was burning a hole through his body.

Yelling helplessly after the men, a deep suspicion slowly grew in his mind. 'Ho-ho. So that be it, is it?' he screamed. 'Not satisfied with putting muck on a man, you want to rub it in, do you?' Putting all his strength and weight into his back, he straightened his legs and tried to press the tram up the incline, howling all the while, 'Think I'll bend to ask for help, eh, you lousy lot of useless bastards?'

Squeezing and straining, he at last felt the tram move a

little. This and his fury urged him to greater efforts, and he pushed it another yard, when the weight forced his feet back down the slippery roadway and they again jammed against the sleeper where they were when his mates left him. Panting and gasping for breath he was forced to stop his efforts for a while. He heard the men shove the last empty tram to its place, but was too proud to ask them for help after what they had done to him.

Will closed his eyes to ease the smarting of the sweat that poured into them. He kept them shut for a while till he heard a sudden bang in the tram resting on his back. Startled out of his wits, he turned his head by twisting his neck, and saw two men throwing coal into the tram as if their lives depended upon the speed with which they filled it. His eyes bulged glassily at the sight, and, horrified to the point of tears, he bawled, 'Hi there! What in bloody hell be you doing? Do you know this is my tram?' His voice was hoarse and cracked with fatigue, passion, and self-pity.

The men continued their frenzied filling, apparently deaf to Will's howls. He felt the strain on his back become greater with every lump and shovelful of coal, but he knew if he tried to get away from the tram its weight would overcome him and smash his body to the ground. Impotent and fuming, his only hope was to keep his feet tight against the sleeper and maintain the burning pressure of the cold iron on his back until the men released him. It seemed hours to Will before the tram was filled, but at last it was full. One of the men went round it chalking a number on the sides. When he came to the front he gave a surprised start when he saw the wet, straining body of Will.

'Duw, duw, butty, look what I have found by here!' he cried in feigned alarm. His mate hurried to the spot and both of them looked at the suffering Will for a moment before shouting loudly to the harry, 'Come quick, boys, and see what we've found.'

A scurry of pattering feet followed the shout. Forcing his way to the front, Big Jim looked pathetically at the figure before him. 'Well, well,' he murmured compassionately, 'it is poor old Will Smallbeer. Pity, pity. I wonder what he is doing by there.'

One of the other men replied: 'Poor old dab. Gone off his head sudden, I 'spect. Pity, too, mun. Only yesterday I was telling him he was bound to go one day with all the beer he be drinking.'

This infuriated Will and sent the strength oozing back into his body. 'You lot of dirty whoremasters,' he screamed, 'pull this bloody tram off my back, then see if you can insult me.'

Big Jim looked at him, a pitying look on his face. 'There you are, boys,' he said sadly, 'that do prove he have gone in his head. Fancy him holding a tram by there all this time and there be two sprags in it.'

Will gave a squeal and jumped to the side as if impelled by an electric shock. The tram did not budge. Wide-eyed and motionless he looked at it for some seconds, then broke through the surrounding men like a thunderbolt, frothing and howling incoherently. They heard him hurtling back with gruesome threats of 'I'll chop your bloody heads off,' and scattered before the whirling, razor-sharp hatchet in his hand. The impetus of his stampede carried him past them, and before he could turn Big Jim's huge arms were round his belly. After a short, sharp struggle Will was subdued. Tears of mortification filled his eyes while the men sat round him in a ring.

Len was the first to speak. 'Well, boys,' he said quietly, 'this is the first test of strength between all of us together and one who is not willing to be with us.'

Will struggled to his haunches as he grasped the import of the words, and Len went on: 'No man can be strong enough to do what we all don't want him to do. You remember the blacklegs in the strike?' he asked.

'Ay, ay,' the men replied in chorus.

'Well, the other side of that is no man can refuse to do what we want him to do. One man in our barry thought he could stand by himself against us all and bring disgrace on us in the eyes of the other workmen in the pit. If he still believes this, that is his own look-out.'

Will, much less cocksure after his experience, broke in: 'Say straight what you do mean, mun. You do want me to join the federashon, is that it?'

'Yes,' all the men shouted together.

'Do the federashon mean that workman have got to fight against workmen?'

Len replied this time. 'Yes, when a few stubborn workmen go against what is good for the majority.'

'Huh. If that be it, then I give in, muniferni, and will join next Saturday. But mind you,' he added hastily, 'no man be going to make on my bloody back and no man can rub muck in me, either.'

297

The workmen cheered this speech and Will was allowed to rise to his feet. They all helped to fill an additional tram to make good the one he had lost, and this satisfied Will, although he threatened to have the blood of any man who tried to 'simple' him.

LEN AND MARY ORGANISE THE CIRCLE

About this time Len found himself becoming more and more interested in books, particularly those lent to him by Ron, but though he spent much time with them, they remained as inscrutable as ever. As usual when he was in an intellectual or emotional difficulty, his thoughts turned to Mary and Ezra. Knowing the latter was absorbed in the affairs of the federation, Len did not want to worry him with his troubles, but he wished he could gain the confidence of Mary and break down the cold barriers she placed between them. At last, after pondering over the matter for weeks, he decided to approach her.

Standing outside Ezra's door, he felt the same perturbation as on the first occasion, but plucking up his courage he knocked timidly. Immediately he had done so he regretted it and forgot all he had planned to say, but before he could recover his composure the door opened and Mary confronted him.

She looked stronger and brighter than when he last saw her, and this made him glad. For some moments he remained silent, his eyes unconsciously fixed on her face. But presently, realising that she was blushing under his stare, he pulled himself together and, coughing in an embarrassed manner, he asked if Ezra was in.

'No,' answered Mary; 'dad has gone away since this morning and won't be back for some time. Can I give him any message?'

He paused a second and dropped his eyes before answering: 'Yes... er... well, no. I didn't exactly come to see him, Miss Mary. I wanted to ask you about something that is worrying me. But it doesn't matter now,' he concluded hastily.

Mary looked at him in surprise. She knew he was shy and diffident, but she had never before seen him so completely at sea, and his uneasiness touched a sympathetic chord in her.

'Well, if you have something to talk to me about,' she said, less brusquely than she usually spoke to him, 'why not come in and chat it over, since you are here?'

He followed her through the passage into the kitchen, his heart beating in his throat. Inviting him to take the armchair where her father usually sat, she took her favourite stool near the fireplace. Len noticed that her big eyes now looked blue.

He swallowed nervously and began to explain what was troubling him. 'You see, Miss Mary,' he said, 'ever since your father started telling me about books and the way newspapers are used to tell us what other people want us to know, instead of what we ought to know, I've been trying to learn what exactly we *should* know.' He felt he was tying himself into verbal knots, but went on desperately: 'Ron, of the general store, told me a lot of things before he went to college and gave me some books, but I can't make head or tail of them.'

He stopped, hoping she would show in some way that she appreciated his difficulty, but she continued to look at him gravely without saying a word. Her silence made Len more confused than ever. He felt he could explain no further and decided to come straight to the point.

'I was thinking,' he stuttered, 'that perhaps your father could spare time to teach some of us young chaps all the things he knows.' And as this sounded lame and insufficient, he plunged on: 'What I mean is, perhaps he could take a class of us youngsters same as they do in school. Only he would teach us about the working-class.'

He stopped here, completely at a loss for words, and for some time not another word was spoken. Then Mary said, 'I think I know what you have in mind, Len.' Her rather hoarse voice sounded very sweet in his ears and he quivered at her use of his name. She did not notice this, however, and went on: 'What you want is someone to teach politics to a group of young men like yourself who want to learn things but are groping in the dark for want of direction?'

He nodded his head dumbly, and again both remained silent for some time. Mary was once more the first to break it.

'I don't think dad has the time for such a thing,' she

301

observed. 'And in any case I don't think he would be of great use to you, because he's a man of action rather than of words.'

Len stirred in disagreement but said nothing, and she continued: 'What you should do is to get your chaps, and some of the young girls if you can as well, into a kind of little circle where you can share your problems and discuss them together each week.'

Len immediately saw the possibilities in her suggestion, and feeling suddenly full of confidence, said 'Good. You've hit it right on the head.'

They began at once to make a list of the people who might come to such informal meetings, but Len found that his temperamental unsociability left him with very few suggestions. Mary, however, made up for this deficiency. She seemed to know everyone in the valley, with their tendencies and idiosyncrasies, and between them they worked out a list of over a dozen names, confident that Ezra would be able to add to the number. Mary agreed to interview Ben the Barber, to see if the 'Circle', as they decided to call it, could meet each Sunday in his little back room.

Having concluded these arrangements, Len got up to go, but Mary invited him to have a cup of tea. Shyly but readily, he assented and sat down again, while she busied herself with the dishes. Watching the movements of her body, the dream he had had of her in the arms of Evan the Overman's son again flooded his mind. He pictured the loose breast hanging from its bodice and wondered if her breasts were really like that. A pain shot through him at the thought that, perhaps, she was courting some young man. He knew Ezra wished her to become a school-teacher eventually, and the knowledge maddened him, for he felt that it entailed her moving in circles superior to his own.

He was jerked out of these morbid thoughts by Mary handing him a cup of tea and offering him a biscuit. Ashamed of his thoughts, he stuttered his thanks, but self-consciously he avoided her eyes for fear she should read his mind. She seemed, however, to be oblivious to all he had been thinking, and while they sipped the tea they were both silent. But the turmoil in Len's heart increased with every moment, and suddenly, raising his eyes to hers, be asked 'Do you remember the night you teased me about love?'

Mary was startled for a moment, but she managed to retain sufficient composure to murmur: 'Why, yes. Of course I do. You mean the night you ran away like a little baby?'

Her words hurt Len's dignity. 'I don't think I ran away. You were asking me questions I didn't know how to answer, so I thought the best thing I could do was to get out.'

Mary looked at him more sympathetically, but though she knew he expected her to speak, she found herself at a loss for words.

He waited a while, then, getting no response, continued in a lower voice: 'But since then, I believe I am beginning to learn the truth about myself and about you.'

She looked at him, her eyes filled with doubt and wonder, but let him continue uninterrupted: 'All through the strike, whenever I was worried about anything, my thoughts used to turn to you. Sometimes I thought I hated you for your snotty, cutting ways to me. Then I would always apologise to you in my mind for thinking such things.' Mary lowered her eyes, and he went on, more to himself than to her: 'Ay. Just like that. Often I dream of you, and always they are dreams which make me angry and miserable.' He turned to her with a quaint little shrug and asked: 'I wonder if what I feel for you is love?'

Mary rose from the stool, and, unconsciously imitating her father's habit when he was disturbed or worried, began pacing up and down the room. The restless action brought to Len's mind a comprehension of what he had said. Immediately nervous and penitent, he sprang to his feet, saying: 'Oh, forgive me, Miss Mary. I had no business to say such a thing to you. I'm sorry.' His face was flushed with embarrassment and shame. Mary ceased her pacing, and standing directly before him, looked deep into his eyes.

'Sit down,' she said; and was glad when he did so, because, looking down at him, she felt stronger. Then, slowly and distinctly, she spoke to him, her voice very soft and her eyes becoming moist: 'There have been times when I've really hated you, because I thought you were robbing me of dad. But now I know I was wrong; that you are just a boy groping for something you are not even yet aware of. You probably think what you do of me merely because you have felt my antagonism. Now that's all gone; I see you as a friend and a comrade, who can help me to help dad carry out all he has in mind. Your words tell me you are too sentimental ever to be a serious menace to dad's position. But,' her eyes flashed, 'you must never talk to me again of love. I don't think I am capable of such a thing. Besides,' she added sadly, 'there are good reasons why I should put any such ideas out of my mind even if

304

they were to arise there.'

Len's head sank lower on to his shoulders while she was speaking. He felt the world was suddenly being torn from him, and sensing his mood, she put her thin hand, soft as a butterfly's wing, on his head.

'Don't worry, Len,' she said. 'You have many more years before you than I expect I have, and if you follow dad and your real impulses there will be thousands to love you, thousands whose love will be much more precious to you than mine could ever be.'

Tears trickled down Len's cheeks, and he swallowed hard. But before he could say anything, a knock sounded at the door.

'That's dad,' said Mary, in her normal voice, and a moment later Ezra entered the kitchen. He found Len on his feet ready to go.

'Why the hurry?' he asked.

'Oh, I've been here a good time,' was the answer, 'and I ought to be going or my mother will be getting worried.' And with a brief 'Goodnight,' he left father and daughter alone.

During the following weeks Len did not have much time to brood over Mary's words. He had been made secretary of the Circle, into which Ezra and Mary had succeeded in drawing the most varied elements, and they began organising lectures and debates, bringing in speakers from outside the valley. Slowly the members of the Circle gathered confidence and began lecturing to their fellow-members, each taking his turn.

The subjects ranged from philosophy to music. For the latter a piano was borrowed from Mr. Evans Cardi and

Mary collaborated with the lecturer, the son of Williams the under-manager, illustrating his points by playing for him. Watching her fingers move in obedience to young Williams, Len was consumed with jealousy, and though he joined in the applause at the end, his clapping was false and hypocritical. When he heard the lecturer ask Mary if he could take her home, he burned with fury that she should consent with a smile.

At work next day he hardly spoke to anyone, and only grunted in response to his father's occasional queries. They were standing some huge thirteen-foot timbers underneath a great hole in the roof, and Big Jim swore there had been grass on some of the soil that had been shifted from the fall. Len, being more light and sprightly, straddled the cross-timber, or 'collars', at the top of the upright props, while his father lifted up to him the smaller six-foot timbers. They were wet and slippery and Len, whose feet hung unsupported, had to take the weight in his arms and the small of his back. The strain on his body was terrible, even though Big Jim assisted him as far as possible, cracking jokes all the while in an attempt to raise him from his despondency. Turning his lamp sideways so that the gleam lifted and added to the light from the lamp Len held in his mouth, Jim commented: 'Arglwydd mawr, you do look funny up there, mun – 'sactly like a ape.'

Len took no notice. His breath hissed through his teeth, clenched on the heavy lamp. The strain of handling the long, heavy timber, that twisted in his hands like an eel, began to exhaust him, and he jerked it in an effort to get the further end fixed on the timbers opposite. But it fell short, and swearing under his breath he twisted and strained in the effort to control it. But its slippery wet surface, added to the leverage of its length, defeated him, and forgetting the lamp in his mouth, he shouted, 'Look out, dad!'

The lamp clattered to the ground thirteen feet below and though his father sprang back like a panther, Len heard him moan. A cold chill ran through him.

He looked down and saw Big Jim squatting on the side, rubbing his naked chest vigorously and muttering, 'Oh, my poor tits.'

The sheer incongruity of the scene amused Len, and looking down from his high perch, he began to rock with laughter. But suddenly his father, ceasing his wails, jumped to his feet and roared out: 'Uffern dân! Not satisfied with nearly killing your poor old father, you now make fun to him!'

Len, however, made no effort to control his laughter, and this enraged Big Jim. Running back a short way, he picked up the huge fourteen-pound sledgehammer, and swinging it above his head like a broomstick, he howled:

'Out of that bloody timbers! Come on. Down you come before I hit the bloody lot out.' Then, giving the upright prop a hard blow as an earnest of his intention, he continued threateningly: 'By Christ, you can muck on me, but no man can rub it in. Dangerous man I be when I lose my temper. I have kilt men for half of what you have done to me. Just shows what comes of spoiling your children!'

In a leisurely way, and still laughing, Len began to scramble down from his perch, when suddenly a rattling sound came from the timbers above, and before he could drop to the ground a stone struck him glancingly on the head. Without a murmur his limbs relaxed and he fell headlong, but Big Jim caught him in his huge, sure arms before he touched the roadway, and carrying the inert body some distance back, he laid it gently on the side. Feverishly he examined the sweat-bedewed head. Len's eyes were closed, and, finding no wound or sign of blood, Jim was frightened. A dread shot through his mind that the lad's neck was broken, and drawing him to his body like a mother cuddling her child, the old worker began to cry piteously.

'Oh Len bach, I didn't mean what I was saying. Open your eyes and look at your old dad again,' he pleaded, but there was no response. Len lay limply, his features immobile, and Jim's voice became more pathetically vehement as he begged: 'Come, Len bach, let me hear you laughing at me again.'

Presently Len's eyes twitched, and, Jim, placing him tenderly back on the roadway, ran for the big tin jack of water. He upturned the neck of this to Len's mouth until the water gushed over the lad's face and chest, bringing him back to consciousness with a shudder, and seeing that no vital harm had been done, the old man began to upbraid him.

'There you are,' he scolded. 'That do just serve you right. That's what you get for poking funs to people older than yourself.'

Len's hand wandered to his throbbing head, and at once Jim became solicitous again.

'Is your poor little head paining?' he crooned as if he were talking to a baby. Len nodded, but said nothing. Fortunately the stone had struck him flatwise. Had its edge caught him it would probably have fractured his skull.

He tried to struggle to his feet, saying, 'I'm all right now, dad, let's get on with those timbers or we'll never finish.'

But Big Jim was adamant. 'You sit here for the rest of the day,' he insisted, wrapping Len in shirts and coats. 'There is a day after today. I can go on cropping the sides ready for tomorrow, then we can finish the whole job.' Len gave way because he knew it was useless arguing and he still felt giddy and sore.

A few Sundays after this incident a stranger attended the Circle. He had a letter of introduction from Ron, who had promised to lecture, saying that he was unable to come, but had sent a substitute much more efficient and interesting than himself.

It transpired that the lecture was to be on 'Sex, its purpose, problems, and diseases,' and Len, shocked by the title, took old John Library, the chairman, aside and suggested that the girls should be asked to leave in case they should be offended.

John looked at him quizzically.

'You've still got a lot to learn, Len bach. Why shouldn't the girls have the benefit of this lecture, if there is any benefit to it, as well as yourself?'

Len, taken aback by the old man's answer, could only blurt out: 'There are some things we can't talk about before women.' And then, as if this closed the matter, he added: 'It isn't right.'

But John merely walked to the front of the room and without more ado opened the meeting.

Len kept his eyes on the picture of 'Bendigo in Fighting Pose' that faced him on the opposite wall, occasionally giving a sly squint at the charts the lecturer produced, but hurriedly averting his eyes. His face went red and white in turns and he felt an insane desire to get up and order Mary out. He was not so much concerned about the other girls. 'If they are brazen enough to stay here, that's their own business,' he thought. He fought the desire back. When the lecturer spoke of the diseases, Len was amazed and horrified. He had never realised that people suffered from such ghastly things. He remained throughout the lecture wishing all the time that Mary were not there.

That night in bed he could not rid himself of the terrible pictures drawn by the lecturer. It appeared to him that everything connected with sex left one open to putrefying diseases.

The lecturer had stated that syphilis (Len had always heard the men in work call it 'pox') was brought into the country hundreds of years ago by the Crusaders, and that eighty out of every hundred people now had it in one form or another. But when Len thought of Mary and his own father and mother, he could not believe that any of them suffered from such a thing. His whole being revolted at the idea, and he tried to forget the hideous subject. Nevertheless, his sleep was disturbed by dreams that left him moist with a cold sweat.

The village was now more prosperous than it had ever been. The pits never ceased their throbbing night or day. The 'foreigners' had intermarried with the natives, their children, now young adults, creating a new cosmopolitan population in the valley. Street and mountain fights were no longer so frequent, but the continually extending police station housed more police than it ever had. Each of the four groups of collieries had its separate federation lodge, linked together by a Combine Committee. Mr. Evans Cardi, together with most of the other little tradesmen, extended their premises and their business at the same time. A new theatre was built near the Square. Every Saturday the men and women of the village followed their rugby football team into the neighbouring areas, and the game sometimes turned into a battle of fists. A new railway was laid through the valley to deal with the flow of coal that was too great for the railways already there, and the city by the sea into which this coal was poured became one of the greatest ports in the world. Beautiful houses and buildings sprang up in it. The number of its millionaires increased with the increased number of ships that left its docks with coal for the four corners of the earth. Lord Cwmardy became so wealthy that his daughter could afford to travel the country demanding rights for women.

Early in the spring a joint meeting of the pit committees was held in the Boar's Head, where the inquest on the explosion victims had been held. The big room was packed to suffocation, reeking clay pipes filled it with black acrid fumes, and huge jugs of beer were shared out in little tots among the men.

Feeling stifled by the thick atmosphere, Len drank his in a single gulp, and going out into the bar for fresh air, bought himself another pint, which he took back with him to the meeting-room. Putting the mug under the bench, he began to listen attentively while Ezra explained the purpose

311

of the meeting and the need of striving for a majority on the local council. As the speech concluded, a murmur of applause came from the men present and they began chatting among themselves.

For a while Ezra let them go on, the hubbub adding to the density of the atmosphere, but at last he tinkled the empty glass on the table before him. 'Now boys, we will have a little bit of order and start the discussion. Who's going to begin?'

There was a long pause before a middle-aged man from one of the neighbouring pits got to his feet, and coughing nervously, began: 'Mr. Chairman. I must be quite honest to you all. I don't see what good can come to us if we begin to potch about with these old politics. To me politics is something for rich people who have got plenty of time to spare to play about. We have got our federashon and I do think that is enough for us to go on with, without bothering our heads about things that are no use to us. I do agree that it is all officials and what not is on the council now, but what difference do that make? Haven't they always been there? No,' he went on more slowly, spitting on the floor before he continued, 'I do say let well alone. We are all right now. Don't let us spoil everything by poking our noses into things that have got nothing to do with us.'

He sat down amid some applause, and another coal-scarred veteran jumped up, who, speaking in a high-pitched, excited voice, agreed with the first speaker. As he worked himself up, a little globule of moisture gathered at the end of his nose. This fascinated Len. He watched it growing

312

longer as the old man continued, and held his breath as every nod of the speaker's head threatened to break the grip of the wet blob and drop it on the old man's chin. Unheeding, the latter went on.

'Ay, boys, you can take it from me that the best thing is to stick to our own last and let everybody else stick to theirs. I also do agree that it is all officials and their butties be up there now. But let them be, say I. It do give them less time to run after the firemen's wives.'

A roar of laughter greeted this last sally, and he sat down, wiping his nose on the back of his hand. Immediately three men jumped on their feet simultaneously, each claiming the floor, and began quarrelling as to who was first on his feet. One twitted the other: 'You say you are first; why, mun, you are too slow to be the first of twins.'

This drove the slandered man, who happened to have a twin brother, into a frenzy.

'Say that again,' he howled, 'and I'll knock your bloody face to the back of your dirty bloody neck!'

The man thus challenged made no reply, but rushed past the intervening benches, pulling off his coat as he went. The delighted committee-men made no effort to stop him. They cleared the benches out of the way and formed a ring round the fuming contestants.

In a flash the meeting had split into two groups, who were all mixed up in a tumbling mass of fighting bodies. As benches and tables went crashing to the ground and blood was splashed about the room, Ezra remained still and silent in his chair, but the tumult brought men rushing in from the bar, Big Jim leading them.

313

Jim caught a glimpse of Len standing white-faced and trembling near the door, and without waiting to ask questions, he jumped to the conclusion that the lad had been hit. Roaring like a bull, he flung himself into the mass of bodies, hitting indiscriminately at everything that came near him. Dai Cannon rushed after his mate and met a crack on the ear that tumbled him over before he had struck a blow. Holding his ear tenderly, Dai slowly crawled to where Len was standing watching the scene with eyes that betrayed his fear.

Len smiled, despite his alarm, at Dai's comment. 'By Christ! They're hitting hard here, Len.'

For some minutes the fight continued, but at last the men began to tire and, as one by one they dropped out, others began to drag the chairs and benches back into place. When this was completed and the men once more seated, Ezra continued with the meeting.

'Now you have all enjoyed yourselves,' he said, 'perhaps we can go on. Who wants the floor next?'

The same three men who had started the row at once sprang to their feet, but before the argument could begin again, Ezra said: 'Tom Davies has the chair,' and the other two immediately sat down.

Wiping the blood from his nose with his coatsleeve, the speaker started: 'Mr. Chairman. I don't agree with the other two speakers, much as I respect 'em. What I want to know is, why for should the company have all the say in our valley? When we was on strike it was the council who brought the police here. I have always said this and no man can make me believe different. If Ezra is good enough

314

for us in the Federashon he is good enough for us on the council or anywhere, I do say.'

This speech had the loudest applause of the evening. The reference to Ezra seemed to focus the whole matter for the men, and they saw the issue no longer as an abstract thing between themselves and the Company, but as one between Ezra, their leader, and Mr. Hicks, the representative of the Company. It turned the tide in favour of fighting the elections, and after Ezra had still further explained the matter, a vote was taken, and all the men, except those who had spoken against, put their hands up for contesting, Big Jim looking around too see what Len was doing before raising his.

More jugs of beer were sent for and shared in the little tots among the company. But, although Ezra went out immediately the meeting was concluded, Len remained behind with his father, for fear he might start another fight. In spite of some critical moments, however, the night passed off without further disturbance, and presently an impromptu concert had started.

Everyone present was expected to contribute to the programme or sacrifice the price of a pint of beer for the pianist, and by the time Len's turn came he had drunk sufficient beer to shatter his usual shyness. He felt he could sing better than any who had performed before him, and at last the self-elected chairman, his eye already black from a blow he had received in the fight, announced in a grave, urgent voice: 'And now gentleman, with your kind attention, I am going to call upon our great friend, Big Jim's boy, to oblige the company.'

315

Len blushed and fidgeted in his seat, as he had seen the other artistes do. Big Jim shifted a lump of tobacco into his cheek and buried his nose in his pint mug; and the pianist struck up a preliminary chord that ran from one end of the piano to the other. When Len hesitated, the crowd grew restless and the chairman shouted: 'Order, gentlemen, please, the singer is on his feet. Give him a clap, boys.' Big Jim hastily replaced his pint on the table to participate in the encouraging applause, and Len walked self-consciously to the piano. Bending his head, he turned his back to the audience and hummed a tune into the pianist's ear. The latter's fingers ran over the keys, but he failed to get the pitch of Len's voice. Finally he muttered: 'It's alright, kid. Kick off. I'll follow you.' Len turned round and faced the noisy, smoke-filled room. Again the chairman raised his hand warningly.

'Now gentlemen, please, the singer is on his feet. Now then, Dai,' he continued, addressing someone at the back, 'if you can't 'preciate good singing, there is a room downstairs where you can drink your beer without disturbing nobody else.'

This statement was greeted with loud applause, and the pianist again struck up a chord while Len, swaying slightly, clasped his hands before him and fixed his eyes soulfully on the ceiling. Something in the back of his mind told him this was the correct posture. Drawing his breath in deeply he began to sing, 'A fair-haired boy in a foreign land at sunrise was to die', and finding he had pitched it too high had to force himself to the top notes, each of which threatened to burst the veins in his neck.

316

Big Jim gazed at him with open mouth; he thought he had never heard such a beautiful voice. As Len slowly entered into the mood of the ballad, his voice sank naturally to its proper pitch. In his drink-hazed brain he pictured the incidents on which the words were based. He saw himself in the condemned lad's place, and a quiver of self-pity gave his voice a pitiful vitality. Then as he imagined his mother in Sunny Bank, weeping for him as he sat in the death cell, he felt manly and brave, and his voice echoed the mood. In the last stanza, where the pardon came too late, he saw his mother and Big Jim bringing wreaths to put on his grave.

When the last quavering tones were silenced, a burst of applause greeted his effort. Tears flooded the eyes of the men present. Loud shouts for encore rose from all parts of the room to be drowned in the stentorian shout from Big Jim.

'No, no. Blast an encore. Let us have the same song again.'

The chairman appealed for order. 'After that very fine rendering,' he said, 'I am sure you all agree with me that we ought to ask our young friend to oblige us again.'

Len was embarrassed. He did not know any other songs, except hymns, and the words of these even he had forgotten. He felt very proud of his first effort, but was at a loss how to accede to the request.

Turning from the piano, his face flushed and eyes burning, he looked at the people before him. Their features, shrouded in a thick haze of smoke, looked blurred and indistinct, but when the chairman again called for order, Len gave a little preliminary cough and said: 'Fellow

317

workers, I don't know any more songs, but if you like I will recite a poem entitled, "The Oration of Spartacus to the Gladiators".'

Loud applause greeted this announcement, and Len continued: 'It tells of a band of Roman slaves who escaped from their masters and hid themselves in the mountains where, for three years, they beat back all the attacks of the whole Roman army.'

The pianist struck a low chord and Len commenced the oration. His brain was now so muddled that he forgot half the words, and he substituted anything that came to his mind. At the end neither he nor any of the audience knew what he had said, but the latter applauded as if this made no difference.

Later that night Big Jim and Len returned home. Both felt very happy until they reached the house, where Siân was awaiting them.

One glance at their faces showed her what had happened.

'For shame,' she said to Jim, 'teaching your young son to drink!'

Len went straight to bed. He lay down and felt the ceiling falling. When he closed his eyes the room ran madly round him, and his stomach turned with it. He swore never to drink again.

WAR

As summer turned into autumn, Len and Mary devoted themselves with even greater assiduity to the Circle. The subjects they discussed took on an increasingly Socialist bias, and under the guidance of John Library the Circle organised private and public lectures at which well-known Liberals and theoretical Socialists spoke. The experiment proved very popular, and political interest and discussion began to develop in the valley.

Large numbers of young men joined the Circle, the cleverest among these being Tom Morris, who came from the neighbouring valley. Eventually lack of space made it necessary to close the books to many who would have liked to become members. The informal homeliness of the whole proceedings, together with the camaraderie between the members, made newcomers anxious to remain.

Discussions commenced in the Circle were carried into the pit in such a way that the Circle became a big factor in the life of the valley. Marx and Socialism slowly became the chief topic of discussion and debate, and many of the Circle members, led by Tom Morris, were ready to believe that Marx was God's second name. Len was voracious for information and knowledge. He began to comprehend a little more of the books given him by Ron.

Ezra advised him to leave Marx alone. 'Besides being out of date,' he said, 'his books are too heavy and dry for you.' And Len took his advice.

One Sunday Mary suggested that the Circle should have a holiday fund for the purpose of spending one day a year together at the seaside. This was agreed to, and each week the members subscribed to this, and it was decided to go to Blackpool on the following August Bank Holiday. Len and Mary were delegated to look after the arrangements, and when at last the day arrived, beautiful and warm, each member of the Circle put on a red tie or scarf as the symbol of their vaguely defined beliefs.

The journey and the scenery reminded Len forcibly of his first excursion to the seaside. The long train journey made him depressed and morose, but Mary, who seemed more sparkling and lively that day than he had ever seen her, tried to lift him out of this despondency.

Someone in the carriage pulled out a large bottle of whisky from his case, and the spirit was offered round. Len felt it would be churlish to refuse, particularly when he saw Mary swallow her portion in a single gulp, and as the fluid ran through his veins like mercury, his eyes began to shine and his taciturnity was dissipated by the softening influences of the liquor.

During the day Len, for the first time in his life, met girls who had not been reared in the valleys: robust, boisterous women from the factories of Lancashire and elsewhere. Their free-and-easy camaraderie bewildered him and, noticing some of them linked arm-in-arm across the street and looking the worse for drink, he asked Mary shyly if they were loose women. She gave him a biting, scornful glance and replied shortly: 'They are hard-working girls having a hard-earned holiday, exactly the same as you are today. The only difference is that they are enjoying themselves and you are not.'

Len subsided at the snub, and soon the company began to break up.

Mary refused many invitations to join particular groups, excusing herself on the plea of a headache, and eventually she and Len were left alone.

She suggested a stroll, and they wandered away from the crowds. The sparkling sea fascinated Len, and he became absorbed in emotional daydreams which led him gently and logically to Mary walking at his side. They sat down at a spot from which they could look out over the ship-speckled sea, soaking its rim in the vast impenetrable horizon.

Len felt intoxicated with the scene and the proximity of Mary, who sat clasping her knees and staring into the distance. The heat rose in little hazy bubbles before his eyes. It oozed into his body, and he started to speak, but closed his mouth before uttering a word. Turning on his side, he looked at Mary. Her profile was straight and delicate, reminding him of pictures he had seen in books. Without turning her head she remarked, each word like a soft tinkle of a bell in his ears: 'Isn't it lovely here? The world is a beautiful place, and worth living in after all.'

The last phrase startled Len for a moment.

'Why do you say "after all"?' he asked.

She made no reply, and Len, rising from her side, crawled on his knees until he was facing her. He looked deep into her eyes and brought them back from the limitless distance which had for the moment stolen her from him. He saw his own eyes look back at him from hers, and his bones turned to liquid and his muscles to steel. He leaned sharply forward, his face slightly moist, his body vibrating.

'Mary,' he said, and in his voice was the essence of his desires. 'Mary, dear, why do you lose yourself outside a world which you say is good to live in?' But before she had time to answer, he rushed on as if each word spontaneously gave birth to a hundred others. 'The world is beautiful, my dear, because of the people, the children. Because of you.' A slow blush dyed his face, as Mary looked at him. The sunbeams in her hair burned Len's body through his eyes. Something hard and impelling quivered in his nerves, and taking hold of her hands, he drew them from her knees, disarranging her skirt as he did so. He squeezed the thin, delicate hands to his chest, which heaved spasmodically in the tumult of his emotions.

'Mary, my love,' he whispered, 'I want you.'

She did not answer, but lay back upon the long grass that curled around her. Len looked down on her, his eyes stripping her body of its garments, and tiny bubbles of froth gathered at the corners of his mouth. His elbows either side of her head, he lay on her body, his own vibrant with desire.

His voice was low and husky when he whispered: 'You are my love. Now I know what has been tormenting me. I am not complete without you. I want to squeeze you to my body, into my heart, until we become one.'

His hand stole slowly to her blouse. He undid the buttons and thrust his hands through the opening until his fingers touched her flesh, and a tremor ran through him at the contact.

Mary looked at him with dilated eyes. His pulsing fingers sent trickling electric currents racing over her, and slowly, like a thief before a newly-opened safe, his hand crept forward until it closed on her breast. She gave a momentary sigh, closed her eyes, then sprang up at the burning touch, rolling him to one side. Panting for breath, she allowed the sun to kiss away the burn of Len's hand as, unwilling to release what it had found, it drew her bosom free from its sheltering blouse. The pink, crustling nipple made him giddy, but as he leaned towards it, she halted him.

'I'm sorry, Len,' she said quietly, in spite of the throb in her voice. 'It was all my fault. I shouldn't have forgotten and led you on. Forgive me and forget if you can that I have been so foolish.'

Len looked at her amazed. 'But you've done nothing,' he exclaimed. 'If there is anyone to blame it is me. But I don't see what wrong we have done. Oh, Mary, why do you turn from me like this? I'm sure you loved me for a moment just now. Then you break from me as if you were snapping a chain. I can't help wanting you. It's no disgrace, unless,' he added quickly, as if the thought had suddenly leapt to his mind, 'unless you don't think I am good enough for you.'

Mary started. Slowly she covered the taunting breast before looking him in the eyes.

'Len, if you want to remain friends with me, you must never say that again. You were born to our valley and are one of our people, therefore you are good enough for anyone.'

Len started to apologise, but she waved his words aside and continued: 'In this world there are many reasons why we must sometimes crush back our desires. As long as my father lives, I belong to him and he belongs to the people. And if that isn't enough,' she burst out with a sob, 'feel this.'

She caught his hand savagely and placed it on her chest beneath her bosom. He felt the cavity beneath the loose skin, and her ribs were sharp under his fingers.

Without removing his hand, he looked into her face. His eyes were soft with unshed tears, but the tumult of his emotion was quieted and his voice was calm and soothing when he said, 'I understand, dear. Don't let that worry you. Instead of carrying the horrible burden by yourself, we can carry it together. People have got better, although they had the same thing as you. We must try to make you well.'

His voice failed and he could say no more. Silently he circled her head with his free arm and drew it down until his lips were pressed to hers. Gently, without passion, he kissed her, all his body melting into the caress. And when he released her, he saw little shining imps playing happily in the depths of her eyes.

They rose, and sauntered, arm-in-arm like a pair of children, back to the crowded town, and for the remainder of the day they were inseparable.

They heard the paper-boys shouting the news, but they paid little attention. It was only in the train that they learned from the other passengers that Germany had forced Britain to declare war in defence of Belgium, and though everyone was excited, it was the general opinion that it would be a very short one.

The journey back was slow and tedious. On innumerable occasions the excursion train was shunted into sidings or held up in other ways for hours, while trains full of khaki-clad men were given the right of way.

The sight of these men, shouting and singing, stirred something in the hearts of most of the people in the carriage, except a short man with bright eyes and black, bushy hair, who had sat quietly in the corner throughout the heated discussions that had raged in the carriage. Looking out of the carriage window at a passing troop train, he murmured audibly: 'Poor boys. Food for the guns.'

Everyone in the carriage stared at him, and he began to address the carriage in general. 'Those men, now singing and happy in the belief they are going to have an extended holiday, will soon be lumps of clay rotting in the soil of a foreign land.'

A member of the Circle challenged him heatedly. 'Don't you think it right,' he asked, 'that Britain should go to the defence of a little country that is being trampled underfoot by one of the greatest military powers in the world? Don't you think it is the duty of Britons to defend those weaker than herself from the jack-boots of militarism?' He looked around triumphantly when he finished, as if saying: 'That's taken the old geezer down a peg or two and put him in his place.'

Len, though he was deeply interested, said nothing. With the others in the compartment, he felt that the Government could do nothing other than declare war in the circumstances that had been forced upon it. He instinctively believed in the altruistic motives of the Government and thought it only right that England should put a stop to the challenging Germans. In common with most of his own age, he had been taught to despise the Germans as a sly, jack-booted people who spent most of their time hatching plots and spying upon other countries. He was therefore inclined to agree with the second speaker, but no more was said on the subject.

When they arrived in the valley they found it full of excited, gesticulating people, and during the following week nothing was talked of but the war. The pits became battlegrounds. The police station was turned into a recruiting office. All reservists were called to the colours, and they left the valley in a special train, to the sound of band music and cheers. The streets were decorated with bunting and house windows were plastered with cheap, gaudy prints of the foremost generals.

Shortly after the declaration of war, Big Jim and his cronies sat drinking in the Boar's Head. Jim retailed tales of the Boer War, painting a romantic, glamorous picture of the campaign.

Dai Cannon in a surly voice asked, 'If it was so nice

and cushy as that, why the hell don't you join up now?'

Jim, already half drunk, sprang to his feet, shouting, 'Think you I be 'fraid to fight measly, square-head Shermans? If so, Dai, you make a bloody mistake, muniferni. Huh! One Englishman be worth ten of the bleeders. But there,' he questioned sadly, 'what can you 'spect from a man who is forced to fight? That is the beauty of our country,' he continued, 'only those who do want to fight is taken.'

The other men joined in the argument, one of them remarking, 'Ay, boys. After all, our little country is still the best of the bunch. If Big Jim do think it worth fighting for, I be with him.' Dai felt the tide against him and said no more. Actually he felt rather sorry he had spoken at all, because he knew his words had put into Jim's head an idea the latter would surely carry out.

And sure enough, later that night Jim and four of his drinking pals marched arm-in-arm down the street towards the police station. The constable on duty nervously jumped to his feet at the intrusion. He was alone, and feared their intentions. In a conciliatory manner he asked: 'Hallo, boys, what do you want here this time of the night? Not lodgings, I suppose?' He laughed at his own wit, and the others joined in.

When the laughter had subsided Jim said, 'No. We be not come here for lodgings. Ha-ha. We be come to fight for our King and country.'

The policeman immediately grasped the situation.

'Sit down for a minute,' he invited. 'The recruiting sergeant will soon be back. He is only just gone down the road a little way.'

Jim and his mates seated themselves on the bench while Jim regaled them with reminiscences of the numerous nights he had spent in different cells in all parts of the world.

A considerable time passed before the recruiting sergeant returned. When he at last entered, he was staggering a little and his face was flushed. He sat heavily and suddenly in the nearest chair and commenced to snore immediately. The constable leaned over him and whispered something in his ear, shaking him at the same time and bringing him to his feet with a jerk.

'Eh?' he gasped, while his bleary eyes roved the room. 'Men want to join the army of Hish Majeshty the King? Where are they?'

He caught sight of Jim and his pals, and strode unsteadily towards them. 'By Christ,' he shouted, 'what splendid figures of men! The King will be glad to see you, boys. I suppose, like all the others, you want to be in the same crush. Good. I'll see to that. Now come over here so that I can fill in particulars.'

The men followed him, Big Jim in the lead. The latter was the first to be questioned.

'What's your age?'

'Thirty-two.'

'Eh? I asked your age, not the size of your waist.'

'Don't bloody shout at me,' yelled the irate Jim, 'and don't you dare to call me a liar, butty. Don't forget I have seen more service than you have seen years. I was fighting and dying for my country when you was hanging to your mother's tits.'

This outburst cooled the sergeant a little.

'All right, mate,' he said pacifyingly, 'don't take no offence at me.'

Some time later all the men were signed up, given a shilling each, and informed they would receive instructions. Jim went jubilantly up the hill to Sunny Bank, where Siân and Len were awaiting him. They heard him singing before they heard the rattle of the latch. He came in beaming, lifted Siân in his arms and danced a crazy jig round the small kitchen. Siân struggled strenuously and forced him to put her down, then stood for some moments gasping for breath. Jim turned his attention to the silent Len.

'Well, boy bach,' he said, 'proud you ought to be this night with your old dad.'

For a moment Len did not grasp what he was saying, but Siân, as if sensing what was coming, stared at Jim with wide-open eyes.

'Proud? Why proud?' she asked suddenly.

'Well, my gel,' he answered sheepishly, taken aback somewhat by her evident lack of enthusiasm, "in't it something to be proud of that your old man have joined up to fight for his King and country?'

Siân gave a cry and drew the hem of her canvas apron to her eyes.

'I knowed it,' she moaned. 'O God, why did I give you money to go out tonight?' Her voice broke in a sob. 'I ought to have knowed you would get drunk and do something daft.'

She turned on him fiercely. 'Don't you think a man of your age have got something better to do than to go traipsing round the world while I got to struggle by here alone to rear the children? What have the war got to do

329

with us?' she continued despairingly. 'We did not make it. Let those who did fight it out between themselves, not take men from their wives and children. All my life I have been tormented with you. First you run to the Boer War and leave me alone with little Jane bach, now in her grave, God bless her, and Len, by there. Now you are going to leave me again and go God knows where. Shame on you, James. How can you ever hope to find forgiveness at the hands of your Maker for doing such things? Sure as God is my judge, you will come to a bad end.'

She wept bitterly, wiping her dripping nose on the rough apron that left it red and chafed. Then she continued with greater vehemence, while Len and Jim looked on speechlessly: 'For King and country indeed! I have never seen no king, and the only country I know is inside the four walls of this house and between the three mountains of our valley. What have Belgiums got to do with us? I have never done nothing to them and they have never done nothing to me. And now my home is to be broken up again because him who did ought to be caring for me do think more of other people.'

She broke down completely and Len led her to the chair while Jim attempted to defend his action. 'Duw, duw, fenyw,' he said, 'haven't you got no heart, mun? If we don't stop those Shermans getting through little Belgium, mun, they will come over here sure as hell. And think what that will mean. Us 'ont have no homes then. We will have to go and live like dogs in the levels on the mountain-sides. Do you think I want you to go through that, Siân bach? No. I would sooner lie stiff and cold, with

330

ten bullets in my heart, than see any Sherman having you, 'nghariad bach i.'

This somewhat mollified Siân. Raising her red-rimmed eyes to his, she said, 'But, James bach, don't you think you have done enough? You did go all through the Boer War. What more can anybody want? Why don't you let the young men go?' she concluded.

Jim felt her last retort was unanswerable until he caught sight of the whitening face of Len, who had not missed the significance of his mother's words. Siân sensed in a flash the error she had made. The lad's features looked drawn and haggard in the dim lamp-light. The words made him feel he had betrayed his mother, for if he had only joined up his father should have been forced to remain at home. He turned to Siân.

'I'm sorry, mam,' he said. 'If I had joined up, dad would have stopped at home. It's all my fault.' He looked into his mother's worried face. 'Don't nag him any more.' His head bent lower. Siân jumped to his side and pressed his head to her body.

'Don't you dare never again to say such a thing to your mother,' she scolded. 'Your dad is much more able than you to carry a gun and fight. He is used to it and his body is big enough to bring him back safe. Don't you worry your little head, Len bach, and don't pay any heed to my old tongue. It is like a snake's sometimes, but I don't mean half of what I do say. Huh. You join up, indeed,' she concluded, with a deprecating shrug that settled the matter in her mind.

Next day Big Jim's exploit was the talk of the pit. Will

331

Smallbeer snorted, 'Fitter if his son did the clean thing and let his poor ole man stop in the pit for a change.'

Len choked back the lump in his throat, but made no reply. Big Jim however, took up the challenge. Flinging his pick to the ground, he strode up the barry.

'Well,' he asked threateningly, 'what have you got to say about our Len?'

All the men in the barry stopped working in anticipation of some excitement. 'Nothing much,' replied Will. 'Only I do think it only fair that the young uns should have a go at this lot and not leave it to us old uns all the time.'

'What in hell be you talking about, mun?' was Jim's retort. 'You have never done any fighting in your bloody life. The only soldiering you have ever knowed is the militia. Bah! Toy soldiers! You don't know what you be talking about, and I be just as daft as you to waste my breath on you.' He spat heavily, and putting a huge lump of damp tobacco into his mouth, returned to his own place.

That evening Len hurriedly bathed and was preparing to leave the house when Siân stood with her back to the door.

'Where be you going?' she demanded, her voice quivering with dread.

Len looked at her a moment in surprise before he realised the reason for her fear.

'Don't worry, mam,' he reassured her, 'I am only going up to Ezra's house. Before I ever do what you are thinking I will be man enough to come to you and tell you first.'

Swallowing her tears, the distracted woman withdrew from the door, warning him: ''Member now, Len bach, not to be late. I will be waiting for you.'

Len proceeded direct to Ezra's house. Both Ezra and Mary were in. The former looked anxious and worried, but nothing was said until the usual cups of tea were ready and Mary took her seat near the fire. Since the eventful day at Blackpool the young people had seen very little of each other, although both instinctively felt they were in the other's thoughts. Mary opened the subject first.

'It seems,' she said, 'the war can't last a long time with the number of men that are joining the forces. Oh,' she added impulsively, 'I wish I were a man and able to go.'

Len felt the blood rush in waves to his head. He became momentarily giddy, then pulled himself together as Mary's voice seemed to come to him from a distance. 'How splendid it must feel to fight for something that is good and honourable, to fight in defence of someone weaker than yourself.' She looked at Len and stopped when she saw the agony in his face.

'What's the matter?' she asked solicitously. 'Are you ill, Len?'

Ezra glanced up from his brooding at this remark. Before he could say anything Len spoke in a quiet, strained voice.

'I came to you tonight to help me. I feel I have been a great coward. My father has joined the army and everyone is now looking at me as if I'd committed a crime, but I'm not a coward,' he cried hysterically. 'I didn't know what my father intended doing; if I did I would have gone before him. I know that Mary is right when she says that all the young men are joining up, but what can I do?' he asked helplessly looking from one to the other. 'Dad is going this week. If I go as well, my mother will be left

333

alone and she will break her heart.' He turned and spoke directly to Mary. 'Tell me. What am I do to? You say you glory in someone who fights in defence of one weaker. I am ready to fight for you or my mother, but,' he added in bewilderment, 'I don't see you in any danger from the war.'

Ezra looked at him in sudden surprise, but Len hurried on, his words bubbling over each other.

'I don't want to go to the war, although I know I ought to. I hate brutality. It hurts me to see men wilfully maiming each other for no purpose.'

The silence of the other two oppressed him. He asked a straight question to both.

'Do you believe I should kill men I have never seen?'

Ezra hesitated a moment, then replied with another question. 'You say you detest physical violence, Len, but what do you think strikers should do to blacklegs who insist on attempting to break their strike? Take our own strike, for instance,' he added. 'Do you think our men did wrong? Or, again, were our men who fought in the riots wrong when they used physical force and violence to defend themselves?'

Len felt himself in a trap and turned his eyes mournfully to Mary.

'What am I to say?' he asked. 'Of course our men were right in what they did.' Then he added more brightly, as if struck by an afterthought. 'But it was different then. We could see them face to face. Now we are asked to kill men we have never seen and never known.'

He swallowed hard, and Ezra interjected: 'Yes. Isn't it better that we should stop those who want to do harm, before they come here to do it? Isn't it better to stop blacklegs leaving their own homes than it is to fight them on our own doorstep? Not that I believe in war,' he went on hastily. 'In my mind most wars are made by competing capitalist nations, but this time there can be no doubt that we have to defend our own country against a set of capitalists who are more brutal than our own. When a country violates treaties she has solemnly entered into, Len, then we have no choice but to teach her a lesson.' He closed his mouth with a snap.

Len had a deep underlying feeling that the arguments were not real, but he could find no words to express his doubt. His mind wavered, but it seemed to him that Ezra's words were so logical that they were unanswerable, and he bent his head low.

'All right, I'll join up tomorrow.'

Mary started to her feet, but he was gone before she could say anything.

Pain tugged at Len's heart the remainder of that night. His vivid imagination took him to the battlefields even before he had volunteered. Before going to bed he told Siân there was no need to call him for work in the morning. The startled woman looked up from her supper.

'Not going to work?' she inquired, her voice echoing the mental anxiety that immediately gripped her. 'For why be you not going to work, Len bach? Be you bad?'

Len shook his head sadly. 'No, mam bach,' he said, not daring to look her in the eyes. 'I am all right.' His shoe scraped awkwardly on the floor. 'I am going to join up tomorrow.'

Siân gave a little scream and jumped from the table. She staggered to the foot of the stairs and shouted hysterically.

'James, James. Come down quick as you can. Something awful have happened to our Len.'

There was a quick scamper in the bedroom overhead and in a moment Jim rushed down the stairs. He arrived in the kitchen with his trousers in his hand, his short, flannel shirt barely reaching his knees.

'What's the matter?' he growled.

Siân sat in the armchair sobbing. Len replied for her.

'Nothing much, dad; only I'm joining up tomorrow.'

Jim stopped pulling the trousers over his bare legs.

'What?' he shouted. 'Tell me what you be saying again, boy.'

Siân looked up at the tone of his voice. 'That will do, James,' she said sharply, while the tears rolled unheeded down her drawn cheeks. 'Don't you shout at the boy like that; he is not a dog.'

Jim looked from one to the other in amazement, then finished putting on his trousers, grunting to himself the while. Siân began to moan.

'Not enough for me to lose my gel and then to get my man to leave me for the sodgers once again, but now I have got to lose my son. O dear God! Pity you did not take me to the grave when you did take Jane and her baby bach. My life have been nothing but work and misery ever since I did first come to know James. Better if I had died in my poor mother's arms before I see the light of day.' She sprang to her feet, shouting to Len. 'But you shan't go. You are not twenty-one yet, and the law do say I have got control over you till then.'

At the look in Len's eyes, she started to wheedle. 'Why for do you want to leave your mam by herself in her old age, Len bach? Have I not been a good mother to you? Haven't I worked my fingers to the bone to put food in your little belly? Haven't I often gone without a shimmy to my back to rear you 'spectable and clean?' She hesitated as her love conquered her self-pity. 'You can't go!' she exclaimed. 'You aren't strong enough to be put about like your father. You have always been a delicate child. Three months of sodgering will kill you. You won't have a nice soft bed to yourself in the army. No, you will have to sleep with bad men and drunkards who do not know what a decent home is. You won't have your mother to get up at four o'clock in the morning to light the fire for you and warm your pants before you come down.' She exhausted herself and wept quietly in the corner.

Jim took up the cudgels. 'Your mother's right,' he said. 'The army is no good to boys like you. You have got to be strong and tough, like me, to stick it. And, mind you, once you jib in the army you are finished, because the men will make your life not worth living. You stop at home, my boy. If there is any fighting to be done, Big Jim will do it for you. I am used to it. You listen to me. Your old man won't tell you wrong.'

Len wilted at the pathetic attempts to win him from his resolution. His heart responded to all they had said, but his mind was made up. Mary's silence when her father had challenged him had been the deciding factor, stronger even than the loneliness he felt when he saw all the other

337

young men of his own age leave the valley for the war.

'Your words grieve me,' he said to his parents. 'But I must go. Everyone else is already gone and very soon people will be calling me a coward, as Will Smallbeer did today.'

'Who the hell is Will Smallbeer, anyhow?' broke in Jim. 'He have never done any real sodgering in his bloody life. It do only prove what I have always believed. If there is any killing to be done, let the old uns go first; they can be spared better and they won't be missed so much.' His big, thickly veined hands clenched. 'Don't worry about a useless old snot like him, Len boy. 'Member I have joined up for you, and if you go now it do mean that you let your father down.'

This new line of action galvanised Len.

'What?' he shouted. 'Do you mean that you joined up so that I could stop at home?'

'Ay, of course,' answered Jim without hesitation.

Len persisted. 'Tell me the truth, dad, did you and the other boys join up when you was all drunk?'

Jim struck a dignified posture. 'I never thought,' he said reproachfully, 'that I would ever rear a son who would tell me to my face that I be a liar, and that Big Jim do not know what he be doing after he have had a pint or two.' He sighed deeply as if the thought were too heavy a burden to bear.

Siân came to his rescue. 'That be it, Len bach,' she said excitedly, ignoring the latter part of Jim's statement. 'Your father did join the sodgers for you to stop at home. It wouldn't be fair for the two of you to go, and the gov'ment ought to be satisfied with one of you. There now, let's leave the nasty old business there. Come to bed and forget all about it, Len.'

Each argument they adduced strengthened Len's belief that he had no business in the war, but he was too weak to face up to the situation that would follow his refusal to volunteer. He pulled off his boots and made for the bedroom, saying, 'It's no good, mam and dad. I have got to go. Perhaps you will understand one day.'

Next day he found that his father also had remained from work. The only reply Len received to his query on the matter was a brief, 'I be coming with you, Len, to see fair play. If you are bound to go, then you must come in the same crush as me, so that I can look after you.'

Shortly after breakfast both men presented themselves before the recruiting sergeant at the police station. A long queue of other young men was there before them, and they waited their turn, Len listening vaguely to the conversations taking place around him. He knew practically all the men and marvelled at their breezy nonchalance, on the verge of what they regarded as a new life, but for himself he was nervous and fidgety. Eventually he and Jim were welcomed by the doctor who had attended Jane before she died. The sight of him brought sudden tears to Len's eyes.

The office was crowded with young men, many of whom were stark naked. Len's mind revolted at what he saw and heard. The recruiting sergeant, with a satisfied smirk, brought him back to the work in hand with the words: 'Ah, a fine young man! I can see now you are going to be a credit to the forces.' He asked Len for his name, age, and address, then handed the lad over to the doctor, who curtly bade him undress. Len unconsciously looked around the crowded room as if mutely asking for some privacy, but no one took any notice of his appeal, and he began to strip. The doctor kept him waiting a while, then thumped his body about, and after a lengthy examination, grunted to the sergeant, 'No good. Cardiac and traces of lung trouble.'

In a maze and hardly knowing what he did or what was happening around him, Len dressed and went out with his father. He felt a sudden despair tear at him, for he was the only one among all those he knew who had been turned down. His repugnance of the army suddenly evaporated and he wanted, more than anything, to become a soldier with the others. A strong feeling of inferiority began to consume him as he walked slowly, without a word, back up the hill to Sunny Bank.

Jim broke the news to the weeping Siân, who had not moved from her chair since they had left the house. Her eyes immediately brightened up and a soft smile played around the corners of her mouth.

'I knowed it,' she said triumphantly. 'Something told me they wouldn't take my boy away.'

'Huh,' grunted Jim. 'You can thank me for that. If I did not give a tip to the doctor he would have passed the boy all right, never fear.'

Both Len and Siân knew he lied, but neither contradicted him. That night in bed Len wept tears of sheer impotence. He wondered what Ezra and Mary would think of him, and pictured the valley denuded of all young men except himself, scorned and despised by the women and the older people. For the first time the glamour of the war began to grip him. He imagined himself performing valiant deeds that won Mary's approbation and the applause of all the people. He felt himself an outcast, and his old taciturnity grew on him again.

Before the week was out, Jim and his mates were called up. After the leave-taking in their separate homes, they proceeded to the Boar's Head, where they all got drunk before making their way to the railway station. Even the staunchest adherents of the chapels gave them bright greetings as they made their way singing and staggering down the hill. Len, however, did not accompany his father. He could not bear a parting in which he thought he should have been the central figure, so having bade his father 'Goodbye and good luck' in the house, he went up the mountain and for hours wandered there aimlessly, like a person who has lost all interest in life and merely drifts on.

The days that followed were like a nightmare to him. The newspapers published reports of the horrible atrocities being committed by the Germans, and his blood ran cold when he read in one account that they had crucified a baby to a door. But the horror that filled him was turned to rage when he read later that the Germans were slicing the breasts off the living bodies of the Belgian women they captured.

One morning Mr. Hicks rode to the colliery yard and called upon all the men below the age of forty – he was forty-one himself – to join the colours and avenge the atrocities.

Scores of men responded to the appeal, marching down the hill behind Mr. Hicks, and next day a recruiting office was opened at the end of the bridge leading to the colliery.

The following Sunday the big theatre was taken over for

341

a recruiting meeting. Len was drawn to this like a fly to a web. All the week the streets and the pits were buzzing with talk of the revelation of atrocities and cruelties that were going to be made. Huge placards covered the hoardings and sidings of the valleys, and empty trams came down the pits with chalked slogans advertising the meeting.

When Len arrived a long queue was already formed half-way up Main Street. He noticed Mary, who beckoned him beside her. They found the huge theatre a mass of flaunting Union Jacks, and photographs of stern-looking men in military uniforms. On the platform were a well-known Trade Union official in the uniform of an officer, a short, fat, clean-shaven man who edited a famous journal and was later imprisoned for swindling, the bishop in his robes, Mr. Evans Cardi, a few local preachers, the vicar from the church, Lord Cwmardy, Mr. Hicks, and some military officers, together with a man in a blue-flannel nondescript uniform who had been brought specially from the military hospital a hundred miles away to be presented at Cwmardy as one of the first heroes wounded in the war.

The meeting opened with the singing of the National Anthem. When this was over the Trade Union official stepped to the front of the stage.

'Men and women of the valley,' he said, swelling out his chest, 'I want you to show our distinguished visitors how you can sing the ancient hymns of Wales. Put your hearts into "Hen Wlad Fy Nhadau", boys.' He began the tune himself, his beautiful voice filling the hall and stirring the audience into emulation. At its conclusion Mr. Hicks and Ezra stepped forward as joint chairmen of the meeting, and

342

the latter having outlined the procedure, continued:

'I am on this platform today not because I believe in war but because I believe in right. When right is threatened, then we are justified in using might to protect it. If this were a war of aggression on our part I should oppose it with all the strength in my power, but as a man and a worker who has suffered, I cannot stand aside and see all the democratic traditions for which men have died being trampled underfoot by unscrupulous rulers of other nations. If the people of these nations cannot see how they are being misled, and take up arms at the behest of their rulers, then our reply must be sharp and emphatic. For every one of them who takes up arms against right and justice, we must have two to defend it.'

When the cheering had subsided, Ezra called on the editor to address the meeting. 'You have all heard or read of our famous friend,' said Ezra in his introductory remarks. 'Therefore I have no need to explain who he is, other than to say that his fearless exposition through his journal of all that is unfair and unjust demands the appreciation of every decent man and woman of our valley.'

The fat man stepped forward to a storm of applause. His greasy face shone in the glare of the footlights and his breath came in wheezy gasps from the strain imposed on his over-full paunch.

'Ladies and gentleman,' he said, wisely clearing his throat, 'I am indeed pleased to know my little efforts in the sacred cause of humanity are appreciated by you. Today that humanity is in the melting-pot. An octopus of horror creeps over the world in the guise of men. Heartless monsters rape the virgin soil of Europe with obscene jack-booted feet. Today our country is called upon to defend humanity, to defend righteousness, and all that is good and pure from the onslaught of Hunnish barbarians. I have come specially this night with proof of every word I utter.'

He kept on for an hour retelling tales of torture and lust inflicted on innocent people by the Germans. His eyes glistened and his jelly-like flesh quivered in an ecstacy produced by his own words and thoughts. The speech lifted the men and women in the meeting to a pitch of furious indignation. Howls of execration and sharp cries of bitterness and hate filled the hall as he unfolded horror after horror.

Mr. Hicks took the chair at the conclusion of the speech and immediately called upon Lord Cwmardy. The latter made a brief statement during which he remarked, 'All those of you employed in the pits of my company – and that means all the pits in the valley,' he added as an aside which met with responsive applause – 'well, those of you, I repeat, who do your duty to your King and your country in this time of common danger and crisis need have no worries about your homes. More than this, every man who leaves my pits for the war will have his place in that pit sacredly safeguarded, so that when he returns home he can step back into his work as if he never left it.' A storm of clapping greeted him at the end of the speech.

The trade union leader was next called upon. Solemnly holding himself as erect as possible in his uniform and holding the sword with untrained hand to his side, he marched to the front of the stage to the accompaniment of wild cheers. The people rose to their feet, singing and shouting. Red-faced and awkward, the speaker waited until the tumult had subsided before saying, slowly at first, then with increasing tempo: 'Men and women of this glorious valley, the civilisation and freedom built up by the untold sacrifices of the forefathers of our land is being menaced by the iron heel of war and destruction. The whole world today is looking at our country, and every eye in the country is looking at this valley. Shall it ever be said that, for the first time in our history, we have been found wanting? I say no, a thousand times no. Our nation is today united as it has never been before. All sections are blended in the common desire to save democracy in the name of our holy God. Tonight on this platform you see with me Lord Cwmardy, my Lord the Bishop, and the other good friends. What is is that has brought me, a true son of the people, into the same harness as those we used to think our enemies? It is the common human urge, my friends, to sink our petty little quarrels when the cause of justice and freedom is threatened. After all, when danger threatens it is then we realise that we are all brothers. Tonight, in humbleness and sincerity, I am asking every one of you who is eligible to join up with me. Let me lead you on the battlefield as I have led you at home. I do not ask any of you to do what I am not prepared to do myself. The King has graciously given me a commission, not in honour to myself, but in honour to you whom I represent. "Go," said His Majesty to me, "back to those wonderful people in your vales and in your pits. Tell them the Empire is calling them to its defence." Yes, friends, our empire, our country, our homes are in danger. Who will follow me in defence of all they love and hold dear?'

His voice lifted into a dramatic tension on this last appeal.

For a moment there was breathless silence, then a roar of 'I will' surged through the hall as a mass of men rushed down the aisle towards the platform. In a second the recruiting sergeant, blazoning with medals, sprang from the wings to the stage. The bishop beckoned to Mr. Hicks, who, after a few whispered words, walked to the edge of the platform and held up his hand. It was several minutes before a measure of calm asserted itself and the long line of men on their way to the stage halted.

'Hem,' began Mr. Hicks, 'our bishop thinks that so solemn an occasion should not be allowed to pass without thanking the Lord for putting courage into the hearts of these men who are now ready to defend the faith and asking Him to extend to them His grace.'

All present bowed their heads while the bishop stuttered a prayer interspersed with hiccoughs. This over, Mr. Hicks proceeded, 'As our men are joining up in the army of justice and truth, it is the bishop's wish we should give praise by singing the hymns "Onward Christian Soldiers" and "Abide with Me".'

The trade union leader lifted his voice in the opening notes, and as everyone took up the hymn, the men were swept towards the recruiting sergeant who, sweating and silently swearing, took their names and addresses. He was overcome by the numbers and called upon the other people on the platform to help him. Before the meeting concluded, Lord Cwmardy again walked to the front of the stage.

'It is fitting,' he announced, 'that I should report that five hundred and ten men have volunteered in this meeting to enter battle on the side of the just and the right.'

Both Mary and Len were overcome by the fervour of the whole proceedings. The lights, emphasising the glamorous colours of the decorations, seemed to dance in the vibrations of the mass singing and swept the people forward on waves of hysterical emotion.

LEN WORKS
FOR PEACE

When Len returned home he missed his father from the usual chair and, without thinking, asked Siân: 'Where's dad, then? He's late tonight, i'n't he?'

Siân looked hard at him for a moment, then began to cry. Len realised his mistake and tried to soothe her. But to no avail.

'Your dad be gone, Len bach,' she moaned. 'Perhaps he will never come back to us. The good Lord alone knows what he have gone for. I don't. They do say the Shermans are cruel. Perhaps they be; I don't know. But wasn't our own sodgers cruel that night they did shoot down our men for nothing? Them was supposed to be our own flesh and blood, but that did make no difference. When their guns went "bang", our men did drop just as sure as if it was Sherman guns.' She lapsed into silence, but her words brought Len back to himself.

The vague revolt in his heart seemed to find a focus-point in her words. He began to wonder vaguely how the country could be in danger when the supposed enemy was the other side of the water. He brought back to mind incidents he had witnessed during the strike, and pondered the difference in men when they wore different clothes. He thought to himself that his mother was right when she questioned the distinction between English bullets fired at Englishmen and German bullets fired at Belgian people. He was not quite clear or fixed, but nevertheless he was beginning to find a mental balance.

In the weeks that followed he came to see the situation more clearly, and he was helped by a lecturer who came to the Circle to explain what the war meant. The lecturer stated it was a difference between robber states, each of whom was intent upon exploiting its own people and each other. He used the words 'cannon-fodder' and this reminded Len of the dark-haired man on the excursion train. The lecture as a whole made a great impression upon Len's outlook, and a new vista of thought and understanding opened up before him. He learned that the young lecturer called himself a revolutionary and believed that nothing would come right until this revolution had taken place. He had heard of revolutions before, but never in such a positive way as that presented by the lecturer, and at the conclusion of the lecture he asked:

'What does the lecturer actually mean by the revolution? Does he mean that we have got to have civil war and slaughter each other?'

The lecturer smiled. 'Not quite so crude as that,' he answered. 'What I meant is that the workers will have to be armed in order to overcome the resistance of the capitalist class, who will never give up their power by peaceful measures. Even if we had a majority in Parliament,' he continued, 'the capitalists would use the armed forces of the State against the government of the day, if that government was against their interests.'

Len failed to see how this contingency could occur. He believed that the government was the final authority and that whatever measures it decided were final and binding upon everyone. He did not agree that it would be necessary to have a mass slaughter in order to maintain the conditions of the workers. He was appalled by the thought of his fellow countrymen doing to each other what they were all now doing to the Germans. But in spite of Len's opposition on this matter the lecturer had cleared, to a large extent, the fog of doubt which had assailed him in relation to the war.

Later in the evening John Library suggested that the Circle should organise a public meeting at which the lecturer could put his point of view against the war. This was enthusiastically agreed to, and Len and Mary were deputed to make the necessary arrangements. They failed to get the theatre for the meeting and had to content themselves with the huge baths that were hidden in a corner of the valley practically inaccessible after dark.

Len continued to ponder the problem of the war. He began to mentally query how Ezra could find it possible to stand on the same platform as Mr. Hicks and Lord

Cwmardy after all they had done against the workmen during the strike. In Len's mind nothing could wipe that out. He felt Ezra's action to be an insult to those victims of the soldiers' bullets who now lay resting in the cemetery. He kept brooding over the matter and thought to raise it with Mary. But he feared risking her displeasure, because he knew once the subject was broached it could only end in a condemnation of Ezra.

Despite his introspective doubts the arrangement for the public meeting went on apace. Mary painted attractive posters to advertise it, which Len pasted on the hoardings and the walls in the early hours of the morning.

Two days prior to the meeting Len received a message in the pit that Mr. Hicks would like to see him at the end of the shift. Throughout the remainder of the day Len wondered why he was wanted. He finished a little earlier than usual and was among the first to ascend the shaft. He proceeded directly into the colliery office, the lamp swinging on his belt.

Rapping on the inner door that led to Mr. Hicks' private room, he waited nervously. He heard a cough and a rustling of paper inside, followed by an authoritative 'Come in.'

Hesitantly Len opened the door and walked across to the smiling Mr. Hicks, seated at a desk in the centre of the room. He heard the door close behind him and glanced around abruptly. The police inspector, his back to the door, stood facing him, and Mr. Hicks greeted him with the remark: 'Well, my boy, how are things with you? I hear you have a pretty good place now.'

Len nodded without saying a word.

'Hemm,' went on Mr. Hicks, 'I am glad to hear that, because nothing pleases me more than to know that my men are contented. By the way,' he added, 'I understand you are one of the youngest men we have working a place of his own.'

This pulled Len together. 'That may be so,' he answered, 'but I don't think it necessary to call me into the office specially to tell me that, Mr. Hicks.'

'Quite so, quite so,' commented the latter. 'As a matter of fact,' he added, 'I didn't send for you for that purpose at all. Inspector Price would like to have a chat with you.'

Len turned to the huge man who was now sitting on the chair near Mr. Hicks.

'Yes,' said the Inspector. 'Just a few words, Len, without prejudice to anyone. They tell me that you were a pretty big figure during the strike.'

Len did not reply, and the other went on as if he had made no pause. 'Yes. I was told you did a lot of things then that in ordinary times some of us would have to take notice of. But we must let bygones be bygones, eh? Now, what I want to speak to you about is this meeting I'm told you have in the Baths next Sunday. Something to do with the war, isn't it?' Len made no answer, but the reason for his summons to the office slowly dawned on him.

'Well, well,' went on the Inspector, 'fancy you mixing up with things like that, Len. Indeed, I'm surprised at you. I'm sure your mother would be shocked to know your intentions, especially when your father is risking his life at the front to defend all the good things you are now enjoying.'

Len could stand it no longer, his blood was at boiling-point.

'Look here,' he burst out, 'what are you driving at, Inspector? Why don't you tell me straight what you have got in your mind instead of beating about the bush like this?'

The Inspector was taken aback for a moment, but soon regained his urbane equanimity.

'Yes, that's it,' he said quietly. 'Let's have it straight, and here it is. A young man like you, working in a good place with good money, while men old enough to be your father are fighting and dying, has a right to ask for things straight. But,' he flashed out, 'they should not have the right to organise meetings for the purpose of spreading sedition and adding further danger to those now fighting. One would think that a man like you would be satisfied to skim the cream off the good things other men die to give you.'

Len went white. He tried to stutter a reply, but the Inspector hurried on, his voice getting louder and more threatening with each word.

'You ought to be damn well ashamed of yourself, skulking here at home when you should be carrying a gun in defence of your country!'

Len braced himself. 'What about yourself?' he retorted. 'You are bigger and more able than I am to carry a gun and you are much younger than my father, who is already there. I tried to join in the first week, but they refused to accept me because of my heart and chest.'

His effrontery infuriated the Inspector, who sprang to his feet and shouted:

'You bloody little whippersnapper, how dare you talk to me like that? For two pins I'd make you glad to stop in bed for a month!'

354

Len cowered before the huge, raised fist, but the Inspector recovered himself before the blow fell, and Mr. Hicks drew him to a corner of the room out of Len's hearing. For some minutes they talked rapidly, and when they returned to their places both were smiling again.

'Excuse me losing my temper, Len,' said the Inspector. 'I have not been too well lately and my temper is a bit short. Actually I have taken a liking to you. I wouldn't, for instance, like to see Mr. Hicks throw you out of a good place because you are mixed up with a gang who are using you for their own purpose. No,' he went on, 'nor would I like see the military authorities grabbing you in spite of your health and drafting you straight to the war with very little training. Think, Len. If you carry on with this meeting you will only land yourself in trouble and I won't be able to help you. Remember, I cannot be responsible for anything that happens in the meeting if you persist in it.'

No more was said, but Len understood what was implied. He turned and left the room, his heart throbbing against his ribs. In his perturbation and excitement he could not even wait to go home and bath before seeing Mary, but went straight to her house. She gave a little gasp of surprise when she saw his blackened face and pit clothes.

'Great Scott,' she exclaimed. 'Has anything serious happened, Len?'

'No, no,' he assured her hurriedly. 'In any case, nothing very serious, but something very important.'

She led the way to the kitchen without another word and laid an old newspaper on a chair for him to sit on. Gingerly seating himself, Len related all that had transpired.

Mary listened in silence. When he had finished, she paced the kitchen agitatedly.

'I never thought of such a thing,' she murmured. 'They as good as called you a traitor to your country, Len, if you continued with the meeting.'

'Ay. But they did more than that, Mary. They said that you and other members of the committee were bigger traitors than me and were using me for your own ends.'

This had not struck Mary until Len's words brought it to her mind with a jerk.

'No man can call me a traitor to my country,' she blurted out indignantly. 'I agreed to the meeting because I believe it fair that everyone should have the right to their opinion, even if it happens to be against my own. I believe in this war,' she continued more vehemently. 'Who can read of those poor babies and those helpless nuns being slaughtered by the Germans and think they shouldn't be stopped, whatever' – she quoted the next phrase from the recent speech of a famous statesman – 'whatever it may cost in blood or treasure?'

Her bosom rose and fell under the pressure of her emotions. Len felt her magnetic strength pull him, as it always did in moments of excitement, but he checked himself.

'I don't agree with you,' he said bravely. 'The Germans are only men like those who have gone from our pits to fight them. I can't believe that any men, whether they are Germans or no, can do the terrible things we read about.'

She turned on him with a sneer. 'Perhaps you think all the papers are saying lies, that all the preachers and parsons are liars, that only you yourself know what the truth is.' The pain that suddenly lined his face checked her. 'Think, Len,' she pleaded more softly, 'you saw that man in the meeting showing us photos and other proofs of what is being done.' She snatched a paper from the little sideboard as if she wanted to excuse her words yet convince him he was wrong. 'Look at this, where it says the Germans are boiling down the corpses of their own dead soldiers to make grease for the guns.'

Len looked and sickened. His faith in his own opinion wavered.

'Well,' he asked unsteadily, 'what shall we do about the meeting?' She hesitated to give a definite reply. Something told her she had been on the verge of appearing a coward in his eyes.

'Perhaps we had better wait till dad comes home,' she answered cautiously.

He assented, saying he would go home for dinner and bath and return when he was clean.

Mary's words had startled him, but even in the turmoil of conflicting thoughts he began to feel himself more strong and firm. He felt confidence and a determination welling up in him. The feeling was something new. Always, in the past, when he had been unable to answer arguments or solve problems he had capitulated either to Ezra or to Mary. Now he began to question earnestly whether he had been at fault in blindly following the opinions of others.

Siân met him at the door, her face was haggard and her eyes looked weary and heavy.

'No letter today again, Len bach.' Her voice had in it a

tone of hopelessness. 'Something must have happened to him. He have never kept me so long without writing before.'

Len tried to console her. 'It's all right, mam,' he said, although he hardly knew what to think himself at the fact that not a single letter had yet been received from Jim. 'There is nothing wrong with him. I expect they are pretty busy out there now and they haven't got much time for writing letters. You can venture, mam,' he added, 'if there was anything wrong we would hear quick enough.'

'Let's hope you are right. Many is the time I've nagged him over nothing,' she murmured, weeping softly into her apron.

Len did not take long bathing, and was soon back at Mary's house, where Ezra was already waiting.

'Well,' commenced the latter, when Len was seated, 'I understand you and Mary have been having a squabble over the war.'

'No, dad,' broke in Mary, 'I didn't say we had a row.'

'Well,' said Ezra, 'let's say you had a few words. Now let me see, as far as I can gather the police desire that your meeting on Sunday should be called off. You and Len disagree on this. I am of the opinion that the meeting, for Len's sake, should be abandoned. What is the position?' he continued. 'In the present state of public opinion any statement against the war, in which so many of the men from our own valley are engaged, would result in a riot. The people who would be held responsible for anything said would not be the ones who actually said them, but those who organised the meeting. Will Morris can say what he likes and get away back to his home, but you, Len, will have to remain here and face the music. No, apart from anything else, I think for your own safety you should call it off. You will understand that in these circumstances I can't allow Mary to risk being a party to this. I'm very serious about the whole matter, Len, and I hope you have sufficient faith to believe that what I'm telling you is for the best for everyone concerned.'

Len looked at him a moment, then turning his eyes to Mary, said to both of them: 'I think you are wrong. Although I don't know what it is and can't explain it, something inside me tells me that we must let the people know the two sides of the war. Wherever we turn now we only hear one side. Everybody is wrong and terrible and cruel except our own people. I can't believe this. There are bound to be some decent people among the Germans. We are told that they do this, that, and the other, but I can't forget what our own soldiers did to us during the strike. No,' he added, as if soliloquising with himself, 'I love and respect you both, but I can't do something which I don't believe to be right. I hope,' he pleaded 'you won't think any the less of me for this.'

A strangely warm light crept into Mary's eyes at the words, but neither she nor her father said anything more as Len, with downcast eyes and bent shoulders, made for the door.

The next evening Len saw John Library, and as a result of their chat went across the mountain to the other valley where Will Morris lived. The latter was very pleased to see him, and they discussed the meeting until late in the evening. When Len left it was dark as death, but he knew the mountain better than he knew his own mind and arrived home safely.

Siân's pain-shadowed eyes told him she had received no letter from Jim, but she made no remark while Len ate the frugal supper. When he had finished she asked him if he would wait in the queue for the pound of margarine ration allocated to them. Although he was tired and anxious to go to bed he immediately assented, and putting on his overcoat, he bade her good night. The night seemed blacker than ever as he made his way towards the main street. When he reached the general stores of Mr. Evans Cardi, some fifty or sixty men and women were already queued up. This was not the first time Len had kept the queue all night for his mother to get the rations in the morning. He sat on a window-sill tucking his arms round his chest to keep it warm. Soft snowflakes were beginning to spangle the black air, and seemed to quiver in the throb from the pits before they finally settled on the ground. Soon everyone in the queue was covered by a snowy surplice. Many of them had learned, after much practice, to fall asleep on their feet, but the cold that penetrated his clothes prevented Len from doing so. He shook the snow from his sodden garments and found its absence made him feel colder. His feet and face went numb, an excruciating pain gripped his toes and he felt the muscles of his face tighten into rigidity. He tried to loosen them by working his mouth, but a slow shiver spread from his legs until it seized his whole body. The pain became intolerable and he gave himself a vigorous shake, which sent pins and needles rushing through him. Clenching his teeth, he began rubbing his legs, but the damp cloth in contact with his flesh made him more uncomfortable than ever. He had an insane desire to leave the queue and go back home. He pictured the kitchen and its big fire warming the armchair, which had become his favourite seat since his father had gone to the war. The thought of a cup of hot, unsweetened tea and a slice of warm, unbuttered toast moistened his mouth and nearly drove him frantic. Unconsciously he moved forward, but with an effort of will he restrained himself, for he knew that if he returned home Siân would take his place in the queue.

Throughout the night he waited with the others. He started to count the minutes and dropped off into a standing, half-conscious doze in which he saw Mary looking at him from the curb, and at last, about five o'clock, Siân and other women came to relieve their men. Peering at every face, Siân eventually spotted Len sitting erect against the wet window-pane. She gave him a gentle shake.

'Come, Len bach,' she ordered. 'It's time for you to go back up the house and change for work. I have left the toast lovely and warm in the oven for you and the teapot is on the hob. All you got to do is put the water in it.'

Len felt unable to get up from the sill. He desired more than anything in the world to remain where he was without moving, and it required all his mental strength to drag his body away. His chest burned and thick mucus stuck in his throat. He coughed and spat it into the gutter.

'Take care of yourself, mam,' he bade her. 'Put the shawl over your head. Good morning.'

When he reached Sunny Bank his breath came in gasping sobs that hurt him. He thawed his body before the huge fire Siân had left him and drank the tea, but he could not eat the dry, toasted bread. It crumbled like dry sawdust in his mouth, nearly making him sick, and he spat out the half-masticated lump that looked like a black pebble in the grate. His shivering fingers drew on the pit clothes, disturbing the dry coal-dust on them, which blew about in a little thin cloud. Putting his hand in his trouser pocket he felt something squirm, and he pulled out a huge red cockroach, which he immediately threw on the fire. He gazed abstractedly at its brief, futile struggle and at the tiny green, crackling flame that forced its way with a hiss through the red glow, then stooping under the table he picked up his boots. Immediately there was a rush of squirming black beetles. The floor became black with them as they headed for their nests, and as Len squashed them with the heel of his boot, each blow made a wet-sounding squelch. He caught the broom from the corner and swept the black patches towards the grate, but their white entrails remained on the floor and he left these for his mother to remove.

Throughout the day he had to fight to keep his eyes open in the pit, afraid to sit down for dinner in case he fell asleep. Most of the other men in the barry were in the same predicament. His movements were those of an automaton, and at the end of the day he did not know how many trams he had filled or how much work he had done. He felt no desire to leave the pit, all he wanted was to lie down and sleep. Dragging his feet behind him, he followed the long trail of tired, silent shadows making for the pit bottom. The air on the surface, sweeping over the slushy black snow that covered the valley, revived him, and his feet became lighter as he hastened down the hill towards Sunny Bank.

Siân was sitting near the fire, her head bent on her hands, when he entered.

'Hullo,' he said in surprise. 'What's wrong, mam? Have you heard from dad?'

Without looking up she answered, 'No, Len bach. Not a word have I had from him yet.'

He tried to comfort her, but he felt himself a hypocrite and a liar even as the words passed his mouth. He knew that each morning she waited, full of forced, happy anticipation, for the sound of the postman's feet entering the street, that she followed each step with a bursting heart, her breath coming more quickly as he approached, but ceasing entirely for a moment as he passed the house. If he paused a moment for some reason outside the door she would quiver in a flutter of excited agitation, but when he passed her whole body would relax. Len knew that every woman in the street dreaded the sight of the old man who carried telegrams and that when he entered a street everyone was overcome with nervous anticipation.

Siân brought him from his thoughts.

'It is not that this time,' she said. 'You know I did take your place in the queue this morning. When half-past eight come, Mr. Evans pulled the shutters from his window and started to serve the people who was waiting. Before he had served half of us, he said that the food was nearly all gone and that he wouldn't be able to serve us all till more was sent in. Everybody did look stunned for a minute, then, before I knowed what was happening somebody behind gave me a push and in a flash everybody there was

363

pushing and shouting and rushing. Like wild animals they was, Len. I be 'shamed of them. They broke the window and stole ev'ry scrap that was in the shop.' The tears again filled her eyes.

'Never mind, mam annwyl,' soothed Len, 'We will manage somehow. Perhaps he will have some more rations in by tonight, and he is bound to give us what is coming to us on our ration cards.' Even while he spoke a pang of hunger tore at his stomach, giving him spasms of giddiness.

Siân looked up from her shawl. 'Oh, it's not so bad as that. When they did rush, I did not let them have all their own way. Oh no. I was never a woman to stand being pushed about. So I did push with them, and when they broke the window I was close enough to have this packet of saccharin and some margarine.'

Len smiled a little at her words and sat down to drink the potato soup she had made for his dinner. The saccharin made his tea sickly and left a bitter after-taste in his mouth, but it was better than no sugar or sweetening. On Siân's advice he ate dry bread, because she thought she had discovered a method of turning a small quantity of margarine into three times as much butter.

After Len had bathed he helped her bring out the large earthenware pan in which she made bread. She put the lump of margarine into this and poured about two quarts of milk on top of it, then stirred the mixture vigorously with the wooden spoon that she used to turn the clothes in the boiler. When her arm got tired and heavy she handed the spoon to Len, and for hours they kept this up, until at last Siân declared the flaccid, greasy-looking yellow mass in the pan was butter. Len was glad to hear this for his back felt as if it were broken and his arms were like lead.

The days that followed passed slowly. He heard no more from Mr. Hicks or the Inspector about the meeting, nor had he seen Mary since the day he declared his intention of carrying on. The arrangements were now completed and from scraps of conversation he picked up in the streets and in the pit he knew it would either be a packed meeting or that there would be so few present that it would have to be cancelled.

When the Sunday arrived, Len was quivering with excitement. He put on his best suit, which he had not worn since the excursion with the Circle, and in the late afternoon John Library and the speaker came to the house. Their appearance flustered Siân, who immediately began dusting the chairs with her apron, at the same time apologising because she had nothing nice in the house to offer them.

'But at the same time,' she averred, 'you are welcome to what ever we have got.'

The two men calmed her flurry and in a short time they rose and went off with Len to the meeting. When they arrived at the Baths they found the doors had been smashed in and that the huge place was packed to suffocation with a mass of people singing patriotic songs at the top of their voices, their faces hidden in a cloud of blue tobacco smoke.

John Library took the chair. His snowy white hair glistened in the light, throwing a dignified halo around his thin, austere face. Ben the Barber, whom they met near the entrance, insisted upon coming on to the platform, and just as Len was settling himself in the chair he heard a whispered voice calling his name from the front. His heart gave a leap as he peered through the smoke and saw Mary sitting in the front row of seats beckoning to him shyly. He quickly went towards her.

'Something forced me to come tonight,' she said softly, not looking at him. 'I felt I couldn't remain away and leave you fight this out alone, even though I still believe dad is right.'

Len caught her hand in his and pressed it to his chest, suddenly forgetting where he was and oblivious to everyone but himself and Mary. He tried to say something, but it stuck in his throat. Instead he bent his head and looked her straight in the eyes with a glance that burned into her consciousness the pleasure her presence and words had given him. But a cough from behind brought him back to the meeting, and he resumed his seat.

John, speaking quietly, opened the proceedings.

'Fellow working men and women,' he said, 'we are met here tonight to listen to a speech on a matter that concerns every one of us.' A deep silence of expectation fell over the audience at his first words. 'I know that in many parts of the country it would be very dangerous to hold a similar meeting to this and say what is going to be said here. But I have faith in the people of the valley. I believe that even in your sorrows and worries, even in your love for your country you are sensible enough to listen to every sincere point of view, even if that point of view should be opposed to yours at the moment. The strike has proven that there is a very strong sense of fair play among our people and that we always incline to take the side of the weak and defenceless. Already young Len here, who has done a lot to make this meeting a success, has been threatened by certain people. He has been told that if the meeting goes on he will lose his job in the pit, will be drafted, in spite of his health, to the war, and that possibly physical violence will be done to him.'

Loud cries of 'Shame' from all parts of the hall greeted this information, and John continued: 'I don't believe our boys across the water are fighting and dying for such things as that. They are there, rightly or wrongly is not for me to say, defending democracy and freedom, where every man has the right to his own opinions and liberty to express them. You will have noticed that not a single policeman is near our meeting tonight, whereas if it had been a meeting to recruit our boys to the war, they would be all over the place.' A gust of ironic laughter and shouts of 'That's so' swept the hall. 'But although they are not here in uniform,' continued the chairman, 'among us is a stranger in ordinary clothes who has been sent specially to take notes. We welcome him and hope he will put down what is actually said by the speaker and not what he would like the speaker to say.'

A thin thread of applause circled the audience when the black-haired young man with a cadaverous face and self-confident manner walked to the front. 'Comrades,' he said, 'I have been warned and advised that if I came here tonight it would be the last meeting I would ever speak at, and that I would be taken out feet first. If such is to be my fate, if I am to be maimed at the hands of my fellow workers, so be it. I shall be content to know that I die for principles that are dear to my heart and at the hands of people whom I love. All that I ask you tonight is that you listen to me patiently when I am speaking. When I finish the matter is in your hands.'

Sympathetic applause broke out, mingled with shouts of 'Good kid. Spit it out straight; you won't be hurt here.'

The speaker paused a moment and put his right thumb into the armhole of his waistcoat, leaving the other free to gesticulate. He spoke coldly and dispassionately of the causes of the war as he saw them. Then he began to warm up as he came to the war itself. 'What is actually happening?' he asked. 'While the papers and the propagandists are patriotically howling in the names of God, King, and humanity for the defence of their country, while the business people of the land are shouting of the sacrifices they are making, the capitalists of this country, anxious to make profits wherever they can and however they can, not caring how many die, are selling munitions to the very countries we are fighting against. Our men are left torn and mangled on barbed wire exported from our country to the enemy. Preachers declare that God is on our side – and our men are rotting in the swamps of Gallipoli, shot down by bullets made in England.'

This statement was followed by a wild hubbub throughout the hall. The speaker waited till the noise died down, then went on. 'The war is a war of competing capitalists and conflicting interests. We are merely pawns in the horrible game; flesh and blood whose very destruction becomes profitable. Each bullet that finds a bed in a human breast is a bullet that carries a profit. In order that our minds are prepared to take our bodies to the slaughter, our emotions are whipped up into a frenzy. Every lie, every distortion that can help to achieve this mad end is used in press and on platform, ay, and in pulpit. They try to prove to us that God is on our side, just as the German capitalists are telling their people that the same God is on their side. Our rulers strangle freedom in the name of democracy, they kill Christianity in the name of religion; they slaughter millions of the cream of the world in the name of peace. Oh, my friends, can you not see that these vultures prey on us living and dead?'

He paused in the dead silence, his chest rising and falling with emotion, before he concluded, 'I want to say that I would sooner die here and now, at the hands of my own people, than I would carry a gun to destroy my fellow workers, in the interest of our joint enemies.'

The fervent force of his words captured the people; it shocked and startled them. For some moments there was complete silence, which was eventually broken by isolated claps here and there that rose higher in increasing numbers until the applause was taken up by everyone. It seemed that the spell which had gripped the people ever since the war had started was broken by the words. The very thing he had accused the capitalists of doing he had, consciously or unconsciously, done himself. He had appealed to the people through their emotions, had played on their feelings and their deep subconscious desire for the war to end. But, after lifting them to heights of emotional enthusiasm, he had left them dangling with no foundation for their feet. He had not told them what they could do to end the war. His speech had been a declaration of personal faith and not an exposition of policy, and though everyone in the meeting was thrilled, when they left they were completely in the dark as to what they could do.

Len was elated that nothing untoward had occurred and that the speaker had not been heckled or interrupted. He had followed every word of the speech avidly and, like everyone else, had been shocked at some of the horrible implications of the speaker's remarks. He felt half-satisfied, like a starving man who eats a small sandwich; and the problem of how the war could be stopped confronted him more sharply than ever after the speech.

On the way home he asked Mary how the speech had affected her. She told him:

'I felt horrified when he said that the capitalists are selling munitions to our enemies. I cannot believe that men can be so inhuman. I believe the speaker was quite genuine and believed all he said, but that he is being misled and makes desires into facts.'

Len made no retort for a while. His arm was round her shoulders. Occasionally a harsh cough shook her and he felt her tremble beneath his arm. His own body responded as if to an electric shock, and pressing her face to his shoulder, he murmured incoherent caressing endearments into her ear. After a while she asked what he thought about the meeting. He took a little time to gather his thoughts before he replied: 'I think the speaker spoke the truth; that every word was gospel. But what worries me is how can we stop it all? Oh,' he wailed, turning her round till she faced him and both stood still, 'how can we stop these men of ours being slaughtered as they are? Day after day more of them are killed, and the post office has had to put extra boys on to carry the telegrams from the War Office.'

Mary rested her head on his chest. She felt lost in a maze of contradictions. She wanted to believe with her father that the war was in defence of all that the people held dear, but Len's convinced attitude and the words of the speaker had shaken her more than she cared to admit even to herself.

'Even if it were true,' she remarked, 'it wouldn't make the war wrong or our cause less great and worthy.'

Len nodded in silence, but did not feel capable of arguing the matter out. He was himself floating in a mental whirlpool, unable to find equilibrium, and though they did not discuss the matter further that night it remained the chief thought in their minds.

In the pits next day the speech was on everyone's tongue. It had sent a wave of horror through the valley, but the resentment was not so much against the war as against the people they were told were making a profit out of it. Len however, heard no more of the threats that had been made. He knew that John Library's exposure of them had made them too obvious and glaring to be put into effect. For both Mr. Hicks and the Inspector had anticipated and desired a different outcome to the meeting.

THE WAR DRAWS
TO AN END

A few days later Len heard that the speaker had been arrested at his home the previous night and had been tried for sedition that morning. John Library told him that he had been given the alternative of paying a £20 fine or doing two months in prison, and his old eyes shined brightly as he added: 'When he heard the magistrate pass the sentence, he lifted his chin in the air and said, "You may as well take me down now, because I shall never pay twenty pounds for speaking the truth!"'

Len was proud he had been associated, if only for a few hours, with such a man. He felt it was the same action he himself would have taken in similar circumstances, and the fact that the other had already done it and issued his challenge in open court thrilled him.

Mr. Hicks and the Inspector organised another recruiting

campaign in the valley. The chapels took the matter up, and for a whole week special prayers were offered for victory on the battlefields. Preachers called upon the men to join up in defence of God's laws, that were being violated so ruthlessly by the Germans, and girls sent white feathers through the post to the few young men who were still at home. Len, who received a few of these, felt they were doubly unjust because, as he reasoned, even apart from his growing convictions, he had offered himself for service during the first week. In spite of this he failed to console himself when he saw boys of fifteen and sixteen joining up. The terrific campaign that was waged for the war made him, as it made most men still wearing civilian clothes, feel guilty of something cowardly, and in spite of his reasoning he could not rid himself of the feeling.

At last, when this campaign had practically denuded the pits of all young, able-bodied men, a famous man, sent specially from London, appeared in the valley. He told the people they had served their country well and that no more men could be taken. 'The pits,' he declared 'have become part of the battle-front and are as important as the first-line trenches. You can all regard yourselves as soldiers fighting on the side of right against might. You can look upon your working clothes as uniforms of honour and the pits as key positions.'

This change of attitude considerably encouraged those who were left at home, and they redoubled their work in the pits. They were told to regard every lump of coal as a bullet, and the more bullets the country could have the sooner would the enemy be defeated and the war ended.

Presently Len began to notice the abnormal number of strange officials and under-officials who were started at the colliery. Most of them were young men, and he inquired from John Library who they were. The old man, with a twinkle in his eyes, answered: 'Oh, they are the sons and other relatives of the people who are urging our men to the front. Mr. Hicks' son is among them, and so is Lord Cwmardy's.'

One day when he handed his pay over to Siân she grumbled: 'I don't know what I am going to do with this. It isn't half enough to go round.'

Len looked at her in amazement. 'Why, mam,' he said reproachfully, 'I am earning more money now than I have ever earned, and I am not getting half the food I was having when dad was home.'

Siân bridled at the insinuation she thought she saw in his remarks.

'Think you I be wasting your money?' she demanded. 'Because if you do you can put it out of your mind now. I do know you are bringing in more, but it do take a lot more than the extra you do have to pay for the little bit of food we are allowed. Everything is gone up three and four times in the last months, and I can't stretch the little extra to meet it all.'

Len was immediately sorry for his words. He saw how he had neglected her since Jim had gone to the war and how he had left her to her own devices, with the result that he did not know how things were going in the house. He thought it peculiar that, following upon this conversation with his mother, he should notice for the first time that most of the talk in the pit centred on the question of the cost of living. Week after week it was the same. Will Smallbeer summed the matter up nicely when all the men were having dinner back on the roadway one day. 'By Christ,' he said, 'a pound note do go under your bloody nose now. All you got to do is to buy three penny apples and it is gone.'

'Well,' remarked another, munching a lump of black dried bread that looked like half-chewed tobacco, 'we can't 'spect to be in a great war like this without knowing it.'

Len felt impelled to intervene. 'That's all right,' he said, 'but I bet the rich people are getting everything they want, high prices or no, and in spite of all rationing cards. If our wages have been highered it is nothing compared to the way which the cost of living have gone up. Not only that, but the company are now charging more than five times extra for coal and we don't get twice as much pay for filling it. Once the price of coal rises everything else follows, and the little bit of extra money given to us is swamped before we have it.'

The men in general agreed with these sentiments, and that night Len called on Ezra and reported what he had heard in the pits, suggesting that a meeting of the men should be called to discuss the whole matter. Ezra pondered a moment before saying: 'I agree with you, Len, that something should be done, but I don't see where a meeting of the men could help us in any way. The matter, you see, is now in the hands of the Federation Executive and the Government. We cannot go over their heads in any way at this critical stage in the war.'

'I don't see where that is against us,' retorted Len. 'The

owners use the war to force up the price of coal and I don't see why we can't use it to get more wages. They have got us like soldiers as it is. We work like dogs, and they have made our committee into a ways and means committee for getting more coal instead of what it used to be during the strike.'

The bitterness in his voice surprised Ezra.

'I can't understand you, Len,' he said. 'Only recently you declared you were in favour of producing more coal to end the war quickly. Then you said you were not concerned who won the war. Now you want to use the war to improve wages – in other words, for your own ends. I can't see what is in your mind.'

This linking up of statements he had made staggered Len, for it showed him to have been inconsistent. He bowed his head a brief moment, saying: 'I never thought I was such a twister. Yet,' he added, in a puzzled way, 'I have been sincere in everything I have said and I have really believed and felt every word. I can't understand it.'

Ezra helped him. 'It's merely because you don't understand things yet. You just see things as you want them to be at the moment and don't face up to things as they are.'

Len was flustered by the severity of the blow and made no more mention of the subject, but he persisted in asking for a meeting of the men. Determinedly he told Ezra that if he were not prepared to call a mass-meeting then he would himself hold a meeting of the men in his own district, on the parting where meetings had been held immediately following the strike. Ezra capitulated to this threat, knowing Len's obstinacy in matters which he felt keenly.

The meeting was held in the theatre. Len looked around from his seat in the gallery and was amazed to see how few of the 'natives' were present, while large numbers of strangers, who had started at the pit since the outbreak of the war, filled the places of those who had been recruited.

Ezra opened the meeting with a brief explanation of its purpose, and immediately he had finished men jumped up from all parts of the hall. The chairman singled out one man and permitted him to speak, assuring the others that they should all have their turn. All the speakers were vehemently in favour of demanding an increase in wages, but Len, who was the last to speak, wanted to test the feeling of the men before he put his point of view.

'I agree with all those who think the time has come when we have to get our wages nearer the cost of living,' he said. 'What is the good of five or six pounds if it only buys a quarter of the necessities we had with our smaller wages before the war? It is nonsense for anyone to say that the company has no money. All of us here can remember when our Federation leaders offered the Company that if they wouldn't raise the price of coal during the war, we wouldn't ask for an increase in wages. What was the owners' reply to this patriotic offer, made for the sake of the old country that the owners claimed they loved so much? Their answer was that they couldn't possibly think of not using the war to raise the price of coal. In other words, my mind tells me, rightly or wrongly, that the owners saw the war as a chance to get very big extra profits for themselves. No one inside or outside of this meeting can say that they have not succeeded in this.'

His voice rose louder as he entered into the spirit of his words. Everyone in the meeting listened to him intently. 'No; patriotism to them is a very paying thing. The longer the war lasts the more money they make out of it. I know they will say that we are traitors to our country and that we are betraying our boys at the front if we ask for more wages. I know they will do a hundred times more against us now than they did during the strike even, but we have got to face it some time or other. As it is now, we are slogging ourselves to a standstill for a lot of shillings that don't buy half of the food we need to give our bodies strength to keep on working. I say,' he concluded, 'that our leaders should put it to all the miners in the country that we should be prepared to strike if we cannot have more wages. Why should we work and starve and our brothers at the front fight and die while other people are piling up mountains of money from our sacrifices?'

Ezra put the resolution that the Federation Executive should organise national strike action in the event of wages not being increased in line with the increased cost of living, and it was carried unanimously.

At the end of the meeting Ezra called Len to him, and they walked up the hill together. With biting sarcasm Ezra informed Len that the speaker in the meeting against war who had made the defiant gesture in the police court had paid the £20 fine out of his mother's savings. The shock stopped Len in his stride.

'What?' he gasped. 'You don't mean to tell me honestly that he has betrayed his principles?'

'Just that,' retorted Ezra calmly. 'Either he lied in the

meeting when he propounded what he said were his principles or he couldn't face up to the test.'

Len said no more. He had thought of making an excuse to drop in at Ezra's purposely to see Mary, but changed his mind when he learned of the new development. He felt at the moment that all men were liars and that such things as principles did not exist. He brought back to his mind Ezra's exposure of his own culpability in this regard and, feeling ashamed, began to look for excuses. They came to him readily after he had realised his own weaknesses and vacillations when it was a matter of weighing up fundamentals. He remembered Ezra's words, 'You see things as you desire them to be at the moment instead of as they actually are.' Here, he felt, was the key to the whole problem, if he could only understand it and work it out in his own mind and emotions. He began to realise that he was more of a nervous being than a consistently thinking individual.

When he reached home he found Siân awaiting him in great excitement. The sheet of paper she waved in her hand gladdened his heart, for he guessed immediately that his father had written at last. Hastily taking the letter, he read to himself the hardly decipherable words. Siân interrupted him sharply.

'Think you, Len bach, that your dad have only wrote to you? Read out loud for your old mam, my boy.'

Tears of joy made her tired eyes soft and misty.

Len read aloud:

'Dear Siân and Len and all at home,
Just a few words hoping they will find you all well as it

leaves me at present. I am very sorry being so long writing to you, but I have been very busy. My old general is out here. When he did hear that I had joined up he told his orderly, "Now, 'member, sergeant, as soon as Big Jim do land tell him I do want to see him!" Now, Siân bach, what do you think to that? You 'on't half be able to swank to Mrs. Thomas next door now. Don't worry 'bout me. Everything in the garden is lovely out here. The only things I do miss is the beer in the Boar's Head and those cakes you used to make for tea every Sunday. Nobody can make cakes like you, Siân bach. The general did tell me only yesterday, "Don't forget, James, when the missus do send you cakes I want some of them." True as God is my judge he did say that. Tell Len when he is writing back to let me know how the old place is going. I do miss that old barry somehow or other. He will never have 'nother butty like his old dad. What say you, Siân? Well, I must close now, with love and kisses to all at home from your ever loving

James and father,

Jim.

P.S. – I hope you are getting the army 'lotment all right. We are short of fags out here.'

When Len had finished, Siân was openly sobbing.

'What a lovely letter your father do write, Len bach. Anybody can see he is a edicated man. Fancy the General 'membering him. But there, James was always like that; everybody do take to him as soon as they see him.'

The letter helped Len to forget for a while the mental

turmoil of the evening. He felt relieved now that he knew his father was safe.

That night, as he lay awake thinking over the events of the past few weeks, it suddenly struck him that the letter had probably been written at least a week or a fortnight before it was delivered and that he was no more certain that his father was alive now than he had been before receiving the letter, but he resolved to tell Siân nothing of this.

The heavy work in the pit together with the terrible food he had to eat was beginning to take toll of his health. He developed a racking cough very similar to that which tore Mary on occasions. Strangely enough, this did not alarm him. He accepted it as something that drew Mary nearer to him, and felt he was now in a position to bear her burden. Despite this mental reaction, he found the hurried drive in the pit to fill more and ever more coal telling on his strength. His face grew gaunt and yellowish, while his body became more thin and bony. He dreaded his mother's call in the mornings, and he had to exercise all his determination to respond to it. Each morning the long procession of black-clothed, silent shadows up the hill became an ever greater nightmare. He rarely went out in the evenings now, and often fell asleep with his head in the bathing tub. On these occasions Siân would tenderly try to swill his naked top half without waking him.

Ezra noticed the symptoms and urged him to take a rest at home. Len thanked him for his sympathy, but pointed out that it was impossible if he and his mother were to eat.

Ezra knew the truth of this, and said no more.

One evening Len went down to Ben the Barber's for a

haircut. As soon as he entered the shop Ben looked up from the face he was shaving and, as if he had been expecting Len, remarked caustically: 'Would you like to know what other people think of you and your sort?'

Len was aware of Ben's quaint mannerisms of speech and knew that deep down the man was a rebel against all conventions.

'No, why?' he asked casually.

'Well, just look at that newspaper over there. No, not that one on top; the one underneath,' and with this Ben went on with his shaving, whistling quietly as the razor flashed in his hands.

Len sat down and read the paper. He turned over the numerous pages and pictures dealing with the war. He was sick of reading about the perpetual and ever-recurring great victories that were being won each day, none of which seemed to bring the war any nearer an end. He found he had opened the paper in the middle and so he turned the pages back. Ben watched him from the corner of his eyes, still whistling and wielding the razor over the lathered face. Suddenly Len's face went white. In a streaming headline across the front page he read:

MINERS BETRAY SOLDIERS AT THE FRONT

At the moment of our country's greatest peril, certain elements in the ranks of the miners are advocating a strike for an increase in wages. While men are laying down their lives in defence of the nation, these people talk in terms of cash and threaten to deprive the navy and the gallant forces who are so heroically fighting of coal. If the perpetrators of such an agitation lived in one of the enemy countries they would be shot offhand as traitors. We cannot believe that the miners are themselves responsible for this. Rather do we think they are being misled against their desires by people who are no friends to this country and who are prepared to go to any lengths to ensure the defeat of our glorious army and navy.

Len read the remainder of the article, becoming more indignant with every word. When he had finished he raised his head and looked at the chuckling Ben. The latter spoke casually.

'Now you know what you and your tribe are, and what you should be getting.'

'But it isn't true.' A flush dyed Len's face. 'Our men are not against those who are fighting. All we are asking is that the coalowners sacrifice a little for the war as well as us and the forces. I agree we have got to make sacrifices to draw the war to an end, but let it be sacrifices on everyone's part, and not only us bottom dogs.'

Ben intervened with a grunt.

'Huh. What's the good of talking like that. This is a war in which there are no classes. If the Germans conquer, what have you got to lose? Nothing. Absolutely bugger all. But look at the owners. If the Germans win the war they stand to lose their pits and everything they have sacrificed so much for in the past. Don't you think they deserve a little compensation now in face of the risk they are running? Let me put it to you like this. If we lose the war you lose nothing unless it's your life – and that does not alter the fact you lose nothing. The owners, on the other hand, stand to lose everything: therefore they have got to insure themselves against this. So it's only right and fair they should get as much profits as possible now in case they get none later on. See?' he concluded quizzically.

Len said nothing. He knew Ben's penchant for sarcasm and was aware of his cleverness in argument, for Ben's irony intrigued him.

Some time after this Big Jim and some of the other men of the valley came home on leave unexpectedly. Len saw them walking up the hill from the station. They were all drunk. Their puttees hung in dirtied, bedraggled strings round their legs. Their hungry-looking, pinched grey faces were shadowed by the rims of steel helmets, and they carried their deadly-looking rifles in their hands. Singing bawdily and staggering from side to side of the pavement, they attracted the respectful and awed attention of all the people who saw them, and when they met a group of men standing on the corner of the street directly facing the main entrance of the Boar's Head, the soldiers immediately entered, followed by the others.

Len was torn between two desires. He wanted to hurry home to tell Siân that Jim was home. Yet he wanted to let her have the full joy of surprise when Jim would walk in the house. But, lest the shock of Jim's sudden appearance would upset her too much, he decided to tell her without delay.

When he reached home he asked casually:

'When did you get the last letter from dad?'

'Well, well. What be coming over you, boy?' she asked, giving him a queer look. 'You ought to know that without asking me, mun. You did read it out for me in this very kitchen.'

Len pretended to recollect himself.

'Ay, of course I did, now I think of it,' he said. 'Only I was wondering perhaps he have sent you a sly one and Mrs. Thomas next door read it out for you. But never mind. Duw, wouldn't it be fine, mam, if he was to walk into the kitchen now, without letting us know he was coming?'

Siân hesitated as the tears bubbled in her eyes.

'Ay, it would be,' she said. 'How I would like to see him! It be nearly three years since he did leave us, and he have not been home once. 'Tain't fair. Nearly everybody else have been home four or five times already. But there, I would forgive everything if he was to walk in now. Many a time I have nagged him for nothing, Len bach. I do regret it all now and often wish I could draw many a word back. Poor old James. I 'ood have to go a long way to find a man half so good as him.' She lifted the canvas apron to her eyes.

Len interjected quickly:

'Well, mam, there is no need for you to cry. Dad is home already.'

Siân jumped to her feet like a leaping rabbit.

'What say you?' her voice was incredulously high. 'Don't you dare to tease your poor old mother, Len.'

'Mam,' Len faced her reproachfully, 'you know I wouldn't do that for my right arm. I spoke the truth. Dad is home and he is now in the Boar's Head having a little drink with the boys before coming up.'

Siân's eyes flashed.

'In the Boar's Head before coming to see his only wife, the 'ooman who have reared his children for him! What do you think of that, Len? He don't think more of your mother than mud.'

Hastily putting her shawl over her head, she opened the door and made her way down the hill. Len made no attempt to prevent her. He knew that her temper would evaporate when she faced the exuberant Jim, but it was hours before he heard his father's voice raucously singing some obscene ditty. All the people in the street came to their doors or their bedroom windows at the noise. They shouted greetings to Jim, who waved salutations to them, totally unaware that they could not see him in the darkness. Siân kept exhorting him to be quiet, but the only answer she received was: 'Quiet, muniferni? Let the world know that Big Jim have come back home,' followed by his trying to sing louder than ever.

Siân felt proud as she held his staggering form erect. He wanted to enter every house in the street and she only prevented him after calling for Len's assistance. Eventually they got him to the house, and he sank with a bang into his armchair. Len had stoked the fire, and its gleam threw Jim's bloodshot eyes into sharp, glaring relief before he fell asleep. Between them, Siân and Len pulled the uniform and other military paraphernalia off the recumbent, snoring body, Siân sobbing the while:

'Poor boy. I 'spect he be fair worn out with what he

387

have gone through.'

Len felt a thrill run through him when he grasped the rifle. He felt an insane desire to pull the trigger and hear the explosion of a shot. He suggested they should take Big Jim to bed immediately, but Siân was opposed to this.

'No,' she said. 'He must be waking when he come to bed or he will be thinking in his sleep that he is not back in his own little home.'

She poured hot tea between the clenched teeth while Len rummaged through the haversack and other bags that Jim had brought with him. From the depths of the former he pulled out a dirty paper bag greasy with half-melted butter, some uncovered sausages with grains of sawdust sticking in their skins, and a tin of corned beef. The sight of the food immediately set his stomach turning and bubbling with hunger. Saliva filled his mouth in spite of his attempts to swallow it back, and suddenly feeling faint, he went to the back door to get some air.

When he returned to the kitchen Siân had succeeded in waking Jim. Len thought his father looked even more huge than before he went away. He noticed long red streaks such as are made by vigorous scratching on Jim's chest. Jim made long smacking sounds with his lips.

'Ah,' he said thickly, 'it is good to be home, mun.'

His eyes roamed longingly over Siân's body.

'Duw, duw. You do look more beautiful than ever, Siân bach. Ay, indeed you do. Better than the gel in the 'staminet.'

Siân perked up at this.

'What gel be you talking about, James?'

'Oh,' he replied, dimly realising the mistake he had made, 'just a ole bag of a 'ooman, you know, Siân,' confidentially lowering his voice, 'a common ole cow. Ay, that's it. An old tart who do live by robbing the boys.'

'Hush, James bach,' Siân's voice was thin and her expression shocked. 'Don't say that 'bout any 'ooman. 'Member your mother was a 'ooman.'

Siân cooked some of the sausages for supper. For the first time in years a feeling of satisfaction rippled through Len's body, sending warm glows through his blood.

After supper Jim vociferously asserted he was remaining in the kitchen for the night.

'No bloody bed of feathers for me,' he declared. 'Me an my ole love will sleep by here on the floor better 'n any bed, an' a damn sight more helfy.'

'Sleep on the floor?' Siân stared at him aghast. 'Duw, duw, man. Have the beer turned your brains? You do know that as soon as we put the light out the black pats will cover the kitchen floor with their dirty, crawling legs. And more than that, James, you ought to know after what happened once before that black pats be very fond of beer and will always go for where they do smell it, and you do know very well that you do sleep with your mouth wide open.'

Jim rose unsteadily to his feet, holding on to the brass rod under the mantelshelf for support.

'Black pats! Black pats!' he said with slow dignity, inflating his enormous chest. 'What be black pats to me, who have slept with millions of rats as big as dogs every night that God sent for the last two year or more? Black pats, indeed!' he said contemptuously drawing his hand from the rod to strike an imposing attitude and falling ignominiously backwards into the chair. Although neither Len nor his mother said a word, he shouted: 'Don't think I be drunk and don't know what I be doing. A man who have killed hundreds of square-headed Jerries do always know what he be doing. Where is Siân?' he asked suddenly.

She immediately came to his side and without further fuss she and Len took him upstairs to bed.

It was many hours before Len went to sleep. Groans, grunts, and creakings from the next room were hardly intercepted by the intervening wall. The sounds made him think of Mary, and again he felt the soft contact of her body, as he had felt it that day at the seaside. Little flushes of heat ran through his flesh at the memory. Then his thoughts turned to the bayonet his father had brought home. He shuddered as he recollected the rust on it, which he thought must have been blood. He imagined the point sinking into a man's body and the entrails being drawn out with the suction of the grooves at the sides. He felt a peculiar kind of blood-curdling pleasure at these imaginings, but at last, with the creakings and groans still in his ears, he slowly drifted to sleep.

The next morning Len was surprised to see how the street was decorated with gay bunting bearing in bold letters words of cheer and welcome to the local heroes who had so unexpectedly returned on leave. Bright flags hung from the windows of the ugly houses making cheerful splashes of colour.

For some days he had no opportunity to talk with his father. He was in bed when Len went to work in the mornings and in the Boar's Head when he returned. But on Sunday, after breakfast, he had a chance to raise the matter that was foremost in his mind.

'Well, dad,' he said, 'what do you think of the war?' He tried to make his voice as casual as possible, but its quiver betrayed the intensity of his emotions.

Stretching his long legs to their full length, Jim broke wind and lit his pipe before replying, after Siân had scolded him for his lack of manners. He addressed himself first to Siân:

'Wherever you be,' he quoted sententiously, 'let your wind go free.' After this shattering remark he turned to Len and rolled off on a long recital of the heroic deeds he had performed.

'Ay,' he said, 'us in the front lines do do all the fighting and the dying and some little puppy-dog of an officer, with goose-down on his face instead of whiskers, do come along behind the lines and pick up the medals and the leave.'

Len was interested.

'So it is very much like the pit,' he asked, 'only instead of being called workmen you are called soldiers and the officials are called officers? '

Jim gave a loud guffaw. 'Haw, haw, haw,' he roared, and it took some time for him to recover sufficiently to say: 'Not quite like that, Len. We can tell the officials to go to hell. You tell that to an officer and you get to hell first. Officials be sometimes wrong, but officers are never wrong.'

Jim monopolised the conversation for the remainder of the day, Siân and Len listening interestedly to the account of his many varied experiences. This was the last occasion on which Len had an opportunity of talking to his father, for Jim spent the greater part of the few remaining days of his leave in the Boar's Head.

When the day came for him to return to the front Siân clung to him like a baby, and cried. She wanted to accompany him to the station, but both Jim and Len were adamant, and they bade goodbye on the doorstep.

During the months that followed life in Cwmardy became a monotonous routine to the people. The owners granted the demands of the miners and so averted a strike. But the cost of living immediately jumped up and balanced the advance.

One evening a telegram was stuck on the window of Mr. Evans Cardi's stores:

'GERMANS ASK FOR ARMISTICE. THE WAR IS ENDED.'

Huge crowds of people tried to force their way to the window to see the telegram with their own eyes. Having seen it, they dashed off in all directions to spread the news. Musical instruments appeared from nowhere, and in a very short time the whole valley rang with music, laughter, and noise.

CWMARDY
TEACHES LEN
A NEW LESSON

Inside twelve months after the conclusion of the war most of the miners in Cwmardy who had gone to the war and had returned were again at their places in the pit.

On his first day down Big Jim told Len, 'Duw, duw, boy bach, being down in the old pit agen do make me feel as if I now be home real, mun.'

Len laughed. 'Ay. It is funny how the pit gets hold of us and we are not satisfied when we are away from it. Must be something in the air, I suppose.'

It was not long before the men had adapted themselves again to the life of the pit, but their experiences in the war had made them carefree and assertive, and they took little heed of the officials, who did not dare to question their conduct.

Meanwhile the Company was introducing mechanical

methods of cutting and conveying the coal, Len's barry being one of the first to be put on the new technique. The conveyor consisted of a number of long iron troughs, bolted together and fastened to a tiny engine driven by compressed air, which took the coal in bucking jerks from the coalface to the trams. And in this way the men were able to more than double their output.

One day the men, naked to the waist as usual, were crawling up the long conveyor face, squirming their way like snakes, sometimes on their bellies, sometimes on their sides, until they reached their working places. Whenever their bodies touched the cold, damp roof it seemed like a burn upon their hot flesh, and the tiny lumps of loose coal and stone on the floor rubbed into their sweating flesh like pins, so that they were not anxious to have more of this than was absolutely necessary. Once they had reached their places they stayed there till the end of the shift unless some urgent reason obliged them to move.

When they had all arrived, the workman at the top end sent the order down the line of crouching men, 'Right you are. Let her go.' The order passed from mouth to mouth until it reached the man at the bottom end, who responded by jerking a little lever attached to the engine, which, after coughing and rasping for a few minutes as if clearing its throat, gathered power, and presently, with a clatter and a clang that deafened the men's ears to everything else, the iron troughs of the conveyor had begun their spasmodic bucking jerks. The loud and regular 'phot-phot, phot-phot' of the blast engine beat time to the rattling clamour of the conveyor, and conversation became impossible in the tumult.

The men got to work with their picks and shovels. Resting on their knees to give greater power to their arms, they tore great lumps of coal from the solid face, and breaking them into smaller pieces, heaved them with a turn of their shoulders and a twist of their arms into the conveyor. But however much coal they put in, the conveyor was always empty when they turned to it again.

'Duw,' said Big Jim, 'it be like throwing coal down the pit and losing it.'

Gradually the rhythmic, discordant din gripped the men's muscles and their movements began to keep time with the noise. Streams of perspiration oiled their joints and made them operate smoothly, and within an hour after the conveyor had started the men were immersed in a universe of coal, sweat, and clamour. If anything happened to stop the machinery they felt that the world had suddenly become void, and their ears would be filled with a strange blobbing sound, so that they were glad when the tumult began again. The silence felt like something tangible pressing on their skin, and it was on their sense of touch that they had to depend to ascertain if the roof were weakening.

After five hours of this Len felt as if his spine was on fire and his limbs had been amputated. To save moving his body too much he tugged and strained to tumble a larger lump of coal than usual into the trough, but each time he got it on the rim the jerking edge tore it from his grasp and threw it back to the ground. Len cursed and grunted under the strain, which was all the greater because the limited space did not allow him to use his full strength. The coal put on by the men above him kept dancing and jigging before his eyes as it bucked downwards towards the tram. Big lumps, small lumps, funnily-shaped lumps pranced noisily before him like a rushing, rock-strewn river. The glittering mass fascinated him and made him giddy, and the thought flashed into his mind that the strain had driven him insane. He bent until his face almost touched the jumping coal, staring until his eyes bulged in glaring concentration. Then he screamed wildly, his sharp hysterical falsetto cutting through the mechanical clamour like a knife. The thin piercing agony of the notes rose higher.

'Stop it! Stop it! For Christ's sake, stop!'

With the speed of a flashed signal the words passed from mouth to mouth till they reached the ears of the man near the engine, and in an instant the coalface became deathly silent. Men looked at their nearest neighbours in mute query, to meet the dumb echo of their own bewilderment. Len was now scrambling like a madman in the coal on the conveyor. His hands tore at the gleaming lumps until his nails hung loose. Big Jim sprang forward to see what was the matter, and in a few moments they had uncovered a naked arm that had been ripped out of its shoulder socket. The two men gave one horrified glance at the limb, then frantically turned and squirmed up the conveyor face, shouting at the top of their voices: 'Quick boys, quick. Something awful has happened up above.'

Men who had become momentarily lifeless with amazement flung themselves into revitalised motion at the call. Their sweat-slimed bodies gleamed like oil and outshone the brightness of the coal as they frenziedly slithered past it. Len and his father were the first to reach the scene of the accident, the latter gasping and heaving with the mad rush in the enclosed space that was too small for his huge body.

Alongside the still conveyor they saw the silent form of a young lad who had only recently started work. His body twisted and squirmed as if with convulsions, and his wide-open, staring eyes glittered queerly in the light of the lamps that showered their beams on him. His lips kept moaning: 'Bring my arm back, bring my arm back. Why did you take it from me?'

Len caught the lad to him, cuddling him like a baby across his chest. The single arm kept flailing helplessly, emphasising the empty socket where the other had been. The gleaming bone winked wickedly through the blood that spouted from the shreds of torn flesh.

By the time the other men appeared, panting and gasping, the lad had ceased his weak struggles, but Len felt the nerves still quivering like soft jelly in a shaken dish. The boy turned his head and asked in a low, supplicating tone: 'Did one of you bring my arm back?'

Big Jim swallowed something and blew his nose before replying, 'Never you mind 'bout your arm, now, boy bach. That be all right, you can venture.' He took the frail body from Len and stretched it out along his own, so that the men could quickly press their fingers and thumbs to the torn arteries, to prevent the blood pouring away.

The boy remained conscious all the time they were waiting for the officials to bring the first-aid material, and though he seemed more satisfied about his arm, he insisted upon seeing it.

Big Jim tried to dissuade him. 'What for do you want your old arm, boy bach? There be plenty of time for that, mun, when the doctor do see you. Duw, duw, he will look at it and look at you, then he will tell you to shut your eyes quick like, and when you open them again your arm will be back on.'

The lad did not seem to hear him, and began to moan: 'I want my arm. I want my arm.' Len whispered to one of the men near by, who crawled away, and in a short time returned with the dismembered arm sticking out from beneath his own. The ghastly sight turned Len's stomach, but he could not take his eyes from Big Jim as the latter took the limb and tied it to the boy's body.

'There you be,' he said, in what he intended to be a jubilant voice. 'There be your little arm, boy bach, safe and sound with you agen.'

The boy sighed heavily, then asked, 'Will I be able to play football any more, Big Jim?'

The latter, still on his back with the lad lying on him, laughed boisterously. 'Ha-ha-ha. Ho-ho. Now what do you think to that, boys? What a question to ask! Ha-ha. Play football agen? Of course you will, mun. You will be captain of your team a hundred times yet, 'on't he boys? Duw, duw. You be worth ten dead men, easy, mun.' Jim turned to the other men, tears bubbling in his eyes, and they all hurried to confirm his words. The lad seemed satisfied, and settled himself more comfortably on the body that held him. His eyes closed and he seemed to drift into a sleep.

The officials fussily hurried up and the lad was tied and

bandaged in preparation for the journey home. They tried to select the men who were to carry him out, but no one took any notice as they all put their clothes on and left the conveyor to itself.

That evening Len could not remain in the house. The horror he had felt when he saw the arm still filled his mind. He wanted to be violently sick, but his stomach would not respond. The arm dangled like a monstrous marionette before his eyes, even when he shut them. He paced the small kitchen like a tomcat in a storm, and eventually decided he could stand it no longer. Leaving the house, he curtly informed Siân he would not be long.

Len's thoughts cleared a little in the fresh air, as, quite unconsciously, he walked in the direction of Mary's house. When he reached the door he looked up in surprise and paused for some moments while he argued with himself whether he should go in. Before he had made up his mind the door opened, and Mary and Ezra came out.

'Hallo,' said Ezra, 'if you've come to see us you are unfortunate, as Mary and I are going for a little walk up the mountain.' Len felt that such an excursion would soothe him, and he shyly asked: 'Would you mind if I came with you? I can't bear to be inside after what happened today.' Mary looked at him sympathetically and nodded a glad assent.

The three made their way slowly up the rugged breast of the mountain till they reached the summit. Here they sat down and watched the smoke from the pit drift and spread until it covered Cwmardy with a filmy blanket. The glow from the furnaces shot streaks of red into the black smoke, and for some reason the scene made Mary sad.

'Isn't it awful that we have to spend our lives with smoke to breathe and coal-dust to eat?' she asked.

For a while neither of the men answered her.

Although they had heard the remark both appeared engrossed in their own thoughts. But at length Ezra turned to Len. 'That makes me wonder how far the atmosphere of the valley is helping to break your father. Have you noticed how thin, bent, and slow he is becoming, Len?'

'Yes. I have noticed him in work. But there, what can we expect? When a man works over thirty years in the pit it is bound to tell on his body in some way or another.'

A hooter from below sent its wailing note up the mountain. Len started, as if the sound were strange to him.

'There it goes,' he muttered bitterly. 'Hear the whip crack? I wonder if all those who respond to its lash tonight will come back up in the morning.'

'That is a matter for fate to decide,' said Ezra.

Len sprang to his feet excitedly. 'Fate, fate? What is that? Do you say that fate tore that boy's arm out this morning? Was it fate that blew our men to bits in the explosion? Did fate smash Bill Bristol to a pulp? No; I can't believe that, Ezra. It wasn't fate that brought us into the strike or into the war. You did the first and the capitalists did the other.'

Ezra betrayed no emotion at this sudden outburst, but Mary rose to her knees. 'I agree with Len,' she said. 'We are ourselves responsible for what happens. The pity is that we follow events instead of trying to determine and mould them. Our fate is in our own hands. Take Russia, for instance. In spite of all that the papers say, I would like to see how those people are shaping their future. Whether they succeed is another matter, but at least they will have made the attempt, which is more than we are doing.'

Len was encouraged by this support although he did not entirely agree with the sentiments. 'You can't say we aren't trying to better things,' he said. 'What was our strike but a battle by our people to improve conditions?'

Ezra broke in. 'Yes, that's right. It was part of a war, a war that will never end while there are masters and men in the same world.' He pointed his finger to the pits where the red glow was becoming deeper in the encroaching dusk. 'Who sunk those pits and mined them? Who made those lines into rivers of coal? No one but our people. And what have they in return? Nothing but poverty, struggle, and death.'

The three got to their feet and watched the little pinpricks of light that were beginning to stab the darkness over Cwmardy.

'You are right,' said Len slowly. 'But if our people have the power to win strikes even against bullets and batons they have the power to do away with their poverty, to put an end to the struggle and begin to live clean, healthy lives.'

Ezra looked at him as he caught Mary's arm, and they began the descent. 'Hmm,' he said. 'When you two have lived so long as I have you will learn there are some things in life the people can never abolish. The struggle for a living is one of them.'

There was no reply, but as they carefully negotiated the rocky path that led back to Cwmardy, Len, unseen by Ezra, squeezed Mary's arm with a warm confidence.

WE LIVE

WE LIVE

CLOUDS
OVER CWMARDY

The wind howled over the mountain and swept down on Cwmardy as though chased by a million nightmares. Dark corners roared and whistled when they encountered the onslaught, while telephone wires twanged under the pressure. Street lamps turned the moisture into miniature rainbows that glistened on the slimy road. The tumult echoed high up over the valley, where the tempest spied the fissures in the mountain and battered its way in, to return with increasing fury on the village beneath.

A tall smokestack stuck its head through the ruddy glow of the pit furnaces, too proud to notice the clamour of the storm, above which sounded the 'chug-chug' of the pit engines, broken at short intervals by a 'clanketty-clang' as the pit spewed two trams full of coal into the storm and sucked two empties out of it. The wind howled more loudly still at the theft, but to no avail; for immediately the empty trams were in the grip of the cage it tore them from the elements and plunged them into the blackness of the pit. The heavy wooden droppers on the shaft-head beat back the chasing wind and rain, which sought revenge on the houses lower down the valley.

The little lights in the cottage windows of Cwmardy winked at the storm, inviting it to burst open the doors and share with the family inside the cosy heat of the open fireplace. Behind one of these windows an old woman sat patiently darning a sock. Her drawn face, with its yellowish skin, reflected the shadows from the fire, before which she sat with parted knees. A huge man was stretched languidly in an armchair nearby. His slightly bowed shoulders and silver-streaked hair betrayed advancing age, and his face was remarkable for its long, stiff moustaches and the black scars that emphasized its lines.

For about the twentieth time in as many minutes the old woman raised her eyes from the wool in her lap and looked towards the window, down whose cracked panes the water streamed.

'I wonder what in the world our Len and Mary do want out on such a night as this?' she muttered disconsolately. 'They will be sure to get wet to the skin, and with her bad chest that will mean pewmonia so sure as God is my judge.'

She stopped for some moments and listened to the squealing storm, while the old man grumbled a curse at the smoke which every now and then belched from the chimney into the kitchen where the old couple were sitting. After a while she turned her attention to her companion.

'Fitter if you went out to look for them, James, instead of sitting by there on your backside, like if they was safe and sound in the house and you didn't have a worry in the world,' she complained. Jim looked at her a moment, then spat heavily into the fire before replying.

'Huh! What you talk about, 'ooman? If the son of Big Jim is 'fraid of a little drop of water and a little puff of wind, it is time for you to ask what is the matter with you,' and with this trenchant remark he placidly resumed his pipe.

The steel-rimmed spectacles on the tip of her nose quivered with her indignation. 'Shame on you, James, talking 'bout your only son like that! But there, I do only waste my time talking to you. Huh! It is all right for you to talk, with your body so big as a bull's and your head just so dull as one.'

She got up from the chair and went to the door, which she opened just wide enough to push her head through; but though she shouted her son's name at the top of her sharp voice, it got lost in the wind even as the cry left her lips. Big Jim turned his head and growled.

'Shut that bloody door, Siân fach, or this smoke will make me into a kipper. There's nothing for you to worry 'bout, mun. I 'spect they have gone to a meeting and 'on't call here 'cos it is too rough to come up the hill.'

Siân banged the door and shuffled back to the chair, her unlaced boots flapping on the stony kitchen floor with every step.

'That's how you men always is,' she grunted. 'Always your own comforts first, never mind 'bout nobody else. No, not even your own flesh and blood. Well, well! There have never been such a night since the 'splosion, and there you be, James, so happy as a tomcat on the tiles, knowing all the time that they are out in the middle of it.'

This brought him erect in his chair. 'Hell-fire, 'ooman! Have I not told you they is safe enough? You be nuff, mun, to give a man the bile and diarrhoea all in one. And you do call this a storm – ha, ha! It is nothing but a sun shower. Good God! I 'member once in Africa—'

Siân forestalled the threatened reminiscence. 'I don't want to hear nothing 'bout your old Africa or your storm. No. Pity it hadn't took you then; it 'ood have saved me a lifetime of worry and trouble.'

She bent her head and went on with her darning, raising her eyes every few minutes to glance at the ticking clock, whose rhythmic monotone for some time dominated the kitchen. Big Jim went on smoking contentedly, occasionally spitting into the grate and twisting his soap-stiffened moustache with a slow, dignified twirl. He looked up once at the garishly painted almanac on the mantelshelf, and a distant look stole into his eyes when he remarked:

'Duw, duw! The years is slipping by pretty quick now, Siân fach. Only the other day us was in the middle of the 'splosion, and here it is 1924 already. The years are going over our heads like months, muniferni.'

Siân glanced from her darning to reply softly: 'O Aye; you are right. Us is getting on now, James bach, and the earth will soon be calling to us.'

Outside the house the storm seemed to have swept the streets clear of humans, but the structure known as the

Fountain on the village square glistened as the lights from the Boar's Head chased the shadows over its body of rusted iron.

Ben the Barber's doorway looked like a black blob painted into the darkness stretching beyond the rim of light cast from the windows of the Boar's Head. But occasionally the blob was pierced by a tiny gleam as the two policemen crouching within the door exposed a button. Both were well protected from the storm, but this did not prevent the moisture dangling from the end of their noses. The taller of the two raised his head from the keyhole for a moment to whisper excitedly: 'I'm sure I heard something about lock-out.'

His mate merely growled:

'Huh! I wish they'd pack up for the night. Perhaps we could sneak into somewhere dry, then.' He noticed the other's head still lifted from the keyhole, and broke off his grouse to say: 'Keep your bloody head down, mun, or we might lose something important, 'specially if you heard right about the lock-out.'

The other obeyed, at the same time retorting: 'Huh! What do that matter? We can always put it down in the station the same as if we have heard it, can't we?'

A shuffle of chairs came from the room and he sprang erect immediately, with a sibilant warning. 'Sssh! They've finished and are coming out.'

His mate, draping the cape more closely about his shoulders, hastened towards the Fountain to be pulled up sharply.

'Not that way, you fool. You'll be right in the light there.'

He hurriedly retraced his steps and the two had hardly pressed themselves into the black recess of another doorway when a number of people came out of Ben the Barber's.

One of the men muttered to the woman next him, as he buttoned his coat up to the neck and watched her do the same: 'Good God, what a night, Mary!'

'Aye, Len. Terrible, isn't it? We'd better run or we'll be soaking long before we reach your mother's.'

He caught her arm and both ran into the driving rain, burying themselves in the darkness beyond the Fountain. Half-way up the hill they came to an involuntary stop, panting and dripping. Len put his arm round the thin shoulders of his wife as he heard her breath wheeze in her throat, and gently drew her small form into the shelter afforded by the pine end of a house. A racking cough suddenly tore at her chest, and he helped her wipe away the stained sputum that wetted her lips, his slim body nearly hiding hers.

After a while she broke the silence that had followed the fit of coughing, her voice still harsh with the strain.

'I'm sorry I went to that meeting.'

He stooped a little to peer more closely into her face as he voiced his surprise. 'Sorry? What have you got to be sorry about, Mary?'

'Oh, I don't know. Only I thought, when you asked me to come, we were going to hear something definite about all these rumours of a lock-out. But instead of that, all I've heard is blabbing about revolutions and politics.'

He drew himself up in a hurt manner, his arm still about her shoulders. 'Half a minute, Mary. Don't say that politics

410

is nonsense. Didn't you hear the chairman say that politics is everything for the workers? Good God! If we had more politics we wouldn't be in the hole we're in now.'

She interrupted him petulantly. 'Oh, shut up for goodness sake! You take everything that Harry Morgan tells you as if it was gospel. You make me sick, Len. Here we've been talking all night about revolutions, when very soon we might want all our strength to face the lock-out that is coming if what our women say is true.'

Her words stung him and he lost his temper. 'Aye, women's cackle – with their arms folded on their bellies, while we are in work! Huh! You'd sooner listen to rubbish like that than to sense the same as you had tonight. But I don't care a hang! You can say what you like, I'm glad I joined the Party tonight.'

She looked up into his face, and even in the darkness he saw the whites of her eyes gleam as she said: 'Aye, I know that. But what else could I expect from a husband whose head is as soft as his heart?'

Len swallowed audibly and tried to say something, but the words wouldn't come. He was used to her vehemence, particularly when she felt something deeply, and had only asked her to the meeting in the hope that Harry Morgan, the Party leader, would have shaken the convictions bred in her by Ezra Jones, her father, the local miners' leader. He was himself susceptible to the same influence and always hesitated when they combined forces against him in an argument, although he never admitted this fact even to himself.

To cover his discomfiture he suggested that they proceed, and neither of them said any more as they plodded up the hill. They entered Siân's house without knocking; but the old woman looked up from her darning when she heard the latch rattle.

'Huh! Fine time of the night, indeed, for a young stripling of a boy to be out,' she began, at the same time making place for them near the fire. 'When I was your age, my boy, I 'oodn't dare to be out after seven o'clock, and here you strut in with Mary fach and her bad chest at 'leven 'xactly like it was first thing in the morning. You ought to be ashamed of yourself, Len.'

He said nothing, and squatted comfortably in a chair, but before he had time to settle down properly she ordered:

'Come here. Leave me feel if your clothes is wet.'

'Oh, let me alone, mam. We've only been to a meeting, and it's bad enough to have Mary nagging without you helping her,' he replied petulantly.

'Ah, answering your only mother back, is it? Don't forget my boy, when I was your age I 'oodn't dare to look at my mother twice, let alone answer her back, God bless her!' She raised the canvas apron to her nose. 'But there. What is the use of arguing? Children today is too big for their boots and half of them don't know they are born. Huh!'

She turned to Mary. 'Take your wet clothes off, my gel, and put them by the fire while I do make a cup of tea.'

'Don't bother, mam. We'll be going before long,' Mary replied, at the same time drawing her chair up, and continuing: 'What do you think have happened tonight?'

Siân interestedly cocked her ears up at once and Mary went on, without looking at Len, who wondered what on

412

earth she was driving at.

'Our Len have joined Harry Morgan's Party.'

Siân gave a little scream: 'What? Joined those infidels?'

She was overcome with emotion for some moments, during which Jim slyly opened one eye which he immediately closed when he saw her looking at him.

'Wake up, James,' she demanded. 'Something awful have happened to our Len. Oh, Duw! After me rearing him tidy and 'spectable all these years and taking him to chapel every Sunday like a clock and now to come to this!'

She covered her eyes with her apron, and did not see Jim stirring awkwardly and blinking his eyes like a man suddenly awakened from a deep sleep.

'How be, Mary fach. What is all this bloody fuss about?' he greeted them.

'Our Len have joined the Party,' Mary informed him.

'Huh! Well, that's better than joining the militia, in't it?'

Len smiled at the remark, knowing by it that his father was siding with him against the two women.

Siân turned to Mary. 'There! What did I tell you? The man have got no shame in him. You can see now what I have had to put up with all these years. No wonder my hair have gone white years before its time.'

This statement stung Jim, and he drew himself erect in the chair. 'Don't you listen to all she do tell you, Mary fach. I have been man and wife to her for more than forty years, and she have got nothing to say against me.' He lost his temper. 'Hell-fire! What can I help if our Len have joined the Party. He haven't kilt nobody, have he? No, by damn, and if I was only twenty years younger, I 'ood do

413

the same as him.' The challenge brought no response, so with many sighs and groans he stood up, and Mary let him take off her wet coat and arrange it on the brass rod over the fireplace.

Siân was busily buttering some bread when her wandering glance noticed thin spirals of steam ascend from Len's trousers. She stared hard for a moment and bent her head to have a better look before declaring triumphantly:

'There you are! Whatever I do say is always wrong, but now you can see for yourselfs. Look at that trousers, Mary. It is wet to the skin. Come on, my boy, off with it this minute.'

There was some commotion while Len, realising the futility of argument, changed into an old pair of his father's trousers, which hung about him like a blanket. Thus satisfied, Siân called them to the supper table, and it was some time before the rattle of crockery and the crunching of homemade pickles was interrupted by her abrupt query.

'How is your father, Mary fach? I haven't seen him since old Mrs. Davies, Ty-top, was buried.'

Mary hastily swallowed the food in her mouth. 'He's not half well.' Then, turning to Big Jim, she said: 'I believe he's worrying about all this talk of a lock-out. He went off early yesterday morning to see somebody or other, and he's been moping like a bear ever since.' She sighed. 'I wish I knew what is the matter with him, but he won't tell me or Len a word.'

Jim sucked the drops of tea from the end of his moustache with his lower lip, then commented: 'Well, I don't know what you do say about it, Len, but there's something in the wind. Look how us was on stop today for more than an hour waiting for trams. It never used to be like that. No, muniferni! Aye, gels; I heard Shenkin the fireman tell Sam Dangler that they have closed two of the pits the other side of the mountain and have rosed the horses.'

'Why is that, Len?' asked Siân, now anxious to placate him. 'I thought they did only rise the horses when there is going to be a strike or something like that, and I have never heard of a strike over the mountain. No, nor have Mrs. Jones, Number two, either, because she was talking to me today and she never said a word, although she have got brothers working over there.'

'No, mam. The men are not on strike, but the owners say that they have shut the pit for good and are sending some of the horses over here and selling the others.'

Mary had remained singularly quiet during this conversation, but she now broke in sharply: 'That's what makes me so mad, and why I went to the meeting with Len tonight – worse luck. They'll find work for horses. Aye, they'll see to it they are not left to wander about the pit; but they don't care a hang what happens to the men.' Her voice rose passionately. 'No, they'll be left on top with no one to find work for them or to see that they are fed.'

Big Jim leaned forward in his chair and tapped her shoulder patronisingly with a huge forefinger. 'Aye, aye, Mary, my gel, you is quite right. If old Cwmardy and the company do close down our pit, they will see to it that the horses is all right, but us will have to look after our bloody selves. That's the way of the world, my gel. It have

415

always been like that ever since I have knowed it, and always will be. What say you, Siân?'

It was Len who answered. 'That's one of the things for which I joined the Party tonight,' he declared, glad for some reason to justify his action. But Siân only glared at him, and Mary opened her mouth to say something when the donging tones of the clock interrupted her. They looked at it simultaneously and Len got to his feet in a flurry, the ends of the trousers dragging under his boots. 'Come on, Mary,' he pleaded; 'five o'clock in the morning will soon be here. I can call for my trousers tomorrow night after I come home from work.'

They all rose to their feet and the young couple, after bidding the others good night, left, with Siân admonishing: 'Now, be careful where you do tread, 'cause it is the easiest thing in the world to break your necks on a night like this.'

Meanwhile two policemen in the station were slowly removing their waterproof leggings. One was too fat to bend sufficiently and had to wait until his mate could help him.

'Ah,' he gasped, straightening his tunic, 'thank God that lot's over.'

'What lot – your leggings?'

'No, you silly fathead! I'm talking about that bloody meeting.'

A head poked itself around the door of the mess-room in which the two officers were sitting, and a voice hissed: 'Look out, boys. He's just come in.'

The fat policeman gulped nervously, then said: 'Funny for the old man to be around this time of the night. I

416

thought he'd be safely tucked up in bed with one of his dames by now.'

'Don't you worry about them tales, mate. Old long 'un is more concerned about his duty and these bloody Bolshies that are springing up all over the valley than he is about women.'

The door opened and the two men sprang to attention as the inspector, followed by another uniformed individual, walked in. Their salute was barely acknowledged by the painfully elongated man who walked direct to the fireplace and then turned his back to the flames. From this point he scrutinised the remaining inmates of the room with eyes that were red-rimmed, as though he slept little or drank much. A short, bristly moustache emphasised the thickness of his lips, and he stared at his subordinates for some time with a fish-like, glassy look. When he spoke his voice was as thin as the hair he tried to spread all over his head.

'Well, who was at the meeting?'

'Harry Morgan, Fred Lewis, Len Roberts and his wife, sir—'

'Yes – yes, hurry up and don't eat your words!' he snapped, gently stroking his posterior as the heat warmed his flesh.

The man so addressed coloured and hastened his recital of names. When he had finished, the thin man remained thoughtfully silent for some moments before saying: 'Hmm. Len Roberts and his wife, eh? It seems this chap Morgan is beginning to spread his wings. Hmm.'

He looked up sharply to ask: 'What did they say?'

The two policemen looked uncomfortable and fidgeted

uneasily without speaking.

'Come, come. Haven't you heard what I said?'

The fatter constable drew himself erect and saluted again. 'Well, it's like this, sir. It was such a dirty night and the wind was howling so much that it was impossible to hear a word of what was going on inside except a blur of voices.'

The thin face before him turned from red to purple and a little time elapsed before the lips parted to bark out: 'What? Do you mean to tell me you heard nothing? That you listen to a nest of Bolsheviks plotting sedition and have nothing to report?'

He swallowed hard, then turned abruptly from the flabbergasted constables: 'Inspector, I want a full report of that meeting first thing in the morning.'

The inspector saluted and both left the room, but the discomfited policemen remained standing for a long while, both looking miserable and awkward.

At last the taller gave a deep sigh. 'Ah well. The old man must have been upset about something. Perhaps he's had a row with his old woman.'

'Maybe. But that's no reason why he should have his bang out on us. No good arguing about it now, however. The best thing we can do is to prepare that report.'

They pulled their coats off and drew the table nearer the fire.

Outside the station the wind still howled round the streets of Cwmardy, seeming to gather greater fury because the rain had deserted it. A group of men, their heads bent to the beating wind that ballooned their coats behind them

418

like bustles, battled past the police station and its two busy occupants.

'What a hell of a night!' one remarked, his words partially strangled by the wind.

'Aye, but we can be thankful the rain have stopped, or we'd be soaked long before we reached the pit,' another remarked.

'Not much odds about that. You want to see Dai Cannon's heading. The water pours down from the top, and bubbles up from the bottom. Gee! And the stink – ugh! It's like a thousand lavatories and polecats all in one. He's got to work under zinc now to keep the water from his body.'

'Ach! Zinc be damned! What bloody use is that to a man? He can't carry it about with him from the face to the tram. Better for him to stick the water than try to dodge something that can't be dodged.'

They continued to fight against the wind and presently one of them asked: 'What's all this talk about us going to be locked out?'

The reply came instantly: 'By damn, they might as well shut the bloody hole for good for any use it is to us on the wages they pay now.'

Further conversation was lost in the noise of the pit-hooter, which suddenly split the air with reverberating blasts that echoed through the crevices of every house in the valley. The group of men hurried their pace in response to the command, and in a short time Cwmardy was left to the mercy of the wind as the clanking of hobnailed boots on stone died away.

419

ANOTHER VICTIM

The following afternoon Len wearily dragged his feet out of the pit-cage and was glad to find that the storm had blown itself out and a yellow sun was poking its thin rays through the murk of the valley. The sight and the cool air invigorated him and he wasn't long reaching home, where Mary was busily cooking his dinner.

Before pulling off his dirty coat he asked: 'Where's your father, Mary?'

She looked up from the saucepan over which she was bending, and although her face was flushed with the heat from the fire, he noticed that her eyes were sad in the dark shadows that circled them.

'I don't know, Len. He's been out again since early this morning.' She paused and stirred the contents of the saucepan, then continued, without looking at him: 'I've

421

told him you joined the Party last night.'

Len stopped short, his coat hanging loosely from one arm. 'What did you want to do that for?' he demanded sharply. 'But there, what does it matter? He was bound to know sooner or later.'

He went on with his preparations for dinner, and while she was serving it up he asked: 'What did he say?'

She waited until she had shared the dinner on three plates, one of which she put on the hob, then answered: 'I don't know what he said altogether. Here, eat your dinner; we can talk after.' She sat tiredly in the chair beside him and pecked at her food, leaving half of it untouched. Having finished his dinner, he noisily moved his chair back and reached up to the mantelpiece for a cigarette, while Mary poured him a cup of tea. He puffed away silently, trying to look unconcerned, but all the time watching her through the smoke that left his mouth, as she patiently began clearing the dinner things.

At last his impatience bubbled over and he again asked: 'Tell me, Mary, what did he say?'

Her hands trembled fretfully when she replied: 'Oh, for God's sake don't let's bother our heads about that nonsense now!' She went on with her work and after it was finished sat down, drawing her hand across her forehead.

Len became immediately solicitous, and tried to soothe her. 'Your head is bad, my dear?' he queried. 'Why don't you take a powder and have a lie down. I can manage by myself now.'

The gentle tones made her ashamed of her irritability, and she looked at him affectionately as she replied: 'It's all right, Len. Only I'm worried about dad.'

She paused to wipe her perspiring hands on her apron. 'I don't know what's coming over him. He's getting more miserable every day and hardly touches a bit of food. Oh, Len, he's breaking up fast and is not the same dad I've known in the past.'

Len, conscious of how deeply she loved her father and how she was affected by the change taking place in him, hardly knew what to say, but managed to murmur: 'Aye, I've noticed him myself these last few weeks. It must be his age,' he added consolingly. 'Look at my old man – he's getting so miserable that it's hellish to work with him. We'll be the same ourselves when we're their age, I suppose.' He tried to laugh, but the half-hearted attempt drew no response from his wife.

Len knocked the light off his cigarette and carefully put the stump back on the mantelshelf before going out into the backyard to fetch the tub, which he placed in the centre of the kitchen. This done, he pulled off his dusty shirt and wet singlet; then, naked to the waist, lifted the boiler of hot water from the fire and poured it into the tub, where Mary cooled it with panfuls of cold water. Bent double over the edge of the tub, he began bathing, and Mary gathered together the discarded pit clothes.

His head was a mass of black lather when he heard her say: 'There have been more compensation cases here for you today.'

Len hurriedly swilled the soapsuds from his head and sat on the tub-rim while she handed him a towel. He wiped himself, but his hair was still damp, although his face was pink with rubbing.

'Who's been, Mary?' he asked.

'Oh, old Reuben and the boy with the broken back,' she answered, washing his back vigorously, then taking the towel from him to use it herself.

Len stood up and, unbuttoning his trousers, let them fall about his feet before stepping naked into the tub.

'Well, well,' he said while he soaped his legs. 'It's a shame the way they're mucking about with the compo people.' Mary watched the ripple of the skin over his ribs as he raised water with his cupped hands to swill his legs.

'Yes, you're right, Len,' she commented bitterly, her mind focused on the thin body before her. 'The company have now offered them a lump sum each to square them off.'

Len's amazement was demonstrated by the way he let his hands drop limply to his sides and looked at her, utterly unconscious of his nakedness. 'What? Offered them a lump sum?' He clicked his tongue against his teeth in audible disgust. 'Well, well. That means the rotters want to wash their hands of them, now the poor dabs are no use. No wonder your old man is worried, by damn.'

He came out of the tub and began dressing in his evening clothes. He had already pulled the clean shirt over his head, when a new idea entered his mind.

'But why do they want to buy the compo men off, now?' he asked in bewilderment.

Mary shook her head. 'I don't know, unless it's something to do with all this talk that we are going to be locked out,' she replied hesitantly.

Len shook his head, as puzzled as she was, but he made

424

no further comment as she helped him take the tub back out.

A further smoke revived his spirits and he asked her to come to the pictures.

'I'm sorry, Len, but you know I've got a Woman's Guild tonight, and I can't let them down,' she replied.

This upset him again, and he muttered half savagely: 'I don't know, but whenever I ask you to come with me, Mary, you've got this, that, or something else on. I tell you straight I'm just fed-up.' He began to shout. 'I would be treated much better if I was a lodger.'

Mary seemed to compress her body into knots as he continued his tirade, but she kept control of herself until he said, 'Only last night, you were nagging me about joining the Party, but you don't say a word about yourself and this Guild, which is only a bloody gossip-shop, I expect.'

This brought her bounding to her feet. 'Don't you dare say that about our Guild, Len Roberts! Those women do more work in a month than your Party, as you call it, can do in twelve.'

'Aye,' he sneered, 'they'll work blue hell organising mystery tours and trips round the coast in a charabanc, but when it comes to anything that counts, they're all blab.'

Mary's face went white. 'Oh, so that's what you think, is it? Now we know where we are. But let me tell you this, you and your Party will be glad to come on your hands and knees to our women for help before you'll be any good.'

Len laughed loudly. 'Ha-ha-ha! That's a good un! Ha-ha, the best I've heard for a long time! Come to you for help – there'll be something wrong with us when we do that.'

The sneer stung her deeply. 'I don't know so much

425

about that. You are all pretty good talkers. Aye, you'll talk all night about revolutions and Russia or anything that doesn't concern our people. But when it comes to a lock-out or something about the pit you're all dumb.'

She challenged him with a direct question. 'Tell me, how much time was spent last night talking about conditions in Cwmardy?' She answered herself without giving him time. 'Five minutes and not a second more. Bah! Fitter if you and Harry Morgan thought a bit less about people in other countries and a bit more about your own.'

This was unexpected and caught Len awkwardly, but he tried to defend the position. 'Half a minute, Mary. You've got to understand the conditions all over the world, mun, to know how to alter things here. Good God! Haven't we got something to learn from the Russian revolution? You're talking like a sledge, mun.'

She made no reply other than with her eyes, which looked at him pityingly as she rose from the chair and prepared herself for the Guild. When she was ready, he put his coat on and took his cap from the peg near the door.

Mary smiled quietly to herself and asked: 'Where are you going, then?'

'Oh, I might as well come with you down the road. I might see Will Evans or some of the boys,' he replied in tones that made Mary regret her sharp words, but neither spoke again as he accompanied her down Main Street and left her at the house where the Guild held its weekly meetings.

Len continued his way aimlessly, his mind occupied with the row he had just had with Mary. But he soon forgot this and began to think of the work he had to do next day. He planned to go down earlier than usual so that he could stand some timbers before the haulier came. Having settled this, his thoughts wandered to the compensation men and the talk in the pit.

'It's a funny thing,' he mused. 'Ten years ago next August the Great War started, and now, nearly exactly ten years after, there's all this talk about the pit shutting down and all of us being thrown out of work. It's like as if things go in waves every so often.'

He was deep in meditation of the problem when his attention was attracted by someone shouting his name. He stopped and looked behind to see two young men hurrying towards him, whom he recognised as Will Evans and Fred Lewis. The former was slim, but even with his clothes on his body gave an impression of sinewy strength. His cap, pushed carelessly to the side of his head, and the blade of grass which dangled loosely from his mouth were symptomatic of his whole approach to life. He never troubled about his appearance, and his eyes gleamed with a mischief which prompted him to see the humour in everything. He had a habit of bursting unexpectedly into a loud laugh that rolled in recurring gusts and rising resonance from his mouth in a manner that made it irresistibly infectious. Fred Lewis, his companion, was the opposite in every way. Rather tall, his black hair made his face sallow and exposed the fallacy of the 'hail, fellow, well met' demeanour which, in a patronising way, he deliberately cultivated. Fred boasted to everyone that he was among the first to join the Party and was no less assertive in declaring that he was its foremost theoretician. But he never told anyone he hated Ezra, the miners' leader, because of the latter's influence over the workmen, and detested Harry Morgan because of his growing ability and eloquence. All other men he regarded with contempt, as nincompoops made to follow people like himself. Will had long ago at work detected these weaknesses in his mate, and never failed to take advantage of the fact, secure against all retort in his extreme lack of self-consciousness.

The pair came up to Len, who greeted them with a casual 'How be, boys?' But Will was bubbling over with impatience and made no attempt to return the salutation.

'Is it true what I have heard, that you have joined the Party?' he asked.

Len merely nodded his head and Fred said, 'There you are. Will you believe me now?'

Will Evans looked at Len with open mouth, then began to laugh unrestrainedly. 'Well, by damn, I never thought you had nuff sense, Len, to do a thing like that. Ha-ha! Ho-ho-ho!'

Len appeared hurt by this doubtful compliment, but had no time to say anything before Fred interjected: 'Oh, I don't know about that, Will. Len has got the average intelligence, and in any case he can always turn to me for help when he's in a knot.'

Will turned to the speaker, his eyes filled with admiration. 'By damn, Fred, if you keep on you will so sure as hell land up in Parliament one day.'

Fred unconsciously expanded his chest. 'Well, there's many worse and less clever than me there, so I don't see why not.'

Will glanced at Len's face, but the misery he saw on it made him change the subject. 'You're looking like a dog with the colic. Buck up, mun,' he remarked.

'Oh, I'm all right,' came the dejected reply. 'Only I thought to go to the pictures tonight, but Mary went to the Guild instead, and I was wandering about on my own till you chaps came up.'

Will burst into another guffaw of laughter, which impelled a passer-by to ask: 'Happy, tonight, in't you, Will? Have the old man lost a leg, or what?'

'You mind your own bloody business, Twm. Len by here have lost his missus in the Guild, and he don't know what to do with hisself.'

The newcomer, although uninvited, joined the company, and the conversation continued for a long time. It was only eventually interrupted when Fred's restless eyes saw a cortege of men in pit clothes slowly coming towards them down the street.

'Hush, boys, somebody has had a tap.' In an instant the whole street was silent but for the sharp 'tip-tap' of iron-shod boots as the men, four of them carrying a stretcher covered completely with brattice cloth, passed by.

Someone whispered: 'Who is it?'

To be answered in a softer whisper: 'Si Spraggs. He was caught by the journey, poor dab, and never had a chance.'

The news passed from mouth to mouth as quickly as a telephone message, and even before Len reached the door of the Guild-room the women were already coming out, their eyes full of fearful queries till he told them who it was. They immediately became relieved and solicitous.

429

One stout woman who had reared a houseful of children, all of whom were now working, muttered disconsolately: 'Well, well. There have been nothing but worry and trouble in that house ever since I have knowed it.' She outlined the history of the bereaved family while the other women listened attentively, at the same time inwardly congratulating themselves that the corpse did not belong to them.

When the recital was finished, one asked, 'She is going to have another baby, in't she? I fancy I saw her looking like it the other day in the shop, but I didn't have much time to notice.'

They went back into the house and continued the discussion there. Before they finished they had planned to provide a wreath, and had allocated themselves in pairs to be responsible for the widow's house and to keep her company until the body was buried.

Len felt like following Mary, whose face had gone grey when she heard the news, into the Guild-room. Common sense held him back, and he retraced his steps up the street, to find his mates had disappeared. This did not worry him, however, because the tragedy had swept everything else from his mind and he automatically followed his feet while his imagination ran riot.

His first conscious knowledge of direction came with the increased palpitation of his heart. He stopped to rest and looking around saw below him the narrow strip of valley which Cwmardy headed like a black bonnet. The evening was now brilliantly fine, and the air on the mountain clear as he slowly continued his way to the top.

But the thought of the corpse followed him and stamped itself more deeply into his brain with every step he took across the mountain, till he sighted the valley on the other side. He sat down, and after a while his thoughts drifted and he began to appraise the scene before his eyes. He compared the gloom of the village beneath and the thousands of dark lives it contained with the bright sky and clear air above in which the larks tinkled their tunes. Len followed the ascending music and wondered if the larks sang because they were happy. The people he knew mostly sang hymns, which were always sad and seemed to harmonise with their sorrows. He let his eyes wander down the length of the ragged valley and saw the smokeless stacks of the idle pits near its end, a sight which prompted him to wonder how soon Cwmardy pits would be equally silent and dead. It seemed that everything he saw and heard was a portent of impending dereliction and despair, a thought which made him mentally forgive Mary the quarrel for which he was at least equally responsible. He sighed and turned in the direction of the Channel, which glistened in the distance like a ribbon of light.

His boyhood's romantic ambition to become a sailor had evaporated with the passing years, but a strange tenderness and longing still surged through him whenever he caught a glimpse of the sea. It always took his mind back to the time his mother had taken him on the chapel excursion and to the day in Blackpool at the beginning of the War, when he had first made love to Mary. Musing in this manner, he lost all consciousness of time until the

431

night began to wrap him in its cold blanket. Presently he began to shiver, and rising to his feet, he slowly made his way home down the mountain.

THE LOCK-OUT

The Big House, perched on a jutting crest half-way up the mountain, brooded whitely in the dusk. Its windows, already reflecting the lights behind, shone through the trees that surrounded this mansion belonging to the colliery company. From its altitude it looked down on the pits and valley its occupants dominated.

Lord Cwmardy, head of the company controlling the pits, rose from a chair and looked at the three men who sat with him in the drawing-room of the Big House. They sat in different postures, but each of them accepted the warm invitation of the cushioned chair which nearly buried him. Cwmardy's square, clean-shaven face with its silvered hair and the poise of the broad shoulders demonstrated the strength and the self-confidence of the man. Pouring himself a glass of liquor from the decanter

433

on the table, he sipped it appreciatively, then began to speak in deep tones that fitted in with his general build. He told his listeners the banks were pressing and that nothing faced the company but liquidation followed by complete reorganisation of the pits. His voice shook a little when he explained that the working conditions and price-lists would have to be drastically altered. He had been born in Cwmardy and reared with its people, and always felt a vague sentimental attachment to them, but he soon gripped himself as he concluded his report.

Mr. Higgins, the representative of the banks, stretched his long body more comfortably in the chair and carefully stroked his grey moustache, with a hand noticeable for its slender whiteness, before saying, 'I believe Lord Cwmardy has explained the position fully. I don't pretend to understand the technique of mining. That is your business, gentlemen; but I do understand it is high time something was done to ensure payment of interest on the money we have invested.'

He kept on for some time, and when he finished his statement there was a long silence which was eventually broken by Mr. Hicks, the general manager of the pits.

'I don't believe the men will accept lower price-lists,' he commented hesitatingly.

Mr. Higgins drew himself from the chair to say coldly: 'That is their responsibility. We have done all we can,' and the conversation drew to an abrupt close.

There was an awkward pause; the bottles on the table glowed in the firelight, some blood-red, others bright yellow, like gold. At last Mr. Higgins introduced a new subject.

'What is this affair I understand you are presiding over, Lord Cwmardy?' he asked with assumed interest. The coalowner's eyes sparkled immediately.

'Oh, it's a kind of musical festival, a gymanfa ganu, as our people call it,' he replied. 'We usually get some very good singing, and I enjoy attending them.'

Once started on this subject he was in his element and for a long time entertained his listeners with anecdotes relating to it. When his guests retired, Lord Cwmardy strolled to the window and watched for many minutes the twinkling lights of the valley. Something like a sigh escaped him as he turned back to the room.

Next morning Len was sleeping like a log and Mary had to shake him roughly before he woke. Once down the stairs, however, he soon recovered his faculties and began dressing in his pit clothes, while Mary, her nightdress covered with Siân's shawl, prepared breakfast. Before the meal was finished they heard sounds from her father's bedroom, followed by his entry into the kitchen. Ezra's hair was bushy but grey, and the ends of his once-trim moustache were ragged, as though they were continually being gnawed. His eyes, dark like Mary's, were sunk into his head. The brows were so thick that his eyes appeared to be half closed; but the shortish, broad body showed the essential alertness which, together with a stubborn tenacity in doing what he regarded as right, irrespective of other people's opinions, were his main characteristics.

Mary hastened to pour her father a cup of tea as he took his seat in the armchair at the side of the fire. This helped to ease the tightness in his chest a little, and he asked: 'Did you hear anything particular in the pit yesterday, Len?'

Before he could receive a reply, the old miners' leader hastened out at the back, where he coughed painfully for a while then returned to the kitchen.

'Ah, that's better,' he gasped, licking his moustache. 'Hand me that cup, Mary.' He took a sip of tea and continued: 'What was I talking about? Oh, I know. Yes, there's something big in the wind. Lord Cwmardy is down again. That's the third time now, and he doesn't come here for nothing. I wish I knew what was in his mind.'

His voice had become puzzled, and he stuffed his pipe with the herb mixture which Big Jim was prepared to gamble his life was the best cure for asthma.

Len looked over the rim of the saucer he held to his lips, gulped down the tea in his mouth and nodded his head as he commented: 'Aye, Will Smallbeer was talking about it yesterday. The trams have been coming pretty slow these last few days, and he said we can expect short time before very long now.'

Ezra looked up sharply. 'Will Smallbeer? What does he know? What he says isn't worth taking notice of. But, all the same, listen to what the men are saying, Len. Their guesses are never far off the mark.'

Len rose and put his coat on, wondering what Ezra was driving at, but he made no further remark. When he was dressed he kissed Mary, bade the two good morning, and left them alone together.

Big Jim was ready and waiting for his son when the latter reached his parents' house, where, as usual, Siân insisted on his drinking the cup of steaming cocoa she had waiting for him. As the men left the house she warned them: ''Member to take care of your selfs.'

Jim merely laughed and waved his hand airily as he joined the long line of silent men making their way to the pit. Before they had reached half-way a whisper ran back through the line. 'No work today. Stop trucks.' The men stopped and looked questioningly at each other, as though someone had pulled a lever that tied their feet to the paving-stones.

The spell was broken by a loud shout from Jim: 'Good God, couldn't they have told us before we put our dirty clothes on? Now us will have to bath all over for nothing. Blast 'em!' He spat disgustedly into the roadway. A group of men came down the hill, pouring water from their jacks and loudly declaring: 'It's no good, boys. The sidings is full of coal; not a bloody empty to be seen anywhere, and the lamp-men have been ordered to give no lamps out.'

Dai Cannon, one of the local preachers and Big Jim's close friend, indignantly pulled his overhanging belly back under the leather belt, while his loose lower lip dangled wetly beneath his moustache.

'Why didn't they blow the hooter to let us know there was no work?' he demanded of no one in particular.

All the men now began pouring their water into the road and some of the younger ones started to sing lustily as they turned and retraced their steps to the strains of:

Mae bys Mary Ann wedi gwiwo
A Dafydd y gwas sy'n cael y bai.

437

(Mary Ann's finger is swollen
And David the servant gets the blame.)

Bedroom windows were hastily lowered and tousled heads pushed through to see what was the matter, but the men shouted reassuringly to the women folk.

'Don't worry, gels. It's only stop trucks. Go back to bed; the old man will soon be with you. Ha-ha!' The laughter at these quips rippled through the ranks like wind through grass.

For three days in succession the men had to return home. On the third occasion they did not pass jokes at the expense of the women; the useless trudge up the hill each morning had made them too resentful.

'Bloody wasters, drawing us out of bed like this for nothing!' said one loudly. 'By gum! In the trenches they ought to be, where we was. We'd soon bring them to their senses, or blow out the bit they've got.' This statement met with general approbation.

Siân knew the men were returning even before Big Jim and Len opened the door. The miners made sufficient noise to advertise their coming. She looked up when her men entered and waited until Jim had pulled off his coat before asking: 'What, again? However do the company think we are going to live?'

Her hair hung in graceless wisps over her nightdress, deepening the lines in her face. 'Three turns in one week. Oh dear, dear, it is more than a poor 'ooman can bear.' Neither of the men replied to her wail, but Len stayed to prevent the quarrel he thought was brewing.

The silence got on her nerves. 'Can't you say something, dyn jawl?' she asked Jim. 'Or have your tongue got tied to your head? But there, what do you worry, so long as you do work sometimes and have your pocket-money regular. Huh! It is me who have got to ponder my poor brains out how to stretch the little bit of pay twice so far as it is 'sposed to go.'

Jim could stand her accusations no longer, and began shouting back: 'Hell-fire! Think you us have come back for fun, 'ooman? What think you us is, mun – tomcats to go up and down the hill as you do shout to us? By damn, if you do think that you is thinking wrong, my gel. Take that from me, muniferni!'

He caught a glimpse of the fire kindling in her eyes and changed his tones. 'Don't blame us, mun, that there is no work. Us can't help it,' he cajoled. But Siân knew his tricks and was not deceived.

'Oh, no! Nobody is to blame, I 'spose, but it is me who will have to face the peoples who have been good enough to put food in our bellies. What to tell poor old Evans Cardi the good Lord alone knows. I can never do it.'

She wiped her eyes in the hem of her nightdress, exposing her withered legs. Her tears always affected Jim, and he now reluctantly tried to soothe her, grunting: 'All right, left it to me. I'll go down and see the old ram.'

Siân withdrew the nightdress from her eyes and glared at him. 'For shame, using them words before your only son! Huh! You, indeed.' There was a world of contempt in her voice as she repudiated what he had thought a

439

magnanimous offer. 'Clever man you are to see anyone. No, James. The best thing you can see is in the Boar's Head, where there is plenty of rams every night, more shame on you.'

Jim started to make an indignant protest but she gave him no time. 'And don't you never think you can wear the trousers and the petticoats; one of them is quite enough for you. You look after your own business and leave mine to me, if you please.' She drew her bent form erect with great dignity and her eyes flashed a challenge at him.

Jim looked at her with open mouth, into which the ends of his moustache drooped, but he had no fitting retort and the matter dropped when Len said: 'Don't worry, mam. Dad can't help it. I must go up the house now. So long.'

During the idle days rumours of the impending lock-out had spread like fire, and the people could talk of nothing else, everyone professing to have inside information, although actually all of them were completely in the dark. On the fourth day the pits began again. Len and his father were among twenty-seven other men and boys who worked the same conveyor face. On the day of the restart the men chatted to each other as they cleared the stones and rubbish that had fallen on the iron troughs during the stoppage.

Will Smallbeer gave his opinions to Len while both were engaged in lifting a huge stone that had fallen flatwise on the conveyor. 'There is something funny about all this business, Len, you mark my words. I have been working in this old pit for going on forty years now, and have never knowed her having stop trucks for nothink.'

440

Len was as puzzled as the old man, but did not like to expose his ignorance. 'Perhaps the company is going to go bankrupt because they can't make the pit pay,' he suggested hesitantly.

Will Smallbeer lost his temper and let the edge of the stone he was holding drop back into the conveyor with a bang, as he straightened his back the better to say: 'Ach! Don't pay to hell! No man can never get me to believe that. Why! Here us is filling coal for shilling a ton, when us can get the trams, and the company do charge twenty shillings for the same bloody coal on top.'

'That might be,' Len retorted, unwilling to be beaten in an argument now it had started, 'but the company have got much more to pay than our wages, mun.'

Will lifted his lamp to the level of Len's face and looked into his eyes. 'Poor boy,' he muttered as he lowered the lamp again. 'Poor dab! You do want to have your head read. Pity!' He sighed like a man deeply grieved.

The conveyor began to clatter into life and further conversation became impossible.

Len's limbs tugged wearily on his body when he entered the kitchen after the shift was over. Mary was busy preparing his dinner, but he noticed she looked ill.

'What is the matter? Have you had another pull?' he asked anxiously.

She shook her head somewhat wearily. 'Don't worry, Len. I'm all right. Just a bit of a cold.'

He knew she had avoided his question, but, aware of her obstinacy, he did not pursue the matter. Ezra was sitting in the armchair in exactly the same attitude as when Len had set out for work in the morning. His white hair gleamed in the glow from the fire. He did not say a word till dinner was over, and while Len bathed and dressed merely resumed his pipe, the peculiar stench from which nearly choked the other two. At last the miners' leader casually looked from the fire to say: 'I've found out the company's little game at last, and what our men have been talking about isn't far off the mark.'

Len sat down and gazed with deep interest at his father-in-law as the latter continued more slowly and seriously: 'Mr. Hicks sent for me this morning to tell me that the pits will close down unless we are willing to meet the company half way.'

Len's eyes opened wide. In spite of all the talk about a lock-out he had never thought of the possibilities in such a tangible way as Ezra was now putting them, but the elder man gave him no time for conjecture or comment.

He had bent again towards the fire and it seemed he was now musing rather than talking. 'Clever, clever! Shut the men out just as winter is coming on us – huh! We've had six years of peace since the end of the War, but it was too good to last.'

He raised his head and they saw that his face had become drawn and his eyes sad when he asked: 'Will you go round the committee-men, Len, and tell them there is a special meeting tonight?'

Len did not question him, although he glanced in a puzzled way at Mary, who turned her head away. He had shut the door behind him before she noticed his cap still

442

hanging on its peg. She pulled it off and hurried to tell him about it. He was already half-way down the street when he heard her shout and looked behind to see what was the matter.

'You've forgotten your cap, Len.'

His hand went automatically to his head and found it bare. 'Never mind,' he shouted back. 'I shan't be long, and a bit of fresh air 'on't hurt me.'

When Len had notified all the committee-men he made his way to Ben the Barber's, hoping to have a haircut before the meeting started. He found the shop empty, but sharp whistling and the noise of chairs being shifted in the inner room urged him to peep round the door. Ben was hobbling about, preparing seating accommodation for the committee meeting. Chairs, benches, a table, and an old-fashioned stove with a stack that penetrated the centre of the ceiling occupied all the available space.

Ben stopped whistling when Len asked: 'How's trade, Ben? I see you're busy.'

The voice that replied was as sharp as the whistle that preceded it. 'Huh! It's on tick, like that clock by there,' pointing to the mantelpiece.

'Never mind, times will soon get better,' Len soothed.

The lame little barber continued his hopping between the chairs, grunting all the while: 'Better? Better? Ha-ha! That's good, hmm! That's why the committee is meeting special tonight, isn't it? The last time it met here was during the strike, and take it from me there's more trouble brewing. Aye, my old nose can always smell it.'

The shop door opened to admit members of the

443

committee and he kept silent as they sat down with various salutations. Len forgot his haircut and joined the conversation which Dai Cannon started. Ezra was the last to enter, and the miners' leader wasted very little time before taking the chair and beginning his report. He told the committee how the company was unable to hold its contracts on the market because of the high cost of production in the pit and the competition from other countries. His report did not take long, and he concluded with the remark: 'That is how the position was put to me, fellow workmen. The company says it can't keep the pits going as things are. Either we lower the cost of production – that means we fill more coal for less wages – or the pits close down. The matter is now in your hands.'

Whenever Ezra did this, the committee-men knew from long experience he had already come to a personal decision which was distasteful to himself.

Len sensed the man's mood and wondered why he had not hinted in the house what he intended doing. He saw the glare from the fire deepen the lines in Ezra's face and fancied his eyes had become dismal; but his attention was quickly drawn back to the room by a shuffling of chairs as Dai Cannon rose heavily to his feet. Dai's bottom lip hung lower and wetter than usual as he growled: 'Huh! I seem to have heard that yarn before. Going bankrupt, eh? That's always the tale when they want something from us.'

Ezra stopped him with a wave of the hand, and his words exposed the decision he had come to. 'Either that, Dai, or close down the pit for good and get no work and wages at all.'

The discussion now became heated and bitter, Harry Morgan being particularly vehement as his voice rang through the room like a bell.

'That's the new line of leadership,' he declared raspingly, staring hard at Ezra. 'Because the company say "more work for less wages, or no work at all" we are expected to tell the men that half is better than nothing. Bah! In this way the company can get everything it wants and our Federation becomes the agent for giving it to them. If that's all the advice Ezra can give, he'd better go over to the company openly. That would be cleaner than acting as their servant in our ranks.' His voice rose passionately as Ezra's face went whiter. 'No, we can never accept this. If we do, we destroy our Federation and play right into the hands of the boss. We must fight the lock-out as we fought the strike; and if the company can't keep the pits open, then let's force them out of the way and get on with the job ourselves.'

This challenge was greeted with a burst of applause and Ezra's chin sank more deeply on his chest as he felt the temper of the men vibrate in the close air, but when he rose to his feet he was his old indomitable self, and his voice, though deeper, was as cutting as Harry's when he replied to the latter's accusation: 'I was fighting this company when Harry was in petticoats. Yes. I lost a wife and a home through it, which is more than Harry has ever done or is likely to do. It's quite easy for a man with the pride of a peacock and the brains of a sparrow to strut bravely for a short minute in this room, and easier still for him to use a soapbox to slander better men than himself; but let him tell us what to do without hurting our own

445

people more than we hurt the company.'

Harry bawled out, 'Struggle or starve.'

Ezra laughed in his face and remarked: 'You mean struggle and starve.' The others now joined in, and the place became a bedlam of conflicting and challenging voices.

Across the road Mr. Evans Cardi was slowly putting up the shutters of his stores. The corrugated iron sheets which had been placed over the windows during the big strike were now stiff and heavy. His wife came out to help him, and in a short time the windows were covered and the light blotted out. John's shoulders drooped as he walked into the kitchen; the high forehead that jutted over his eyes made them look even more morbid and sunken than they actually were. The old couple ate in silence the meal she had prepared, and after she had cleared the dishes away, she sat opposite her husband and began knitting. This, for some reason, seemed to irritate him and he peevishly exclaimed: 'Put that knitting down, Maggie, it gets on my nerves!'

She obediently dropped the wool into her lap, with a patient gesture, and asked: 'What is coming over you, John? You get more miserable every day.'

He looked at her queerly before rising to his feet. 'Do you know how much we have got left in the bank?' he asked, his voice hoarse from the fatigue induced by worry.

'I don't expect we have much, John.'

'You are right. We haven't got enough to meet our bills this week.' He rose to his feet, agitatedly ruffling his hand through his sparse hair. 'But how can we help it?' he groaned. 'Big Jim's wife and many others didn't pay anything off their bills this week again.'

'Did you let them have more credit, John?'

'Of course I did. You see, Maggie fach, if we don't give them credit they won't come to deal with us when the pit is working full, and that means that we lose their custom and what they owe us,' he explained apologetically.

'But how are we to carry on, John? There's Ron's college fees due again.' She clasped her hands and dropped them helplessly on her lap where they tangled themselves in the wool. 'Oh, God! What are we to do?' she moaned in a frenzy of self-pity. 'I can see nothing before us but the workhouse and my poor boy on the parish, after all we have done for him.'

Her head dropped until her eyes were on a level with the fire, in whose flickering tremors she saw the shattering of her dreams. Her attitude alarmed John, and he tried to soothe her. 'Hush, my gel. Things are not so bad as that. Ron will surely get a job as a teacher or something when he finishes his studies. Don't worry; everything will come all right yet.'

The harassed woman rose and, placing her hands on his shoulders, while the wool made a pool about her feet, looked him squarely in the eyes.

'Do you really believe that things will ever come better in this valley, that puts a blight on everyone that comes to it?' Her voice was an echo of the incredulity that consumed her.

John tried to brighten her and answered reassuringly:

447

'Of course they will. Once we are over this depression, and the company conquers the foreign competition threat, we will be drawing dividends again from our shares in the pit.'

The poor woman's eyes warmed a little, but her tones were still sad when she said: 'I hope you are right, John bach. Yes, I hope you are right.'

The night pressed darkly on Cwmardy as two uniformed men left the Fountain, where they had been watching what transpired in Ben the Barber's, and methodically paced their way up the Main Street, focusing their lamps on every doorway they passed. Before they reached the hall of the chapel, next door to the police station, their heavy tread was lost in the sound of singing. Lights streamed through the painted windows in a variety of hues that seemed to quiver in the caresses of the music.

The two officers hesitated a moment, until one exclaimed, 'It's the gymanfa ganu that Lord Cwmardy is leading. Let's go in for a bit to hear it.'

The other agreed, and they tip-toed into the chapel, which was packed with miners and their families. The men sat on one side of the aisle, and the women, dressed in their Sunday best, lent a brightness to the other.

Lord Cwmardy stood in the pulpit, his face beaming with pleasure as he led the singing. The beautiful voices seemed fastened to the end of his baton, as it lifted them into ascending crescendos, then dropped them into deep throbs. Occasionally the sopranos rode the heavy basses like a flock of seagulls on a wave.

Lord Cwmardy's baton flashed more quickly and his face became a mask of concentrated hope as he worked the choristers towards the final stanza of the hymn they were singing. The initial mournful hopelessness of the tune was lost in the tempo of the finale, which swept the voices together into a vocal unity that awed the policemen at the door.

Wiping the perspiration from his forehead and rolling the sleeves of his white shirt more firmly over his elbows, Cwmardy looked at the languid form of Mr. Higgins, with a glance that seemed to whisper: 'What do you think of that? There is nothing like it in the world!' The coalowner was very fond of music, and thought his work-people the finest choral singers in the world.

Whilst the festival was still in progress, the committee-meeting ended and the men came into the street, where a heavy drizzle was beginning to fall. Each raindrop, impregnated with fine coal-dust, became a lump of mud before it fell on the earth of the valley, where the rain had all the effects of a deep fog smothering the lighted windows and pressing drearily on those it touched.

Len and Ezra walked quietly home, their coat-collars buttoned tightly to prevent the black moisture running down their necks, but Len's bare head was dripping before they had gone twenty yards. The ascent made Ezra wheeze and his chest bubbled wetly as he fought for breath. What the miners took to be asthma was now demanding a heavy toll from his one-time vigour.

They were in the house before either spoke, and Mary solicitously took the wet coat and hat from her father, at the same time scolding Len for going out without his cap. He merely grunted in reply, and she turned impatiently to her father to ask: 'Tell me, dad, what happened in the

449

committee tonight?'

Ezra kept on gasping, while his eyes bulged with exertion, and it was Len who answered: 'We have decided that we can't accept the terms offered by the company. The only man in favour was your father, but I don't blame him. Let every man stick to his opinion.' He became enthusiastic: 'By gum, Mary, you ought to have heard Harry Morgan.'

Mary looked at him while she gathered her thoughts. His reference to Ezra had stunned her for a moment; but at last she muttered: 'So we are in for another spell of misery.' Then her eyes brightened as she went on: 'But, duw, Len, it's good to know the spirit of the big strike is still in us, even though so many years have passed.'

Ezra recovered his breath, shook his head disapprovingly, and said: 'It's easy to talk like that, my gel. But there, I suppose it's natural for youngsters like you. Aye, I used to be the same myself once, but a lifetime of fighting against the company has taught me it's useless running your head against a stone wall.'

Len squared his shoulders. 'I don't agree with you, Ezra. I believe the committee is right and that Harry Morgan hit the nail on the head when he said that this was a new stunt by the company to get rid of their debts and smash down our wages and conditions.'

Ezra, with his customary astuteness, let Len run on, knowing this was the surest way of finding out all he was thinking. Len's eyes were gleaming as he entered into the spirit of the argument.

'I know it is hard, but isn't all our life hard? I understand what it will mean if they shut the pit; but we can't let them use the pit like a sledge against us, just to make us accept everything that they say. Oh no! Don't forget, Ezra, hundreds of our men were hurt and some died so that we could be where we are today.'

'Aye,' said Mary, 'that's right, Len. But we can't get from the pit something that's not there, can we?'

She always sided with her father, feeling his wider experience to be a surer guide than Len's exuberance. Her outburst startled Len. 'Something that is not there? What do you mean?' he asked.

'What she says,' answered Ezra, a smile softening the lines of his face. 'If competition makes it impossible for the company to pay the present wages, then it means, as far as they are concerned, that the wages are not in the pit and therefore the men can't have them. Mind you,' he added, somewhat hurriedly, 'that's the argument of the company. But there is something deeper in the whole business than you see on the surface. It's all right for Harry Morgan to tell us we must fight or go down. Aye, it's all very well for him to say we should do as they've done in Russia, and take the pits over for ourselves. That's very brave talk, but no one yet has told us how to do this.'

Mary tried to help her father. 'It took ten days to do that in Russia; but it's taken us hundreds of years to build a trade union in this country.'

Len turned sharply in surprise. 'What? Ten days? God Almighty, mun, it took Lenin a lifetime to plan with his comrades what happened in Russia!'

'Ha! So it took more than ten days to shake the world, then,' she scoffed.

451

Ezra cynically interrupted: 'There you go again, wandering all over the world. We started talking about the pits and now you two are bothering your heads about what happened in Russia.'

He stopped pacing the kitchen and stood facing Len. 'Listen. You know that no one wants to smash the company more than I do, but, my God, to do that I'm not prepared to smash the people. What I see in the future if we let the company lock us out is our men slowly drifting back one by one to the pits, after they have reached the end of their tether – and that won't take very long, believe me. No, Len, you must learn that there is a time to fight and a time not to fight. If I could only see some hope of winning, I'd agree with what the committee decided tonight; but I can't, I can't. All I can see in front of us is collapse, and when that time comes I hope I will be dead, because our valley and our people will be finished.' He bent his head on his hands as though he wanted to blind his eyes to a picture they saw.

The hopelessness of the words tugged at Mary's heart, and she put her arm round his neck with a protective gesture which showed her whole mind was fixed on his sorrow and not his outlook on the future.

But Len, with no bonds of blood to bind him to sentiment, although he felt deeply the breakdown of confidence implied in the words, sprang restlessly to his feet. He was one of the workmen and knew their every whim and mood.

'I don't believe you,' he stated abruptly, even while he felt amazed at the manner in which he was addressing his

452

old mentor and leader. 'You know I have got every respect for you, but if what you say is right, then there is no hope for us. It means that, after all we have done and worked for, we have now got no future except misery.' The very thought of this outcome to the struggle of the people made him offensively assertive and his voice shrill with disbelief. 'No, Ezra; I don't believe you, and I wouldn't believe anybody else who said the same thing as you.'

Mary felt she wanted to challenge him and defend Ezra, who had again recovered his composure, and was now lighting his pipe with a long spill of paper, quantities of which he always kept on the hob; but Len gave her no time.

'It's no good you standing up for your father, Mary. He'll be the first to tell you that you have got to think for yourself, as he told me years ago. Gee, mun, use your common sense. Isn't it us that sunk the pit? Of course it is, Mary, and by gum it's only us can save the pit.'

Len was always like this. Whenever he was engaged in a tussle with Ezra, he vented his spleen on Mary and carried the fight to Ezra through her. She knew this, and its effect was to make her more determined in her support for her father even when, sometimes, she sensed he was wrong, as she did on this occasion. But she said nothing as Len continued expounding his convictions.

'Why, if we give in to the company now, it means that we really end where you don't want us to. Harry was right when he said our only chance is to keep on struggling. How do we know,' he demanded, glancing at Ezra, then hastily turning back to Mary as he saw the hot eyes fixed on him, 'how do we know that if we give in at the start the company 'on't come after us again in six or twelve months with the same yarn; and down we go again. And so it will carry on, down–down–down until we reach the farewell rock, then everything will be finished and we can put our tools on the bar for good.'

Len's face was flushed and his eyes were bright with emotion as his own vehemence strengthened the convictions in his mind.

Mary rose and began clearing away the supper things, remarking at the same time: 'Oh well, it's no good arguing now, I suppose. The committee has decided, and we'll have to put up with what's coming.'

The words bred a new idea, and after a short pause during which she flicked the crumbs from the tablecloth into the grate, she turned with the cloth in her hand and demanded passionately: 'Why is it we have got to suffer like this year after year? We are no sooner out of one thing than we are bang into another, and all our lives is nothing but trouble and strife.'

'It's the way of the world, Mary; and neither you, or I, or anybody else can alter it,' Ezra replied.

Len shuffled restlessly in his chair before saying: 'I can't agree with that. The world, after all, is only what we let it be or make it.'

No one replied to this and the conversation languished, each becoming preoccupied with the thoughts generated during the evening. At last Mary reminded Len: 'You had better get coal and sticks ready for the morning, or we'll be forgetting.' He went out of the back door, and after a time returned with a bucket of coal in one hand and a bundle of sticks under his arm. By the time he had put the sticks in the oven to dry and had washed his hands, Ezra, with a muttered 'Goodnight, both,' had gone to bed. Mary and Len followed shortly after.

Mary waited uritil her husband was in bed before stating quietly: 'So you are still siding with Harry Morgan and his communists against my father.'

He raised his head from the pillow and, reaching up, took her small face in his two hands.

'It's not that altogether, Mary, but I'm bound to agree with anybody who thinks the same as me, in't I?' he queried half regretfully, for the first time realising how deeply he had hurt her.

She made no reply and shook her head free from his hands, turning her back to him when she came to bed and falling asleep with nothing more said.

During the remainder of the week, life apparently went on as usual in Cwmardy, but when the men came up the pit on the following Saturday they were confronted with a huge printed poster, pasted on the end of the bridge that separated the colliery from the village. The miners nearest read its contents out loudly, so that those behind could hear. Every two minutes or so the number of men increased as the cages brought them to the surface, but the whispering voices soon acquainted them with the news.

CWMARDY CONSOLIDATED COLLIERY CO., LTD., (1924)
PUBLIC NOTICE.
The official receiver herewith announces to all

455

concerned that the affairs of the above company and all its undertakings are now in the hands of Sir William Wheeler, who has been appointed the official liquidator to wind up the company.

All who have claims upon the company must make them to the liquidator within one month from this date. No applications can be considered thereafter.

The collieries will be open for work on and after next Monday on the following conditions and price-lists.

The surrounding men listened avidly, many of them with their mouths open, to the recital that followed. The items passed from mouth to mouth as they were read, so that even the miners on the fringe of the crowd were aware of the new conditions almost at the same time as the readers. When the words 'Any workman not prepared to accept these conditions need not present himself at the Colliery' were read, a roar of anger deadened the sound of the pit engines. It was heard in Cwmardy, and women rushed to the doors with frightened eyes to ask each other what had happened.

Big Jim looked furiously about him. He and Len stood practically in the middle of the angry mass of shouting miners.

'Ha,' howled one, his voice ringing sharply above the others, 'so this is the new way of robbing us, eh?'

'The frigging blackguards! Put a bit of lavatory paper with words on the bridge and think we will say "pity" to ourselves, and then go back to the pit for whatever they do want to give us. Huh! Babies in dirty napkins 'ood jib at that.'

Another loud roar stopped him. 'Bankrupt to hell!'

'The swindlers are running away!'

'Bloody robbers!'

'Let them keep the pits!'

This latter cry grew louder and more insistent. It was taken up by increasing numbers, until nothing else could be heard.

'Let them keep the bloody pits!' and with this challenge the miners marched down the hill to their homes.

When Monday morning came the hooters blew their raucous command through Cwmardy as usual, but no lights suddenly responded in the cottage windows. Before 6 a.m. John Evans Cardi stood staring through the bedroom window of his stores into the empty darkness outside. He drew the curtains a little further apart and squinted up the street in the direction where the pits were silently brooding as though they had missed something they wanted very much; but the only light he could see was the one which gleamed from the police station. John shivered as the cold air played about his bare legs, and a groan gurgled in his throat.

His wife drew herself from the sheets and beseeched him: 'Come back to bed, John bach. It's no use you worrying and catching your death of cold standing by there.'

The old man slowly retraced his steps and got into bed, making her shrivel as the cold clamminess of his flesh touched her own. 'Duw, duw, you are freezing,' she complained.

John paid no heed to the remark, but Maggie heard him murmur: 'At last it has come. This is the end of everything.'

She shook him sharply. 'Come, come, one would think the end of the world was here.'

He turned his head and something bright dripped from his eyes and glistened for a moment in the lamplight.

'Well, what is it, my gel, but the end of our world? Every penny gone out of our savings, the company bankrupt, and our last hope killed by this morning's silence in the street.'

He hesitated and looked hard at her with misty eyes, then moaned: 'Tell me, Maggie, how are we going to live? We have nothing left. Nothing. The men have made their minds up and the pit is dead.' He turned on his belly and buried his face in the pillow while she tenderly smoothed the thin hair on the back of his head.

About a fortnight after the beginning of the lock-out, Len called at his parents, a practice he had whenever he was worried or had time to spare. He found them quarrelling; Siân was dabbing her eyes with the corner of her apron. The old couple paused while Len made himself comfortable, then Siân began where she had evidently left off.

'How on earth us is going to live after this week the Lord alone knows,' she moaned. 'Poor old Mrs. Evans Cardi was crying to me only yesterday about the money they have got out and nothing coming in, poor dab. Well, well, between everything, I don't know what the world is coming to, no, not I!'

She began weeping into her apron again, hoping by so doing to provoke Jim. She succeeded.

'Hell-fire!' he bawled. 'You do talk to me, mun, as if I was boss of the bloody company. What can I help if they shut down their frigging pits – they don't belong to me, do they? Why the hell don't you go up to the Big House and nag Lord Cwmardy – not have your bang out on me all the time?'

He turned appealingly to Len, the sight of whom seemed suddenly to give him a new line of defence. 'Ask Len,' he demanded. 'He have got a better head than me and can answer you back in your own brass.'

This gave her the opportunity she wanted. 'Ha! That's the sort of man you are, is it? Willing to put your burdens on the back of your own poor boy that have got enough to do to carry his own, what with this lock-out and his wife dying on her feet with her chest. Ach! Call yourself a man, indeed! Huh! I have seened better ones in old Sanger's circus before now. Duw, even a dog will fight for his own! Shame on you, James!' Her face was both pitying and contemptuous when she turned away from him.

Jim leapt to his full height like a bouncing ball, at the same time involuntarily squaring the droop in his shoulders and inflating his chest the better to express his indignation as he shouted: 'No man can call me a dog, specially you, Siân. No, by damn, I am a better man than all your family put together, and don't you forget it!'

She interrupted him, anger in her very poise. 'Don't you dare to say anything 'bout my fambly, James Roberts. They are too good for their names to be on your tongue. Yes. Where would Len bach be,' she demanded, 'if they didn't look after him and our Jane, now in her grave, God bless her, when you runned to the Boer War, not caring if us had a crust to share between us.'

459

Big Jim collapsed under this tirade, and sat down, his moustache now drooping wearily. 'All right,' he announced, 'I will go over the mountain tomorrow to look for work somewhere else, and I do hope when I get it that my body will be smashed to bits by a fall. That will bring you to your senses, and you will be sorry for all that you have said to me.'

Len burst out laughing at the sheer incongruity of the remark and the manner in which Jim said it, but there was no mirth on Siân's face.

'What,' she queried like one who could not believe she was hearing aright, 'you will leave your own home, your wife, and children, so that you can be buried by a fall, God knows where? No! Never! Not while there is breath left in my poor old bones.'

No more was said after this, and a little time later Len bade them good night and went home.

CONFLICTING LOYALTIES

The weary weeks dragged on until the lock-out was in its eighth month, without either side making any move to re-open the pits which moped stagnantly at the head of the valley. Relief stations had been opened in the chapels, and once a week long queues of people waited patiently for the food-notes doled out to them from the rates. Lack of cash made it impossible to buy clothes or pay Federation dues, and each week the people became more shabby. Women looked enviously at the smoke curling from the stacks of pits surrounding Cwmardy and silently longed for the day when theirs would once more be pulsating with similar life.

Coal was as scarce as cash, and one evening Len told Mary: 'Put my working clothes out to air tonight; me and dad are going up the level for some coal in the morning.'

Mary looked sadly at the lines marked deeply into his thin face and the weary posture of his body.

'We can manage for this week again, Len, if I go careful with what we've got. I hate to see you going up that level,' she burst out. 'Your body can't stand it; you are fading away before my eyes and are looking like an old man. Nobody would ever think you are only twenty-four next December.'

Len understood her solicitude and was glad of it, but he tried to ease her mind when he replied: 'Don't worry about me; I'm all right. Let's get as much in as we can now, before the company blows the levels down, as it has threatened to do.'

Mary did not answer, but before going to bed she dragged the box containing his working clothes from the dark hole under the stairs and arranged them on the brass rod fixed to the mantelshelf.

Early next morning, as the dawn was being spawned in the smoke that fogged the valley, they rose from bed. Mary prepared the breakfast of dry toast and tea, which was all the relief-note enabled them to obtain since the lock-out, while Len donned his pit clothes.

'Is that old tater sack still here?' he asked. She fetched it from the back and laid it down on the mat before the fire.

Len looked through the window and remarked: 'It's not worth drying it, Mary. The weather don't look at all too good.'

After breakfast he kissed her and, advising her to go back to bed, wearily made his way towards his father's house, where he found the old man waiting on the doorstep staring at the heavy sky with its restless clouds.

'It's looking pretty dark, Len bach, and us had better

hurry up,' he announced.

Before they reached the summit of the mountain, the mist had turned into a drizzle that soaked through their clothes in spite of the sacks draped across their shoulders.

Big Jim spat disgustedly into the air and muttered: 'Huh! Every time you and me do come for a bit of coal, the rain do come pelting down 'xactly like if someone is watching to spite us out.'

Len said nothing, the clammy clothes clinging coldly to his body making him too miserable for words, but followed his father up the steep path towards the mine level, driven horizontally into the side of the mountain. Several men passed them before they reached their destination, each bent nearly double beneath the sack of coal straddled lengthways across his shoulders.

'How is things up there today, boys?' Jim asked.

'You'll find plenty of muck and water, but bloody little coal!' was the grunted reply as the men gingerly made their way down the mountain.

Len and his father continued the climb towards the level, and when they reached its mouth they sat on the sopping grass to recover their breath. The hole into which they intended to go was driven flush into the earth, and seemed hardly big enough to admit a sheep. An endless torrent of water tumbled noisily out, swirling round the heavy wooden box on sleigh-like runners that obstructed the opening to the level.

Len was the first to rise to his feet, and, shaking the wet sack from his shoulders, took hold of the rope attached to the box, at the same time remarking: 'Come on, dad. We might as well get going.'

Big Jim grunted, took a huge lump of half-chewed tobacco from his mouth, carefully wrapped it in paper which he put into a brass pouch, then followed Len into the level.

They crawled on their hands and knees, Len pulling the box while his father pushed. Before they had gone a dozen yards they stopped to light a candle each, which they then stuck in the tin holders fastened to their caps. The tiny glimmers glinted on the black water as the two men went more deeply into the entrails of the mountain. By the time they reached the small seam of coal, both were exhausted and half sat, half lay in the water for some minutes to recover.

Big Jim took advantage of the rest to look about him, but a glance was sufficient to send him into a temper.

'Muniferni! Same bloody trick agen! They have tooked all the loose coal and have left nothink but stiff dead ends and muck to us. By Hell, call themselves butties, mun jawli! Huh! They don't know what the name do mean!'

'Never mind about that now,' Len interrupted peevishly. 'Let's get on with the job before the other men come, or we'll be here all day!' Thus admonished, Jim stopped his grunting and helped Len get the tools from the bar on which they were locked. They each took a mandril and shovel and went towards the coalface, which was a little drier than the roadway.

For hours they punched with all their might at the hard overhanging roof that prevented their getting to the thin vein of coal underneath. But eventually they hammered it flush with the coal, then took it in turn to fill the box with the stones and rubble. Each time the box was full, Len pulled it to the mouth of the level, where he unloaded the rubbish, occasionally watching the larger stones roll down the mountain with increasing momentum. When the rubbish had all been cleared away, they started working the coal. The idleness enforced by the lock-out had softened the men's bodies and made their muscles less supple. Len felt his hands burn intolerably. The mandril became a red-hot iron that seared more deeply into his flesh with every blow he struck, while the confined space forced him to contort his body until it lost all human semblance. His posture added to the strain on his shoulders and drove pins and needles into him in currents that made him long to scream. He turned on his belly, stretching his limbs in the water that covered them as he lay. This eased the cramp for a little, but his hands burned even more ferociously when he took hold of the mandril again.

He was glad when they had sufficient coal to fill the box. Even the crawl through the foot-deep water with the rope tearing at his shoulder as he dragged the loaded box behind him was better than the paralysing cramp of the coalface. By the time they had finished filling their sacks with coal, more men had come to the level. These helped to lift the loaded bags on to the shoulders of the two men before going into the level themselves, leaving Len and Big Jim to get down the mountain as best they could.

Before they had proceeded far, Len began to feel the weight on his back grow heavier with every stride. Each lump of coal became a nail that stuck into his flesh with maddening persistence. He jerked the sack to shift the pressure and pain from a particular spot, only to feel others that were even more agonising. The weight forced his shoulders nearer to the ground and pressed his feet more deeply into the wet earth, making it a strain to drag them from its grip. When he lifted a foot to take a step forward, he felt he was lifting the world with it. The pressure on his body forced his mouth open, and he sucked in the air with audible gasps like a swimmer in a heavy sea.

They had not covered half the distance down the mountain before Len was in a state of collapse. He closed his eyes, hoping thus to shorten the distance to his home, but when he opened them again, Cwmardy seemed further away than ever through the dull skeins of rain that dangled from the skies.

He groaned, and only the sight of Big Jim steadily plodding ahead prevented his dropping to the ground with the sack of coal across his neck. Although his brain was numb, the red-hot needles in his back forced him to break the shackles that held his feet to the earth. He thought each step he took would be his last, but somehow the last was always the next. His knees lost rigidity and his bones seemed to melt so that his feet dragged along the ground, at no point entirely leaving it. He lost all sense of space and time until he bumped into Jim when the latter stopped by the wall that separated the colliery siding from the road leading to the village. His father helped him lift the bag of coal onto the wall so that he could rest.

Len felt his body float in the air and a lifting sensation fill his head. He sat down abruptly and closed his eyes.

Presently he heard a sudden clang of iron and Siân's voice saying: 'You haven't got much further to go now, Len bach, and us have brought two buckets to help you.'

He jumped to his feet and saw his mother and Mary before him. Pride made him ashamed of their action and he blurted out savagely: 'What the hell did you want to bring those buckets for? Do you think I'm still a little kid, mam, and haven't grown up?'

Siân looked at him reproachfully, the wet shawl, swathed round her head, dripping moisture on her face. Len turned away and rested his arms on the wall while he looked at the long lines of coal-filled wagons the other side. Here and there he caught sight of a policeman on guard. Big Jim remained squatting on the ground, placidly chewing the tobacco he had so carefully saved before entering the level. Suddenly Len turned to his wife and pointed to the pit sidings.

'Look, Mary. In't it a shame? Those thousands of tons of coal, that me and dad have helped to fill, now rotting in the rain, have been there since the lock-out began, while we have got to kill ourselves to get a bag full from the level. It's bloody maddening! Aye, and we're all mad. Why the hell don't we all get together and empty those wagons, instead of slogging our guts out in the mountain?'

His voice became squeaky with excitement and exhaustion, and Mary, knowing his moods, did not reply, but Big Jim, looking at his son slyly for a moment, remarked: 'Aye, aye, Len bach. You are quite right, my boy. Big Jim's son must always be right, muniferni; but be careful the bobbies don't hear you or catch you looking at

467

that coal on the sidings, or you will have a summons, sure as hell! Ha, ha!'

Siân felt it necessary to add her quota. 'Aye, indeed, Len. Many a poor old dab have been fined or put in jail when they tooked coal because they didn't have no money to buy some.'

This sentiment found a responsive chord in Len's mind. 'By gum,' he said, 'I'd never seen it in that way before, mam. They lock us out of the pit; then give us food-notes instead of money; and when we take coal because we haven't got money to buy some, they make us pay twenty or thirty times its value in fines, and when we can't pay that they make out that we are criminals and send us to clink.'

Big Jim looked at Mary with a glance that seemed to say: 'There's a clever man for you, my gel. Not many scholars in Cwmardy could put it together so quick or so good as that, eh?' But he confined his remarks to: 'And who is on the bench to send you down? Why, Mr. Hicks, the general manager, in't it?' No one replied.

When they were ready to go Len resolutely refused to allow the women to fill their buckets from his sack.

His mother looked for some moments as though she were prepared to use force to compel him, but she cooled down sufficiently to say: 'All right. You will come to your senses one day. But you shan't spite us out. No, not if us have got to go round the back lanes and scrape cokes from the ashes to fill our buckets. Huh! You have comed a big man all of a sudden, haven't you?'

Len knew from past experience how advisable it was

that he say nothing, so he worked himself under the sack, which now felt heavier and more painful than ever, and followed dumbly in the wake of his father. Siân noisily rattled the empty buckets, and Len prayed that none of his mates would see the two women before he reached the house. He clenched his teeth and kept his eyes fixed on the ground until he came to the little tin chapel and heard a murmur of voices.

Big Jim stopped and turned round to ask: 'What is on there, Len? It can't be a service or your mother 'ood be there.'

Len was too exhausted and miserable to answer, but he also wondered as he slowly dragged his body and its burden towards the house.

Inside the chapel a congregation of preachers, shop-keepers, and others was listening to a prayer offered up by Will Smallbeer, who had been converted during the lock-out. The sound Big Jim had heard was the deep 'Amen' from those present when the prayer was finished. This was soon followed by a lament about conditions in Cwmardy, and Mr. Evans Cardi summed up their feelings when he said: 'This lock-out is taking us to ruin. I can't see any hope of our getting back the debts the people owe us, and now, after eight months, we are no nearer the end of the stoppage. It's bankruptcy, it's ruin!' he wailed despairingly.

The village doctor, whose double chin hid his tie, helped the discussion that ensued. Clearing his throat, he rose to his feet, and was immediately given a respectful silence which enabled him to say without lifting his hoarse voice: 'Yes, gentlemen. It's ruin for all of us unless something happens very soon. The people expect me to treat them just as they did when they were working and paying for my services. But I must live. I have to pay for the powders and medicine I give them, but it is impossible to carry on any longer, impossible.'

A bitter moan ran round the chapel, whose tin walls made the echoes even more melancholy. After a while, Mr. Hughes, the preacher from Calfaria, the chapel where most of the officials worshipped, rose from his seat.

'There is no sense in it, friends,' he began. 'The men are being led unwisely. No one can say there is a dispute on, yet Ezra persists in treating it as one. The Communists are using Ezra's stubbornness to further their own political ends, and he is too weak to stand up against them. I say there should be no politics in the union.' Another moan, interspersed with cries of 'Shame!' interrupted him for some moments. 'O God! If we could only gain the ear of the people and show how his obstinacy is bringing despair and dereliction to Cwmardy,' he was continuing, when Will Smallbeer jumped up excitedly.

'I know, I know!' he shouted. 'Why not go up the Big House to see if the company have got something new to offer? We can then go to the people, 'specially those who go to chapel, with something definite that many of them 'ood be only too willing to accept. Once we can get a few of them going back to the pit, the rest 'ood soon follow. I say the same as Mr. Hughes – keep politics out of the Union and the pits.'

His beer-drenched waistcoat glistened queerly in the dull light of the sacred edifice.

A few evenings later, a group of men with hats pulled down and coat collars turned up, made their way slowly up the tree-bordered drive leading to the Big House. The trees, bending in the cold wind, seemed to beckon each other to listen to the subdued tramp of ascending feet and the request they were taking to the company.

Will Smallbeer shivered and whispered to the preacher: 'Cold night, in't it, Mr. Hughes?'

The latter's acquiescing nod could not be seen in the darkness, and no more was said, although the wheezing breath of Evans Cardi was audible through the leafy rustling. The men paused a while when they reached the main door of the Big House before ringing the bell, but the speed with which the ring was answered showed they were expected.

'Round the corner to the servants' entrance,' the footman announced without any preamble or explanation.

As the flunkey shut the door in their faces, Will's eyes glared in the lights pouring from the windows and he swallowed noisily.

Mr. Hughes broke the tension when he said, in what he obviously intended to be a propitiating manner: 'A small misunderstanding, I expect. Lord Cwmardy will probably explain when we see him. Come, let's go round the back.'

The others docilely followed him, although Smallbeer continued snorting as though a straw were tickling his nose.

It was late in the night when the men came back out through the front door, where Lord Cwmardy shook each of them, with the exception of Will, by the hand. The deputation was half-way down the drive when the dogs guarding the grounds began to howl mournfully, the echoes running between the trees with eerie reiteration.

Mr. Evans shivered coldly at the sound, but Smallbeer seemed to find it stimulating.

'The dirty sods!' he cried vehemently. 'They know they got us in a vice now we've been up to them, the rotten bastards!'

'Ssh,' whispered Mr. Hughes and Evans Cardi together in shocked sibilance.

'You forget yourself, William, but don't forget the friends who are with you.'

'I know!' bellowed Will. 'You think because I have stopped drinking since the lock-out and attend the services regular, that I have forgot where I come from and the butties who fought with me in the strike. Never, never!' he shouted, his voice rising in temper with every word. 'Give me Big Jim and Len before the bloody lot of you!'

He quickened his pace before they could reply and his curses, floating back to them through the night, mingled with the moaning of the dogs and was soon lost in the distance.

Len left his chair and went to the door when he heard the tramp of heavy feet hurry past the window, but all he could see was the back of the man running up the street. Something peculiar in the gait puzzled him.

'What was it?' Mary asked when he returned to the kitchen.

'Someone running. I couldn't make out who it was, yet I could swear that I know him.'

The puzzled frown remained on his brow for some time

472

after they resumed their conversation, then suddenly he remembered.

'It was Will Smallbeer!' he declared dramatically. 'I wonder what he's been up to?'

Mary supplied the answer in a moment. 'He was one of the deputation picked in the chapel meeting to see Lord Cwmardy. More than likely they've finished and have come back,' she said.

Both remained gazing into the fire for a long while after this, until Mary looked up at the clock and queried:

'I wonder what is keeping dad. It's not often he's out so late as this.' She paused, then moaned: 'Oh duw! He worries me more with every day that passes.'

Len shook his head and both resumed their meditations, until Mary again broke the silence.

'This will finish him. If the chapel people have made an agreement with the company, it will mean that dad will have reached the end of his rope. Aye,' she added bitterly, 'it would have been better if you and the Party had listened to him in the first place. All this misery wouldn't have happened then, and our men would be working and solid in the Federation, instead of as they are now, split up and ready to go back to work on the conditions offered in the beginning.'

Her thoughts turned to Ezra again and her eyes filled with tears. Len watched the shadows play over her face, and they reminded him of the reflection of moving clouds on the mountain. She grasped his arm tightly. 'Oh, Len, I'm afraid this will change dad altogether. He doesn't seem to have his old strength to fight both the preachers and the men who want to go back to work.' She began to weep quietly, at the same time wailing through the fingers that covered her eyes. 'Oh Len, I wish the men would decide to go back, all together, and put an end to this poverty and worry that is slowly killing us. If it keeps on much longer, there'll be nobody left in Cwmardy; those of us who are not in the cemetery will be tramping the country looking for work.'

Her words and demeanour worried Len. He had never seen her so completely broken up before and so obviously a victim of her emotions. But he said nothing in case his remarks should further disturb her, although he felt that matters were reaching a crisis. His mind switched back to the discussions in the Party, particularly the one where Fred Lewis advocated that the Party should support Ezra and urge the men back to work. The scene which followed Harry Morgan's taunt that Fred was ratting lived again before his eyes, and his mouth unconsciously shaped to the arguments he had himself used to prove the accusation.

He forgot the kitchen and the softly weeping Mary near him, and his eyes became blind to everything but the indignant form of Fred, when he rose to his full height and walked out, flinging back over his shoulder the retort: 'Call yourselves Communists! Bah! If you were in Russia, the bloody lot of you would be shot as anarchists!'

An impatient rattling on the door-latch brought him back to his immediate environment, and he turned his head to see Ezra walk in. The miners' leader looked like a very old man who had lost all vitality, and he hardly glanced at his son-in-law as he sat down wearily. Mary wiped her eyes hastily, hoping the tears had left no betraying signs upon her face. The silence that followed the elder man's entry was heavy with unspoken thoughts until Ezra himself gave them voice.

'We have now got to make up our minds. Either the committee takes the men back to work, or the preachers and shopkeepers will.'

There was at once a hopelessness and yet a kind of desperate determination behind the statement that egged Len on to say something, but Ezra stopped him with a wave of the hand that seemed to sweep the whole of Cwmardy into its grip.

'It's no good arguing now. Everybody knows the position, and like cowards we have all been keeping it to ourselves, hoping that something would turn up to prove us wrong. Aye, cowards.' His voice began to quiver with a passion that was unusual in this stern man, and it rose a little as he went on. 'If you had only listened to me at the beginning, these months of hunger and sorrow would not have been. But no; it was easier to call me a renegade, as Harry Morgan did in the committee, than to face up to reality. But now, all of you, do you hear... all of you, have got to face it,' he shouted. 'There is no committee, the men are not paying the union, and unless we give the terms for going back to the pit, the others will; and that means the end of the Federation in Cwmardy. Already there is talk of a new non-political union, and there are many of our own people who will welcome this – yes, welcome it in the hope it will smash the Federation for good.'

Mary grew alarmed at his vehemence, and hurriedly rose from the chair to place her arm about his neck when he drew his hand across his eyes like a man whose sight is fading.

'Oh, dad, don't take it so hard,' she implored; 'no one will ever make me believe that the people are not behind you now, as they were during the strike.'

Len, who had been a silent listener to Ezra's outburst, saw her gulp back the sob in her throat and came to her aid, although he sensed that words would no longer have weight with her father. He hardly knew what to say in the circumstances, but forced himself to declare half-heartedly: 'All of us who count are behind you, Ezra; and you can bet on it the Party will back you all the way against those who want to give in to the company. You can have faith in that,' he concluded rather apologetically.

Ezra lifted his head sharply, letting them see the dull glow in his pouched eyes. 'Don't talk to me of faith,' he almost snarled. 'That's what the preachers you condemn say they have, but I've got none of it. No! I've always had to go on facts, not faith. Nine months of semi-starvation is enough sacrifice for our people, and rather than see others, who have no business to interfere, put an end to it, I'll do it myself. Yes. There is nothing for it now, any more than there was in the beginning. When there are two evils that we have got to choose from, we must always choose the lesser.' His voice was husky when he concluded and he caught Mary to him, making her sit on his lap as though the contact brought consolation.

Len felt himself devoid of argument in face of the crisis as Ezra had presented it, but faith in the Party persuaded him that there was a solution somewhere, even though he couldn't grasp it at the moment.

He was saved further pondering by Mary, who said quietly, in tones showing she had a complete grip of herself once more: 'I agree with you, dad. You are right and we must put an end to this lingering. I'm sure the most sensible of the men who used to be on the committee will agree as well when you put the position to them.' Both men immediately saw a glimmer of hope in the sentiment, although each hoped a different outcome.

Ezra lifted her from his knee and, rising himself, stood near the fire with his back turned to it. He recited a number of names and asked Len if he'd go round their houses in the morning and invite them as old committee-men to a discussion on the new development. Len agreed, but insisted upon adding Harry Morgan's name, which Ezra had for some reason omitted. There was an argument over this, and Ezra only finally gave way when Len threatened to drop the whole matter if Harry wasn't invited.

Next day most of the invited men turned up to the committee. Dai Cannon, Sam Dangler, and Big Jim sat near each other; the latter commenting audibly about the others present.

'How be, Reuben?' he greeted a coal-scarred veteran, who at the beginning of the lock-out had been given a lump sum in commutation of the weekly compensation he had received for an affiiction to his eyes, which the doctors said was nystagmus. The man so addressed turned around to look at his questioner. His eyes were large and seemed to be all pupil, that blinked and quivered in the dull light of the room. He carried his head slightly sideways on his hunched shoulders, as if this made it easier to concentrate his gaze.

'Hallo, Jim. Glad to see you,' he growled.

He had no time to say more before Fred Lewis strode in, walking arrogantly past the men already there and squatting himself in a vacant chair near the table, from which he turned round to nod patronisingly to his acquaintances.

Jim bent down a little to whisper in Dangler's ear: 'That's a clever chap for you, mun.'

Sam nodded his head disparagingly. 'Aye, he's clever all right. So clever that he do always look after number one first, never mind a hell about anybody else. One day he'll leave all of us in the dirt, 'spite of all his big talk.'

Jim did not like to be contradicted in this manner, and hastened to defend his position. 'Hell, mun! I didn't say anything 'bout that, did I, Dai?' turning to the latter, who shook his head in confirmation. 'All I did say was that he is a clever man. As for the other thing, why, you do know so well as me that any man born above the Boar's Head can look after hisself without asking anybody for help. In't that right, Dai?' turning again to his mate for support, then immediately adding: 'Mind you, I don't say he be so clever as our Len. Duw, there's a scholar for you! I bet he's the smartest man in the four pits, muniferni. It is a pleasure to hear him arguing with Siân when she is in her tantrums. Duw! He do blind her with science.'

Fred Lewis sensed he had something to do with the conversation, and hearing the word 'clever' turned round and smiled at Big Jim, who solemnly nodded his head as a greeting, at the same time twirling one end of his moustache.

478

Ezra now rapped the table and Jim hurriedly whispered to Dangler: 'Give me a bit of the 'bacco you do owe me, Sam, before he do start.' He rubbed the proffered lump carefully on his patched trousers to loosen it as Ezra began quietly speaking.

Len sat next to Harry Morgan, whose high forehead and large spectacles made his face appear all eyes as he listened intently to the miners' leader. During the first half of his statement, Ezra stressed continually the poverty wrought in Cwmardy by the lock-out, until old Reuben grunted loudly: 'Cut it out, mun. Don't us know all about that, without you preaching by there about it?'

Harry clapped the interruption loudly, and Big Jim, thinking it was Len, did the same, although the latter remained perfectly quiet. Ezra, always intolerant of opposition, immediately threw aside the factual sternness with which he began the meeting.

Fixing his attention on Harry and not even glancing at Reuben, he raised his voice heatedly. 'Can't you forget your politics and your prejudice for a while, man?' he demanded. 'Or have you come here with your usual tactics of disruption, not caring what will happen to the workmen so long as you and your Party have their way?'

Harry jumped to his feet to make an indignant repudiation of the charge, but Will Evans' loud, rolling bursts of laughter were before him. 'Ha-ha! Ho-ho-ho! That's a smart 'un! Hit the other bloke first when he's pulling his coat off. Ho-ho! Ha-ha-ha!'

Will's thin cheeks rippled with the laughter, but he soon became quiet again when he saw the serious faces around him remain impervious to the attempted joke. But it had served its purpose, because Harry had resumed his seat during the brief interlude, leaving Ezra's statement unanswered.

The miners' leader continued his speech where he had left off before the interruption, and when he reached the end he was pleading vehemently that the committee should ask the company for the terms and advise the men to accept them.

'Unless you do that,' he said tonelessly, like a man to whom talking has become a sudden burden, 'we will destroy even the little organisation we have left, and rather than that, I am prepared to admit defeat.'

He suddenly noticed the tense look in the men's eyes, and his own filled with a pain that he tried to hide in an outburst of temper. 'Don't stare at me like that!' he cried. 'It hurts me more than it does you to have to say these words. I never thought I would see the day when my own men would leave me and follow others.' His voice quavered, but he had hardly time to sit down before Harry Morgan began speaking.

Len listened to the Communist leader, following every word with an intensity that made him oblivious of the fact that the other men were equally interested. The high-pitched voice sounded louder than it actually was as the words rebounded from the walls of the small room. Harry always addressed a dozen men in the same manner he did a thousand and this occasion was no exception. With a bite in every sentence, he explained the tactics of the company ever since the strike, how they began by separating mates in the pit, then introducing strangers to further estrange the men.

'And when they had done this,' he continued, 'what after? They came to us in seam after seam saying we would have to lower the price-list and give them more output or the seam would have to be closed.'

Ezra started to his feet but Harry hurriedly checked him with the remark. 'I know I will be called a disrupter and all the rest of it for what I am going to say, but that won't stop the Party of which I am proud to be a member from speaking what it thinks is the truth.'

Fred Lewis jumped up excitedly. 'I'm as much, if not more, a Communist as you are, and I say we must always be prepared to change our line. I believe we are wrong and that Ezra is right.'

Big Jim guffawed loudly. 'Ha-ha! If I do know my P's and Q's you 'on't be a Communist after today, mun jawli.'

No one took notice of him, and Harry continued as though there had been no interruption. 'Ten months ago they flung their bombshell. They said accept what we give you or finish in the pit till you do. That was an ultimatum, a threat that tried to rob us of our voices and make us puppets of the boss. And after sticking it for nearly ten months, Ezra now wants us to give in because a few preachers and what-not are interfering. I say no; and if Ezra says differently, he's of more value to Lord Cwmardy than all the officials in the pit.'

As he developed the argument, his passionate utterances electrified the men present. There was a momentary pause when he finished, until Len cried out: 'That's it; Harry's right. To give in now will be to play

481

right into the hands of the company.'

He went on at some length, repeating the arguments already made until he sensed a restless fidgetting among the committee-men, one of whom shouted: 'We've had enough speeches. Let's vote.'

Big Jim was on his feet in a jiffy. 'Don't you shout my boy down, if you do know what is good for you,' he howled. 'Fair play for everyone I do say and don't none of you forget it.' Dai Cannon caught the tail of his coat and jerked him back to the seat, but not before Len also sat down.

When Ezra put the matter to the meeting, the vote for standing firm was decisive. His face went even paler and he opened his mouth to say something, but changed his mind and rose from the chair without another word. He turned when he was near the door and looked back at the silent men, whose eyes were fixed on his. Hot saliva rose to his throat and he swallowed hard, his drooping shoulders looking pathetically lonely as he left the room.

Len did not return until late that night, and when he at last entered, Ezra was already in bed, but Mary sat crouched over the fire. Her posture was sufficient witness to the despondency that consumed her. It hurt Len to see her in this frame of mind and he put his arm consolingly round her neck, at the same time using his free hand in an effort to turn up her face so that his eyes could look into hers. But she avoided him with an impatient motion that made him halt involuntarily.

After a while, during which he stood awkwardly near her, not knowing what to do or say, he muttered: 'Let's go to bed; the fire's going out and you'll only catch a cold down here.'

She made no effort to answer him or to move, and when he realised her intention he became impatient. Bending down, he put one arm under her legs and the other round her shoulders, and, although she struggled feebly, carried her up the stairs.

He knew that Ezra had already prejudiced her regarding the night's decision, but her attitude had stirred his pride too much to permit him to ask what his father-in-law had actually said. Both of them silently undressed and went to bed.

Len was up early in the morning. He pulled on his trousers, then glanced down at her sleeping face, bending to kiss her softly on the lips. The tightly drawn little wrinkles about her eyes told him the depth of her worry, and he felt sorry he hadn't tried to coax her during the night. She stirred restlessly, but did not wake as he quietly closed the bedroom door behind him. He lit the fire, made tea and some toast, which he took up to her. She was awake when he entered.

'I'm sorry, Len, I was so nasty to you last night,' she apologised, taking the cup from his hand.

'Never mind, you are worried.'

She hurriedly put the cup on the chair near the bed as he said this. 'Oh, Len. Yes, I am worried,' she emphasised. 'I'm sure dad won't accept the decision you took last night. I'm sure he won't.'

Len looked hard at her. He felt she was hinting something to him, but could not grasp it. Mary saw the puzzled look in his eyes and longed to tell him what was bubbling on her lips; but, instead, she hastened to console.

'Don't bother your head, Len. Everything will come all right in the end.'

He left her in bed and went to meet Harry Morgan and the other Party members, who had planned to chalk the roads and poster the hoardings with slogans. It was so early that the streets were practically deserted, but Will Evans and another man posted themselves at each end of the street to watch for any wandering policeman while Len and Harry hurriedly chalked huge letters on the roadway: 'People of Cwmardy, don't go back to the pits till the old conditions are granted. Stand solid behind the committee. Demand the council feed our children in the schools. Don't listen to those who want to break our resistance.'

In every street the same advice was written, while posters with much the same message were pasted on the pine ends of houses and other places. The continual bending put a pain in the small of Len's back, but he refused all requests from the watchers to change places. He felt more proud of his handiwork with each slogan he chalked, and was determined to finish the job on his own.

He little thought while he was doing this, that Ezra, with Mary at his side, was making his way up the drive towards the Big House. Half way the miners' leader stopped abruptly and grasped his daughter by the shoulder. Mary could feel in his fingers the conflict which gripped him, but she faced him without flinching when he stared into her eyes. His voice sounded like a croak when he spoke.

'Tell me, Mary. What else can I do?' Before she could reply, he rushed on: 'I know you are against my seeing the company now the committee has decided, but that's not good enough for me. No. If it wasn't for Harry Morgan and Len, the others would have seen the same way as I do and we would now be doing the right thing. Remember that, Mary,' he pleaded. 'If there is anything wrong in what I am doing, the committee is to blame and not me. They should have been men enough to do what is best for the people instead of letting themselves be influenced as they were.'

He drew a hot hand across his brow and Mary led him gently to the grassy verge of the drive, where he sat down wearily. The poverty and the deadly inertia of the last ten months made her believe with all the strength of her mind that her father was right in his desire to call the lock-out off. But the long experience of discipline and obedience to leadership which he had carefully nurtured in her forced her to disagree with his present action. The very training he had given her throughout her life was the instrument which now made her condemn him, although she took care not to let him know the extent of her opposition.

Mary took the bent head in her hands and pressed it to her bosom, but the contact seemed to acquaint him with her innermost thoughts and he hurriedly shook himself free.

'I know what you are thinking, Mary,' he asserted hoarsely. 'Yes, I know.' He paused a little to recover himself and when he continued his words came more slowly and deliberately. 'You believe that the committee is right, and that I am weak. That's what Len and the others think. But you're all wrong. Do you hear me? All wrong. I have led the people of Cwmardy for thirty years, and I know their every mood. Ha! If I let them dribble back to work one by one until the return became a rabble, you would think I was strong eh? But I've led too long to fall into that trap and I know – are you listening? – I said that I know the only way to lead is the way the people want to go, and you must take them altogether or you'll be left on your own.'

The despairing monologue appealed to Mary's desire and emotion, but she failed to efface completely from her mind the consciousness that she had heard similar statements from him before in a crisis. The continual conflict of opinions between Len and her father was slowly developing an independent outlook in her, but this was not yet strong enough to beat back the devotion she had for Ezra, which always made her support him when she failed to convince him.

Without being conscious of it, she now tried to reconcile her love with her opinions. 'I don't agree that the committee is right, dad,' she declared sadly. 'But I don't believe the people won't follow you now as they have always done, if you ask them to. What I can't understand is why you are going to the company in spite of the committee, instead of going to the men. Oh, dad, I'm sure they'd do what you want them to, never mind what the preachers say.'

He stopped her sharply. 'That will do, Mary. You are too young to know what is best.' His voice became softer as he begged: 'But in your ignorance don't you also desert me, Mary. No, don't you do that, my dear, because that would mean the end of everything.'

His plea conquered her and the tears in her eyes made them scintillate when she answered. 'However can you think such a thing, dad? Whatever happens and whatever anybody says, where you go I'm coming, never mind where it is.'

She helped him to his feet, and the windows of the Big House seemed to grin maliciously at them as Ezra left Mary waiting, and went to the front door with bent head and heavy feet.

Half an hour later he returned and dumbly handed her a document which she subconsciously knew contained the terms on which the men could restart work. She read as she walked, and her eyes were flaming by the time she had finished.

'The men will never work on these terms,' she exclaimed.

Ezra did not look at her when he replied: 'Too late now. I've already agreed to them, and all that is left is to explain them to the men.'

This shook her severely, for she had not for a moment thought he would have gone so far as this, and she stopped to blurt out: 'But, dad, you shouldn't have done that. You ought to have let the men see the agreement first, since they are the ones who will have to work under it. At the very least you ought to have showed it to Len and the committee.'

His silence quieted her, and she said no more as she followed him down the drive, but, buried in meditation, Ezra failed to notice that she made no attempt to return the document.

During the remainder of the day Mary burned to show the agreement to Len, but she restrained herself till they were alone in their bedroom. Len knew her moods and lay quietly in bed watching her undress, although his heart beat more quickly each time he saw her thin body.

When she had finished she sat in her nightdress on the edge of the bed and handed him the document, saying: 'Here, read this.'

He sensed by the throb in her voice that something serious had happened, and, in a sudden surge of emotion, he drew her backwards across his body, pressing her to him.

She struggled from the embrace and gasped: 'Read that first, perhaps you won't be so anxious after.'

Len forced his eyes to the paper, but before he was half-way through he sprang out of bed and began pacing excitedly, his shirt swishing like a kilt about his bare legs, while he muttered to himself.

His movements got on Mary's nerves, and she grasped his shirt. 'For God's sake, sit down, Len. You give me the creeps talking to yourself like that.'

He glanced down at her. 'Creeps, to hell. I know somebody else who will have the creeps when the workmen know about this lot,' he declared, at the same time sitting on the bed beside her, while he read the agreement again.

'Good God, the men'll never accept this!'

'They have already been accepted,' Mary said quietly.

Len jumped to his feet, stared at her for some moments, then burst out as though he doubted his ears. 'Accepted? Who's accepted them?'

He was obviously bewildered, and she averted her eyes when she replied. 'Dad agreed to them with Lord Cwmardy today. I was with him.'

Len took her face in his hands and fixed his eyes on

hers in spite of her efforts to avoid him. When he spoke, the words were hard and incisive. 'If your father did that he is a traitor.'

A muffled sound came from Ezra's room, followed by a groan. It galvanised Mary into sudden life, and tearing her head free she jumped up, her heaving bosom betraying the tumult the accusation induced in her. She forgot all her previous doubts as the blood love in her body clouded her intellect and forced her to her father's defence.

'You coward, to slander your best friend, the man who has taught you all you know!' she shouted passionately. Len came towards her and would have spoken, but she checked him with a gesture that showed her contempt. 'Don't come near me,' she gasped, and the cough that lingered in her throat made her words sound more bitter when she continued: 'You, of all men, ought to know how much my father has sacrificed for the people and the Federation. I was there when he told you how my mother died of a broken heart when the owners sold her home up because of dad.'

Len nodded mutely. He felt uneasy, but she gave him no time for words, as she went on with her tirade while the tears rolled down her cheeks. 'My father has always in every way been a man of the people; and now when he is in the greatest need of help, they snub him and turn from him.'

A spasm of coughing racked her chest and checked the torrent of words. Len picked his trousers from the bedrail and extracted a handkerchief, with which he wiped away the phlegm that stained her lips. He drew her tenderly to the bed, where both sat for a while as she regained her breath.

489

When the spasm was over, she took up again the threads of defence, but her voice was now more subdued.

'You've told me scores of times, Len, that the workers never desert their own,' she said.

Len immediately saw what she was driving at. 'That's true,' he stated categorically, as though there was no room for doubt. There was a pause before he took the initiative and challenged her. 'But you can't expect them to stick to a traitor, can you, Mary? You're not soft enough to believe they'll stick to somebody who's got no faith in them. If you are, then you'll believe any bloody thing.'

Mary coloured and asked, in tones that were again beginning to quiver with temper: 'If what you say about them is right, why have they turned from dad after he has given everything, his life, home, and happiness, to them?'

Len looked at her pleadingly. He had known this fight was bound to come off sooner or later, and dreaded it because he was aware it could lead to a lasting cleavage between himself and Mary. Her passionate devotion to Ezra had often raised jealous queries in his mind, but he had always evaded the issue. Her words showed he could do so no longer and must face it whatever the ultimate result. He drew himself together with a tremor and said with all the gentleness he could command:

'Mary, my love, why don't you try to listen to reason. You know how hard it is for me to say these things, but they have got to be said, mun, or I'd be less than a man and not worth any love you might have for me.' He swallowed bitterly as the thought flashed through his mind that she had very little love to give anyone after Ezra

490

had had his share.

The pause encouraged Mary to believe he was weakening. She also knew the issues at stake, but confident from past experience, she felt herself stronger than he on vital matters and had already made her mind up for him. She began to plead: 'Oh, Len, if you can say these things about dad, what can we expect from those who don't know him so well?'

Len realised she was trying to keep him on the defensive, and the knowledge gave him courage to protest. 'I don't agree with you that either me or the people have deserted your father. No, by gum, Mary, the boot's on the other foot, if it comes to that. You know as well as I do that ever since the big strike and the shootings, he has drifted further and further away from the struggle and the principles he used to believe in. Be fair, mun, and don't shut your eyes to things they ought to see.'

Mary jerked herself taut and her eyes flashed into his. The essential truth of his remark had struck her like a blow, but she stubbornly continued to challenge him.

'You have got to prove that,' she declared harshly.

Len looked at her helplessly. He ached to catch her in his arms and his head hummed with the effort he was making to control his emotions, but the love he had for her, which had often been a weakness, was now the source of his greatest strength. He shook his head slowly before saying in tender tones that none the less showed the depth of his conviction:

'It is for you to see the facts, Mary. You will find all the proof you want in them. Think, girl,' he pleaded, 'only for a little minute. Isn't it true that ever since the strike he believes that the men can never beat the company, that it is always better to meet them half-way than it is to fight them? Of course it's true,' he answered himself. 'He has lost faith in the people, and, because of this, thinks the company is invincible. That is why he always tells us that half a loaf is better than nothing. You have heard him say that yourself a dozen times, haven't you?'

She nodded her head without thinking what she was doing. He saw the gesture and it gave him confidence to go on. 'Oh, Mary, I know you love your father to the bottom of your heart, but don't you also love all the people who have suffered the same as you from the lock-out? Haven't us all sacrificed as much as each other to beat the company and make the pit fit for men to work in?'

Mary's head dropped slowly while he spoke, until her chin rested on her chest, and she sobbed quietly to herself.

There was silence for some minutes, during which she gathered new energy. 'The Party is jealous because dad has got so much influence over the men,' she challenged him. 'They want to break him so that they can have control of the Federation.'

Len caught her shoulders and bent his head sideways until her eyes looked into his. 'You are saying anything now, Mary, because you are too weak to give in. You are only telling me something that your father has told you, and you know in your heart that it is a lie.'

The downright assertion and his manner of making it conquered her, and she made no effort to continue the argument. Len's face flushed when he realised she had capitulated, and a warm glow ran through his body. He drew her head towards him while he murmured in her ear.

'Don't worry, Mary; it's always better for us to face reality than to run away from it. Your old man has often told us to look at things as they are, and not only as we want them to be. And he was right, although it often hurts us to the bone to do it.'

Her submissive acquiescence spurred him on, and he felt her tears wet on his cheek as he carefully turned her body until it rested recumbent upon the bed.

'Oh, my dear, it is only by our love for the people that we can measure our love for each other.' Without conscious effort he caught his silent wife to him and squeezed her body to his flesh with hot intensity.

Mary sighed softly and Len felt desire sweep over him from head to feet as she relaxed herself in his arms and her upturned face looked trustingly into his eyes. With excited haste he pressed her backwards on the bed and his kisses stole the blue from her lips, replacing it with a living red. Her head now rested on his arm and her flesh quivered with vitality as his hand sought its intimacy. Though neither spoke a word he saw the smile on her lips melt the shadows in her face before he clasped her to him and both were buried in each other.

Some time later, he turned on his side and carefully covered her with bedclothes, before drawing her body tenderly to his and stretching his hand to extinguish the light.

BACK TO WORK

Next day Len reported Ezra's action to a special Party meeting which he called for the purpose. It was decided that if Ezra did not call a meeting of all the people, the Party would, with Len as the speaker making the report. On the other hand, if the miners' leader convened the meeting, then Len was to be chief spokesman in opposition to the terms.

The news of what had been done soon filtered through the doorways of Cwmardy, and for the remainder of the week nothing else was talked of. Ezra sent a crier round to announce a mass-meeting on the Sunday, and the message gave delight to the preachers and shopkeepers, the vicar going so far as to liken Ezra to Moses leading his people out of the desert.

Many of the miners, however, wondered what was wrong with their leader, but the increasing torment of their poverty together with their inherent loyalty inclined them to his support.

Mr. Evans Cardi rubbed his hands gleefully when one of his customers told him what had happened, and a smile parted his lips as he hurried into the inner kitchen to let Maggie know.

'We have reached the end of this misery at last, thank God,' he said. Her face was flushed when she looked up from the account books and waited while he told her what Ezra had done. When he had finished, she gave a little sigh.

'He is a good man, but pity he didn't do it little bit sooner; we could have let our Ron finish his studies then,' she remarked. Her husband, looking years younger already and the lines on his face seeming less harsh, interrupted her. He was anxious that nothing should spoil the joy induced by the knowledge that Ezra was leading the workmen back to the pit.

'Don't worry about that,' he consoled. 'I have been talking to some of the councillors about him, and if we use our heads and scrape some money together, they might find him a job as a teacher when he comes back.'

'But you know, John, that he doesn't want to be a teacher,' she retorted.

'Tut-tut. He will get used to it in time, and perhaps later on he'll be able to look round for something better.' A knock on the counter took him back into the shop, where Siân and another woman with a baby in a shawl were waiting. Evans could not conceal his exultation and greeted them with: 'Better times ahead now, eh? Ha-ha!' At the same time washing his hands in invisible water.

496

The woman with the baby grunted. 'Hmm. From what I can hear, I don't know so much about better times. Our Si told me that the only difference will be that we will be getting parish pay just the same, only now we will have to work for it.'

'Tut-tut,' Evans interrupted impatiently. 'Hard work will never hurt nobody.'

Siân cocked her ears up. 'What? Never hurt nobody? Well do I know that it 'on't, if a man can get a bellyful of good food and a clean home after doing it! I don't believe in these old strikes and lock-outs no more than anybody else, but I don't believe in a man working for nothing, neither. Oh no! Come you, Mr. Evans.'

The grocer hurriedly served them, then went back to the kitchen, where he and his wife planned their son's future in every detail before retiring for the night, happy in the belief that they were on the brink of a new prosperity.

Very early Sunday morning, three buses droned through the drizzly rain towards Cwmardy's police station, waking many of the inhabitants long before their usual time. An occasional eye squinted through carefully parted window curtains, but none saw the buses unload their cargo at the police station. One of the higher ranks surveyed the newcomers critically as they stood rigid and awkward in the cramped space of the station. His eyes were coldly vacant as a carp's when he told them: 'We don't expect any trouble, now that Ezra Jones has come to his senses, but those Bolshies may try to turn the people against him.' He spoke at some length before he allowed

497

the tired men to rest on the benches and chairs brought in for the occasion.

Ezra had spent a restless night, and after tossing about for hours he rose from bed and quietly made his way to the kitchen. The cold dampness made him shiver, and he hurried to light the fire and make some breakfast for himself. He had not finished this when Mary came down, her nightdress covered by an old shawl of Siân's.

'Where are you going, dad?' she asked in surprise when she saw her father.

'Just for a little walk, my girl. A bit of fresh air will do me good.'

He tried to hide the turmoil which was consuming him, but Mary's senses were too acute to be deceived. 'You can't go out in this weather, dad. It's raining, and you'll be soaking wet long before the meeting.'

He gave her a quick glance as he put his coat on and when he was near the door turned to say heavily: 'It's not the rain that harms, Mary. Life would be easy and happy if we only had to contend with that. Yes, easy and happy and men could die in peace.' Without another word he opened the door and went out.

Later in the day Len tried to persuade his wife not to come to the meeting. She had told him nothing of what had transpired between herself and Ezra; but he guessed there must have been something, and the fact worried him. She made no reply to his hesitant request, but he knew by the drawn expression on her face that she was intensely worried and he longed to console her in some way, although he felt

498

that words would sound empty in the circumstances. He had already told her of the Party's decision to fight Ezra's policy in the meeting and this helped further to estrange them, so that he left the house alone.

Len found his father impatiently waiting for him. The rain had now stopped, although the sky was full of buffeting clouds, which neither of them noticed as they joined with the others who were making their way to the meeting place on the rubbish dump. The turmoil in the sky found an echo in the valley, where, louder than the drone of countless voices, the pit engines filled the air with a preparatory 'chug-chug' that beat on the bent heads of the people.

'What think you is going to happen today, Len bach?' asked Jim in his deep guttural voice, before suddenly bending his huge body and dismally emitting a curse. 'What in bloody hell is the matter with me these days? My back and legs do feel like they are on fire and I can't walk two cams without wanting a whiff.' He checked himself with a groan, his face contorted with pain and disgust.

Len always felt unhappy when he witnessed these periodic evidences of his father's decline, and he now paused sympathetically, hardly knowing what to say.

'Why don't you go to the doctor, the same as mam have asked you?' he demanded rather curtly.

Jim looked at him a moment as though he thought he had to deal with a man who had suddenly become deranged, then he roared out loudly enough for everyone in the vicinity to hear.

'Doctor to hell! What good can his powders and water

do for a man like me, who have looked after hisself all his life and can work better'n any two men in the pit any day of the week. Doctor, muniferni!' He spat contemptuously on the ground, rubbing it viciously with his foot before saying: 'Come on. It is only a touch of the bile after those chips your mother maked for dinner.'

He thought over this for a while as they continued their walk. The words had implanted a new reason in his mind for the pains he was enduring. He was immensely proud of his once magnificent body and always loath to admit that excessive work and age were now beginning to take toll of his strength.

'Aye, that is it,' he muttered, 'chips.' He stopped again and looked at Len queerly. 'Huh! I can see taters in your face as well, my boy. And no bloody wonder. For the last ten months us have had nothing but chips in our guts come day, go day. By hell, it's a wonder our skins is not like tater peelings by now.'

This explanation appeared to invigorate and anger him at the same time. 'Hell-fire! How can you 'spect an' old sodger like me, who have fought in two wars, to thrive on bloody muck like that? Ha-ha, tinned dog and taters. Ha-ha!'

Len said nothing, but Big Jim chuckled all the way to the dump near the sewage-contaminated river, where thousands of people were already assembled.

Ezra sat alone on the lorry that was to be the platform. His posture, with his chin cupped in his hands as he drearily surveyed the mass of faces before his eyes, denoted the melancholy and solitude which enveloped him. The white patches in his hair gave him a pathetic appearance, although his face still conveyed his dominant strength even in defeat. The delay began to make the waiting people restless, and an impatient murmur eddied through their ranks, breaking into Ezra's thoughts and bringing them back to the job in hand. He appeared a weary man when he rose to his feet, but the upraised hand, commanding silence, betokened the same power he had carried in moments of victory.

The characteristic gesture thrilled Len as it always had done in the past, and for some reason it made him think of Mary. He wondered if she had remained at home, even as he realised this was impossible for one of her temperament. More or less unconsciously he looked around for her, and saw scattered here and there amongst the crowd of hungry faces a number that looked healthy and well fed; but before he had time to ponder the problem, his wandering eyes caught sight of Mary and Siân, and he immediately started edging his way through the throng until he reached their side.

Mary's whole being was fixed with staring concentration upon her father, and Len knew by her attitude the struggle going on within her. He touched her gently on the arm and she started at the contact, although she tried to smile when she recognised him.

'Oh, you frightened me for a minute, Len,' she apologised. He made no answer other than to clasp her arm more tightly to him as Ezra's husky voice broke through the dead air.

The miners' leader explained the misery that had followed the lock-out and the hopelessness of expecting to defeat the company by adamant inaction that only prolonged the agony for the people. His whole demeanour tanged with hate as he outlined step by step the measures taken to break their ranks.

'Men who have lived on your backs for so many years now interfere in your pit affairs and want to break up the Federation. They have been doing all in their power to turn you against me and have divided you in such a way that the only hope left is to go back to work together and admit we are defeated,' he declared bitterly.

Will Smallbeer's heavy voice flung itself into the momentary silence that followed these words: 'That's right. Back to work, boys, before they put strangers in our places,' he boomed with all the force of his lungs.

The cry was taken up and rolled through the crowd. 'Back to work!' 'Back to work!'

It rose higher and mightier until another cry, which gathered impetus and volume with every second, began to chase it: 'What for?' 'Let's know what for.'

For many moments the two impulses shook the mass of people until they swayed like trees in a tempest. Len, still holding Mary's arm and followed closely by Jim and Siân, pushed his way to the lorry, on which he immediately clambered, leaving his family pressed against the wheels.

But as Len climbed up a messenger ran to the man who waited patiently in his car on the main street for news. He listened to the hasty report, then gave curt instructions to the messenger, who hurried back to the field where Len, having succeeded in getting some measure of order among the people, was shouting at the top of his voice:

'Ezra is betraying us. His words show he is becoming a deserter.'

Ezra clenched his fists until the knuckles drew the skin so taut that they looked as white as Mary's face. But Len saw neither.

'Let's know in shillings and pence what the new terms mean. Let's know the exact conditions before we start,' he cried, his voice cracking with the strain.

Someone shouted: 'Get down, you bloody Bolshie!'

Others howled: 'Give the chap a chance. Let him speak. Go on, Len.'

In a flash the air became electrified, and Len's further statements were drowned by the noise.

Mary looked nervously around the excited mass, and the hollows in her cheeks became deeper as she hesitated. Then she scrambled on the lorry before Jim and Siân could check her. The wind billowed her skirt over the back of her knees, but no one took any notice of this as they recognised her haggard features and she rushed towards her husband and caught his wildly waving arm.

'Stop. For God's sake stop. It is madness. Madness!' she cried. Len did not hear what she said, but he read her lips when she shouted: 'Leave it to dad. He's the only one who can handle them now.'

The big men who were scattered about drew closer together as Ezra once more rose slowly to his feet. He had made no effort to calm the tumult while Len was trying to speak, and now waited until it subsided, which it soon did as the people became aware that he intended speaking again when they made order.

When at last he spoke, the words throbbed in his throat. 'You've heard what Len and his Party have to say and will think what you like. I have a duty to you and intend doing it whatever is said. The pits will be open tomorrow for all of you that want to go. Those who don't can stay away. I have finished.'

With this he gave Mary a glance that bored into her bones, gulped hard, then abruptly jumped off the lorry and left the field.

The people looked in amazement after his retreating form, until the big men started to hustle and order them to move on. Slowly they began to drift away, muttering and arguing as they went, until only Len and Mary, Big Jim and Siân were left on the deserted field that had become as silent as a cemetery. They looked at each other dumbly for some moments, then turned and followed the people as the pit-hooters blared the fact that the pit had found new life.

Len and Mary went home to his mother's, and when they were all seated Siân asked in a casual manner: 'What do you think to it, James? Do you think the men will act sensible?'

Jim said nothing, the long stand had made his body sore, and Len's failure to get a hearing had increased his irritation. But at last, seeing that no one spoke, he condescended to say: 'I don't believe they do know their bloody selves what they are going to do.'

This knocked Siân off her mental perch for a moment, but she soon recovered herself. 'Huh! Don't know what they is going to do, eh? And the hooters blowing like it

504

was New Year's Eve. But there, perhaps it was you was too dull to understand what Ezra said.'

The words made Mary's cheeks go even whiter, a fact which the old woman immediately noticed. Repenting the effect of what she had said, she put her arms round the girl's neck and tried to console her with flattery.

'There, there, my gel. What are you worrying about? Your father did do quite right, as everybody with sense do well know.' She looked significantly at Len and Jim as she said this, but neither of them took up the challenge, though Len began to feel very awkward and wished he had gone straight home. He was on the point of suggesting this course when his father asked: 'Do you think they will work tomorrow, Len?'

'Yes, dad. I'm afraid they will,' nodding his head sadly.

''Fraid? How comes that, Len bach?' asked Siân with assumed surprise.

'Hell-fire! Don't start nagging the boy so soon as he do come in,' shouted Jim in exasperation.

Len stemmed the impending storm. 'It's all right, dad. Mam and Mary are worried about the shop and the rent. It is they have got to stand the brunt of that; we know nothing of what it is.'

He bent down to pick up a black beetle crawling over the sand near Mary's feet, and threw it into the fire. They all watched the squirming form turn the hues into blue and green, which worked up through the red of the flames.

'Duw! That was a pretty sight, mun,' said Jim admiringly. 'See if you can catch some more, Len.' And he looked at the soot-grimed wallpaper in case any should be crawling there.

505

Siân resumed the conversation with a plea. 'Tell me, Len bach, what is you and your father going to do tomorrow?'

Len had feared this direct question and looked at her before answering. The worry he saw in her face put a grief in his heart, and he hardly knew how to reply. He turned to Mary for support, but her gaze was fixed on the fire, and it was obvious by the droop of her body that the events of the day had robbed her of what little strength she had. Bracing himself, he huskily tried to placate his mother, at the same time hoping his words would justify his action in Mary's sight.

'I know it is hard for the two of you, mam. But what else could I do? We can't go against our principles and go back to work tomorrow after we have told the other men not to, can we?'

Siân, as usual when she was deeply upset, raised the corner of her canvas apron to her nose and moaned, 'O God, bach, where is it all going to end?'

The smoky air in the kitchen weighted the words in the ears of the two men when she continued. 'Whatever can us do? Ten months without a penny piece and head over heels in debt, and me without a shimmy to my back! Oh dear, dear! There is nothing before us in our old age but the workhouse.' She stopped her moaning and turned sharply to Len to declare bitterly: 'But I knowed it! Yes, so sure as God is my judge I knowed it 'ood come once you started mixing with those old Bolshies!'

She paused and sniffed, hoping Mary would come to her aid, but the latter did not appear to be listening to what was going on in the kitchen, so Siân continued on her own, her voice rising with her temper. 'Don't you dare to bring that Harry Morgan, with his nice tongue and sly ways, inside my door agen. No, and if you are wise, Mary fach, you will keep him from yours too. It is him that have turned the head of our Len.'

None of them interrupted her and she stopped of her own accord, only to resume, with greater vigour, in a direct attack on Jim, who had been silently congratulating himself that he was out of it.

'There is nothing stopping you to go to work like other men, James, because you did never have no principles, whatever the old things is!'

The sudden turn in events shook Jim, but he squared his chest indignantly and his eyes flashed red in the fire-glow as he retorted: 'Be careful what you tell me to my face, 'ooman. Don't you never dare to say that Big Jim have got no principles. Huh! Many a better man than you have lived to regret those words all their lifes. But there,' he added resignedly, as though it had just struck him that the argument was beneath his dignity, 'what am I bothering to you about principles for? There have never been one in your fambly, so what can us 'spect?'

Siân stared at him with open mouth as he went on. 'Let me tell you, once for all, Siân, that if Len and Mary is Bolshies, then, by damn, I am one as well, and a bigger one than the two of 'em put together! See?'

With a dignity amounting to arrogance he raised his hand to his moustache and twirled its stiff ends about his fingers. The action thawed the glare in Siân's eyes as she sensed the rigid loyalty of her husband, and looking at

Len, she saw the same pride there.

'All right,' she sighed. 'Have it your own ways this time agen. But so sure as God is my judge, one day they will have to break the door down with sledges to find our dead bodies starved to death on the floor.'

Big Jim, whose pride was stung by this last remark, interrupted her. 'If any man will ever find me starved to death, it 'on't be on the floor, but decent and tidy in bed like every 'spectable man did ought to be. Yes, muniferni! If you do want to die on the floor, Siân, you will have to do it by yourself, and I tell you straight now.'

When Len and Mary eventually left the old couple and went home, they found that Ezra, after leaving the kettle on the hob, had gone to bed.

THE BREAKING OF
A FRIENDSHIP

On the Monday morning after the mass-meeting Mrs. Evans Cardi was awakened long before her usual time by the sound of singing. For some half-dazed moments she failed to understand what was happening and her hands groped aimlessly under the bedclothes, until she suddenly realised that her husband was not beside her. She sat up in a frenzy of alarm, and when she bent over to light the candle her fingers were trembling.

The singing seemed to get louder and she fancied she recognised the voice. Gathering her courage she got out of bed and went cautiously down the stairs into the shop, where she found John, his nose pressed against the windowpane as he peered into the street, happily humming:

'At five in the morning,
As jovial as any

The miners were leaving
Their homes for their work.'

Accompanying the tune like a staccato baritone was the 'tramp, tramp' of hobnailed boots.

'Whatever are you doing down by here, John?' she asked in amazement.

He did not take his face from the window, but called over his shoulder: 'Come here, Maggie fach. Come and see them going to work. Ha-ha.' He laughed with the exuberant happiness of a child. 'Our troubles will soon be over now. Come, look at them going up the hill to the pit. Ha-ha! We won't have long to wait now before trucks of coal will be rolling down the line, and the ships in the docks will get up steam and we will have dividends on our shares in the pit.' He began to shout as the picture gripped him. 'Then, Maggie, we can pay off the mortgages, get rid of our debts, and have enough money to get our Ron a better position than teaching on the council.'

Maggie's eyes gleamed with joy, but she urged him back to bed and he reluctantly left the window, unwilling to lose sight of a single unit in the long line of black-clothed men silently trudging their way to the pit. He was enamoured of the tiny pin-pricks of light that stabbed the morning darkness through the cottage windows, but her exhortations reminded him that the hair on his naked legs was stiff with cold and excitement.

He followed her upstairs into bed, marking each step with a happy little chuckle. She tucked him in beside her, stiffening her limbs involuntarily when he wound his cold legs about hers and fell to sleep like a baby with his face resting on her bosom. She had followed him before the hooters howled the news that the last man was down the pit.

The echo of the hooters had died at the bottom of the valley before the specially imported police had left their hiding-places in the dark corners and alley-ways of Cwmardy.

On the way to the station one of them said loudly: 'Good job that's over. We'll be able to sleep in peace now.'

Someone muttered a warning. 'S-sh! Do you want all the men who haven't gone to work to hear you?' They spoke in quiet whispers after this.

'About how many do you reckon went to the pits?'

'I should say about four thousand.'

'Huh! That means there's over a thousand that listened to that bloody red Len Roberts, and are now in bed while their butties are working.'

Another butted in: 'Aye, it's a shame. I say all these bloody Bolshies ought to be rounded up and sent to Russia. They wouldn't be long finding out which side their bread is buttered then, and would be damn glad to come back to the old country to work.'

They slithered in single file through the half-open door of the police station and carefully drew the blinds.

The police officers had hardly settled down to sleep after their all-night vigil before the sun poked its rays across the sky and into the black pall belching from the smokestack which threw them back at the windows of the Big House, where Lord Cwmardy sat with the earpiece of a telephone pressed to his ear.

He seemed very interested in what was being said from the other end on the colliery yard, and when the voice had finished, asked: 'How many did you say, Mr. Hicks?... Hmm. Very good. Better than I thought for the first day. Yes. Eh? What did you say? No, no, man. Don't delay. Put the notice up immediately. Give them till Saturday to present themselves for work and let them know if they're not there by then their places will be filled with men from other areas... Oh, by the way, Mr. Hicks, have you seen to it that the old partnerships have been broken up and the working places interchanged?... Very good. Very good, indeed, Mr. Hicks... No, there is nothing more, good morning.'

He replaced the receiver with a smile and made his way to the dining-room, where his daughter, a robust young woman, sat awaiting him. Lord Cwmardy patted her hair affectionately as he passed her on his way to the chair she had ready at the breakfast table. He settled himself comfortably while she poured the coffee, after which he remarked.

'Well, my dear, the men have come to their senses at last and we can look forward to some tranquillity in this valley.'

His eyes became reminiscent and his voice strangely soft when he said: 'Do you know, Margaret dear, I love this old valley and the people in it? It was here your grandfather sunk his first pit and laid the foundations of the company as it is now. Yes, your grandfather was a fine man. Strong enough to know not only what he wanted but also how to get it. Often is the time when I was a little boy he took me down the pit and made me sit on the side while he helped a collier to fill his tram if there was a rush for coal.'

He sighed at the memory, and his daughter looked at

512

him from under her eyelids.

'Do you think the men will quietly accept the new price-lists?' she asked.

He squared his shoulders abruptly, spilling a drop of coffee on his trousers, but taking no notice of this.

'Accept? Of course they will. We have broken the backbone of their resistance and need have no further worry. You see, my dear, these pits here have always been a storm-centre, our people being the first to fight and the last to give way. But we have ended all that now Ezra Jones, their leader, has become more sensible. A fine man, Ezra. He used to be a firebrand and caused us a lot of trouble for many years, but he's getting wiser as he's getting older.' He strangled another sigh in his throat and asked her to pass the marmalade.

While Lord Cwmardy was having this conversation with his daughter and the hooters were blasting the valley with their blare, Big Jim was trying to light the fire in the kitchen grate. It was only after persistent nagging that Siân had persuaded him to get out of bed first. Her deliberate restlessness while he was sleeping made him grunt continually and had at last awakened him.

Rubbing his eyes, he sat up on his haunches and growled: 'What in hell is biting you, Siân? I thought you had poisoned all the bugs. For hell's sake go to sleep, 'ooman, or get up and let a better man sleep in peace.'

'Fitter if you got up yourself for once, like other men. There 'ood be some shape on living then,' she retorted.

Jim remembered looking at her for some moments in

513

amazement before bursting out: 'What? Me light fire? Good God! What is coming over you, my gel. Don't forget I am a man, not a bloody dish-cloth. Huh! It has always been against my principles to do a 'ooman's work.'

He had begun to curl up under the bedclothes again, but her next words brought him back to his haunches with a jerk.

'Bah! Principles indeed, what are they? I have never seened one and nobody else have neither. Will a principle put food in our bellies or clothes on our backs?' she demanded of her dazed spouse. 'No, never in your life. It is only work will do that.'

This shot compelled Jim to remark with ponderous slowness, as though she had committed sacrilege: 'A principle is like God. It is something you can't see, but it is deep down in your heart all the same.'

Siân had looked at him scornfully before replying: 'Huh! Your heart 'on't take you far when your belly is empty of food.'

It was this final remark, spoken caustically, that had sent Big Jim shamefacedly down the stairs in his shirt, vainly trying to maintain his dignity by flinging back with a grunt over his shoulder what he thought was a crushing retort:

'For shame on you, 'ooman, for thinking a man's guts is more 'portant than his heart. If somebody heard you, mun, they 'ood think you have never been inside a chapel in your life. Huh!'

He now tried to analyse her statements as he held a sheet of newspaper before the fire to draw the flames more quickly up the chimney. He felt that somehow she

514

had got the better of him, and, pondering over the problem, forgot all about his work until a draught of air tore the paper from his hands and sucked it up the chimney, where it set the soot on fire with a roar.

The noise startled him for a moment, and he sprang back just as Siân, half-dressed, came rushing down the stairs to see what was the matter.

Jim immediately grasped his chance and shouted at the top of his voice: 'Hell-fire! Is this bloody house witched, or what?'

She gave a glance at the fireplace, then began to pull her skirt over her head while he made frantic efforts to extinguish the flames, howling instructions all the while.

'Get some salt, Siân! Quick, now!'

'There is none in the house,' she moaned, at the same time unconsciously patting her disordered hair.

'Hell-fire! This is not the time to prink yourself up, mun. Get some sand, then!'

'That is all gone too. Oh dear, dear. This will mean a summons so sure as God is my judge, and us without a penny in the house. Why for was a man so useless ever brought into the world?'

She sat resignedly in the chair and muttered: 'Ah well, us might jest as well be burned to death as starve to death. It is quicker, anyhow.'

The neighbouring women rushed out into the street and saw the dense fumes of smoke and flame pour from the chimney. They gazed sympathetically at the sight for a while, then one said: 'Poor old Siân will have a mess to clean up after this.'

515

'Aye,' another replied, looking at the curling smoke and folding her arms aggressively on her stomach. 'And no need for it at all, if Big Jim did only do the same as our Dai and sweeped it down once and agen with the cane brush, it 'ood never catch fire. But there, what can you do with a man who do always say, whenever you tell him anything: "One man, one job"?'

This started an argument, and the fire died down while the women gossiped.

Later the same morning Len took a stroll through the main street, nodding here and there to the various groups of men scattered about. All of them were opposed to the new terms, and their resentment was expressed in their thin faces and the heat with which they discussed the position. Each time a strange policeman came near they turned their backs to him and audibly spat into the roadway as he passed.

Dai Cannon was the centre of one group that hailed Len, who returned the greeting and joined them.

'Aye,' the irascible old man was saying, 'Not so very long ago they was shouting like anything for the Federation and now the twisters have sneaked back to work like dogs scrounging after a bitch in heat. Ach, they do listen to Ezra like as if he was God.'

The keen attention which the listeners paid to his words encouraged him and he spoke more loudly: 'No man is good enough for that. No. What have Ezra done for us after we have paid him well all these years and gived him a nice house and enough money to wear collars and ties every day of the week?' He blew his nose before answering himself. 'Nothing. He have turned on us like the

516

rest. I tell you, boys, it's every man for hisself these days.'

Will Evans, a muffler dangling rakishly from his neck and his cap stuck at an angle on the side of his head, thought it time to help. 'That's right. They're all the same, self first and everybody else last, from what I can see of it. Look at Fred Lewis. He's supposed to be in the Party and have been preaching revolution like blue hell for years; but now he's crawling round licking Ezra's arse. Bah! I wonder what Ezra had from the company for this sell-out,' he concluded insinuatingly.

Len felt his face go red, then white, and was about to break into the conversation when someone warned: 'S-sh! Here they come. Talk about the devil, muniferni!'

Ezra, his head bent and his hands behind his back, came slowly towards them. Fred Lewis was with him, talking volubly, his hands in continual motion as he tried to emphasise something; but Ezra did not appear to be taking any notice of him. The miners' leader quickened his step a little as he came near the group and his head sunk more deeply between his shoulders, until he heard someone hiss: 'Traitor!'

The word jerked him erect, and he stopped to scan the faces before him with glittering eyes. He stared at them, one after the other, until he saw the white face of his son-in-law. For some seconds the two men's thoughts were centred on each other and completely oblivious of anyone else.

Len felt a vague pity run through him and he would have given anything if he could have apologised for the remark, but Ezra's features were set with a hardness that allowed for no compromise. His voice rasped like a saw on steel when he said: 'Did you hear it? "Traitor" was the word they used. And you and your gang taught them to use it. Huh! After what you have said and done behind my back, you should know what a traitor is.'

His voice broke for a moment but his eyes were more adamant than ever when he shrugged his shoulders and without another word walked on, leaving the men gaping on the kerb. Lewis, nonplussed by the suddenness of the incident and feeling very awkward, sheepishly followed, but the attack made Len feel giddy. His head swirled, making his mouth dry and his stomach sick. Will Evans saw the emotional strain he was undergoing and patted him sympathetically on the back.

'It's no good worrying, Len. That have just about finished everything between you and your father-in-law,' he consoled.

Others joined in the talk that followed, but Len had lost all interest in what they were saying. During the afternoon most of the men who had stopped from the pit again gathered round the street-corners to see the others return. Len sensed the cleavage between the two sections as the black-faced men walked past the groups. He saw one-time mates look bitterly at each other and pass in silence. The sight sent a thought flashing through his brain.

'Good God,' he muttered to himself, 'we have forgotten all about the company and now see each other, instead of Lord Cwmardy, as enemies.' He continued to look on helplessly and all the time the conviction grew on him that something new had developed in the valley overnight. He began to wonder if the Party were right when it advocated

518

that the men remain out in spite of all that had happened. Wouldn't it have been better to keep the men together and accept the inevitable, rather than have them turn on each other as they were now doing?

These and other thoughts crowded themselves on him until he heard a shout.

'You'd better all get back, boys, because they're starting strangers next week if you don't.'

The news beat into Len's mind like a blow, and he hurried away. By the time he reached the house he had gripped himself somewhat, although his hurried entrance betrayed the tumult still within him.

Ezra sat quiet and morose in his customary place, and did not even raise his head when Len entered. The latter ate the food that Mary had prepared even while he noticed that her downcast eyes seemed to lengthen her face, giving it an appearance of loneliness. She motioned him to a chair near her when he had finished his food, and the action bore out his feeling that something unusually serious had happened. He tried to catch her eye, but she avoided him and all he saw was the twitching of her face. He sat down and for a time the only sound was that of heavy breathing. Then Ezra broke the silence and his words dripped like melting icicles into Len's heart, where their very coldness sent hot flames through his body.

'Len Roberts; there is no room in this house for you and me together. One of us has got to get out.'

Len sprang to his feet, but Mary's look dragged him down before he could say anything, as Ezra went on without raising his gaze from the fire. 'Well can you look

519

to Mary – you, who have made her father's name a byword in Cwmardy!' The miners' leader rose to his feet and rested his hand on the mantelpiece. 'You heard what I said? Either you or me are leaving this house tonight. Too long have I stuck all the sneers and taunts that have been flung at me, and the time has now come when it's going to be ended, inside these doors at least.'

Len felt like a child tossed into a flood. The words buffeted about inside his head and he was unable to grasp their import clearly, although spontaneously he thought of Mary. He was unable to conceive of anything happening to himself unless it happened to her, and the first question that broke from him was a puzzled: 'But what about Mary, then, Ezra?'

The very innocence of the query shook the elder man, who had prepared himself to face a scene and never expected this. He hesitated, then answered: 'Mary will do what she thinks best. She is old enough to think for herself, but all I hope is that she will stick by her father for the short time that is left to me.' Something in his throat clouded the last words and nearly made them inarticulate.

Len looked from father to daughter dazedly, then something hot simmered within him and he jumped up as for the first time he became aware of the full weight of Ezra's ultimatum. His chest was heaving when he shouted: 'Ha! I see what you're driving at now. You want me to leave my home. You want to kick me out like a dog, and think I'll go with my tail between my legs!' He swallowed hard and went on more hurriedly, as though the words were bursting in his mouth: 'But you're thinking wrong. Yes, by gum, you're thinking wrong.' His arms were now beginning to wave wildly and Mary tried to pacify him, but he only cried: 'Don't interfere, Mary. If your father isn't man enough to stand up to opposition, then he's not man enough to lead the Federation. Do you think that because I am your husband I have got to believe everything he says and do everything he wants me to? No; not on your life! I have got a home to go to, don't worry – the one I had before ever I came here, and I'm always welcome there.'

'Hush, Len,' she implored. 'Dad's bad and don't mean half of what he's saying.'

Ezra had now resumed his seat, and his dejected demeanour had the effect of dampening Len's temper as quickly as it had flared up. This emotional volatility was one of his main characteristics, and it always found expression in his relationship with Ezra and Mary. All his mature life had been influenced by the miners' leader, and even now, despite their many differences, he regarded Ezra as the strongest and most dominating man in Cwmardy. Coupled with this was his intense devotion to and pride in Mary. They had been reared together in the village and drawn into the struggles of the people from early childhood. This had the effect on Len of mentally fusing father and daughter together as an indissoluble unit, and he could never think of one without at the same time thinking of the other. He wondered now what she would do in face of what Ezra had said, knowing that the ultimatum applied to her as well as to himself.

Throughout the scene, Mary had remained practically silent, although she was aware of the personal issues at stake. She was her husband's superior intellectually, having the capacity to think more coherently and feel less acutely, and when she now spoke it was obvious to both men that she was expressing her deepest convictions.

'Dad, Len. I'm sorry that this has happened, especially when all of us know there was no need for it.'

Ezra shuffled restlessly, but she gave him no time to intervene.

'I know what you feel, dad, about what's happened, but you can't blame Len for that, although he belongs to the Party.'

'Can't blame him, Mary? Don't talk foolish, girl. Isn't he one of the leaders and isn't he the one they always put up to fight me on every issue?'

'I know, dad, I know,' she patiently assented. 'And I wish in my heart he had listened to me and never joined it. But what's the good of talking about that now.'

Ezra stopped her curtly. 'There's every reason why we should talk about it. His Party called me a traitor and it's a lie. A lie!' He shouted the last words, but gained control of himself immediately. 'I have spent a lifetime in this movement, Mary, and your mother got buried in it. Yes, I know the struggle from A to Z, and I won't allow any man to call me a traitor because I won't do what he or his mates want me to do. What I have done I have done with my eyes open, and the people have listened to me. I am sorry there are still a few soft enough to follow Len and his Party.'

Len's temper began to rise again, but Mary intervened hastily.

'Don't start quarrelling again, we've got enough to

worry about without that.'

'But he told me to leave the house, Mary, and I want to know if he means that.'

Mary knew immediately that Len had precipitated the crisis in spite of her efforts to avoid it, but she tried to mitigate the effects by taking the offensive from Ezra's hands at the beginning.

'Yes. That's true, Len. Dad told you to go.'

'No, I didn't, Mary, I said one of us would have to go.' The tones in which Ezra said this were as heavy as lead, but they acted on Mary like a stimulant.

'Oh, why do we beat about the bush like this?' she asked. 'Both of you are feeling nasty and bitter, but tomorrow you will be sorry for what you are saying now.' She gulped a little. 'Listen, the two of you. Both of you know how much I think of you, but you are asking me to choose, dad, and it's not fair. There's room in this house for all of us, as there has been ever since Len and me were married, and I don't see why you should talk to him as you did just now because you have quarrelled about something else.'

Ezra stirred in his chair again. 'Don't talk so lightly, Mary,' he said sharply. 'This is not a simple quarrel. For years you know that Len and me have been getting further apart on everything that counts, and now we've reached a point where there can be no harmony between us while we are together. That's what I mean when I say there is no room in this house for both of us.'

Len felt obliged to interpose and, turning to Mary, he exclaimed: 'That's just the point, Mary. Your father and me can never agree on many things. Anybody can see that after what he's done about the lock-out. Good God, I'd say the same thing about my own mother if she did the same thing as that. So what's the good of arguing? I've followed Ezra through thick and thin all my life, and it cuts me to the bone that it's got to come to this. But it's not my fault. Neither you or him can expect me to bury all my thoughts in what he says and does. No. He has taught me to think for myself, and what I haven't learned from him I've learned in the battles of our people and in the pit from my butties. And that's good enough for me.' His voice became bitter as he took down his coat from the back of the door. 'Your father has told me to leave. How easy he said it, knowing it's his house and I've only been here on sufferance all this time! I can hardly believe I have been so blind as not to see it before. Never mind. We're never too old to learn.' His anger got the better of him, although he had been trying to control it, and he blurted out: 'But I remember the time when he left us all without being told to go. Aye, left us when he thought we were in a hole and the company was beating us. That's the sort of leader he is... good when everything is going all right, but cruel and selfish when the odds are against us and he can't get his own way.'

He put his hand on the latch and was about to lift it when Mary sprang up with a little cry. 'Don't, Len. Don't go and leave me. Dad doesn't mean what he says. Do you, dad?' She appealed to Ezra, but he made no response. She went to him and took his head in her hands, while Len stood immobile, hardly knowing what to do at this new development.

It was obvious that Mary had made her mind up during the last few seconds and was now tensed to express her opinions whatever the consequences.

'Dad,' she challenged gently, 'you are not only nasty with Len because of what's happened about the lock-out, but also because you are jealous of him.'

This stung Ezra to retort immediately. 'Jealous? Jealous of him? Ha-ha!'

'Don't laugh, dad. I'm very serious, more serious than I have ever been in my life. You are jealous because you are afraid that Len and the Party are going to get more support than you from the people of Cwmardy and because you believe I think more of him than of you. I don't believe in the Party any more than you, but I'm bound to say, dad, that I think you did wrong when you didn't give the men a chance to have a say about the agreement, although in everything else I believe you were right.'

The two men were now listening intently to what she was saying, each conscious of the fact that she was determining their future.

'But, dad, when you tell Len to leave the house it means you are asking me to leave either him or you. Yes, you are asking me to choose which I love most, and I can't, I can't,' her voice broke and she paused while she recovered herself.

'Can't you see, dad, that I love the two of you equally as much, but in different ways. I'm not a little child now, only doing what I'm told to do. You have reared me to think like a woman and have always taught me to have an opinion of my own. Oh, dad, don't you remember when you used to take me to the workmen's committees and meetings because I was too small to be left in the house on my own after mam died?'

Ezra knew what was coming and his head slowly sank until it had slipped from her grasp, when she went on very softly.

'Don't you think, dad, that had an effect upon my mind? Of course it had. When the men used to challenge you on something, I used to hate them in my childish mind for daring to say anything about you. I used to be thrilled when you and them would be talking of the strikes and the other things connected with the pit. I was happy when I was old enough to join with our other women and do something myself, as well as listen to others. Yes, all of these things you've reared me up to, and that is why, dad, Len can never steal me from you, but neither can you steal me from Len.

'That's something you must both learn. You tell Len that he must go. That means that you are throwing me out as well, because if he goes, I go with him – not because I love him more than you, but because I have to take his part when you are unfair, dad, and take advantage of him. I know now as sure as the morning will come that if I choose to stay with you after Len has gone that you will want me to agree with you in everything, as you now want Len to do. You will want to rob me of the independence that your own training has given me. You will love me so long as I agree with you in everything. No, dad. That's something Len has never asked me to do. If he goes, I go with him.'

Her eyes filled and she caught Ezra's head to her breast

and felt his heaving shoulders as her words sank home. She silently nodded to Len to go to bed. Before the door had properly closed behind him, Ezra broke down completely and she heard him sob for the first time in her life. Her own tears fused with his as she tried to soothe him.

SPEED-UP

Len was glad that the threatened domestic break-up had
not matured, but he was very worried about affairs in the
pit, and during the days following the quarrel, his mind
was concentrated on the problem of work. He felt uneasy
and wondered if he and the others who remained out were
doing the right thing; but he dreaded the thought of going
back to work after the stand the Party had made against
the terms and the restart. He hesitated to tell anyone of
his thoughts in case he would be regarded as weak, but
towards the end of the week he determined to seek
Ezra's advice, although there was still a certain tenseness
between them.

The opportunity came one night at the supper-table
when, instead of asking Ezra direct, he asked Mary: 'What
do you think me and dad should do? I don't fancy it's

right for us to go back to work just because the company says it will put other men in our places.' He paused. 'But somehow I feel unless we do something quick, they'll keep us out for ever. I don't know what to do for the best,' he concluded dolefully.

Mary looked dubiously at her father, but the latter appeared to be deep in thought. All along she, in common with many of the women, felt there was no purpose served in remaining out now most of the men had restarted; but she had mentioned nothing to Len about her opinions. His straight query and evident puzzlement, together with Ezra's apparent lack of interest, prompted her, after a brief hesitation, to be frank.

'I hardly know what to say, Len,' she muttered, looking at him helplessly, then blurting out: 'But one thing is sure, we can't carry on for ever with nothing coming in. Oh, I wish to God the men had never got divided like this.'

She knew she was on dangerous ground even as she uttered the words, but both men fortunately seemed to miss their import. Her outburst, however, brought Ezra from his abstraction, and he raised his head with a tired motion.

'There's two lessons I've learned in life. One is that the next best thing to victory is to know when you're beaten. The other is always to keep with the men wherever they are.'

Len looked at the man and wondered what was coming next, but he made no effort to say anything, as Ezra went on, his dark eyes a little less moody: 'And no one can question that we've been beat this time. How can we expect to win,' he demanded, 'when we are fighting not only the company but the Government as well?'

He paused, realizing immediately the slip he had made, but Len, impelled by the opportunity, gave him no time to recover before asking: 'But it's a Labour Government, Ezra, and how can they be against us?'

The miners' leader coughed, pretending to clear his throat, then said: 'Yes, it's a Labour Government, but what power has it got? It's only there on sufferance and can be put out at any minute.'

'But, Ezra, if it's kicked out for doing something for the people, then that's just the way in which the people will put it back with full power, isn't it?'

Len was getting excited as he began driving his points home, and Mary became a little anxious as she saw his exuberance. 'Let's stick to the point and not start talking about politics that will lead us nowhere,' she advised in an effort to avoid the argument she knew was brewing.

Ezra willingly followed her cue. 'You're right, Mary, and the point's perfectly clear, in my mind at least, and I should think to every other sensible man or woman.'

Len opened his mouth, but he had no chance to speak, as Ezra interrupted his unspoken thoughts.

'Oh, I know all about principles and what not, and I know it's very nice to feel oneself to be a martyr. Ay, indeed, very nice and comfortable. But I've never yet seen what good it's done anybody, least of all the people it's supposed to help. That's why I advised the men to go back to work.'

Len could hold himself in no longer, and he broke the momentary silence that followed Ezra's remark. 'But, Ezra, the position's different, mun. You told us to go back when we were all united, and by telling us that you broke us up, as you can see for yourself now.'

'Yes, Len. But that would have happened in any case because of what you and the Party did. If you'd only listened to me and put those wild theories out of your head, the men would have gone back together and there wouldn't be any of this bitterness.' His eyes became hard again and his face set. 'You can thank the Party for the present position in Cwmardy.'

Len hastily swallowed the food he had put in his mouth, while Ezra was speaking, but Mary interrupted him before he could make himself articulate. The partial reconciliation between the two men had given her a happiness she had not felt for a long time, and she knew whatever she said would be accepted by both as her honest opinion, even if she were wrong.

'I don't think you're right, dad,' she said, 'I believe you've got enough influence with the workmen to hold them, especially when you have the committee behind you, as you did.'

Ezra started to say something, but she went on: 'All the same, I believe the same as you about Len going to work. His place is there with the other men, and even if they were wrong that's no reason for deserting them.'

Len rose agitatedly from the table: 'You can't say I'm a deserter!' he exclaimed. 'There's such things as principles that one must stick to through thick and thin.'

A slow smile passed over Ezra's face, softening it for a moment as he said: 'That's where you're wrong. When I was your age I used to think the same, but experience –

and you will agree it has been a fairly wide one – has taught me that principles which go against the workmen must be put on one side.'

The argument now became more heated and continued until very late, but at the end of it Len agreed to apply for his work back if the Party and the workmen still out agreed.

Early next morning Len went round the homes of all the Party members he could get hold of, and it was decided to support Ezra if he called a meeting. This was done; Len and two other Party members going round the streets with a bell to announce the meeting, which was held the same afternoon.

After much bitter recrimination and bad feeling, all the men decided to go up to the pit the next day and apply for their work.

Before the first hooter had started to blow the following day, Siân was out of bed and had lighted the fire in the kitchen. Her face was glowing with happiness when Jim came down, and she fluttered around him like a hen.

'Ha-ha, James bach, it is good to see you in working clothes once agen. Aye, indeed, mun.'

'Huh! I do agree with you,' Jim grunted in reply, at the same time bending to pull his trousers over his feet. 'Don't be long with that toast; our Len will be down any minute now.'

'Tut-tut! Don't you worry 'bout my business. This is not the first bit of toast that I have made. Oh no.'

The old couple were seated at the breakfast table when Len walked in. Siân immediately jumped from her chair to wet the cocoa she had prepared for him. 'There, Len bach,

533

put that down your little belly.' Len never refused this, because he knew it gave her pleasure.

In a short time the men were ready to leave and, as they were about to go, Siân warned them. 'Now, 'member, mind to take care of yourselfs today. You have been a long time from the pit now, and 'on't be so quick as you did used to be.'

Big Jim's happy laughter rippled round the kitchen like a drum beat. 'I have worked in that old pit going on for forty years and you can venture there is not much about her that Big Jim don't know, you take that from me.'

With this, they both kissed the old lady and left the house. When the two men presented themselves at the lamp-room they were told to wait outside the manager's office, or 'insulting room', as Jim always called it.

'Funny bloody game this, in't it, Len?' he asked bewilderedly, as they made their way across the colliery yard towards the office where a long queue of men were already lined up.

Len did not answer, although he was equally surprised by this unusual procedure. They fell in at the tail end of the queue and waited, while they watched the twinkling lights jogging from the lamp-room to the pit-head. The indignity of the wait galled Jim, and at last, unable to contain himself any longer, he bawled out to no one in particular:

'Frigging hell! What do they think we are – doorboys, or dancing fleas, or what? I have never seened such a insult in all my born days.' No one replied, and this drove him frantic. 'By damn, they can spit on me, but no bloody man breathing can rub it in, muniferni.'

The words were hardly spoken when a rustle ran through the ranks as the office door opened and the colliery sergeant came out, shouting at the top of his voice: 'Only fifty wanted today. First come, first served.'

The waiting men stood immobile in amazed silence until the sergeant bawled: 'Come on there. Who's the first to start?'

In a flash the ranks broke and the men rushed for the door. The fifty men required were signed on in a very short time and made their way to the lamp-room, while the remainder were advised to come up again next morning, when perhaps more men would be needed.

Jim looked dazedly at Len, hunched his shoulders, swallowed hard, then turned his back to the office and walked away, saying deep down in his throat: 'Len bach, they got us by the short hairs.'

Next day the rain swept Cwmardy in gusty spasms that soaked all it touched, but men were waiting at the pit-head long before the first cage went down. Len and his father were drenched when they reached the office, water streaming down their faces and the backs of their necks. Jim wanted to remain at the front of the queue, but Len urged him, grunting and swearing, to the end. Everyone waited tensely for the sergeant's voice, each man ready to rush for the door at the first sign. When it opened, however, both Mr. Hicks and the sergeant came out. The two proceeded along the line of anxious men, Mr. Hicks occasionally calling a man out and feeling his biceps. If he was satisfied with the result he sent the man to the lamp-room; when he was not, he sent him home with the advice to try again some other time.

A number of men had already been instructed to start before Mr. Hicks reached Jim, but he unhesitatingly told the old workman to get his lamp, without bothering to ask him questions or feel his muscles.

'The fireman will tell where you are to work,' the general manager advised, as Jim started on his way to the lamp-room like a man in a trance. But before he had gone far, he turned sharply on his heels and demanded, 'What about our Len?'

'Oh, we'll find something for him later,' was the complacent reply.

Jim snorted. 'Later to hell! That is no bloody good to me. Either he do start now with me, where he have always beened, or not one of us will start.'

Mr. Hicks knew this was an ultimatum and that it would be no use blustering, but he was anxious to have Jim back in the pit because of his capacity as a workman.

'Oh, all right. As a special favour, you can take him with you.' Without another word the two men fetched their lamps and made their way to the pit. Before entering the cage, Len looked back at the queue of waiting men, then took a sigh with him into the iron carriage.

The 'bang... bang-bang' of the wooden droppers falling into place as the cage dropped out of sight sounded strange to Len and the hot, foetid atmosphere of the pit, after the long period of fresh air on the surface, made him choke. He tasted it thick in his mouth and retched like a man who had never been down a pit before. The sensations took his mind back to the day when he had

536

first started work, and his imagination ran more quickly then the falling cage. He felt glad he had been destined for the pit and laughed inwardly at his one-time longing to be freed from it. The dangers and the struggles, the hatreds and the humour had become part of his life. His body and mind had been moulded in the pit by his fellow workmen, and without them he knew his world would be empty.

Big Jim beside him in the crowded carriage, groaned, then growled: 'I wish that engine man 'ood be more careful with his brakes, instead of jerking our guts into our mouths like this. If his back and legs was paining like mine he 'ood have a bit more care, muniferni.'

The darkness of the pit-shaft did not enable Len to see the man who answered. 'Aye, you are right, Jim. But what can you 'spect from these crots of kids that they have brought in to work the engines? Bah! The old 'uns who have worked this cage all their lives have been chucked on one side like muck. I tell you, boys, this old pit is going all to hell.'

There was no time for further conversation before the carriage floor bumped on the wooden planks that covered the water sump at the pit bottom. The men got out, separating according to the side of the pit in which they worked. Len waited for his father and they walked in company with other men towards the stable a hundred yards or so from the shaft bottom. They had nearly reached the heavy planked door which covered its entrance when Jim pulled up sharply and whispered, 'S-shh! Didn't I hear somethink in the stable then?'

The men stopped and listened. Above the whistle of air

537

through the cracks in the door came sounds similar to those made by wildly scrambling hoofs, then a muffled voice: 'Hold his head, mun! Keep his bloody arse in towards the manger!' A short silence, then: 'Whoa! What the bloody hell are you doing? Whoa, boy, whoa!' Then more excitedly, 'Get hold of that twitch. Quick now. Ah that's better.' The scrambling ceased and the men looked at each other, their faces dull shadows in the darkness that pressed on them.

One remarked: 'They'll have a job with old Dangler today. It's his first day down since the lock-out, and I pity his poor haulier.'

'Huh! You can keep your pity for yourself. He's working your heading today,' remarked another voice, adding as an afterthought: 'You needn't worry about the haulier. Sam's got him and you can bet your life that he knows how to handle Dangler. They're old butties.'

Suddenly the noise of the whistling air stopped as the huge stable door was tugged open by those inside.

Someone shouted: 'Hide those blasted lamps and get out of the way.' The waiting men hurriedly clambered on the sides of the roadway as a file of horses, each with a haulier at its head, came out. The horses were restless and excited, the whites of their eyes shining wickedly in the semi-darkness. One of the hauliers warned in passing: 'Watch Dangler. He's the last. Keep well away from his arse if you're wise.'

Big Jim picked from the roadway a short piece of stick as thick as his forearm, and muttered to Len: 'If he do try any of his funny trickses on me, I'll put him down so flat as a pancake.'

538

Len did not reply as Sam, clinging tightly to Dangler's head and talking in his flattened ear, led the horse past with swishing hoofs that made the air rustle like a ballet dancer's skirts. The men kept a respectable distance behind the horses, whose feet disturbed the coal-dust and lifted it in fine clouds through the enclosed air, where it tickled their nostrils like snuff.

Will Evans sneezed loudly, blew his nose, and said for all to hear: 'I'm sure old Sam do train Dangler so that nobody else can drive him. That's the only way he can stick to his extra turn a week for working a dangerous horse.'

'S-shh!' came the sharp warning. 'We are near the locking hole and the fireman might hear you.'

The men's lamps were examined in the big hole driven into the side of the roadway, and they were given separate instructions by the fireman before proceeding on their way.

The official welcomed Jim with a smile. 'Hallo, Jim. I'm glad you're back, mun jawli. It's about time they sent some real workmen down, instead of these strappers that are here.'

Len cocked his ears up at this but said nothing as the fireman went on: 'I have got orders to send you to Mockyn Bobby's heading, Jim.'

Before he could say any more Jim's surprised voice interrupted him. 'Mockyn Bobby's? What the bloody hell do I want there? Me and Len have got our own place, without going to anybody else's. Ha-ha! Come on, Shenkin bach, stop pulling my leg, mun.'

'Indeed to God, I'm not pulling your leg, Jim. I have got more respect for you than that, and well you do know it.

539

But them's the orders I have had from the big boss.'

Jim bewilderedly pulled his cap off and wiped it over his face as he asked. 'But what's the matter with my own place? I have droved it in from the engine parting, and I am not going to leave it for any big boss.' He lost his temper and began to shout. 'No, I 'oodn't leave it for the Devil hisself, and that's telling you somethink, Shenkin.'

'Come, come, Jim bach. Don't be so stubborn, mun, you know that I can't help it. Another man is working your place and you have got to shift, that's all about it.'

Jim, his eyes bulging in his blackened face, held his breath a moment when he heard this, then gasped, as though he doubted his ears: 'What did you say? Another man working in my place! Arglwydd mawr! If any man have touched my coal and my timbers, I'll chop his head off with his own hatchet!' He swallowed hard then howled: 'Who is it? Come on, tell me quick. Who have got the cheek to work my place while I am idle in the bloody house, standing Siân's nagging because I am man enough to fight for a principle?'

The fireman became alarmed at his vehemence, but he felt he had to carry out his instructions whatever the consequences. 'It is not your place any more than it is mine,' he asserted. 'All the pit do belong to the company, and they can do what they like with what they own, can't they?'

'Not my place?' Jim challenged. 'Who the hell droved it in? Who ripped it down and timbered it?'

His voice became shrill with thwarted pride. 'Who risked his body and slogged his guts out to keep it tidy so that there was always a tram of coal ready on the road and two in the face? Not my place, indeed. If it is not mine, who the bloody hell's is it?'

The fireman did not attempt to argue further. 'Them's my orders, Jim,' he said, 'and if you don't like them, then all you have got to do is to go back up the pit; and I would be sorry for you to do that.'

This ultimatum shook the old workman and put a glazed glare in his eyes like that in a cow's that has just been poleaxed, but pulling himself together he hurriedly thought out another line of action in defence of his place.

'If us have got to go to Mockyn Bobby's, then where is Mockyn working?' he asked.

'Oh, they have sent him the other side of the pit,' was the reply.

Len had been silent throughout this argument, although he saw the new tactics the company was adopting to break the men apart and scatter them among mutual strangers in various parts of the pit. He caught his father by the arm.

'Come on, dad. There's nothing for it but to go where we are sent.' Jim looked like refusing, but after a brief hesitation he responded to the appeal and walked away from the locking hole with his head bent and his lips cursing.

After twenty minutes' walking in the humid air, the clothes sticking to their bodies with sweat, the couple reached the place where they had left their tools before the lock-out. The clamour of coal being thrown into a tram stopped as they drew near and Jim walked up to the man who was working, at the same time tilting his lamp so that the light fell full on the stranger's face.

There was an awkward pause while Jim scanned him up

541

and down before asking heavily: 'What for did you come here and work another man's place, butty?'

'What else could I do? I either had to start here or not at all.'

'That's right, dad. It's not his fault,' Len broke in, fearful that the old man would lose his temper again.

Jim sighed. 'Ah well. Perhaps it will all work out square in the end, Len bach.' He turned to the stranger and advised: 'Take care how you do work that face, butty. It is hellish funny and you have got to keep your butts clean and cut the right-hand side in front of you all the time if you want to work her as she ought to be worked. And you want to watch the top. It is very sly and you can't trust to test it with a mandril, because it will ring like steel one minute, then, before you can blow your nose, it will drop "bump" like a shower of lead.'

The man thanked him for the advice and the couple, sharing the tools between them and bent double beneath their weight, left him. By the time they reached their new work place, Big Jim was again in a temper generated from weariness. He rested for a while to look about him, then spat viciously at a passing cockroach before saying disgustedly: 'Huh! I thought so. Rippings behind, coal worked square till it is left so hard as concrete, muck all over the place. Huh! A navvy have been working here, not a collier. In a muck-hole he ought to be or digging trenches on the tip.'

Len took no notice and began pulling off his clothes. The heat was intolerable and the percentage of gas in the air made the blood pound at his temples. He felt exhausted already, although he revived a little when the upper part of his body was naked to the hot air.

The two men had half-filled their first tram when the fireman came round to inspect the place.

'How many is this, boys? Your third?' he asked.

Jim threw his mandril violently to the ground. 'Who the flaming hell do you think you are talking to – white mice or what? Three, muniferni! Ach, that little fireman's lamp have gone to your head.'

'Gone to my head or no, Jim, you can depend on it the Big Boss will expect eight a day from this place.'

'Eh, eight a day? Ha-ha, you have made a mistake, Shenkin, you are talking to men now, not donkeys. There's no man in the pit can fill eight a day in this bloody muck-hole without pulling the roof in on him, and you can venture Big Jim is not going to do that. Ho, no! When I will be buried alive it will be up in the sun, where I can enjoy myself.'

The fireman grunted uncomfortably, and stroked the moustache over his mouth with a thick forefinger. 'Ah, well. If you 'on't do it, you can bet the buttons on your coppish they'll find somebody who will, Jim.'

This put Jim on his dignity, and swelling his chest he declared: 'You can tell the Big Boss from me that he can get to hell out of it, and if he can find a better workman than me there, let him send him down. Till then, tell him to keep his chops shut when he is talking to men who was working when his father was carrying him about in his trousers pocket.'

The fireman gave it up and went on his way, his lamplight getting progressively smaller until it looked like the red-hot point of a needle.

Len and his father kept on working in silence for a

while after the official had left, until the former, who was heaving shovelfulls of coal into the tram, asked: 'You can see the game, dad, can't you?'

'See it? Of course I can. Clear as ink. They are going to try to break our hearts, boy bach. Make us do twice so much work for half so much pay. Bah! A tadpole could see it, mun, if he had eyes.'

Putting his hand to the small of his back the old man bent his body and groaned. 'Ach! What is the matter with me? To hell with everything! Aye, and myself as well.'

For the remainder of the day he worked with less haste, and Len noticed that he made no effort to lift the huge lumps of coal into the tram without first breaking them up into smaller pieces. At the end of the shift both men felt sore and tired, and although the fresh air on the surface revived them a little, it was some weeks before their bodies again became inured to the strain and cramped positions of the pit.

STRIFE
IN THE VALLEY

Nearly twelve months passed by, but hundreds of the original workmen at the pit were not restarted. Their places were taken by families who lived outside Cwmardy, many of whom moved into the valley when the menfolk found jobs. The native unemployed drifted to the rubbish dumps and mountain sides to dig for coal during the winter, while some unloaded the rubbish wagons on the pit-head, displacing the men who had been paid wages for this work. Overtime became rampant and new divisions and bitternesses developed among the people.

During this period the cleavage between Ezra and the Party on the issues of the lock-out had widened until they now embraced nearly every issue that rose in the pit and the valley. Ezra was made a J.P., an honour which, the Party claimed, proved he had irretrievably betrayed the people, and as a result Harry Morgan was put up against him as candidate for the former's council seat. Harry was defeated, but he continued to attack Ezra on every possible occasion. The logic and arguments of the Party's fight had Len's full approval, although he was allowed to keep in the background as much as possible to avoid further crises in his domestic life. The uncompromising attitude of the Party, and the statements its members made against him, embittered Ezra, and he came to regard them as greater enemies than the company. Len, on the other hand, found that the struggle against his father-in-law widened his ideas and gave him a better appraisal of Socialism and all that it meant. The old illusions bred in him by Ezra, and later by Fred Lewis, regarding revolutions and politics were shattered, and, altogether, he gained a basis of knowledge that made him an able lieutenant for Harry Morgan and a formidable opponent for the miners' leader. Mary unconsciously helped him a great deal to get this mental balance and clarity.

Since the quarrel she had tended to become more critical of everything that was said and done by her father and Len, and found herself, without knowing it, being drawn nearer to her husband not only emotionally but intellectually. But she would not join the Party, out of loyalty to her father, who, she felt, was fast breaking up in every way.

One day Ezra was called to London by the Federation. He remained there a week, and on his return looked gloomier than ever.

The discontent in Cwmardy seemed to be common throughout the country, and rumours began floating about

546

that there was to be a General Strike of all the workers in the land against the threat of the coalowners further to reduce the miners' wages and conditions. Ezra confirmed the rumours at a mass-meeting, and this brought men back into the Federation. His report of the discussions in London became the foundation of definite discussions in the pits and the meetings. Len's experiences in the pit, apart from what he learned in the Party and the Federation, made him convinced that the time for action was again approaching. The knowledge made him introspective as he thought of the poverty Mary and his people would have to endure once more, but he brushed this mood away when he visualised the possibilities of victory for the men.

Despite this, he came home from work looking unusually gloomy on one occasion. Mary noticed his depression, but waited until he had had his dinner and bathed before asking:

'What's the matter, Len. Have you had a stiff day? You look more than tired out.'

He stretched his legs wearily before him and lit a cigarette. 'I expect I do, Mary. I'm just about fed up with the pit since I started after the lock-out. None of us know from one day to the other what job we will be expected to do once we get down the pit. If the officials ask us colliers to unload muck, we've got to do it or they'll say, "There's plenty of men on top of the pit who'd be glad of the chance!"'

The light on the cigarette burned his finger and he bent forward to flick the dead ash into the grate before querying, almost hopelessly: 'Can't you see what it is all leading to,

Mary? The men are afraid to trust one another for fear anything they say will go back to the boss and every week the company is quietly dropping our money, until they don't even pay the price-list they themselves forced on us. Good God! I remember before the lock-out all of us used to pass our pay-papers around, but now you can't get to know what the man next to you is having for his work.'

Mary shook her head disconsolately, but tried to encourage him as she sensed the despondency beneath his words. 'It's no good worrying, Len. We'll get nowhere by doing that. It's rotten, I know, but the men are bound to turn one of these days.' She sighed and drew her chair nearer the fire as though she felt a cold chill fill the air. 'It's a wonder to me how they stick it,' she went on restlessly. 'They must be smouldering on the quiet and one day that will burst into a flame again, then something will have to move.' A pause, then: 'I hope something real will come from this General Strike which dad is talking about. I fancy it's not so hard and cruel when we're all fighting together as it is when we're on our own.' Another thought came to her and she whispered: 'Remember Black Friday, Len?'

He nodded his head and she rose from the chair and sat on his knee. His hand aimlessly caressed the strands of her brown hair, which reflected the brightness of the brass candlesticks on the mantelpiece. The contact suddenly awakened something within him, and he pressed her close to his body. Her eyes softened as she continued: 'But one day our people will get their own back on the company and the traitors; then dad will be back where he belongs... with the people as their leader. It's bound to come, especially if the Federation can get the other unions to take part officially in the General Strike.'

Len felt her vibrate with feeling and her body magnified itself despite the sunken chest hidden beneath her blouse. Her assertiveness in some vague way made him aware that power did not depend alone on bulk.

At the next Party meeting, a few days later, Harry Morgan gave a report of what the Miners' Executive was doing to further the General Strike. 'We must make the national leaders agree to stand by us for a strike against the demands of the owners,' he declared, his high forehead gleaming in the lighted room and his spectacled eyes looking as large as an owl's. 'That's the first move – get all the country into action. Then our Party will have to help the Executive to work through the other unions and industries so that all the people will know the justice of our case, and when the attack comes, they will be ready to meet it with us.'

The large room in the library where the meeting was held was crowded with people, all of whom were blended in a tense anticipation of what was to come. When Harry continued, his voice kept rising into a falsetto as the excitement gripped him: 'Yes, comrades. For the first time all the people in this country will fight together in a common cause against a common enemy.'

A murmur rolled round the room, and one old man, who was the founder and deacon of one of the local chapels, rose to his feet. Even above the subdued whispering, his chest could be heard rattling like a bag of marbles. Numerous blue scars were scattered over his hands and face like tattoo marks, but when he spoke, his voice, though hoarse, carried a timbre that made it sweet in the ears of his listeners. Job Calfaria, as he was known to the workmen, had won the respect of the people by his devout efforts throughout his life to practise in the pit and in Cwmardy the principles he preached each Sunday in the chapel. He was now tremulous with emotion as he said:

'Twenty years have I waited for this. Twenty years of work and pain as I have seen my butties go one after the other down the hill to the cemetery, each poorer after all he had done than when the good Lord first sent him into the world. And now, when my own race is nearly run on this earth, what I have prayed for so long is about to come. Oh, my fellow workmen, how glad I am to know that these old eyes of mine will see you free and happy before they close forever on the sins of our masters!'

The eyes he spoke of bubbled over and the tears ran unheeded down the furrows in his cheeks, wetting his moustache.

The murmur that had preceded his speech now become a rumble of sharp claps and stamping feet that brought the meeting to a close.

Outside in the street, groups of men and women were gathered heatedly discussing a special article in the evening paper. Len bought a copy and with a single glance at the glaring streamer across the top of the page hurried home to show it to Mary and Ezra. He handed the paper to his wife before pulling off his coat and waited while she read it aloud.

REDS PLAN GENERAL STRIKE.

Agents of Bolshevism, who have been allowed with impunity to preach their pernicious doctrines in this country in spite of numerous warnings we have given, are now plotting a General Strike as the first step towards a revolution which they hope will take government out of the hands of the people. They hope to bring about a dictatorship in place of the democratic parliament which has for untold years been the heritage of British people. They want to bring their pernicious political creeds into the trade unions of the nation.

Much now depends upon the statesmanship of the trade union leaders, and we are not without hope that they will again come to the rescue, and prevail upon their men to undertake no foreign methods in this country to settle disputes which can always be disposed of by machinery already set up for that purpose.

Ezra laughed broadly when Mary read this with due emphasis on the relevant paragraphs. 'Ha-ha! The usual red herring, and we should have expected it. You take it from me there will be much more before the strike begins... if it ever does.'

Len took the paper from Mary's hand and remarked: 'They want to split us up at the start by making people believe that we miners are only a bunch of agitators paid from Moscow to make trouble here. Ach! What a bunch!

Harry is right when he says that from top to bottom, from the Government to the colliery company, they are all linked up like stinking sausages on a string.' He flung the paper into the grate with a gesture of disgust. 'The dirty hounds. They'll sink to any depths and say any lies to get their own way over the people.'

He hung his coat behind a chair before sitting down. Mary's eyes glinted wickedly as she saw that his anger arose from agitation and not thought.

'Oh Len, for shame,' she twitted, 'fancy a Communist losing his temper because he thinks the capitalists and the Government are unfair – ha-ha!'

Ezra joined in his daughter's laugh at Len's discomfiture, and this checked Mary immediately. 'Shoni Fairplay is dead in this world long ago,' she declared. 'Aye, ever since one man began like a bug to live on the back of another.'

Len caught the spirit of her new mood and entered into it with a gusto that was strange to him. 'But bugs feed so much, Mary, that they get helpless and easy to kill. My old man have often told me, Ezra,' turning to his father-in-law, 'that he would sooner a flea a thousand times to a bug, because a flea will have a go for his life, but a bug after he have been feeding on you for hours will stand and stare you out as brazen as brass.'

They all laughed at this, until Mary, unwilling to be beaten in this debate of similes, continued: 'But don't forget, Len, that many a bug has saved himself by the stink he makes from his own rotten body. Oh yes, he takes blood from us and this makes him so fat and lazy that he can only lie back and smell, but he always comes for more when the first lot is gone. And that's what happens with the capitalists. They can't either live or protect themselves without the people. After they have robbed us, they protect themselves with those they have taken from our own ranks.'

Ezra leaned forward as the significance of this struck him. He fancied he saw its full implications and wanted to divert the others from this.

'Take what happened during the last strike, as a start,' he broke in. 'As soon as the Government saw we were beating the company, they sent the police into Cwmardy; and when they found that police and batons couldn't drive us back to work, they sent soldiers and guns.'

Len's eyes sparkled as he saw his chance. 'So you believe in revolution, Ezra?'

'Not at all, my boy. I believe in the ballot box and democracy.'

The reply was somewhat hesitant, as though Ezra felt himself off guard, but Len pushed his advantage further. 'How can you say that when just this minute you said that the Government sent in soldiers against the people of Cwmardy after we had with a single voice said we didn't want any more cuts in our pay.'

Ezra had now recovered himself. 'Ah, that's a different question. The police and soldiers were sent here because we haven't yet learned how to vote in the right way. That's it, my children; if we put our enemies in power when we have the chance to shift them peacefully, then it's no use grunting when they whip us.'

This last remark drew Mary upright in her chair, and

her chest heaved as a new idea grew in her mind. Even the ticking clock seemed to hush itself when she spoke, her husky voice adding emphasis to the words. 'But the people put a Labour Government there in 1924, daddy, and the police were used as much against us then as under any other government. If parliament is power, why did our labour leaders take sides with the owners in every strike that took place?'

Ezra's face went grey at the question, until he bent his head to poke the fire into a red glow. When he rose he was ready to answer.

'That was not the fault of the Labour Government; they were only in office and didn't have any power.'

Len felt that the lameness of the answer made it an apology, and he hastened to turn the subject before Mary could continue the argument.

'Never mind about that now. The big thing is to bring this General Strike off; then we will settle the question of power.' He became reminiscent and asked: 'Do you remember, Ezra, when you used to tell me that power wasn't something on top of the pit only, but that it was also underground. You said it's not enough to have a good Federation; we must have unity underground in the coalface as well?'

'Yes. And I still believe that. But government is a different thing.'

There was a long silence after this, before Len rose from his chair. 'Let's go for a walk before bedtime, Mary.'

She consented, after telling her father they would not be long.

The young couple walked slowly up the path that ran gently from the foot of the mountain to its summit. Half-way up, they stopped to sit down and look at the black mist that already hid the valley from sight. The gleam from the pit furnaces broke through the darkness and covered the mountain with a blanket of red in which were streaks of yellow. A thought, generated by the recent discussion, sprang to Len's mind at the sight.

'Funny, isn't it?' he began rather sadly. 'During the strike we all carried the red flag in our demonstrations and meetings and every one of us was proud to do it. Somehow or other, it seemed to be the spirit of our struggle, but now the only people who still cling to it are those who believe the same as the Party. Aye, for some reason the others have put yellow into the red, just like those beams that are bursting from the furnaces.' He pointed in the direction of the pits.

The analogy appealed to Mary, who was still somewhat upset. 'Yellow is the symbol of cowardice,' she remarked slowly, then stopped, as though the words had given birth to a new idea. She folded her arms across her breast and squeezed them tightly to her before resuming hesitantly: 'But I can't believe that dad is a coward today, any more than he was when he led the strike. No, no. He can't ever be a coward. It must be that the yellow is the sign of compromise which you say the Party believes to be his policy. Yes. That must be it.'

She shivered and, rising to her feet as she turned up the collar of her coat, bade him come. They descended the mountain a different way from that they had climbed, and soon found themselves in Main Street, where Mr. Evans Cardi was idly standing in the doorway of his darkened stores. His voice was heavy when he greeted the couple: 'Goodnight!'

Len noticed the old man's hands were trembling and would have passed after returning the greeting, had not the other pleadingly asked him: 'Do you think they will come out on strike again, Len?'

'Yes, of course they will, Mr. Evans. There is nothing else we can do, is there?'

The shopkeeper said no more, and with lowered head retreated into the shop, where his wife, seeing the hunched shoulders, asked plaintively: 'What is the matter with you now, John?'

He told her and there was a stillness for some moments before she said in desperation: 'But it can't last long, John. It can't. You have told me that the men are divided and that the Federation is smashed. How can they go on if that is true?'

John gloomily shook his head without looking at her, and muttered: 'That won't stop them. Ezra is with them again and the Communists are supporting him, so that they are all behind him and will fight so long as he tells them to.'

Agitation conquered his wife and she expressed in words the dominant desire of her mind, when she exclaimed: 'But the Government is bound to step in. They can't let these people ruin the valley in this way. Oh God,' she wailed in a spasm of despair, 'where is it all going to end? First the explosion, then the strike, then the lock-out, and now this.'

Her emotion affected John deeply. He had no answer to her plea, so placed his arms on the table and buried his face in them, moaning all the while more to himself than her.

'We will have to get our Ron from college now. The bank manager was telling me only this morning that we can't get any more advances from him. Oh, Maggie fach, we are worse off than when we started forty years ago.' He jumped angrily to his feet and shouted: 'If the people would only pay what they owe us, we could carry on. But no; they are going to the Co-op and the big shops after we have fed them all through their troubles.'

He broke down and cried like a child in sheer impotence while she tried to console him even as her own tears dripped on his sparse hair.

NIGHT ON THE
MOUNTAIN

The pits in Cwmardy once again became hot-beds of agitation, which the officials failed to check, as renewed confidence from the prospect of a General Strike swept the men nearer each other than they had been since the lock-out.

The headquarters of the Party at the library was too small to hold the men and women who joined, and at each meeting numbers had to sit on the floor and window-sills to make room for all who wanted to enter. Even the elder men and their wives generated new life and entered into the arguments with as much vigour as the younger members.

The Party held regular street meetings, where they took it in turns to explain what was happening to the people elsewhere, and why the Government was already preparing to take sides with the owners against the working men and women. Sometimes miners from other parts of the country were brought in to speak to the miners in the valley. Everything helped the people of Cwmardy to prepare for the strike with vigour and determination, confident that this time they would be victorious.

Dai Cannon, who had again broken the pledge, summed up the general feeling very neatly one Saturday night when he and Big Jim were drinking in the Boar's Head.

'What think you of the big strike that is coming off, Dai?' asked the latter.

'Short and sweet, like a donkey's gallop,' was the terse retort.

Jim thought the reply a very good joke all through the weekend and was still chuckling over it as he made his way to his working place on the Monday morning. He had to wait some time in the face before Len arrived. The old man was in the middle of his recital when a light appeared back in the roadway and jogged its way towards them. Jim ceased his story-telling and gazed with open mouth at the diminutive form that confronted them.

The little lad, his lamp nearly dragging the floor, broke the silence first: 'Shenkin the fireman have sent me to work with you,' he declared categorically, as he began pulling off his coat. The sight of his puny body drove Len suddenly frantic. It revived memories of the day when he had himself started to work in the pit and all it had meant to him since. He remembered his mother telling him, when he left the house that first morning: 'You be starting, Len bach, what only the grave can take you away from.' The thought made him wonder how long this little lad would be a slave to the pit.

'Is this your first day down?' he asked the boy, only to receive a contemptuous reply, uttered in a pitying voice.

'Duw, duw, no, mun. I have been working for going on three months now.'

Len lifted his lamp to have a better look at the boy's face. 'You must be gone fourteen, then,' he remarked, 'if you have been working this last three months.'

'Oh, that's easy, mun. Don't you 'member my old man? He was kilt about five years ago; and ever since then my old 'ooman have been having compo for him. Oh, aye, the company have been very good to us. They let me cheat my age a bit, see, so that I could start to work sooner than the other boys and help my mother. Aye, aye. I'm boss of the house now, of course,' he added in a confidential tone.

'Oh. Are you a good workman?' asked the discomfited Len, while Jim looked on with admiration in his eyes.

'Good workman, indeed. I should just bloody think so! If you don't believe me, ask my last butty.'

He lowered his voice confidentially. 'That was a good butty, mun. He thought I was the best boy in the pit and gived me trumps regular as a clock every week.'

Len smiled at the subtle hint, while Jim covered his desire to laugh with a gruff: 'Arglwydd mawr. They be sending them down these days before they be tucked properly, muniferni!'

The two men ordered the lad to remain near the tram and made their way to their respective places in the coalface. Some time later a number of lights gathered around the tram and both men squirmed back through the face once more to see who the visitors were. They found

Mr. Hicks with three other officials and a tall, healthy-looking young stranger awaiting them. The little lad unconcernedly went on putting coal into the tram until Big Jim stopped him. The lad's body oozed sweat, which washed the coal-dust off his chest and soaked into the waist of his turned down trousers, making them shine oilily. Jim gave the lad a glance and bade him sit down, then turned his attention to the officials.

Mr. Hicks coughed, and said: 'This is David, the son of Lord Cwmardy. He has come down to see the pit and you boys at work.'

The tall young man held out his hand to both Jim and Len, saying at the same time, 'Pleased to meet you. I've heard a great deal about the two of you.'

Len said nothing while his eyes examined the magnificent body before him, but Big Jim was ready with a reply.

'Glad to meet you, butty. I hope you will never come so bad as your old man.' The officials were flabbergasted at this retort, and Mr. Hicks indignantly took Jim to task.

'For shame, James, talking like that to the son of the man who employs you,' he stated.

Something cold ran through Len's body and chilled his blood. He raised his lamp, showing up in white relief the fresh, well-filled features. His voice was hard as the steel wedge he used on the coal when he asked quietly: 'Where do you work, mate?'

'I don't work. I'm at college,' came the good-natured retort.

'At college, eh? How old are you?'

'Twenty. But why do you ask?' There was surprise in the query, but Len took no notice.

'Hmm. Twenty years of age, at college, and not working. Hmm!' The officials stood silently by, but Cwmardy's son kept smiling good-humouredly.

'If you don't work, how do you live?'

'Oh, my father pays my college fees and gives me an allowance.'

'I see. Yes. I see; your father keeps you.' A brief pause, then: 'But where does your father get the money from?'

The sudden question, put so artlessly, swept the smile from the young man's face. He took a step towards Len, clenching his fists tightly, but he stopped abruptly when he saw Big Jim also move forward.

'What the devil has that to do with you?' he demanded, his voice shrill with indignation.

Len's words ran into each other as he replied, pointing his fingers at the boy, who was sitting interestedly on the big heap of coal near the end of the tram.

'That's where the money comes from to keep you in college with an allowance at twenty years of age. That child has got to come down this damned muck-hole day in, day out, year after year, until he gets too old and weak to fill more coal. After that, if he's not killed before then, he'll have to rot on top of the pit until he pegs out and is ready to be buried in another hole.'

Len's chest heaved as he made his denunciation, and the officials stood motionless, like rabbits facing a stoat, so that without interruption he continued: 'Your father makes that little boy by there work eight hours a day for

563

thruppence an hour so that you can live without working.'

Mr. Hicks broke the spell and sprang to the aid of his discomfited charge, shouting loudly: 'Stop these insults. If it were not for Lord Cwmardy giving the boy work, he'd have no wages and he and his mother would starve. You should be glad he's been given something to do.'

Len looked wistfully at the manager when the latter was speaking and replied gently: 'Aye, you are right, Mr. Hicks. I can see it now. When we won't work, we starve whatever our age or size.' He paused a moment as though he were mentally trying to solve a puzzle, then continued: 'Yet Mr. David by there don't starve although he don't do any work. His body is bigger and stronger than mine can ever be, yet he can get a new kind of thrill by coming down the pit to see us and that little boy working. Aye, a thrill, more shame to him!' He began to shout with rage. 'That's it. We work and sweat and slog our hearts out to fill the rotten guts of louts who think that work is beneath their dignity.' He lost all control of himself and howled: 'Go! Get back to where you came from. Spend the allowance your old man gives you from the last ounce of our strength. See the blood on every pound-note you change, taste the battered bodies on every bit of food you eat, see the flesh sticking on the coal you burn. Aye, and when we refuse to work to keep you fat and idle, send your police in to baton us down.'

The outburst staggered all his listeners, and Mr. Hicks murmured hurriedly to the officials: 'Come. Let's go. The man's mad.' They obediently followed him till they came to a huge lump of coal Big Jim had levered from the face, and which now obstructed their passage.

One of them shouted back: 'Break this up for us to pass.'

'Break it your bloody selfs,' Jim replied, throwing his mandril towards them. The crestfallen officials and their important charge retraced their steps, and without another word or glance at the two workmen made their way up the road, followed by Jim's exultant shout: 'Ha-ha! Ho-ho! That will show you that our Len is so clever as any of you, college or no college. Put that in your pipe and smoke it. Ha-ha!'

Len and his father sat silently for some time after the departure of the visitors, while the boy looked at them with awe and admiration. Unable to contain himself any longer, he rose to his feet, swelling his little chest in such a way that his navel became a pool holding one bubble of sweat which shone in the light from the lamps.

'Gee,' he exclaimed, 'that did take some doing, mun, to tell the boss's son off like that, and in front of his own face, too! In't you afraid to have the sack? But there, I 'ood have done the same myself if he gived me any of his bloody cheek.'

Len burst out laughing, then ordered: 'Let's forget it, and get on with our work.'

At the end of the shift Mr. Hicks was awaiting them as they stepped from the carriage.

'Get away to hell out of it,' he screamed, spitting out the words and waving his stick frantically. 'Here I go out of my way to get better relations between the men and the owners and you turn round and insult the very man I bring down to do it. Yes, that's the one,' he shouted to the interested workmen who had gathered round, at the same time pointing his quivering stick at Len. 'That's the man who wants to spoil everything.'

His anger got the better of him and stepping forward he raised his arm threateningly, but not before Big Jim had barged between them, with the quietly spoken command to the manager:

'Put that stick down. Come, quick now, before I splash you against that bloody wall.'

His fierce demeanour cooled the general manager, who slowly lowered his arm and walked back into the office. The excited men gathered round, began asking questions, but after a brief explanation, Len led the way to the pay office, where Big Jim picked up their joint wages, from which he took some coins before handing the remainder to his son with the remark: 'Here, take your pay from this and give the rest to the old 'ooman. Tell her I 'on't be long, but I must have a pint before ever I can walk up that bloody hill.'

Len was long accustomed to the procedure and the excuse, so he made no reply and went alone to the house where Siân was waiting. He gave her Jim's wages and waited for the inevitable question, which she always answered herself.

'Where is your father? In the Boar's Head, I s'pose. Huh! One day he will repent all that he is doing and will be glad to sit quiet in the corner by there with me to tend on him hand and foot. Ach! One of these nights I will lock him out, so sure as God is my judge.' She placed the wages in her purse, which she then replaced deep in the bosom of her dress before turning to Len again.

'I wonder how many more pays us will have before the strike will be on us?'

He looked into her eyes. 'Don't worry, mam fach. It won't last long this time, because all the workmen in the country are behind us.'

'I know, Len bach. I know,' she replied quickly, as though she wanted to dispel a doubt. 'Don't think I am downhearted. Oh no, my boy. When it is a fight, your old mam is with you all the way.'

Len left her and slowly made his way home to Mary, where he soon forgot his weariness as he recited the events of the day. Dinner was over by the time he had finished, and he anxiously waited for her comments while she emptied boiling water into the bath-tub. But she said nothing as he pulled his shirt off and he was on his knees leaning over the tub before she remarked softly:

'There's a silly thing to say to the boss, Len. You are asking for the sack. Yet I can't help feeling it was splendid to stand up to them like you did.' The warmth of her words soothed him as she went on. 'How is it you are so kind and gentle and patient in most things; yet you have these sudden spasms of temper?'

He would have replied, but she stopped him with a laugh as she pictured the lad making his defiant challenge after the officials had gone. The laugh ended in a sigh. 'Ah, well. Never mind about those things now, Len. Bath. Then we can talk about the strike.'

Len hurried over his bathing, wiping his head while she washed his back, and in a short time the couple were immersed in an argument during which Len explained why the strike must necessarily be a short one. His old pessimism was evaporating as the strike drew nearer, and he could see nothing but complete victory before them.

Mary shook her head and looked into his eyes, where she saw her own face in miniature. 'I wish I could believe the same as you, Len,' she began. 'But somehow I don't think it is going to work out so easy as all that.'

'Of course you don't, mun. You are a woman and don't understand these things. But tell me why you don't think we are going to have a quick win?'

'I can't say, Len. Oh, dear, there's something in the back of my mind that makes me think of what dad did during the lock-out.'

Her tones were sad and he tried to comfort her with an off-handed: 'Ach, we all make mistakes one time or another, and your father is a different man now.'

'That's just it,' was her retort. 'But you see, Len, what mistakes can lead to. What happened in Cwmardy during the lock-out can happen again in the strike. Not all of those who are going to lead it want it, and those who don't want a strike they are leading will always look for a way to end it.' She paused a moment, then continued more vigorously: 'Look at Fred Lewis for a start. I know he's in the Party, but no one will ever make me believe he is sincere. Give him half a chance and he'll use it to push himself on.'

Len laughed. 'You're miserable tonight. I'd like to see the leader who'd dare to break this strike. Why, the people would kick him right out of the movement for ever.'

'I'm not so sure. There's so many ways of doing a thing, and don't forget we'll have the Government against us,' she replied slowly; then shook her head and added in dismissal of the subject: 'Come. Let's go for a walk before it gets too late.'

It was already dusk when they left the house, and a few pinpricks of light, breaking through the murk, rimmed the streets of Cwmardy as the pair sauntered along the edge of the mountain. When they were nearing the railway line that ran from the pits through the valley, Mary suddenly stopped and gripped Len's arm tightly.

'Did you hear anything?' she asked nervously. He shook his head and strained his eyes to peer into the blackened distance. Then he heard a sound like a low moan creep towards him, and pressing her arm to his side he whispered: 'I heard something then. It was like someone moaning.'

'Yes. It came from over by there, near the quarry.' A pause, then: 'Oh, Len, perhaps some poor dab has tumbled over it.'

He swallowed hard before saying, 'You stop here while I go and see.' But she still grasped his arm as he cautiously groped towards the sound. Their feet loosened a large stone that rolled before them with increasing speed. Len stopped again and pointed excitedly to a vague black shadow that seemed to skim the dusk on the right of the quarry.

'Isn't that someone running?' he asked, a quiver in his voice.

'Yes,' was the hurried reply. 'Look, Len – that was a button shining.'

They hastened their descent till they reached the quarry, from which the moans now came more clear and piteous. Len lighted the way with matches, taking care that Mary kept near him. They had only walked a few paces when Mary, her voice shaking with apprehension, whispered: 'Hush. There's somebody talking!'

They both heard it simultaneously: 'Oh mam, mam! Oh, my poor head.'

'Come quick, Len, it's over there,' Mary darted off with Len close at her heels. He nearly fell over her when she suddenly bent down to scan a form at her feet, her hands moving quickly and impatiently over it.

'Light another match, Len.'

He immediately obeyed the low muttered command, carefully shading the flame in his cupped hands. The flickering light fell feebly upon the body of a boy in working clothes, who lay stretched out upon the stony floor of the quarry. The match-light died and buried itself in the surrounding darkness before Len could strike another. Mary became impatient.

'Get some paper, mun. Look through your pockets.' He found an old pocket-book and hastily tore out some pages, which he twisted and lit. The increased light shone on a black face with closed eyes and slowly moving lips. Mary caught the head to her, gently resting it in her arms. Len brought the light nearer and saw the blood flowing through the hair until it ran down the boy's face, streaking it with red. All the time, the lad's lips kept moving.

In a frenzy, Len lit more paper, and parting the dirty hair saw the gash that split the boy's skull. He felt his stomach turn and his head go light, but pulled himself together when he heard Mary say:

'Pull my petticoat off. Quick! I mustn't move or he'll

bleed to death.' Len fumbled at the end of the garment trying to tear off a piece, but it was too strong. Mary slowly bent her head till it touched the earth behind her, arching her body. 'There – hurry,' she gasped, all the time trying to keep the lad's wounded head still and steady.

Len hastily put his hands under her skirt and tore the fastening of her petticoat loose from the waist, pulling the garment intact from her body.

'Rip some strips off,' she ordered. Len did so and between them they cleaned and bandaged the wound, after which they both remained stupefied for some moments, neither knowing what to do next. The continual moans flayed their nerves, while the flame licking at the remaining end of the paper died down, then suddenly flickered to life again. As the light finally faded into the night, the moan took shape. Len hurriedly bent his head to the lips and heard them whisper tiredly:

'Oh mam, mam! Oh, my poor head.' A long silence, during which Len and Mary held their breath, then: 'He hit me and run away. Oh, mam, mam, where are you?' The low plaint ended in a sob that brought tears to Mary's eyes, but Len nearly pressed his ear on the cold lips in his anxiety to hear every word that oozed from them. He had to wait some time before the limbs stiffened in Mary's arms and the lad burst out explosively: 'The rotter hit me, then run away. But I saw him, it was a b...' The last word died on the first syllable and the body relaxed again.

'Oh, he's dead, Len, he's dead,' Mary moaned, and Len frantically put his hand on the chest beneath the wet shirt.

'No,' he said somewhat hysterically, 'his heart is going

a bit, although it's very soft. Oh, Mary, my dear, what can we do?' he asked.

Mary shuddered. Her arms were cramped and her body quivered with the strain. 'Go down quick,' she muttered. 'Fetch your father and mine. Fetch anybody you can find.'

Len jerked himself erect and replied sharply: 'No; I can't leave you here by yourself in the dark.'

He could not see the flash in her eyes but he felt the harshness in her voice when she said: 'Don't be childish. Do what I tell you, Len. Can't you see that perhaps this boy is dying and every minute counts?'

Len said no more and hurriedly scampered from the quarry.

When he returned he was accompanied by a crowd of people, many of whom carried lamps, and a stretcher borrowed from the surgery. They took the lad from Mary's arms and tenderly placed him on the stretcher, while Big Jim picked up the cramped girl like a baby. The procession then slowly retraced its steps down the mountain to Cwmardy, Len holding Ezra's arm and helping him over the steep track that snatched away his breath.

The people left in the village were waiting to receive the procession with its burden, and their excited muttering faded into silence as it approached. The stretcher was taken straight into the surgery where the doctor prevented the entry of everyone except Big Jim and Ezra.

Very few people slept in Cwmardy that night, they were too busy wondering what had caused the injury to the boy, who had not opened his mouth since the last statement Len heard. The general puzzlement found an echo in

Mary's home. Len confided in his father-in-law, and when the recital was over Ezra began pacing the kitchen, as he always did when perturbed.

'Whoever did it, did it for the boy's pay,' he asserted. 'But what I can't understand,' he continued, stopping to look hard at Mary, 'is who could be so low and brutal to rob a lad of his wages?' He turned to Len. 'You are quite sure you didn't hear the last word he said?'

Len shook his head. 'No, Ezra, but it sounded like something that begins with a "B",' he replied.

Ezra went on with his pacing, at the same time muttering, half to himself, 'B? B? What can that mean? Bowen, Bevan, Brown?' Len interrupted him. 'I don't believe it was a man's name he wanted to say because an A came before the B sound, didn't it, Mary?' turning to his wife who now joined the conversation.

The excitement of the night had affected her deeply, but when she replied her voice, though low, was emphatic.

'I believe he wanted to say: "But I saw him. It was a Bobby".'

Ezra's face went grey as she asked Len: 'Do you remember the shiny button we saw for a minute on that running shadow?'

Len nodded his head and she continued: 'That might have been one of the silver buttons that only policemen wear.

Ezra interjected harshly: 'Hold your tongue, Mary. For God's sake keep such thoughts to yourself. You can't prove anything, and if somebody heard you say such things as that, you'd get us all into serious trouble. And in any case,' he added as an afterthought, 'what would a policeman want with a boy's few shillings?'

Len, who had taken umbrage at Ezra's tone, answered: 'When he heard us running down the mountain he might have pinched the pay packet to make us think it was a common thief who had beat the boy about.'

'No, no, Len. It doesn't work out so easily as that and you and Mary had better wait until you have definite proof before you ever speak of the matter again.'

But Mary, having started on this train of thought, was not satisfied, and despite her father's strictures took it further. 'The wicked scoundrel might have been waiting for one of our men who take coal from the trucks and carry it down the line in the dark, dad,' she asserted.

'There, there. That'll do,' commanded Ezra brusquely. 'Don't let's have any more loose talk that might land all of us in prison.'

This closed the discussion and little more was said before Len and Mary went to bed, leaving Ezra staring into the ashes that cumbered what was left of the fire.

Next day, Ezra had a telegram calling him to London again for a meeting of the National Executive, at which a final decision was to be taken regarding the contemplated General Strike. He was away for some days, during which the main topic in Cwmardy was the strange accident that had since resulted in the boy's death. Most of the people were convinced there had been foul play, and they were quite ready to believe the rumours that somehow began floating around to the effect that a policeman was responsible.

At the inquest Mary tried to give her opinion, but was abruptly silenced by the coroner who told her: 'We want

574

to know what you saw, not what you think.' Siân voiced the general opinion when she told Jim after the inquest:

'I think our Mary fach is quite right. There is nothing too bad for those pleece to do, and I 'oodn't trust one of 'em not a inch further than I could throw him. That's gospel for you, James.'

The talk and gossip soon died down after Ezra's return, with the announcement that the General Strike would begin in a fortnight's time if the owners still insisted upon reducing the miners' wages. This news revitalised the people and meetings were held almost every other day to make preparations for the coming fight. But in the minds of many, the lad who died in the quarry was not forgotten.

PREPARATION
FOR STRUGGLE

A short time prior to the strike Harry Morgan, who had been speaking all over the country on behalf of the Communist Party, urging all people to support the miners and the coming strike, asked Len: 'How would you like to go to the city for the Party, to help the comrades there?'

Len did not answer for some moments. The request made so abruptly took his breath away. When at last he spoke, both his words and face expressed incredulity.

'What, me? Go to the city? Good God, mun, you're talking through the back of your neck. How can I help the Party or the people there? Ha-ha, that's a good un, Harry!'

Harry smiled, a twinkle glinting behind his spectacles. 'You can help them all right, Len. Your experience in the last strike was second to none, and since you've been in the Party you've become a passionate speaker who can win the people to our point of view when you try.'

The compliment made Len laugh again, but he checked it as another implication of the proposition struck him. 'Are you asking me to leave my own butties in a fight?' he asked incredulously.

Harry's smile widened. 'Why not? Do you think they can't carry on without you?'

The quick retort abashed Len, and he blushed as he replied: 'I didn't mean that, Harry, and you know it. But my place is with my own people, and there I'm going to stick in spite of all your sneers.'

Harry's smile vanished. 'Your place is where you are wanted most,' he declared sharply. 'You see, Len, this fight can lead to great things that some of us can only dream of now. Think of it,' he exclaimed, his voice rising with enthusiasm, 'the whole working class entering into action together, behind the miners, against the bosses and all that it means. The Government is bound to show its hand as the agent of the capitalist class. It will take sides with them against us and expose the fight to our people for what it really is – part of a struggle for political power. It's possible for us to do what Lenin and the Russians did – that is, get rid of the parasites for good.'

Harry went on in this strain for a long time, giving Len no chance to say a word until he had finished, by which time he had drawn a word picture of such immensity that it frightened Len, although the logic of his life experiences forced him towards it.

He made no reply, but turned away with a muttered: 'So long. I'll see you again.'

Harry was astute enough to make no attempt to detain him or say any more.

For the next few days Len could think of nothing but what Harry had said. He pictured all he had heard and read about the Russian Revolution, and tried to apply the conjured images to Cwmardy. But always he checked himself with a plethora of mental queries. Would the owners and the Government give way peacefully to the desires of the people? Would the army refuse to obey its generals if the Government tried to use it against the people? What about the Air Force, manned by men like Lord Cwmardy's son? These and other questions tumbled through his mind incessantly, keeping time with his mandril as he drove it into the coal. Accompanying these questions and running through them were thoughts of Harry's request that he should go to the city during the strike. He wondered what he would have to do there if he went, and who he would meet. He felt he could do nothing once he was away from his own people and, subconsciously, feared things would go wrong if he were not with them during the strike. Already he was beginning to sense his own power and influence.

He sought Mary's advice on the whole business and they talked it over for hours one night, but failed to reach any definite decision. Already extra police were being drafted into the valley and the atmosphere was getting tense, but the workmen and the Party were once more solid behind Ezra, who was confident the strike would be short and successful and that, as a result, the Federation would be united under his leadership again. He had continual discussions with the railway and other union leaders in Cwmardy, and a joint strike committee was set up.

The people of the valley echoed this confidence, a fact which found expression in the Boar's Head on one occasion when Will Smallbeer and Big Jim were the centre of a group of drinking pals. Jim had already drunk sufficient to make him patronisingly philosophical. 'Aye, boys. It is just like Buller and the Boer War. He let them do this and do that till they thought they was beating us, muniferni; then all of a sudden, after he had drawed 'em where he wanted 'em, bang-bang, just like that, and the war was over!' He shifted a lump of tobacco to his cheek and placed the half-empty tankard of beer to his lips, while Will Smallbeer wiped the ale that dripped from his moustache to say ponderously:

'Strategy. That's the thing, strategy. Us might have to lose two or three or four, aye, perhaps more battles before us get into position to win the big 'un. But it is worth it in the end, and that's where us is now. For years and years we have been fighting here and fighting there, but never all together at the same time.' His eyes gleamed with memories and beer, as he went on. 'But we are there at last, boys bach. Ha-ha! This time all together at the same time, and nothink can stop us winning now. Our Lord's words are proving true – "Righteousness shall always prevail".' He closed his eyes to repeat the last statement, then took another drink from his pint mug.

The conversation became general after this, and young Will Evans struck a discordant note when he said: 'Huh! Us is all bragging like blue hell tonight. Make sure us isn't

580

barking at the wrong dog. I heard stories like Will Smallbeer's during the lock-out. Aye; us was all big men then and thought we was cocks of the walk. But don't forget, boys, what happened in the end. Mark my words, some waster will so sure as hell let us down again.'

'Don't talk so bloody soft, mun,' was the reply he received from several quarters. 'Isn't the T.U.C. calling us all out this time? There can't be no selling now, and Smallbeer is quite right.'

Will closed an eye in an impish wink, looked at the fire and spat into the grate with a smacking sound before saying, without raising his head: 'That's it, boys. Old Smallbeer is quite right, in't he? Of course he is. He always was, wasn't he? Even when he went up the drive to the Big House during the lock-out, eh? Ha-ha!'

His queerly pitched laughter rumbled round the room as he raised his head triumphantly, and Will Smallbeer slowly and with great dignity got to his feet. The old man's whole demeanour showed he had been greatly hurt, but that he was prepared to forgive because his traducer did not understand. Everyone became silent as he chided them.

'For shame, boys, to kick a man, and a butty at that, when he is down. Everybody with any sense in his head do know full well that what I done in the lock-out was quite right. If us hadn't gived in then Ezra 'ood have kept us out forever and our bellies 'ood by now be fast to our backbones. Aye,' he continued in a paternal manner, gratified by the attention being paid to his remarks, 'a good fighter must always know when to give in just so much as he must know when he is winning, in't that so,

Jim?' He turned to his mate for support.

Thus appealed to, Jim twirled his moustache and nodded. 'Aye. That's right, Will bach, only that a good fighter have never got no need to give in.' This unexpected statement brought a loud laugh from all present and the discomfited Smallbeer sat down without another word.

The week immediately preceding the strike, Mr. Evans Cardi called a meeting of all the tradesmen in Cwmardy. His tall form looked thinner than ever and his thin moustache dropped loosely over his mouth when he rose to address the meeting.

'I have called you together, friends, so that we may decide what we intend doing during this strike. Most of us have now reached the end of our tether and, speaking for myself personally, I won't be able to give any more credit to the strikers.' He broke into a wail he could not control. 'My God! We have suffered enough. Our savings gone, our investments useless, and now our business ruined. This valley and its people are like a blight.' His sentiments were repeated by most of the other speakers, but when it came to deciding action, none of them knew what to do. They were lost in a wilderness of conflicting emotions and interests which crushed each other at every point of contact.

Davies, the butcher, tried to survey the position for them. 'The multiple shops that have come to Cwmardy will not give credit, but they will bring in cheap stuff and sell it at a price that would ruin us. The Co-op, with its huge capital and backed by the Federation, can afford to give credit, knowing it is guaranteed. That's the position,

582

gentlemen. If we don't give credit we are ruined, because the people won't come back to us after the strike; and if we do give credit we won't be able to pay our wholesalers because the people will never be able to pay us.'

He brushed his fingers through his hair like a dazed man, still trying to find something he could not see.

Late that night, when Mr. Evans Cardi returned to the stores, he heard voices in the kitchen and vaguely wondered who was there, but he was not unduly curious because his mind was still fixed on the problem of credit and the final ruin that faced him. He pulled off his hat and coat and quietly opened the kitchen door, but before he had time to look about someone clasped him round the head, pressing it passionately, at the same time murmuring:

'Dad, dad. I've come home. Look at me.'

The arms released the old man's head and he looked up to see the square, well-set form of his son, Ron. Mr. Evans turned, and through the wet haze blinding him saw Maggie sitting quietly near the fire. He walked unsteadily to her, putting his hand affectionately on her shoulder before again looking at Ron.

Gulping back his tears, he exclaimed: 'Ron, how well you look, and how glad I am to see you, my boy!' He paused and his face clouded. 'But what brought you home so soon?'

Ron laughed happily. 'Why, I wanted to see you and mam, didn't I?'

'Yes, yes. I know. But there is something more than that.'

A further hesitation while both men looked each other in the eyes, then: 'Don't hold anything back from me, Ron

583

bach. If you have done something wrong, you have no need to be afraid to tell me.'

Maggie, her face a series of interlinking lines, interrupted. 'Don't worry, John. Our Ron couldn't do anything wrong. He came home because he felt there was something out of place here. I told you not to tell him anything in your letters,' she added petulantly.

The old man brightened for a moment. 'Is that so? Good, very good indeed.' Then another cloud covered the happiness on his features. 'But what are you going to do, Ron? Have you got a position anywhere?'

Ron sensed how the conversation was developing and could almost feel his father's rising hysteria. He took a vacant chair, and placing it near the old lady, pressed his father into it, before saying as he stood before both his parents:

'Mam and dad, you know I love you two more and owe you more than anyone else in the world. I could read in every one of your letters, although you did your best to hide it, how things were faring with you in the shop, how everything has been going out each week and practically nothing coming in. Do you think, knowing this, I could stick at my studies while you were suffering here with no one to help you?'

The old people looked up at him and pride made their features soft when he continued: 'No, dad and mam. My place is by your side, helping you through. I have won a degree and am now a certificated teacher. With these qualifications, it won't take me long to get a position.' He stopped when he saw the gleam in John's eyes and coughed.

'Wait a minute,' his father said slowly, dragging every

word from his throat. 'Don't think for one minute that qualifications are enough to get you a decent position in Cwmardy.' He began to shout a little. 'No, they don't count a lot here, although you must have them as a matter of form.'

His shoulders drooped, and his next words were without bitterness or anger. 'To get a position here under the council you must buy it.' The last two words were whispered, as if he feared someone would hear them.

Ron looked at his father in amazement, then burst out indignantly: 'What? Buy a position? If that's so, haven't you paid enough, haven't you and mam scraped and slaved to pay the rates and give me education enough to win qualifications?'

His mother checked him. 'That is so, Ron bach. But we are not the only ones who have done that, and you are not the only boy in Cwmardy who has got degrees and is now looking for a job. Your father is right.' She became slightly hysterical. 'To get a position we will have to pay for it, and we have no money, my boy, no money at all. Oh God,' she moaned and suddenly buried her face in her hands.

As the full implications of what they were saying struck Ron, he turned white. 'Well, if that's so, there's nothing before me but the pit.'

His mother jumped to her feet, letting the tears run unheeded down her cheeks. 'There will be no pit for you while there is sight in my eyes and blood in my body,' she hissed. 'Your father and I have not sacrificed all these years to see you end in the pit.'

The wailing tones of John followed immediately. 'Besides, how can you go to the pit when the men are on strike?'

585

'Oh, the strike won't last long,' Ron asserted, although all his ideas were crashing to the ground. 'Once it's over, your old friends among the officials will be able to squeeze me in somewhere.' His father looked at him earnestly for some moments, then rose from his chair to confront him.

'Ron bach, forget the pit. The officials have no more authority under this company than doorboys. No, less than that, because doorboys have the liberty to stay away from the pit.'

He quietly resumed his chair, leaving Ron erect. The young man felt himself standing in solitude astride a world that was crumbling beneath his feet.

The fire crackled in the hearth and drew his attention. He looked into its depths and slowly forming in the flames he saw a picture of the pits. This changed even as he watched and he saw it become transformed to a likeness of Len's face. He sighed and sat quietly near his parents. Neither of them moved till the fire had burned out and the glow from the cokes had died in the ashes.

Very early next morning the police station hummed with subdued excitement. The police officers had been awakened sooner than usual and were busy polishing their boots and brushing their uniforms in readiness for a special inspection. The imported extras marched from their various billets in squads, and in a short time all the police were paraded in the large yard hidden by the high walls behind the police station. Most of the imported constabulary had never been in the valley before, although all of them had heard of it. Its reputation made them nervous and fidgety. One half-turned his head towards the officer next him and whispered from the corner of his mouth:

'What sort of men are these miners of yours? I've heard a lot about them, and if half of it is true they must be pretty hot.'

'Yes. They're hot all right, and tartars at that. But we manage them all right when there's no trouble about, and that's— ... sssh.'

He broke off abruptly as a group of men came out of the station into the yard. The paraded police instantly drew themselves to attention while the inspection took place. They looked an imposing body of men with their bright buttons, erect posture, and huge bulk. The inspection over, they were addressed by a squeaky voice that seemed to add emphasis to the uttered words.

'Shortly you may be called upon to keep the peace in this valley. Those of you who have never been here before, need to know now that you will be dealing with men of violent passions and extreme views, men who don't care to what extremes they go in times of crisis like the present. Among them are a number of agitators and Bolsheviks who are always ready to take advantage of every opportunity to stir up trouble. At the first sign of this I want you to take stern measures to avoid repetition. When you strike, strike straight and strike hard. It may save a lot of trouble later on. If the first blow is insufficient, keep on until you have done your work. Remember these men fight to the last and are always dangerous while they have strength. I don't ask you to go out of your way to look for trouble; on the

587

other hand, don't avoid it or try too hard to prevent it.'

Later the same day Len coaxed Mary to come with him for a walk. He always tried to keep her as much as possible in the fresh air, because her chest was getting worse and was really alarming him, although she never mentioned anything about it.

'Let's go up the mountain,' he pleaded as she wiped the dishes after dinner. 'We must settle the whole business one way or the other today, because Harry's been on to me again about it and told us to make our minds up,' he added as a clincher.

Mary looked at him and saw the shadows in his eyes. The sight put speed in her hands, and in a short time she had distributed the dishes in their places on the dresser and was ready to accompany him.

They made their way up the street and out of the village towards the quarry where they had found the injured lad. When they reached it they stopped to rest while the emotions of that night once more swept through them. Stretching before them countless spirals of chimney smoke rose lethargically into the air and the barking of dogs came gently from the distance. The occasional sharp, long-drawn cry of a mother calling her child split the air like the flight of a bird, but the other sounds floating from the valley were mellow and round, like the strumming of a giant harp.

The placid serenity of the panorama enthralled Len and he placed his arm round Mary's shoulder, at the same time becoming reminiscent and sentimental until she checked him with a remark: 'Don't be silly, Len. You know those pimpers with their spying glasses are everywhere,

588

and very likely are watching us now.'

He responded to the admonition, sitting with his chin on his knees and fixing his attention on a procession of small figures in single file slowly winding its way up the incline towards the quarry. He gazed for some moments, then drew Mary's attention to it.

'Look! Can you see them?' he asked, pointing with his finger in the desired direction. She nodded her head and he went on: 'They are walking as solemnly as if they were in a funeral.'

Both continued watching the procession come near enough for the individuals to be distinguished, when Mary said: 'The boy in front looks as though he is dragging something, Len.'

'Yes, and some of them look to me as if they are crying. I wonder what's the matter,' he queried in reply.

The problem was too much for them, so they waited for the mysterious pilgrimage and the burden so solicitously being dragged with it.

At last the procession reached the mouth of the quarry, where it stopped while the children scanned the unexpected occupants. After a brief hesitation the boy who appeared to be the leader recovered his courage and silently led the way over the stones to the grassy rim, pulling an old pram covered with sacks behind him. The other boys and girls followed him in single file, as they had done up the hill, paying no further attention to Len and Mary, who looked curiously on. When the leader stopped they all gathered around him. Suddenly a small girl began to sob pitifully, but this was the only sound that broke the silence as one of the lads lifted the edge of the sack on the pram and drew out a big ball of tightly rounded paper, a broom handle, an old rag doll, a bag of something that rattled like marbles, and then a fire shovel.

With this latter implement he began digging vigorously into the soft earth while another lad reverently extracted another rag-covered bundle from the recesses of the pram, and held it rigidly in his outstretched arms until the first boy had dug a hole.

Len wondered what it was all about, when Mary nudged him and nodded towards the weeping girl. They saw one of the boys look at her hesitantly a few times as though he wanted to say something but was too shy to make the attempt. At last he pulled himself together and, walking towards her, put his arm about her shoulder before bursting into tears himself.

Len felt a lump rise in his throat and turned his head away. The hole was now ready and the leader tenderly lifted the rag from the form held by the other, and exposed the battered carcass of a small puppy. Taking it in his own hands, he very carefully placed it in the little grave. The children now filed past the hole, each looking down at it before walking on; then they all waited while the grave was refilled and the puppy covered in. When this was done one of them took a short piece of stick and a piece of cardboard from the pram and, tying them together, stuck the improvised monument on the grave. After this ceremony had been completed, the sacking, fire shovel, and all the other paraphernalia were bundled back into the pram, the weeping girl lifted astride the lot, and the procession began its trudge back into the valley.

When it was out of sight, Len and Mary bent down to read the crudely written epitaph in white chalk:

Our Toby.
Kilt by a Kart.
All the gang is greefed.
By order.

Mary glanced into her husband's eyes, not sure whether it was his or her own that were misty, and they continued their walk in silence.

Presently she said: 'Isn't it wonderful, Len, how our children copy what older people do.'

He did not reply for some moments, and when he did, it was slowly and thoughtfully: 'Yes, Mary, it is. And if they can grieve like that for a dog, how deep is their desire for love.'

It was a long time before either spoke again, but when they left the mountain they had agreed he should go to the city in the morning.

'You see, Len,' Mary had persuaded him, 'one day the people will want you as a leader, and you must have as much experience as possible, not only in Cwmardy but all over the country, like Harry Morgan. After you have been to the city seeing new people and new ways, you will know much more than you do now. That will come in useful for us later on. And it won't be for long,' she twitted him, 'because you yourself believe the strike will be a short one.'

Len had argued no more after this shot. 'Take care of yourself while I'm away, and write to me every day to let me know how the strike is going here,' he muttered, rather hurt by the fact she had said nothing about being parted from him. It began to drizzle as they walked home and the lights from the Big House winked coldly through the drops.

Next morning Len and Mary were up early, the absence of hooters and the throbbing of the pit leaving the dawn dead. Breakfasts and other preparations were soon completed and they made their way to his mother's house, where Siân fussed about him like a broody hen.

'Now 'member, Len bach,' she warned. 'You are going to a strange land among strange peoples who you have never seed before. Look after yourself and mind to keep away from the public houses, although, fair play, I have never had cause to worry about you and that, different from your father, thank God.'

Big Jim stopped soaping his moustache and raised his head from the cracked mirror into which he had been peering. He glanced round at the company and chuckled deeply in his throat.

'Ho-ho! Telling Big Jim's boy how to look after hisself! Ho-ho-ho! That's good, mun jawli! Why, Siân fach, you did ought to know by now, mun, that it is like putting water on a duck's back, it do go in through one ear and out through the other.'

Saying which he bent hurriedly to the mirror and thus escaped the glare Siân cast at him.

The old woman nearly broke down when Len caught her to him and kissed her cheek before leaving the house.

Her eyes followed him till he turned the corner by Evans Cardi. Big Jim airily waved his hand to her as he followed Len and Mary out of sight, and Siân went indoors with her apron to her nose.

During the wait for the train Jim, with Mary hanging tightly to his arm, advised Len what to do in the city. 'Take heed of your mother's words,' he warned, 'they be good and sound. But don't never be a mollycoddle – no, by God, don't let it never be said that Big Jim made and reared a jibber. If a bit of fun come your way, take it and care not for no man.'

'But I'm not going for fun, dad. I'm going to help the Party in the fight,' Len interjected.

His father looked at him with patronising affection and drew himself erect, at the same time inflating his once magnificent chest. 'Aye, aye, boy bach. I do know that well enough without you remembering me. But you must 'member you will never be so old as me so long as I live, and I do know better than you of the ways of the world. Duw, duw, aye. Did I ever tell you of one day on the Rock?'

Len heard a puffing in the distance and hurriedly interrupted the threatened reminiscence. 'Come, dad. The train is just in.'

Jim picked up the little attaché case that contained Len's one change of underclothes and a few handkerchiefs, and pretended to fumble with the carriage door while Len caught Mary tightly to him and tried to crack a whispered joke that died on his tongue. The guard blew his whistle, there was a quick scramble, and before either of them knew it Len was in the carriage leaning through the window and pressing something into his father's hand, with the words:

'Here, dad. Take this and have a pint while I'm away.'

The train moved forward as Jim gazed at the coin and then at Len. 'All right,' he said with a kind of sigh. 'Since you do press me so hard to take it, I will, because I have never been a man to go against his own children.'

The train was now half-way out of the station and Len shouted above the din of the engine: 'So long, Mary. So long. Look after her and mam, dad. Tell Will Evans I'll write to him as soon as I get a chance.'

He kept leaning further out of the window, waving his hand until a bend took him from sight and he sat down to watch the houses and the valley he loved float past the window. A lump rose to his throat and he wished he had not undertaken the task. He began cursing Harry Morgan and the Party for taking him away from Mary and his people. This mood did not last long and he soon dozed off to the drone of the wheels, asking: 'What's before me? What's before me?'

THE BIG STRIKE

During the next ten days Cwmardy seen from the mountain looked like a dead village on which the silent pits frowned as though in disgust. But in the streets the aspect was entirely different. Squads of police periodically paraded the entire area, seeming anxious to find an excuse to break through the suppressed excitement of the people, who met in huge meetings each day to receive reports of what was happening throughout the country and in Parliament. Groups of men and women gathered in every street to read and discuss the latest *Labour Bulletin* dealing with the strike. Everyone felt that the testing time had come and that the owners of the pits were about to suffer a severe defeat.

Mary helped the Party members to distribute leaflets from house to house, in each of which they explained how the Government was solid behind the owners and against the workpeople. This activity gave her new strength and put a glow in her cheeks. The close contact with her people made Mary a different woman and helped to dissipate the pessimism that had grown in her following upon the defection of Ezra during the lock-out.

In one mass-meeting, called to receive a report from Ezra of the latest discussions in the Executive, a man whom Mary hadn't seen before began asking questions. He sat a few seats in front of her, and something in his manner of speaking drew her attention to him. She felt in a vague way that his sentences were not uttered in the same manner as they would have been by the people in the valley. Unable to see his face, she watched his waving arms as he addressed the meeting, and thought it strange his women-folk allowed the padding in the shoulder of his coat to be visible through a big tear in the cloth.

'Perhaps he's only a poor lodger on his own,' she thought to herself, and sympathetically concentrated her attention on what he was saying.

Ezra had adopted his customary posture, elbow on knee and chin cupped in his hands, as the man started to speak, but he jerked himself erect when he heard:

'I say the time has come when we have got to do something. What's the good of being on strike and just sitting about twiddling our thumbs? That's just how our leaders like to see us... nice and peaceful like rabbits in a field.' Loud clapping and stamping feet interrupted him for some moments, and when he continued it was with more vigour and confidence. 'The Communists are just as bad. Harry Morgan is away in another part of the country, pleading there is a danger of a section of the men breaking away and forming a new union. I say a leader's place is in his own home, not traipsing about the country. Take Len Roberts – he's gone away as well, and who sent him? Not you, no not on your life; he had orders from his Party and had to obey, whatever you might have thought.'

Someone started applauding again and Fred Lewis shouted: 'Hear, hear, a Communist's place is with his own men.'

This brought Big Jim to his feet immediately, his moustache bristling. 'Don't you dare to speak bad of our Len behind his back,' he bawled. 'If you have got anything to say when he is not here, say it to his face.'

Loud laughter silenced him and the speaker continued. 'What we want is action. Why should we put up with all these strange police? That's what I want to know. I say we should march from here to the police station and hound them out of Cwmardy.'

The unexpected sharpness of the challenge sent a momentary shock through the meeting, until a few jumped to their feet shouting: 'That's right. Action – that's what we want!' Others sprang up at the call, and in a short time the meeting was in an uproar, some scrambling for the door, others bawling for order, and a few hesitantly advising prudence.

Mary felt the excitement press on her and she wanted to shout with the rest. Through her mind flashed the thought, 'Why should we have them here? We didn't ask for them and everything is peaceful.' The knowledge increased her indignation, and she was on the point of rushing to the door with others when she caught Ezra's eyes fixed on her. He was now on his feet with fists tightly clenched and face white as the patches in his hair.

'Stop!' he shouted, and the one word ran through the hall like a bell bringing to a standstill those who were milling towards the doorway.

He waited a moment, then went on harshly: 'Do you want to play into the hands of the Government? Do you want to give them an excuse for batoning and shooting, when our national leaders are calling for cool heads and public order?' He paused again, but no one replied, and a number began to sit down. This action soothed the others and a sort of sigh crept into the air.

Ezra felt he was again master of the situation, and his next words showed this. 'You are men, not sheep to follow the whistle of any shepherd. Who is the man that called for riot?' he demanded. The people looked round to the spot where the first speaker had stood, but his place had been taken by someone else during the excitement. Mary glanced suspiciously about her, but failed to see the torn coat. Uneasy thoughts entered her mind, but she had no time to ponder them before her father's voice again cut through the hall.

'Did any of you know him?'

There was no answer.

'I thought so. A stranger sent into our midst to provoke us to disorder – yes, I thought so. We should have expected this.'

The assertion was followed by a noisy hubbub, and the temper of the men rose once more as the full import of the incident came to them.

Ezra closed the meeting shortly after, but the discussion continued on the streets and in the houses. Jim and Mary reported the affair to Siân, whose legs were too bad to enable her to walk to the meeting.

Jim concluded his recital with the sentiment: 'I knowed there was somethink wrong about him as soon as I clapped eyes on his dirty chops. Muniferni, if I had him by here now, I 'ood bust him between my finger and thumb like a monkey-nut.'

Siân snorted. 'Yes, easy for you to say that now, but I 'spose you was jest so ready as the others when he spoked his nonsense.'

Jim looked at Mary like a man deeply hurt. 'There, what did I tell you on the way up?' he demanded.

Mary had no time to conjure up the imaginary conversation before Siân broke in. 'Never mind 'bout that. What is in the soup kitchens for dinner tomorrow?'

Mary took advantage of the question to change the subject. 'I believe it's corned beef stew, mam, but I'm not sure.'

'Huh! Corned beef stew agen. Fitter if they gived us enough money to buy our own food decent.'

Mary listened to a long harangue, in which Jim joined, on the difference between food values and cooking in the good old days and now, then made her way home to make tea for her father, who, she knew, would be tired and irritable after the strain of the meeting.

On the tenth day Cwmardy was again in a ferment. The clang of hobnailed boots ran in repeating echoes round the streets, adding to the clamour of voices.

Ezra, with Mary at his side and a telegram in his hand, paced the kitchen, his face putty-coloured and pitiful. Suddenly he reached for his cap, stating abruptly: 'I'm going out to them.'

'Wait. I'm coming with you,' she replied.

Together they made their way through the village to the Square. To every excited query, Ezra, the telegram still clutched in his hand like a death-warrant, declared: 'Yes. We are smashed. The strike is over.'

The people fell in behind and followed them to the Square. On the way down the growing procession was met by some policemen, one of whom shouted:

'Stop. You can't demonstrate without a permit.' The words were drowned in a roar: 'Permit to hell! Get out of the way! Chuck them in the Fountain!'

The Square was soon packed with people, and Ezra climbed onto the Fountain bowl and, turning slowly to face all the people, read the telegram: 'Strike called off. Advise your men return to work without delay.'

A short silence generated by mass paralysis followed the words, then a shout that increased in volume with every second as the strikers grasped the significance of the instruction. The shout rose to a roar that broke through the walls of the Big House and the police station before bounding back to run round the valley in reverberating challenge.

'The rats!'

'They've sold us!'

'We refuse to go back to work!'

'Our strike goes on!'

The slogans grew louder and higher, became more incoherent and confused as they reached a climax, then became clear again as they fused into triumphant song:

> 'Though cowards flinch and traitors sneer,
> We'll keep the Red Flag flying here.'

The tumultuous chorus struck Len's ears just as he left the carriage in the railway station. The sound sent the blood pumping to his head. Without thinking he dropped his case and rushed to the Square, where the people were already forming up in preparation for a march round Cwmardy.

Big Jim, now alongside Ezra, who was still on the Fountain, was the first to see Len. He stared hard for a moment at the unexpected vision, then began to howl at the top of his tremendous voice:

'Whoa, boys! Whoa! There's our Len, back from the city.'

Mary hastily pushed her way nearer the Fountain at the news, and another roar swept the air: 'Len! Good old Len! Let him speak.'

Flushed and panting, Len pushed through the mass of people, until, impatient with enthusiasm, some of them lifted him on their shoulders, where he was held in a vice despite his struggles. By the time the new tumult had died down, he had recovered his wind and his voice was clear and vibrant as, catching sight of Mary, he began to speak.

'Comrades. I just want to say how proud I am to be back again among you, in the valley to which I belong. It is true that the General Strike has been betrayed by a small group of politicians who call themselves leaders of Labour. Yes, it's true – they went round the back door of Downing Street to sell us, like butchers with cat's meat.' He was interrupted by a storm of booing:

'The traitors!'

'Kick 'em out!'

'White-livered rats!'

'They're no more labour than my arse!'

When the uproar had spent itself out, Len continued. 'But our fellow workers haven't let us down. They are still behind us to a man and a woman.' Again he was interrupted, but this time by cheers, which continued for several minutes. 'Yes, comrades,' he went on, when he had a chance, 'the Government, as our Party said all along, sided with the capitalist class, but let the Labour Party and the councillors use the local council to feed our kiddies in the schools, and our fellow workers in every part of the country will see to it that we will not starve. Let us keep on fighting until victory is won and this Government brought down.'

Again the stormy cheers moulded themselves into music that helped to marshal the ranks for the delayed march:

> 'Then raise the scarlet standard high,
> Beneath its shades we'll live or die.'

The rhythm timed the marching feet, whose heavy 'tramp-tramp' maintained a sonorous monotone to the song. Len kept close to Mary all the way, pressing her closely to his side in the crush.

'This is life,' she whispered, stretching herself to bring her lips near his ear.

'Yes,' Len replied, 'because it shows the way to revolution and freedom.' Her hand sought his, and they both joined in the singing as their feet took them on.

The strike of the miners continued throughout the country. Things got worse each week that passed for the people in Cwmardy. The Federation funds became exhausted and no strike pay could be doled out. The local Co-operative Stores came to their help and gave credit to the soup kitchens which the committee opened in the chapel vestries and the school yards. The men supplemented this by occasional raids over the mountains after wandering sheep.

In the meantime Len had renewed his boyhood friendship with Ron, and they spent hours together discussing how the Labour Party could save the position through Parliament and the council. The discussions sometimes became very fierce, when they differed on matters of policy, but always they met again to pursue the argument. Len was adamant that no solution to the troubles of the people could be found through Parliament and was fond of reiterating a statement:

'You can depend on it, nothing will ever come to us except through the trade unions and revolution. The pits and factories are the fortresses of the working-class and only through them will we free our people.'

Ron was equally adamant that if the Labour Party worked correctly and sincerely in Parliament there would be no need of a revolution. 'Before you capture the pits,' he asserted on many occasions, 'you have got to capture political power.'

This always stumped Len, particularly if Ron accompanied it with a challenge. 'After all, isn't your Party a political Party, striving to organise the masses to take power out of the hands of the capitalists?'

Ron's parents kept much of their poverty away from him, but even so he had a fairly shrewd idea of their circumstances, and the knowledge tore at his heart until he dreaded the chasing thought that never left him. He had tried everywhere to find work, only to find in its stead that his father's words were true.

One day in sheer desperation he asked Len: 'Do you think, Len, if I explained to Mary she would use her influence with her father to get me a position somewhere under the council? I understand he is the chairman this year, and a word from him will go a long way.'

He coloured self-consciously when Len looked at him, but tried to cover his confusion with an apologetic explanation. 'You see, Len, my position is entirely different from yours and the other men's. I am not a workman, have never been trained for one. My parents thought to make me a cut above that. Do you remember,' he asked wistfully, 'when I used to boast of my going to college instead of to the pits?'

Len nodded sympathetically, his heart aching at the tragedy unfolding itself before him.

'Well, I've been there for years, as you know, and have now come back with all that education can give me. Yes, knowledge, degrees, and all that these things mean. But when I come back to my own home, where it was intended my training should make me a big figure, I find myself unwanted and useless. Oh, God,' he moaned in a spasm of realisation, 'if my father doesn't find enough money to buy me a job I must remain idle all my life.'

He paused for a moment to regain control of himself, but before he could continue Will Evans strolled along, his cap set rakishly on the side of his head and a blade of grass in his mouth.

'Hallo,' he casually greeted them, 'how be?'

Both returned the salutation, after which Len asked: 'What's on tonight, Will? Anything important?'

He noticed Will scanning the street uneasily even as he answered. 'Aye, of course. There is something important every night if I can find one.'

He pulled the blade of grass from his mouth to spit and, lowering his voice, whispered confidentially: 'You haven't seen Will Smallbeer about, have you?'

Len replied, while Ron shook his head: 'No, he haven't passed us and we've been here about half an hour, Will.'

A dreamy look came into Will's eyes and he muttered, more to himself than the others: 'I wonder where the old blighter is gone to?'

A brief pause followed, during which he appeared to be making up his mind about something, then, with a resigned shrug: 'I s'pose I'll find him after he have spent the bloody lot.'

He turned to Ron. 'You see, butty, we sold a bag of coal to the doctor yesterday and put it all on a horse, and it

605

have come in at a big price.'

Len tried to console him. 'Don't worry, Will bach. Old Smallbeer is as honest as the day and wouldn't do you down for the world.'

'Yes, I know that, Len, only once a man gets four or five pints in him he do forget what honesty is. Ah well, no good worrying, I s'pose, only next time us will sell a bag of coal I'll make bloody sure who'll handle the money.'

Len turned the subject. 'Me and Ron have been talking about a jam he's in, Will. Perhaps you can give us some help.'

'Oh, aye,' Will commented interestedly. 'Well, you can depend on it, butty, when you fail, I 'on't, although I admit you are a bit cleverer than me in most things.'

Len and Ron laughed loudly at the complacent back-handed compliment.

'All right,' said the former, 'let's see what you'd do if you was in Ron's position.'

Ron repeated his statement, and in the telling forgot everything but his own woes. Will listened with exaggerated intentness until the recital was finished, then, like a professor propounding the solution to a problem, he commented:

'Hmm. Yes. That is a tough 'un, to be sure.' He turned his attention directly on Ron to whom he addressed his next remarks. 'You see, they do say – I can't prove it mind you, but it is common talk all the same – that to get a job on the council you have got to give the councillors your first year's wages. Huh, 'scuse me,' he apologised, 'I mean salary. But even then you can't be sure of a job, because somebody else might give more than you.' He screwed his eyes up and continued. 'But even then, once you've got in it's a pretty good bargain, for you are right for life afterwards.'

The sheer starkness of the statement battered at Ron's last hope. 'But my father hasn't got any money to give them,' he complained bitterly, realising his friends were unconsciously digging a grave to bury his past. 'There have been so many strikes and lock-outs and so on in Cwmardy and he's given so much credit that he's now ruined and doesn't know where to turn.'

Will glanced at him with the same quaint look. 'Oh, aye, so that's it, eh? Your father is further back than when he started. Nothing left after all he have done, like Len's old man and me and all of us in the pit. Hmm. Pity, pity.' He closed his eyes like a man deep in prayer, then suddenly opened them again to say: 'I know, Ron. Tell him to come out on strike with us.'

The two men looked at him in amazement, Len being the first to recover his composure. 'Don't talk soft, Will mun,' he pleaded. 'How can Mr. Evans come on strike when he's not working for anyone except himself and his family?'

Will took some time to absorb this. He screwed his face into furrows, then looked into the dirty air before stepping forward a pace to aim a kick at a lump of horse-dung in the roadway. He watched it smash in pieces and let his gaze follow one bit that travelled towards Ben the Barber's window. He sighed disappointingly when it fell short, then resumed the conversation as though there had been no interruption.

'Well, there might be something in what you say, Len, now I come to think of it. Aye, I do give in to that.' He turned abruptly to Ron. 'Look here. If your old man haven't got no money the best thing you can do is fight with us,

607

see? When we got money, everybody have got it, because it is no bloody use to us unless we spend it.'

With this parting shot he fixed the cap more tightly on his head, gave them a nod, and strolled away with a final remark: 'If you see Smallbeer, tell him I haven't forgot about the bet.'

Len looked after the retreating form of his mate with amusement which he failed to conceal, but Ron's look expressed amazement.

At last he asked: 'So you think nothing can be done, Len?'

'No, Ron. Nothing except what Will said – struggle or starve.' He paused, as though sorry for the pain he was going to give his friend, then went on with greater vehemence: 'Look at my people. They have lived on bread and taters and tea for months, yet not one of them complains or talks of giving in. We are fighting not only the owners and the Government but our own leaders, who are a majority on the council. We asked them to feed our children in the schools, and they refused, Ron. They refused because they say there is no money there, and even if there was they wouldn't have power to use it in this way.' He saw the sad hopelessness that crept over Ron. It melted the hardness of his words and turned them into a plea. 'Don't think I am harsh, Ron. It's the last thing in the world I want to be. But I must tell you the truth, mustn't I? I know my people are blamed for bringing the valley to ruin, but all they are doing is what you are trying to do, only in a different way. They are trying to get a living from their strength, just as you are trying to get one from your education.'

608

Ron looked hard into the far recesses of the sky for some minutes before replying softly, like one who had found sudden conviction in momentary contemplation.

'Of course you're right, Len. Didn't I study the theory before sending the books to you? But the study was so easy, comrade, and the necessity that now makes me put that theory into practice is so hard. Yes. Very, very hard.' He shook himself sharply, then said: 'Forgive me, Len. I have been selfish and cowardly.'

Len caught his hand and pressed it warmly. 'Don't apologise to me, comrade bach,' he begged. 'I'm not worth it. How often have I lost faith because I didn't understand? How often have I failed because I wasn't strong? Don't worry, Ron. Keep close to the people. When we are weak they'll give us strength. When we fail, they'll pick us up and put us back on the road again.'

The intensity of his emotions robbed him of further words for a while and both of them stood silently awkward until Len somewhat lamely suggested: 'I tell you what, Ron. Let's tell Mary that you're prepared to join the Party if she will. Then the three of us can fight together now, like we used to play together when we was in school.'

Ron shook his head slowly. 'I must think it over, Len. I have to consider my father and mother, and you know what their feelings are regarding the Party. You see, Len,' he added apologetically, 'dad has to be friendly with the councillors and he must be careful, particularly now when the Party is fighting the council.'

Len's face dropped in disappointment, and the other, noticing this, hurried to make amends by saying: 'I know I must come to it some day, but they have done so much for me that I can't bring myself to hurt them just yet.' He felt the lameness of his answer, hesitated a while, then blurted out: 'But I'll come with you on the demonstration for school feeding and parish relief at the end of the week.'

This news brightened Len, and he began explaining what the Party intended doing on the demonstration. The two friends talked of this for some time before parting.

On the day of the demonstration Ron rose early and had cleaned the house and lit the fire before his parents had got out of bed. He toasted some bread and went into the stores to look for something to go with it, then he called them from the foot of the stairs. A lump had risen to his throat when he saw the empty shelves, that made the shop look nude and obscene, but he choked this back as he heard his parents shuffling about in the bedroom. He was worried about the old people. His mother was obviously ill, and on a number of occasions he had caught his father looking vacant and strange, like a person who had lost his memory or his mind. Ron hastily brushed the thought away as they came down the stairs and entered the kitchen. After the frugal breakfast was eaten he kissed his mother and patted his father's shoulder affectionately before reaching for his coat. He had put this on when he heard the rough scrape of a chair hurriedly shifted. The sound, so unexpected, awakened a hazy fear and he turned round to see his father standing at the side of the table with one hand outstretched and a finger pointing accusingly.

'Where are you going, Ron?' The tone in which the question was put made it more ominous than the words.

The old man's eyes were fixed on his son in a stare that frightened Maggie without her knowing why. She rose unsteadily to her feet and put her hand on the sleeve of her husband's coat.

'What is the matter with you, John? The boy is only going out for a walk.'

He made no answer other than to shake her hand away. Ron felt his flesh pucker as he caught the stare of his father.

'Why do you look at me like that, dad? I'm only going for a stroll, as mam said.'

'Don't lie to me, boy. I asked where are you going?' The old man spat the words out as though they were venom on his tongue, and Ron knew further evasion would be futile. Still clutching his cap, he took a chair and sat down near his mother, who bent sideways a little and put her arm protectively round his neck. The brief period of suppressed emotions that followed got on Ron's nerves and made him reckless. The stillness in the kitchen was so deep that when he spoke he thought he was shouting, although his voice, apart from a little quiver, was quite normal.

'If you want to know, dad, I'm going on the demonstration to the council.'

John wrung his hands, slippery with sweat, then slumped to a chair, only to spring up again immediately. 'I know. Yes, I knew it all the time. Oh, God! Oh, Maggie fach, our only son has been deceiving us all the while.'

He clasped his head in both hands and squeezed desperately as though hoping in this way to crush certain things from his brain. Maggie grew alarmed and tried to soothe him.

'Leave the boy have his fling for a while, John. He is young and will soon come to his senses.'

'Young, young! Don't tell me that. He is older in knowledge than both of us put together.' He started pacing the kitchen, his temper increasing with every stride, until he could no longer contain himself. Turning abruptly on his heels, he flung himself towards Ron and tried to tear the coat from his shoulders, at the same time shouting in a snarling voice:

'You shan't go out! I won't leave you disgrace the family that has sacrificed its all to give you education. Let me go, Maggie,' he screamed as the latter, frantic with fear for the safety of her son, tried to drag him away.

Ron rose to his feet, slipping his arms free from the coat so that it dangled loosely in his father's hand.

He felt again the same helplessness as on the night when he had returned from college and had been told there was no hope of work for him in Cwmardy. His cheeks paled as he realised that battle was simpler and less harsh than the one that now confronted him. Then it had been economic desperation that had caused the scene, but now it was ideological hatred. He felt the world, that had suddenly come between himself and his parents, swirl about him like a fog and wondered vaguely where his feet would land. A voice from miles away impressed itself through his thoughts. It reminded him, for some reason, of the bell tolling in the cemetary as the gates opened to admit a corpse.

'To think that we have reared and kept close to our hearts an infidel, an unbelieving Communist, a son that

612

associates with the scoundrels who have ruined Cwmardy and our home! Oh, God, what have we done that this should be our final tribulation?'

Maggie helped her husband to a chair into which he slumped like an empty sack. Her own face had hollowed during the short time the scene had already lasted, and Ron knew that deep in her heart she felt the same as his father, but that love for her offspring was greater than her faith.

John weakly raised his head from his arms and looked again at his son, who stood so immobile and silent nearby. Their glances met and fixed for a while before the old man's eyes dropped as they melted with pathos. 'Ron, Ron.' The name, so slowly repeated, seemed to ooze from his heart.

'Tell me, my boy. Tell your mother, whose body bore you safely through the travail and blood of birth, tell us, whose lives were fused in yours, that you'll mix no more with that crew of atheists.'

Ron shuddered coldly and came out of the trance that had gripped him. He fought desperately for arguments to justify his actions, for reasons that would destroy the intolerant prejudice of his parents. Although they had never mentioned a word to him he knew that his boyhood association with Len and the contact between them ever since had been a painful knowledge to his parents, who had aspirations that transcended such friendships. Being aware of this he could not help sympathising with them, even now in this crisis, as he thought of the tremendous shock they must have suffered with the realisation that the friendship had now become not merely personal but political. Up to this moment he had been prepared to drift along on the fringe of the movement, as his reply to Len's plea had implied, but the sudden outburst from his father had involuntarily destroyed all his emotional vacillations. He now squared his shoulders and faced the old couple, whose stares burned through him.

'Why are you so bitter against the Communists, dad? They have done nothing to you.'

'Done nothing to me? Ha! Haven't they ruined this valley and my business? Don't they always and everywhere advocate strikes? Don't they preach disorder and revolution? Haven't they drawn the people from their chapels and religion?' He began to get excited again, but checked himself with a moan.

'Oh, Ron. We reared you to become a decent, law-abiding citizen. We held out hopes that you would become a leading light in the life of Cwmardy. Yes, a well-respected man. And here you have linked yourself to everything that is foreign to our people and their beliefs. You are a friend of the riff-raff in the valley.'

This sneer stung Ron to a hasty retort. 'You can't say that, dad. Len's people have been dealing with you all their lives. His mother goes to chapel as regularly as anybody, and Len himself is as gentle as a lamb. It's your blindness and the narrowness of your life that makes you so intolerant of any opinion that happens to be opposed to yours.' He spoke very low, but each word was emphatic as he continued. 'You want things to remain stagnant, to be today as they were in your boyhood. You are not willing for people to learn, not prepared to see them struggling. You want them to be like a river that doesn't flow. But it can't

614

be. No, it can't be, whatever you may feel or think. As water, to be clean, must keep on flowing, so must the people keep on struggling to get security and happiness in this world. How can it be otherwise?' he entreated them both. 'Water that is stagnant is foetid and deadly, and people who won't struggle are dull, apathetic, and sordid.'

Both the old people gazed at him dumbstruck, silent in the pause which preceded his next words. 'I respect your faith, mam and dad. I know you are sincere in them, but so also I know that other people are equally sincere in their principles, although you do not agree with these. They are not wrong because you disagree. Oh no.'

John could stick the indictment no longer, and sprang to his feet, his whole body quivering as he shouted: 'That's enough. Get out of this house with your infidel ideas! Go to those you call your friends and see if they can help you in your poverty – see if they will do and suffer for you as me and your mother have done for thirty years. And when you find out the truth, come back here and see what you have left.' His voice cracked and an odd look crept over his face. Maggie was now openly crying, and Ron half started towards her, but changed his mind, and hesitantly putting on the coat he had retrieved from his father, he turned and slowly walked out.

The old man and his wife waited until they heard the door slam, then looked at each other in silence, each seeing a face that was lined and worn. Maggie saw strange fires glowing in her husband's eyes, but was too weary to wonder why they came or what they portended. The scene had robbed her of volition and they sat pensive

615

and practically motionless for some hours, once or twice letting their glances wander round the room.

In spite of extreme poverty, their pride had forbidden the sale of any of the furniture, each piece of which they regarded with an affection second only to that which they had felt for their son. The various wooden articles filling the house symbolised for them the stages and episodes in their married life, and they now reminded Maggie of the past. A tear worked its way down her withered cheek, following every intricate groove till it reached her chin, from which it dropped when she coughed. John placed his arm round her bony shoulders, pressing her head to his breast, while the glow in his eyes deepened, as did the furrow on his brow.

'There, there, Maggie fach,' he crooned in her ear. 'Don't take it so hard; it is no good grumbling or grieving at our lot.' He paused a second and tried to lighten his tones. 'Ron will come to his senses again, when the people who owe us money pay their debts and make it possible for us to get him a position.'

She was seized by a fit of coughing which left her gasping, but she at last gathered sufficient breath to groan: 'What is the good of talking like that, John? You know the people can't and never will pay us.' She stopped again to cough, then began to moan. 'Oh, Ron, Ron! Whatever is to come of you? I had such lovely dreams of what you were going to be. I saw myself as the proud mother of a great man and now, oh dear, dear.' She turned to John, and repeated: 'Yes, a great man, and here we are as poor as church mice not knowing where to turn. It's enough to make anyone a Communist.' She relapsed into silence and John shook himself restlessly. He seemed to be struggling with some idea, and eventually said with infinite slowness, as though he were answering a difficult question that had been put to him.

'No. We can never go to the parish for help, and we can never lift our heads while Ron is an infidel. Better for us to die here and now than face that disgrace.' His face seemed even thinner and the shadows more numerous as he whispered the thought and his fingers dug passionately into her shoulder.

Maggie looked into his eyes and her own opened wide at what she saw there. He seemed to read her thoughts before she hoarsely spoke them, nodding her head in time with the words. 'Yes, John. You are right. Better that than the other thing. But how?' She exclaimed sharply as the idea began to fix itself in her mind. John lifted her tenderly to her feet and they stared at each other with an intensity that made them alone in the world. She felt a pain in her chest as though rats were gnawing at the bones, but watching his look become more fixed and horrifying, she did not cough. The visible tremor of his body told her he was trying to fight away some inevitable action, but she felt no fear.

At last he spoke, every word deliberate and emphatic. 'Maggie fach, we have lived together many years now, and have seen many ups and downs, but through it all we have stuck together as man and wife should. Yes, my dear, that has been our life.' A sob came into his voice but he checked it immediately and clasped her head in his hands.

'Oh, Maggie fach, as we have lived, that is how I want to die... together.' He flung his arms wildly into the air and his voice rose hysterically as despair conquered him. 'Yes. Ron has left us alone and we must die together. And now.' He screamed the last words twice, before staggering to the ornate sideboard, where he began frantically searching for something in the drawers.

Maggie watched his every movement but she made no effort to hinder him. Instead, she slowly sank back into the chair, looked into the dying flames that gasped in the grate, and sighed. A smile clung to the corners of her lips and her eyes grew bright. She scarcely seemed to notice that he had left the sideboard and was now standing over her with an open razor in his hand. His whole body was trembling and he kept mumbling incoherently, but Maggie paid no attention. Once or twice she shaped her lips to say something, but the words did not come. Then presently, almost as though she were crooning gently to herself, she whispered:

'John. John bach. So this is the end.' It was not a question but an assertion. There was no sadness in her voice and her face was placid.

Suddenly she caught the hand that held the razor and dragging it to her lips kissed the open blade. 'There is no room for us any longer here,' she murmured, 'but God has provided a place for us somewhere else where we won't be a burden on our little Ron.'

John bent his head and she felt his hot lips burning through her hair. 'Come, John bach,' she coaxed him, 'there is no need for us to wait. I'm ready to come with you.'

618

He appeared not to hear her, for he continued muttering to himself, blind to everything but the loose skin on her neck. With passionate eagerness his fingers traced the veins and sinews whose throbbing seemed to fascinate him. He closed his eyes as his hand jerked up and drew the razor across her throat. He felt the blade slice through her flesh, but when he opened his eyes again, Maggie's were still staring at him, though blood was pouring from the wound. He fancied she wanted to say something, and bent his ear to her lips, unconscious of the spurting blood that drenched him. But all he heard was a whimpering gurgle. He lifted his head a little, wondering what she wanted, when her fingers closed over his hand and slowly lifted it to her neck.

The action flashed to his brain knowledge of what she desired and he carefully searched for the wound with his fingers. Finding it, he parted the edges, placed the razor inside and slashed again, her hand still gripping his and following the sweeping stroke. He felt her grasp tighten convulsively on his wrist, as her head sagged forward on her chest.

John freed himself from the clasp and stood back a pace. 'I'm coming, Maggie fach, never fear,' he muttered, and, hearing no response he caught her head in his hands, heedless of the blood streaming down her dress to the floor beneath his feet; then, seeing the razor which he still clutched, he flung it with all his strength into the grate. His glazed eyes stared at it for a long time as it lay resting in the ashes, and the only sound was the mocking 'tick-tock, tick-tock' of the clock on the mantelshelf. This eventually forced itself in upon his senses and he raised

619

his head to look again at Maggie, whose eyes were now closed. He went to her and stroked her sticky hair with his lips for a time, then suddenly jerked himself erect and his feet slipped in a puddle of blood.

He looked at this helplessly for a while, then sprang to the back door through which he hurried, returning in a moment with a length of rope, used to tie orange boxes. Jumping on the table he fastened one end of the rope to a hook in the ceiling, leaving the other looped end to dangle about a foot lower. Then he scrambled off the table, each action becoming more hysterical, and made for Maggie's slumped body. He lifted her head and gazed at her. The lips were already curled back from the teeth, but he kissed them, while he mumbled to himself: 'I'll soon be with you.' He closed his eyes for a moment, then jumped back on the table and placed the loop about his neck. Its touch sent a cold shiver through him, but he bent his knees to allow the full weight of his body to fall on his neck, and scrambled with his feet to find the edge of the table and kick it away even as he heard loud shouts in the street and Ron's voice calling: 'We are marching for bread and extra relief.'

The table crashed over and the old man felt his chest bursting. He opened his mouth, but no air came. He began to kick wildly and his body swung like a pendulum on the rope, which swayed for a long time after the demonstration had passed the shop.

LEN GOES TO GAOL

While this was happening in the stores of Evans Cardi, the drizzling rain curled over the rim of the mountain and swept down on Cwmardy in visible gusts as the people gathered about the Square for the demonstration to the council chambers. The wind moaned along the telephone wires, lashing the people's faces and bending their heads to the muddy earth. Harry Morgan and Len stood on the Fountain, with Ron and Mary nearby in the centre of the crowd. Harry's arms waved wildly and his voice crackled through the rain as he shouted:

'Where are those who are supposed to be our leaders? Where are those we put in Parliament and the council? Here we are about to march, not to the Big House against the owners, but to our own leaders who we have put in power on the council. We are marching for relief and school feeding. I ask again, where are they now?'

A loud howl followed this:

'Where are they now?'

'Where is Ezra?'

'We gave them power. They must give us bread.'

Len saw the skin on Mary's face twitch, and it made his burn. Pulling Harry's sleeve, he pleaded: 'Don't keep them too long, comrade. Let's start the march. Our people are getting wet, standing here.'

Even as he made the request Mary had left Ron's side and was pushing her way to the Fountain, which willing hands helped her to mount. The waves in her brown hair shone wetly in the wind, which ruffled the strands across her face. Brushing them aside and paying no heed to the surprised couple with her on the Fountain, she began to speak, her words vibrant with feeling.

'Our leaders have deserted us,' she declared, 'because they think the fight is only in the pit, between us and the company. Yet they once asked us to put them on the council and in Parliament because the struggle is everywhere. When they were only a few on the council they pleaded with us to give them more seats, to give them more power, because they were helpless. We gave it to them – all the power they wanted. We put them in control, and now they tell us that although they have power they can do nothing because they have no money.'

Someone shouted harshly: 'Don't forget your father is one of them.'

She went white as she turned in the direction of the sneer and for a moment Len thought she was about to fall

622

off the Fountain, but before he could move to help her, she had recovered herself and began speaking again, although a little huskily: 'I know he is one of them, but I also know he doesn't agree with the others. If he felt there was any way to help us, I know he would take it. But what can he do alone? Although he is true, he is helpless.'

The struggle between filial love and the objective reality of the present situation weakened her, and Len caught her arm as she stumbled. His voice was harsh with affection as he said: 'That will do, Mary. Don't kill yourself. We'll start off now.'

He never remembered the exact statements she had made, but he understood the changed outlook behind them and marvelled as his glance roamed over the crowd that faced him. He saw glimpses of the police at the rear hustling the people, and knowing what the action portended, he immediately took command, shouting as loudly as he could:

'Keep together, boys! Don't let anyone break your ranks and don't let anyone provoke you.'

He jumped from the Fountain, Mary and the others beside him, and the march to the council chambers began, the people clamouring and shouting as they followed their leaders. A red banner was hoisted into the misty rain, which soon soaked it into limp sogginess.

Mary was the first to notice the number of police that fell in alongside the demonstration from every street and lane. She mentioned it to Len, who looked around and saw the truth of her remark.

When he turned to her again, his look was worried, but

he tried hard to be casual when he said: 'Well, we expected them, didn't we?'

'Yes,' she retorted urgently, 'but can't you see what it means, Len? During the long strike they came to protect the company; then they came to protect the blacklegs, as dad often told us; but now they come to protect our own leaders.'

He paused momentarily as the full effect of her words struck him, but the pressure from behind pushed him along again as he replied: 'By gum, you're right, my dear.'

They kept on marching without saying any more for a while, during which he appeared to be gathering his thoughts. Then quite unexpectedly he said to her: 'Of course, that's right. It's the logic of the whole struggle, although I never saw it that way till you showed it to me now. The councillors start off by being our leaders against the company. The Government sends its police in to help the company and the blacklegs, in the name of law and order. This makes our leaders lose faith in our ability to win the fight, and because we won't listen the police are sent in to help them. Well, I'm damned,' he concluded, 'it's funny how the struggle sieves us out, in't it?'

No more was said until the council chambers were in sight, by which time all the demonstrators were drenched to the skin; but the banner was pushed higher into the air when they saw the strong cordon of police blocking the entire road.

Len went white and his lips closed tightly for a moment. Then he grasped Mary's arm and grimly warned her: 'Now, remember. You say nothing. Leave this to me and the other boys.'

Mary did not reply, but a defiant look flared in her

eyes. The procession only stopped when the front ranks were right up against the cordon, but it was near enough to the council chambers for the strikers to see the ashen faces of the councillors through the windows. A loud howl immediately broke the air.

'Come down here where you belong!'

'Baby starvers!'

'Traitors!'

The police ranks drew in ominously and each constable grasped the looped strap that dangled from his trouser pocket. The inspector in charge stepped forward a pace and faced Len, whose body looked insignificant against the other's.

'Come on! Break up!' came the harsh command. 'You can't march any further.'

'We don't want to march any further,' Len retorted. 'All we want is to send a deputation into the council.'

The inspector hesitated a moment and the shouting became more wild. It seemed to irritate the police officer.

'That'll do,' he said. 'I don't want any of your bloody cheek, and you can't send a deputation, because the council has just told us it doesn't want to see you.'

The strikers near heard this and the shouts grew into a roar at the news. A wild movement began to sway the people, and without any warning the fight started. The police charged into the crowd, hitting madly at every head within reach. The councillors hurriedly retreated from the windows of the chamber as the bodies began to flop to the ground, where they tempted heavy booted feet.

Len felt himself hurtled about like a log in a flood. He

looked about frantically for Mary, and seeing someone grasp her roughly by the arm, the world went dark and he snarled at the top of his voice: 'Keep your dirty bloody paws off her,' at the same time furiously pushing and fighting his way towards her. A sudden pain brought him to his senses as he felt his arm being twisted behind his back in agonising jerks. He moaned with the pain and shouted hoarsely: 'Let me go, you cowards. Give me a chance.' A further twist brought his head down till it nearly touched the ground and he heard from far away someone saying harshly: 'Take him inside.' He kicked wildly behind him, then felt something crash upon his head, and as he crumbled up he fancied he saw a huge black boot coming to meet his stomach. But he did not hear Mary scream wildly: 'Oh, my God, they're smashing Len up and taking him in!'

Hours later Len was lifted roughly from the stony floor of the cell into which he had been flung. He vaguely sensed he was being dragged along a dark passage, but didn't take much notice. He wondered if he had two heads and how far apart they were from each other. He knew they were on fire because of the fierce burning in them. His eyes pricked him like red-hot needles and he was afraid to open them, but the bright light in the room to which he was taken seeped through the lids and forced them open. The momentary glance showed him, through a steamy mist, a large number of uniformed men. He raised a heavy hand to his head, then dropped it again, wet and sticky, to his side. A murmur of dim voices came to his ears, but he made no effort to distinguish what was said

626

as his knees began to wobble and he crumpled face down upon the floor.

The next thing he remembered was the sound of low moans and a trembling that shook his limbs like jelly. He slowly gathered his thoughts and drew himself to his knees, all the time wondering what had happened and where he was as he rose unsteadily erect. His head still throbbed, but the burning agony had gone, although his ears were filled with a funny buzz that somehow made him think of the mountain in summer. He stood swaying for some seconds, then thrust his arms before him and stepped out – one pace, two paces – before his knees touched an obstruction. Bending down, he let his fingers run over the coarse cloth that covered something like a bench. Straining his eyes to see what was there, he fancied the air became lighter, and looking at the floor behind him he saw a shadowy pattern beginning to form on it. He kept watching this, his whole soul in his eyes, until he distinguished black bars with panes of light between them.

Slowly lifting his head, he saw the small window high up on one side of the cell wall. Turning away, he gazed around the cold emptiness that surrounded him before wearily making for the bench to sit down. The clammy air made him shiver, but he did not think of the blanket beneath his body as, with his head clasped in his hands, he drew to his mind all that had happened. His eyes filled with tears as he again saw Mary in the grasp of the huge policeman and the bodies of his mates upon the wet earth.

A thin, squeaky noise, percolating from the street into the cell, disturbed the painful soliloquy. Len listened and

627

heard a newsboy shout 'Special Edition.' The sound made him happier in a moment, as it gave him contact with the world outside. He thought it sweeter than the music of his mountain larks and walked hurriedly to the cell window the better to catch every syllable.

'Russians imprison British subjects.' He stretched himself taut at the words and breathlessly waited for the rest. 'No free speech in Russia. Englishmen in danger. The Government takes stern measures.'

Len wondered what had happened and for a moment forgot his own predicament. He slowly resumed his seat upon the plank, and as he thought more deeply over the newsboy's cry a bitter smile curled his lips.

He never remembered how long he sat without moving, but he suddenly felt the cold steal through the flesh into his bones. He shivered and pulled the solitary blanket over his shoulders in an effort to keep the cold at bay. Finding this insufficient and his muscles beginning to quiver involuntarily, he rose and paced the cell, the blanket dangling to his feet like a robe. The rhythm of the walk began to work itself into his brain, which made a song of each step. 'Eight steps up. Stop. Five steps across. Stop. Eight steps up. Stop.' He sat down again to get away from the maddening reiteration, and tried to retrace the events of the day. But tales he had heard of what policemen did to prisoners in the cells insisted upon intruding into his thoughts. The affair of Syd Jones the wrestler came to his mind with stunning force. He remembered the night Syd was frog-marched to the station and brought out next morning dead from heart failure. Big Jim always insisted the man had been beaten to death. Other incidents and anecdotes crowded into his mind, where they became a panorama of living pictures that bred in him a slow-developing fear. He looked about the cell for a weapon, but saw nothing, and suddenly realised it had become pitch dark. He sat down again, closing his eyes tightly in a vain attempt to shut out the pictures that passed before them.

He began wondering what the police intended doing with him. His imagination illuminated the cell and he saw the iron-studded door open to admit a number of great hazy forms. He jumped up in a frenzy, only to find the darkness more intense than ever. Fearing to sit down again, he paced the cell once more. This time the thud-thud of his tramping feet made him think of boots and he smiled when he remembered the old saying that all policemen had big feet. But the smile faded into a pitiful twist of the lips with the thought that boots made fine weapons. Better than batons, he thought, when a man was down. He saw them, big, black, and shiny, staring at him from all parts of the cell, and their cold, glittering hardness appalled him. He felt them driving into his head and body, and closed his eyes to sweep them from sight. But they followed him, scores of them, lifting, falling, kicking, thudding. 'No-no,' he shouted hysterically, burying his face in his arms. 'Not that, not that. You can't kill me here.'

His breath came in gasping sobs and he sat down to steady himself. The thick darkness seemed to press on him, but when he raised his head he fancied the walls had drawn closer together. Perspiration ran in trickling streams down his face and the hair on the back of his neck bristled. He stopped breathing and tried to brace himself, but all the time the walls came nearer and nearer, until he felt they were nearly on him and ready to crush him in a clammy embrace.

He sprang erect in a panic and raced to the door, which he missed in the darkness, flattening himself against the opposite wall. Rebounding from this, with increasing panic he hurled himself in the opposite direction, and sensing he was against wood began to kick madly at the door, at the same time screaming: 'Let me out! Let me out! For God's sake let me out! I'm smothering.'

There was no answer and he kept on kicking and screaming until, when he was nearly exhausted, he heard the shuffle of feet outside the door and the clanging of keys. He felt the door pressed open against his body and retreated more deeply into the cell, where a flash of light suddenly blazed full on his eyes, completely blinding him.

'What the bloody hell is all this fuss about?' he heard a voice ask roughly.

The sound and the knowledge there was another human being with him sent Len's courage back to him in surges. Still seeing nothing, he pulled himself erect and answered:

'Nothing. I only wanted some company.'

For a second there was amazed silence, then:

'You cheeky little bastard!' came the indignant retort. 'Who the hell do you think you are, Lord Muck or what?' Another pause before the voice continued: 'Here, mate, we'll soon put a stop to his damned nonsense. Anybody would think he was in a public house or something, making all this damn noise. Help me to pull his boots off.'

Before Len could make any remonstrance he was pushed flat on his back, while one policeman sat on his stomach and the other pulled off his boots. In a short time Len was again alone. He wrapped his feet in the blanket and tried to sleep, but his mind was too restive.

After what seemed hours he heard the clang of keys and the door open again, but, thinking it was the police, he did not move or open his eyes. Then a small hand, soft and cool, pressed upon his burning forehead, and springing to his feet he caught Mary to him in a clasp that melted her body to his. She eased herself gently away with a blush as she saw the grinning policemen.

'Hallo, Len my dear. How are you?' she asked, trying to speak casually although her voice was trembling. She looked at his face, where she saw the dried blood and bruises. Tears clouded her vision, and this time, heedless of the presence of anyone else, she kissed him hungrily. What she had seen for some reason flashed her memory back to the battered lad on the mountain, and something told her that her suspicions were correct.

The waiting police grew impatient. 'Come on, hurry up,' said the sergeant, 'we can't stop here all bloody night to watch you two spooning by there.'

Mary looked at him indignantly.

'It's your fault we are here at all,' she retorted heatedly; 'and now you've got to wait till I finish my business.'

'Pretty bloody cocky, in't you, missus?' he replied with half a smile. 'But never mind. Get on with your business and don't be too long.'

Mary turned to Len and inquired what he was charged with. He told her he didn't know and began explaining all that had happened when he was interrupted.

'Cut that out. That's not business.'

Mary bridled up again, but Len checked her with a weary gesture. 'Never mind about that, Mary my dear. We'll know soon enough. Tell me, have any of the boys been hurt?'

She told him a few had been badly battered but he was the only one arrested. His eyes subconsciously travelled over her body, but she showed no signs of injury. Clearing his throat and drawing her into the far corner of the cell, he whispered in her ear. 'Will your father be on the bench tomorrow?'

She went white at the question and was some time before answering. 'No, Len. I've tried to coax him, but he says if he sits on your case it will show he's taking sides and would do you no good.'

Len's body jerked and he would have shouted out but for the pressure of her hand upon his wrist. Controlling himself, he mumbled bitterly: 'Huh! When he asked the committee to let him accept the position as J.P. he said he'd be able as a magistrate to see that our people had fair play when they were brought up in court. And now the very thing he'd do if he had the position, he says he can't do because he's got it.'

He saw the pain in her face and hastened to soften her palpable grief. 'There, there. Don't take no notice of me. We're all unfair to you, my dear. Whatever your father does we throw up to your face as if you could help it; and all the time you are fighting with us, not only against the company and the police, but against your love for your

632

father. Oh, Mary, forgive me,' he begged.

She patted his bent head caressingly.

The sergeant bawled out. 'Come on there, time's up. No more sloppy bloody nonsense.'

Mary looked him straight in the eye before saying: 'One day, my friend, you'll get what you deserve. And you'll find it will be something very different from what you desire.'

She kissed Len again and walked to the door, where she turned to say: 'Cheerio, Len. Keep your spirits up. All the boys and your father and mother are thinking of you, and one day our turn will come.'

He strained his ears to listen for the patter of her little feet, but the heavy thump of her escort's drowned it. His emotions had been soothed by her visit, and shortly after her departure he fell into a deep sleep.

He was still asleep when the door was opened early next morning, and the policeman had to shake him roughly before he woke. Len looked up with a start, then remembered where he was, and, stretching himself, he rose. Although he still felt sore all over, his mind was clear and alert and he was prepared for what was to come. The policeman placed a mug of dirty-looking tea and a piece of dry bread near him, with the remark:

'Don't be long shoving this down. It's nearly time for the court to open.'

Len looked at the stuff contemptuously, then at the police officer. 'You can take that stuff back to where you had it from,' he replied. 'All I want is a wash and a shave.'

'Ho! Want to be a bloody swank, do you? Well, you

can't have a shave, see.'

Len looked the surprise he felt. 'Why not,' he asked innocently.

'Because we don't want you cutting your throat, the same as some of the others have done in my time,' was the astounding answer.

Len's eyes filled with horror, and the policeman, repenting the confidence he had intended as a barb, begged: 'Don't let on that I told you that, or I'll get into trouble.'

His words went unheard by Len, whose mind was busily traversing the possible reasons why people should commit suicide. 'Poor devils,' he muttered to himself, and sighed, then visibly pulled himself together before telling the policeman: 'Don't worry about me cutting my throat. There's too much rubbish needs cleaning from this world yet.'

The officer took him to the lavatory where Len swilled his face under the dripping tap. This done, he returned to the cell, where he was left alone with his thoughts. But he did not have much time for further meditation before the door opened once more and two brightly polished constables marched in and, placing themselves either side, led him down the narrow passage and up some stairs, whence he emerged into a small box-like structure in the middle of a strange room.

Len peeped over the side of his cage and saw that the court was half full of people, among whom he immediately noticed Mary and his father and mother. They looked at him yearningly when they caught his glance, and Siân half rose from her seat to come to him, but Mary tugged her skirt and made her sit down again. Big Jim waved one hand airily, while the other curled his moustache, as much as to say: 'Don't worry, boy bach. Big Jim is with you now.'

Somewhere from without the court came a deep muffled drone of voices. Len wondered what it was even as he noticed the hasty passing backwards and forwards of the numerous police in the building. The drone grew louder and heavier until it seemed to shroud the building like a shawl and he heard the strains of a song battering against the walls:

> 'Then comrades, come rally,
> And the last fight let us face.'

Something swelled in his chest and he felt the air swirling about his ears. He momentarily forgot the courtroom and, lifting his musical voice, he joined in:

> 'On our flesh too long has fed the raven,
> We've too long been the vulture's prey.'

His action electrified the people in the public gallery, who, as though drawn by the music of his voice, instantly rose to their feet and accompanied him, Mary's sweet soprano riding Big Jim's deep bass. After a momentary paralysed silence there were loud howls for 'S-s-silence' and posses of police, white-faced and fearful, stormed into the court, where they looked at each other stupidly, none of them knowing what to do.

Len stood square and erect, his head thrown back a little and his eyes glistening proudly as the last notes faded into silence and three men entered the court from behind a heavy plush curtain. Police sprang rigidly to attention to a loudly barked 'S-silence!' and the magistrates took their seats on the raised dais that faced the court.

Len scrutinised them with interest, realising they were the persons who held his liberty in their hands. The one in the middle had a pinky bald head, a clean-shaven face with hanging cheeks, and a pair of rimless pince-nez which he carried on the tip of his nose. The other two Len knew as the alderman who had read the Riot Act during the long strike and Mr. Higgins, the financial advisor to the company. The man in the middle, whom Len assumed to be the chairman, bent across the desk to whisper something to a small awkwardly built man in the well of the court, who had to stand on his toes to get his ears near enough to listen. When the conversation was finished, the latter, screwing up the muscles of his face to give himself an appearance of sternness, addressed himself to Len.

'You are charged with unlawful assembly, breach of the peace, riotous behaviour, assaulting the police, and impeding the police in the execution of their duty.'

Len's eyes grew larger with each statement and he looked dazedly at Mary, but the only consolation she could give him was a wan smile which put a blight on her own even as she gave it. He heard the small man ask sharply:

'Do you plead guilty or not guilty?'

Realising the question was addressed to himself, Len pulled his wits together and answered heatedly: 'Not guilty, of course. I'm a working man, not a criminal, and it's all lies.'

This created a sensation and the police looked at each

636

other with shocked faces, as if something indecent had been said.

The chairman rebuked Len. 'Please answer the question and don't make political speeches.'

For some time after this Len hardly followed the proceedings, his brain joined with the singing outside, until a policeman went into the box and gave evidence of the violent assault that had been committed upon him. Len looked at the huge bulk of the man with interest, then began to realise as he followed the evidence that it was he himself who was supposed to have maliciously battered the witness.

At the end of this evidence he was asked if he wanted to cross-examine the witness. The question startled him for a moment and he blurted out: 'Yes, of course I do. It's lies, wilful lies.'

A dozen police gathered round the dock as his voice began to rise, and Big Jim fidgeted restlessly in his seat. The chairman rebuked Len again. 'You can ask any question you like on the evidence,' he warned, 'but you can't use this court for propaganda. Don't forget we are men of experience on this bench and know how to deal with stubborn people.' The police and officials laughed heartily at this quip, the other magistrates joining in.

More witnesses went into the box to repeat the evidence of the first. The monotonous repetition sent the alderman to sleep. At length Len was asked if he wanted to go into the witness-box or preferred to make a statement from the dock. After a brief hesitation, during which he tried to decipher the difference between them, he elected to remain where he was. Despite several interruptions from the chairman and the clerk he managed to recount the events of the day up to the time of the fight. By this time his modulated voice was firm and distinct, every word as clear as a music note.

'You don't want us to believe that the police were responsible for the riot, do you?' asked the chairman in amazement.

'Yes, I do,' replied Len sharply. 'They carry batons, not wings, don't they?'

Big Jim laughed loudly and it was immediately taken up by the other people in the public gallery. The police rushed about like hens, bawling: 'Silence! Order!' as loudly as they could.

The chairman, his face purple with injured dignity, warned those present: 'If there is another such unseemly outbreak I shall order the court to be cleared at once.'

Len took no heed of the threat and continued his statement. 'This court has already made its mind up against me,' he declared. 'You are biased from the beginning because I am one of the strikers, and are ready to accept as God's truth every lie that the police have brought against me. This is the first time I have ever been in a court of law, but I've been here long enough to know that no working-man can ever hope to get justice in such a place as this.' He was interrupted again but he took no notice and began shouting to get himself heard above the others. 'If justice is fair, why am I tried by a coalowner instead of by my own fellow workmen?' A policeman stepped into the dock and gripped his arm tightly. This calmed him a little but he gave one parting shot: 'This bench and the police work hand in hand.'

His tirade had electrified the people present and Big Jim was already on his feet when the chairman looked at the other magistrates, slyly nudging the alderman, who had dozed through it all. Each of them nodded assent to something that was unspoken. The chairman then beckoned to the chief constable, who had sat quietly near the clerk throughout the proceedings.

'There are no previous convictions,' he stated, then coughed and rubbed his forefinger along his little moustache, 'but the police know him as a desperate character who associates with revolutionaries and other disorderly elements. He is in the forefront whenever there is any trouble among the workmen, and is always the first fomenting them to acts of violence.'

The magistrates looked sternly at Len during this recital, at the end of which the chairman addressed him. 'We are sorry to see a young man like yourself in this position, charged with such serious crimes against the peace. But we can't tolerate foreign methods of agitation in this country, and in all the circumstances we are agreed that you must go to prison for six months with hard labour.'

An unearthly scream cut through the court like a sword, followed by a mad roar, but Len did not see where the police rushed, as he was hustled down the steps back into the cell out of sight.

MARY JOINS
THE PARTY

During the remainder of the day Len was like a man in a dream. He heard the shouting that continued outside rise on occasions until it became a wild roar that hammered his ears. His whole being yearned to know what was happening; at the same time he wondered how long it would be before they took him from the station to the prison.

It was very dark when at last the cell door opened and he was taken into the charge room, which was full of pale-faced policemen. The chief stepped towards him in an ingratiating manner, saying: 'We want you to be reasonable, Roberts. We are taking you to the railway station, but there are many people outside waiting and we want you to see that they do nothing foolish.' Len sensed at once that the delay in transferring him was due to the fact that the police were afraid of the people. He warmed at the

641

thought, but he said nothing as he fell in between two sergeants, one of whom bent down to whisper:

'If you try to make a dash for it, I'll bash your bloody brains out before you go two steps.'

Len looked up at the threat. 'Don't worry,' he answered; 'I won't run away. If you think I will, why not handcuff me?' holding out his wrists.

The sergeant was about to follow this advice when the chief yelled: 'Put those things back, you damned fool. Do you want the people to tear you to bits?'

Abashed, the sergeant returned the handcuffs to his pocket. Len could not see how many police surrounded him as the procession made for the door and entered the street, where the people were waiting. The lights from the lamps and shop windows seemed to flow with the water on the road and the sight fascinated him, but he raised his head when he heard a terrific shout:

'Here he comes!'

He caught glimpses of the densely packed mass through occasional gaps between the police escort which swayed under the pressure as it slowly forced a path to the railway station, where the train was already panting impatiently.

The police each side of Len gripped him tightly as though they feared he would float away from their ranks on the crest of the shouts that vibrated all over Cwmardy. As they neared the station, outside which a cordon of police was lined, the ranks were broken by a sudden rush and Len found himself surrounded by his own people, among whom were Mary and his parents.

Siân, tears streaming down her cheeks faster than the rain that dripped from her hair, flung her arms about him like a hen covering her chicks before a barking dog.

'They shan't never take you,' she declared, her eyes flashing as her body swayed in the undulating movements made by repeated police dashes into the crowd to recover their prisoner. This only made her crush Len more tightly, and his body had to follow the motions of her own while, his face pressed flat to her breast, he struggled for breath.

During the tumult he felt someone press his hand, and bursting free, he saw Mary beside him, both women guarded by the towering bulk of Big Jim. Mary glowed with excitement as she asked: 'What shall we do? Make a dash for it?'

Len hesitated for a moment, then said: 'No, comrade bach! It will only mean postponing what is bound to come and it will mean more pain for us all. No! Better for me to go now.'

She nodded agreement and kissed him passionately before forcing her way, Jim close behind, back into the middle of the crowd. Len heard voices raised in song; and still clasped tight in Siân's arms and surrounded by people, he began again the walk to the railway station, where the engine was puffing and blowing like a fat man who had run far. The cordon of police opened, then closed behind them; but not before Big Jim and Mary had dashed through and fallen in alongside Len and Siân. The remaining police came running up, and in a short time the platform and waiting-room were full of them. The same two sergeants hurriedly got hold of Len and tore him from

643

Siân's grip, bundling him into a reserved carriage. The other passengers craned their necks through the windows, anxious to see what all the excitement was about.

Siân fought like a mad dog to get into the carriage with Len, but Jim caught her by the shoulders and held her in a vice despite her kicks and threats. The engine gave a piercing scream and the people lifted their song to even greater resonance and strength. Siân wept tears of sheer impotence.

Mary chokingly cried: 'Don't worry, Len; we'll get you out before your time's up.'

Big Jim waved his free hand, and the train slowly gathered a puffing momentum that took Len away from Cwmardy and his people.

Before the people reached their homes, they knew what had happened to Ron's parents. This knowledge and Len's imprisonment pressed on them like a physical weight.

Mary lay awake for the greater part of that night. The heavy air gave her a choking sensation and forced her out of bed. She paced the room for a while, casting an occasional glance at the pillow where Len's head used to rest. She opened the front of her nightdress to let the air cool her chest, but the action only made her think of his hand, and increased her misery. At last she made her mind up, and, picking up the candle, went into her father's room. When she entered, Ezra, still dressed, was brooding over the little fire which he always kept going all night. His hunched shoulders and drawn features made him look very old and ill, and Mary felt for a moment something of the tremendous emotional strain that was tearing at him. The little dancing flames from the fire played over his bent head, giving it a lurid life which his dull eyes, when he looked up at her, betrayed as false.

Mary's heart went soft and moisture dimmed her vision, but she quickly regained control of herself and asked quietly: 'Why in't you in bed, dad?'

Ezra merely shook his head and replied: 'I can't sleep, my dear. My brain is burning with thoughts of Evans Cardi and Len, so what's the good of going to bed?'

She sat near him for a while, laying her head on his shoulder before beginning softly: 'Yes, it's awful. The world is upside down somehow.' She sighed and went on: 'We must get our Len out of jail as soon as possible, dad.'

She felt his bony body quiver when he answered: 'Yes, quite right. But how, my dear, how?'

Mary rose to her feet, the helplessness in his voice astounding her so much that it took her some time to reply. 'We must ask the Federation and the people to have protest demonstrations.'

'But that is the very thing he's in prison for,' was his quick retort.

The words struck Mary like a blow, sending a cold anger through every vein. 'Yes, that's true,' she almost shouted. 'But he wouldn't have been locked up and beaten about if you and the other councillors had done your duty and had been with us on the march.'

The look that leapt to his eyes frightened her, but she went on, although more quietly: 'Oh, dad! Can't you see our Len's in jail because he led a demonstration to you and the council, to his own leaders, and you told the police you didn't want to see us. Didn't this give them the excuse they wanted?'

The gravity of her challenge appalled her after she had made it, and she dropped to her knees near him. 'Oh, dad,' she moaned. 'Can't you see where you are going? Don't you know that Len and the Party are right when they say you are being driven closer to the company and the police every day because you have stopped being a fighter with the people? I have followed you blindly all my life, but now I'm beginning to see how right Len and the Party have been. I know you are still as true, dad; but things have gone beyond you.'

Ezra shook himself like a dog whose coat is full of water or fleas. 'You don't understand, my dear,' he said bitterly. 'The councillors know better than you or Len or his Party what our people are suffering, and no one feels this more than us. Don't forget that Len hasn't got a monopoly of sympathy for the poor. But our hands are tied at every turn. Yes.' He paused awhile and bent to the fire again, to continue sadly: 'It's true we have a majority on the council, but we can do nothing with it, because we have no money and the Government hems us in at every point. Hundreds of pounds are spent in relief for the strikers and income from the rates is falling every week.'

Mary felt the room go black and rose agitatedly to her feet. Ezra's gaze followed her, and he saw the thin limbs shadowed dimly on her nightdress as she paced the room. A hard lump rose to his throat, breaking through his efforts to keep it down. To cover his discomfiture he tried to speak harshly and aggressively.

'Why should Len help those Bolshies to bring the people against me just because I am a councillor? Isn't he concerned any longer about the company, that he wants to fight me and the other leaders? None of us can do the impossible, and he has only got himself to blame for what has happened. I've told him times out of number to come away from Harry Morgan and the gang mixed up with him, who think of nothing else but disorder, and everybody but themselves as traitors.'

His daughter stopped her restless walking and drawing near looked steadily into his eyes. 'So your enemy isn't the company any more, dad?' she grated through her teeth, even while she hated what she was saying. 'It's now your own workpeople, like Len and Harry.' She broke down and stopped, although no tears came to help her; then went on pleadingly: 'Oh, dad! Why don't you join forces with them instead of thinking them to be wasters and enemies?'

Ezra caught her by the shoulders rather roughly, his mouth a thin strip that added to the shadows on his cheeks. 'How can I join with people who have nothing in common with me? All that I believe in and fought for they think is "Social-Fascist" and "reactionary". In all their meetings they say openly that everything I have done has helped to betray my people.' The gall in his words thickened. 'How can I join with people who believe in violence and revolution, who want to use the Federation and the whole Labour movement to this end, who act like spies in every organisation?' He lowered his voice. 'No, Mary; to join with them would be to betray all I have lived and struggled for.'

647

Mary drew herself from his grasp and made quietly, as though she were afraid of disturbing something, to the door, where she turned to say sadly: 'All right, dad. Let's hope that by refusing to work with them you'll never find yourself in the position of having to work with the company and all that it stands for; although, God help me, whatever you did, I would still love you.'

Ezra half started forward, but she closed the door and went back to her own room before he could say any more.

Next morning she got out of bed flushed and heavy. Her chest burned with a cough that tore her lungs and left her listless. But despite this she hurried over her housework and prepared breakfast for her father, who had not yet come down. She thought once of going out without seeing him, but changed her mind and went upstairs to his room. She saw at once that he had not slept all night, and a wave of solicitude swept over her.

She bent down and kissed him on the forehead. He began stroking her hair and presently his fingers were caressing the lobe of her ear. The old affectionate touch revived sentimental memories and she murmured softly: 'Forgive me, dad, for speaking like I did last night. You see, dear, it isn't my fault, is it, if I now see things with different eyes? But whatever happens I'll always love you as much in the future as I have in the past.'

He drew her to him and whispered half sadly, half triumphantly: 'I know, my dear. I know that you will never desert me. But I can't understand. I have tried to teach you all I know, and now it looks as if the very things I taught you are weapons you use against me.' His brow puckered into a puzzled frown. 'Something strange is happening. Things are moving too fast for me,' he sighed, and added: 'Let's leave it all there, Mary. Let's keep as father and daughter and keep politics outside the front door.'

He followed her down the stairs and looked wistfully after her when she went out, leaving him alone with his breakfast.

Some hours later, she saw Harry Morgan walking towards Ben the Barber's, and, quickening her pace, she caught up with him before he entered the shop.

'I've been looking for you all the morning,' she exclaimed a little breathlessly.

He made no reply, but waited for her next remark.

'I want to see you about our Len.'

'Well, what about him?' was the curt retort, which took Mary aback somewhat. But she soon recovered her composure, although she went a little paler.

'I thought he was a comrade and that you and the others would be worried about what's happened to him.'

He softened when he realised how she was suffering. 'We are, Mary. In fact, I have called a special Party meeting to discuss it now, and that's why I can't talk about it with you, because you are not a Party member and we haven't yet worked out a line on it.'

Mary looked perplexed. 'Can't discuss it?' she repeated questioningly. 'Why not? In't I interested in the business as well as you, and haven't I got the same principles as your Party?'

Harry laughed shortly and retorted: 'That's what they

all say. But you can't be a Communist outside the Party.'

Mary started to say something, stopped, then said something else. 'But Len always told me that Communists are not born, they are made. Experience, knowledge, life, struggle is necessary to make us into Communists, and it is your place to help us into the Party, not put obstacles in our way.'

Harry blushed a deep red at the reproof, and Mary, turning her back, walked away with her head held high and her teeth clenched hard.

Later in the day, Mary called up to see Siân, whom she found busily washing clothes. The old woman was flushed with exertion and heat from the steaming water in the tub, when she rose to greet her daughter-in-law. She hastily wiped her hands in her apron, while Big Jim sat morosely in the armchair, smoking his favourite clay pipe, which sent Mary into a racking cough.

Solicitously knocking out the hot ash, he invited her to sit on the stool near the fire, with the kind advice: 'You will find that big enough for your little arse, Mary fach.'

Siân glared at him, but he took no notice, and in disgust she turned to Mary.

'Why are you washing so early in the week, mam?' the latter asked, more to gain time than information.

'Oh, my gel! I must do something to forget our little Len in that awful prison, as if he was a fief or a murderer, God bless him.'

She raised her apron to her nose and began to sniffle.

Jim grunted audibly, and said to Mary: 'I hope to Christ your nose will never come like Siân's, my gel. It is worse than a bloody tap that is leaking before you touch it. I never seed such a 'ooman in my life for crying, muniferni.'

His own eyes looked a little wet as he said this. Mary feared that Siân would take up the challenge and start a quarrel, so she joined the conversation.

'I must start washing as soon as I can, too, so that our Len can have a change of underclothes. He's had the ones he's got on for over a week now.'

Jim growled: 'It's no good your doing that, because they 'on't let him have them. You see, he's in a jail, not a infirmary.'

Siân dried her tears and stared at him as though she thought he had suddenly lost his senses. 'What you said? 'On't let my boy have his own clothes? Huh! Why not, James? Don't forget that you are not boss of the jail yet, big man though you think you are.'

Jim tried to patiently explain to her, but she interrupted him with a snarl. 'The jawled! God forgive me for saying such words! To smash my boy up, then put him in jail for nothink, where he will have to mix up with all the old riff-raff that I have never reared him up to.'

Jim interrupted her. 'Shut up, mun! Good God! What if he was in a military jail, like his father have been? It 'ood be time enough to make all this fuss, muniferni.' He turned to Mary. 'Did I ever tell you, Mary fach, about the time they put me in jail on the Rock?'

He went no further with his contemplated anecdote. 'It is all right for you to talk,' Siân interjected. 'You are big enough and dull enough to take care of yourself; but our Len have only once been away from his own home, and is

651

not used to roughing it like you old rodneys in the militia.'

Jim stretched himself to his full height. 'Don't you dare to say to my face, 'ooman, that I was in the militia! I am a guardsman and have been all my life.'

Mary warded off Siân's ready attack. 'It's no good us worrying,' she told the old woman, who again put the apron to her nose. 'It won't do Len any good and would only make him miserable if he knew.'

She remained with them for some time longer, and, after she had sipped down the tea which Siân insisted she should drink, she went wearily home.

She did not go outside the door for some time after this visit. She felt ill and depressed, but one day while doing some shopping she heard someone shouting, and hurried her steps till she came to a meeting being addressed by Harry Morgan. This was the first time Mary had seen him since their altercation. He stood on a beer box, borrowed from the Boar's Head, and she noticed there were very few women among the crowd of fifty or so that listened to the speaker. Harry's face was shining with the perspiration induced by the vigour of his gesticulations, but Mary would have passed on had she not heard him refer to her father.

'The Reformists have become Social-Fascist,' he announced, 'and Ezra is the leader of them.'

Something cold clutched at her heart, and she felt her whole body shrink as Harry went on.

'If the councillors fed our children in the schools, if they had joined with us on the demonstration, Len would now be among us instead of rotting in a prison cell.'

The truth of the statement paralysed Mary for a moment, until she saw Ron standing near the box, holding a red banner. The tragic death of his parents recurred to her immediately, and she scrutinised him more closely. He looked much thinner and taller than when she had last seen him, but he bore himself in the same proud manner as hitherto. She had heard he was now lodging with Will Evans' mother, but that he intended going away shortly to look for work.

When Harry had finished speaking, Ron took his place on the box. His cultivated voice and calm demeanour gave added weight to the sentiments he expressed, sentiments which were echoes of what had already been said. But his presence upon the box excited Mary and turned her thoughts to Len, who was responsible for this transformation in Ron. She kept thinking of this all the way home, and was unusually quiet for the remainder of the day. Ezra noticed this and attributed it to her depression.

'Come with me to the public meeting organised by the Labour Party tonight?' he asked her.

She was on the point of refusing, then remembered it would give him pleasure, and consented with a thin smile. Ezra found a place for her in the gallery of the theatre where the meeting was held, then left her to take the chair. The platform was full of local notabilities, among whom she noticed the M.P. for Cwmardy; but for some reason her attention was mainly fixed upon the dress and appearance of the people on the platform. They looked so prosperous, and she could not help comparing them with the strikers and the street-corner meeting in the afternoon. She glanced about and noticed that Ron, Harry, Will

653

Evans, and other members of the Party were scattered about the hall. Ezra opened the meeting and welcomed the M.P., who had just arrived.

The latter spoke of the strike and what he had done in all parts of the country to bring it to a victorious end. Then he complimented the people of Cwmardy on their patience, and deplored the action of the Communists, that had brought Cwmardy into disrepute and had landed one of their number in jail.

Mary's blood coursed through her like hot lead, and she sprang to her feet, waving her arms wildly, while she shouted: 'Withdraw that. You are talking about my husband.'

The speaker smiled tolerantly and tried to continue as though he had not heard the interruption, but from various parts of the hall other cries arose and drowned his voice.

'Withdraw that statement! Give the girl a chance!'

This support gave Mary strength and made her more determined. She rushed from the gallery, down the stairs, and entered the floor of the hall, by which time Ezra was on his feet trying to get order. After a while the noise subsided and the speaker began again, only to be checked by Mary's voice.

'Withdraw that statement. Let me come on the platform!'

The Party members edged towards her and uproar broke out once more. Mary kept on shouting, hardly knowing what she said in her excitement. She saw those on the stage hold a hurried consultation with her father, and forced herself forward towards them; Ron and Harry, although she was not aware of it, were at her side. She reached the front

654

of the stage, all the people now on their feet and shouting, and with the help of Harry and Ron scrambled up. As she did so, the others on the platform, including Ezra, left it, so that when she looked around it was empty.

She gazed dumbly at the huge blur of faces that confronted her, and her courage oozed away as she realised that, having captured the platform, the people now expected her to say something. She opened her mouth and heard a pitiful little squeal which made her close it again sharply.

Harry, who had scrambled on the platform behind her, growled: 'Go on, mun. For God's sake say something, or let me do it for you.'

The remark made Mary brace herself, and she stepped forward to the edge of the stage, where, for the first time in her life, she made a speech.

Her concluding words were accompanied by a burst of applause, after which Harry took control of the meeting, making it one of protest against the imprisonment of Len. Mary remembered very little of what happened after this, but before she reached home, she had joined the Party.

About two months after the meeting and Mary's entry into the Party, she went with Big Jim and Siân on a visit to Len. Siân spent the whole morning making little round cakes on the bakestone, and insisted on packing these up despite all advice that Len would not be permitted to have them.

The massive, stony aloofness of the prison awed the two women, but Jim strutted up to the huge iron gate as though it belonged to him. The bell he rung announced their presence with a sonorous austerity that chilled Siân's blood.

While they waited for the gate to open, Mary read aloud the big printed notice informing visitors of all the things they could not do if they wanted to come back out. Siân listened attentively, and when Mary had finished handed the parcel of cakes to the first child that came along.

They entered the little cubby, where Len was waiting for them. His face was sallow and thinner, but his eyes were clear and his whole body seemed to beam a welcome when they entered. Siân tried to touch his feet with hers beneath the table that parted them, but it was too wide and she had to give up the attempt, at the same time squinting from the corner of her eyes at the warder who stood rigidly at the end.

Len explained: 'We are meeting in by here as a special favour from the governor. I asked him not to let you come to the usual place because I knew it would upset you to see me behind glass and bars, like they have in the other place for visitors.'

His words were hurried and excited, as though he had to say something quickly to maintain a grip upon himself, but after the first spasm of emotion generated by the sight of them, he held himself in check.

Mary told him all the news and he supplemented her information with questions which he shot at her like machine-gun bullets. While this was taking place, Jim, trying to whisper quietly, but every word audible to the others, was telling the officer of the time when he was himself a warder in the military prison at Gibraltar.

'Aye,' he said reminiscently, with a faraway look. 'I have spent most of my time in gaol, between one thing

656

and another. But, mind you, butty, I am not sorry for it. No, indeed! Not by a long shot. There's many a poor old dab in the cemetery who 'ood be glad of the chance to be in gaol now.'

But Len did not hear this. His whole attention had been diverted by Mary's news that the strike was on the point of collapse, and he felt heavy as lead when she told him that one of the coalfields had broken away from the strike and made a separate agreement. There was an awkward pause after this.

No one knew what to say until Mary tried to relieve the tension by saying: 'Oh Len, I've joined the Party,' and plunging into an account of the eventful meeting.

This lightened Len's despondency, and the little gathering became more cheerful. Not a word was spoken of Ezra, although Len was bursting to know what he was doing.

All this time Siân had been eyeing his clothes, and on several occasions had opened her mouth to say something, but thought better of it. Now, however, she could contain herself no longer. 'What is them old sacks they have put on you, Len bach?' she queried.

Len gave a hasty and somewhat guilty glance at his suit before replying: 'Oh, this is the clothes they give to all prisoners, mam.'

Jim was about to add something, but Siân silenced him with a look. 'Well, I am going to see the manager of this place about it. I have never reared a child of mine to put on clothes from other people's backs, and I am too old to let anybody start doing that to my own flesh and blood now.'

Len hastened to placate her, but only finally succeeded

657

after he had told a few lies about the good treatment he was having.

'It is like being home,' he asserted with a twist of his lips that he thought was a smile. 'All I do miss, mam, is the sight of you and dad and Mary. And what do you think? The first day I came here they put a lovely Bible on my table, and I've got it ever since.'

This finally dissipated any doubts she had. The warder now announced that their time was nearly up, and this news damped their spirits like a wet blanket. Mary sensed the loneliness induced in Len by the information, and choked back her own tears in an effort to cheer him up.

'It won't be long now,' she consoled, 'before you'll be with us again and back in the fight. All the people are waiting to welcome you, and Cwmardy will be like a flag-day when you come out.'

Len saw through the attempt to cheer him, but it warmed his heart. 'Don't worry about me, comrade,' he said. 'Look after mam and dad. I'm sure of food and shelter here, but our people outside are sure of nothing.'

They caressed each other with their eyes before they parted, and Len was led away.

One day shortly after the visit to Len, and twelve months after the beginning of the strike, news reached the valley that the national leaders had called the strike off, and were advising the men to make the best terms possible in their own areas so that they could restart work immediately. Ezra and the committee called a general meeting where the position was explained to the people, whose haggard faces were bitter. There was no singing or cheering as Ezra pronounced their defeat, and when the meeting ended the people walked home with the same slow, measured steps they took at a funeral.

BREAKING POINT

When Len was released from prison he found Cwmardy like a cemetery, although he received a joyful welcome at a meeting organised by the Party for this purpose. He had only been out a few days before he felt a weight press on him as the deadly blackness of the valley caught hold of him, and made the 'chug-chug' of the pit engine sound like a wail. Mary was also affected by his depression, especially the night she told him all that had happened since his imprisonment.

'The company is only taking its favourites back,' she reported. 'And they are bringing in scores of men from over the mountain to work the pit. Our own men have left the Federation and the company is forcing them into its own non-political union. Everything is topsy-turvy, with everyone fighting for himself. They tell me,' she continued, when he made no remark, 'that things are worse than they have ever been and everybody is afraid to open their mouths for fear they'll be sent up the pit.'

She made no mention of her father, and although he noticed the omission he did not comment on it. When she had finished, he remained silent for a long while, then caught her in his arms and buried his face on her shoulder. She knew the mood, but left him alone with his thoughts, while she stroked his hair. He trembled at the touch and raised his head to look at her. The shadows he saw on her face darkened his own, and he murmured huskily:

'Mary, my comrade, what's going to happen to our people? To think, after all the battles they have fought and the things they have suffered, that they are now beat and broken up makes me sad.' He turned away as though this helped him to think better, then burst out: 'But it's not them who are to be blamed; it's those who let them down and betrayed them.' He lost his temper and began to shout angrily: 'This is what comes from lack of faith. Aye, by gum, this is what compromising with the company means – no organisation, no confidence, every man for himself and to hell with everybody else. No wonder the company is doing what it likes with us.'

She eventually calmed him with the reminder that moaning would help no one. Her coolness strengthened him, and they talked of other things till it was time to go to bed.

They had hardly finished their breakfast next morning, when Harry, Ron, and Will Evans walked in after a preliminary brief rap on the door. Len was glad of their company, although he hardly knew how to talk to Ron in case he said something that would revive the terrible tragedy. But after the first awkward preliminaries Will, as usual, gave the conversation a light turn.

'By gum, Len,' he said, looking him up and down with his head screwed on one side to get a more comprehensive view, 'prison have done you good, mun. You look more like a man now than I have ever seen you.'

Len laughed and turned to Harry, who was placidly poking the fire, while Mary cleared the breakfast dishes.

'How is the Party going, since I've been away, Harry?'

'Very good,' was the reply. 'Mary is a trump and is fast getting one of our best speakers.'

Len blushed and went warm all over. He hoped Harry would keep on talking about her, but the latter changed the subject.

'There's not much chance of the company taking you back to the pit, now they've got an opportunity to keep you out,' he said.

Len started forward in his chair, but the other gave him no time to say anything.

'That means you'll have to sign on the dole, like the others who're not likely to start back again. We've been talking about it, haven't we, boys?' turning to the others, who nodded acquiescence, although they didn't know what he had in mind. 'And we think your Party job is to get the unemployed organised on the exchange.'

'But what about the Federation?' asked Len in a puzzled voice.

'Oh that's finished as far as the unemployed are concerned.'

Len still looked dubious, but made no further comment other than to ask, 'What do you expect me to do?'

Ron helped him. 'Since you've been inside,' he explained, 'we have been holding meetings outside the exchange each signing day. Most of the speaking has been done by myself and Mary, because Harry is away in other parts of the country very often now. We've had some of the unemployed to join up, but we must get them all. The Party thinks you can do this better than any of us.'

Len sensed the implied compliment but for some reason did not feel flattered.

Shortly after this they left, Ron remaining behind for a moment to say he intended leaving the valley at the end of the week, as some friends were hopeful of getting a position for him elsewhere. The news saddened Len, but he made no effort to dissuade his friend.

Late the same afternoon, Len strolled down to see his father, who had just bathed and was beginning to enjoy a smoke when he entered.

Siân bustled to get her son a chair, and after he had settled himself, Len asked: 'How's things going in the pit, dad?'

Jim drew the black clay-pipe from his mouth, looked at it a few moments, then spat in the fire before saying:

'Hellish, Len bach. Hellish! The company is making it a proper bloody muck-hole. Aye,' he went on prophetically, 'one day, there'll be another blow up; then everybody will be saying "pity the poor miner". Pity to hell!' he shouted in sudden temper, while Siân glowered at him reprovingly. 'There is no need for it, if the company 'ood only work the pit as she ought to be worked. Huh! I hope you will never come back to it, Len bach. It's not fit for a dog, let alone decent men.'

He paused, then added confidentially: 'Do you know, Len bach, they have got spies in the pit now, and if us won't join the new union, they give us the sack. What think you to that, my boy?'

'Ha! So that's it, is it, dad? Well, I'll be up with you in the morning to get my old place back.'

Jim stared at his son in amazement, then burst out laughing. 'Your place back? Ha-ha! There is no bloody place there for you now, mun. We work here today, there tomorrow, and God knows where the day after. Not only this, mind you. If you do say anything about it, the officials get shirty straight away and are not behind in telling you that if you are not willing to do it, there is plenty on top of the pit who 'ood be only too glad of the chance. No, Len. There is not much hopes of you getting back, and if you did, you wouldn't be there a day, muniferni.'

Jim painfully eased his body from the chair, tapped the bowl of his pipe on the hob, and made his way to the stairs, where he remarked: 'I'm going to bed. Bring my supper up, Siân.'

Len said nothing as he watched the bent bulk of his father go up the stairs, but Siân sighed.

'Your dad is breaking fast, Len. Aye, indeed, fancy going to bed this time of day! Well, well! He have had his best days and will never again be the man that he was. The work is killing him now. Well, well! And to think I do 'member the time when he could eat it.'

665

Len rose with the first hooter at five o'clock next morning. Mary was already down, warming his working clothes and making breakfast. She looked more frail than usual, and her actions as she moved about were eloquent of weariness. 'All this is waste,' she grumbled. 'Why can't you listen to sense, Len? We could be in bed now, instead of potching about down here for nothing.'

He took no notice of her plaint and after he had finished his breakfast caught her to him and kissed her. 'Go back to bed, my dear, you're tired,' he said.

He found his father groaning and grunting as he struggled to pull a singlet over his head, unnecessarily shaking it and paying no heed to the cloud of dust which scattered all over the little kitchen. Jim looked for his pants among the remainder of the pit clothes drying on the rod before the fire, but failed to find them.

'Arglwydd mawr,' he howled, 'do you 'spect me to go to work naked, that you haven't put out my pants to air?' Siân glared at him, but made no reply as he flung the clothes from the rod to the floor, increasing the dust that was already heavy on the furniture.

Len helped him. 'You are sitting on them, dad.'

Jim rose from his chair as though it contained a pin, looked down dazedly for a moment, then said half apologetically: 'Well, well. Whoever 'ood think of that, now. Fancy me sitting on my own pants and not knowing it. Ha-ha!' The laugh sounded empty and Siân knew it to be an attempt to cover his discomfiture.

Before leaving for the pit, Jim warned his son: 'You are only wasting your time, Len. There is no work there for you, and you will only have to bath all over agen for nothink.'

'Perhaps you're right, dad, but there's no harm in trying.'

They bade Siân good morning, the latter responding with the remark, 'I will wait down till you come back, Len.'

The two men silently joined the long human line winding up the hill to the pit. Len noticed a large number of strangers, but said nothing until half-way to the pits, when a hooter suddenly blasted the morning. He looked at his father in surprise.

'What hooter is that, dad?' he asked, unconsciously quickening his stride.

'Oh, that is a new stunt by the company. All the men have got to have their lamps out ten minutes before the last hooter do blow or they shan't go down.'

Len would have asked more questions, but he had to save his breath to keep pace with Jim, whose gasps were mixed with curses as he practically ran to the pit, all the other men doing likewise.

They had passed the colliery office and were about to go across the bridge when someone shouted harshly behind: 'Ay, there. You by Big Jim. Where the bloody hell do you think you are going to?'

Len stopped in surprise and looked back to see the colliery policeman hurrying towards him with waving arms. Big Jim stopped with Len, but the other men hurried on their way and took no notice.

The sergeant hustled importantly up to Len, and caught him roughly by the arm. 'Come on, where are you going?'

It was Jim who replied, 'If he's coming the same place

as me, butty, it's to the bloody workhouse.'

'That's enough of it, Jim. Nobody's talking to you,' said the sergeant before turning his attention to Len. 'Come on. Back past that bloody office you go, and quick if you know what is good for you.'

Len saw his father's face go white as snow, then red as blood, and knew something was about to happen.

'Ha,' said the old man. 'At last. Just the chance I have been waiting for, muniferni.' He placed his box and jack carefully on the ground and began pulling off his coat, talking gloatingly all the while like a man about to experience a long-desired pleasure. 'You is a hell of a big man and thirty years younger than me, but never mind about that, because you is just about my dap. Aye, butty. You have had your fling long enough. Now one of us have got to pay the tune, and you can venture it 'on't be Big Jim that is going to pay.' His coat was off by now and he pranced up to the sergeant with his fists outstretched, but the latter, seeing the move, had drawn his baton in readiness. Len stepped between them.

'Don't be silly, dad. You'll only get the wrong end of the stick in the long run. Put your coat back and hurry or you'll lose the pit. He won't do anything to me.'

Jim reluctantly obeyed. 'Better not for him to, mun jawli. Huh! A big man like that pulling his truncheon out like a babby. But there, I always did say they have got no guts and that us can beat 'em every time, man to man.' He continued talking to himself as he made his way over the bridge. When he neared its end he turned and shouted: 'If you do fancy your hand, butty, wait for me on

668

top of the pit finishing time and I will be with you. Good morning, Len bach. If he do say anything out of the way to you, us will settle it tonight.' Len saw him put his hand to his back and walk painfully out of sight.

He paid no further heed to the sergeant and retraced his steps down the hill. Siân was waiting for him, as she had promised, but he told her nothing of the occurrence.

'Us did tell you that you was wasting your time,' she scolded.

'I know, mam. But it was better for me to see for myself, wasn't it?'

When he got home and had bathed, Mary tried to coax him to go to bed for a while, but his brain was too restless to permit him to lie down. All day he was tormented by the transformation that had taken place in Cwmardy. He likened the pit to a fortress which had to be besieged before entry could be gained, and even then it could only be done if he allowed himself to be chained and guarded. The thought galled him, because all his life had been spent in and around the pit and its every throb palpitated through him like blood. He remembered the books he had read and the speeches he had heard since he was in the Party, and subconsciously he began to tell himself that the pits really belonged to the people and not to the company. This reminded him of some of the arguments he had had with Mary before she joined the Party, and again he thought of the struggle for power.

'That's what it means,' he mused to himself. 'And the Party is right. Power to take over the pits for the people who work and die in them.' He paused a moment, then told himself: 'That means revolution, because Lord Cwmardy and his tribe will never give them up.' The conviction soothed him, somehow, and he felt happier because of it.

For many months after this he devoted himself to propaganda on the labour exchange, trying to get his old workmates organised as unemployed. Every signing day Mary and other members of the Party stood on the little wall that separated the exchange from the row of ramshackle houses facing it. From this vantage point they addressed the queues of unemployed, until Len eventually became known as the mouthpiece and leader of the local Communists. The people found his direct statements and eloquence very attractive, and always listened attentively to all he had to say. The long unemployment was painting a premature oldness on him, but these activities prevented his becoming demoralised. Every Tuesday evening he and the other Communists met in a room lent them by old John Library, who had always prided himself on his advanced views and was affectionately regarded by the people as the philosopher of the oppressed. At these meetings, the Communists discussed for hours the problems confronting the workers and themselves. Each year these became more complex and confusing, until the Party was forced to intensify the political training of its members. Len was given the role of trainer in Cwmardy – a role that was the logical outcome of his tremendous influence with the people and prestige in the Party.

Always during the summer months, Len, whenever he had an hour to spare from his activities, tried to coax

Mary to the mountains. Sometimes she refused for some reason, and on these occasions he went up alone and wandered aimlessly about, always eventually finding himself on a spot overlooking the Big House and the pits. One day, when the whole world was centred on Leipzig, Len, his thoughts fixed on Dimitrov, reached this point. He sat down in deep meditation for a while, before he saw what he thought was a familiar figure slowly make its way up the drive to the Big House. The more he watched, the more convinced he became it was Ezra, and began to wonder what reason prompted the visit of the miners' leader to the den of his enemy. He failed to find a motive, and was at last urged by the encroaching darkness back into the valley, where he met Mary, who said she had been looking all over the place for him. He noticed her wildness and broken breath, but asked no questions until they found a secluded spot where they could talk without being overheard. Something in her attitude bred a faint uneasiness in him, and he felt half afraid of the news she had, before she told it. He tried to soothe her, but she brushed the effort away impatiently, at the same time saying: 'Don't, Len. I've got something awful to tell you, and we can't run away from it.'

The words killed the impulse beginning to work within him, and he waited quietly for her to explain. The humid air, heavy with dampness, hung over the valley like a weight, emphasising the turmoil of the life it contained. The people who occasionally passed were silent, like bent shadows emerging from the darkness only to be buried in it again a moment later.

671

Mary sighed and her hand searched for Len's, the thin fingers pressing his convulsively. At last she spoke again. 'I can't tell you up the house, Len. I've got to be outside, the house seems to be a part of what I want to say. Oh, Len, dad has been up to Lord Cwmardy, who's given him a job in the office if he'll finish with the Federation.'

The last words left her mouth in one burst, after which there was silence, while the young couple watched the burning glow from the pit furnaces. It seemed to crush the darkness with a grip that made the Big House look like a castle cut out of the hard bosom of the mountain.

When Len spoke the tones were low and emphatic. 'It can't be true. I don't believe it.' He suddenly caught her to him and felt the broken breathing that shook her body. The tremor made him weak, and he tried to avoid the fact contained in her words. 'No, I'll never believe it. Ezra would never take a favour from his greatest enemy and sell his own fellow workmen to get it.'

Mary shook herself free from the hard clutch of his hands and said resignedly: 'Come. Let's go up the house to see him. Perhaps it's not too late even now,' she added hopefully.

On the way up he kept muttering: 'Good God! To think what our comrades in Germany are suffering, while we have to fight such things as this. Good God!'

They found Ezra pacing the kitchen in a manner that reminded Len of himself in the prison cell. He saw the struggle that had taken place pressed into the lines and furrows of the old leader's face and in the once vitalising eyes whose flame was now quenched.

672

The tragedy of the transformation gave Len the burning sensation of a bile and made him regret his mutterings. He walked towards the chair into which Ezra had sunk on their entry, and without any preamble pleaded: 'Ezra, don't leave us. Don't let all that you've done for our people be buried in a colliery office. Remember you still belong to them and they'll come back to you again if you have patience and faith.'

Ezra rose to his feet and began pacing the room again as Len went on: 'Hell, man, don't sell out to the company after all these years of fighting. Think of Dimitrov facing the might and horror of German Fascism on his own.'

Ezra stopped with a quiver at these last words, then turned sharply round to face his son-in-law. 'Who are you to talk of my actions and my future?' he demanded harshly. 'You and the gang you follow! Haven't you publicly branded me as a renegade and a rat before the people you profess to love? In't you responsible for making them desert me and –' he hesitated a second and fixed his gaze on Mary, then concluded – 'yes, turned my own daughter against me. Would Dimitrov have done that?'

Mary started to say something, but her father paid no attention as he continued in tones of implacable conviction: 'I have been deserted because of the dirty lies bred in the mouths of your Party members, and I'm now, after forty years' service, alone, friendless, and penniless. This is the reward for my devotion.'

Len stepped nearer him with an eager interruption. 'But if you hang on a bit longer, Ezra, I'm sure the men will come back to the Federation. They're bound to. It's in their bones and their hearts.'

Ezra looked him deep in the eyes before replying. 'Must I live till then on air?' Or do you want me to use my influence to get a job that belongs to other people? No,' he answered himself with a shout, and the next words came with increasing momentum, 'I'd sooner go to the enemy and say, "I'm defeated, Cwmardy, and helpless. My fight is over and I ask you to let me do something for the short time that is left to me".' He paused to gather strength, then said: 'This need never have been if you and Harry Morgan hadn't brought your foreign theories into our valley.'

Mary raised her gaze from the fire to say sadly: 'That's not fair, dad. If Len is a foreigner, then I am one, because the both of us and yourself have been reared with the valley. All we have been through, all we know and do comes to us from the valley and the people. If the Party thinks different from you, dad, it's not because we are against you, but because we believe you are wrong. There's nothing foreign in learning to do the right things for the struggle of our people, is there? Oh, dad,' she moaned, rising to her feet and catching his arm affectionately, 'there's no need for you to take this job that Lord Cwmardy throws to you like we throw a crumb to a dog. You know we can live happy together by here for the rest of our lives.' Her voice broke and she began to sob softly.

Ezra's head bent lower with each sentence. The silence that followed made the cracking flames roar like thunder. At last he shook himself and looked up to say: 'It's no good, Mary. I don't want anyone to keep me. I can keep myself in the future as I've had to do in the past, ever since that day I took your mother to her grave and came back with you in my arms to an empty world. Yes, just like that, Mary. To a world whose very fullness made it empty of happiness and peace. That's what I want, what I've been hungering after for years... peace. All my life has been a fight, and the little that is now left me I want for myself.'

Some of his old strength found expression in the adamant finality of these last words, and the others, realising this, said no more. Shortly after, Len and Mary left the kitchen like people leaving a tomb.

When the men left the pit next day and filed in a long, ever-lengthening string across the bridge, they looked in amazement through the office windows at the bowed shoulders and grey hair of Ezra, with a pen in his hand and a huge ledger before him. He did not raise his eyes from the book and he was deaf to the remarks that spanged against the window panes. On the way to their homes the men could talk of nothing else. Will Smallbeer was the most vociferous.

'Leaders, muniferni,' he growled to those with him. 'What did I tell you years ago? Didn't I say put a beggar on a horse and he'll gallop to hell? By hell! You can all see now that old Smallbeer was right, mun jawli. They're all the same, give 'em half a chance and they'll sell you.'

Big Jim thought of Len, and grunted: 'Huh! Us can't blame a man for that, mun. It is human nature. A man have got to live whatever he is, and you can't throw blame on Ezra when rotters like you do leave the Federashon and let him starve in the gutter. No, muniferni. I tell you boys straight, I 'ood do the same my bloody self if you played

675

that trick on me.'

Most of the older men felt Jim's sentiments were correct, but the younger ones were equally vehement in their condemnation of Ezra's action.

EZRA'S DEATH

For many months Len could not bring himself to concentrate on the significance of the change in Ezra's outlook and action. He subconsciously felt the tremendous personal tragedy embodied in the event, but hesitated to put into words the forces and ideas that had shattered so strong a man as Ezra. Len was pulled two ways, by his affection for his old leader and by the logic of the struggle against Fascism and war developing throughout the world. His own experience in the Party showed him the one way out, but the fact that he was still living in the same house as Ezra tended to make him subjective. At the same time he was worried about his own position. It hurt him to know that his father came home from the pit each day more bent and painful, while he himself remained to all intents and purposes idle around the streets and in meetings.

The horrible sense of dependence and inaction made him morbid. His body had been moulded in the pit and he felt it calling him like the pangs of hunger, a feeling he tried to escape by throwing himself even more vigorously into the work of the Party. The clear division of the people into employed and unemployed and the chaotic state of disorganisation among both sections appalled him. These things and the collapse of the official Labour Movement in many parts of the world became the basis for most of the discussions in the library. It became increasingly evident there was not unanimity in the ranks of the Party. One or two, led by Fred Lewis, concentrated on local affairs and were of the opinion that the only way to save the Federation and unite the employed and unemployed was by fighting for the appointment of a full-time agent in place of Ezra. The others, led by Len and Mary, thought the first thing to be done was to explain the dangers of Fascism to the people of Cwmardy, to get them back into the Federation as a basis for other things. The controversy lasted for weeks and became very bitter. At one meeting Fred Lewis accused Len and Mary of being influenced by the fact that they were related to Ezra and were jealous of anyone else taking his place.

Mary got up immediately the accusation was made and asked: 'All right. Assuming your line is right, Fred, who do you think we should fight for to be the miners' agent?'

Without hesitation, just as though he had already decided and the answer was involuntary, Fred replied: 'Myself, of course. Who else is there in the Party who could do it?'

678

This brought matters to a head, and Harry Morgan, who now worked for the Party nationally, was sent for to help. A special meeting was held to thrash the business out finally. Will Evans was elected the chairman, and opened the meeting with the statement: 'This is going to be a most important meeting, comrades, because what we decide here tonight will be the policy of our Party that all of us will have to fight for in Cwmardy. I call on comrade Mary Roberts to give a report of what have happened up to date. After she have finished, we will have a statement by Harry. Then there will be open discussion, and we hope none of you will keep anything back. If you have got anything to say, let's have it straight out on the table, so that all of us will know where we are.'

Mary spent very little time tracing the changes that had taken place in Cwmardy and the consequent differences in the Party. Harry Morgan followed with a survey of the political situation in general and its bearing upon the position in Cwmardy and the line of the Party; but he did not commit himself on the issue before the meeting.

Len was the first to take part in the discussion. There was a tense feeling of alertness among all present when he asked for the floor. Mary inwardly prayed that he would keep calm and remember he was not in a propaganda meeting.

'Our Party,' he began, 'is based on loyalty to majority decisions, even if we in the minority are against that decision. This in my opinion is the only way we can work as a Party that has got to organise a revolution. But this revolution is not a thing of a moment; it doesn't float down to us from the air or bubble up from the earth. No.

679

It is made in the struggles and tribulations of our people, it is born in the conditions that are imposed upon our people by the capitalists, conditions that can only be altered by taking power out of the hands of the ruling class. But the problem for us is, how? Yes, that's the problem, because what we do in small things will determine the form of the big ones, and what we do in Cwmardy on this issue must be done in such a way that it helps all the people forward into organisation and unity, not only against the company but against the Government.' He stopped a moment to clear his throat, then without taking his solemn eyes from the chairman he continued: 'I say, before we can begin talking of new officials, we have got to build organisation to such a pitch that full-time officials will be necessary. We are not there yet because our people have lost faith in the leaders who have let them down so often. And we can't blame them. Let's build the Fed, smash the non-pols, and get the people to elect a committee to lead them. After we do this, then perhaps we will be able to think of another miners' agent instead of Ezra.'

He sat down, to be followed immediately by Fred Lewis, who wasted no time with preamble. 'If we follow Len's line, we'll neither have a Federation or a Party,' he declared. 'How can you expect organisation unless you have leaders to build it?'

A voice asked: 'Isn't our Party the leader?'

Fred retorted promptly: 'Yes it is, but our Party is made up of individuals, of men and women, not rag dolls, and that's why I say we must put one of our members forward for this position.'

The discussion went on for hours before Harry summed up all that had been said. 'I think Len's line is the right one. Build the organisation first, then the people can elect their leaders after.'

Everyone had been careful to omit mention of Lewis's individualist stubbornness on other occasions, but when the motion was put to the vote Fred's hand was the only one that supported his present contention. When he saw this he jumped up, put his cap on and made for the door, shouting over his shoulder, 'I'm not leaving the matter here. I'm going to take it further.'

Several members urged him to come back but he paid no heed and slammed the door behind him. Those left looked at each other blankly, before the chairman announced:

'Well, that's that. We know where we are now, and all I hope is he'll do what he said. The meeting is now closed.'

But it was some time later before the Party members left the library and made their way home.

Memories of this discussion and Fred's attitude lingered with Mary for a long time. Her health was becoming worse each day, and on occasions she had the greatest difficulty in breathing. As a result, she could not devote so much time as she desired to the Party, particularly as she was further handicapped by the fact that her father was getting more morose and intolerant, while his whole body seemed to be fading away before her eyes. Len was hardly any consolation to her during this period, most of his time being spent with the other Party members, holding meetings, distributing leaflets, and campaigning to get the people back into the Federation. Mary, knowing this, never complained, and kept from him as much as possible her fears regarding Ezra.

But one night she was awakened by a loud knocking on the wall that separated their bedroom from her father's. She hurriedly shook Len, who sprang to his haunches in drowsy alarm. Before he could ask any questions, he heard the knocking that had alarmed her, and without even waiting to put on his trousers, ran into Ezra's room.

In a matter of seconds, Mary heard him call out: 'Come quick, Mary, something's wrong with your father.'

Pale with dread, she hastened after him, and saw Ezra struggling painfully to gulp air into his open mouth. Len held the old man's head in one arm while he used a newspaper as a fan.

'Dress quick, Mary,' he urged his frightened wife. 'Run down the house and tell mam and dad to come up at once.'

Without hesitation she left the room, and the next thing he heard was the slamming of the front door.

Siân woke when the first pebble rattled on the window-pane. Pressing her nose against the glass she recognised the dim shape of Mary, and hastily began pulling her skirt on, at the same time waking Jim.

'Quick, James bach. Somethink have happened to our Mary.'

Jim needed no second bidding before he was out of bed and half-way to the kitchen, stubbing his toes against the stone stairs on the way down. He strangled the curses that rose to his throat and opened the door to admit the dripping Mary, who, instead of dressing as Len had advised, had merely flung an old coat over her nightdress. Siân, stumbling into the kitchen, saw this with her first glance, and drawing it off replaced it with her great woollen shawl.

'There now, gel fach. Sit yourself down and take your time,' she tried to console. But Mary was too agitated to dally.

'No, no. There is no time to sit down. You must come up the house with me at once. Oh dear, dear,' she burst into sudden tears and moaned. 'Something terrible is happening to dad. He is groaning and fighting for air while his eyes are fixed on Len in an awful stare.'

She brushed her hand across her forehead and hurried to the door, the old people close at her heels and Siân muttering: 'I knowed there was somethink wrong. This is my dream working out. There, there, Mary fach, don't take it to your heart so much. The Good Lord do always do what is best, and everythink will come all right in the end.'

Outside the howling wind clutched savagely at the rain, throwing it against the houses, where it smashed into running streams. The tears on Mary's cheeks were washed away as the three people stumbled through the storm towards Ezra's house, where a solitary light blinked in the sweeping rain and beckoned them to hurry. They found the miners' leader sitting up in bed with Len at his side. His eyes were fixed on the window with an intensity that was frightful in its obvious blindness, and his moustache was thick with the saliva that dribbled to his chin as he muttered incoherences to himself. His face shone with the perspiration that oiled it. Mary sprang forward and put her wet arms around him.

'Here I am, dad,' she whispered chokingly. 'You'll be all right now. Big Jim and Siân are here to help you. Cwtch up now and go to sleep.'

She tried to press the bony body back into the bed, but he struggled against her efforts, gasping feebly: 'Don't tie me down; let me be free to fight.'

His glaring eyes roamed the room when she released him, and Jim stepped up to take her place.

'Come comrade bach,' he crooned, gently as a mourning mother. 'Big Jim is with you now, and there is no need for you to fight while us is here.'

Ezra looked at him and his stare softened a little as it focused on the bent form of his old workmate. His words came from deep in his belly when he said: 'Ah, Big Jim. He'll not desert me like his son did. No. Old Jim will fight with me to the last.'

He paused a moment, then began waving his hands weakly above his head, at the same time crying helplessly: 'Let me get to my feet. Don't let it ever be said that I lay down when there was a fight to be won!'

Jim forcibly held him in bed while Len rushed for the doctor and Siân went down to the kitchen to light the fire. Ezra's eyes became glazed and he breathed in choking gasps that stuck in Mary's heart like daggers as she sensed the outcome of the struggle taking place. All the passionate love she bore him now surged through her with a force that dried the juices in her body as he fought to get out of bed.

It required the joint strength of Jim and Len to hold Ezra down while the doctor examined him. At the end of the examination the doctor took Mary on one side. 'There is nothing I can do for him,' he said with professional hardness. 'You must prepare yourself for the worst. I'll give him something to keep him quiet for a few hours, and I'll call again in the morning.'

The storm outside the room shook the house with frenzied blasts that mellowed the moans of the man on the bed. He began calling for Mary and paid no heed to her mournful protestations that she was with him.

Siân's red-rimmed eyes were wet when she said: 'Get into bed with him, Mary fach. Perhaps his body can tell him what his brain cannot.'

Mary obeyed, and the moans ceased for a while as some subconscious faculty told him his daughter was near. His face lost some of its putty pallor and the pain-filled lines smoothed out, giving it again some semblance of its old strength. Len looked on and felt a new confidence creep over him at the sight. Siân busied herself making a cup of tea and Big Jim stood near the bed, watching every restless motion of the form beneath the clothes.

The night slowly dragged out its storm-wrenched hours, and when the pit-hooters called the men to work in the early morning, their blare startled the people in the silent house. But the noise seemed to connect Ezra with the life in the valley, and he stirred impatiently before eventually opening his eyes to look about the room. He appeared more normal, although his skin had a peculiar yellowish tinge. He felt Mary at his side and turned to her, smiling wanly when she pressed her hot lips on his forehead. A knock sounded on the front door and Jim went down to answer it. When he returned he replied to the query in Ezra's glance.

'It was Sam Dangler's missus wanting to know if Sam could do something to help before he went to work.'

Ezra's face brightened, and Jim helped him rise to his haunches as Mary left the bed.

'My people still think of me,' he whispered.

'Of courst they do, mun. They don't never forget those who have been good to them,' Jim answered confidently.

A sudden spasm of coughing seized Ezra, and it seemed about to choke him until Jim cleared the mucus away with a huge forefinger. For some time after this the room was silent except for Ezra's terrifying gasps.

At last the dying man beckoned his daughter to him and whispered weakly: 'Open the window, my dear. I want to hear the men going to work.'

'But you will catch your death of cold,' she protested.

His features hardened as of old when anyone tried to thwart him. 'I said open the window,' he insisted. 'Chills or anything else can't affect me now.' Mary obeyed, and as she returned to the bedside the loud tramp of hobnailed boots followed her.

They all fell in with Ezra's mood, and for an hour listened silently until the hooters again blasted the dawn with their announcement that the last man was down the pit. Ezra sighed and whispered feebly, each word like a burden he was unwilling to relinquish.

686

'There goes life, creation. They will give their bodies to the pit all day, and their strength will be turned into coal. Yes. Black lumps of coal which will be turned into gold at the docks.' He became reminiscent as he sank back on the bed. 'It is the flesh and brains of our people that gives life to the world. Without them the world is dead. Dead as I'll be in a very short time.'

Mary sprang forward with a cry. 'Oh, don't say that, dad. You're looking better already.'

Ezra gazed at her and gulped hard as she buried her head in the clothes that covered his breast. 'Don't grieve for the dead,' he admonished, while his fingers with slow tenderness wound through the strands of her hair and wandered to the lobes of her ears. The familiar caress filled her with longing, and he went on more softly and weak: 'No, my daughter. And don't grieve for the living. Fight for them. Yes, that's the thing.' He borrowed sudden strength from somewhere and jerked himself erect, while Mary passionately clasped his hand to her bosom as he shouted: 'That's right. Fight, fight, and keep on fighting until...' A dry rattle followed the last word, and his body relaxed limply in Mary's arms.

Siân quietly led the sobbing woman from the bedroom and left it to the two men and their dead leader. Len looked down silently on the white face that had suddenly become placid, and it danced in the tears he tried to blink away. Big Jim blew his nose loudly before gently straightening the cooling limbs and drawing the sheet completely over the still form. This done, the old man turned to the window through which the daylight was

687

struggling to enter and muttered brokenly:

'Poor old Ezra is gone for good. The company have broked his heart so sure as they have broked the Federashon and the spirit of our men.'

Len looked at him, drawing the back of his hand across his brow. 'Yes, he's gone, dad. He's gone.'

Siân took control of the household during the following week, sleeping there at night so that Mary should never be alone. Jim made all the arrangements for the funeral, and Len received the visitors who came from everywhere with condolences. It had been Ezra's wish that his body be cremated, and the knowledge that Mary intended being true to this desire excited the people of Cwmardy, because it would be the first cremation that had ever taken place there. A further cause for speculation and gossip was provided by the Party announcement, on behalf of Mary, that there were to be no prayers and it was to be a red funeral with the Party in charge. Lord Cwmardy sent a letter which Mary read, then put in the fire. Len never asked what it contained, being too much concerned with her health to be interested in anything else. Her restraint and inner strength amazed him and made his love for her even more all-embracing than hitherto.

The miners kept out of the pit on the day of the funeral and from early morning began gathering about the street where Ezra had lived. Harry Morgan came down from London to speak on behalf of the Party. He brought with him a huge red banner with a gold hammer and sickle emblazoned in its centre. All the Party members in Cwmardy and many from outside turned up with red rosettes pinned on their breasts. Towards the afternoon large numbers of rich-looking cars rolled into the village, each containing top-hatted occupants.

The first intimation that something was happening in the house came when Harry Morgan beckoned six of the Party members inside. The huge crowd swayed forward as the coffin, covered with a red flag, came into sight through the window and was placed on trestles in the middle of the street. The mourners gathered around, Mary standing on the doorstep, with Siân at her side, and her eyes large and black in the dead-white flame of her face. Harry Morgan spoke a few words, which were followed by the rising cadences of the 'Red Flag'. Six Party members lined up on one side of the shrouded coffin and six old members of the Federation committee on the other. When the signal was given, they bent down simultaneously, and when they rose again Ezra's body rested on their twelve shoulders. The mass of people lined off in front and the mourners followed behind the coffin for the march to the crematorium, eight miles away. Lord Cwmardy walked with Big Jim at the head of the procession.

Len had a hazy memory of what transpired during the slow walk down the valley. He remembered seeing the lined streets and covered windows, but it all seemed like a passing panorama that floated by on a stream of hushed voices.

His faculties returned inside the crematorium chapel as he stood beside Big Jim and saw the coffin placed on the conveyor that led to a hole in the wall.

Harry Morgan went to the pulpit and his usually sharp voice was quiet as he began the people's farewell to Ezra.

He pictured Ezra's life as steps in the struggles of Cwmardy, each incident and action irrevocably leading to a certain outcome.

'He weakened at the end,' he declared, 'but which of us dare say we would not do the same in similar circumstances? He failed to see the struggle as a river flowing on against ever stronger dams placed there to stem its progress and divert its path. He took our people through many of these dams, but reached one that could only be broken through by a collective leadership, by a revolutionary Party that, knowing the strength of the obstacles, could mobilise the people into a unity powerful enough to overcome all barriers. Our Party did not regard Ezra as an enemy. We loved him for what he had been and what he had done. We grieve for him today, but we also glory in the knowledge that the foundations that he laid are safe in the keeping of the Party and the people.'

His voice broke and Big Jim suddenly bent to Len, white and staring as he whispered: 'Look, Len, look, the coffin is moving.'

Len looked and saw the words were true. Every eye in the chapel watched the slowly moving encased body of the miners' leader advance towards the hole in the wall. The movement was eerie and awe-inspiring, and there was deathly silence until, at a signal from Harry, the Party members began singing the Internationale. The red-draped coffin went out of sight as the words:

> 'Then away with all your superstitions!
> Servile masses, arise! Arise!'

filled the building, and two little doors closed on the hole that took Ezra from the world.

When Len got outside he saw everyone gazing up, and, following suit, watched the heavy, ugly-looking black smoke that came through the crematorium chimney and mixed with the air of the valley. He went home alone and found Mary and Siân sitting quietly near the fire. He said nothing to disturb them, and was soon in a reverie himself.

LOCAL POLITICS

The old woman remained that night and the following week in the house.

'Not for the poor gel fach to think she is all alone with only Len, now that her father have gone, God bless him,' as she remarked to Jim one night when they were disposing of Mary's domestic future. They tried to get the couple to give up the house and come and live with them, but Mary was adamant against this.

'It isn't because of the sticks and stones here,' she said sadly, when they approached her on the matter. 'They don't make a home. But the memories bound up in them do. That's why Len and me must stop here, where my father lived and reared me.'

The old people grudgingly gave way to her, but Big Jim kept worrying about it.

One Saturday night he returned home from the Boar's Head leading a savage-looking bull terrier. Siân jumped from her stool and looked at the animal with startled eyes.

'Whatever have you got by there, James,' she demanded, as Jim took the stool she had vacated and betrayed by his attitude that he was affronted by the welcome accorded his dog.

Len and Mary were sitting on the sofa, but he paid no attention to them when he replied: 'What think you it is – a broody hen – that you do ask me so silly a question? But there,' he added resignedly, 'whatever I do is always wrong in this house. I am fed up with trying to please everybody. After I give the last four pints I have on me, this is the thanks I get.'

Siân softened at once. 'Don't take it like that, James. I didn't mean to simple you, and you do know that, but the last time you brought a dog home it did nearly eat us out of house and home, and times is not so good now as they was then by a long way.'

'Ha! Don't worry, my gel, this is a different breed altogether. This 'un,' bending to pat its head, 'is a house-dog. You know, one of those that will let a packman or policeman, or somethink like that, come in the house, but won't never let them out, not while there is blood in their bodies.'

Siân listened interestedly to this explanation, then asked: 'But what is the good of stopping a man to go out, James? I 'ood think what you want is to stop 'em coming in.'

Jim turned to Len and Mary, who had not said a word, and the disgust in his look made them smile. 'Now what do you think to that? In't it like a woman all over?'

'But what do you want a house-dog for, dad,' asked

Len innocently.

Jim lost his temper and shouted: 'It's not for me, mun; I can look after myself. I buyed this for you and that little gel who have got no father in this world.'

The implication hurt Len, and he felt impelled to challenge it. 'Don't you think I can take care of Mary, then?'

Jim snorted, then laughed. 'Ho-ho! You, indeed. Huh! I 'ood like to see you in front of half a dozen burglars. Why, a puff of wind 'ood blow you from here to Africa, mun, in less than a minute. No, I can't be with you all the time, but Bonzo by here can – can't you, butty?' He took the willing dog on his lap.

When Mary and Len left the house for their own that night, the dog accompanied them.

It was months before Mary got over the shock of her father's death, and even afterwards she occasionally ached for his presence. Everything about her conspired to bring back memories of him, and she detested being alone in the house. She accompanied Len as often as possible on his Party activities, and when for some reason she was unable to do this, she found a strange solace in the savage demeanour of Bonzo, who came to understand her every mood.

Siân spent much time with her, although, as she complained one day: 'This old hill is getting too much for my poor old legs these days, Mary fach, and I do dread the thought that perhaps I 'on't be able to come here so often before long.'

She came up specially on one occasion, bursting with news, and happened to catch Len in the house.

'What do you think?' she asked, after she had squatted down and recovered her breath. 'Your father, Len, have joined a club. You know, those drinking dens where, not satisfied with having beer in the weekdays, when they can get it, they do have it on the Lord's days, which was never made for such a thing.'

Len understood his mother's agitation and tried to placate her. 'Don't worry, mam. Since the old man must have a pint now and then, he might as well have it in a club as in the Boar's Head.'

'Yes, yes,' she interrupted impatiently. 'He have told me all about that already. But what is worrying my heart out is that he will want to go there on Sundays, and you know the deacons is all eyes, Len.'

Mary took up the cudgels on Jim's behalf. 'Don't worry too much about them, mother,' she exhorted. 'Your Jim is as good as all of them, even if he will drink a pint or two on Sundays while they are in chapel.'

'I don't agree with you, my gel. James might be so good as them, but he could never be better than old Thomas Jones. There's a Christian man if ever there was one,' she piously exclaimed.

Len agreed with her. 'That's right, mam. He's a real man that do practise what he do preach. It's men like him I would like to see in our Party.'

The conversation was hushed as a rattle sounded at the door and Big Jim entered. Len got up to make way for him near the fire.

'Don't bother, my boy,' Jim thanked him, at the same time taking the chair. 'I will manage all right.'

He stretched his legs towards the grate and pulled out his pipe, puffing at this until it glowed, then said casually: 'The old 'ooman have been telling you 'bout the club, I s'pose.'

Mary nodded acquiescence and Len added: 'Aye, dad. Mam is afraid you will use it to go boozing on Sundays.'

Jim drew himself erect in the chair to say with impressive dignity: 'If I can't carry beer respectfully on a Sunday like any other day, then it's time for me to peg out. Yes. And let me tell you in front of your mother's face, Len,' turning his own to the fire, 'that if she do think them bloody deacons—'

Mary hastily changed the subject. 'How are things in the pit, these days, father?' she asked.

Jim took the cue immediately and began a recital of woes regarding the pit. 'It's more like a muck-hole than anythink else,' he declared categorically. 'I have worked underground for more than fifty years now – that's right, in't it, Siân fach?' looking at his spouse, who nodded agreement. 'And I have never seened such a shape on it all my born days.

'Colliers, muniferni!' he paused to spit disgustedly into the fire. 'Huh! Give 'em a shovel and plenty of loose coal and they're all right, but ask them to dress the face and they don't know what you are talking about.'

He bent down to relight his pipe, then spoke directly to Len. 'It's a shame to see all your old butties who have been reared in the pit now on the streets, while strangers is working their places. Do you know,' he added, 'that nearly everybody except some of the old-stagers have all signed to be in the industrial union, instead of in the Federashon?

697

There is going to be a hell of a stink about it one of these days, 'specially if they try to make me join it.'

Len cocked up his ears at this, but said nothing, as his father rumbled on from subject to subject. After supper he and Mary accompanied the old couple down the hill, Siân declaiming against the bad times all the way; but Len heard very little of it, his mind being absorbed in the information his father had given.

At the next Party meeting only two matters were discussed: the election of a councillor and the development of the company union. Fred Lewis attended the meeting and took part in the discussion, although it was his first appearance since his last disagreement with the Party.

Len, in the chair, explained the issues involved. The people in the crowded room listened intently to every word, and it was obvious they regarded the matters as very serious. The Party was a very strong influence in Cwmardy, and any decisions it took had far-reaching consequences both inside and outside the pits, a fact which made the discussion even more important than it would have been otherwise. A new member of the Party was the first to take part in the discussion. He was a small-framed, excitable, and quickly moving man who had originated in Berkshire. When he talked, his words came so quickly that they tumbled over each other, and occasionally he had to pause to re-adjust his false teeth which persisted in dropping.

'What we want,' he declared, 'is more news in the *Daily Worker* about Cwmardy. We can expose to everybody what is happening in the pit and nobody will know who's responsible. On the top of that, if we had such news, we could duplicate little leaflets to put in every one of them, asking the men in the pit to join our Party.' He stopped a moment, then seemed to remember something else he had planned to say, and went on: 'I for one would be willing to go to the pit-head to sell the *Daily Worker* if we could get this news in. You used to go there with the old pit paper, didn't you?' he demanded. 'And if you could do it then, I say we can do it now.'

Fred Lewis followed, his sallow features and long body commanding attention.

'It's no good talking like Frank Forrest at this stage. Let's get down to fundamentals first. We can never tackle the non-pols until we build the Federation, and we can't do that until we have a miners' agent. You all know what I think about this, but let's leave it at that for a moment and turn our attention to the election of a councillor. This is the second vacancy since Ezra died, and I think the time is ripe for us to fight the seat again.'

This focused the discussion, and after he had finished others took the cue and it was eventually agreed that the Party should contest. Then came the question of candidate. The qualifications and eligibility of each member present was measured, and it was at last moved that Mary be the candidate.

Lewis went white as a sheet and, jumping to his feet, exclaimed excitedly: 'I'm opposed to Mary. We are only making our Party into a laughing-stock by giving our enemies the chance of saying that we are putting Mary forward because she is Ezra's daughter and should be supported because of this. I ask you,' he pleaded, at the same time looking round the room, 'is the council to be a family affair, such as the Labour councillors have tried to make it, or is it an institution we can use on behalf of the people? If it's this, then we want a mass leader and a responsible comrade there, not a woman, good as Mary might be in other directions.'

When he sat down Len checked the following clamour. 'Let's be clear before we go on,' he began. 'None of us in this room is concerned about Mary as Mary. What we are discussing is our Party and what best we can do in the interest of our people. If this is so, then we must ask ourselves is it good that our people should have a Party woman in the council? That's the first thing we have got to answer. If we say yes, then we must ask ourselves, does comrade Mary Roberts understand the line of the Party and does she fight for it? As far as mass-following goes, she has as much influence as any of us.'

Will Evans got up next and asked: 'If Fred thinks Mary shouldn't be our candidate, who else have he got in mind?'

The man to whom the question was addressed answered without hesitation: 'Although I've got enough to do as it is and I don't want the position, I don't think anybody else can win the seat for the Party.'

The colour had come back to his face and his whole attitude was now aggressive. After further discussion, Len put the two names to the meeting and for the second time on an important issue Fred was alone in support of himself. Without waiting for further discussion, he rose and left the room, deaf to Len's entreaties that he stop for the other matters. The meeting went flat after this, and the only other decision taken was in line with Frank Forrest's suggestion regarding leaflets in the *Daily Worker* and the selling of them on the pit-head the following Friday. Will Evans and Forrest were instructed to help Len and Mary get the leaflets out.

Neither of them had done this work before, but Frank assured them that he'd soon get into the knack. The Party typewriter and flat duplicator were taken up to Len's house the next day, and for the remainder of the week the latter was transformed into an editorial board-room and a printing shop as they plodded through the initial drafts of the leaflet. Will's pencil was more often in his mouth than in his hand, but between them they had the leaflet ready eventually.

'By the shades of Moses,' Will stated with a sigh, 'I'm glad that's over! I 'ood sooner handle a mandril and shovel than a pen, muniferni.'

The task of cutting the stencil fell on Len, who gazed dubiously at the old rebuilt typewriter, that looked more like a mortar-mill than anything else. He scratched his head and sat uncomfotably facing the machine for a while before getting to work. He used one finger like a hammer, which fell on the keys at long intervals as he looked for the letter he had to hit. Mary, in spite of her protests, was sent to bed long before the stencil was finished.

Dawn was breaking its way into the kitchen by the time, coatless and hot, they began the last stage of production. Will Evans separated the sheets of red paper and handed them to Frank, who put one inside the duplicating frame, jammed down the cover, which Len rubbed vigourously with a roller, then shouted: 'That'll do. Let's have a look at it now!'

The three men crowded round the little frame as Frank carefully raised the lid and pulled out the paper. They all held their breath while this operation was taking place, until Will, thinking his mate was too rash, hissed: 'Careful there, butty. Steady or you'll be so sure as hell to tear it.'

No one took any notice, and at last the paper was through. Frank turned it over carefully and for some moments they stared at the blank sheet as though it were a skeleton.

Will was the first to break the silence: 'Holy hell!' he blurted out. 'Us have been printing leaflets for blind men.'

Poor Frank still held the paper in his hand, staring like a paralysed man at its blank surface.

Len sighed. 'Perhaps we had better sit down for a minute,' he suggested.

His advice was taken, Will's glance alternating between the sheet and the duplicator. Suddenly he jumped and picked up the press to rub his finger over its skin.

'Got it!' he declared dramatically. 'Got it! Frank put the ink on the wrong side. No wonder nothing come through. It's like cutting coal arse-backwards.'

Len became puzzled. Frank's eyes glinted viciously.

'It can't be that,' he said pitifully, 'because the comrade who had it showed me how to do it hisself.'

'Huh!' Will grunted. 'Perhaps you had your eyes shut when he was showing you.'

Frank started to his feet at the insinuation, but Len

interrupted: 'Come on, boys, or pay-day will be over before we start. Let's try it Will's way.'

Will grabbed the roller with the command: 'Hand me that tube of ink,' and with one squeeze of the tube followed by a flourish of the roller he placed the paper in position. Again the trio watched, anxiously impatient, while the paper was taken away.

Before it was half off, Will looked up to announce triumphantly: 'There you are, boys. Plain enough for a bat to read.'

He switched the paper away and held it before the others. Their dazed look surprised him, and he slowly turned the sheet around, stared hard at its black, inky wetness for a moment, then exploded in a tirade.

'Hell fire! Who done that?' he howled, looking at the other two, as though he had just caught them committing murder.

The incongruity of the situation appealed to Len, and he burst into laughter, the others eventually joining him. The noise woke Mary, and wrapping a cloak over her night-attire she hurried downstairs. She was unable for some time to make head or tail of what they were trying to tell her, but Len at last managed to blurt out the whole story coherently. They cleaned the machine carefully, and, after an examination of the screws and other paraphernalia, Frank discovered what was wrong and they began again.

Mary was preparing breakfast and their hands were all blistered by the time they had printed all the leaflets they had planned, but everyone was happy in the accomplishment. That afternoon, all the available members of the Party gathered at the colliery offices with bundles of *Daily Workers* under their arms. It was pay-day, and for a time the home-going miners provided a brisk sale until Mr. Hicks stepped out of the office to show he was present. His appearance slackened the sales appreciably, but they went up again when he returned to the office. A few minutes later two policemen hurried up the hill towards the sellers.

'Here they come,' Len announced casually to his mates.

'Let 'em come. To hell with 'em! Because they wear brass buttons, they don't own the bloody world, do they?' Will replied, raising his voice to shout more loudly: '*Daily Worker*, one penny. Read how the Government is helping the blackshirts.'

The two policemen, who were now quite near, stopped to consult each other, all the time watching the sellers from the corners of their eyes. Len kept close to Mary, and whenever she moved, he followed. The police appeared to have made up their minds, and approached him.

'Do you know you are on private property?' the senior officer asked. The question was entirely unexpected, and Len floundered for a suitable reply. Mary filled the breach with a counter.

'Since when has this public highway been private property?' she asked.

'It has never been a public highway,' came the retort. 'From that mark there,' pointing back towards Cwmardy and away from the pits, 'belongs to the company.'

Mary said no more, but beckoning the others, she led

them the other side of the mark, where they continued their selling.

The new move had the police guessing, and the sergeant went into the office. When he came back out, he went straight to Mary. 'You can't stop here. You're causing an obstruction,' he stated abruptly.

Will's jaw dropped for a moment when he heard this ultimatum, then his temper got the better of him and he shouted in disgust: 'Well, if this isn't the bloody limit! Put me back in a muck-hole and bury me. Us can't go on the other road because it's s'posed to be private, and now we can't stop on a public road because we obstruct it when there is nobody about but ourselves, the sky, and the smoke. If that's justice, I give in, muniferni.'

This annoyed the policeman, who ordered brusquely: 'Come on there, quick now, and none of your bloody cheek either, Will Evans, or we'll put you inside.'

Frank bridled up at this ultimatum to his mate. 'Ho! So that's the game, is it?' he asked, prancing challengingly before the two officers, and glaring defiance. Before he could say any more, the others herded round and shepherded him away.

The sergeant gave a final shot: 'Don't forget we're booking you all for this.'

He was true to his word, and in the middle of the next week each of them received a summons to attend the police court, where they were fined £1 each and costs for wilful obstruction.

Things developed quickly in Cwmardy after this, as the time for the council election drew near and the Party sent a number of letters and deputations to Fred Lewis, asking him to attend the meeting to define his position. He did not acknowledge any of the letters and was never at home when the deputations called. Hours were spent discussing what was to be done about the matter, and just prior to nomination day it was decided to make a final effort to get his viewpoint. Len and Mary were deputed to watch for him and invite him to a meeting of the Party which would be organised to suit his time and convenience. They failed to find him for some time, and it was Len who eventually saw him in Ben the Barber's where he was waiting for a haircut. Len broached the subject that was uppermost in his mind, and when Fred met him with a curt refusal began to coax.

'Good God, mun, you've been in the Party ten years or more. Don't let all the good work you have done in the past be wasted just because of this.'

The other man scowled. 'Don't lecture me. I was working for the Party when you was toadying around Ezra.'

Len kept his temper. He was older than Fred and certainly more experienced, but he tried another tack.

'Perhaps that's true, but it's all the more reason why you shouldn't jib now, just because you don't agree with our line.' More customers entered the shop at this moment, and the discussion was held over until both of them got outside, where, after a long argument, Len finally persuaded him to come to the meeting that night.

The Party meeting began promptly at six, and to avoid any semblance of partiality Len was removed from the chair and John Library took his place. The first thing he did was to ask for the minutes of the meeting where it was agreed that Mary should be the candidate. This was duly read out, after which Fred Lewis spoke.

'I think that decision is wrong and against the interests of the Party. In a personal sense I don't want to be a councillor, but I feel there is no one in the Party better fitted for it than myself. I want to say here, now, that if you insist on that resolution, I shall leave the Party, because I don't believe it is any longer fit to be called a Communist Party.'

This statement created a temporary uproar, which the chairman soon quelled before asking a series of questions which he put directly to Fred.

'Why did you join the Party?'

'Because I believed it was the only Party with the correct policy for the people.'

'You know that the policies of the Party are worked out on the basis of a majority vote after exhaustive discussion?'

'Yes.'

'You know majority decisions are binding upon the minority, although the latter have the right of trying to convince the others where they are wrong?'

'Of course I know that. I've been in the Party ten years.'

'Do you think that has been the right method of deciding policy in the past?'

Fred sensed the trend of the questions and began to hedge. 'Yes, but what was good in the past isn't always good for the present.'

John was very patient, and his clean-shaven face with

its snowy thatch of hair almost beamed as he went on. 'Tell us, Fred, where it is wrong today and give us a better method of doing our work.'

Fred stammered, then coughed and lost his temper. 'Don't cross-examine me. I'm not a kid. I know you are wrong, although you've all made your minds up against me. But that doesn't worry me. I'm still a Communist, which none of you have ever been, and I'll go to the people and tell them so. And as far as the election goes, I'm standing as a workers' candidate on real Communist principles. Goodnight.' With these words he straightened himself and walked with as much dignity as he could muster towards the door. Len caught his hand as he passed.

'Don't do this, Fred. You know what it means,' he beseeched.

Fred roughly brushed his hand away. 'You can take my resignation from the Party here and now,' he declared as he closed the door with a bang.

The silence that followed made the room seem dead. Those present looking at each other dumbly, until Mary, rising to her feet, broke the tension with the determined declaration: 'There can be no resignations from our Party, and if he does what he threatened, there's nothing else for us to do but expel him and make it an issue for the election.' This statement led to a further long discussion, which John Library skilfully directed until the meeting became a committee of ways and means to win the election.

Over supper that night Mary betrayed the anxiety she had tried to hide. Len had drawn his chair away from the table and was bending to light a cigarette when she said slowly, as though not sure of her words:

'I wonder what makes Fred so bitter about me, Len?'

Len looked up sharply. 'Huh! He's only using you because you happen to be the candidate. He'd do the same if it was anybody else, and don't make any mistake about that.'

She stopped wiping the plate and asked: 'But he put it in such a way, Len, that he made me think he had a personal grievance against me.' Len smiled. 'Aye. He's got a grievance against the whole Party, because he can't use it as he wants.' He suddenly lost his temper. 'He's a rat and, you watch my words, he'll end up by being our bitterest enemy.' He paused a moment and again bent down to light the cigarette. When he raised his head he had regained control of himself. 'Come, Mary fach. Let's forget him and go to bed. We've got a hectic fortnight before us if we are to win this fight.'

Mary hurried her washing up, but they did not go to bed for a long time after this, being too concerned with talking about the campaign, until the dead ashes in the grate reminded them of the late hour.

A SEAT
ON THE COUNCIL

For the next fortnight Len and Mary, together with the other members of the Party, devoted all their time to public meetings, leaflets, and the other work connected with an election. This culminated in a mass rally on the eve of the poll. Will Evans and his mates had specially decorated the hall for the occasion, draping the front of the stage with a huge red streamer on which was inscribed:

'VOTE FOR MARY ROBERTS, PEACE AND PROSPERITY.'

Long before the time for officially opening, the hall was full of people, who whiled away the time singing songs and hymns until they became impatient and began stamping on the floor and clapping their hands to the refrain: 'We want Mary! We want Mary!'

The clamour made Mary self-conscious, and when she accompanied Len, Harry Morgan, and John Library on to the platform, she was as white as the silk scarf around her throat. The entry of the quartette was marked by a further burst of singing which drifted from tune to tune until it ended with the 'Red Flag'.

By the time John Library had risen and opened the meeting, Mary had recovered her composure a little, but still failed to distinguish individuals in the yellow mass that stared at her through the blue haze that filled the air. She was glad of this, because it gave her strength to concentrate. John's voice came to her from miles away, and its music slowly stirred her imagination, making her fuse all the faces into one, that of Ezra, her father. She saw again the dark eyes and strong mouth, and fancied she heard the echo of his voice in John's. By the time she was introduced, the strange thought seized her to speak as though she were arguing with him. She did so, and when she had finished her address the people were on their feet cheering wildly.

Next morning she and Len were up very early, Bonzo gazing curiously at them as though he wondered what they were up to so early in the day. Breakfast was a hurried affair, and it was not long before both of them, trying vainly to look unconcerned, were ready to go down to the school to examine the ballot boxes, prior to the voting taking place. Bonzo eluded Mary's attempt to keep him in, and she looked piteously at Len while the dog sat down contentedly some yards away and waited for them to move. Len looked at him helplessly for some moments, then shrugged his shoulders and turned to Mary with the remark:

'There, you've done it now! He'll keep us busy all day watching he don't fight.'

'But it wasn't my fault, Len. I thought he was safe on the mat and never expected him to dodge us like that. Try to coax him to you,' she added as a bright after-thought. Len bent down and snapped his finger and thumb.

'Come here, boy. Bonzo, good old Bonzo!' he coaxed, at the same time sidling nearer the dog, who casually kept moving backwards as though he enjoyed the sport. Mary became impatient at last.

'Oh, leave him there. We'll have to put up with whatever happens now, I suppose. Come on or the boxes will be sealed before we get there.'

Len disgustedly gave up his efforts to wheedle Bonzo and followed her, at the same time trying to keep an eye on the dog, who now bounded and pranced before them. When they got to the school where the balloting was to take place, they found Will Evans and other Party members already there, the former answering, in reply to their suprised query: 'We wasn't taking any chances and wanted to be here early to make sure there'd be no funny tricks at the start.'

'But you've lost a turn to be here, Will,' Mary expostulated.

'Turn – bah! What's a turn in a man's life? And, anyhow, what's a turn if we win today? Do you know, Mary, I had a couple of pints last night and when I went to bed I had a funny dream, mun.'

Len shuffled uneasily. He had heard some of Will's dreams before, and was now nervous as a consequence.

713

This one, however, proved to be quite innocuous and amounted to the fact that it had given Will an unflinching conviction that they had won the election already. The returning officer, who stood near, smiled grimly at the recital, but said nothing as the little group, satisfied the ballot boxes were empty when sealed, went outside, where they met the first voter coming in. She was an old woman over eighty years of age and had never voted in her life before, but had made her mind up to do so this time, 'Because it is the only chance I have ever had in my life to vote for a woman, my gel,' as she had told Mary when the latter was canvassing. She waved her hand as she entered the booth and turned her head to shout in her cracked voice: 'Don't you worry, Mary fach. You do know where my vote is going, sure enough.'

Things were very quiet throughout the morning, but towards the afternoon groups of children came to the parlour which was rented for the day as a committee-room and begged for red tissue paper and copies of Mary's election address with her photo on it. These were readily given, and for the remainder of the day the children paraded the streets singing:

'Vote, vote, vote for Mary Roberts,
Drive Fred Lewis out of town.'

Fred, on his way to his own committee-rooms, a huge red and yellow rosette adorning his coat, passed them. He went white, although he gave a sickly smile as the children booed him lustily, until another procession of children, coming from the opposite direction, wearing red and yellow tissue-paper hats, swooped upon the first lot with wild shouts and a free fight ensued. After this he continued his walk in a better mood.

In the meantime Len was busy before a huge chart he had stuck on the wall of the committee-room. It contained the polling number of every voter in Cwmardy, and opposite every number was either a red, black, or blank square to denote the probable result of the canvassing and whom the number was likely to vote for. A party member kept running between the polling booth and the committee-room with a paper containing the number of each vote recorded. Len hurriedly checked these on the chart. He found it very difficult work, because large numbers of people hung about the room all the time, anxious to do something to help. On one occasion he got exasperated and shouted to some Party members:

'For heaven's sake get out on the streets, not hang about by here. Can't you see our people are not turning up yet and the time is getting on?'

Thus stimulated, the people filed from the room and gathered round the polling booth, their bright rosettes giving a splash of colour to the scene. Mary kept walking from house to house, accompanied by Will Evans, and urging the people to vote as soon as they could.

During the late afternoon, after the workmen had left the pits, a steady stream of voters entered the school. After voting the people gathered in groups and discussed the chances of the respective candidates. Jim and Siân came down arm in arm to record their votes, the former urging

715

his wife even when they were at the door of the booth:

'Now 'member, Siân fach, don't make no mistakes. The last, do you hear? The last name on the ballot paper.' This done, the pair strutted out into the street as though they had just been crowned and all the people were there to cheer them.

Jim heard someone remark: 'I don't think Mary have got much of a chance. She's a 'ooman, you see, and Fred Lewis is too well known.'

The old man turned his head sharply to say: 'What you said? Our Mary have got no chance? Huh! She is in already, mun, and everythink is over bar the shouting.'

'Don't talk so daft, mun,' was the reply he received. 'She haven't got a bloody earthly.' Jim strode back at once, his hand digging into his pocket.

'Come on then, butty. If you be so sure as that, stand up to your beliefs like a man. I'll bet you five good pounds that our Mary have won by a thousand majority easy, muniferni.'

'Right,' came the quick retort. 'Put your money down.'

Jim opened his mouth in a pitiful gape and looked longingly at Siân who was again at his side. The people around became silent as they wondered what the old man would do in face of the challenge. Jim sensed the feeling and it helped him to grip himself. Drawing his body arrogantly erect and twisting one side of his moustache, he announced to all and sundry: 'Huh! It 'ood be a pity to take the man's money so cheap, and I was never one to take advantage of anybody. No, butty. Keep your money. I don't want to take it from you – not that I couldn't put my

716

hand on five hundred pound this minute if I wanted to, let alone five pounds.' He said this with an air of superior contempt that left his challenger dumbfounded, then went on with magnanimous generosity: 'But if you do want a little bet, just for the fun of the thing, I will bet you four pints. And if you win call in the Boar's Head or the club, and have 'em on my name.'

The amazed man held out his hand helplessly to clinch the bet, and Big Jim, his head high in the air and humming a little tune, went proudly towards the committee-room, at the same time trying to make his rosette larger by spreading its folds. Once out of hearing of the people he bent to tell Siân: 'Five pounds, indeed! Huh! He never seed more than five pence in all his life. Trying to take the rise out of Big Jim, see, Siân fach; but I was too old for him. Oh, aye, it will take more than a pup to frighten me with his bark.'

He stopped to watch Mary's children supporters pass, cheering them loudly as they sang her praises. But before he reached the committee-room where Len was, Fred Lewis's supporters came along.

Jim scowled at them savagely. 'Fitter if their mothers kept them in the house,' he grunted to Siân, 'instead of letting 'em strut about the place like hooligans. Huh! Come, let us go in from the noise. I don't know what Cwmardy is coming to, between one thing and another.'

They entered the room and found Len in his shirt-sleeves swearing under his breath. The old man listened silently for a while, then asked sharply: 'What is the language you are using before your father and mother,

717

Len? Haven't you got no respects left, or have you forgot how I reared you?'

Len looked from the chart and a grin spread over his face for a moment, to be replaced by a worried frown. 'I'm afraid we're down, dad,' he muttered. 'Our people are not turning up half so well as the others, and if they don't buck up we'll lose.'

'Sit down, mam,' he added, hurriedly reaching for a chair. Jim remained standing, a puzzled frown on his forehead.

'Losing? Losing? How comes that, my boy? Good God, us have winned it already, mun! What are you blabbing about?'

The words sounded unconvincing and showed that Len's statement had shaken him. He drew his hand across his forehead and repeated: 'Losing. Good God! Four pints.' Len began to grasp the significance of the disjointed statements, but said nothing until Mary came in looking worn out, although taut with excitement.

He immediately went into the kitchen and came back with a jug of tea and some sandwiches, which he shared out between her and Siân. While they were eating, he explained the position.

'Unless our boys keep on the doors, Mary, we're down the drain,' he declared. A sudden thought struck him, and he turned to his father.

'Look here, dad, fetch all the boys except those in the booth here straight away. Tell them I want them very important.' Without the slightest hesitation Jim obeyed.

While he was away, Len frantically jotted down names and addresses on to various strips of paper, and when the

Party members came in he gave each of them a slip with the instructions: 'These are our votes that haven't come in yet. Get after them and if necessary carry 'em to the booth.' His excitement spread to the others, and Will asked:

'How are we standing, Len, by the chart?'

Len hastily added up some figures and when he raised his head again there was a desperate look about him.

'Nine hundred and twenty of their votes have come and seven hundred and eighty of ours, and we've only got three hours to go,' he declared, at the same time looking at the clock. The sight of it inspired him, and he turned again to the full room.

'Nothing for it but cars, boys. If we've got to carry every bloody vote we'll win this election.'

Mary looked up in alarm. 'No, no,' she said determinedly. 'We are not going to chance anything, Len. We've got to play for safety. We don't want the election declared void by the police.'

Len glared at her as though he itched to strangle her where she sat. 'Playing for safety to hell!' he howled. 'We're fighting to win. Fred Lewis has got cars flying around all day, and is sweeping 'em in from the cemeteries and wherever he can get 'em.' He caught Mary's cool glance fixed on him, and calmed down immediately.

'All right, don't get your hair off,' he pleaded, then turned again to the Party members. 'On the streets, boys. Whip 'em in. We've got three hours and can do it yet if we get down to the job.'

He put his own coat on and went out with them. Half an hour later three cars bearing glaring red streamers were

719

racing to the booth, dumping voters there, then racing off for others before the first load had recorded their votes.

As eight o'clock drew near, the atmosphere became more tense and the main street crowded with people, many of whom paid frequent visits to the Boar's Head while they waited. Both Len and Mary had forgotten the chart, realising that everything now depended upon getting to the booth those supporters who had not yet voted.

Sweating freely and at the same time trying to smile at everyone, they scoured the streets of Cwmardy to make sure no possible vote was lost. When eight o'clock came they were both nearly exhausted, but Mary brightened to a startled thought.

'Where's Bonzo?' she asked. 'I haven't seen him since this morning.'

Len grunted wearily. 'Oh, he's been courting, I expect, or we would have heard him before now.'

Mary frowned at him and led the way to the booth, where the people packed around the doorway. A police inspector politely made way for the couple to enter, closing the door tightly behind them. They found the four Party members selected to be present at the count awaiting them, each with a wide smile. Fred Lewis stood talking to the returning officer, his supporters grouped around them, but he came forward to shake hands with Mary.

'May the best man win, but I think I'm there,' he stated with an uneasy smile.

Mary merely nodded her head and made no observation as she turned to her comrades, to whom Len was earnestly talking. Before the conversation was over, the returning officer and his clerk announced the procedure, and the supporters went to their places each side of a long table. They were placed alternately, a red rosette next a red and yellow, and so on round the table; the returning officer and his clerk sat at the end.

The room became silent as the first box was turned upside down and a little avalanche of ballot papers spread over the table.

'Now count them into bundles of fifty,' came the command, and immediately eight pairs of hands were buried in the papers and the counting began.

When this was over, there was another momentary silence, then: 'Pass them down towards the right and check them as they come.'

This was done, each supporter glueing his eyes on his neighbour's hands as the latter checked the number of papers in each bundle. The returning officer then checked the total with a number he had on a bit of paper and found both tallied. All the papers were again strewn over the table and he ordered the counters:

'Place all votes for Roberts in bundles of fifty on your left and votes for Lewis in the same numbers on your right. Pass spoiled votes down to me.'

The atmosphere became tense, and Mary, standing on one side near Fred Lewis, felt her mouth go dry. Fred said something, but she failed to comprehend what it was and merely nodded, hoping this would serve instead of words. She saw the little bundles of paper mounting until she thought those on the right were like mountains. A grim little smile began to pucker the corners of her mouth, and, shrugging her shoulders, she began quietly walking about the room while the counting proceeded.

Len's whole being was concentrated on the papers that covered the table. He not only watched those of himself and his immediate neighbour, but let his attention wander all round, never for a moment losing sight of what was happening elsewhere. On one occasion he drew the attention of the returning officer to a bundle at the bottom of the table.

'I think there is a mistake there,' he stated. 'There's a Lewis on top of that bundle, but all the others are for Mary.' He blushed and apologised, 'Excuse me, I mean Roberts.'

The bundle was investigated and the mistake rectified. The little error made everyone suspicious and more alert.

When the first box had been counted, the officer in charge ordered that the various bundles of fifty for each candidate be sent down to him. This was done and another box emptied, when the whole process was gone through again.

The piles mounted up slowly, but Mary kept her gaze away from them, although it required all her determination to do so. As the count neared the end she caught a glance from Len and hesitantly walked over to him. She saw a piece of paper with a mass of figures on his knee, and bent down to scrutinise them more closely. What she saw made her throat contract and she swallowed noisily, at the same time raising her eyes pitifully to Len and whispering: 'Oh, Len, it can't be true. Over five hundred majority for us? No, I won't believe it. It can't be true.'

Len caught her hand and pressed it silently to his side.

'Pull yourself together, Mary, and get ready. He'll be announcing the official figures in a minute.'

Even as he spoke a restless tremor ran through the people in the room. The man in charge coughed importantly and the others, with varying degrees of anxiety, watched his mouth. Fred Lewis's face was streaked like a ghost's, and Will Evans, thinking he felt sick, solicitously offered him a peppermint, with the remark: 'Buck up, Fred, my lad. Better luck next time. Here, take this. It will help the bile from your belly.'

Fred did not even turn his eyes from the returning officer as the latter announced. 'I declare Mary Roberts elected as the councillor.'

Mary felt the room twist about her, but Len's arm about her waist steadied her.

'What will I tell the people, Len?' she muttered half incoherently.

'Thank them for their faith in the Party and tell them you don't represent any section or group now that you are a councillor, but that you are at the service of all the people in Cwmardy,' he answered. The others grouped around her with congratulations, and Will Evans gave her a kiss that resounded through the room.

Mary felt the room swirl round and her knees melted, but the arms of her comrades kept her erect as they slowly escorted her, together with the official, out of the door and towards the little iron railing that separated the school from the road.

The clamouring people became suddenly silent as the returning officer climbed on a pillar and, with a sheet of paper held imposingly before him, read out the result. His final words were lost in the roar of cheering that could no longer be restrained. Big Jim burst through the crowd and lifted Mary bodily on to the pillar, so that all the people could see her, while Siân, alternately laughing and crying, waved her arms about like a marionette.

After a while Mary checked the quiver running through her body, and, holding up her hand, called for silence. Then she began speaking, quietly and hesitantly at first, then more strongly as the situation gripped her. Standing above the people, her little form with its thatch of gleaming hair looked twice its usual size as she exhorted them to use her victory as a weapon to fight against the enemies of the people and as a warning to traitors.

When she had finished, another prolonged shout shook the air, and she was swept off the pillar on to the shoulders waiting to carry her triumphantly up the street to her home. Hours later the singing and shouting still lingered over Cwmardy, and it was early morning when the last echoes buried themselves somewhere in the mountain.

THE UNEMPLOYED

The election victory and the return of Mary to the council changed completely the domestic conditions in Len's household. He had now to help with the housework so that Mary could attend the various committees and meetings which her new role entailed. But he was not sorry for this, because the demands on her time forced her to concentrate on other things than her health, with the result that the latter improved each month that passed. Nevertheless the changed routine in his life occasionally made Len irritable and fretful. He felt Mary's intense preoccupation in council work robbed him of her emotional company to a large extent. On the other hand, he felt she was overstressing the importance of council work when she insisted on raising the matter in every meeting of the Party. But it was Will Evans who brought this latter matter to a head one night about two years after the seat had been won by the Party.

Mary was demanding a special public meeting at which she could report something that had happened at the previous council meeting, when Will jumped restlessly to his feet and asked:

'Is this a political party or a council clique, or what? It's just about time we found out exactly what we are. All we hear in every meeting is council this, and council that, and there's no time for discussions on anything else.'

Mary had remained on her feet during this outburst, but she saw the little smile that Len gave when he heard this echo of his own thoughts. The sight stiffened her against the challenge.

'I'm glad Will has had the courage to say what's on his mind,' she began, 'because it's obvious that more than him are thinking the same thing. I agree we mustn't concentrate the Party on one phase of the struggle but neither must we neglect any phase. And all I've been trying to do is to get you comrades to see the importance of council issues to the people. It's these little things, such as parish, housing, child welfare, and so on, that affect the lives of our people in the quickest and most living way, and it's because of this the council can be made a mobiliser for bigger things and actions.' She warmed to her subject as she saw the intentness with which the others followed her words.

'Take the question of unity between ourselves and Labour. Where are the leaders of the Labour Party?' she asked; then answered: 'In the Federation and the councils,

726

isn't it? They are united with us in the Fed against the non-pols and the company, but they are miles away from us in the council. And that's just our problem. We've got to break down their opposition to us politically in one way or another, and I think the council is one way of doing it. If we can get Labour and Communist councillors marching together, on behalf of the unemployed for instance, I'm sure the mass of people would follow.'

She kept on for some time and when she finished, three or four jumped to their feet together, each anxious to be first in the discussion that followed. Before the meeting finished, a better understanding prevailed and a clear plan of action was worked out.

During the afternoon of the next signing day at the exchange Len walked into the back kitchen with a weary droop to his shoulders. He pulled off his coat and placed it behind the chair before sitting down. There was a hopelessness in his actions that saddened Mary. She knew how keenly he felt the fact that since their marriage he had been unemployed most of the time and life had been a continual battle to maintain existence on insufficient means. She went to him and her hand dropped on his shoulder.

He buried his face in his hands and moaned: 'Don't, Mary dear. You make things harder with your patience and courage, when your whole body yearns for things to prevent it wasting as it is.'

She did not answer, but ran her fingers through his hair as he fixed his gloomy eyes on the fire. They remained in this posture for many minutes, until presently he took his unemployment pay from his pocket and handed it to her, with a gesture that seemed to ask for forgiveness and brought a sob to her throat.

'Oh, Len,' she pleaded, 'why do you worry so much about me? Don't you realise if things were different, if we were not so poor as the rest of our people, we would not be together.'

He started at her words, then answered slowly: 'But Mary comrade, why need our people suffer this poverty when there is so much being destroyed and wasted in the world?'

'Len, Len,' she reproved him, 'you are a Communist and should know all about the struggle and what it means.' She sighed, then continued: 'Dad always said you were more emotional than intellectual, more moody than rational.'

This stung him to retort: 'That may be, but it is only because I am made of flesh and blood, not stone.'

She wormed her way to his lap and sat down, drawing his head to her bosom and soothing him with endearments. 'There, comrade, have your bang out. You'll be better after.'

She nursed him like a baby for a while before saying: 'Think of the thousands in Cwmardy who are worse off than us. Then think of what they must do to save themselves from the ruin other people are making.'

Her tones became softer as she let her mind roam through the realms of her political convictions. 'Yes, as dad used to say, we must see things as they are in order to make them what we want them to be. Our poverty and misery is the expression of our class condition, but it is also the foundation of the unity that will sooner or later destroy both.'

The confidence in her statements shook him, and placing his arms about her frail body, he pressed it to his

728

and kissed her, before rising from the chair, still holding her in his arms. 'You are right, Mary. We must not grieve over our condition, but fight against it. That is the way and that is what the Party is for. Forgive me, comrade, for being so childish. I couldn't help it for a moment when I came in and saw the suffering in your face, but you have given me sense again and I can see more clearly now.'

He brushed a sleeve across his mouth and told her of the cuts in benefit that had been made in the unemployment exchange that day. 'The people are in a ferment,' he declared, 'but no one seems to know what to do. It's all come so sudden that even the Party is not prepared.'

Mary released herself from his arms and began to pace the kitchen, muttering to herself: 'But someone *must* know what to do, our Party must *find* a way for the people.' She stopped her pacing and faced him. 'Len, we must call a Party meeting at once. You go round the comrades, now, while I make dinner; then we can discuss the whole business.'

The room in the library where the Party held its meetings was packed to suffocation, even people who did not belong to the Party thronging the corridors to hear what was going on and to take part in the discussion. Len, as chairman, opened the meeting with a brief explanation of what was happening on the exchange.

'Our people don't know where to turn to make ends meet, with the sudden and vicious cuts that have been made in their benefit,' he declared; 'and as a Communist Party we have the duty of organising and leading them against it.'

A shrill shout from the corridor floated into the room: 'That's right. Tell us what to do and how to do it, and all

729

of us will be behind you.'

The people applauded this statement, which was followed by another from a middle-aged man. 'That's right, fellow workers. I haven't been home with my dole yet. I have been cut ten shillings and am ashamed to take it to the old 'ooman. What can I tell her,' he wailed, 'when she'll ask me what's to be done?'

This focused the problem for the people present and a loud hubbub of excited argument developed and held up the proceedings for some time before Len could obtain order and throw the meeting open for discussion.

Mary was the first on her feet asking for the floor. She wanted to direct the ideas and opinions of those present in a concrete way, so that the discussion could be positive from the beginning. Her quiet voice failed to carry beyond those in the immediate vicinity for some time, but as it rose higher and stronger it spread its resonance over the room and brought silence that enabled everyone to hear when she said:

'The problem is, what is to be done? Our Party has the task today of solving this, and the first need is unity. Whatever we do must be done together. We have called some of our leaders many things in the past and they are now full of bitterness, but this must be buried in face of this new attack so that we can go forward with them against those responsible for these cuts. I believe we can get the Labour councillors to come with us in this.'

The applause prevented her continuing for some time, the women present clapping vigorously and stamping their feet on the wooden floor until the air in the room rumbled like thunder. Mary waited until the noise died down, then went on somewhat nervously. 'But the first thing is to get all our unemployed together, so that we can find out how many have been cut and by how much. We must then take this to the combine committee so that we can bring the men in work on our side, then we should leave ourselves under the leadership of the combine and ask them to call all the people, with their M.Ps. and councillors, together next Sunday when we can decide what to do next.'

Mary sat down and her beating heart made her deaf to the tumult that followed her words. Men and women clamoured to be allowed to speak in support, but Len wisely asked only those to speak who had different points of view. There were none, so he called for order to put the proposition to the vote and it was carried by a show of waving hands. Someone struck up the 'Internationale', and the meeting closed with the last of its stirring words.

The road outside the library was alive with excited people, waiting for someone who would give a practical lead. Len got on the balcony, Will Evans and Frank Forrest either side of him, and shouted at the top of his voice:

'There will be a mass-meeting of all unemployed men and women on the tip tonight.' The announcement spread in wider circles till all were aware of it.

Without invitation and as a matter of ordinary practice the Party members accompanied Len to his home, where Mary immediately busied herself making tea for them all, putting hot water on the already used leaves in the teapot and pouring out the anaemic fluid without apology. Will Evans paused in his sipping to remark: 'I think we ought

731

to have a leaflet out straightaway; this will force the combine to move.'

Frank Forrest put his cup on the table, pressed his thumb against his loose artificial teeth to keep them fixed, and replied: 'That's not the way to work. If there is to be a leaflet, the combine itself should have one out officially. We have comrades on the committee and it's their job to see to this.'

'Aye,' retorted another, 'if we start monkeying about now, we'll drive the Labour people further away from us instead of bringing them nearer, as we must do if this fight is to go on.'

Mary, sitting on the stool near Len, asked: 'What about our meeting tonight? I believe there'll be thousands there, and it's from there the drive will have to be made. The best way of building unity is not by being content to talk about it and condemning those who don't come our way, but by getting the masses into motion. This will force the others to follow, or force them right out of the movement.'

A wisp of smoke curled out from the chimney and, catching her throat, caused her to cough. The others remained respectfully silent till the spasm passed, Len patting her back the while. Then Will stated:

'I think Mary is right, but who's going to speak in the meeting and put our line forward?'

'Why not yourself?' came the immediate response from many quarters.

Will stared at each of them in turn before saying pitifully: 'Me? Good God! No, I can't speak, mun, and those who said I should, are talking all balls.' He blushed suddenly and turning to Mary in the silence that followed his last words said hesitantly: "'Scuse me, Mary, I forgot about you.'

Len laughed and this eased the momentary tension. After this little interlude the discussion became heated until it was finally agreed that Will should take the chair and Len do the speaking, with Mary in reserve.

Will Evans remained after the others had left, to get a few tips on what to say. He appeared excessively nervous, and this was all the more noticeable because it was in such contrast to his usual devil-may-care demeanour.

Mary chided him. 'What's the matter, Will? You've chaired concerts in the Boar's Head – in fact, all your butties say you are a star turn – and here you are like a little baby with the belly-ache, because you have to chair a meeting.'

'Aye, it's all right for you and the others to talk, Mary, because you haven't got to bloody do it, see. It's one thing talking to your own butties in a pub, but it's another talking to hundreds you don't know.'

Len began saying something, but before the first word left his mouth Will turned on him. 'Don't you say anything, Len. I remember the time when you was like a bloody kid because you had to speak.'

'Oh, well,' Len replied to the challenge, 'it's no good arguing now; the Party has decided, and that's an end to it.'

Will glared at him as though he wanted to strangle him, but he said no more, and shortly after the three went to the meeting place, calling in at the Boar's Head on the way to borrow a box for use as a platform.

The rubbish dump was already dense with people when the trio arrived, and there was a loud hum of excited conversation in the air. Will took the box directly to the centre of the throng, then waited hesitantly.

All the time the Party members were urging him to open the meeting, he was swallowing awkwardly, until the impatience of the crowd, acting as a stimulant, drove him in desperation on to the box, where he stood for some moments looking wildly about him before saying: 'You all know what the meeting is about and I now call on comrade Len Roberts to address you.'

He abruptly stepped off the box, his face steaming with perspiration, to make room for Len, who got into the heart of the subject without any preamble. The added height of the impromptu platform enabled him to see many of the councillors and members of the combine committee who were present, a fact which encouraged him to say: 'There is only one body that can lead this fight successfully, and that is the combine. We must follow it loyally when it gives us its lead.' He then continued with a recital of the things the combine should do immediately, chief among them being the calling of an official meeting of all men and women the following Sunday. The people present, when asked if they agreed with this, made no mistake about their consent.

That night Harry Morgan called a Party meeting, where the whole plan was discussed and decided down to the smallest detail, with the result that in the Sunday meeting called by the combine everything went smoothly, in spite of the fact that Fred Lewis refused to attend on the plea that the whole project was a Bolshevik manoeuvre.

During the remainder of the week Mary and Len spent

734

most of their time outdoors advertising with chalk, poster, and bell the mass demonstration that had been decided upon. Party members and committee men from the combine joined forces with Labour councillors to distribute leaflets round all the houses. Long before the time for the demonstration arrived everyone in the valley knew about it.

After supper the night before the protest march, Mary lay back in her chair and closed her eyes. Len saw the twitching of her cheeks, which he thought had become even thinner since the beginning of the week.

'What is the matter, my dear?' he asked somewhat sadly.

She looked up and smiled at him, but the drooping lips still kept her teeth hidden, and he knew the effort was forced even as she said: 'Nothing, Len, nothing. I am just a little tired.'

He refused to be hoodwinked in this manner and rising from his chair went to her, taking her slim hand into both his own and bending down to bury his mouth in her hair. 'Why try to hide things like this, Mary, when you know that your every mood affects me like an electric current?' The mumbled words came clear to her through the strands of hair that tried to strangle them, and she shook her head slowly as though afraid to reply.

Len waited a while, then finding she made no further attempt to reply, he continued: 'I know how hard you have worked this week for the demonstration and how your chest is troubling you because of this, so why do you keep so aloof when I ask you something? You seem sometimes to be miles away from me, and it is always when I want to be closest to you, Mary. You are a comrade and my wife, and there must be something very deep between you and me, so deep that you are afraid to cross it.'

She caught his head and drew it level with her eyes, which, dilated, stared into his with an intensity that robbed them of vision. The hand on her breast involuntarily withdrew itself when she said in a deep whisper: 'Len, there is so much for you to do in the movement and I am afraid.'

He jerked his head away from the grip of her eyes. 'Afraid?' he queried, as though not sure the word had been used. 'Afraid of what?'

Before answering, she rose from her chair and went to the settee, drawing him with her, and the two, half-sitting, half-lying, faced each other.

'You love me, Len.' The words were at once a statement of fact and a query, to which he nodded a humble acquiescence like a boy caught pilfering. 'Yes,' she went on, 'and that is the danger.'

Again something in her words and tone alarmed him, and he stiffened his limbs although making no reply.

'You see,' she went on, 'if I let you see the world and the struggle as something centred in myself, what will happen to you if you were to lose me?'

He jumped to his feet like a startled hare, and the whiteness of his face emphasised the blue veins in his forehead and the pouches under his eyes.

'Lose you?' he gasped incredulously. 'Lose you? What on earth do you mean?' An idea gripped him even as he asked the question and he hurried on without a pause: 'You are in love with someone else.' He flung himself back on the settee heedless of where he fell, and catching her roughly by the shoulders let his eyes bore deeply into hers. What he saw there made him blink and when he spoke again his voice, though quiet, was infinitely sadder.

'Don't be afraid to tell me, comrade. I know I am not the only man in the world, and that most men can give you much better than I ever can.' A lump rose to his throat at the thought, but he forced himself to say what his whole being was fighting against. 'Yes, my dear. Men and comrades who can give you all the things you have been used to with your father, and the comforts which your poor little body calls for.' His head drooped and he felt a tear trickle down his cheek as he said: 'Forgive me, Mary my dear. It is all my fault. I have been selfish and unkind. I have exploited your patience and your energy. It is only right that I should pay the price before it is too late.'

He rose and stumbled to the fireplace, leaning against the mantelshelf and looking into the fire with eyes that were now dry as the cinders in the grate. Mary did not move after his outburst, but she watched his every motion while the tip of her tongue played about her lips, wetting them for the words bubbling there.

'So that's the sort of man you are! So those are the ideas you've been nursing in your heart!' She shot the statements at him with the momentum of bullets that twisted him half round to face the full blast of what was to follow. 'You coward! To believe such things for one moment and keep them to yourself, while all the time you were talking to me of love, pretending to be so kind and open when the other comrades were here and in the Party meetings.'

737

The blood rushed to his head in waves, changing the white of his face to a flushing red. He made a mute appeal for silence, but she paid no heed to it and went on with increasing vehemence.

'You call yourself a comrade... and I believed you!' Something clutched her throat like a talon, changing her words into hacking coughs.

Len sprang to her side and began rubbing her chest with his hand until she had recovered. Then he stood aside again and bent his head to wait for her further attack.

His action and his posture after the seizure melted the ice in her heart, and a tiny smile crinkled the corner of her lips when she realised how deeply she was misinterpreting his motives. 'Let's forget what both of us have said,' she pleaded softly, 'and get back to what began it all.' He nodded gladly and she continued. 'What I was trying to say was that if we love each other to the exclusion of everything else, even while we are working for the Party, then something would be bound to suffer if one of us lost the other.'

He followed the soft reasoning for some moments without appearing to understand its meaning, then it burst upon him like a flash what she was driving at. 'You have been to a doctor?' he demanded. 'Come on. Tell me what he said.'

She curbed his impetuosity with a glance. 'Yes. I have seen Dr. Barnard, the specialist, and he says if I won't go to a sanatorium very shortly, I'll be in the cemetery inside two years.' She tried to make the statement casual, but failed hopelessly, and the last words were moist with sobs, which acted on Len like petrol on a flame.

'Don't believe him,' he shouted defensively. 'Doctors

pretend they know things when actually they don't understand more than you or me what is wrong.'

'Hush, Len. You know better than that, and it is no good trying to run away from facts. For years both of us have been trying to hide what I showed you years ago in Blackpool.'

Len bent his head and remained silent for a long while. At last he looked up and spoke to her in the deep musical tones that always came to him in a particular mood.

'My love, what can we do? If you were penned up in a home, away from the workers, out of the struggle, you would die as quickly and surely as though you were poisoned. Your life does not exist only in your body, but in what your body and brains do for the struggle in which your father reared you.' He broke down for some minutes and buried his wet face on her shoulder, eventually raising it to continue, without looking at her. 'If I thought there was the least hope you would be cured or even get a little better by going to the sanatorium, I would gladly tell you to go. You believe that, don't you, comrade?' he asked pleadingly.

She answered with a nod, knowing he was putting her own ideas into words without being aware of it himself.

The confirmation excited him and he spoke more hurriedly. 'Yes, yes. What we must do is to plan your work in a better way. So much rest, a little activity, only the most important council committees, choose your food, then watch your weight. Aye, that's the thing. Weight is now life to you. We musn't let you lose an ounce one day without making it up the next.' He laughed to hide his desperation, and she smiled in company. 'If we maintain your weight we can't go wrong. And to do that I will pour my strength, this exuberant energy of mine, into you.'

It was her turn to laugh now, as she ran her hand over his frame, but the spirit behind his remarks heartened her, even though she knew it would be eventually a losing fight.

'Come,' she said, 'let's leave the matter there and clean the supper things.' They both rose, and he wiped the dishes as she washed, both working with happy smiles.

Later that night before she dropped to sleep he took her in his arms and, working her mouth open with his lips, he kissed her with an intake of breath that emptied her lungs and left her gasping, while he fought savagely to take the disease from her body into his own. The vigour of his continued caresses warned her of his intention, and she violently turned from his lips. He had extinguished the candle and failed to see the happy glow on her face as she bade him good night.

Early next morning both woke like a pair of children and he passed joking comments as he watched her dressing. 'We'll soon have to buy a corset for you,' he twitted when he saw her small body exposed by the intimacy of her underclothes.

'What on earth for?' she asked in feigned surprise, drawing another garment over her head.

'Oh, to stop your belly bulging out,' he answered, at the same time breaking into a chuckling laugh, which she joined happily.

But he immediately became serious when she began pulling strong elastic garters over her stockings. 'Huh! Those have got to come off,' he declared categorically.

'What have got to come off?' she asked innocently. 'My stockings?'

He glared a moment, letting his naked legs dangle over the side of the bed before saying, in a dignified manner that reminded her of Big Jim: 'Of course not. Do you want to catch your death of cold? I mean those garters.'

Mary was in a happily wicked mood. 'If I do that my stockings will come down, and I may as well go without any as let that happen, Len.'

He swallowed noisily and came off the bed towards her, at the same time asking in what he intended to be a superior manner, although he would have died rather than go into a draper's shop: 'Have you never heard of suspenders?' Then he entered into an exposition of the harmful effects of garters, that act as ligatures and prevent the blood flowing freely. Mary laughed inwardly at him, but every simple word stamped into her the impress of the love behind it. When he had finished, she flung him a caress with her eyes and later in the day made herself a pair of suspenders.

CWMARDY
MARCHES

During the week Mary had been busy among the women in the street, all of whom had pledged themselves to come to the demonstration. She had been particularly anxious about this, as she believed that each street should come into a demonstration as a contingent with its own banner, and not in the usual straggling individual manner. So, immediately after dinner, when Len had gone down to fetch his father and mother, who were to start from the same street as themselves, she went from house to house getting the women ready. In every home she was welcomed either with a smile or a joking remark, the little children, many of them with bare backsides, running to the door to greet her.

Half an hour before the demonstration was timed to start the women and children and the unemployed men in the street were lined up with a red banner at their head with:

'Sunny Bank Women want Bread not Batons'

sewn in white tape. Mary forgot her chest and the conversation with Len on the previous night as she looked behind her at the ranks of men and women who were ready to march. Each pair of eyes gleamed as brightly as her own and every mouth wore a smile, even the little babies', clutched tightly to their mothers' bodies in heavy woollen shawls. One of the Party members from the next street came up with a clarinet and two kettle-drums. The ex-servicemen present soon selected two drummers, and in a very short time the air was ringing with the strains of popular songs. The sharp notes of the clarinet kept everyone in tune and the tremor of the drums made feet itch to get into stride. Occasionally the clarinet gave a shrill scream as though its innards were twisted, but no one took any notice of this and kept on singing with unflinching gusto.

At last the music was interrupted by a cheer as Len and his parents came round the corner of the street. Big Jim, failing to walk erect, pretended he was doing so by stretching his head unnaturally far back and twirling his moustache arrogantly. But, not noticing where he was going, he stumbled against a stone in the roadway and would have fallen had not Siân gripped him tightly.

'Holy hell!' he growled under his breath, while at the same time trying to regain his dignified posture. 'These bloody roads are not fit for a dog to walk on, muniferni. It

744

is time that the council do something about it.'

No one heard his words in the excited clamour as the people prepared for the march off. Jim and Siân were given the place of honour in the front rank because they were amongst the oldest inhabitants of Cwmardy. Len and Mary stood either side of the procession to marshal it. The men with the clarinet and drums waited for the signal, everyone held their breath for a moment, then three rolls on the drums, the clarinet blared into action, and the people began their march to the main demonstration. At each street-corner numbers of people saw friends already in the ranks and tried to break in to join them, only to be firmly told that they must go behind as the ranks were not to be broken. Whenever anyone was persistent, the women became vociferous and let the delinquent know, if he was not prepared to go to the rear of his own volition, he would be placed there. Siân and Big Jim, right at the head of the demonstration, with the blood-red banner streaming directly behind them, walked silent and erect, like soldiers, Jim jealously watching every stride she made to make sure she was in step. She stumbled once and, not knowing how, was unable to change her step to answer the music before Jim saw her.

'Change,' he hissed, without turning his head. 'Change, fenyw, for God's sake. You are a disgrace to the regiment, mun.'

Siân felt deeply the indignity of her position. 'I can't, James bach, I don't know how,' she moaned quietly so that no one but he could hear.

'Uffern dân, do scotch with both feet at once,' he

instructed. She misunderstood him and gave a little hop which only took her slightly in front without bringing her into step. Jim's eyes went blood-shot as he glared at her.

'Fall out,' he ordered. 'Fall out quick to the rear before anybody know you are with me.'

Siân squared her drooping shoulders and planted her feet more firmly into the earth with each stride.

'Never,' she declared emphatically, not caring now who heard her. 'No, not for all the sodgers or sailors in the King's or anybody else's army will Siân fall out. Huh!'

Len happened to come to the front of the procession at this moment and one glance at his parents told him what was brewing. He blew a whistle sharply, the impromptu band stopped playing and the people came to a halt.

'Just a whiff for the stragglers to draw up, so that we can march into the Square in order,' Len shouted, at the same time trying to convey with a glance a message to Mary on the other side. She unostentatiously made her way to him and he whispered in her ear. When the signal was given for the restart, Mary was marching between the old couple.

Sunny Bank contingent was the first at the starting point on the Square on top of the hill near the pits, but in a very short time hundreds more had gathered and before the pit-hooter blaringly announced that the men were about to come up, the Square was packed with men and women. Red banners and streamers speckled the air as the mournful strains of the drum and fife band floated up the hill. Miners in their working clothes and with coal-soiled faces joined the unemployed people, for the march round the valley.

The air was blasted by a roar like thunder when the gallant little group of bandsmen, puffing and blowing, staggered over the crest of the hill and came into sight. Their thirst was quickly quenched by the women, who ran into nearby houses and fetched out jugs of tea, water, and small beer, or whatever other liquid they could get. The lodge officials, some in working kit, now formed up in front with Len and Mary. Jim and Siân fell in the rank immediately behind, their temporary difference forgotten. The people of Sunny Bank made sure their banner was next to the one belonging to the combine committee, this being the only one to which they would grant precedence.

The signal was now given to the band leader, the drums rolled, the fifes began to wail, and the long demonstration against the cuts inflicted on the unemployed began its march around the valley.

At the bottom of the hill, before turning into the Square which led to the rubbish dump where the other pit contingents of the combine were waiting, Len looked back. His eyes glowed with what he saw. The street behind him looked like a flowing river of human beings, on which floated innumerable scarlet banners and flags. He looked far into the ascending distance, but failed to see any end. His eyes began to water with the strain and he allowed his ears to continue where the former failed. Although directly in front of the band, he heard running beneath its thrumming wails the deep monotone of countless boots tramping rhythmically on the hard road. The potential power in the sound tickled his throat, sending saliva into his mouth. He had to gulp before he could say in an excited whisper to Mary: 'It's the greatest thing that's ever been. Everybody is on the march. Everybody.' His emotion became too deep to allow for more.

Mary, pride in her every gesture, murmured: 'This is the cure, Len, for me and the people. Unity. Unity in action.' Her voice rose into a shout on this last phrase, and in a moment it was taken up by some young people until it spread all through the ranks like thunder.

'Unity. Unity in action.' The sound of the marching feet was drowned in its tremor.

Mary turned to look at Siân and Jim. The old couple were tight-lipped and silent, but they beamed with happiness, although in Jim's eyes there was also a look of dignity and discomfiture, as though his pride was beating back something he badly wanted to do.

Mary sensed the situation and whispered to Len, who immediately stepped back to his father's side and said: 'There's a urinal lower down, dad. You had better drop out by there and join us on the field.'

Jim kept his eyes fixed on the man in front of him and screwed his mouth up to say: 'What in hell think you I am, Len? Do you think I can't carry three pints without falling out? Huh! I have drunked twenty-three before now and marched eighteen miles afterwards without ever thinking of losing a drop, muniferni.'

Len felt abashed at this retort, particularly when he glimpsed the proud smile on his mother's grim face, and he hastily stepped forward to his own place, where Mary glanced at him inquiringly. He shook his head as an answer to her unspoken query.

By this time the head of the demonstration had reached the Square, which was dense with people cordoned off to make way for the demonstration to pass through to the assembling field. Uniformed ambulance men, lining each side of the street, took their places alongside the marching men and women, and in this manner for over half an hour the people of Cwmardy poured through the Square which was their ancient battle-ground, into the field where most of their vital decisions had been taken.

A short rest was taken there, while the various bands competed for the loudest playing. The valiant little fife band was lost in the din of different marches blared with brassy resonance into the air, which shook in the martial strains. The various committees now took charge of their own contingents and began marshalling them up, after Mary had had a conversation with the leaders, who agreed that the women should head the march from the field. There was some initial confusion while the people were being sorted out, some women preferring to march with their menfolk, but eventually everything, as far as possible, was in order and ready for the next stage. The bands, each with its own vivid and distinctive uniform, were scattered at regular intervals through the length of the demonstration, adding to its vivacity and colour. A bugle sounded, drums rolled once more, the bands took up the refrain, and the procession began to unwind itself from the field.

The leaders of the combine committee marched in front of the leading band, which was followed by the women, but Siân and Big Jim still remained in the second rank, having with adamant curtness refused to be parted or shifted. The procession marched twelve abreast through the main street, most of whose shop windows still wore shutters as mementos of past battles.

When the front of the demonstration was two miles advanced, and on the summit of the hill to the east of Cwmardy, people were still pouring from the assembling field. Len lifted his head sharply into the air when he fancied he heard the distant strains of music in the direction left of the demonstration. He turned to Mary and the workman next her.

'Can you hear anything?' he asked.

They both looked simultaneously past Len, and he, seeing their amazement, turned his head to look in the same direction. He drew his breath sharply and his perspiring face went a shade whiter. The mountain which separated Cwmardy from the other valleys looked like a gigantic anthill, covered with a mass of black, waving bodies.

'Good God,' the man next to Mary whispered, 'the whole world is on the move.'

Mary did not reply for some time, unable to take her eyes from the scene, although her feet kept automatically moving her forward in time with the band. Then she murmured, 'No, not yet. But the people are beginning to move it now.' She said no more, and even the bands were quiet. The people seemed overwhelmed with the mighty demonstration of their own power, which they could now see so clearly. Their voices suddenly became puny, and articulation was left to their feet, which rattled and sang on the roadways with music more devastating in its strength than all the bands in the world.

Len momentarily felt himself like a weak straw drifting in and out with the surge of bodies. Then something powerful swept through his being as the mass soaked its strength into him, and he realised that the strength of them all was the measure of his own, that his existence and power as an individual was buried in that of the mass now pregnant with motion behind him. The momentous thought made him inhale deeply and his chest expanded, throwing his head erect and his shoulders square to the breeze that blew the banners into red rippling slogans of defiance and action. Time and distance were obliterated by the cavalcade of people, whose feet made the roads invisible.

The head of the demonstration now began to descend the other side of the hill which led to the road leading back to Cwmardy. As it passed Fred Lewis's villa, he ran out, hastily pulling his coat on as he ran.

'Hallo,' he greeted them, waving his arm the while in a gesture of welcome, although his shaven face looked even sallower than usual under its dark skin. 'All the people in the two valleys seem to have turned out today.'

No one answered him and the band struck up another vigorous march. He tried to sidle his way into the front ranks, but was silently elbowed from one to the other until he found himself helpless on the side, dumb and open-mouthed in face of the flood that swept past him. At last someone took pity and allowed him to join in the ranks, where he was immediately lost to sight like something ephemeral that had come and vanished instantly.

Len's heart was now pounding madly as the significance of the incident gripped his imagination, and he turned again to Mary, who sensed his mood immediately.

'Like a moth around our bedroom candle,' he told her softly, clasping her hand in his. 'It comes and fusses about the flame, concentrating attention upon itself while it is buzzing around, then a little puff and it's gone again. Devoured by the very thing that drew it and gave it momentary prominence.'

'Yes, Len. The people are like that flame. They give life, security, fame, and power to some. But they always give it on loan. And always, sooner or later, they collect the debt; and the day they do that is the day that welshers disappear. Like a star falling in the sky, it comes out of nothing and for an instant the whole world that can see looks up to its radiance, and watches it fade and die, to be swallowed by the very void by which it came.'

They both became silent again, while the men either side looked at them queerly, probably wondering if the demonstration had suddenly affected their minds.

'That is how the Party came,' she mused to herself, although Len, hyper-sensitive where she was concerned, heard her muttered thoughts. 'But the Party can never melt,' she continued, unconscious of Len's interested attention. 'It is moulded in and welded with the body itself, so that only the weakest and rottenest parts of it can ever drop off and be discarded.'

She was suddenly attracted by a big building some hundreds of yards in front, and she more or less subconsciously recognised the old mansion that housed the officers and staff of the new unemployment board operating the cuts. Little figures on the veranda scuttled

752

out of sight as the procession came into view. The action gave her an idea and turning sharply she tried to spring past Len without disturbing the marching step of the demonstration. He heard a sound like something tearing beneath her skirt and his eyes opened wide with a quick-born suspicion of what had happened, but before he had time to question, she was past him and hastily whispering something to the foremost ranks of women, all of whom, he noticed, nodded their heads in agreement. When she returned to her place by his side, he was so curious that the incident of Fred Lewis completely slipped his mind. He noticed the determined twist that had come on her mouth and was too impatient to wait.

'What's in the wind, now?' he asked.

She looked at him and the other men slyly, then replied loud enough for them all to hear: 'The women are going in to see the chief unemployment officer.'

The men stood stock-still for a moment, amazed at the casualness of the statement and the implications involved in it. But they were soon forced forward and had to argue their opposition to the project while they were marching.

'You can't do that,' said one. 'The committee never decided it.'

'No,' said the other. 'This is a demonstration against the Government and I'm not one who is prepared for any hanky-panky bloody tricks. Everything has gone all right up to now, and we don't want you women kicking up a shindy for nothing.'

Mary changed colour and Len started to defend her when she said determinedly: 'I agree with you. But the

Government isn't only a number of people in London. Government is of no use and can't act unless it has agents and officers and staff in every village of the country.'

'That's it,' Len implemented, unable to restrain himself any longer. 'Isn't Parker, the new unemployment bloke, an agent of the Government carrying out Government orders? Of course he is,' he answered himself. 'An Act of Parliament on a bit of paper with a king's seal stuck on it in London is of no more value than the paper itself and a spot of red wax. It is only when what it says is acted upon in Cwmardy and all the other places in the country, by people who are paid to operate it, it is only then that an Act of Parliament is of use to the Government. I think Mary is right,' he concluded. 'The Government in London don't make us suffer in London. No. It's here they make us suffer, and it's here we've got to fight them and the suffering they inflict on our people.'

Before the other men had time to reply to this argument they were outside the offices. Mary and Len silently stepped on one side and let the band proceed, unaware of what was being discussed. The other men in front went with them, but the leading rank of women had stopped, their action followed in turn by every rank that closed up. The motion worked quietly back through the demonstration like a slow ripple receding to the rim of a pond. Police, white-faced and trembling, seemed to spring from nowhere, and their chief came hurrying towards Len and the others in the front.

'You can't stop here, Len,' he declared. 'Permission was only given for the march and the meetings in the field.'

The air immediately became filled with excited clamour which drew the police together into a more solid phalanx between the demonstration and the building. Big Jim worked his way to Mary's side, followed closely by Siân, who kept her eyes on Len.

'We don't intend harming anyone,' the latter told the inspector. 'All we want is to send a deputation in to see Mr. Parker about these cuts.'

The inspector hesitated, but only for a moment as the pressure behind began to force the front in. 'Wait a moment,' he asked nervously. 'I'll inquire if a deputation will be received.' He returned in a matter of seconds.

'I'm very sorry, but Mr. Parker can only see deputations by appointment.'

'That's not for him to decide,' said Mary.

She looked behind her and sighed before turning again to the inspector.

'There are women in this demonstration who have carried babies more than ten miles already,' she said. 'And I don't believe they are willing to do that for nothing. If you don't believe me, ask them,' she invited, secure in her faith that the women would stand and that the men would stand with them.

The inspector looked at the mass of people, who stretched beyond reach of sight, and very wisely did not accept the invitation. Instead he shook his head resignedly, then warned her: 'You will be held responsible for all that happens here today.'

Big Jim, standing near, pushed himself between them. 'Oh no, not quite so quick, boy bach. If anybody is to be blamed for what haven't happened, it's me, and don't you forget. Huh! Fancy a bloody lump like you trying to put the blame for nothing on a little gel like that.'

Mary caught his arm before he could say more.

'Don't worry,' she told the inspector. 'We shan't hurt anyone if your men keep their hands still.'

The long pause while the conversation was going on made the people impatient and restless, particularly those too far off to see what was happening. They began to press forward and the weight increased as a shout rose: 'Don't let anybody stop us. Right on now and no turning back.'

The noise stimulated them, and they surged forward with such vigour that the front ranks were through the police cordon before anyone knew what had occurred. The inspector made a grab for Mary as she was swept past him, but the pressure tore her from his grasp. In a matter of seconds the mass of women had surrounded the officers, and, helped by the men nearest them, were lustily shouting for the unemployment officer to come to the window and speak to them. But no reply came from the house, so the women rushed into the silent building, only to find all the doors barred against them.

A shrill voice, rising clear above the din, shouted: 'Round the back.'

In an instant the women poured out of the building and streamed with the remainder of their mates to the rear, where Mary, helped by numerous hands was already being lifted to the window. She had gripped the sill and was scratching wildly with her shoes on the wall to get a foothold, when Len saw her stocking slowly drop down over her leg, leaving its whiteness bare to the eyes that watched.

He was about to shout a warning when other women rushed forward; at the same time a crash was followed by the tinkle of falling glass. No one ever knew who was first through the window and in the office, but the next thing the crowd outside saw was a dozen women waving and cheering from the room above.

The demonstrators responded and the cheering swept through the ranks until it resounded all round Cwmardy as the mile upon mile of street-packed people took up the shouts, although only a small proportion of them could possibly know what had happened in front. Mary, one stocking sagged over her shoe, looked at the women about her, and pride made her forget for some moments what they had come for, until a loud noise at the door the other side of the room drew her attention. The women all turned in that direction, and for the first time saw a slight, pale man, with a small moustache hardly the width of his nostrils, standing fearfully with his back to the wall furthest from the window. Some of the women began to laugh at the sight, but the noise at the door became more loud and imperative. 'Open this door,' a muffled voice was shouting. 'What for do you keep me out here in the cold when you are all in there?'

Mary recognised Siân's voice, and in a very short time with the help of other women she drew the bolts, undid the chain, and opened the door to admit as many of the people crammed in the passage as could enter the room.

Siân, quivering with temper, demanded to know who had dared to lock her out. Mary, putting her arms round the old lady's shoulder, soon succeeded in placating her, before turning to the man with the moustache, who was begging the woman nearest him: 'Don't touch me. I have got my duty to do even if I dislike it.'

He shook pitifully as he made his plea. Mary stepped forward and the people noticed a sneer on her lips when she replied: 'Duty? That's what the policeman says when he kicks a woman he's batoned to the floor. And that's the excuse you make when you rob her of bread.'

She paused to regain her breath after the exertion of climbing into the room and the passion that was now beginning to overcome her. Another woman, her eyes as heavy with fatigue as her stomach was from bearing too many children, filled the breach.

'We haven't come here to touch you,' she declared, her voice still carrying traces of the music that once used to stir concert audiences. 'But neither do we want you to hurt us, whether you call it duty or not.'

'But what can I do, what can I do?' he wailed, rubbing his hands helplessly through his hair.

'Don't operate any more cuts and send a wire to the Government telling them of our demands,' shouted Mary.

This excited the other people in the room, and they all began shouting together. The people outside thought something was happening to them and the shout spread in wider circles until the unemployment officer thought the world was being deluged. A look of absolute fear came into his eyes and when he saw a group of men wildly clambering about the window to get inside, his heart gave way and he dropped to his knees moaning like a child being cruelly beaten. Mary glanced at the crouching form and a spasm of pity ran through her for a moment, till she saw Len and Will Evans with other men, sitting astride the shattered window-sill, from which point of vantage they could see all that was happening both in the room and among the mass of people outside, who now began to sing again.

She bent down, and putting her hand under the official's arm helped him to his feet, where he stood, swallowing hard, as Mary asked him in quieter tones: 'Well, what is your answer? We don't want to be here all day.' She glanced round the room. 'Some of these women still have over ten miles to march before they get home.'

The man looked helplessly at her, then managed to whisper: 'What if I refuse?'

The answer came from all the women simultaneously: 'You'll stop in this room till you change your mind.'

Mary began making her way to the window. He sensed her intention and stopped her with a cry that seemed to stick in his throat. 'All right. I'll do as you say.'

The women could hardly believe their ears for a moment, and looked into each other's faces as though seeking answer there, until Mary rushed to the window and, with a flurry of skirts, was lifted bodily by Len and Will on to the sill, where they held her safely while she told the people outside what had transpired.

Like an electric current the news flashed from mouth to mouth so quickly that it seemed all the people in Cwmardy knew of it in an instant.

The air crackled in the shouts and cheers, while Mary and the other women left the building and took their places back in the ranks. The band had now returned, and striking up a Welsh battle march the demonstration started on its final trek to the field where the meetings were to be held.

For hours the people remained on the rubbish dump, listening to speeches, singing, and cheering themselves hoarse, before black shadows creeping slowly over the mountains warned them it was time to begin the tramp home.

Len and Mary went home with his parents. They found the fire burned out and the coal nothing but a white ash.

Jim started to swear miserably. 'A man can't leave his own house for two minutes, muniferni, without the bloody fire do try to spite him out.' He was tired and sore and wanted to vent his spleen on something. He chose the fire knowing it couldn't answer back, but Siân was also tired.

'For shame, James bach,' she scolded. 'If you haven't got no 'spects for me, you did ought to have it for these children by here, who can hear every dirty word that do leave your mouth.'

Jim grunted and lowered his huge body very slowly and carefully into the armchair while Len with some paper and sticks drew the fire into a new blaze on which Mary soon boiled the kettle and made tea.

The supper revived their spirits and their eyes flashed again as they recited the various happenings of the day and competed with each other which was the most stirring thing that had occurred. Big Jim thought it was the march of the Sunny Bank contingent up to the meeting place.

'Only one thing did spoil it,' he commented. 'If it wasn't for your mother by there, with her bad legs and what not –

I told her 'nough not to come out – it 'ood have been a better march than any guardsman could make.'

Siân half rose from her chair, but Len forestalled the threatening storm.

'I don't know, mum and dad,' he said, 'but the best thing of it all to my mind was when our Mary climbed up that window with her stocking hanging down over her shoe. Ha-ha!' He laughed boisterously at the memory, while the others looked down in surprise at Mary's bare leg, which in her astonishment she lifted without thinking what she was doing.

Big Jim chuckled wickedly at the sight. 'Well, well,' he remarked like a professor stating an unchallenging thesis, 'that's a lovely little leg for you, Siân fach.'

But Siân did not hear this remark. 'There,' she declared. 'Now I know why you do cough so much. How do you 'spect your chest to be helfy when you do leave your legs naked like that?'

Mary blushed, but had no time to make any reply before Siân continued. 'How come it you is like that, my gel? Tut-tut! No wonder half those men was mad.'

'Oh, mother,' Mary eventually managed to blurt out, her face red as the fire, 'I didn't know it was down.' She turned to Len and began to upbraid him. 'Why didn't you tell me?' she demanded.

He burst into another laugh. 'I knew, but I forgot all about it in the excitement,' he answered.

Big Jim broke in. 'I am not the only man who do forget things then! Ha-ha! That's one for me, Siân.'

He suddenly stopped laughing and doubling up in his chair

761

began to groan. 'Oh, hell! This bloody back and the rheumatics will be the death of me. Help me, Siân,' he growled out, 'not stand staring by there at a man dying, mun.'

Siân sprang to the cupboard, bringing back with her a bottle of something which she shook vigorously.

'Pull his shirt off, Mary fach,' she commanded.

Mary went to the old man, who continued to grunt as they helped him remove the shirt and exposed the huge hairy chest beneath.

'I have told you before, Siân,' he grunted, 'that that stuff is like dog's piss for all the use it be.'

Siân took no heed of his grunts and began rubbing the evil-smelling stuff into his chest, after which she turned him round and did the same to his back. He twitched his shoulders once when she happened to be a bit rough.

'Holy hell! Trying to kill me on the sly, are you? Don't forget I have got witnesses here if you start any of your bloody nonsense.'

'Hush, James bach,' she retorted placidly, 'don't draw sin on your head without need. You have got enough there as it is.'

Before the treatment was finished, the sound of singing came from the mountain that separated Cwmardy from the other valley. It was so sweetened by the distance that they looked at each other.

'It's the people going home from the demonstration,' Len said.

Without another word they all went to the door and looked at the black sides from which crept the music of the men and women still making their way homewards.

Other people in the street heard it and were drawn out of their houses to the doorstep, where they silently listened to the slowly receding harmony, that brought odd little twitches to their throats. Suddenly, Big Jim, still without his shirt, strode into the middle of the road and waving his arm in the air, let his voice boom out: 'Three cheers for unity – hip-hip!'

The 'Hurrah' that followed spread over the valley like a blanket, and was repeated till the sounds of singing were lost in the distance.

STAY-IN STRIKE

The action taken in Cwmardy against the Government's attempt to lower the standards of the unemployed spread through the country like a flame. The Government grew alarmed at the growing heat and strength of the protest and issued a 'Standstill Order' that restored the cuts already made.

This victory acted like a tonic upon the people, particularly those in the pits. The prestige of the Party increased tremendously as a result of the struggle, and many of its members were made officials of the Federation, Harry Morgan becoming chairman of the combine and Will Evans chairman of the lodge.

Strengthened in this way and now having to act as administrators as well as agitators and propagandists, the Party members held many discussions on how best to get rid of the company non-political union.

One Friday, the men themselves brought things to a head. A hurried phone message sent Harry and Len scurrying to the pit-head, where they found the men who had just come up holding a meeting. Although Will Evans was busily addressing them, the men were broken up into little groups each discussing something that appeared to upset them considerably. Big Jim was the most vociferous, and the only one whose words were decipherable above the din.

'Do they think I am a dog,' he bawled, 'that they give me boy's pay after a week's work? Muniferni, if Hicks do think he can do that to me, he is climbing the wrong pole, and he can put his shirt on that. Good God, if I tooked this pay home to Siân, she would chuck it and me out through the bloody window!'

Will Evans tried to get order. 'Come, boys,' he pleaded, 'let us have some sense about it. Let's know first of all how many of you are under your money.'

Into the air went a number of hands each holding a pay sheet.

'Hold 'em up, boys, while I count 'em.'

This done, he asked for the amounts the individuals were short of, and immediately the din rose again.

'Ten bob. Twelve and six. Fifteen bob.' The shouts came from all parts of the crowd.

Harry and Len had worked their way to the improvised platform by this time and the former got up alongside Will. His uplifted hand, commanding silence, for some reason reminded Len of Ezra and took his mind back over twenty years when the fight for the minimum wage began. But he had no time for meditation before Harry's piercing tones broke into his thoughts.

'The first thing to do, comrades, is to appoint a deputation to see Hicks straight away.'

This was speedily done, Harry, Will, Big Jim, and Len being appointed for the interview.

Mr. Hicks hastily dodged back from the window through which he had been watching the scene, and when they entered the office they found him surrounded by his officials. He did not invite them to confront him, but addressed them over the heads of his subordinates.

'Well, what do you want now? And why in hell is it those men have not gone home? If they were doing justice to their work they'd have gone long ago.'

Harry started to speak, but Big Jim got in before him.

'Pull your feet off that table, mun, when you are talking to better men than yourself, and meet us face to face, not with this pack of bloodhounds between us.'

'Let me alone, Len,' he continued when the latter tugged his sleeve to calm him. 'Do you think I have put my body into this pit all my life to have a pay like this after a full week's work?' He dragged his hand from his pocket and exposed a ten-shilling note and some silver, flourishing it around his head so that all could see. He grunted disgustedly. 'Huh! I have pissed more than this against the back wall of the Boar's Head on a Saturday night before now.'

Mr. Hicks rose from his chair and the officials opened out to admit the deputation to his sight. The heavy pouches under his eyes quivered with temper when he spoke, and he clutched his stick so tightly that his knuckles were as white as his face.

'So that's what all the fuss is about, is it? You expect me to pay men for loafing about all day, do you? Well, let me tell you all now, that those days are over for good.'

Harry interrupted him. 'Don't forget, Mr. Hicks, there is a minimum wage Act, that some of our men died for, still in existence, and you can depend on it you'll pay that whatever goes.'

Hicks turned on him in a fury. 'What? Are you threatening me? Get out.' He turned sharply to the official nearest him, and snarled: 'Here, phone up the police. Tell them I'm being intimidated.'

Jim's bent shoulders straightened so erectly that his body seemed to fill the room. 'Police, police,' he stuttered. 'Ah! They 'on't be much bloody good to you. You had to send for sodgers when us fought for the minimum wage in the first place, and you'll want 'em now before you make us work for nothing.'

It was obvious by now to all present that Mr. Hicks was not in a condition to negotiate anything with the deputation, and Len nodded to his friends a hint to leave. As they were going out Mr. Hicks raged like a lion losing a prey it thought secure.

'All right,' he roared, waving his stick like a baton. 'If you won't listen to sense, Jim Roberts, call in the office for your cards. There are plenty of better men than you waiting and willing to do your work, and that goes for the others as well.'

Jim, who was on his way to the door, turned at this to snarl: 'Aye, I know. The Federashon have been a bone in

768

your guts for a long time now. That's why you have brought these non-political foreigners in to take our places, and you do think now you will sweep all the old hands out and fill the pit with non-pols. Bah!' Spitting his disgust. 'I have seened better things than you in a dog's bile. Ach! But don't you think you have winned. No, us have still got a couple of cards up our sleeve.'

With this the deputation went out to the men who were impatiently waiting.

Later that evening a meeting was held in Len's house. Party members looked their perturbation. They knew Mr. Hicks had precipitated the inevitable, but were not sure how best to counter his move. They discussed the position for hours, Len remaining silent for a long while until an idea breeding in his mind reached maturity. When he spoke it was in a whisper, as though he were afraid of what he was saying.

'Comrades, we've been bullied and battered for staying up the pit. What about staying down for a change?' The brief sentence was followed by a momentary pause, then a gasp of surprise as the audacity of the idea made itself felt. When the Party meeting broke up, the decision was made and worked out the same night in a secret emergency committee of the Federation.

During the small hours of the morning the throb of the pit engines seemed more subdued and hesitant, and the black air quivered as though with the suppressed excitement. Shadows slipped silently from house to house leaving a message in each, but no word leaked out from the quickly closed doors. Police officers, smelling trouble as a fox smells fowl, snooped around the street-corners and back lanes vainly trying to pick up information.

Mr. Hicks, rather more subdued, had called all his leading officials together in the consulting-room on the pit-head. The general manager's face shone white in the sooty atmosphere of the overheated office as he addressed his subordinates, most of whom were in their pit clothes.

'It's strange,' he muttered disconsolately, 'that none of you know what the men are up to. Usually when they are going to strike we know all about it, but this time everything seems so still and ordinary, yet we know there is something in the wind.' He rose from his chair and restlessly scratched his head as though the contact of his fingernails with his scalp would give him inspiration. The faces of his listeners emphasised his own bewilderment when he asked: 'Did none of you hear the men say something in the pit today, just one little hint?'

Williams, the under-manager, his black moustache drooping over his mouth, shook his head slowly. 'Yes. It was shameful to hear what some of them were saying. A stranger would have thought they were pounds under their money instead of a few paltry shillings.'

Evan the Overman interrupted. 'But a funny thing, they seemed friendly with the company union members. I can't understand it at all.' He pulled a brass box from his waistcoat pocket and put a huge wad of tobacco in his mouth.

Mr. Hicks watched him, with an absent look, and when the pouch was replaced, the action seemed to fix something in his mind.

'All right,' he declared, 'we will know soon enough. All of you be up half an hour earlier than usual in the morning. I have told the police to stop those reds distributing any leaflets on the pit-head, and all you want to do if the men try to hold a sudden meeting is to urge them down as quickly as possible. That's it,' he declared, his eyes beginning to gleam with enthusiasm, 'get them down.' The officials left the office with this exhortation echoing in their ears.

Next morning, as the men queued up to await their turn for going down the shaft, a whisper ran through their ranks. It was as delicate as the swaying of a rose in a breeze and was inaudible above the rhythmic intonation of the machinery to all but those interested. 'Be careful with your grub and water today, boys,' it ran sibilantly from mouth to mouth, never becoming louder as it slipped through the ranks, but manifesting its existence by a restless tremor. The men seemed unusually anxious to get down out of the daylight, which as a rule they were loath to leave for the blackness of the pit.

Officials scattered here and there about the surface were amazed at the eagerness with which the men filled each cage and sank out of sight. When the wooden droppers had banged loudly after the last human load, Mr. Hicks came out of the consulting-room. A broad smile split his face as he approached Williams, the under-manager.

'Well, it seems our suspicions were unfounded, Mr. Williams. Very good. Very good indeed.'

He twirled his walking-stick happily as the under-manager replied: 'Yes, Mr. Hicks, they went down, thank goodness, and we are right for today again.'

The colliery sergeant butted in. 'Not even Roberts and his Bolshies troubled us, sir. We were expecting some nonsense from them.' Mr. Hicks nodded, but made no reply as he turned and made his way back into the office accompanied by his under-manager.

Meanwhile the men in the last cage lingered a little on the pit bottom, but not long enough to cause suspicion. They fancied the trudge to their working places, past huge roof-holes and overhanging rocks, had become much shorter, and many of them sang quietly as they walked with bent heads and bowed shoulders. The hymns they sang were old and mournful, but the voices, though deep, were happy. The younger men were especially exuberant, galloping noisily down the steep inclines, making the men in front scamper hurriedly to the rubbish-plastered sides in the belief that the horses were stampeding. Will Evans, however, seemed to have lost his playfulness, and he walked quietly behind Dai Cannon and Big Jim, hardly listening to the remarks flying around him.

'I don't like this new stunt we are planning,' Dai told Jim, a blob of sweat dangling precariously from the end of his nose. 'I always like to see a straight fight, and not these foreign affairs that sound all right but don't lead nowhere.'

'I don't know, mun Dai,' Jim grunted, his huge body bent nearly in two under the low roof. 'Us have always got to find new ways of fighting if us do want to win. And, any fight is better than the pay I had yesterday. You ought to have heard Siân when I gived it to her!'

'Huh! New ways, muniferni. The old ones was good enough for my father and his father before him, and they are good enough for me too.'

Jim unconsciously lifted his head to reply, hitting it sharply against an overhanging piece of rock. 'Hell fire!' he roared, forgetting all about his answer as he rubbed the injured spot vigorously. 'This bloody pit is getting more like a muck-hole every day. They will want dogs to pull the coal out before long if they don't do some ripping to this blasted top.'

Will Evans noisily shifted a lump of tobacco into his cheek. 'Aye, you are right, butty. The company have forgot all about repairs. So long as we give them all the coal they want, never mind a hell how we get it. This old pit will soon only be good for swopping for a broody hen. They tell me,' he added confidentially, 'that they are going to get rid of all the horses and are going to buy mice to pull the trams out because the roof is so low.'

'Mice,' growled Jim. 'Huh! No decent mouse would work in the bloody hole. It's only daft beggars, like us, will do that, and fight each other for the chance. No wonder the bosses are laughing, muniferni.' He kept on grunting and swearing for the remainder of the distance into the face.

Once there, the men were not long stripping to the waist, and in a very short time the signal passed down the face: 'Let her have it.' After a few preliminary coughing 'phot-phots' the conveyor began its voice-shattering jerks that always kept it empty. The air became heavy with coal-dust that added to the heat and made it more intolerable.

The diffusing light from the lamps was blanketed by the dust, which left nothing but green pin-pricks to stab the darkness. Bodies, gleaming with sweat, lost tangibility and became emphasising shadows in the blackness. Big Jim lay flat on his side, slicing through the coal with deep, reiterating blows from his needle-pointed pick, while Will Evans, on his knees and bent in two, shovelled the product on the troughs, which he fancied were always shouting: 'Fill me up quick... Fill me up quick.'

Suddenly the terrific clattering of the conveyor ceased, leaving the men dangling helplessly in an aural void until a heavy voice boomed up the face.

'Who the bloody hell put this muck on the troughs? Do you think I am a cockle girl, or what, spending all my time picking stones off the conveyor? Play the bloody game, you up there.'

An authoritative voice sounded from the roadway. 'What's the matter, boys bach? Why the hell is the conveyor on stop? Do you know you are losing coal every minute and the journey is waiting for you?'

Big Jim could not stand this; flinging down his mandril, he lifted himself on his knees until his naked back touched the roof. 'Coal! Coal! That's all I can see and hear,' he shouted. 'That's all my bloody life is. Never mind about money. Never mind about food. Give the company coal and the world can go to hell.' He exhausted himself, picked up the mandril and started hacking the coal as a vent for his temper. The conveyor began again as suddenly as it had stopped, and for the remainder of the day it dominated the bodies of the workmen.

At the end of the shift the men lay back on the roadway for some time, stretching their limbs to cure them of the cramp induced by their work, but Will Evans seemed to have gathered a sudden excess of energy and ran from place to place like a rabbit, saying a few words to the men in turn. When he returned to his own road the workmen there were already dressed and waiting for him, Big Jim whiling away the time with yarns about Africa and Gibraltar.

'I 'member once in Gib,' he said, while Will put his clothes on, 'an old Dutchman who owned all the oyster beds, mun jawli. One day he comed to our commandant with tears in his eyes as big as dog's balls. I was batman to the commandant at the time and knowed all that passed.' "Somebody is pinching my oysters," he did say, "and I do want you to put a stop to it." He said a lot more than this, waving his hands about all the time like if he wanted to chuck 'em in the air and bring the fief to him there and then. Our C.O. didn't say a word till he had finished, then he said, short like, "All right, butty. I will put a guard on the beds." But next day the Dutchy comes up agen with the same tale, only worse. The chief did scratch his head funny-like and grunt to hisself: "Hmm. Peculiar. I will put another sentry on." And he did too, muniferni, but on the third day the Dutchman comed up agen with the same yarn and crying real this time like a man whose dog has been poisoned. After he finished – and it was a hell of a long time before he did, mind you – the C.O. said stern-like: "All right. There is nothing for it but to double the guard." The Dutchman gave him one look for a minute then let out a yell that nearly broked the windows, and beginned to dance about like one of those dolls us used to see in the circus, shouting all the time at the top of his voice: "Double the guard! No, by damn, take the bloody lot off before they eat the beds and all!"' All the workmen joined in the laugh that followed.

On the way out Dai Cannon asked, 'Was that true, Jim, or one of your usual?'

Jim stopped in his stride and turned round, at the same time lifting his lamp to have a better look at his mate. 'Have you ever knowed me to say a lie, Dai bach? No, never in your life. That yarn is so true as I am standing by here this minute, God strike me dead.'

Dai said no more as they continued their way with the other men towards the pit bottom. At every road junction and parting others joined the progressively lengthening line until the pit seemed full of veins pulsating with men. Each step forward intensified the quiet excitement that had developed in the ranks. Tired feet became lighter and gave a jogging motion to the swinging lamps that made the long stretch of light look like an undulating streamer of ribbon. The scampering hoofs of the horses in front sent dust whirling in the air; but no one noticed this or seemed to be inconvenienced by it, as the men turned off the main roadway and silently followed the horses into the stable, letting the compressed air close the door behind them with a bang.

Mr. Williams, the under-manager, and Evan the Overman stood waiting on the pit bottom. The last tram of coal for that shift had whirled up the shaft five minutes ago, and the two officials were now uneasily waiting for the men. Ordinarily the latter were ready to go up before the last trams had left the pit bottom. Williams looked at his watch, then turned the whites of his surprised eyes to his subordinate.

'Good God! It's gone three o'clock!' he declared, like a man who sees an unexpected and unpleasant vision. 'What on earth can have happened?' he asked helplessly.

'I can't make it out,' answered the equally puzzled overman. 'If there had been an accident, we would have heard of it long before now. Let's ask the hitcher.'

The two men strode over to the workman responsible for loading and unloading the cage and handling the lever controlling the knocker on the surface.

'Funny the men haven't come out yet, Tom.'

'Aye, mun. But perhaps they are having a whiff somewhere.'

The under-manager lost his temper. 'Whiff to hell!' he blurted out. 'This is a pit, not a bloody hospital.'

'Aye, I do know that, but funny things do happen in a pit sometimes.'

The manner of the reply convinced Williams the man knew something. 'Come on,' he ordered brusquely. 'Out with it. Where are the damned fools?'

Tom carefully wiped his face in his cap before replying. 'Well, if you look in the stables perhaps you will find something there.'

The two men looked at the hitcher for some moments as though they thought he had suddenly gone mad, then a slow suspicion began to form in the under-manager's mind. His face went pale beneath its coal-crusted blackness.

'Come,' he ordered. 'There's something fishy about this business and I believe I know what it is.'

The two officials stumbled hurriedly towards the stable,

leaving Tom unconcernedly squatting at the pit bottom. Before they reached the stable door, they heard voices above the clamour of the wind squeaking and howling through its cracks. Without a word they put their shoulders to the planks and burst the door open.

The whitewashed stable, with its row of stalls in which the horses were placidly munching, looked like a huge circus in the lights of the lamps hung about its timbers. The men were gathered together in a compact mass listening to one of their number who was mounted on a tram of manure. They all turned their heads when the door opened and the two officials entered. After a brief hesitation Williams and his mate walked towards the figure in the tram, the men quietly making way for them to pass, then equally quietly closing in behind them.

Williams confronted the man who towered above him on the foundation of horse-dung, and from force of habit raised his lamp to have a better view, although its light was indistinguishable in the scores of others.

'Well, what is this damn nonsense?' he demanded. 'Do you know it's long past the time you should have been up the pit?'

Someone began laughing, and in a matter of seconds it was taken up by all the workmen and the stable quivered with hilarity.

'Ho-ho,' Big Jim exclaimed, the echoes of his voice booming in the enclosed space like pebbles in a drum. 'Fancy Williams worrying 'bout us being down after time. Ho-ho! Life is worth living, muniferni, if it was only to hear that!'

Williams sensed the determination and all that it implied

in the laughter, and began to cajole immediately he could make himself heard.

'Come, boys. Don't be silly now. You will only make things worse for yourselves if you have any grievance.'

There was no reply, and the stable became like a vault in the stillness. Williams swallowed hard, then tried again. 'Be reasonable, boys. If you have any grievance, elect a deputation to discuss the matter with Mr. Hicks in a proper way.'

Someone in the crowd shouted out: 'Be reasonable be damned! Haven't we been reasonable and patient for months, trying to get the management to pay us our proper wages and withdraw the blacklegging non-pols or make them join the Federation?'

'Aye,' broke in another. 'And what have been our thanks? Scores of us getting the sack, forced to join the scab union, spied on and summoned by the police, and no pay after doing our work!'

A deep murmur began to drone round the stables. Its intonation turned Williams' face even whiter beneath its coat of black, and he started to stammer. 'B-b-b-b-but w-w-what good can you do by stopping d-d-d-down here?'

Will Evans, on the tram, answered him. 'That is our business. Yours is to get out and tell Hicks we are stopping here until he cleans our pit of scabs.'

Evan the Overman, who had been silent all the while, felt it was now time for him to intervene. 'But you can't do that, mun. You'll starve to death and your lamps will all be in the dark before much longer.'

Big Jim inflated his magnificent chest. 'Huh! Funny to

hear you worrying 'bout us, Evan. Don't bother your head, mun. Us can look after ourselves and the pit without your help, take that from me.'

Will Evans began laughing. 'Ho-ho! Boys, this is good. When we don't come to the pit they send their bobbies running like blue hell to drive us down and their magistrates make us pay for stopping on top. Now they are falling over each other to get us up. Ha-ha!'

Again a wave of laughter flooded the stable and the two officials retreated through the door and back to the shaft bottom.

While this scene was taking place underground, Mr. Hicks looked through his office window on the surface. The noisy clang of passing trams had long since ceased, its place being taken by a strange silence. Mr. Hicks' uneasy eyes saw large numbers of pale-faced men in pit clothes scattered about the colliery yard, but what surprised him most was the large proportion of other men who walked about excitedly. His grey moustache looked limp when he turned to the chief clerk at his side.

'Quite a lot of men looking for work today,' he commented dubiously. The other man did not reply for some moments, then: 'I don't understand it,' he said. 'They can't be looking for work, and even if they were, what are all those women doing here?'

The general manager looked again, screwing his eyes up to have a more accurate view. He stared hard for some moments, picked his stick up from the corner where it rested, hastily ordered his clerk to get in phone communication with the pit bottom, and strode out into the crowd.

He spied Len, with Mary and Siân at his side, in the middle of the throng, and made his way directly to them. 'What are you doing here?' he demanded. 'You know you have no right on these premises.'

'Huh! Who are you then? Lord Muck?' asked Siân indignantly. 'Anybody 'ood think to hear you, mun, that you do own the place.'

The people gathered around the little group, the women immediately siding with Siân. 'That's right. Let him have it,' exclaimed one. 'It's through him and his sort that our valley have been ruined and our men are now down the pit till God knows when.'

This stung Mr. Hicks into a frenzy. 'What?' he howled. 'Aren't the men coming up today?'

His only reply was a joint yell from hundreds of throats. 'No. And they won't come up until you get rid of the scabs and pay them their wages.'

The noise of the challenge struck the air like the detonation of artillery and swept down the valley, bringing men and women to their doors and into the streets, which they hurriedly left as they made towards the pit. In a short time Cwmardy had emptied all its occupants, except the invalids, on to the pit-head. Even dogs, barking joyfully into the vibrating air, scampered between the tramping feet of their owners and added to the noisy multitude that now filled the colliery yard.

The frantic general manager, accompanied by other officials and hardly conscious of what he was doing or saying, strode among the men in working clothes.

'Get down at once,' he ordered, 'or go back home for good.'

'Go down your bloody self and stop there!' was the only reply he received.

He turned to his officials. 'Don't stand there like damn clowns,' he shouted, while his eyes glared. 'Get those idiots up at once.' He would have continued his raving had not the clerk come from the consulting-room with a message that he was wanted on the phone at once by Williams the under-manager.

He had some difficulty in forcing his way through the crowd, but sweating and swearing he eventually accomplished the task and grabbed the phone.

'Hallo. Hallo there,' he growled impatiently into the mouthpiece. 'Yes – yes. It's me. What the hell is wrong down there?'

A long pause during which he turned from white to purple then back to white again, as the under-manager explained the position. Before Williams had finished his report, Hicks' body was rigid. He turned to the officials who had followed him into the office, staring as though he could not see them, the receiver still dangling from his hand. At last he pulled himself together and swallowed hard, before saying to no one in particular: 'That's finished it. They're going to stay down... Stay down.' He lingered over the last two words as though they stuck to his tongue and their taste was bitter. He walked slowly to the window, his head bent and his hands behind his back, looked at the mass of people surging outside, then seemed to gather new rage.

'Phone the police. Clear the yard. Phone Lord Cwmardy,' he yelled in one burst of words, at the same time flinging his stick into the corner and himself into a chair. Outside the people were shouting: 'Where's Fred Lewis, our Executive member?'

Down in the stable the men were holding a meeting with Will as their chairman. They were all both confident and jubilant with the exception of Dai Cannon, who now demanded the platform of dung, which was immediately vacated for him by the chairman. Willing hands helped the old man mount the tram, where the lights turned his greying hair to silver, as his deep voice rolled round the stable.

'Boys,' he began, Big Jim looking up at him with open mouth, 'you all know me, and know when there is a fight on I am in it with all my heart.'

'Aye, aye, Dai bach,' someone shouted, 'especially if there is a pint behind it.'

The quip put Dai on his dignity immediately. He pulled his overhanging belly back under its leather belt. 'This is not the time for tomfoolery,' he declared with great and emphatic solemnity. 'At this hour of destiny, only fools and donkeys dare to guffaw. All of you think the company will give way in a very short time. I want to warn you – and me and Big Jim know this company better than any man alive now that Ezra has gone.' Jim nodded his head in proud confirmation as his mate continued: 'I want to warn you that this company will be prepared to starve us to death rather than give way on this vital principle, but I believe they will give us the back money without fighting at all.'

A loud shout greeted this remark, 'Tell us what to do,

783

mun, not gabble by there like a bloody goose.'

Dai lost his temper. 'Don't you shout at me,' he yelled, lifting his foot and stepping forward over the edge of the tram. Before he could say any more his arms rose in the air for a moment then followed his head as he plunged off the tram into the waiting clutches of Big Jim. He tried to get back again, but impatient shouts of 'Put it to the vote,' prevented him.

Will Evans got on the platform. 'All right,' he declared. 'If you are all ready we will vote. Every man take his lamp in his hand and we will decide by a show of lamps. I believe that will be better down here.' The light in the stable seemed to bubble frothily as the lamps were hastily taken from the various resting-places.

'All in favour of going up the pit and appointing another deputation to see Hicks, please show.'

A moment's pause, then a solitary light lifted itself above the others as Dai declared his conviction against them all, in a silence as deadly as that of a cemetery.

'All in favour of fighting it out down here, please show.'

Immediately the lamps went up, burying the ground in darkness but turning the roof into a light-drenched sky.

A loud cheer followed the vote: 'Good old Cwmardy.' It broke in shattering echoes on the timbered walls and dug itself deeply into the hearts of the men. The last notes were slowly dying in the shuddering atmosphere when someone took them up and moulded them into song which sprang simultaneously from throat to throat, pouring into the stable a flood of melody that emptied the enclosed space of everything else:

'The land of my fathers,
The land of the free.
The home of the harp,
So dear to me.'

The sweet tenors seemed to draw the baritones with them like magnets, lifting them up, then drawing them down, as they ran longingly over the notes of the anthem.

At last it was finished, and Will from his point of vantage carried on with the meeting.

'I have been told to say on behalf of the Party to which I belong and on behalf of the combine committee,' he declared, 'that we believe that all boys under eighteen, men over sixty except Big Jim, and those whose health is not so good ought to be sent up the pit.'

The men became divided instantly, those affected by the suggestions being opposed to them, while the others agreed.

The chairman was about to put the matter to the vote when a fracas in the middle of the crowd sent ripples of excitement through it.

'Half a minute, Mr. Chairman,' someone shouted. 'There is a fight by here and we want to see there will be fair play all round.'

Will forgot the dignity of his position and immediately jumped off the tram to be nearer the combatants, pushing his way forward until he was close to them. Big Jim, however, was before him and was already holding Dai Cannon's coat, as the latter, his fists extended, pranced about like a young cockerel in front of Will Smallbeer, who was hurriedly pulling his shirt over his head.

'What is the matter?' Will asked in bewilderment. Dai did not stop posturing as he answered.

'Nothing much, boy bach. Nothing much. You leave this to us. No man can insult me. No, not if he is so big as two houses.'

'But what is it all about that two butties have got to fight to settle it?'

Dai stopped a moment to spit disgustedly. 'Don't call that man my butty,' he pleaded dramatically.

Will looked helplessly at Jim, who was complacently chewing a lump of tobacco.

'What is it, James?' he asked.

'Oh, Will said Dai was years older than him and would never see sixty agen if he lived to a hundred. Dai called him a bloody liar and Will offered to fight him for it, the loser to give in that he is more than sixty and the winner to stay down with the boys.'

Smallbeer had by this time relieved himself of the shirt and stood with his head bent nearly to his knees and practically hidden by his whirling arms. Occasionally the bald pate shone through temporary gaps in the defences.

'Come on,' he challenged. 'You are very good with your tongue, let's see if you be half so good with your fists. And after I finish with you,' he added, 'I will fight any two who do say I am more than forty-five at the most, barring Big Jim, who have got more sense in his little finger than all of you put together have got in your bloody heads.'

Before he could continue, Dai let go his fist and a howl at the same time, as the former landed smack on the bony head. He danced about more vigorously than ever, rubbing his injured knuckle the while.

'Stand up and fight like a man, not twt down by there like a monkey,' he beseeched. His adversary only laughed at the taunt.

'Ha-ha! Bit off more than your mouth can hold, eh?' he gloated, at the same time advancing cautiously towards Dai, while the human ring drew in more closely about the combatants.

Fred Forrest pulled Will's sleeve as the latter, interestedly and oblivious of anything else, waited for developments. He turned at the tug and bent his ear to the whispering of his Party comrade. 'You've got to stop this.'

'Stop it? What in hell for? Let the old men enjoy themselves, mun.'

'We can't have the men fighting each other, Will. We want to keep all our fighting for the boss.'

Will seemed on the point of refusing to interfere, hesitated a moment, then a second thought determined him.

'All right,' he declared, 'leave it to me.'

He pushed his way back to the tram and began shouting at the top of his voice: 'No more fighting among ourselves, boys. Let's carry on with the meeting. Make those two put their clothes back on. Give a hand, Big Jim.' His sharp command pierced the air like a stiletto, and the words brought the men back to the fact there was important work still to be done. The two loudly protesting battlers were unceremoniously bundled back into their clothes, after which the meeting went on.

The youngsters and old men were rounded up and dug from the hiding-places into which many had retreated during the excitement. They were marshalled in front of all the others, the huge door was opened and the procession wound out of the stable towards the pit, its progress marked by the dust that floated around it.

Half-way out Will Smallbeer suddenly burst into tears. 'It's not fair,' he sobbed, 'to send a man out like this. I can work and fight and drink as good as any man half so old as me, and here you send me up the pit like a baby to be a laughing-stock for everybody. But I 'on't go,' he howled, flinging himself headlong on the side, where he crouched up like a ball.

Big Jim looked at the prostrate form sympathetically for some minutes before saying: 'Pity, mun. Pity. Don't he look 'xactly like a hedgehog by there when a dog is nosing it.' No one laughed.

Far away came the sound of a cage in motion, followed a very short time later by two lights that floated towards the waiting procession of men.

'Who the hell is this?' Will asked of no one in particular.

'Must be old Hicks coming to see us,' someone else remarked.

'Whoever it is, no giving way now without a signed agreement,' came from a score of whispering voices, as the lights stopped at the head of the long line. Will Evans, accompanied by Big Jim and a few others, made his way to the front, where he was surprised to see Fred Lewis and a stranger squatting down comfortably on the side.

'Hallo, boys,' the former greeted them affably. 'Made your minds up sudden, haven't you. I have been away, as you know, and only heard this morning at the Executive. This is Jack Hopkins, our area member,' he added. 'They have sent him up with me to help in this affair.'

'Oh aye. That's good,' said Will. 'But what sort of help are you going to give us?'

The stranger replied: 'Well. We first of all want all of you to know how much we admire what you are doing. But now you have made a demonstration and shown your spirit, we think you should come up the pit and let us tackle the business constitutionally.'

The message slipped from mouth to mouth till all the waiting men were soon aware of it, a fact that found expression in a groan that grew louder.

'Constitution to hell! Now we're down we're sticking down till Hicks gives in.'

Will turned again to the leaders. 'That's how it is,' he declared.

'But listen to reason, mun,' Fred pleaded. 'You can't keep down any length of time without serious harm to some of you, and when you are finally forced to the surface you'll be worse off than you are now, and we'll be further away than ever from smashing the company union.'

The listening men began shouting again their disapproval, and Will, encouraged by this, declared: 'If the Executive is not prepared to help us in a better way than that, ask them to keep their hands off and leave the fight to us.'

The stranger became desperate, his squat, burly figure shaking with the feeling that gripped him. 'If you come out,' he promised, 'I guarantee we will get your money tomorrow and clear the pit of scabs within a month.'

'Who telled you that?' asked Big Jim. 'Cwmardy or Mr. Hicks?'

'No. Not yet; but they will be bound to when you have the whole weight of the Executive behind you.'

'You tell that to the marines, butty. I knowed old Cwmardy before you was pupped and he's not so bloody simple as you think.'

'No,' commented Will to loud cheers from the men who were impatiently waiting for a definite statement. 'We'll come up when you have it signed in black and white that our money is there and that the company union have finished forever in this pit. And mind you,' he went on, 'we 'on't take it from no one except Len Roberts.'

A burst of applause made further conversation impossible, and the men lifted Will Smallbeer from the side and carried him bodily to the pit bottom.

The two miners' leaders went up with the first batch of old men to convey the news to the waiting people. Fred Lewis jumped on a coal tram and held his hand up for order, which he soon got. All eyes present were fixed upon him with concentrated attention, and Mr. Hicks, watching from the office window, felt his heart gladden when he saw the black-grimed men who had ascended with the leaders.

'He's persuaded them to come up,' he whispered to his subordinates, as Fred Lewis's voice crept through the closed door.

'Fellow workers,' it rang in the air which was already beginning to carry the germs of dusk, 'they have decided, despite the advice of the Executive, to stay down until the scabs are cleared out. They are now sending all those too

790

young, too old, or too weak up the pit.'

There was a moment's breathless silence, during which no one seemed to breathe, then a roar swept the valley: 'Hurrah! Hurrah! The fight is on. Down with the company union.' Fred looked mutely at Jack Hopkins, and the eyes of each showed the other that further argument was useless. The former jumped off the tram and the two were soon lost among the people.

Mary's eyes shone happily as she clasped Siân's arm and looked at Len, who stood erect as a dart nearby. The pride and happiness in the demeanour of all the people stirred her heart.

'Isn't it wonderful, mother, the way our men fight?' she asked.

Siân nodded her head nonchalantly, although her posture betrayed how deeply she was gripped.

'Aye. They have been reared to it, you see, Mary fach.'

The dense crowd of men and women began to sway spasmodically, and suddenly, without a word or warning sign, Len felt himself lifted in the air and carried to the tram, where he was gently placed down feet first.

'Speech. Speech,' came the insistent demand. Although taken by surprise, Len remembered the discussion in the Party the previous night and knew exactly what to do.

'We must all go home now,' he declared, 'and prepare for the morning, when we must all be ready to be on the pit first thing with hot tea and food for our boys down below. There is no need for anyone to worry,' he exhorted, 'if we stand fast we can depend on it our boys in the pit will stick.' Loud cheers interrupted him for some minutes,

791

then he went on. 'Perhaps it would be well if we picked a deputation to go down and see exactly how the boys are fixed.' This was agreed to, and Len, with half a dozen others, was selected for the job.

Mary squeezed his hand as he made his way to the cage, and Siân instructed him to tell Jim: 'Mind to keep his flannel shirt on. I will send him a blanket and some 'bacco tomorrow morning.'

The cage with its little party of emissaries dropped out of sight as quickly as a falling bomb, and Len once more tasted the pit in his mouth. The hitcher was waiting for them on the bottom with a greeting.

'Hallo, boys, come to pay us a visit in our new home, eh? You'll find all the family quite well, thank you.'

Len smiled and asked: 'Where are all the boys?'

'Oh, you'll find them in the bedroom.'

'Bedroom? What do you mean?' lifting his lamp to have a better look at the man.

'Aye, aye, mun. They have turned the stables into a bedroom.'

Without another word, Len and his mates made their way towards the door behind which they now knew the men were settling down. The whistling air tried to prevent them jerking the door open, but with a concerted tug the men broke its grip and stood for some seconds looking in amazement at the scene before them. All the available brattice cloth had been hastily gathered, shared out, and was now being used as blankets. With a sheet of this under them three men were squeezed closely together on the manure tram, sleeping as peacefully as babies. Many of the younger men had taken possession of the mangers in the stables and were nestled down to rest while the horses' lips moved wetly about their bodies, hunting the stray fodder scattered about. The remainder of the men had made their beds on the floor of the stables, using fodder sacks, old timber, and whatever they could find as pillows.

Many, unable to sleep in the strange surroundings, were quietly whispering yarns or chatting, when Len and his party opened the door. Immediately the stables became silent of everything but the whistling air and the occasional clang of a chain as a horse restlessly shook his head. The scene struck Len with majestic force. The silence turned the stables into a cathedral where anything but whispers and bared heads would be sacrilege. He had known the pit and the men in all their moods, but never had he imagined the former as at once a battle-ground and a home for the latter.

He blinked away the moisture in his eyes and called out: 'How be, boys. It's only me and a deputation.'

Big Jim sprang to his feet like a catapulted ball. 'Hurrah,' he howled. 'It's our Len and his butties. Up to it, boys.'

Instantly all the reclining men were on their feet and gathered about the little group of pale-faced emissaries.

One, still rather suspicious, asked: 'Come down to try and get us up, have you?'

The deputation felt the resentment and determination in the words and hastened to explain. 'No, no, boys. We have been sent down by the men and women on top to help you carry on the fight.'

A roar of cheering drowned the remainder.

Then another asked: 'What are the women doing up there?'

'Oh, they turned out to make sure that everything is all right with you.'

Another burst of cheers followed this remark, and Big Jim's voice rose above it: 'By damn, those gels is good boys, muniferni.'

Will Evans, who was one of the three ensconced on the dung, now came forward.

'Hallo, Len. Glad to see you, butty.'

Len looked his mate up and down. 'Good old Will. What do you intend to do now?'

Will scratched his head for some moments and was then about to speak when another of the men forestalled him. 'We are going to make this stable our headquarters. Then tomorrow we'll divide up into squads, to keep the place clean, fetch the water, and what not. We have already decided to have an Eisteddfod tomorrow, and Big Jim is going to be the adjudicator. There will be four choirs and variety turns as well.'

The determined sangfroid of the man amazed Len and it was some moments before he could ask another question. At last he managed to inquire: 'But won't your lamps all be in the dark by then?'

'Ay. We 'spect so,' Will replied off-handedly; 'but that 'on't make any difference to us. If horses can manage in the dark, I'm bloody sure we can.'

Even now many of the lamps were beginning to lose their power and the light in the stable was like the smoky dusk of the surface. Len bent his head and could find nothing more to say other than: 'Stick to it, boys, and don't worry about the people up above. They'll play their part.'

Another member of the deputation continued: 'Aye, you can bet on that. We'll have food and hot tea down to you in the morning.'

Someone shouted: 'Don't forget some 'bacco, butty, and the *Racing Special*.'

The remark gave Len a new idea. 'Boys,' he shouted out, 'I'm going to stop down with you.'

For a moment there was complete silence, then Will replied: 'No bloody fear, you don't. Your place is on top, seeing to things there.'

'Who'll stop me staying down?' demanded the crestfallen Len.

'You'll see now,' was the quick retort, as Will jumped back on the tram, from which position all the men saw his dim form.

'Where is Len's place, boys? Up or down?' he asked them.

'Up,' came the unhesitating response, like a roar of thunder over the mountain. Len sensed the men were right and made no further effort to persuade them otherwise. After some more discussion, the deputation, escorted by all the men, left for the pit bottom. When they ascended the shaft, they heard singing fade slowly as they left it in the earth, but immediately the cage burst the wooden droppers from the pit-head it seemed the same singing was born again as those on the surface welcomed them. The deputation reported the position, and the people, their minds contented, slowly made their way over the bridge and down the hill to their homes.

A VICTORY
FOR THE WORKERS

That night Mr. Higgins and Lord Cwmardy, hurriedly
called from London, held a conference in the Big House
with their chief officials. There was a bright gleam in
Cwmardy's eyes as Mr. Hicks excitedly reported the events
of the day. When he had finished Mr. Higgins stopped his
restless pacing to remark:

'Scandalous! The men must be evicted from the pit at
once, by whatever means are necessary to accomplish
this.'

Cwmardy, his pipe clenched tightly in his teeth, nodded
his head slowly. 'Yes, that's so. But what men, what men!'
He became reminiscent as he went on. 'It's their courage
and audacity that makes them such splendid workmen.'
He gave a short sigh, then entered into the discussion that
followed. The conference did not break up until the red

797

streaks of a new day began shooting over the mountain.

Throughout the night Mary and Siân, with the other women, remained up cutting bread and butter, making sandwiches and tea. Siân was as excited as a young girl about to be married. She supervised the proceedings from her seat in the corner of the canteen, got up by the Co-operative, occasionally rising to do again something not done to her satisfaction.

'Pity they did send old Smallbeer and Dai Cannon up,' she remarked. 'I am sure the both of them do feel it awful.'

The women ceased working for a moment, while one of them remarked: 'The men did quite right. Us can't risk any chances now, and God knows what 'ood happen to old men like that if they was kept down for long.'

'Aye,' said another sympathetically, 'They could have fits easy.'

This started a buzz of conversation in which Mary joined. After a while the conversation took a serious turn as the women let their thoughts drift to the menfolk underground. One middle-aged woman sighed deeply and looked on the verge of tears. Mary noticed her and queried, 'What's the matter, Mrs. Davies?'

The woman gave a little sob, lifted her apron, and replied: 'Only yesterday afternoon my little Ianto, God bless him, asked me for a shilling to put on a horse, and I wouldn't give it to him. And now he's down in the pit and perhaps I'll never see him again. Oh dear, dear.' She broke down completely and it was some time before she controlled herself sufficiently to add: 'But he shan't suffer. Oh no. He shall have the racing paper down every day like the clock, and I will never refuse him a brass farthing again as long as I live.' This pledge consoled her, and they all continued with their work.

Early next morning the people of Cwmardy, led by the band and a lorry full of food, made their way to the pit-head, which they found surrounded by police and officials. Len tried to pass the cordon, but was grasped roughly by the shoulder and pushed back. 'No one is going near that pit today,' remarked the police inspector. The people looked at each other in amazement for some moments, until Mary, with Siân clinging tightly to her heels, brushed past Len and the inspector and, without looking back, shouted over her shoulder: 'Come on. Our men need food.' Her action electrified the people; and in a second the crowd plunged forward with a roar and burst through the uniformed barrier that vainly tried to hold them back. Siân, her fists flailing wildly in all directions, fought like a tigress.

'Want to starve my man, do they?' she grunted to herself as she ploughed her way towards the pit.

One of the policeman lost his head and, drawing his baton, began lashing at the unprotected heads. For some moments he had it all his own way and a number of men and women lay around him stretched on the dusty earth. Then something caught him behind the ear and he collapsed like a deflated concertina to join in the squirms of his victims. Without leadership or organisation, but driven by a common urge, the people fought their way to the pit-head. Apart from the thudding of blows and an occasional groan, the battle was eerily silent. Food parcels, burst open and their contents exposed during the melee, were scattered all over the colliery yard and crushed by trampling feet into the mud.

Mary felt herself pushed and huddled till she became giddy in the moiling crush. Her eyes lost focus and turned sightlessly in her head, so that she failed to see the truncheon land on Siân's shoulder, but she heard the moan as the old woman sank slowly on her knees into the black mire. The world seemed to burst into a red blaze for a moment, then she flung herself around the old woman, screaming at the top of her voice.

'Oh, Len, Len, they've hit mother.'

Siân, half-squatting, half-kneeling, opened her eyes and looked dully at her daughter-in-law for some moments before asking: 'What is the matter, gel fach? I am all right, mun. It'll take more than that to upset your old Siân.' She closed her eyes again, her face the pasty whiteness of dough, as the pain from her damaged shoulder spread down to her fingers, stiffening them into rigidity. Mary cuddled her more closely as Len pushed his way through to the crouching couple.

Hatless, his face streaked with coal-dust, his breath short and rapid, he eventually reached them and carefully placed his arms around his mother's shoulders, drawing her erect. Mary got the other side and between them they worked a passage through the fighting people to some timber nearby, where they sat down.

Siân was quickly recovering her usual composure, although a few tears trickled down her skinny cheeks as she thought of what Big Jim would have done had he seen her being struck. She shook these away with a sharp nod and catching Len's head declared: 'Us will never get food down to our boys.'

Len looked about him at the police and officials, who were once again between the people and the pit. The showers of stones and sticks which darkened the air seemed to melt about the attackers, giving them greater vigour to charge with lashing batons, forcing the people back upon each other until everything became confusion and pandemonium.

'Come,' he gulped, 'or we will be left by here at the mercy of the police.'

They skirted their way around the timber and behind some waggons until they again found themselves mixed up in the mass of people.

In the pit the men were making preparations for the Eisteddfod and concert. All the lamps had exhausted their light and the company had cut off the electric current that normally lighted the pit bottom, so that everything was done in a darkness more dense and heavy than black ink. It seemed to break into bubbles when the men spoke, and location became a matter of sound.

A voice, which could only belong to Big Jim, rose above the murmur of the others: 'Are you ready, boys?'

The question came from the roof, and betrayed the fact that Big Jim had mounted the tram of manure as a platform from which to conduct and lead the singing.

'Right, boys. Now 'member, no funny tricks and fair play all round, because this is more 'portant than any 'Steddfod in a chapel. Us will go by numbers. Are you ready, number one?'

'Aye,' came a deep responsive chorus from one part of the stable.

'Right then. When I do count three, start off. Now! One, two,' a long pause then, 'three.'

Before the word had interred itself in the darkness it was caught in the wave of melody that came from choir number one. The men not participating listened attentively to the rippling air that broke harmoniously on their ears. The universe was drowned in pleasing sound and made them hold their breath lest they disturb it. No one spoke for a while after the conclusion of the song, then a clamour took its place as the men discussed the merits and otherwise of the choir. The occasional clanging of horse chains made it appear that even the horses wanted to join in.

Big Jim eventually took charge again. 'Not so bad, boys bach, not so bad. Damn, they is worth a clap, mun.'

The hint was taken and a loud clapping of hands followed in which the choristers were as vigorous as any.

'Now us will have number two.'

A shuffiing of feet resulted, then silence followed by: 'Same thing agen. One, two... three.'

Half-way through the second piece a loud voice, peculiarly like Will Evans', shouted disgustedly: 'Those tenors are all to hell, mun. Damn! They are swamping the baritones.'

No one took any notice except Big Jim, who hissed: 'S-s-sh! Fair play all round, boys. If anybody think they can 'judicate better than me, they can come up by here, muniferni.'

After the fourth choir had competed, the men remained quietly awaiting the verdict of the invisible adjudicator.

Jim took rather a long time before starting, then began: "Scuse me, boys. I have been looking for some 'bacco, but my pouch is empty. Anybody got a bit to spare? What about some of you boys I have been keeping in 'bacco for years?' He sensed the hands stretched towards him and cautiously felt them. His fingers closed on one that appeared to have a bigger lump than the others.

'Thanks, butty. I will do the same for you some day,' drawing himself erect again immediately to roar, 'Fire in hell! Who was it who gived me that lump of horse dung?'

A rumble of laughter made his further words inaudible until someone shouted: 'Come on, let's have the bloody 'judication. We is all waiting.'

The laughter died down and Big Jim, spluttering and cursing, was again heard. 'Some men are not fit to die, muniferni.'

'Come on, let's have the result.'

'All right, all right, keep your bloody hairs on. There is nobody here afraid of you, whoever you are.'

A further short silence then, after spitting loudly, Jim began the adjudication.

'Well, boys, us will start with number one. Very good song and very good singing with this one, but they raced the tram a bit too high, eh, boys? All of us do know if you build a tram too high to pass the low timbers, the whole bloody thing is ruined. Now number two did not do that, but what they did do was not to put enough coal in the bed of the tram, so that all the time it was sounding like loose T-head rails under a journey running on wild.'

A loud surge of laughter prevented him going on for a

while. When it had died down into spasmodic gurgles from various parts of the stable, he went on.

'Choir number three was very good, too, on the whole, but sometimes I did fancy I was listening to somebody sawing a empty tram in half, mun jawli. I think, putting it all together, and fair to everybody like, that number four was about a pair of rails in front of the best. What say you, boys?'

There was loud clapping and boos for a while. Then Will Evans took charge, blindly groping his way to the tram and stumbling over bodies to do so. 'Now we will start the concert.'

For hours the men took it in turn to sing and recite, even while there was growing a vague unuttered uneasiness in their minds. The promised food had not yet arrived, and the men sent back to the pit before the lights went out to await its coming had not yet returned. Mingling with the music was this wonder of what was wrong. Fred Forrest quietly opened the face of his watch and let his fingers follow the hands, trying thus to estimate the right time. He thought he had it and immediately his stomach became empty and began to rumble for food. The chairman found ever greater difficulty in getting volunteers, and at last gave it up when someone shouted: 'Cut it out, it makes us more thirsty.'

This focused the thoughts of all the men and hands groped towards water-bottles to discover that the contents had been finished long since in the belief that more was coming.

The stable became silent but for the restless stamping of horses' feet.

804

A voice shouted: 'The poor things are hungry.'

'Aye,' broke in another, 'who had the feed-sacks last night?'

The men concerned immediately got up and drew the bags which had been their beds from stall to stall, filling the manger in each before leaving to the sound of teeth crunching oats.

A further long period of quietude followed, during which many of the men dozed off, their eyes tired of the darkness which made it impossible to know if their lids were open or closed.

Will Evans stumbled and crawled about until he found Big Jim. 'Something must have happened on top, James, or Len and the boys would have grub down long ago.'

A loud grunt and a movement prefaced Jim's reply. 'I could fancy my back is broked, mun, but there,' resignedly, 'what do backs count if the heart is good?' A pause followed while Will meditated on this.

'You must be getting on a bit now, James.'

'Aye, my boy. Gone sixty-five and over fifty years underground, and not a bald hair on the whole of my head. What think you to that?'

'I don't s'pose I will ever live to that age and still be of any bloody use.'

'Huh!' patronisingly. 'Don't break your heart, boy bach. You have got plenty of time to grow old yet, and don't forget my father was so young as you once.'

A loud shout interrupted the conversation. It ran through the stable like a wail.

'Can't anybody stop this bloody snoring by here?'

A number called out: 'Get to sleep and forget it.'

'Sleep to hell. How can a man sleep when that bloke makes me think the missus is in bed with me?'

More joined in. 'Watch him, boys. If he's got strength to think of his missus in bed, he must be picking grub from somewhere.'

'Order, boys. What time do it go dark?'

The question was answered by a chant: 'It never goes dark till your eyes are shut.' Everyone joined in this, after which there was quiet for another spell.

Jim took advantage of this to whisper: 'I'll go back to the pit bottom to see if there is any news. Tom, the hitcher, is sure to know something.'

'I'll come with you,' Will replied.

'No, no! You stop by here to make sure that nothing out of the way do happen. If anybody say they are thirsty or hungry, tell them to chew timber.'

Back came the retort: 'If us chew much more timber, muniferni, us will be shitting sprags.'

This left Jim somewhat crestfallen, and without another word he quietly made his way to the stable door. He was on the point of tugging it open when a sudden panicky scrambling and a muffled yell stopped him.

'Quick boys, quick!' came the hysterical plea, as someone stampeded violently at the bottom end of the stable. 'A mouse have got inside my shirt and I can't get him out!'

Laughter covered the open door and Jim's retreat through it.

Slowly, hands outstretched each side of him, Jim went

towards the bottom of the shaft. He lifted his knees carefully with each stride before jerking his foot out so that the toe of his boot should be the first to make contact with any obstacle in front of him. Mice and cockroaches scuttled wildly among the timbers at the noise of his approach. Winged insects droned past him like miniature aeroplanes. The darkness was impenetrable. Unable to stand the strain any longer he began to shout.

'Hallo-o-o-o! Hallo there! Is there anybody about?'

The echoes battered their way about the timbers, until another shout from far off chased them away. 'Aye, straight on.'

Thus encouraged, Jim soon reached his objective.

'Well, what have happened?' he asked the invisible men.

'Nothing. We have been clanging blue hell on the knocker, but not a bloody sound or a move have us had in reply.'

Jim pondered this for some time, then commented: 'Huh! That's funny, because our Len said there would be food and tea down in the morning, and here we are with another night nearly gone already, if my guts know anything about time.'

He would have carried on, but the iron knocker above his head suddenly brazened out the 'clear-away' signal which meant the cage on the surface was about to descend.

'Ha-ha! That is Len so sure as hell. He do know what I say if I was a million miles away, muniferni.'

No one answered him, and they all listened to the roar of the air as the cages, rushing in opposite directions, crushed it into wild squeals. They faintly heard the crash when the ascending carriage struck the wooden droppers and lifted them from the shaft-top as the other cage came into sight on the bottom.

The men's eyes were instantaneously fixed on the two lamps it contained. Their light failed to illuminate, and the white beam only made the darkness more dead. A long pause while the men wiped the wet mist from their eyes, then Jim grunted impatiently: 'Come on, Len bach. Let's see what you have brought with you, mun. Don't stand by there like a lump of paralysed mutton.'

'Len isn't here,' came the reply. 'It's Mr. Hicks and Fred Lewis.'

'Oh,' the monosyllable sounded like the moan of an expiring martyr.

The two men came out of the cage, their swinging lamps throwing more shadows than light round those waiting on the roadway.

'Ah,' the comment came from Mr. Hicks as he squatted down near Tom, the hitcher, while Big Jim, still standing, towered above both. 'Now we can talk sense.'

Apparently without noticing the general manager, Jim asked Fred Lewis: 'What have happened to the food that you was going to send down?'

'Oh, there has been a bit of a squabble on top,' the latter replied uncomfortably. 'But we have not come down to discuss that,' he added hastily.

'Huh!' broke in one of the men who had been sent back to wait for the food. 'What squabble do you mean?'

Thus faced with a direct question, Fred hesitated a while, then blurted: 'The police refuse to let our people send food down, and there's a riot up above.'

This was followed by a gasp of amazement from the expectant men.

Big Jim was about to say something, when Will Evans' voice exhumed itself from the darkness behind. He had followed Jim in spite of the latter's injunction.

'The rotten bastards!' A pause, before he continued in a sharper tone: 'But it's not the police, it's Hicks and the company, who, not satisfied with half-starving us on top, are now trying to starve us down here.'

'Listen, listen,' pleaded Mr. Hicks. 'I don't want to starve any of you. I want to live in harmony with you all.'

'Ha-ha!' the laugh broke in cackles. 'Want to live in harmony. Ha-ha! And want us to live in harmony with non-pols, who are cutting our throats and ruining our pit. That's what you want – harmony in everything that is best for you and the company.'

Jim's bent shoulders painfully squared themselves erect. 'That will do, butties bach,' he declared. 'If these men want to talk, let them come into the stable to do it, where all the boys can hear what they have got to say.'

The men accepted the advice, and the little procession, one lamp in front and the other behind, made its way from the pit to the stable, obliterating its progress with the dust that followed.

The beams of light that stabbed the darkness through the open stable door brought all the men to their feet with a bound, but nothing was said as Mr. Hicks walked straight to the tram of manure, Fred Lewis close behind him. From all quarters black bodies merged into the lighter shadows cast by the lamps and eyes became blobs of liquid whiteness glaring at the two men.

The miners' leader spoke first, clearing his throat noisily before beginning. His lank form and dark features fitted into the general surroundings, making the latter appear to an onlooker like the picture of a meeting in hell.

'Well, boys, as you all know, I give way to no man for militancy and support for those I represent.' He paused, as though expecting applause, but the deadly silence urged him to continue more quickly. 'But there are times when leaders must do things which the men don't like at the moment, but which are best for them in the end.'

This brought an uneasy shuffling of feet in the dusty manure of the stable floor, and a low growl from many of the listening men.

'We are in that position now,' went on the speaker. 'I speak with the full authority of the Executive when I say we are united in asking you to come up the pit and trust us to settle the matter to your complete satisfaction.' Again the silence egged him on, and he began to plead. 'Think boys. Our people on top are being battered about and our women are grieving for you while you remain here. Damn it all, if we are to fight, let's all fight together.'

A loud howl followed on the heels of this statement.

'We are fighting!'

'The Executive wants us to give in!'

'Our leaders are ratting!'

The slogans rang in the air, stirring it into a fermenting turmoil, that made nerves quiver with excitement. An old workman jumped on the tram alongside Fred Lewis, his black face glistening. 'Fellow workmen,' he bellowed hoarsely, 'when we put a rank and file executive in the Federashon, we all thought that everything would be all right, but here we are now again faced with the same tricks and the same old lies. Bah! All of 'em are the bloody same. Put a beggar on a horse and he'll ride to hell.'

Claps and shouts completed his statement. Mr. Hicks raised his hand and tried to get a hearing, but the shouts swelled into a roar through which came the reiterated demand: 'Pay us our wages and clear the pit of non-pols and we'll come up.'

Its repetitive insistence dominated everything else for a while. It crowded upon Mr. Hicks, bowing his shoulders and putting deep lines and dark shadows into his face. He turned to Fred and whispered something, but the latter shook his head as though he could not hear in the din. Both men, worlds apart but dominated by the same impulse, looked with mutual desire upon the scene beneath. Each movement gave birth to monstrous quivering shadows that chased each other all round the stables. Faces seemed to be detached from the bodies to which they belonged as they dangled from and merged in the moving shadows.

Only eyes appeared fixed as they threw back the glare from the two solitary lamps. One of the men suddenly threw his arms above his head and sunk slowly to his knees, moaning as he subsided.

'O God! Give us the light of day, which the company has taken away. Give us food, give us water. O Christ, give me my family.'

811

The last words ended in a scream that silenced the other men as those nearest bent down to lift the sobbing man to his feet.

'There, there,' they soothed him as though he were a baby. 'Don't take it like that, mun. Perhaps you have got a touch of 'flu.'

The last word spread till everyone knew it. It became an entity of its own, robbed of its context.

Again a slow, dim murmur rose steadily into a roar.

'Up the pit with him.'

'Send him home, he's done his bit.'

Fred tried to take advantage of the incident. 'There you are, boys,' he shouted. 'That's what will happen to all of you in this damned hole. Let's go up together,' he pleaded.

Will Evans flung himself into the ensuing silence.

'Give us the agreement and we'll come.'

This was immediately taken up. 'The agreement. The agreement in black and white!'

Will felt something gnaw inside him and turned away to be sick, but nothing except thick, sticky mucus rose to his mouth, burning his throat like acid as it came up. When he recovered, the men were already lining up, Mr. Hicks and Fred in front, followed by two men holding the man who had collapsed, then all the others in ranks of two. He fell in with them, vaguely wondering what they were about to do, while his feet rose and fell automatically. The roadway widened near the pit bottom and enabled him to get nearer the front just as the general manager, miners' leader, and disabled worker were stepping slowly into the cage. He felt the rush of air that followed the clang

of the knocker and saw the two lights jump suddenly up
the shaft and disappear like two bubbles on a pipe. The
men around him were immediately transformed into
intangibility that found expression in sound, which lifted
in ascending tiers until it filled the black air with
invigorating ripples:

> 'Bread of Heaven,
> Bread of Heaven,
> Feed me now and evermore.'

The plea became a defiant challenge as voices moulded
into moods. The final stanzas were repeated twice before
someone shouted: 'Home, boys,' and they all turned so
that the rear became the front as they slowly stumbled
back to the stables.

Very late that night two meetings were held in Cwmardy,
one in the colliery offices, where Lord Cwmardy presided,
and the other in the new workmen's institute, where Harry
Morgan chaired. Harry's usually beaming face, with its
high, glistening forehead, was now drawn and puckered as
he faced the mass of men and women whose features
betrayed the agony of the past hours. Siân, her shoulder
still helpless and painful, sat with Len and Mary near the
first row of seats. The latter's eyes looked twice their usual
size in the unnatural pinkish glow on her face, the muscles
of which twitched spasmodically whenever she moved her
head. Len, nervous and irritable, sought her hand on the
seat against his side and pressed the fingers between his,

knowing the contact would help to settle his frenzy.

'I'm opposed to the line,' he whispered. 'The men are in the mood to fight and we have negotiated and played about long enough with the problem of the non-pols. Our Party dare not act as strike-breakers now the men have taken action.'

'S-s-sh,' she replied equally quietly, as Harry rose from his chair and Fred Lewis bent forward with his elbows on his knees. 'Fellow working men and women,' the chairman began. 'We have reached a decisive moment in our history. Our men have given us the responsibility of leadership, but this does not mean they have no responsibilities themselves. If they trust us to lead, we must lead in everything that concerns the pit and the Federation.'

Someone in the back of the hall shouted out, 'Well, lead right then. When the men are fighting, don't try to lead them away from it.'

Loud applause from all parts of the building greeted this, and Harry's eyes gleamed behind their spectacles as he felt the indomitable courage of the people. He held up his hand, but for some time could not get order. When he did he went on calmly, as though there had been no interruption: 'That spirit, that courage which our people now display can be used in certain circumstances to defeat us. It is not sufficient to fight; we must always know how to fight to win. Perhaps what seems defeat at the moment is necessary to take us to eventual victory. As it is now, we are not only fighting the company, we are fighting each other. It is anarchy,' he shouted excitedly, as the din provoked by his words grew more emphatic and vociferous.

'Let the Executive lead, not rat,' the people shouted.

'You are as bad as the old bunch once you get in power – you forget all you used to stand for and preach.'

This stung Harry and he went white, but he waited until there was silence before replying. 'You have made me chairman of the combine and because of that I have to see all the people and not only those in one pit. Believe me, boys,' he cried dramatically, 'the Executive will never betray its trust, come what will. We are pledged to sweep the non-pols from the coalfield and we intend to do it. But we cannot do it in the way the men are acting now.'

Another loud howl of dissent swept the hall, during which Harry, waving his hand despondently, retired to the chair and began a conversation with Fred and the others on the platform.

Len watched them dully. He knew from the Party meeting earlier that evening what Harry was saying, and his heart burned within him. He turned again to Mary.

'Oh, my dear, our line is wrong,' he moaned.

'Never mind,' she consoled. 'Right or wrong, it is the line and we have to be true to it.'

'But it means we have to become strike-breakers.'

She swallowed at the implication, but straightening up, said: 'If that is necessary for final victory, then it must be done. Don't forget, Len, we must sometimes swim against the stream, although that is much harder than going with it.'

He gulped and turned his attention to the meeting which was now out of control, the people on the platform appearing to be lost in the wilderness of noise that surrounded them. Len looked at his immediate neighbours and met wild staring appeals that he say something for the men below.

His own eyes grew momentarily misty and blind, then something swept through him like fire and he sprang to his feet with a jerk, still clasping Mary's hand and half-dragging her with him. Mary understood his mood and, sitting down again, let him feel her body near his, knowing her close presence would check any tendency to irrelevant wildness on his part.

His sudden action had run through the crowd like a current and commanded attention. Harry saw this and immediately took advantage of it, recognising his Party comrade even through the smoky fog that hung over the hall.

'Order,' he shouted with upraised hand. 'One of your fellow workmen wants to speak.'

Others took up the cry. 'Order, order,' until the appeal became more noisy than the previous uproar, but it died slowly until at last silence took its place and Len began to speak.

'Comrades,' his voice low and tremulous, 'we are called upon tonight to make one of the most serious decisions of our lives. Our Executive and our chairman, Harry Morgan, have told us what they think. Our men down in the pit since yesterday morning without light or food are also showing us something, and I want to say now that, right or wrong, I am proud of them.' His voice rose into a crescendo of passion with this last phrase, lifting with it a tumult of cheers that lasted many minutes. Mary, sensing what was happening, let her hand creep upwards till it felt his and he clasped it tenderly in his firm fingers.

Someone in the middle of the hall began weeping loudly, causing a little stir in the immediate vicinity until someone shouted: 'It's all right, Len, carry on.'

Len did not heed the exhortation, but it heartened him for what had to come. 'Yes. Proud of them, as we all are. And what are they doing, comrades?' He paused, then answered himself. 'They are fighting to keep a principle which they and their fathers won through suffering many years ago. They are there in the blackness of the pit so that we above it can keep our freedom and the right to join what union we desire without asking the company.'

The whole gathering was now tensely silent and alert to every word as it came from his quivering lips.

'Our pits were swept clean of blacklegs in the big strike, but since then the company has been clever and used the poverty of our own people to turn some of them into scabs. They have forced us out of our own Federation into their union if we wanted work and wages, bread and home. They have kept our men down the pit through fear of starvation on top, unless we accepted all the conditions the company imposed on us through its union. Yes,' he went on bitterly, as his memory traversed the past in quick panoramic flashes, 'they made us sell our freedom for a job.'

The people on the platform, led by the chairman, clapped their hands vigorously, but Mary began to get nervous as she saw the trend of Len's remarks. Her adamant loyalty to all Party decisions made her on occasions fear her husband's vehemence when he felt a thing deeply. She tightened her grip on his hand and tugged it softly, sending a message through it to his brain in the hope that the latter would calm the tumult she knew was boiling in him. It appeared the effort was successful, because when he continued, it was much more quietly.

817

'For months and years our Executive has been negotiating and pleading with the company to let us choose our union without fear of victimisation or reprisals, but each time they have been scorned and called dictators; and now our men have lost patience and taken things into their own hands. Think of it,' he beseeched, 'during the strike, some of us wondered why the police should be sent in against us. But since then, we have learned the Government doesn't keep them just for chasing criminals. No. They keep them to maintain law and order and everything that we do that is in our own interest and against that of the company is illegal and disorderly. They use the police to smash us with their batons; then summons us for a riot which they themselves have made. And after this, before we know where we are, they use magistrates and judges to twist the law and turn us into criminals, then send us to jail. Isn't it true?' he shouted, his face red with the pressure of words, while Harry Morgan began to fidget uneasily, even though he felt his flesh tingle with the stark truth of the assertion.

'Yes,' the speaker went on. 'We have nothing to expect from the company, from the authorities, from anyone. No, nothing can serve us but our own strength, determination, and unity.' The last word seemed to awaken a new line of thought in his mind. 'That's it – unity. Whatever happens, we must be united. Never mind how we differ in other things, we must be united against the things we suffer in common at the hands of the boss and his government.' His voice broke a little and became sad as he continued: 'That is why I believe the Executive is right and we ought to ask our men to come up the pit. Look,' he swept his arm dramatically through the air before him, 'everywhere our men are split. Some are fighting underground like ours, others are on the surface and working. That's what Harry means by anarchy. That's what he means when he says we must on this issue fight together or lose the fight.'

He sat down abruptly and unexpectedly, leaving the people in a welter of surprise and conflicting emotions. Most of them had expected anything but this from him, and his actual pronouncement left them clammy with disappointed expectancy. The meeting continued in an atmosphere of dull apathy for some time, but it ended in an uproar of dissent and indecision.

As the people left their meeting and poured into the lamp-lit darkness of the main street, they spontaneously hushed their voices when a line of buses filled with blue-uniformed and bright-buttoned men passed by on its way to the pit-head, where the meeting in the colliery office was still proceeding. Lord Cwmardy's white hair made his face look softer as he said:

'Mr. Higgins is quite right. We can't let the men confiscate the pit in this manner.' He bent his head as though he were meditating over some deep thought. 'No, the day shift of loyal men must proceed to work as usual in the morning, and the rebellious elements must be removed.'

He drew his hand across his brow and sat down tiredly, leaving his underlings to work out the details.

Big Jim carefully moved his recumbent, pain-filled body to a more comfortable position, whispering curses beneath his moustache as he did so. Will Evans, whose squirming entrails refused to let him sleep, felt the slight movement and closed nearer to the old workman.

'What time is it, Jim?' he asked in what he tried to make jocular tones, but his weariness made the effort a hopeless failure.

'Oh, it's not dark yet and the barmaid in the Boar's Head haven't shouted "Stop tap!"' was the nonchalant retort.

'Hell, Jim! Don't talk of the Boar's Head. I could drink a pint as big as a barrel now.'

Jim's tongue unconsciously ran over the dry rim of his long drooping moustache, leaving it moist enough for his lips to smack with longing as he said:

'Ah! A barrel full as big as a pond, muniferni.'

Both men let their minds wander for some time until a new thought struck Will.

'I wonder what won the three o'clock that day we came down,' he asked wistfully.

'Hmm. What race did you say, my boy? You see, my remembery is not so good as it did used to be, these days.'

'The three o'clock.'

'Oh, aye. I heard you first time, mun, but I did want to make quite sure, you see, because Siân have turned that set of ours into a proper chapel goer, muniferni. That's all you can hear on it – sermons and hymns. Only a deaf man can understand anything else it do say, mun jawli.'

Will became invigorated with the indomitable courage and optimism of the old man. He laughed loudly and woke other restless sleepers, although he was not aware of it till some of them shouted: 'What the hell is the matter? Have

820

the bloody circus started or what? Have a bit of respects for other people, mun, whoever you are. You're not in a workhouse or a gaol now.'

Will laughed more loudly than ever at this, and others joined in, waking everybody up and filling the stable with confused sound that made the horses neigh restlessly.

Someone rose to his feet and the tremor in his voice exposed the weakness in his limbs when he shouted hoarsely: ' Come on, boys. Time to feed the horses.'

When this was done the men crawled more closely to each other, each finding his way to his own group of mates by the directing voices that led him over reclining and squatting bodies. After this everything became quiet for a while and a vague common desire filled all their minds. Everyone kept it to himself even as the longing urged him to open his mouth and speak. At last the desire broke its bonds in an initial sibilant whisper that slowly seeped its way through the ranks and fixed everyone's thoughts.

'Water, water. Where can we get it?'

The intensity of the need that gripped the men killed its vocal expression for some time after this first outburst, when an idea shaped in their minds and again the thought was given life.

'There's water in the pipes between the stop tap and the boshes.' The elementary simplicity of the fact that only now had dawned on them stupified everyone until Big Jim began to laugh clamantly.

'Ha-ha! That's good! The next thing us will forget is that there is always coal in a coalpit.'

This broke the tension, and arrangements were made

for tapping the pipes and filling the empty water-bottles.

Bottles were being passed from groping hand to groping hand, jokes and laughter accompanying the operation, when the stable door suddenly banged open and disclosed a large number of lights. Men stood still with outstretched hands, in stupified amazement at the unexpected sight. Pit-blinded eyes became blinder still as the lights from the lamps struck them with pain-inducing beams.

A voice, emerging sharply from the ring of light, ordered: 'Get ready, there. All of you have to go up the pit, and the quieter you go the better for yourselves. This pit is going to work today, and we've got men ready to work it.'

The lights began to move forward in a solid block that was harder than the blackness which tried to crush it. The strikers involuntarily began to retreat before the menacing advance, until someone shouted from the rear:

'We can't go back any further, we're up against the end.'

But still the lights advanced with nothing but their motion to mark their coming. Will Evans felt his hair bristle uncomfortably as his quick temper began to rush the blood to his head. He had understood the new move even as he heard the order, and the despairing call from behind now snapped something in his head.

'Pick up something for a weapon, boys,' he howled, 'and let us fight for the door. The officials and non-pols are trying to beat us out of the pit.'

The cry was followed by a flurried shuffling as the men stooped to pick up from the floor pieces of wood, iron, and whatever else they could get hold of. Then the strikers stood, wordless and immobile, waiting for the outcome of

822

the new development. The lights they had prayed for now became their greatest enemy, making everything invisible to their eyes, filling them with tears and making their heads throb. But the menacing halo did not stop its advance until it came and broke on the first wave of strikers, who lashed out in all directions without knowing what or who they were hitting. The action ran through the stable with electrifying speed and effect.

The attackers had never expected such a determined resistance, and their first ranks, which of necessity had to take the brunt of the onslaught in the confined space, pressed back upon those behind them, throwing the latter into increasing confusion as the strikers bore on. Groans and grunts mingled with thuds and curses. Lamps were whirled wildly in the air and used as weapons which fell like shooting stars upon the soft flesh in the way of their descent.

Suddenly a whistle shuddered through the stable with a shrill squeal, followed by a warning:

'Look out there!' as a long nozzle peeping through the ranks of the attackers burst into a roaring crackle. The compressed air thus released, drove itself like a solid wall against the men before it, sending some squirming to the ground and the remainder into a panicky retreat to the sides or anywhere they could escape its annihilating fury. Screams found company with appeals as the blast did its work.

'Fair play, boys, fair play. For God's sake give us a chance!'

The answer seemed to come from the very nozzle of the pipe: 'You've had it, you bastards, and wouldn't take it, now take this,' and the terrifying tumult rose higher still as the tap was opened fully.

The strikers felt that everything was lost and were on the point of declaring their readiness to go up the pit when a loud clang of rolling iron challenged the blast for noisy supremacy. The dung-filled tram, released from its wooden anchors and driven into greater momentum by the strong hands of Big Jim and the energetic ones of Will Evans, plunged wildly into the swaying mass of men behind the blast pipe. The latter gave way immediately and ran headlong for their lives towards the pit, the tram hurtling after them like a tornado in which was merged the cackling laugh of Will Evans as he picked up the blast nozzle and switched off the air.

Lamps scattered about the floor of the stable acted as footlights for the grotesque scene. The noise of the battle had stampeded the horses, who were now kicking wildly in all directions, driving the men into bundles on the sides until some sprang on the wooden fences that separated the stalls. Unloosening the chains which held the horses' heads, the men turned the steeds round so that their hindquarters pressed against the mangers and the walls.

Then the survey of casualties began. Wounds were bound with shirt or singlet strips and no distinction was made between friend or foe. When the ambulance men reached Big Jim they found him squatted on the floor clutching a man to his body as though he were nursing a child.

'Good God! Is he badly hurt, Jim?' one of them asked.

'No. Not much yet. But he will be unless he use his head from now on. He tried to run away with the others when the tram went on wild, but I had him, muniferni, before he could get far.

'Who is it?'

Jim's mysterious demeanour filled the others with a curiosity that made the query more than an ordinary question.

'Oh, you will find that out soon enough. I bet you 'on't guess, none of you, in six times.'

The men grew impatient and bending down, took the man from Jim's grasp, raising him erect so that they could all see him. A gasp of astonishment echoed round the stable as the white features of Mr. Hicks reflected the light from the confiscated lamps.

'Holy hell! Big Jim's collared the big boss!'

The men held an immediate meeting to discuss the new developments, after which all the non-pols, officials, and badly hurt miners were sent to the surface with a message to the authorities that Mr. Hicks would remain down with the strikers until a satisfactory settlement was made by the company and that no harm would come to him if food was sent down immediately. This done, the men began to discuss the next moves. Big Jim never moved from Hicks' side, and it was Will Evans who declared:

'That have settled it, boys. No more bloody stables for us. It is nothing but a death-trap. The only thing now is to get inside to the double parting and make that our home. Put out all the lamps except one. We don't want to be in the dark agen if we can save light.'

The men agreed and all available sacks, brattice cloth, and other soft material was taken along as they made their way to their new earth-embowelled home.

The solitary lamp turned the line of men into dim shadows that quivered and danced on the timbered roadway. The eeriness of the tramp stole into Hicks' heart, and he whispered to Jim in a trembling voice:

'What are they going to do to me, Jim?'

'Nothing, boy bach, nothing, if you will keep your head and do what you are told.'

'But why do you keep me down?'

The manner in which the query was made implied a deep fear that tickled Jim, whose reply became a gloat: 'Ah! That's the puzzle, see. Ha-ha! Before now you was the big boss, shouting and ordering and sacking. But the boot have shifted to the other foot. Yes, catching you have made us the bosses, and for once in our lives we will do the ordering and you will do the listening.'

Something in the statement and the silence that followed it turned the manager's blood to water. He began to plead, raising his voice so that the other men could hear: 'Let me go, boys, and I'll see you get fair play.'

There was no reply other than the stumbling, muffled tramp of feet and the quickened tremor on the shadowed walls.

Hundreds of police surrounded the pit-head when the injured came up, but the ranks of people who pressed upon their outermost ranks saw that a battle had taken place underground. They burst into wild cheers when they saw that most of the injured belonged to the non-pols and officials, and the police made a baton charge to clear them from the yard. This action was followed by a shower of

826

stones and coal lumps that precipitated another fight which lasted for hours before the people were finally driven down the hill into the streets of Cwmardy, which became tremulant with exultant shouts: 'Our boys have captured Hicks. Now it won't last long!'

Siân's eyes shone brightly at the glowing embers in the fire grate of her little kitchen.

'Dear, dear,' she mused proudly, 'our James is the oldest man down, yes, the very oldest, and I am so sure as this hand is fast to me,' holding it out for Len and Mary to see, 'that he will be the very last to come up.'

Neither of them answered her, so she turned again to the fire.

'Him and me have been together a long time now. Yes, forty years or more, and it is 'bout time he left the pit for younger men. He have done his share and did ought to have rest and comfort in his old days.'

Mary stirred on the chair and placed her hand on the old woman's shoulder with a gesture that was itself a caress.

'Never mind, mother. One day we will put this old world of ours right and use the good and beautiful things it has for all the people and not for the few who now take it all.'

She changed the subject abruptly and turned to Len. 'What is the next move?' she asked sharply. He shook his head despondently.

'It is out of our hands,' he replied. 'Everything now depends on the boys down below and what the company will do about Hicks. One thing we can depend on, and that is there'll be no more fighting down below, and they'll let food go down now if only for Hicks' sake.'

Each morning during the five days that followed the people of Cwmardy plodded up the hill to the pit, with food and material for the strikers. They remained until nightfall, only leaving when they knew there were sufficient pickets to ensure all necessary information reaching them in the shortest possible time.

A mass-meeting was held on the eve of the morning which marked the tenth day of the strike. A report was here given to the people of the latest negotiations between the Executive and the company, after which Len was appointed to go down with Harry Morgan and Fred Lewis to interview the strikers. On its way to the pit, the deputation was inundated with flasks of hot tea and packets of food. Siân handed them a tin of tobacco with the solemn injunction:

'Now, 'member, you must put it into his own hands and nobody else's, because I do know it is the only thing he is worrying about... and me, of course,' she added as an afterthought.

The tramping feet reminded Len of the Big Strike and Ezra. He wondered what the once dour body now looked like in its earthy blanket. The thought made him shiver, and he automatically looked for Mary in the following throng. He saw her with his mother, the latter limping doggedly to keep pace with her people. His body again warmed at the sight of his two loved ones trudging together in the lines of their fellow workers. He smiled grimly as he noticed Ezra's heritage of determination stamped indelibly into Mary's features, and his heart beat more quickly in its significance.

The setting sun sent blood-hued rays to linger over the

valley as the members of the deputation stepped into the cage, where they dangled on the thread that was to drop them to their mates. A loud heartening shout followed them into the pit and the rush of the carriage was accompanied by a rush of the people, which broke through the police cordon and gave them possession of the pit-head, where they waited patiently for news from below.

Meanwhile Harry and his colleagues had passed the now empty stable and were dragging their feet through the dust to the double parting where Tom, the hitcher, had told them the men had established themselves. Their lights were seen a long time before they reached their destination. A husky voice halted them.

'Stop there and don't move another step till we know who you are.'

The trio immediately obeyed, holding their lamps still so that the others could see they had stopped walking. Some minutes passed before two shadows broke through the darkness into the lamplight, both walking slowly and hesitantly, like babies just learning painfully to stand erect for the first time. Len looked, and recognising his father and Will, his eyes became dim. But neither of the two saw anything, for their eyes were closed tightly, the compressed lids drawing wrinkles all over their faces. The couple walked on until Big Jim bumped into his son, when he stopped abruptly and threw out his arm to grasp Will and prevent his going into danger.

'Well?' he asked in a voice that he strained up from his belly. 'Who is there and what do you want?'

The very weakness of his tones implied a challenge

which the deputation sensed immediately.

'Dad, dad,' Len cried, 'it's me and Harry and Fred.'

Will felt his body melt away from his head, leaving the latter whirling around even as he maintained his senses and wondered what was wrong. He gave a little moan.

'Oh, God! What is the matter with me?' and began to slither weakly to the floor, but before he reached it three pairs of arms were round him, holding his body and bending his head towards his knees. Big Jim rested his shoulders against the sides and dumbly waited while the others attended to Will.

Harry forced a hot sip of tea between Will's clenched teeth. This revived him, and he shamefacedly urged them to let him go.

'I'm all right now,' he declared. 'Keep that tea for the others, who deserve it more than me.'

Harry and Fred, however, insisted upon helping him back to the men, but Jim refused assistance, pretending the heavy hand which clasped Len's shoulder was there to steady the latter, because 'he wasn't used to the pit for a long time.'

In this manner they reached the double parting, where the remaining men, some lying and some sitting, were awaiting them. The lamps were fastened on the high cross timbers to keep the glare from the men's eyes. Big Jim introduced the deputation and a weak cheer welcomed them, but this evaporated into dry coughs that spread like fog among the strikers, whose thin bodies and slack skin began to shape in the light from the lamps.

Harry noticed the pitiful dignity with which the strikers

830

tried to impress the deputation, and swallowed the lump in his throat to say: 'Well, boys, you have done your duty, and the fight is over. Our people are waiting for you with open arms and happy hearts on top. You did the trick when you kept Hicks down.'

He expected, as did his mates, a cheer to follow these words, but none came, and he was astounded to hear after a brief silence the quickly uttered command:

'Let Len show us the agreement. That's what we said on the first day and that is what we say today.'

There could be no mistaking the determined self-abnegation behind the whispered words, and Len wasted no time in arguing.

'Let's be quite straight from the start, boys,' he began. 'We haven't got an agreement for the simple reason that the company thinks it is saving its face if it can get you up first and then let you have the agreement in the office. They want to make sure that Hicks is safe and sound.'

A murmur of disbelief came from the men, and Len hastened to add: 'But there can be no mistake about it. The company is prepared to take a free ballot and let every man join what union he wants to.'

This time a small cheer managed to trickle into the air, and Big Jim quickly stepped into the breach thus offered. 'Us can take his word, boys, because he do know if he said a lie to do us down, I 'ood cut his head off 'xactly like if he wasn't my own flesh and blood, muniferni.' He took his hand off Len's shoulder to give greater vehemence to his words, but the action only made him sway drunkenly. His statement nevertheless decided the men,

831

and a quick vote was taken to clinch the issue.

Then began the faltering walk to the pit. Each of the men refused aid from the members of the deputation and the provisions they had brought with them.

'There is not enough for all of us,' said one as he rejected the offer. 'And we might as well stick it till we can all get some.'

'Aye,' said another, 'and we have had to depend on ourselves all this time, so we might as well depend on each other now at the finish.'

And in this manner, the weaker leaning on the stronger and all leaning on each other, they made their way behind the deputation to the bottom of the shaft, where some officials were waiting for them. This started another upset, the men refusing to ascend till the officials had left.

'Hell fire!' Will tried to shout and in so doing turned his voice to a croak. 'We came down without 'em, and by damn we'll go up without 'em.' Hicks shivered weakly and instructed his subordinates to get up out of the way.

The ultimatum and instructions produced surrender, and the officials stepped into the waiting cage and were whisked away, Fred Lewis going with them to acquaint the people that the others were coming. When the first carriage full of strikers banged its chains against the droppers, the rush of released air was smothered in the terrific cheer that rolled and crashed over the valley. Police and officials were scattered about like coal-dust when they tried to keep the people away from the pit-head. The strikers were tenderly lifted out of the cages and tended by loving hands while they waited for the remainder to come up. Kisses mixed with happy tears and both were lost in the singing and cheers as the cage slowly emptied its final load. The last man to step out was Big Jim; whose trembling hand arrogantly twirled his long moustache. Siân rushed towards him.

'James, oh James bach,' she sobbed, as she flung both arms around him and pressed her face to his black one when he bent down to kiss her. 'I knowed everythink 'ood come all right.'

He raised his head and seeing Mary nearby, stretched out his hand affectionately to stroke her brown hair glistening in the electric lights.

No one ever remembered exactly what followed, everything was excitement and tumult. But the blare of a brass band took command of the situation, and, in step with its lively march rhythm, the people took their victorious strikers down the hill to Cwmardy, where banners and streamers waved a breezy welcome home.

A PARTY DECISION

A few months after the excitement of the stay-in strike news began to appear in the press about an armed insurrection against the Government of Spain. The people of Cwmardy wondered what it was all about until the truth slowly leaked through, and then they began to learn that the insurrection was developing into an invasion. This fact caused furious discussion, and Spain became the main topic of conversation wherever two or more met.

One evening in Mary's house she paused in the act of powdering her nose and looked at the clock; then, with a hasty: 'S-s-sh! It's time for the news' to Len, who was noisily washing his face, she switched the wireless on. The piercing oscillations that accompanied her efforts to find the station startled the dozing Bonzo, who sprang to his feet with a growl and looked disgustedly for some

835

moments at Mary fingering the set, before subsiding back upon his mat in the corner with the stately motion of a dowager at her bankruptcy examination. The dog waited until the voice came over the ether with its deeply intoned announcement: 'This is the first general news bulletin,' then slowly dozed off again with one eye half open.

Len came near the fireplace and continued wiping his face, although he now did so more slowly like one who wanted to deaden any foreign sound. Mary leaned over the table and fixed her eyes on the instrument as though this would enable her to see the words. Both of them unconsciously tensed their bodies when the word 'Spain' came across, and they were afraid even to breathe properly in case they lost one item of the following statements. When it was finished they looked at each other silently for some moments before Len asked in what he thought was a casual manner: 'Do you want to hear about the price of gold?' She shook her head somewhat sharply and he hastened to switch off, leaving the kitchen in a quietude so deep by contrast that Bonzo again cocked his two eyes open to see what was wrong.

Mary bent to pat his head, at the same time remarking: 'It's looking pretty black in Spain, Len, if we can depend on the news.'

Len flung some small coal on the fire. 'Yes, Mary, very black; and we'll have to do something about it soon.'

Both seemed fearful of saying too much in case their emotions overcame them. Mary took a final look round the kitchen, made Bonzo more comfortable on his mat, then said: 'Let's go, Len, or we'll be late and you know how sarcastic

Harry is when there's important matters to discuss.'

They locked the door behind them and hurried to the meeting place, returning an occasional salutation on their way down but not stopping to chat with any of the acquaintances they met. When they arrived at their destination they found all the Party committee already present, with the exception of Will Evans, who was working afternoons.

'Hello. Slept late?' Harry asked as the couple took chairs next each other.

'No, we waited a couple of minutes to hear the news,' replied Mary.

'Oh, aye. Well, we'll get more than the wireless gave before we finish tonight.'

He turned to the others. 'Can we have a chairman, please?'

Len was nominated and carried, and without wasting time he left his seat and went the other side of the table alongside Harry, who whispered something to him for some moments. Len nodded his head in approval, then began the business of the meeting.

'Harry has got a report to give us tonight about the situation in Spain,' he announced. 'It appears there have been some very big developments and we have now got to take some definite and practical steps in the matter.'

The room seemed to go suddenly cold although the air outside was humid and close. Mary felt a queer trickling through her spine, and drew her coat more closely, at the same time bending her head to the table so that only the top of her brown hair was visible to the others.

Harry did not rise from the chair when he addressed

them with slow deliberation. 'Comrades, the civil war in Spain has reached a new stage. It has now become an armed invasion by foreign countries – open intervention by Germany and Italy, the countries of Fascism. Yes, the fight in Spain is no longer one in defence of Spanish democracy; it has become a war for the defence of world democracy and it can only end when we make Spain the graveyard of international Fascism and all that it means.'

He continued for more than an hour giving his report, his voice often shivering with emotion, but Mary never raised her head during the passionate discourse.

An idea germinated by the wireless news was taking more definite shape in her mind with each word Harry uttered. It thrilled even as it drained the blood from her thin cheeks. She knew already that it was what she wanted, even while she tried to drive the thought away.

Suddenly some words of Harry's drew her taut and for the first time she looked up, to see Len's eyes fixed on her with an intensity that drew the blood back to her face in pink flushes that burned her ears as Harry's pronouncements buried themselves there.

'That's the position,' he declared. 'We must continue with protests, we must help financially and with foodstuffs, but more important still, we must help with men. Yes, comrades. We must fill the gaps that the Fascists make. For every democrat they destroy we must find two more to take his place. Our workers have fought in the wars of imperialism. The time has come when they must now fight in defence of democracy and all the ideals that they cherish.'

For a long time after these closing words there was a silence which made the room as callous as a tomb. Harry's report had brought the war from the realms of theory and news and had made it a living individual fact that burst like a bomb in the consciousness of everyone present. Len found his mind fixed on one sentence in the speech. It thrust all other thoughts aside and flayed him like the burn of swishing nettles:

'The national leaders of Labour are dragging the honour of British people in the mud, and it is only the Party and the working class can redeem it in the eyes of the world.'

He couldn't tear himself away from this and the implications it involved. His brain automatically separated the problem into its parts and focused upon the one that posed the question of individual responsibility and obligation. Without thinking of doing so, he let his gaze wander to Mary, who returned his look with eyes that didn't appear to see him.

At last the tension was broken by a voice which asked: 'How can you expect us to recruit workers for Spain if we don't go ourselves? I could never, for one, bring myself to ask another to do what I couldn't.'

Harry appeared to be prepared for this question, and answered without hesitation: 'That's not the point. We shall send our best and most trusted comrades out, you can depend on that. But the main thing is to get workers, particularly those with war experience, to go.'

Mary followed immediately with another question. 'Does that mean that only men who were in the last war can go?'

'No. Party comrades who have no military training

but who have a wide political experience are going to volunteer.'

'Ah.' The sound escaped Mary's lips like the sigh of a mother who suddenly feels again the long dissolved grief of the parting from her child.

Then, for no apparent reason, the room became full of excited voices. From all quarters came the assertion: 'If that's the case, then I'm the man to go.'

Harry raised his hand and for the first time got on his feet. 'Comrades, let's be clear. The matter is entirely in your hands, but I have a suggestion to make which I hope you will seriously consider before coming to any final decision.'

Len had not said a word throughout, but he knew what was to follow as surely as though the words had already been spoken. All his life he had been temperamentally opposed to physical violence, and even now, despite all his experiences of brutal actions against his people, he felt an inward shrinking when it forced itself upon him. It was in this that he differed most fundamentally from his father. Big Jim was urged to violence by the sheer exuberance of his physique, while Len was impelled to it by intellectual realization of its necessity. Because of this Len went into every action with a calculating, cold hardness that was foreign to his normal self, whereas Jim swept into action with joyous whoops that betrayed his pleasure in battle.

Len's thoughts were canalised by Mary's quiet question: 'What is your suggestion, Harry? Who is the comrade you want to recommend?'

The brief hesitation that followed was sufficient answer, but Harry rather nervously replied: 'Len Roberts – he's the comrade I've got in mind, and I think he's the best for many reasons.'

Mary's hand jerked to her breast, which she squeezed convulsively, but she soon calmed herself in the discussion that followed the statement.

'But he can't go, he's wanted here,' said one voice.

'The front-line trenches of democracy are now in Spain, not Cwmardy,' came the retort.

'Let's send a single man. What about myself?' asked another.

'We want the best, the most able,' was the instant reply.

'What about Will Evans – he's just the man.'

'Will's working and we can't draw him from the pit for the time being.'

'But what about Mary? She can't live on air.'

Mary sprang to her feet at this. She felt the question an insult to her whole life and, quite irrationally, resented it. 'I'm not here to bargain about him,' she announced heatedly. 'If he is necessary to the fight I give him freely, whatever the result might be. But don't bargain over him. Don't ask me to sell him.'

The vehemence of the utterance subdued her, and then she realised how unfair she was. No one answered her insinuation, but it put an end to the questions, although Harry tried to put everyone at ease when he asserted: 'Mary'll get what she's having now to live on. The supporters of democracy will see to that.'

Shortly after this the meeting broke up into chatting groups, Harry taking Len and Mary on one side to tell them: 'You'll have to go in three days, Len, so you'd better come down tomorrow to see about your passport and the other things that are necessary. There'll be about twenty others going with you.'

Len's face was hard as stone when he replied: 'That's all right. It'll give me nice time to square things here. What do you say, Mary?' turning to his wife.

She squeezed his hand proudly in hers and looked at Harry. 'Whenever the Party says, we'll be ready.'

'Good. What about having a little private celebration somewhere before you leave?' Mary half started, but Len made the objection first.

'No, Harry. It's not a time for celebrations, and I'd sooner go the same as the other boys. There can't be any fuss made over their going because of the authorities, so I'd sooner if we didn't.'

'Good lad, Len. I'm off now. See you in the morning.'

'So long, Harry.'

The couple waited until he had left the room, then joined the others. They chatted for some time until Len, noticing Mary's impatience, made an excuse and got away.

'Are you worrying, Mary?' he asked as they walked homewards.

'Oh, Len, I don't know what's the matter with me. I've got a funny kind of pain in my belly and yet I feel so proud somehow.'

A wanton thought flashed through his mind for a moment and he expressed it in a whisper. 'Do you think you have gone?' Then he laughed before she could answer. 'Ha-ha! Of course not, worse luck. But, duw, Mary, wouldn't it be nice if you had a baby coming while I'm out there?'

He allowed the pleasure of the thought to control him for some moments, and Mary did not interrupt him. At last he said, as though talking to himself: 'Why not? I know of women who have had babies after twenty years.'

Mary looked at him wistfully, one small hand clenched so tightly by her side that the knuckles stood out white. 'Don't Len. You know it's impossible and you only hurt the two of us by wishing for such a thing.' She could not refrain from adding: 'But it would be wonderful to have a baby waiting for you when you come back. He'd have hair like mine and eyes the same colour as yours, and...' she stopped and a pitiful little smile hung on the corner of her lips.

Len caught her arm and pressed it to his body. 'Never mind, comrade,' he consoled, both himself and her. 'If we can't create anything with our bodies, we can with our minds and the work we do for the Party. That's something to go on with, isn't it?'

They laughed together, then Mary suddenly had another thought. She stopped and stated abruptly: 'Len, you must see your father and mother tonight.'

He coloured a little before excusing himself. 'Oh, we can do that some other time. There's plenty of time before I go away.'

'Oh, Len. How can you say that. Tomorrow you'll be off meeting Harry and making final arrangements. Then the next day you'll be going.'

The reproach in her voice hurt him more than the truth of her statement. He had a horror of fuss and dreaded the scene with his mother, which he knew was bound to occur when she was told what he intended doing. Already he felt his tongue going dry as he vainly tried to find excuses he could validly call reasons. He wished now he could slide away with no one but Mary to know he was going, thinking this would cause his mother less pain. Then hard upon this thought came the knowledge that it was born of selfishness, that it came out of the fact he was himself afraid to face the pain of parting from his parents.

Mary sensed the battle taking place within him, and tried to help. 'Let's go in now, on our way home,' she suggested, and Len somewhat shamefacedly agreed without further comment.

Siân was busily wiping the brass candlesticks when the couple entered, but she immediately replaced the one she had in her grasp and queried with feigned surprise: 'Well, well, fancy seeing you. I thought you had forgot you ever had an old mam, Len, seeing how long you have been coming to see me.'

'I've been pretty busy, mam, between one thing and another,' Len replied as he took a chair and sat down. 'Where's dad?'

'Oh, he's out the back. I don't know how long he's going to be, but he have been there about a hour already.' She bent to whisper: 'Your father is not half the man he did used to be, Len. No, indeed. He is getting more childish every day.' She sighed, then abruptly ordered: 'Here, Mary fach. Sit on this stool. It is better than that old chair.'

Mary did as she was bade and had hardly made herself comfortable when Big Jim came in.

His body was bent slightly forward from the hips and

his hand was pressed tightly to his thigh, but the white moustache still had the arrogant stiffness of the days when it was black. He greeted them with a glad: 'Hallo. Where have you two felled from so sudden? Ah, come to see the old man agen before he peg out, I 'spect.'

He grunted his way to a chair, while Siân looked at Mary with eyes that seemed to assert: 'There, what did I tell you?'

Len, knowing he had neglected his parents in recent weeks, felt a little awkward. He wondered how to frame a feasible explanation, but before he could succeed Jim asked sharply: 'Have you put me in the 'surance, yet, Len?'

It was Mary who answered: 'No, father. And we don't intend to either. You have got years before you, mun, and it would be a waste of money that we can't afford to lose from our dole.'

She tried to laugh the idea away, but Siân pursued it. 'You did ought to, Mary,' she scolded. ''Surance is always handy when something do happen. And, mind you, it can happen to anybody. Yes, indeed. It is back to the earth us have all got to go. Huh! You must put the two of us in before it will be too late. Duw! Think, gel fach – there will be mourning to buy, without counting anything else that you have got to get for funerals if you want to be 'spectable.'

Jim interrupted her with a remark to Len, at the same time puffing heavily at his newly filled pipe between the words. 'Her words is right, Len. But 'member this, the old 'ooman do want a oak coffin; a orange box will do for me. And she do want us to be buried in the same grave, but, muniferni, she will have to alter a lot before ever I will agree

845

to chance my arm to have her nagging me after I am dead.'

Mary laughed loudly, and this prevented Siân making the retort that trembled on her lips.

'Let me help you to make a cup of tea, mam,' the younger woman offered, at the same time rising from the chair and taking the teapot from the hob.

The hot beverage had a soothing effect upon the old people, although Jim tried to depreciate its qualities with a solemn declaration: 'Tea is all right in its place, and that is in a 'ooman's belly. But for a man, ah, it is beer that he should have. Duw, I 'member the time, years ago now, when us could have a pint for tuppence. Beer, mind you, not the muck us have got to pay sixpence for today.'

Siân shrugged her shoulders impatiently and advised: 'Oh, left the old beer there for tonight, James bach,' then immediately remarked: 'Don't you fancy our Len is looking not half well, somehow?'

This query turned the conversation, and for some time they became reminiscent about their offspring.

'Do you 'member the first day he did start school, and us put that lovely new velvet suit on him, James?'

'Aye, my gel. He did look well that day. Just like his old man.'

He addressed himself to Mary, half turning in his chair to do so: 'You are too young to 'member that, Mary fach, much too young. Your little arse was no bigger than a shirt-button in those days. But if your father was alive he could tell you that I was a good-looking chap then. Aye, by damn. Straight as a line, wasn't I, Siân?' He twisted his moustache proudly as the old woman nodded assent.

Len and Mary let their elders wander through the past in this manner, wondering the while how best to break the news that was burning within them. At last Jim made an opportunity when he said appraisingly, looking Len up and down much as a farmer scrutinises a cow: 'Our Len is a pretty smart chap too, come to think of it. Not so big as his old man, mind. No, not by a long chalk. But that is Siân's fault. Still, I can 'member the time when a man like him could make a mark in the army.'

Len and Mary glanced simultaneously at each other and opened their mouths together, but it was her voice that was first heard, as she blurted out: 'That's just what our Len is going to be – a soldier.'

The crash of a saucer as it fell on the floor passed unheeded. Siân sat erect in the chair, her fingers bent as though the saucer were still in their grasp. Her bottom jaw had sagged loosely and her eyes had the same look as a playful dog's that had been unexpectedly kicked.

Jim leaned forward, his shoulders becoming more hunched, and hastily thrust a paper spill into the fire to light his already glowing pipe. But Len saw neither as he kept his gaze on the dancing flames and let his imagination frame pictures in them. The tin clock on the mantelshelf broke into the silence with a hollow 'tick-tock... tick-tock' that beat on the brains of the people in the kitchen.

Suddenly Siân sprang from the chair, her body rattling the table as she rose. 'What did you say, Mary? Our Len going to be a sodger?' Something gurgled in her throat for a moment before she made a pretence of laughing. 'Ha-ha!

Come, don't tease your mam in her old age.'

No one answered and no one looked at her. She glanced at them in turn, her eyes dilated and her face grey, as she waited for the reply. Then she spoke to Jim, her words dropping with increasing impetus from her lips. 'There you are, satisfied now, are you, that your nonsense talk have brought us to this? It is you that have put all these things into his head.'

The continuing silence drove her frantic for a while, but she began to weep in sheer impotence as the reality of the assertion made by Mary forced itself into her unwilling mind.

Mary went to the old woman and quietly led her back to a chair, where Siân could lay her head upon the table. The convulsive sobs that sounded like wet sighs infected the others. Tears began to trickle from Mary's eyes, came more quickly each moment, although she tried to check them, then she broke down completely and, burying her face in Siân's hair, moaned: 'Oh, mam, mam,' at the same time squeezing the elder woman to her own body.

Len gulped and blew his nose to provide an excuse for wiping his eyes, while Jim poked the fire savagely as if seeking revenge for something it had done to him.

For a long time the monotonous song of the clock merged in the women's sobs. Then Siân raised her head, turning it so that her lips pressed on the wet cheeks of her daughter-in-law.

'There, there, Mary fach, forgive me. It is my fault that your heart have come so heavy,' she soothed while her own face burned redly from rubbing with the tear-sodden canvas apron.

848

'That's right,' Jim supplemented hopefully. 'Come, my gel. Wipe your eyes and tell us what have happened.'

This reversal of rôles made Mary feel ashamed, and she kept her head down while she battled against her emotions, leaving the explanation to Len, who made it with hesitant and unconvincing sentences.

Big Jim and his wife remained motionless during the recital, but when it was finished Siân was on her feet again, a defiant blaze in her eyes. 'What? Do you mean to tell me that you are going to fight and die for foreigners millions of miles away from Cwmardy? No, never! If you have got to fight it will be here by your mother's side, where I can look after you. Huh! Spaniards indeed! I have never seened one of them and don't owe them a single penny. No, Len. You stop home by here with your mam and dad in their old age. They 'on't last long now.'

The air pressed heavy as lead and the crunching of Siân's boots on the sanded floor sounded like the crackling of a forest fire as she paced the narrow length of the kitchen. Jim felt impelled to help her, although in his heart he was proud of Len's action and claimed it entirely as a product of himself.

'Good old Len,' he muttered. 'You are 'xactly like I used to be when I was your age. Aye, indeed. But you must listen to your mam now. She do know best. Many a time have I learned that in the old days when I used to be a little bit wild. If it wasn't for her then, God knows where I 'ood have been today. Yes, you listen to your old 'ooman, Len.'

Seeing that Len made no response to this plea, Jim tried another track. 'You can take it from me, butty, those

Spaniards are no bloody use. Duw. When I was in Gib, mun, I comed to know them inside out, and I have never yet in all my born days seened one with any guts. No, muniferni.'

The innocently conceived insult ran through Mary like a burn, and, hastily patting the moisture on her cheeks, she defended the Spanish people. The argument went on for hours, Jim eventually siding with Mary, but Siân remained unconvinced, although she finally accepted the position with the best grace she could.

'Righteousness must prevail one day, I suppose,' she muttered in Welsh, before warning them fatalistically: 'You will find that my words will come true and then you will all be sorry for what you are doing against me now.'

A short time later Len and Mary sadly left the house and went to their own home.

Not a member of the family slept that night. Siân wept while Jim smoked and cursed, between vain pleas that she keep quiet so that he could have the sleep that was nowhere near him. The younger people had also been deeply affected by the events of the evening and especially by Siân's fight to keep her son at home. But they said very little to each other as they prepared for bed. Bonzo seemed to sense something untoward had occurred and kept on petting Len, muzzling his nose affectionately into the latter's hand and springing up to him.

Mary was the first to undress and get into bed, Len sitting on its edge for a time, playing with her hair while he tried to give expression to the emotions bubbling within him. But for some reason he failed, and at last got into bed by her side. Her cool flesh against his hot limbs steadied him, and he began aimlessly fondling her breasts.

'Put the light out, Len.'

He obeyed, and the little room was buried in a blackness which gave both of them courage.

'Do you still think the same about me going, Mary?' he queried. He felt the nod of her head on the pillow, which was her only reply. Somehow he felt disappointed, for although he detested fuss from other people, he found an emotional satisfaction in being fussed over by his wife. He felt her hand creep in tickling motions over his body, and turned on his side to squeeze her more closely to him.

'Len,' she whispered, 'Harry's arguments tonight were right. You are the best man to go.'

'Yes, I know,' he answered, and there wasn't a tinge of egotism in the bare statement.

He let his mind roam among the incidents he had heard regarding the war in Spain and began planning what he would do, although he had not the slightest idea what would be expected of him once he got there. But he knew by the versatility of his own experiences that whatever it was he could fit in. The thought gave him a warm glow of pride, and his fingers, without conscious volition, wandered over her legs. When they reached her buttocks he became sad again, and all his mind centred on her physical condition.

'You are going thinner, you are losing weight,' he complained. 'Oh, Mary. You'll take care of yourself when I'm away, won't you?' he begged.

She did not answer, and a recurring thought made him

nervous of the darkness, so he lit the candle again. The little flame rose and fell in grotesque shadows on the walls.

He watched them for a while and was likening the monstrous shapes to Fascists when Mary gave a horrified little scream and, springing to her haunches, caught him round the neck.

'What is it, Len?' she gasped, her perspiring hands upon his flesh. Len looked dazedly around, then saw a big moth weaving in and out among the shadows. His quickened pulse gave away the falseness of his laugh when he twitted her. 'Ha-ha! There's an old baby for you.'

But Mary, whose face was still squeezed tightly to his chest, muttered in muffled tones that echoed her dread: 'It came from the window. It was big and black.'

Len reassured her and gently raised her face from its hiding-place. 'It's only the shadow of a moth, Mary. What's the matter with you tonight?' The tremor that shook her was sufficient reply, and his body responded to it in a surge of physical desire. Both of them quivered for some moments while he mumbled incoherently in her ears. At last he made himself articulate, although the words sounded far away, as though he were talking to something in his past.

'Oh, Mary, it is not good that a man should love as much as I do, should give himself so completely to another. Everything that was me I have given to you, until now I have nothing left of all that I was. No, not even dignity, or I wouldn't be talking to you as I am.' He sighed as the measure of his emotional capitulation took hold of him, then continued: 'But I am not sorry, Mary.

Everything that I have been you have become. All that I once was you now are. So that our long life together has been creative after all, hasn't it?'

The question was a plea. Mary moved restlessly by his side, but said nothing. She knew all his moods and was aware he was now unburdening the feelings he had been nursing secretly for years. He had turned on his back and, with his hands behind his head, went on musing.

'Yes. By God, I have loved so much that it hurt me more than pain. I have followed your every thought, echoed your moods, and wept in your sufferings. You have become part of me so that I float loosely like a lost balloon when you are not near. Oh, Mary, my dear, I have no life apart from you. My mind always wanders to where you are, and I wonder what you are doing, to whom you are talking. Thoughts creep into my mind and I try to crush them. But they keep on coming until they are too strong for me and I become their prisoner. Yes... their prisoner.'

The last word was said like the 'amen' that follows a prayer.

Mary softly placed her hand upon his head and let her fingers play with the strands of his hair. The touch seemed to give his thoughts a new channel.

'But you have given also, my dear. You have given me your body, have let me have your mind. Yes, your strength has made me stronger, made me more determined, so that both of us have benefited by our life together. Ha! Do you remember, Mary, how I used to tell you that you must have initiative, audacity, and temper as well as political understanding to become a leader?'

Again he felt her affirmative nod.

'Well, it's still true, and you have them all. You are now a leader of our Party, whatever might happen to me. Because of this I shall be happy in my heart whatever I may feel in my mind or my body. What more can a comrade want than to know that the future is safe in the hands of those who follow him, especially when they are the ones he has lived with and loved?'

Something triumphant and stimulating swept over him and he turned abruptly on his side. Clasping her body to his he laughed happily before pressing on her lips the burning moisture of his own. He felt the pulsing of her heart, but did not see the tears in her eyes.

Some time later Mary turned back upon her side and asked: 'Len, are you afraid to go?' The query was put as gently as the echo of a child's song far up in the mountain, but it stung him like the fangs of a snake.

'Afraid? Afraid of what?' he demanded harsly.

'Oh, ever so many things.'

'Such as?'

'Well, perhaps you are afraid to leave me.'

The words were like a blow, stunning him for a few seconds before he could gather his thoughts again. He felt the reproach of the statement and became apologetic, although at the same time he tried to avoid the implied query.

'Oh, Mary, why do you say that? You know I have been to gaol. You know I have been beaten up on demonstrations. You know all that I have done in the struggle, and now you say that I am yellow.' He waited expectantly, but her silence eventually impelled him to continue: 'Yes, I am afraid to leave you,' he challenged. 'I'm afraid something will happen to you while I'm away.'

Mary rose to her haunches. 'I thought so, Len. Yes, I thought so.' There was a happy tremor in her voice, but she pulled herself together before betraying it too deeply. 'Don't worry about me, my comrade. I shall be all right with your father and mother, and don't forget we have the Party. I know it's going to be hard, Len, not only for you but for all of us, but look how happy we'll be when it's over and you're back in the ranks again.'

She caught his hand and rested it against her breast, swaying her body like a mother with a baby. Len let the soothing motion capture him and filled his nostrils with the scent of her flesh as he murmured: 'Yes, Mary comrade. There is no question of fear. It's just another job that has got to be done in order that we can carry the struggle of our people forward.'

There followed a long pause after this till she asked curiously: 'What are you thinking of now, Len?'

Very slowly, as though he were manufacturing the words in his mind before giving them expression, he answered: 'I was thinking of all the little kiddies who think so much of us. Of how they rush to us when they come from school and shout, "Hallo, Len. How be, comrade?" before asking for fag photos. They are so true. They follow us into our meetings and on our demonstrations; and yet, when we go, what will they have to remember us by? Nothing, Mary. Nothing except the fact that they once knew a man who had always been unemployed – a man who wandered from meeting to meeting and street to street always looking for something he never seemed to find. Ah, but now? When they look back upon their youth they'll be able to say: "We knew Len. He fought for us in Spain and Mary helped him." Yes, my love. How much better a memory is that than the deadness of the other. It will help them when they are men and women to be active in the fight. That's what we want, activity that leads to action, not the inertia of pessimism and despair. And what our children see us doing, they do later for themselves. Remember the funeral of the little dog and the passionate loyalty of those kiddies to a playmate that had become a carcass? That's the love and the loyalty we mush cherish.'

His words had become slower as though he was loath to lose them, or let them lead him immutably to the next idea. 'Who knows? Perhaps, when they look back on the past, they'll be able to brag to each other: "Our Len died in Spain".'

Mary jerked her body taut and stopped him. Her breath came in quick gasps as she implored and challenged in a single statement: 'Don't ever say that to me again, Len. You are going to Spain to fight, not to die.'

It now became his turn to soothe and placate. His caresses and endearments helped him, and they were both asleep, clasped in a mutual embrace, when the window blinds leaked the crimson glow of dawn into the bedroom.

Next day, while Len was away making arrangements for his departure, Mary spent all the time with Siân, both of them pretending nothing unusual was about to happen. Siân busied herself making round cakes on the slab of iron kept for the purpose. Len was very fond of these, and the old woman intended them to supplement the food he ate whilst travelling.

Mary scrubbed and cleaned the kitchen. When she reached the fireplace with her bucket, Jim obligingly lifted his huge feet on the hob out of her way.

'Damn! You are a pretty little workman, mun,' he commented appraisingly as she rinsed the moisture off the flags and treated them with blue stone to leave them white.

'It is a pleasure to watch you working, muniferni,' he continued as he put his feet back on the fender, but before he could fix himself comfortably they were all startled by a loud 'plop' that came from the tiny room beneath the stairs.

'Hell fire! Somebody is trying to shoot us,' Jim roared, at the same time looking wildly at Siân, whose eyes were full of apprehension.

Mary had a suspicion, after the first shock, of what had happened, and, with a hurried glance at the old woman, rose from her knees and opened the door leading to the dark, web-strewn cubicle. She hesitantly put her hand inside and withdrew a flagon bottle from whose neck some fluid was frothily gurgling.

Jim gave it one look, then sprang to the dresser for a cup, which he hastily put under the dripping fluid. While the cup was slowly filling he muttered disconsolately: 'Well, well, Siân, I never thought that you could be so mean. Me dying of thirst by here all the week and all the time you have got home-made wine in by there! Huh! For shame on you! Don't never call yourself a butty agen.'

Siân drew herself erect and her face shone with dignity when she replied to the accusation: 'I had thought to keep that for our Len's birthday, and had to hide it away from you or you 'ood have gutsed it long before now, more's the shame on you than me. But since he is going away, us will have it tonight instead.'

A tear dangled insecurely on her eyelid, but she proudly shook it off without raising her hand.

When Len returned late that night he found his people all sitting around the fire in his own house. This surprised him, because he knew Mary had been down to his mother's during the day and that the old couple liked having her there. But he understood the reason for the gathering immediately he saw the bottles on the table and the pile of corned beef sandwiches arranged in neat little tiers in the middle. A lump rose to his throat, but his eyes gleamed happily as the significance of the scene came to him. He fancied Mary looked sweeter than usual, in the dress she only wore on special occasions, and his wandering eyes noticed that his parents also wore what they called the best clothes.

The wooden dresser had been removed and its place was taken by the piano which had been one of Ezra's presents to Mary in the days of his prosperity.

Jim sat in Ezra's chair, a glass of wine in his hand. He held this up to the light appreciatively while he murmured: 'Very good. Very good indeed. But not half so good as a honest pint of beer,' before swallowing the wine in one gulp.

Len pulled his coat off, hung it on the hook behind the door, and turned to find Siân waiting for him. She held a half-pint glass full of wine in one hand and the flagon from which she had emptied it in the other, completely ignoring the empty glass in Jim's outstretched hand as she ordered: 'Here, Len bach. Drink this down. It'll do you the world of good. Better than all your old beers, whatever your father do say.'

Len took the glass and put it to his lips, while Jim pleaded: 'I wasn't meaning *your* wine, mun, Siân fach. Ha-ha! Good God, no. I was talking about that muck Dai Cannon do make. Ach, it is not fit for pigs to drink. Huh! But your wine, my gel, ah, I 'ood sooner have a flagon full of that than a pint of beer any day.'

The sentiments bribed Siân and she refilled his tumbler.

They sat in a ring around the fire, placing the big plate of sandwiches on the stool between them. Then they began talking of old times, carefully refraining, however, from referring to any of the sad occurrences of the past. Mary, whose eyes were beginning to shine wickedly (Len always said they were full of dancing imps when she was in this mood), related the story of the times he had followed the marchers to a certain town, in spite of orders she was not to do so. 'Our Len was like a wet rag by the end of the day,' she asserted, 'and was just crying like a big baby when he brought me to the station to send me back home.'

Len, who was also starting to look a little flushed, took umbrage at this smudge upon his manhood. 'Oh, fair play, Mary. I wasn't worse than any of the others, was I? And in any case, even if I was, it was because I had to lug you most of the way because the back of your shoe had rubbed half your heel off. Fair play now. If we're going to have it, let's have the truth.'

They laughed at his vehemence and Jim bawled out: 'Ho-ho, Mary fach could march your legs off, mun. Haven't

I seened her do it many times on the demonstrations?'

Len thought this an unscrupulous reference to the time he had dropped out of a demonstration because of an attack of giddiness, but he said nothing further about it as he saw his mother beginning to nod drowsily.

'Come on. Let's have a sing-song,' he announced.

Siân immediately opened her eyes and Mary drew her chair to the piano. 'What shall we have, Len?' she asked.

'Let's have something bright and happy that we all know.'

Mary, her thin shoulders swaying to the rhythm, immediately began playing a jazz tune. When she had finished it she asked: 'Did you know that one, mam?'

'Yes, my gel. Of course I did. It was *Bwthyn bach* with some fancy tra-la's, wasn't it?'

'Duw, duw, no. That was "The Blues", mam.'

'Huh. Never mind, Mary fach. Don't worry. I haven't got my specs on and it is quite easy to make a mistake with my eyes so old as they are.'

Len laughed loudly, but after some more tunes the music got into him and mixed with the wine. He rose from the chair and stood by Mary, lifting his voice to the refrains she played. They went through song after song, and, as they exhausted their repertoire of modern music and the wine took more effect, they unconsciously drifted to the old hymns of the people.

Siân became wide awake when the sad tones moaned through the kitchen. She clothed them in their Welsh words, her low contralto throbbing an accompaniment to the voices of Len and Mary, who eventually stopped singing and left the field clear for the old lady.

Jim took the pipe from his mouth and used it as a baton to keep time, smiling happily as Siân crooned her way back into the past where they both immersed themselves to the temporary exclusion of the present.

Whenever Mary was in doubt about the hymn they were singing, she simply paused a second, then let her fingers trickle over the keys and follow the tune as Siân sang it. Len sat down near his father and felt a deep sadness begin to weigh on him. Tears came to his eyes as each song brought back flashes of his youth. Then he became ashamed of his sentiment, and hoping that no one had seen the tears, put his hand out and lifted a glass from the table. It was nearly full, but before he had time to put it to his mouth Jim had taken it from him and, still conducting with his pipe, nodded to the other half-empty glass nearby.

Len took this without a word, looking his thanks at his father over the rim.

The more Len drank the more he worried about its effects on Mary, knowing that wine sometimes made her irritable and excitable. But he need not have bothered his head, because Mary was holding her emotions rigidly in check. Then a wave of new sentiment engulfed him as Siân sang a pathetic ballad. He rose unsteadily to his feet and began by kissing Big Jim, who looked at him stupidly. After this he insisted on stopping the song to kiss Siân and Mary, the tears streaming from his eyes as he did so.

He felt a little more satisfied after this and again let his voice join the others, but when Siân floated into the plaintive melody of *Dafydd y Garreg Wen*, everyone but herself became silent.

The old woman was weeping openly before she had completed the ballad. The last time it had been sung in the family was just prior to the death of Len's sister, and now, although neither of them gave words to the thought, it developed a significance that overwhelmed them.

Siân and Jim did not return home that night. The former slept with Mary and the latter with Len in the bed that used to be occupied by Ezra. They had hardly closed their eyes before it was time to get up. Len immediately went out the back and let cold water from the tap run on his head and bare shoulders. He wanted to be in his highest spirits this morning and was taking no chances. Although all of them pretended there was no need to be excited, they only succeeded in adding to the tenseness of the atmosphere. Siân followed Mary wherever the latter went, fearing, for her own sake, to lose sight of her for a moment. Big Jim strutted around like an unconcerned stag, filling the room with his bulk.

It had been agreed that only Mary was to accompany Len to the station. When this was first mooted Jim had protested, but gave way when Len said it would be necessary for him to look after Siân.

The time slipped by as if it were anxious to steal them from each other, and when everything was ready Mary went out first, unwilling to be a witness of the parting between Len and his parents. Siân caught her son to her with a gentle grasp that slowly developed into an all-embracing passionate clutch that left him breathless. But her eyes were brightly dry when she released him and said: 'Take care of yourself, my boy. 'Member us will be waiting for you. Yes, waiting and watching, and your mam, for one, will be praying for you every night.'

She turned her head away and stooped to lift the hem of her apron to her eyes, but suddenly remembered herself and left it untouched as she stood erect. Len looked at his father, whose hand was already outstretched, and felt his own lost in the grip that bade him a silent good luck.

Without another word and fearing to look again at either, Len followed Mary down the hill to the railway station. At every step Len felt himself pulled from behind, but steeled himself not to look back at the old people, whom he knew were standing on the doorstep watching him recede from their sight. His gaze wandered to the pits instead, and the floating smoke from the stack made him think of the changes that had taken place in his life since the days when he first saw it and heard the palpitating throbs of the pit engines.

He remembered Cwmardy when it was a tiny village made up of smoke-grimed cottages and the pit. Pride swelled him as he now looked at its hundreds of streets and big buildings with bright windows. The Big House looked lonely on its crest, and, instead of dominating Cwmardy, was now dominated by it. He felt run through him the tremor of the life that Cwmardy held, and, catching Mary's arm, he whispered proudly: 'Cwmardy and our people are worth going to Spain for, Mary.' There was no answer, but when they turned the corner that hid them from Sunny Bank they heard a mournful howl from Bonzo as they went out of sight.

The couple had barely reached the station before the

train steamed in with screeches and blasts that unnerved Mary. Len found an empty carriage and, leaning through the window, put his arm round Mary's neck, giving her a long-drawn kiss that was simultaneously a sigh. The wheels were beginning to turn when he released her lips. She bent her head and dimly saw the wheels take him away. Suddenly she jerked up and looked ahead to see him hanging through the window waving his hand in affectionate farewell. Her feet lifted involuntarily and she started to run towards him, her arms outstretched as though she wanted to pull him back. The speed of her feet increased in pace with the quickening revolutions of the wheels and she was deaf when he shouted above the noise of the train. 'Stop, for God's sake, stop.'

She kept on running. The porter who caught her round the waist heard the pitiful murmur that died on her lips as he pulled her back: 'Oh, Len. Oh Len, my comrade.'

For the remainder of the day she hardly knew what she was doing, but her spirits revived in the Party meeting that was held that night. She was made organiser of the branch in Len's place, Harry being unable to undertake the responsibility because of his work as chairman of the combine. This new rôle gave her the feeling she had a two-fold obligation to fulfil, and when she went home she was both happy and weary.

Siân, who had insisted on sleeping with her till Len returned, had supper waiting. Although she had no appetite for food, Mary ate some to please the old lady, who broke down before the meal was over. This helped Mary overcome her own emotions, and she tried to console the other, whose sobs kept time with Bonzo's padding feet as he searched round the kitchen for Len, smelling everything that belonged to him.

A LETTER
FROM SPAIN

Len had been away eight months, during which time Mary had thrown herself completely into the work of the Party, happy in the fact she heard from him more or less regularly. Her health had improved to such an extent that she spoke at more public meetings than she had ever done hitherto, and found no harmful effects. Her infectious enthusiasm impregnated the people and they all came to regard her as their own, belonging to them as surely and solidly as the Square where they had fought so many battles.

They dropped the prefix 'missus' and she became plain Mary to everyone. Even the enemies of the Party had to respect her for her indomitable courage and the *élan* with which she entered every campaign.

Siân tried to restrain her and one day took her to task. 'You are doing too much, Mary fach. What with the council, meetings, committees, marches, *Daily Workers* and what not, your little body will be so sure to break as my name is Siân.'

'Don't worry, mam. What we are doing is nothing to what our Len is going through.'

'Ah well. You will listen one day, when it is too late,' said the old lady before she fatalistically gave way and relapsed into silence.

Mary never put the wireless news on when her parents-in-law were about, but each night before they went to bed she read out the news from Spain, which she had carefully edited beforehand. Quite unconsciously she gave them the impression that Len was responsible for all the Government victories and the Fascist defeats. Big Jim carefully hoarded all she said and every Saturday night retailed the news again over a pint or so in the Boar's Head. On one such occasion, when he had taken more beer than usual, he bragged to his cronies.

'I knewed it years ago. I always did say that boy would be a general one day. Of course. What else could you 'spect from such a father as me? Aye. And I pity those poor dabs of Spaniards if he wasn't out there helping them now against all those Shermans and Bracchis.' No one ever laughed at these statements.

The longer Len remained away the more thrilling a legend his name became to the people of Cwmardy. He came to be regarded as a sort of chivalrous crusader linked up inevitably with the Party and Spain. As a result of this, her own personality, and the work she was doing, Mary had an open entry to most of the houses, being treated as a member of the family. Her smiling presence gave a welcome brightness to some of the drab homes whenever she called at them. She knew the exact circumstances of most families and was aware of the best time of the day to drop in to collect the weekly payment for the *Daily Worker*. Bonzo always managed to catch her up each time she went out, although she took every measure to ensure he was left behind. She was fearful of the many fights he engaged in and also shy because in practically every street were dogs hardly distinguishable from him.

She had been longer than usual without a message from Len, but thought little of it until the weeks became a month, then six weeks, then ten. The long silence began to worry her, and she pestered Harry Morgan each time she met him between his visits to London. But all he could tell her was that the last time they had heard Len was well and doing good work. This news heartened her the first time she heard it, but constant repetition made her introspective and she started searching in her own mind for the real reasons. At night in bed her imagination scoured every conceivable possibility, so that she woke each morning more depressed and listless than she was the morning before. She felt herself losing weight and the cough returned.

Siân noticed the symptoms and watched her like a cat, although Mary had kept her fears from them and always managed to fabricate a story when they inquired about Len.

The Party members saw the change taking place in her and often commented about it, but it was left to Harry to approach her on the matter. He pleaded with her to take a holiday and even offered to arrange everything for this.

869

But she was adamant.

Then, quite unexpectedly, news came through the usual channels that some of the men who had gone out the same time as Len were returning home. The information made Mary's heart skip some beats, then spring with greater vigour into action.

She told Siân and Jim about it the same night and ended with the remark: 'Now we'll know something definite about our Len.'

Immediately the statement left her mouth she realised she had made a mistake, but Siân, rigid in the chair, spoke before she could cover the error.

'Know something about our Len? Whatever do you mean, Mary? Us thought you knowed all about him without this.'

Mary swallowed before answering dubiously: 'Of course we do, mam. What I meant was perhaps Len, who is very important out in Spain, will have to stop there for a bit yet.'

'But you did not put it in that way,' Siân insisted, still not satisfied. Mary felt herself in a trap and tried desperately to wriggle out of it without saying a direct lie.

'But, mam, I was only thinking that if Len is not coming back with the boys, perhaps he's sent a special message with them to us.'

Jim took up the cue and entered the discussion. 'That's it, mun. Like I always used to do, Siân, in the war, when the boys was coming home on leave. Don't you 'member, gel?'

This settled Siân's doubts.

Mary called the Party committee together the following night to make arrangements for the welcome home. There was a full attendance at the meeting, every member alert with subdued excitement. It was decided to organise a demonstration and a mass welcome meeting in the new workmen's hall. Mary agreed to ask the women of the Co-operative and other Guilds to make banners for street decorations. Another Party member, who was also in the town band, stated he knew the latter would turn out in full strength. Harry Morgan, as chairman of the combine, raised the matter in that body, and it agreed to approach all the other organisations in Cwmardy to take part in the welcome home. As a result of all these efforts, a joint committee was formed to take charge of the complete organisation for the day.

Posters were exhibited in the shop windows, leaflets distributed to the houses, and preliminary meetings held in every street. The hall was decorated with red streamers, banners, special Spain prints, and *Daily Worker* posters. The lights were covered with delicate silk so that when they were switched on the whole hall glowed a deep crimson.

Artists belonging to the Party were commissioned to make large canvas paintings of the men who had left Cwmardy for Spain. When these were completed they were fixed on the red plush curtain that backed the stage. Len's wavy hair and big eyes occupied the centre. His picture was painted from a photograph he had taken on one of the marches, and his face looked longer than it actually was in real life.

The intervening days passed like dreams to the members of the Party and the organising committee, but at last the day arrived. The town band was ready to play the battle-hymns of the people. Women had hung banners of every description from their windows and spread long streamers of bunting across the streets, until Cwmardy looked like a lake of waving fire.

The schools were empty of children, all of whom anxiously awaited the street teas that had been organised for them by levies on the wages of the workmen and donations from the Co-operative Society and other organisations.

The men in the pits had already agreed to remain home for the event as a reply to a letter sent to Mary by the chief of police banning any demonstration through the main street.

The people in each street followed the example of Sunny Bank during the unemployed demonstrations, and marched as street contingents, converging on a common point for the mass demonstration through Cwmardy. The police realised it would be impossible to execute their threat and made no attempt to provoke the people.

Long before the train was due the approaches to the railway station were crammed with demonstrators. Most of them heard the train steam in, but very few saw what happened after, until an insistent blare from a motor car urged them to open the ranks for the procession of three cars. The first contained the returned soldiers, with Mary among them. Officials of the committee occupied the other two. The ranks reformed immediately the cars had passed and by the time the latter had reached the Square, they were at the head of a densely packed mile-long stream of people.

The occupants of the cars got out on the Square, the waiting bandsmen formed up before them, the returned soldiers were lifted on unknown shoulders, and, to the deep throb of drums, the march up the hill started.

Mary never knew how the old couple got there, but when her blazing eyes looked round they saw Jim and Siân right behind, the latter waving her arms and shouting at the top of her voice though no one could possibly hear what she said in the deafening tumult that was part of the demonstration.

Mary's heart twitched at the sight and it gave her greater strength to go on, her feet hardly touching the earth till they reached the hall. She managed to get inside, Jim and Siân still following. Those who could not enter were catered for by loud-speakers, which relayed to them every word said in the hall.

Harry Morgan, Mary, Len's parents, and officials of the organising committee surrounded the soldiers on the stage. Harry, who had been elected in charge, beckoned the brigaders to the front, where they stood for many shy minutes listening to the roars of welcome that greeted them back to Cwmardy.

When some measure of order had been restored, Harry called upon them all to sing the Red Flag. The request was heard by the band outside, who immediately struck up the initial chords, which were followed by the massed voices of the people.

When the mighty intonations died down Harry began his speech of welcome. Mary leaned forward, elbow on knee and chin in her hand, the better to follow the proceedings. The faces before her were melted into a huge grey blob framed by the red of the decorations. She heard

Harry's piercing voice cut the air with 'Comrades and Friends,' then felt a nudge. She looked around and saw one of the soldiers beckoning her with his finger. Bending back to hear what he wanted, she noticed subconsciously that he carefully avoided her eyes as he handed her a packet.

'This is from Len, Mary, and there's one from me as well. I thought I might just as well bring it with me, since I wrote it.'

The conversation was carried on in a whisper and as soon as he had finished the messenger sat back and fixed his attention on the meeting.

Mary didn't know what to do for some minutes. Her heart was beating into her ribs with an intensity that added to the glow on her cheeks. She felt it would be a sort of sacrilege to read the letters while the speakers were on their feet and before all the eyes in the hall.

Yet all the time she hesitated her whole being demanded that she read them quickly. Her body began to tremble with excitement and, unable to contain herself any longer, she rose quietly and tip-toed off the stage into one of the ante-rooms behind.

This was in darkness, but the many Party meetings held there had taught her where to find the switch. After a little groping she pressed it, and in a moment the room was filled with a glaring light that hurt her eyes after the subdued crimson of the big hall. She paused to ease the quiver of her flesh, all the time looking with intense concentration at the packet in her hand. She was burning to open it, but reluctant to start doing so. At last she pulled herself together and with a haste that made her

874

fingers clumsy tore open the covering and found two mud-stained letters inside.

She recognised Len's writing at a glance and a pathetic half-smile flickered on her face as she remembered the occasions she had twitted him about his terrible scrawl. She pulled the letter from its envelope and began reading to herself. But in a short time her lips began to move, and she read on half aloud.

Dear Mary and all at home,

I don't know when you had my last letter because postal arrangements are rather wonky, so I'm giving this to one of the boys to make sure that you'll get it, as it looks like he'll be coming home shortly. Well, Mary, I hope everyone at home is O.K. and that the Party comrades are putting their backs into the campaign to help Spain and save democracy.

Obviously I can't tell you much of what is taking place here, but I have been in this hospital for the last few weeks (just a little scratch) and am going back into the line tomorrow. You will be happy to know Ron is here with me. He was one of the first to come out and has made a name for himself as a fighter and a leader. You can just imagine that the two of us stick together as much as possible. He hasn't changed much since the old days, except that he is perhaps a bit thinner. We are gaining the upper hand now and are beginning a new offensive, of which I am glad.

It's marvellous to see how our boys go into action. You know them all and will remember how they were on the demonstrations and marches, but that is nothing to the way they act out here. It makes me proud of our people and of myself for belonging to them.

But it's strange, Mary (or is it?), that while there are certain differences I could swear sometimes I was still in Cwmardy and that the Fascists are not far away in a strange land, but are actually destroying our birth-place and all it means to us. The men who are dying don't seem to be strangers, but our comrades as we know them at home. The same old hills are somewhere around here, and I know the same old smokestack and pit is not far away. The faces I see about me are the same faces as those in Cwmardy. It is only when they speak that I notice any difference.

Yes, my comrade, this is not a foreign land on which we are fighting. It is home. Those are not strangers who are dying. They are our butties. It is not a war only of nation against nation, but of progress against reaction, and I glory in the fact that Cwmardy has its sons upon the battle-field, fighting here as they used to fight on the Square, the only difference being that we now have guns instead of sticks.

Yes, Mary my love. And tomorrow I am happy to go back to them. All our lives we have been together. In our homes, the pit, the streets, the Federation, and the Party. The strikes and demonstrations and marches have led us unerringly to this, the battle-field of democracy.

It is in the nature of things that we can't all come back to Cwmardy, that some of us will be left here with, perhaps, a cross to mark the fact we were once living, but were robbed of life by Fascism.

Yes, that is inevitable, as it is at home that after every action in defence of our rights they stick some of us to rot in prison.

Some of the boys we knew have already gone, but not in vain. They have helped to stamp into the earth an invisible barrier of bodies from which breathes a new spirit of hope and love and invincible courage. Fascism may kill us, Mary, but it can never kill what we die for. No, never! Our very death is creation, our destruction new life and energy and action.

I know, my love, that you appreciate all the possibilities and that whatever happens to me you will carry on building the Party, drawing our masses into a unity that will save Cwmardy for the people. Even as I write I know that you are near and I can almost feel your breath upon my neck as you bend over to read this. I know every throb of that wonderful heart that is too big for your little body.

It seems so long since I touched you with my hands, but I see you in every battle; you are at my side in every action. Remember the day we marched together in the big demonstration, Mary? Well, like that. You are with me wherever I go, whatever I do. And never forget, whatever happens, we were brought together because we belong to the people and it is only the cause of our people can ever part us.

If that should happen, if it becomes necessary, then don't grieve too much, because belonging to the people, you will always find me in the people. Give my love to all the comrades at home. Throw your whole weight into the

Party. Tell mam and dad not to worry about me. Sleep happy in the knowledge that our lives have been class lives, and our love something buried so deep in the Party that it can never die.

So long, Mary, my comrade and love,

Len.

A roar of cheering swept from the hall into the little room and Mary raised her head to see what was the matter, but the lights glistening on the tears that filled her eyes blinded her to everything. She felt there was something within her that wanted to escape. It seemed to clog her body and make it hard to breathe. She lifted her hand slowly to the pocket on the left breast of her coat and drew out the red silk handkerchief with its emblazoned hammer and sickle which had been Len's gift to her from Spain. She looked at it dazedly and saw it dancing in her tears.

Equally slowly and methodically she raised it to her eyes and wiped them, then getting a sudden grip on herself she read the letter again before picking up the other.

It felt heavy as lead in her hand as she opened it. Her eyes fixed instantly on one sentence that stood out before her like a neon sign.

We found him lying among a group of Fascists and brought him away from them to bury him with his own people. He had been with them all his life and we left him with them in death.

Mary read this over and over. She could not tear her gaze away from it until something gripped her by the throat and she could not breathe. She sprang to her feet and the grip was released. When she ran headlong from the room she left a moan behind: 'Oh, Len. You are gone for ever.'

She was on the stage before she knew it and the immediate deep silence that followed her entry brought her to a dead stop. Looking around like a woman in a trance, she saw the blur of faces before her, then the weeping form of Siân with Jim pathetically stroking her hair, nearby.

In a flash she knew that the people had been told that Len was dead and she turned her head to see his portrait stand out among the others with its draping of black cloth. Someone caught her arm and led her to a chair near the table, on which she bent her head. When she raised it again the hall was nearly empty and Siân, red-eyed and heaving, was standing near her, with Jim, who kept swallowing hard all the time.

'Come, Mary fach. Our Len have left us for ever, and this is no place for us. Let us go home.'

Mary looked again at the painting and fancied she saw the lips form into a smile and the sad eyes soften with encouragement.

She stared at it for some moments and the feeling grew on her that Len was saying: 'Go, Mary. Follow the people, they are your hope and strength.'

Jumping up, she caught Siân about the shoulders. 'You go home, mam. I can't come yet; the people's day isn't over and I must be with them till the last, as our Len was.'

Siân straightened her body. 'Us will go, Mary, when

you come and not before.'

They followed the last figures through the hall doors and found the demonstration getting further away every minute, the smoke from the pit curling round it before dissolving into the air and leaving the scarlet banner dominating the scene. They heard the barely audible strains of the band, and the people singing:

'Then away with all your superstitions,
    Servile masses, arise! Arise!'

Mary started to run. 'I must go before they get too far,' she muttered.

Jim and Siân slowly followed, the former shouting, 'Go on, Mary fach. Me and Siân is not quite so quick, but us will be with you at the end.'

Mary stumbled, but kept on her feet. She began mumbling to herself: 'I must catch them up. I must catch them up.' When she reached the tail of the demonstration she thought the beats of her heart were centred in her throat and stumbled again. This time she would have fallen, but eager hands caught her and a cry ran through the ranks towards the front: 'Send the car back. Send a car back.' When it came they placed Mary gently inside and sent it back again to the head of the march.

Jim and Siân limped far behind. He put his arm about her waist. 'Us can never keep step with 'em, Siân fach. Us have got too old. Yes, too old. But never mind, my gel; they have got to come back sooner or later before they can get home, then us can join 'em again.'

Siân halted to get breath. Floating towards them came the voices of the people muted in a common unity:

'Though cowards flinch and traitors sneer,
We'll keep the red flag flying here.'

Foreword by Hywel Francis

Hywel Francis is the Labour Member of Parliament for Aberavon. He was formerly Professor of Adult Continuing Education at the University of Wales, Swansea. Amongst his publications is the classic *Miners Against Fascism* (1984). His father, Dai Francis (1911-1981), was General Secretary of the National Union of Mineworkers (South Wales Area).

Cover image by Jack Hastings

Jack Hastings, or Francis John Clarence Westenra Plantagenet Hastings, fifteenth Earl of Huntingdon (1901-1990), was trained at the Slade School of Art. He painted many murals worldwide, including one at the Chicago World Fair in 1933, and worked as an assistant to Diego Rivera in San Francisco. Hastings took his seat in the House of Lords and served as a Parliamentary Secretary in the Labour Government between 1945 and 1950. He also taught at Camberwell and Central Schools of Art, and served as chair of the Society of Mural Painters from 1951 to 1959.

LIBRARY OF WALES

The Library of Wales is a Welsh Assembly Government project designed to ensure that all of the rich and extensive literature of Wales which has been written in English will now be made available to readers in and beyond Wales. Sustaining this wider literary heritage is understood by the Welsh Assembly Government to be a key component in creating and disseminating an ongoing sense of modern Welsh culture and history for the future Wales which is now emerging from contemporary society. Through these texts, until now unavailable, out-of-print or merely forgotten, the Library of Wales brings back into play the voices and actions of the human experience that has made us, in all our complexity, a Welsh people.

The Library of Wales includes prose as well as poetry, essays as well as fiction, anthologies as well as memoirs, drama as well as journalism. It complements the names and texts that are already in the public domain and seeks to include the best of Welsh writing in English, as well as to showcase what has been unjustly neglected. No boundaries will limit the ambition of the Library of Wales to open up the borders that have denied some of our best writers a presence in a future Wales. The Library of Wales has been created with that Wales in mind: a young country not afraid to remember what it might yet become.

Dai Smith
Raymond Williams Chair in the Cultural History of Wales,
Swansea University